BOUND TO THE SHADOW PRINCE

ALSO BY RUBY DIXON

Ice Planet Barbarians

Barbarian Alien

Barbarian Lover

Barbarian Mine

Barbarian's Prize

Barbarian's Mate

Barbarian's Touch

Barbarian's Taming

BOUND TO THE SHADOW PRINCE

RUBY DIXON

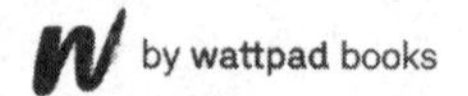

An imprint of Wattpad WEBTOON Book Group

Published in Canada by Wattpad WEBTOON Book Group, a division of Wattpad WEBTOON Studios, Inc.

36 Wellington Street E., Suite 200, Toronto, ON M5E 1C7 Canada

www.wattpad.com

First W by Wattpad Books edition: July 2024

ISBN 978-1-99885-475-2 (Trade Paper original)

Library and Archives Canada Cataloguing in Publication information is available upon request.

Printed and bound in Canada

1 3 5 7 9 10 8 6 4 2

Cover design by Emily Wittig

Images © Surovtseva, Henrique Westin via iStock; © Nik_Merkulov via depositphotos; © Andy Makely via Unsplash; © Pink Linen via Creative Market

Typesetting by Delaney Anderson

CONTENT WARNING

This story contains explicit sexual content, violence and depictions of murder and death, chronic illness, disease, plague, starvation, war and subsequent conquest, sexual harassment, rape, pregnancy, abandonment, infanticide, and slavery that may be upsetting for some readers. Reader discretion is advised.

CHAPTER ONE

The moment I hear the palace messenger is looking for me, I hide in my closet.

It's completely childish. I know it is. It's just that any time someone has a message of "grave urgency" to give me, it means something terrible has happened.

The first time, it was my father's death to bandits.

The second time, it was that my mother had died of sweating sickness.

And the third time, my sister Erynne was told it was time for her to marry my nemesis, Prince Lionel. I still haven't forgiven her for agreeing.

So, any message that's for me and me alone is not good news.

My maid, Riza, enters my quarters and looks around, frowning. "Lady Candromeda?" she calls as she takes a few steps forward, her dark-blue skirts swishing as she strides.

I chew on my nails, hoping she doesn't look in the heavy wooden wardrobe, and if she does, that she doesn't look behind the huge, embroidered pink panniers that I wore thrice last season. They're incredibly stupid skirts, but at least they're easy to hide behind.

Riza gazes around my quarters, her eyes narrowed. "She was just here. And she has to come back soon for her medicine."

Wincing, I wrinkle my nose. Riza's right. I hate that she's right.

I can never get very far because I'm tied to my nurse. She has to administer the potions I take daily, or else I'll get sick and die.

It's the curse of the Vestalin line to have tainted blood. My mother's sister had it. My sister Erynne has avoided it, and thus she's the valuable one. Our youngest sister, Meryliese, was spared the family curse, too, but because she's the youngest, she must be dedicated to the gods. She left when I was a toddler, so I barely have any memories of her.

The Vestalin family is down to me and Erynne.

And I'm tainted.

It's . . . inconvenient.

The Vestalin line dates back to the first kings of Lios. There has always been a Vestalin dedicated to the gods, and there has always been a Vestalin family to bring fortune to the people of Lios.

We are the blood of heroes. The first Vestalin, Ravendor Vestalin, sacrificed herself to save our kingdom, and ever since, we have been held and revered as the best of humankind.

Well, the nontainted ones are.

I'm the tainted one, so I'm more or less forgotten. The taint in my blood, the Vestalin curse, means I'm useless as a bride because I'm barren. Those with the curse cannot have children, and those without the curse have a chance of passing it to their children.

My mother bore six children to my father. Only three of us survived childhood, and I am the only one who was tainted.

Luck was not with me then, and it's not with me today. As Riza looks around, my nurse enters my chambers holding the silver tray in her arms with a vial of medicine on top, steaming.

She sets it down in the usual spot next to my chair by the fireplace and begins the preparation of the potion.

Dragon shite.

"Princess?" My maid calls out again, heading over to my adjoining bedchamber in case I've appeared there. She glances back at the messenger, who lingers in the doorway, straightening his livery. "Your medicine has arrived right on time."

Pursing my lips, I decide to give up on hiding. I kick open the door to the wardrobe and tumble as gracefully as I can from behind the mess of skirts and silks. I throw my hair back and straighten my clothing, lifting my chin as the messenger gapes.

"Have you seen my red silk corset, Riza? I was looking for it," I lie.

She just snorts and moves to my side. "Let me help you with your sleeve, my lady." As I sit gracefully into my chair, she mutters just low enough for me to hear. "Hiding in the closet like a child, and you a lady of four-and-twenty. For shame."

"No one asked you," I mutter as she pulls on the knots of my oversleeve, removing it from my gown while my nurse sits across from me, busy at work.

Once my arm is bare, I extend it out so I can receive my medication, looking away as Riza ties a tight golden band around my upper arm.

I can't look at the needles. Seeing them shoved into my arm makes me feel faint, so I always turn my head. I use this opportunity to glance over at the messenger, who's gawking as my ladies prepare me for my daily medicine.

"What?" I snap, knowing that I'm being unfair to him. "Haven't you ever seen a potion administered before?"

He swallows hard, staring at my nurse.

I glance over just in time to see her pick up a large syringe and a needle as long as my finger. Oh, gods, I had to go and look, didn't I?

I clench my jaw and keep my eyes focused on the messenger as my nurse taps my arm, looking for the vein. "You had a message for me, didn't you?"

"Yes!" he blurts out, wincing just as the needle pricks my skin. His face goes pale, and he fumbles with the letter, showing me the wax seal. "It's from the Alabaster Citadel."

"War foolishness, most likely," Riza comments, holding my removed sleeve. "It's all anyone wants to talk about now."

She's not wrong, yet why would someone send war correspondence to me? It should go to King Lionel, and if not him, then his advisors or my sister Erynne, who rules at his side (or around him when she can). Truly, I'm too far down in the pecking order to be bothered with war updates.

"Are you certain it's for me?" I ask the messenger. "I'm Princess Candra, not Queen Erynne."

"It is for Princess Candromeda. Others were sent to the queen and the king."

Well, that's not good. He holds it out for me to read, but I'm too busy getting my daily stabbing. Plus, I'm not much of a reader. That's Riza. She handles all my correspondence. "Read it out to me."

Looking uneasy, he breaks the wax seal and unfolds the thick parchment, scanning the contents. My arm burns and pinches with the influx of medicine into my veins, then, finally, it stops. My nurse presses a towel on my arm to slow the bleeding.

At least we're done for today, I think to myself.

"To Princess Meryliese's family," the messenger begins, reading my letter. "The esteemed princess set sail upon the *Northern Light* as was commanded by King Lionel last month. Her destination was the Tower of Balance, so she might fulfill her duty to her people now that the Golden Moon will rise soon. I regret to inform you that the *Northern Light* ran into a sandbar—" he chokes on the words.

Riza gasps; my nurse goes still.

"And," the messenger starts again slowly. "The hull of the good ship was destroyed. There were no survivors. Please inform the king that we await news of the Vestalin line and advice as to whom shall take Royal Offering Meryliese's place. Yours sincerely, the Archbishop of the Alabaster Citadel, First of his Line."

I swallow hard. I'm speechless.

At my side, Riza begins to weep quietly while my nurse rubs a cream that prevents infections into my arm. I have no tears. I don't remember Meryliese. But now, only Erynne and I are left in the line of Vestalin.

And one of us has to be the sacrifice to the tower.

I suddenly want to hide in my closet again.

I hold my hand out for the message. The man hands it over to me, and I stare at the important-looking parchment as if it somehow holds solutions to the very real problem of my sister's death.

I want to feel something for Meryliese, but I don't. I have vague memories of a toddler with ebony curls like Erynne's and bright green eyes. I remember my mother's relief upon hearing that Meryliese wasn't cursed. I remember my mother waving her handkerchief bravely as the Alabaster Citadel sent monks and priestesses to come and take my sister away at the age of two so she could be raised to be the Royal Offering, and I remember Mother crumpling the moment they were out of sight.

She cried for three days. Then, she dried her tears and never cried over it again.

"A Vestalin must always do her duty," she'd told Erynne and me. But her focus was on Erynne as she said the words because I'm cursed and useless. I remember that just like I remember Erynne's brave smile.

Poor Erynne. She's just as trapped in her destiny as Meryliese was. I've been the only one with a modicum of freedom, and it's all because of the curse. It makes it impossible for me to carry on our bloodline. I'm too weak, too fragile for childbirth. With the curse in my blood, I have to eat regular meals and avoid strenuous activity, lest the bad blood go straight to my heart.

My sister Erynne has always been the important one. She spent her childhood preparing to marry a king, while I spent mine trying to avoid my nurses and the inevitable needles. Erynne learned to speak four languages and how to ride a horse. I learned that I get headaches if I sit up too quickly after taking my medicine, and it's best to take a brief nap afterward. Erynne can read and write and draw and sing. I read passably but can barely scrawl my name. No one cares, though, because I'm the cursed one.

At least, no one has cared until *today*. Now that Meryliese is dead, I worry what this means for Erynne and me.

I stare at the letter in my hand and then crumple it and toss it aside. "You said this was delivered to the king and my sister a short time ago?"

"Aye, my lady."

Dragon shite. That means they're going to want to see me soon. I jump up from my chair and instantly get dizzy, the concoction racing through my veins with unbearable heat. Immediately, I sit down again, pressing my fingertips to my brow and breaking into a cold sweat.

"My lady," Nurse chides. "You know you must rest for a few minutes after your medicine."

I nod absently, rubbing my brow. "Riza, I need to change to see the king."

"Something elegant, my lady?"

"No, something garish. Pink, I think. And get the panniers." I hate those things, but they do make quite an entrance. "And the yellow chemise that normally goes under the rust-colored gown. Let's pair the two of those together."

"That is . . . quite a choice, my lady," Riza murmurs.

It's a hideous choice, loud and obnoxious and wholly unbecoming of the Vestalin line, but that's exactly the point. I mean to show the king, in very small, subtle ways, that I'm not right for his plans.

That Meryliese's death means he should call off his war. That no Vestalin is suitable to go to the Tower of Balance, and we'll just have to figure something else out.

"Get my jewelry too," I tell her. "And cosmetics."

I aim to be as unpalatable as possible when I see my dear brother-in-law again, just to remind him once more that Candra Vestalin is a disappointment to all.

That no one can depend on her to serve the gods, and that the entire matter should just be forgotten.

CHAPTER TWO

While I'm not the most diplomatic of princesses, I have to admit that I excel at petty court aggressions. Some people are good with lutes; I'm good at getting under King Lionel's skin.

He's an absolute twat and doesn't deserve to be on the throne, but such is fate.

I flick a hand over my wide, heavily embroidered panniers and adjust the puffy yellow sleeves of my chemise. They poke out between the cuffs like lemony tufts and look garishly bright on such a solemn occasion. Wholly inappropriate and absolutely perfect.

Sitting by the window in my room, I toy with the jewel-encrusted belt at my waist and wait to be summoned.

I don't have to wait too long. The king's official messenger arrives, and I pretend to be very interested in the embroidery upon my cuff as Riza harasses him on my behalf. When she finally lets him in, I feign surprise that the king wishes to see me.

My sister has been married to Lionel for all of a year now, and other than official holidays, when he *has* to see me, Lionel completely avoids my presence. It suits me quite fine, as I loathe the boor.

Gathering my skirts, I follow the herald through the enormous keep. Castle Lios should be a place of enlightenment, learning, and joy like it was in the time of my ancestors. But Lionel has taken to ruling things with an iron fist, and he picks endless fights on the rocky borders of Darkfell. Instead of courtiers and musicians, Lios is filled with tense advisors and soldiers. They give me uneasy looks as I swan through the halls in my garish clothing. It's as if my cheery presence offends their war-leaning sensibilities. Lionel is going to drive this kingdom to ruin; I just know it.

And he will drag us all down with him.

"The Princess Candromeda Vestalin," the herald cries as I enter the throne room.

I feign more surprise to see the throne room full of courtiers and ambassadors. I blow kisses and wave at the gathered men as if they're all here to see me. The men in their armor and war cloaks look less than pleased with my antics, but I don't care. I beam at everyone and then sink into a low, perfect curtsy before the paired thrones on the dais.

When I rise, I glance over at my sister, who sits at King Lionel's side. I shouldn't have looked. Erynne's face is blotchy with tears, her eyes red. She dabs at them with a silk handkerchief that matches her dress, and a woeful expression is on her pretty face. Her other hand caresses her heavily pregnant belly, and I'm stricken with guilt.

Here I am, acting the jester, and my sister is weeping over the loss of our sister. I'm filled with a hint of shame that I don't have the same memories of Meryliese that she does. I was too young to remember much, but Erynne is four years older than me and probably remembers a great deal more.

I bite my lip because a princess shouldn't cry in public. At least Erynne's tears can be blamed on her pregnancy.

"Greetings, my queen," I say sweetly, slowly adding, "and my king."

Lionel's jaw clenches, and I just know he wants to say something unpleasant to me. I brace myself, ready for it. We've gotten into such spats in the past. He thinks he gets the final say in all things, and I think he's a dreadful louse, so we've squabbled in front of courtiers many a time. He can't do anything to me as I'm Erynne's sister, and I clearly have the cursed blood of Vestalin in my veins, but I know he'd love to bring me down a notch if he could.

He glances over at his bride, frustration written on his face.

I dislike Lionel intensely. I dislike his florid face, his blond beard, and the way he laughs loudly so everyone will look over at him. I hate his jovial manner because it's fake, and I hate that he married poor Erynne when Erynne is in love with her maid, Isabella.

And I really hate it when Lionel looks over at me. "Who would have thought plump, silly Candromeda would suddenly become important to the court?" He gives me a scathing smile. "Today truly is a day of precipitous events."

"Why, whatever do you mean?" I ask, fluttering my lashes and feigning ignorance. "What has happened, Your Grace?"

Lionel's eyes narrow on me, and for a moment, he looks just like his father. King Balnor was an unpleasant man with cruel eyes. Lionel has the same aggressive, mean streak his father did, and he's determined to have a glorious war again, just like his father. Which is why we're in the situation we're in. He wants a war with Darkfell, and he won't stop until Lios is fully embroiled in a new conflict.

I keep the dumb smile on my face as I rise to my feet and wait for him to tell me the news.

"As you know, the Golden Moon is rising once more."

I nod. "Praise to the Golden Moon Goddess," I say automatically. The Golden Moon, the symbol of the goddess of chaos, appears in the skies every thirty years and remains for seven long years. During those years, the seas are violent, and the weather is full of madness—a sign that the goddess is unhappy with mankind. She has been unhappy since the First War, when Ravendor Vestalin defeated her champion and established the first kingdom, Lios.

To appease the prickly goddess, when the Golden Moon arises, a Royal Offering of bloodlines from both Lios and Darkfell must both be given to the Tower of Balance. There, the best of both kingdoms' bloodlines must remain for seven years until the Golden Moon Goddess disappears from the skies again. To step foot out of the tower beforehand is to anger the goddess once more.

Meryliese was supposed to be the sacrifice from the bloodline of Vestalin. Our ancestry reaches back to Ravendor, and no other bloodline in Lios is as pure.

The blood of Ravendor runs through our veins, evidenced by our pale skin, dark hair, and green eyes in a kingdom full of ruddy-cheeked, blue-eyed blonds. It's rumored that Princess Ravendor married a warrior of Darkfell, and all descendants of her line have Fellian dark hair and eyes.

Even now, we stand apart from the rest of Lios. My sister Erynne is the swan of the court. She is pale and beautiful, her figure willowy and her manner elegant. Her jet-black hair flows down her back like a waterfall, and jewels gleam among her tresses like stars in the night sky. She is gorgeous and ethereal, a credit to the Vestalin bloodline.

Me . . . well, I am more of a plump sort of hedgehog. But a charming one, I like to think. I'm good with wooing people and winning them to my side. Unless you're Lionel—he can rot in the Gray God's dungeons for all I care. I'm deliberately not charming for *him*.

"If we do not send a sacrifice to the Tower of Balance, the land will be in turmoil," King Lionel continues. "The seas will be impossible to sail. Our ships would be dashed upon the rocks. And the crops that feed the people will be decimated. We must send our sacrifice to the tower within the next three days."

Three days. Three days until the Golden Moon Goddess returns.

I am in such danger. My lungs tighten, and I feel a swell of panic, but I tamp it down.

"I trust in the king to do what is right," I say sweetly, all the while mentally flinging daggers at Lionel's fair head. "You will guide the people properly."

"Your sister, Meryliese, was to be the sacrifice to the Golden Moon Goddess," he says. "Her ship was on the way to the tower and was destroyed. There were no survivors."

His bluntness makes me flinch. I recover quickly and affect a pious expression. "And I shall keep her in my prayers, poor thing. She would say to us if she must give her life, that she should give it in the service of the gods."

"Her death poses a new problem," King Lionel says, drumming his fingers on the arm of his throne. "The last two of the Vestalin bloodline are yourself and my lovely wife."

Then, he puts a hand on Erynne's stomach, deliberately touching her very pregnant belly. He goes silent, clearly waiting for me to speak up.

Fresh tears roll down my sister's face.

And I'm neatly trapped because my sister can bear children, and I cannot. She is keeping the Vestalin bloodline alive, and I am the useless one. She is also heavily pregnant with the heir to the throne.

She cannot go to the tower, and Lionel's hand on her stomach seems to proclaim that, even as he gives me a challenging glare.

Well, if he's expecting me to volunteer myself, he's delusional.

I clear my throat. "It will be difficult, but I am sure the people of Lios will be able to endure seven years of hardship if we prepare." I smile brightly. "It is good they have a strong and mighty king to lead them."

A titter surges through the court, and Lionel's face grows florid with anger. "You would rather have your people suffer than volunteer yourself to the tower?"

He's calling me out in front of the entire court, just as I suspected he would.

But still I feign ignorance. Putting a hand to my breast, I gasp loudly. "My lord, I cannot go. I have the blood sickness. I am *tainted*." I do my best to look helpless and woebegone. "I must be administered medicine daily, and we all know that the one that goes to the tower must go alone."

"Your nurse will teach you how to dose yourself. And the kingdom will supply you with food and drink, so your stay in the tower is a comfortable one."

He leans forward on his throne, clutching its arms and glaring down at me. "If you do not go, the ships waiting to bring our men to the borders of Darkfell will be stranded here. The ships that carry grain to our people from across the sea will be unable to arrive. Cities would starve. Children would go hungry. You would sacrifice all of this for your personal comfort? Are you not the line of the hero? Are you not the blood of Ravendor Vestalin?"

Ugh. I hate his sanctimonious tone. I look at my sister, at her red-rimmed eyes, and I hate the sorrow I see there. She's going to be so disappointed in me, and yet I'm not going to commit myself to such a terrible fate.

Seven years in the tower will be a death sentence for me. Even if I learned how to give myself my medication, I couldn't be away from court for that long. I am the eyes and ears for my sister, hearing rumors that she does not. I am busy too. There are holiday feasts and banquets every month until the next solstice. I cannot go to the tower and miss those.

I am . . . too popular. Yes, that's it. "I can't do it. I'm sorry."

"Very well," King Lionel says, his expression full of remorse. "Then your sister must go."

I gasp in shock. So does Erynne.

That rotting *bastard*.

Lionel would send my pregnant, miserable sister to the tower just so he could have his warships? So he could have the offensive in his silly war against silly Darkfell? Who here at court has even seen a Fellian? They keep to their mountains. Why should we war against them?

I grit my teeth, hating the king with every fiber of my being. I fist my hands against my ridiculous pink skirts, furious. "You cannot send her. She's pregnant with your heir!"

The king affects a grieving expression. "It is true. It would be extremely inconvenient, as my love would have to give birth alone."

Erynne begins to weep.

"But once the child is born," he continues, "she can hand it over to us. It is the Royal Offering that cannot step foot outside while the Golden Moon is in the skies. My child can yet be raised at my side here at court."

Monster. Absolute shite-weasel monster. I hate him.

As if sensing the anger bubbling inside me, King Lionel gives me a pious look. "Understand that it is not my choice, Princess Candromeda. But to protect my people, one of the Vestalin line *must* go. Surely, you understand." He looks over at Erynne and takes her hand, kissing her knuckles. "I will sacrifice my queen if it means I keep my people from harm."

"I will go," Erynne says in a wobbling voice, wiping tears from her eyes with her free hand. "You know I cannot let our people suffer."

Oh, this is *such* dragon shite. I roll my eyes. Does she really expect me to believe that she's going to enter the tower, give birth *alone*, and then hand her baby back out to a nurse?

And that she will let Lionel reign, unchecked, for the next seven years?

I sigh heavily and dramatically because I'm cornered and I hate it. I hate all of them right now. "It seems I have no choice, do I?"

"You do have a choice," the king says in a silky tone, looking down his nose at me. "You can plunge the kingdom into ruin . . . or you can act bravely for once in your life."

Everyone in the throne room stares at me.

I truly do hate that man.

CHAPTER THREE

"Are you watching, my lady? You must learn how to prepare your potion." My nurse sniffles and moves next to the fire, where the pork pancreas and herbs are boiling over the flame.

I'm not watching. In fact, I can barely pay attention. I pace in my room, frustrated and panicked at how trapped I feel.

All day, my chambers have been full of people hastily trying to prepare me for my time in the tower. A court scribe is even creating a book for me to take that will have recipes and instructions on how to make food and build a fire . . . how to make tea. How to mend a hole in a dress.

These are all things I have never done. I'm a noble lady. People do these things for me.

Seamstresses rush into my room with different fabrics, holding them up to my body and then racing away again. They will work all night to create a wardrobe sufficient for my time in the tower. And down below in the courtyard, foodstuffs and fuel are being gathered. Tomorrow, the priest from the Alabaster Citadel will depart with me in a carriage so that we might arrive at the Tower of Balance on time. I must be over the threshold before the Golden Moon arises, and we haven't much time.

My nurse tries to get my attention. "My lady—"

"I know," I growl. "Write it all down. I will do the best I can."

"You have to do it right, else you will get sick and die," she replies tartly and then bursts into tears.

I fight the urge to cry myself and move to her side. I squeeze her hand and let her squeeze mine back. She's just trying to help. "I'm sorry," I say in a low voice. "I'm . . . worried."

She nods. "I would go with you if I could."

But she can't. The supplies I will be given are for me and me alone. Only one from the Vestalin bloodline and one from the Darkfell line of princes can enter the tower. It's tradition.

Dragon-shite tradition, if you ask me. But a lot of things are dragon shite lately.

So, I watch as Nurse goes through the act of making the potion again. She has three vials of it already prepared for me, but I need to learn how to make this on my own. I need to figure out how long I must boil the dried pancreas of a pig and how much fenugreek and water to add. I must learn how long to let it cool and how to boil my needles in hot water so I do not get sick. It is all so overwhelming that the knot in my throat seems permanently lodged there.

I'll manage, though. I always manage. Somehow.

There's a knock at the door as Nurse shows me the process for the seventh time. Riza comes rushing toward me, her eyes wide. "Lord Balon from Greenmoor. He wishes to speak to you before you go."

Hmm. Lord Balon has been at court for the last several weeks, flirting with me. He's made it very clear that he's interested in a Vestalin bride, even if I cannot have children. While I'm not in love with him, it's flattering to be courted.

Flattering and slightly annoying that he's showing up now. Does he expect me to ease his fears while my life is being destroyed? Or is he here to tell me he's going to wait the seven years while I'm in the tower? Highly, highly unlikely.

"Let Lord Balon in," I tell Riza. "But he must be quick; there is much for me to do tonight."

I watch as another maid packs away one of my favorite dresses and try not to wince at how wrinkled it will be when it's pulled from the trunks. Then again, I suppose it doesn't matter. No one's going to be there to see my dresses, wrinkled or otherwise.

I fight back the urge to cry yet again. I can't cry. Someone will tell King Lionel, and I'll be damned if I give that man the satisfaction of knowing I'm utterly miserable.

I put on my best smile and rise from my chair, holding my hands out to greet Lord Balon.

The young lordling rushes in, looking as dashing as ever. He loves bright, loud clothing in the latest fashions—something we've discussed for long stretches by the fire. He's a pretty thing too, with bright eyes and golden locks of hair that brush against his embroidered collar.

"My dear, sweet lady," he says, taking my hands in his gloved ones. There's an expression of distress on his face. "I've just heard the news. Tell me it's not true!"

"I'm afraid it is," I say gently. "My sister Meryliese has gone to the gods, and no one can take her place but me."

I bite back all my bitter, angry words. They're useless now. If I don't go into that tower, they'll force Erynne in my stead. It's clear Lionel has no love for her, and if there's one thing I've loved in my vain, selfish life, it's my sister.

I won't send her in my stead, not with her pregnant and wearing the queen's crown. She can do more good here than there, and I hope she can stop Lionel's stupid war before it starts.

Balon's lower lip trembles, and for a moment, he looks incredibly young. I'd forgotten in our flirting that he's five years younger than me. Nineteen is perfectly fine for a flirtation and the occasional bed romp, even some fun—but I'm twenty-four.

I'll be thirty-one when I'm allowed to leave the tower. It's a sobering thought, and it makes me feel old.

"I will speak to the king," Balon insists. "I will tell him he cannot send you. That we are to be betrothed."

"It will do no good." I shake my head and give his hands a tender squeeze. "I appreciate the sentiment, but a betrothal will not save me from my fate. The king means to have his war, and for his ships to sail, I must enter the tower."

"Then we shall wed tonight," he says fiercely, a determined look upon his young, pretty face. "And I will wait for your return."

I manage not to grimace at his words. So, it's not about me, then. It's about marrying my name and my fortune. Of course, it is.

"You will find another lady to love, my lord," I say, keeping my tone as sweet and gracious as I can as I slip my hands from his grip. "But I will make no impulsive actions before entering the tower. You are young. Surely, you will find someone else to wed."

"Yes, but she will not be a Vestalin."

Well, at least he's not hiding his ambitions. I turn back to my nurse and do my best to look busy. "I do this for the good of the kingdom, Balon. If you are yet unwed when I emerge from the tower, seek me out. I will still be a Vestalin then."

He brightens. "Why, you're right." Snagging my hand, he presses a smacking kiss upon it and beams at me. "In seven years then, my sweet lady."

When he leaves, Riza gives me a disgruntled look. "Why do you always flirt with the stupid ones, my lady?"

I sigh. "Because they're usually the prettiest ones. I don't like a man who's too smart. You can't trust them."

"Do you think he'll truly wait for you?" Riza asks.

I shrug. I'm not going to think about that right now. The thought of all those long, boring days trapped in the tower ahead of me is far too much for me to dwell upon. "I'm going to take it one day at a time."

And pray to all three gods tonight that they free me from my impending doom.

I go to bed late after more sessions with Nurse and a few more fittings with the dressmakers. All of my gowns have to be modified to be laced in the front since no one will be there to help me with my sleeves or corsets.

I collapse in bed, only to be woken up by a candle hovering over me, illuminating my sister's beautiful face.

"Wake up," Erynne tells me.

I sit up, completely alert. "Are we escaping?" I ask, a flutter of excitement in my belly.

Are we fleeing King Lionel, then? It's an utterly selfish move because it will doom Lionel's fleet of ships . . . and it will also destroy the crops for the next several years and make food difficult for all.

Yet, if Erynne wants to run, I'll gladly go with her.

My sister shakes her head and hands her candle off to Isabella, who hovers nearby. "No, I'm afraid not. I cannot leave." She gestures at her belly. "Not when I carry the heir to the kingdom."

I collapse back on the bed again and pull a pillow over my face, disappointed. "Then go away. We'll say our good-byes in the morning."

My sister's guilt is likely eating at her, but I don't want to spend my last night in my own bed comforting her.

"We need to talk," Erynne tells me, sitting on the edge of the bed. "And it must be now while Lionel is in with his war councilors."

Groaning, I sit up and give my sister a petulant glance. It's hard not to be a tiny bit resentful of Erynne sometimes. I'm the plump, less pretty one, with a wide smile and one tooth that's slightly twisted and makes me look as if I'm smirking all the time.

Erynne is incredibly beautiful, with a perfect, slender figure. She is clever and talented, and she has the good blood. And the throne. And a baby.

True, she had to marry Lionel for some of those things, but I can still be petty in the middle of the night.

"You have to think about the future, Candra. Promise me that if they take you to the tower, you're not going to run away. That if you cross the threshold, you're going to stay there. If you forsake your duty at the last moment, all of us will suffer."

Did she come here to chide me? I'm not going to let our people starve just because of me—no matter how much I like the thought of getting on the back of a horse and riding away from all my problems. Or how panicked it'd make King Lionel.

His fastest ships are waiting at the harbor for a fair wind, but if the Golden Moon isn't given its sacrifice, the ships will be destroyed, driven against the rocks by the wild winds, and there will be no war with Darkfell.

I like that idea quite a bit . . . except I can't ride a horse.

But other than that, I've thought about it a great many times. All day today, in fact. But of course, I can't do it.

"I'm not going to run away," I say, bitter. "Where would I go? To Darkfell?" I snort at the absurd idea. "They will impale me on a stake in front of their great stone doors as a warning to all Liosians who venture near. I am *trapped*, Erynne. If I go to the tower, my life is over." I spread my hands helplessly. "And if I don't go to the tower, my life is still over. Lionel will make sure of that."

Her eyes glitter with tears. "I know, sister. I know. Which is why you must promise me that you'll go."

"I'll go." I sound as defeated as I feel. "Don't worry. I will take Meryliese's place."

"A shipwreck," Erynne says, fussing with my covers as tears fall down her cheeks. "I cannot believe a shipwreck is taking you away from me, just when I need you the most. Do you know how difficult it is to be queen? To be *his* queen? And with the baby . . . " Her words choke off.

I reach out and rub her arm. "I know. But you'll have Isabella with you. And Riza. She's trustworthy. Please find a place for her with your staff. And Nurse too." I touch her belly briefly. "Nurse would love to take care of this little one for you."

Erynne gives me a faint smile through her tears. "Here I thought to comfort you, and you're comforting me."

"Well, I'll have seven years to weep into my pillow," I say brightly. "So, I'm saving it up. It'll give me something to do in the tower."

She makes another choked sound and then flings her arms around my neck. "I'm going to miss you so much."

Even though I'm trying to be strong, it's hard not to cry as my sister sobs against my shoulder. I hug her tightly, breathing in her scent. It's going to be the last time I get to hug her for seven long years, and we'll both be different people when I come out. Seven years of my life are being stolen away from me for Lionel's war, and I'm so bitter about it that I want to spit . . . except a princess doesn't spit.

So, I just hug Erynne and try not to think about the future. *One day at a time,* I remind myself. *Or you'll collapse before you ever make it to the tower.* "I'm going to miss you too. So much. But you'll have your baby soon. Every time you think of me, just hug her."

"But I'm going to be the last Vestalin," she chokes, hugging me tighter.

My belly clenches. "I'm not *dying,* Erynne. I'm just getting shut away for seven years."

"Right. Of course. I'm sorry." My sister pulls back, and the expression on her face is grave as she studies me. "I brought you something, but you must tell no one you have it."

Well, this sounds properly ominous. "What is it?"

I'm not sure what to expect from my sister. Erynne has always been the dutiful one, the one who is good and sweet and follows the rules. I'm the one who got caught losing her virginity in the chapel with one of the court knights. I'm the one who falls asleep during Lionel's speeches and gets in trouble for embroidering moustaches onto all the important historical tapestries.

What could Erynne possibly give me? A dirty book? A key so I can let myself out? I'm more than a little perturbed when she produces a knife and holds it out to me.

"You want me to kill myself the moment I get into the tower?" I ask, blank with surprise.

"No," she hisses, grabbing my hand and forcing me to take the sheathed weapon from hers. "This is to protect you, Candra. Use your head."

"I would, but right now it's filled with all the recipes Riza has been trying to teach me in the past day," I joke halfheartedly. "What am I supposed to do with a knife? Is it for cooking?"

Erynne gives me an exasperated look. "Don't be dense, Candra."

"I'm not being dense. You're the one giving me a knife!"

"Look." She closes my fingers around it and pushes it toward me. "You're going to be trapped in that tower with someone from the Darkfell bloodline. You must defend yourself if they try anything."

My mouth goes dry, and I stare down at the little knife in horror. There's been so much going on that I haven't given much thought to the fact I'm going to be trapped in a tower for the next seven years with someone whose kingdom has sworn to destroy ours. Someone who Lionel will be declaring war against the moment I step foot inside the tower.

Suddenly, a knife no longer seems like a silly gift. I clutch it tightly to my chest. The hilt can't be more than the length of my finger, and the blade is small and slightly curved.

"It's rather small for a murder weapon," I say.

"You'll be locked in the tower," Erynne says. "Figure out some poisons if you like, and rub them on the blade." The look on her face is intense. "This is the dagger mother gave me on her deathbed. It's infused with magic."

My jaw drops. "Magic?"

Also, I'm hurt that our mother gave Erynne a secret gift as she lay dying. All I got was a pat on the hand and instructions to "be good." I wonder what else has gone on behind my back.

Erynne nods. "The magic of the gods is bound to this blade. It can answer true or false questions. When the answer is true, the knife will shiver in your hand. False, and it will have no response."

That sounds strange. I flip the sheathed weapon over in my hand, eyeing it. It seems rather plain for a magical weapon. "And are you magical, blade?"

The thing positively *shivers*.

I yelp and drop it on the bed. For a moment, it felt alive.

Erynne picks it up again and holds it out to me. "I can't be with you in the tower, but you can ask it questions about us back here. And you can ask it to give you advice about the other person in the tower with you. You might have to take drastic action, Candra. I know you joke that you're a weak thing, but you're strong, and you're determined."

I swallow hard, wishing I felt as brave as she imagines me.

The look in her eyes is fervent as she leans in. "Both you and the Fellian must step across the threshold of the tower, and no one can enter or leave for seven years. But nothing says the both of you must be alive the entire time. Remember the stories of Old Eliza?"

Wordlessly, I take the knife from her again. I do remember.

Old Eliza was of the Vestalin bloodline and served the tower two hundred years ago. She went in at the age of ninety, and after seven years, she did not come out. They went in to find her and found a skeleton lying in bed, hands politely folded over her breast. She had died of old age.

Yet the kingdom had seen prosperity because Eliza had never stepped foot outside the tower.

"So, you're saying I should go to the tower, murder the Darkfell sacrifice, and sit with the body for the next seven years?"

"If it'll keep you alive." Erynne's gaze is hard. "Then, yes. That is exactly what you should do."

I shake my head, horrified at her suggestion. "I'm not a murderer."

"Then you have two days to learn to become one," my sister, the queen, says. "Because after you go into the tower, Lionel's ships are going to sail for Darkfell. And if their Royal Offering has a way to get information from the outside, they might come seeking revenge on you. Seven years is a very long time to be locked away with the enemy."

Staring down at the knife in my hands, I clasp it to my breast and nod.

I hate this. I hate all of it, and the situation seems to be getting worse by the moment. At least my sister wants me to go in prepared for anything.

If it's as bad as she says it is, I might have to strike first, and the thought sends fear racing through me.

CHAPTER FOUR

I'm awoken before dawn the next morning and dressed in a traveling gown. The court is not there to see me off because my journey to the tower must be made in secret, lest we run into Darkfell assassins or even brigands from our own country.

My sister and the king are there to wish me a safe journey, but the goodbye is a tepid one. We hugged and wept last night (or at least, Erynne did). Today, she only touches my hands briefly and gives me words of encouragement for the sacrifice I am making for the kingdom.

Lionel only says, "Go with the gods."

I wish utter disaster upon him. Not Erynne, just Lionel. But I smile sweetly and curtsy because my sister is married to him, and she's trapped just as much as I am.

Then, I'm loaded into a carriage at the head of our caravan, the escort from the Alabaster Citadel riding atop a white steed beside my coach. We move slowly along the coast with trunks of dresses and foodstuffs packed into the wagons behind my carriage, all of which are guarded by the king's military retinue and finest knights.

The journey is faster by sea, but of course, we won't be going that route until it's no longer avoidable.

I think of Meryliese and the terrible shipwreck, and I can't imagine what must have happened. Did she drown? Or was she crushed when the ship was destroyed? Or did the monsters of the sea finish her off? Her body was never found, so I assume any number of horrible fates.

I gaze out the window at the blue waters, trying to absorb every bit of the outdoors and fresh air. I'm told the tower has no windows and that I must be careful with the candles packed for me because they have to last an entire year.

Every summer, the Gray Moon disappears for a day, and then we mortals are without any gods to watch over us. On that day, new supplies will be brought to me so I can continue to live on in comfort at the tower. They will give me no reason to leave.

Not that I *can* leave, of course. The door will be bricked up behind me, and I will be sealed inside. Just thinking about it makes a panicky knot form in my throat.

I stare at the coast, willing something to happen. For the gods to step in. For a monster to rise from the shadowy depths of the waters and knock the tower into the sea.

I give myself a vial of prepared medicine, feeling faint at the sight of the needle entering my arm. I want to throw up, but I force it back, shoving down the plunger on the syringe as quickly as I can. My head swims as the carriage rocks back and forth, dragging me onward to my doom.

We travel through the night, and I do my best to sleep despite the continual jostling motion.

"Will I be saved from my fate?" I ask the dagger, trying it out.

Nothing happens. There's no resultant shiver. I frown and shove it into my bodice, tucking the sheath into my cleavage. Stupid knife. Erynne probably just gave it to me to make me feel better.

The thing shivers between my breasts, and I clutch the front of my bodice. Okay, so the knife can pick up my thoughts. Good to know. Certainly not unnerving at all.

The hated tower comes into sight the next morning, just shortly after dawn. It rises large and menacing over the crystalline blue waters of the sea, like a hand reaching toward the heavens. It's situated on a tiny island where nothing else dwells.

The reality of my fate sinks in, and my breaths become frantic and shallow as I stare out at the spire that blots the horizon. Soon, we'll board a ferry and make our way to the island, where we'll meet the contingent from Darkfell, and the ceremony will begin.

Is it too late to escape?

The knife between my breasts shivers, and I choke back a sob. I won't cry now. I'll cry when I'm locked in the tower.

—

Years of court intrigue have enabled me to keep a cool demeanor as we make it to the edge of Lios's lands. For as long as I can see, the waters along the shore are empty and calm, gently brushing against the tall cliffs.

I know that just to the north, though, the beaches are covered with ships being loaded with supplies; armored men practice drills, and sailors ready the sails for the upcoming departure.

They're all waiting for me. The moment I cross the threshold of the Tower of Balance, the war will begin.

But for now, all is peaceful, and I enjoy the sight of the beaches, as this is the last day I will spend outside for the next seven years.

I watch in silence as a nearby ferry is loaded with my trunks and cask after cask of dried foodstuffs. I have a list that Riza made of all the things they have brought for me, along with meal suggestions to make my supplies last.

She's truly tried to make this easy on me, and I should be grateful. I know she's as anxious as I am because she loves me, but right now, she's with my sister back at Castle Lios, and I'm staring down the Tower of Balance, a spindly, menacing finger on the horizon.

It's hard to feel grateful for anything right now.

When the ferry is finally loaded, one of the knights helps me onto it. I'm immediately surrounded by guards and kept carefully in the middle of the raft. I suppose so I can't fling myself into the waters. Several men take their places at the sides of the flatboat and pole it across the shallow, wide waters of the channel.

The Tower of Balance rises before us, menacing and dark.

I thought it would look more like the Alabaster Citadel, which is made entirely of pale brick and marble. It has gilt edges on all the windows and stained glass everywhere. The Alabaster Citadel is a square, solid building of beauty that priests from other countries flock to in order to pay their respects.

Or I thought perhaps the Tower of Balance would be like Lios Castle: old and stately, with large, rounded turrets, a heavy wall surrounding the keep, and an austere interior covered in banners—made important by the presence of the royal family and their retinue.

Nope. This tower is positively ominous. It rises up, thick and twisting, with no windows or visible brick. Four spaced out, tall battlements protrude from the squared-off top of the tower, and it makes it look as if the tower itself is trying to claw the Golden Moon from the skies.

I hate it. Of course, I do. But I keep myself composed. I'll have seven years inside to crumble and fall apart at my leisure. For now, I have to be a Vestalin and bring honor to myself and my sister.

Honor is *really* annoying me at the moment, though. I'd much rather be a craven coward. At least then, I'd be a coward in the sunlight.

I squint up at the tower, trying to figure out how many rooms it must have. Funny how all the legends say nothing about the living quarters inside the tower itself. Most don't care, I suppose, as they'll never live here.

Lucky me.

I put a hand to my eyes, shielding them from the sunlight I will dearly miss, and I try to decipher the tower as we slowly pole our way across the waters. The base looks much wider the closer we get, and I suspect it could have several rooms on each floor indeed. It's surprisingly huge, with only a tiny bit of beach skirting it and nothing else on the island, not even a tree.

Not that trees matter since we aren't supposed to go outside, but it's just an odd structure. Legend says that the gods themselves pulled it from the ground, and I always thought that was rubbish. Now, looking up at the massive column rising up to the skies, I'm not so sure.

The moment our raft touches shore, I suck in a breath. The men file off immediately, causing the raft to bob. Then, one of the knights offers me his hand. I take it, letting him guide me out to shore.

Once I touch land, my shoes sink into the sand. For a moment, everyone seems to forget about me. The men are busy loading a sled with my trunks so that it can be pulled to the entrance. The priests accompanying me to recite the ritual over my "sacrifice" are busy praying, and I'm left to my own devices.

The wind rips at my skirts as I walk up and down our small strip of shore. I get bored watching the men load my things, so I turn and head down the beach. There's a large, square door in the base of the tower made of heavy wood and covered with swirling iron reinforcements. Nearby is a pile of bricks, and one of the men is mixing what looks like cement.

My tongue glues itself to the roof of my mouth once I realize he's going to brick the door after I'm inside, so I can't get out. Nausea surges in my throat. *Breathe,* I remind myself. *Breathe. Be dignified. You can have a breakdown once you're inside and no one else can see.*

I straighten my spine and keep walking, and as I do, I see them: strange figures stand on the far shore. They've come from the opposite direction we have, and while I stand out in the sunlight with my hair loose and my gown swirling around my legs, they're heavily cloaked in dark colors, hoods pulled over their faces.

They look like ominous specters looming in the lone shadow of the tower.

Darkfell.

For a moment, I panic, and then I remember why they're here. Of course. Their sacrifice must be given to the tower as well. I scan the large, broad-shouldered figures, trying to see if I can make out which is the person who will be their sacrifice, but it's impossible to tell.

One of the figures pauses, then turns toward me, and catlike green eyes gleam under the darkened hood.

With a terrified squeak, I turn and head back toward my people. I remember Erynne's words. *After you go into the tower, Lionel's ships are going to sail for Darkfell. And if their person has a way to get information from the outside, they might come seeking revenge on you.*

Do they know Lionel and his army are waiting to sail even now? Biting my lip, I head back to my group, where the knights stand on shore, watching everything with bored expressions. Part of me wants to tell them that I just saw Darkfell's people, but it seems like a foolish thing to report.

Of course, I saw them. They're here to deliver their Royal Offering to the tower just as we are.

The massive sled is finally loaded, and several men take it by the rope and drag it toward the main door. I follow behind them, frowning at the mountain of crates and barrels loaded atop it.

"You do know I won't be able to pull that into the tower on my own?"

The knight next to me considers, rubbing his bearded chin. "We'll get it up to the door and push it through. Once it's inside, you can unload it slowly at your leisure. Unless you'd like to leave some of this behind?"

"No, I want it all," I reply, trying not to scowl.

I guess I won't have much to do except unload things. The trunks will be heavy, though. Maybe my room isn't at the top of the tower. Has no one ever thought about the logistics of this? It's simply ridiculous. My maids packed me dozens of dresses, as that's what's required in court, but standing here on the beach, I'm tired just looking at the sheer mass of trunks that I'll have to put away.

That's a problem for another day, though.

I watch in silence as the heavily loaded sled is brought to the hefty double doors. They're pulled open with a mighty creak, and the interior of the tower is pitch black. I can see nothing inside. It's like a tomb.

I look around for the Darkfell party, but I don't see them on the beach. Perhaps they've already come and gone, and their sacrifice waits within. I touch the bodice of my dress where my knife is hidden, glad that Erynne sent it with me. She's far more suited for this sort of thing than me.

I'm the court flirt, not the one to handle intrigue, and I'm certainly not pious like Meryliese must have been.

The priests begin their songs to the Golden Moon Goddess, and I know I should pay attention. Instead, I watch, fascinated, as the workmen shove my sled up to the door and then push it deep inside with a loud scrape upon the stone floors.

One of them pushes too hard, and his hand disappears after the sled, swallowed up by the shadows. He immediately cries out in distress and pulls back, clutching his hand to his chest. "It burns!"

"Don't be ridiculous," the knight accompanying me snaps. He casts me an uneasy look. "It's just shadow."

I say nothing. The priests continue on with their prayers, burning incense to the goddess, and as I watch, an acolyte sacrifices a bird, pulling it from a cage and cutting it open from breast to tail. The blood carries in the wind, flecking the face of the knight at my side as if reminding me what horrors await me inside.

"Come, my princess," he says, taking me gently by the elbow. "It's time."

Now? Already?

"Surely the priests have more prayers," I babble, trying to pull free from his grasp. I'm not ready yet. The sun hasn't gone down, and that means the

Golden Moon has a few hours before it rises. I have time, don't I? "I'm sure they have yet another song to sing."

"My princess," the knight says again, his voice kind. "Do not make me carry you."

Dragon shite. Panicked, I let him pull me forward, casting another mute look of distress at the priests.

They give me pitying looks, their gazes straying up to the tower. We move toward the yawning darkness of those double doors, and even the wind seems to die in anticipation of my entombment.

"Please," I whisper to the knight. "Please don't make me go."

"I must," he says. "The king wishes for me to ensure that you are placed safely inside."

Lionel knows I want to run. A hot bubble of panic rises in my throat as we pass by the man seated next to the bricks, waiting to seal the door behind me.

"Please," I say again as we move to the threshold. I grab the doorjamb and try to brace myself. "Please don't do this. I can escape. No one has to know—"

The knight pries my hand off the frame of the door and shoves me inside. Hard. I tumble to the floor next to the heavy sled of trunks, and before I can sit up, the double doors creak closed behind me.

"Bar it," the knight calls out to his men. Then to me, "We will be here in one year with more food and supplies for you, Princess Candromeda. Thank you for your sacrifice."

I sit in the darkness, too numb to even cry. I've been telling myself for days that it'll be all right to cry once the doors are closed and I'm trapped. But now that I'm here, I feel empty inside. Blank.

I stare at the tiny line of sunlight under the doors, listening as the bricks are laid in place, scrape after scrape. Two hundred years ago, the Vestalin woman was pulled from the tower by her lover, who couldn't bear to be apart from her. The goddess's wrath was immediate—raging storms covered the land, followed by intense droughts. The famine was so great that half the kingdom died of starvation. The man's family was hanged—down to even the tiniest of children—as an example to others. The doors to the tower have been bricked up ever since.

Soon, that last bit of sunlight disappears from my sight. It's pitch black inside the tower, and I'm utterly alone. I don't even know where my candles are or where my medicine is.

Or where my enemy is . . . only that they're somewhere in this tower with me.

CHAPTER FIVE

Trapped.

It still hasn't entirely sunk in. I listen to the men bricking the door up behind me to ensure that I won't abandon my post as the sacrifice to the goddess.

If I panic and flee the tower, I doom the war fleet, and I doom the crops for the next seven years. It's vital that I stay where I am. That I do my duty to my people.

Seven years of this.

I can come out when I'm thirty-one.

Yay.

The noise of the bricks being smacked into the mortar echoes inside me. I lean against the sled full of trunks, and it's so heavy that it doesn't budge. I pull myself atop one of the trunks, settling my skirts in the darkness and listening.

It's only when silence greets me that I realize the noise of the bricklaying has stopped. They're done. I'm truly bricked up inside this tower. I'm to spend seven years in this darkness, with nothing and no one. I could be alive or dead, and they won't know until they arrive to bring me fresh supplies next year.

My chest becomes tight.

I jerk to my feet, panting and clawing at my bodice.

I can't breathe.

I can't draw a deep breath, and I desperately need one.

Gasping, I tear at the laces that go up the front of my bodice in such an ugly (but practical) manner until my breasts bounce free, and the entire corset loosens with a rush, my knife clattering to the floor.

I lean against the trunk, sucking in deep breath after deep breath in the darkness.

I can't do this. I can't.

I surge forward, feeling around in the absolute darkness for the wooden doors. My trembling hands hit stone first, and I move along the cold wall until I find the wood of the doors. It takes me only a moment to locate the handle so I can tug on it.

But the doors don't budge. They don't even groan. It's as if they're completely and utterly locked in place.

The anxious knot returns to my throat, and for a moment, I feel as if I'm going to vomit. Or cry. Or both. I give the door another tug, harder this time, but it's useless. With a moan, I press my brow to the wood, collapsing against it.

You can break down later, I tell myself. *I know you want to cry, but you can do that after you pull yourself together. Find your medicine. Light a candle. Get to your room, where it's safe. There's too much to do, and no one is going to help you.*

Right. Okay.

Taking a deep breath, I turn around—and scream.

Two gleaming, shining, *evil* green eyes gaze out from the darkness across the room. The Fellian. The one I need to kill before she kills me.

And she can see in the dark.

Dragon shite.

"Stay away," I cry out in a trembling voice. "Leave me alone!"

I drop to the floor, feeling for Erynne's knife. How could I be so careless as to abandon my only weapon moments after I entered the tower? I'm an idiot.

To my relief, I find the knife quickly and jerk it from its sheath, holding it aloft in the pitch black around me. I look up, searching for the eerie, green eyes, but they're gone. Heart pounding, I stand and peer into the darkness, listening for sounds, but I think I'm alone again. There's no sound but that of my pulse.

With a relieved little sigh, I clutch the knife close. "Am I alone now?" I whisper.

The blade shivers.

"Is she going to kill me?"

There's no response, but at the same time, the air feels pregnant, as if there's a question unanswered.

"Are you sure?" I ask the knife.

No answer. Hmm. That's not a good sign. Either I'm asking the wrong thing, or the knife isn't as omniscient as I thought.

One problem at a time. I need to find my quarters and get situated. I need to make my medicine too. Already, I'm feeling weak and a little sweaty, a sign that I need my dose and that I'll need to eat something to settle my stomach afterward. I know Riza prepared a bag for me for today. I just need to find it.

I run my hand over the mountain of trunks, but finding where anything is stashed feels monumental. Luckily, I have help.

I touch one trunk. "Is there a candle in here?"

Silence from my knife.

"Here?" I touch the next trunk and wait.

It takes four more trunks before I get a positive response. Finally, I haul out the one in question, which just so happens to be underneath a large, heavy garment bag full of my petticoats.

I drag the trunk to the floor and fumble with the latches, pulling it open. I'm relieved when I feel around inside and find a bag of thick candle tapers, a wrapped pair of strikers, and a tinderbox. I clumsily scrape the strikers against each other.

I've never done this before without Riza's supervision, and I all but laugh with relief when I get a spark. When I finally get a candle lit, it feels like a major accomplishment.

Relieved, I settle the candle into a chamberstick holder and bring it aloft, looking around. The main floor of the tower here is huge, the ceiling high above in the darkness. All the sounds I make echo, which tells me it's larger than I expected.

At least I'll have room to move about, I think to myself. I set the candle atop one of the trunks and get to my feet, brushing off my skirt . . .

. . . and I realize my bodice is gaping open, my breasts hanging out. *Whoops.* I quickly stuff them back into place, doing the laces up loosely. After all, no one's here to see me.

Except for the Fellian, I remind myself.

That makes me lace a little tighter because they saw me with my tits out, and the realization is a vulnerable one. I grip my knife tightly and pick up my candle again.

Time to explore my new home. Somewhere out there is the Fellian, but maybe she's just as rattled as I am. Maybe she wants to be left alone too. If this room is any indication, there's plenty of space in this tower for both of us.

I move around the bottom of the tower. There is a large staircase off to one side that goes up and another across from it, going down. Along the wall of the staircase going up are a few old tapestries depicting religious scenes, and along the opposite wall, across from the stairs, is an altar to the three gods, each one depicted in an old-fashioned-looking triptych. There's a scatter of ancient, faded rose petals on the altar, along with a gutted candle.

"You'll forgive me if I don't feel much like praying at the moment," I tell the altar.

If anything, I have the urge to make a crude gesture at the goddess, but that won't win me any favors, either, so I tamp it down and continue on.

I expect to see a lot of dust and cobwebs everywhere, but there's nothing. Maybe someone came in and cleaned this place up for us, but I highly doubt that. Perhaps it's been magically cleaned? Is there even such a thing? I have no idea.

I head downstairs first, and it looks like a kitchen below. I see a large fireplace and hearth set into a wall. There's no wood, of course, and I have a momentary bout of panic as I realize I've got no wood with which to cook my food. How is it that we packed everything but wood?

Then, I think about the trunks and the huge sled and realize I've got that covered. I'll just have to be judicious with how much I use.

That's something to worry over tomorrow.

The hearth is scraped clean of ash and has clearly not been used in a long time. I step inside it and hold my candle up, trying to see if there's daylight at the other end of the chimney. Maybe I can crawl up it and climb my way out of the tower if I get desperate enough.

There's a small hole of sunlight at the top. A very, very small hole. Either this chimney goes up a very long way, all the way up to the battlements. Or it's a tight squeeze. Either way, it's no good to me.

Disappointed, I explore the rest of the kitchen. There are pots and pans, but all of them are battered and ancient looking. I wonder if prior residents left them here over the ages. There's a spice rack and some dried leaves hanging up, but when I touch one, it crumbles to dust.

I find an old root cellar with a few shriveled roots that are probably older than my ancestors, but there's no food other than that. For water, there's a well pump over a large sink, and when I prime the pump like Riza showed me, the thing groans, and a trickle of water comes out.

I won't die of thirst, at least.

I eye the largest copper tub in one corner of the kitchen, and I suspect that's where all the bathing is done. Ugh. At the palace, servants brought hot water up to a tub in my room and poured it out for me when I was done.

I'm realizing the enormity of everything I'll have to do here. Even the simplest of tasks will be daunting.

Cry about it tomorrow, I remind myself. *Keep going—one foot in front of the other.*

I head back upstairs with my candle, and this time I go up the other staircase. This one curves around the steps. It's narrow and tall, hugging the interior wall of the tower.

There are a few more narrow tapestries here, but they're so faded and gray that I can't tell what I'm supposed to be looking at. I count forty steps before I come to a landing, and, panting, I pause at the top to look around.

On the first landing, there's a large wooden door similar to the exterior door and two smaller ones further down the curving hall. After a momentary exploration, I pause in front of the largest door. Is this where the Fellian is? Or is this my room? Or something else?

I'll never know unless I open the door, I reason with myself. And, with a burst of bravery, I push the door open.

It's dark inside, my candle flickering with the breeze the door creates. I hold my light outward, and then the green eyes blink into existence. Before I can suck in a breath, someone hisses at me.

"This chamber is *mine*."

My lips part. I gape in shock and nearly drop my candle.

That is not a woman's voice. It's deep and rich and very, very *angry*.

For a brief moment, I'm terrified.

Fear quickly gives way to indignation, and I draw myself up straight. What kind of fools sent me to live seven years in a locked tower with a grown man? An enemy man? Are they not concerned with my virtue?

I mean, I'm not, but that doesn't mean others shouldn't be.

"Excuse you," I snap back at him. "I live here now too. I'm trying to find out where my quarters will be, so don't get snippy with me."

"It's not in here," he snarls, nothing but a pair of glittering, unholy eyes in the darkness. "You can have the next floor. This one is mine."

"Fine," I retort. With a withering glare, I toss my head and march down the hall.

It's only when the door slams shut again that I can breathe. I inhale a lungful of air as tremors race through me. Fellians are devils. Worse than devils. And I'm trapped in here with a male one.

I've been trying not to think about Erynne's warning but knowing that my companion is an adult man changes things. I might have to kill him after all.

I find the stairwell for the next floor and head up another forty stairs. By the time I make it to the top, I'm dizzy and nauseated, which reminds me that I need to take my medicine soon. The thought of returning down the stairs and digging through all those trunks is daunting, though, and since I'm already up here, I figure I might as well have a look around.

There are three doors on "my" floor, and it seems to be laid out the same as the last one. I open the heavy wooden door, and this time, I'm not greeted by an angry Fellian. This time, all is silent, and I step inside what must be my bedroom.

There's a fireplace, but it's a small one, and there's no way I'll be able to climb up the chimney here. An old, narrow rope bed is against one wall, but there's no bedtick, and I don't know if I have one packed. There's a small wooden table off to the side and a faded gray tapestry hanging on one wall, and . . . that's it.

I think of my opulent quarters back at the palace, with the thick rugs on the floor and my oversized canopied bed. I think of the large window that overlooked the gardens and my attached bathing chamber, and my jaw clenches tight.

Wordlessly, I go to the next room: a garderobe. It's not much more than a creaky wooden seat with a hole cut into it so the waste can splash down . . . somewhere.

And the third door on this floor is a small storage closet, with a couple of old empty trunks left from prior inhabitants and a few discarded pieces of ancient, outdated clothing.

I head upstairs, and the final floor of the tower seems to be nothing but storage for old, broken things. There's a rotting trunk, what looks like scattered armor, a few wooden candelabras, a table with a broken leg, and a book that looks like it might fall apart if I touch it.

Junk. Nothing but junk.

For someone who's supposed to be serving the goddess for the next seven years, this tower isn't exactly welcoming. It's not comfortable. It's got the bare minimum of necessities. And it has far too many stairs for a gently-bred princess with a blood curse.

Already, I'm exhausted, and I haven't eaten, haven't unpacked, and certainly haven't taken my medicine.

I return to my quarters on the floor below. I stare at the rope bed for a long moment, and then, fighting fatigue and helplessness, I set the candle on the table nearby and climb into the bed. The ropes dig into my skin uncomfortably, but I'm too tired and disheartened to care. I close my eyes and curl up as best I can.

Tomorrow, I'll have a good cry about all of this. Once I have everything put away, I'll allow myself to break down.

CHAPTER SIX

I wake up in the darkness to a sour stomach and the uncomfortable watering of my mouth. Oh no. Weak and shaking, I barely manage to crawl out of the rope bed before I vomit all over the stone floor.

Stupid. Stupid. Stupid.

I know better than to skip my medicine. The shaking and sour stomach come first. If I ignore those symptoms, I'll get weak, and my heart will race uncontrollably.

If the bad blood is allowed to continue building up, I'll die in a matter of days, and there's no one here to take care of me.

I'm on my own.

I allow myself a moment of self-pity and then get off the floor. I wipe my mouth with my skirts and fumble for my candle in the darkness. It's gone out, and the striker is downstairs—another problem.

I'll learn from my mistakes, but I'm annoyed that I have to learn from them right now. I just want my medicine and to go back to bed.

Feeling my way forward, I manage to find the stairs again and carefully walk down at a glacial pace. It seems to take forever to find the next flight of stairs and even longer to find my trunks again.

The inky blackness is stifling, and there's not a single hint of light to be found.

I'm alone in suffocating darkness.

It feels like hours before I find the strikers once more, so when my fingers brush over them, I want to cheer with relief. With shaking hands, I just barely manage to light a bit of tinder and dip a fresh candle into the flame.

Once that's done, I reach out to the closest trunk and ask my knife, "Is my medicine in here?"

No answer. Not that trunk, then.

I reach for the next one.

"What are you doing?"

The voice of the male Fellian is near enough that it makes me jump. I drop my candle in surprise, smothering a scream. A moment later, I snatch it back up again before it can go out and glare in his direction.

"Don't sneak up on me!"

"I smelled vomit in the air. Are you sick?" His deep, rich voice is full of indignation.

He melts out of the shadows, just enough for me to see the glint of bright green eyes reflecting the light of my candle and a hulking form wearing a cloak and hood.

"Did the puling Lios king send a sick female to the tower as his sacrifice?"

"Piss off," I tell him. "Go lurk in the shadows somewhere else. I'm busy."

Just because we have to live together doesn't mean we have to get along, and it's clear that we're not going to be amiable neighbors. His room is probably better than mine too. Bastard.

I'm not in the mood to deal with his dragon shite right now. I just want my medicine and a snack. I'll think about the rest of this tomorrow.

"Are you going to leave all your trunks here for long?" The Fellian's tone is insufferable. "You're making a mess."

I turn back to him, glaring, my jaw clenched so I don't vomit again. I take three deep breaths, and when I can speak without getting sick, I manage to say, "I got here today, just like you. When I have a moment, I will take all my trunks and put them away. Until then, you're just going to have to deal with it. I don't want to be here either, understand? So, leave me alone."

He makes a harrumphing sound, and then his big, shadowy form retreats. Ever so faintly, I hear footsteps going up the stairs, and I realize I'm alone again.

Thank the gods.

More bile threatens, so I lie flat on the floor, pinching my nose, willing it to go away because I have to clean up whatever mess I make, and I do not have the energy to clean up vomit.

More vomit. Whatever.

My stomach settles, and with the knife's help, I find the vial of medicine and a package of dry oatcakes that Nurse tucked away for me. I eat one, heat my vial of medicine over the candle flame, and then shoot the syringe into my veins.

I break into a cold sweat and lie on the floor again as I wait for my symptoms to disappear.

Tomorrow, I tell myself.

Tomorrow, I'll panic.

It takes two days for me to decide that the worst thing about being trapped in a tower is the lack of light.

I miss the sun. By the three gods, I miss the sun. I miss fresh air and having light shine on my face when I wake up. I miss looking out a window onto a green lawn and the sight of flowers. I miss all of that so much I ache.

That, or the aching could be due to the fact I'm skimping on my medicine. Nurse's vials will only last for so long, so I'm trying to stretch the concoction as much as I can simply because it's one less thing to do on my overwhelming list of things that I must now do to take care of myself.

In the two days since I've been here, I've gone through sixteen candles and a good deal of my tinderbox. I've managed to put away one garment bag of my dresses and cleaned up the mess I made on the floor in my room.

I dug through my trunks and found a bedtick (thank the gods for Riza and her preparedness) and dragged it up both flights of stairs. I still have to put everything else away, but I've been exhausted and achy, and absolutely, positively unmotivated.

After all, if I make a mess in the lowest chamber and no one is here to see it, does it even matter?

And if it bothers my Fellian neighbor, isn't that even more reason to make a mess?

So, I take my sweet time, curl up in bed, and dream of all the things I had back home that seem like too much effort to do now.

I would love some hot tea, but I don't want to make a fire. A full dose of medicine—but I don't want to take the time to make the medicine. Fresh clothes. A bath.

Gods on high, I would love a bath. It's just that I'll have to do it all myself, and the task seems impossibly daunting.

Maybe I'll just become a dirty hermit the entire time I'm here. Let the Fellian on the floor below enjoy my stink.

A clean dress does seem like it wouldn't be too much effort, though, so I head back downstairs and open one of my trunks, my knife and candle ever-present and at my side.

Riza packed enough dresses for me to change clothes multiple times a day. Sweet, really, but I'd honestly have preferred more prepared medicine or even dry oat cakes. Maybe I can leave a note for next year as to what they should bring me.

It's depressing that I'm already thinking about a year from now. I've only been here a few days. A year is so very far away.

"Your mess is still here."

This time I don't jump at the sound of the flat, irritated voice. I think it brings him too much pleasure when I'm startled, and I'm not in the mood. "I didn't realize it was bothering you."

"Well, it is. You need to clear your things away."

"I'll get right on that," I lie without turning around.

I pull out a thin chemise of butter yellow, wondering if it will match the deep red gown I just pulled out. I suppose it doesn't matter since I'm sitting in the darkness most of the time, but for some reason, it's very important to me that I match my clothes.

I finger the lace on the collar, considering.

"You should know that I have taken half of the root cellar for my food supplies," the Fellian continues in that imperious voice. "I expect you to keep your things clear of mine."

"Of course," I say absently.

Definitely the yellow, I think. It'll be a bold match with the red, but why not be bold if there's only me to please?

I look up, but my shadowy companion is already gone. I guess he just came down here to gripe at me about where he put his food and to demand that I clean up.

Thinking about food makes me wonder about my own stores. I know half (maybe more than half) of the trunks here are goods that I'll need over the coming year. In addition to my medicine, there's probably . . . well, I don't know.

I don't know much about cooking. I confess that in the palace, I'd order cakes and pies and meats and cheeses, but those don't seem like the types of things that will stay good for a long time. And the last day at the palace was so busy I only paid a little attention to Riza's comments about things to cook.

She left me a book. That's good enough.

But I'm curious what a Fellian eats . . . and if he has more food than me.

I use my knife and a few more questions to determine which trunks have food. I open one and find a bag of hard, tiny apples, nuts, and dried meat. I nibble on one piece of jerky as I decide to take my food down to the root cellar and put it away.

After all, my new friend wants me to clean up my mess. So, I'll clean up and snoop at the same time.

A princess thrives on gossip, and if there's no court gossip to be had, I guess I'll make my own sort of intrigue.

It takes some juggling to hold the food and my candle aloft at the same time as I head down the stairs, but the kitchen itself is rather cool compared to above. I set my candle down on the table and open the root cellar door to peer in.

Dear gods. He's got so much food. I get the candle and pull it closer because I can't stop staring.

His "side" of the root cellar is completely packed, wall to ceiling. Wheels of cheese are stacked on one shelf, and another is filled with bags of rounded vegetables. A square crate is full of long, colorful roots and another full of thick, frilled mushrooms. Strips of meat hang down from the ceiling, all carefully tied off onto his side, so there is no question as to whom it belongs.

And down the middle of the cellar, a chalk line has been drawn, clearly demarcating my section from his.

I sniff. As if I'd eat his Fellian onions.

I put my paltry bag on the shelf opposite his and then study his food supplies again. It seems like quite a bit for a single man, even if it's meant to last for a year. Exactly how much does a Fellian eat?

I think of what I've learned of his people. They live under the mountains and eschew the light of the sun. They are warlike and cruel. They devour babies who are considered weak. Well. I suppose there won't be a lot of babies here in the tower, so he's going to have to supplement with onions.

Feeling a little petty, I notice a barrel full of hard, unshelled nuts is close to the line in the center. With my shoe, I reach out and nudge it, tipping it over onto the dirt floor.

Then I feel like an absolute arse because it's food, and no one is bringing any extra to us for the next year. Grumbling, I right the barrel and pick up all the spilled nuts, annoyed with myself.

Once I'm done, I dust my hands off and head back to my sled full of trunks. I suppose I might as well unpack and see how much food I have compared to him. I open another trunk, and as I do, I can swear I hear something.

Candra.

I glance around, holding the candle aloft, but I'm alone. No green eyes gleam out at me from the shadows.

Hm.

I pick through the open trunk. Spices. Nuts. A pouch of something that looks like dirt—

Candra.

I frown again, grabbing the candle once more. "What sort of game are you playing, Fellian?"

There's no response. My neck prickles and I wonder if the tower is haunted by all those who have been here before me. Holding my candle aloft, I circle the large chamber and see nothing amiss. Unnerved, I return to my spot by my trunks.

"Candra!" The voice is barely audible, followed by a quiet scratching. "Princess? Can you hear me?"

I turn in surprise and stare at the sealed doors. Has someone come to let me out already?

Of all the things, I didn't expect to hear scratching and a voice at the sealed door. At least not until next year, when they will return and bring me more food supplies. I thought I was abandoned and forgotten by all.

But someone is here. Someone is here and calling my name.

"Is someone there?" I ask aloud, and the knife shivers against my breasts. "Not you, blade." I press my cheek to the door, listening for the sound of bricks being removed. "Hello?"

"Princess!"

The voice seems to be coming from the bottom of the door. Curious, I drop to my knees and bend over, my ear practically on the floor and my skirts pooling around me. "Who's there?"

"It's me! Balon!"

What in the Gray God's forgotten name? I gasp, hope and delight blooming through my chest. My young lover from court has followed me here? "Balon! You came to rescue me?"

"Rescue you?" He sounds startled. "No, princess. I cannot. But I am here to keep you company. I wanted to show you I have not forgotten you. That I am your faithful man even though we may be separated by the walls of the gods."

Hot disappointment rips through me.

In this moment, I don't care about the gods. I just want to go home. I want out of this endlessly dark tower. I want a bath drawn up by my maids and for someone else to administer my medicine. I want to be taken care of. I want a breath of fresh air.

"I see."

"Do not be disappointed, princess. Even though we must be separated through your sacrifice, I am determined to come here regularly and keep you company. Shall I sing you songs? Tell you stories?"

Tell me stories?! I want *out*. I want out so badly that my skin crawls for wanting it. "How is it you're talking to me? How is it I can hear you?"

"There was a loose brick at the bottom! I scraped it free from its moorings and pulled it out. Even now, I sit here with my cheek to the sands, all so I can talk to you, my love!"

His love. I want to roll my eyes at the declaration. He's been saying that ever since I took him to my bed that one time. He cried all through sex, and I resolved never to bring him back to my sheets again, but he's the only one who cares that I'm trapped here.

There's something sweetly earnest about Balon's eagerness to please me.

"But you can't free me? Please, Balon! I hate it here. It's so very dark."

"My love, I wish I could." Balon sounds distressed. "You are serving the goddess. I dare not help free you, or she will take away her benevolence."

I bite back a sigh. "So, the winds are fair, then?"

"They are indeed. King Lionel has set off for war as of yesterday. The fleet was something out of a song. You should have seen it! So majestic! All of Lios has gone to war. We are certain to be victorious!"

He sounds positively elated.

"All of Lios goes to war, yet you are here?"

"My father will not let me don armor. He says I am far more valuable as his heir. Besides, it gave me the chance to get away and come visit you. Now . . . a song? A story? What would please my love?"

Freedom, I want to say again. I want nothing but freedom. But I bite back a sigh. He's here, and it's something, at least.

"You can tell me a story soon, Balon. Just . . . thank you. Thank you for coming. I appreciate it more than you know."

"I would do anything for you, my darling Candromeda."

Anything except free me, of course. But I don't point that out.

Maybe he won't free me today, but I have nothing but time in which to convince him otherwise. The important thing is to keep him coming back so I can show him how miserable I am and how much I *love* him.

"You're so sweet to come to me. Tell me, how is my sister?"

"About to give birth any day now," he assures me. "And she misses you greatly."

I dig my nails into my palms because I miss Erynne too. We've always been together, the two Vestalin daughters. Well, there were three of us, but Meryliese was always gone—nothing but a distant memory. It's always been Erynne and me.

When she married Lionel, I left our familial, crumbling castle so that I could be at her side. I was to be a trusted advisor . . . but instead, I flirted and partied my way through court while Erynne took on the duties of a queen. I told myself my sister didn't mind and that it was enough just to have me there.

But now I feel a little guilty that I wasn't of more help, that she was forced to lean on her maid, Isabella, more than me.

"Please tell her I love her, and I long to see her again."

"Princess . . . I cannot tell her anything. No one can know I am here."

"Of course, of course," I reply quickly. "Still, it is enough for me that you came."

I smile into the darkness because it's the truth. I've been trapped here for days now with only my own company, and just hearing a familiar voice makes me feel like myself again.

"Tell me court gossip. Tell me anything. Just keep talking."

Balon talks to me for hours until his voice grows hoarse from projecting it enough so I can hear it through the thick door.

He speaks of all the comforting nothings of home. About who wore what colors to a festive ball, what was served, who was found emerging from a lover's bed. A scandalous song written for an anonymous woman that all the court is buzzing about.

It's all utterly frivolous, but it makes my heart happy.

In a way, it's nice to hear that nothing back at court has changed. I thought I would much rather hear that everyone was devastated that I'm trapped in the tower, but it's actually nicer to hear that life goes on as usual—that even without me, a gem of the court and one of its favorite subjects of gossip, everything goes on as usual.

That means it'll all be the same and waiting for me when I get out.

"I must go soon," Balon tells me eventually. "But I shall return to you in two weeks. Is there anything I can do for you, my princess? Anything at all?"

Free me, I want to scream again, but I need him to come back. Maybe after a few more visits, I can convince him that he needs to help me escape.

"It's enough that you're here," I say sweetly. "I'll check for your return constantly."

"I fear it will be two long weeks," Balon tells me. "I cannot return sooner than that. I must see to my duties at court."

"But how will I be able to know if you have returned?" I ask. "There is no way for me to tell time, and it is dark in here constantly. Even now, I have no idea what time it is outside."

He's silent for a moment. "It is near dawn, my lady. When I return, I will bring something to help you! Perhaps a rooster?"

A rooster? What in all the shite am I supposed to do with a rooster?

"If you say so," I call. "Just hurry back." I pause, then add, "I'll miss you terribly."

I wince at the half truth. While it's true that I will miss him, I'd miss *anyone* who would show up to talk to me. I'd happily chatter to the court stableboys if they'd show up and speak to me, just for something to break the monotony of my imprisonment.

Still, though. Two weeks, and he'll be back. I'm touched by Balon's devotion.

Does he truly intend to return for the next seven years, or is he going to break and help me escape earlier? I've always thought of him as, well, an affectionate dolt. Fun for a one-time fling, but not much else. He's young and not the cleverest, but the fact that he's supporting me like this?

It makes him shine a bit brighter in my jaded eyes.

My mood is brighter too. After he leaves, I put away a bit more of the food from my trunks and carry a few dresses upstairs. I'm buzzing with the things he told me—the fact that Lionel is gone from court, off to war. That my sister is there alone, waiting for her baby's birth.

I desperately want to be there. I'll have to play Balon carefully if I want him to break me out. Convince him that I need him so desperately that I will die if we're apart any longer.

Maybe seduction? I consider this carefully.

It's a tool to be used, but one that must be wielded with a delicate hand. I ponder what to say to him when he returns and how I can turn him toward what I want.

CHAPTER SEVEN

The next two weeks drag past.

I unpack my trunks slowly, hauling a few dresses up to my rooms at a time and then hanging them on the hooks left by a prior occupant. When I run out of hooks, I head upstairs to see if any of the trunks there will suffice since it will be far easier for me to drag a trunk down a flight of steps instead of hauling one of mine up a flight.

While there, I break down some of the junk upstairs for firewood and make a fire for the first time since I've arrived.

I've been eating jerky, cheeses, and hard, stale bread since I've been in the tower, but I'm running low on those supplies, and the thought of eating another piece of cheese makes my stomach churn.

I'm also down to the last bit of my medicine, so I spend one day taking apart one of my heaviest trunks that I've emptied and haul the wood, piece by piece, to the kitchen below.

I eye the foodstuffs I have there on my shelf. I've put it all away at this point, and I'm a little alarmed at how much less I have than the Fellian. His shelves are still brimming with supplies, but mine is only half full in comparison.

Is it that I will eat a lot less than a Fellian? Are my supplies more compact? I'm not sure, but it worries me, and I have nothing but time to sit and worry.

I make a fire in the hearth in the kitchen, though it takes a bit of time to get the wood from the trunk to catch, and I end up using far too much tinder. When it's good and hot, I put the ingredients for my potion into the cookpot and add water, watching as it boils.

The dried organs and herbs make a foul-smelling concoction, and the stink of it gives me a wave of homesickness. I think of Nurse and Riza and my sister, and an aching sadness threatens.

Tomorrow, I tell myself. *You can cry tomorrow after you've made your potion and bottled it.*

So, I work instead.

I let the potion bubble, and I flip through Riza's book of recipes, trying to figure out something to cook. She left instructions for a soup with the jerky I've been eating. I'm to make noodles from some of the flour she sent and add a few dried vegetables to give it flavor.

I don't know how long anything has to cook. Her instructions say "until done," but that means nothing to me. So, I let things boil. And boil.

The sludge it ends up making looks heinous. Apparently, vegetables can boil down into nothing and turn into mush. To make matters worse, I still have to eat this.

Grimacing, I choke down a few mouthfuls and cover it heavily with salt to mask the taste, if not the texture.

My potion turns out better. I boil water to add to the concoction and strain it through cheesecloth as I've been shown. Then, I wait for it to cool before pouring it into vials and administering it to myself.

When I'm done, I'm exhausted, and the kitchen is an utter mess. Multiple pots are crusted and filthy, and there's no one to clean them but me. After the fire dies, I have to scoop the ash into a bucket and toss it into the garderobe like I've been told because "you can't let ash build up."

Gods, why did no one tell me it was so much work looking after yourself? This is a nightmare.

Every night (at least, I think it's night), I spend my time by the front door, waiting for Balon's return. When I finally hear him call out again, I all but cry with relief.

"Princess?" His voice is low, near the bottom of the door.

"I'm here," I say quickly, dropping to the blanket and pillow I've set up for his visit. The candle I have with me is low and sputtering, but I don't care. I'll walk back in the darkness if I have to. "You came back."

"I did," he says, sounding pleased with himself. "It was difficult for me to get away, but I managed. I did not bring a rooster, though. Or rather, I brought one, but the moment I opened his cage, he flew away. I do not think he will be of much help."

"That's all right," I say happily. "I'm just glad you've returned."

"I have, and I bring news!" Balon tells me. "Your sister has given birth, Lady Candromeda. She has had a fine boy, and he shows no signs of the blood sickness."

I press my fingers to my mouth. Oh. That's good. That's very good. "And she's well? Erynne? No birthing fevers?"

"She is strong," Balon reassures me. "She was out of bed and back to her court duties within two days. She has named her son Allionel, as the king requested."

I make a face in the darkness. Allionel. The name means "Son of Lionel."

Of course, he'd insist his child be called that. Ugh. How my sister puts up with that pompous boor in her bed, I have no idea. It's not a Vestalin name, but I guess I shouldn't be surprised.

Balon laughs at my silence. "Are you stunned, lady? I am surprised you did not hear the bells celebrating from even here; they were so loud. All over the kingdom, people have been celebrating the birth of a fine, strong heir. I'm told even King Lionel fights harder with the news."

"That's great," I say, even though his words irk me. *Hear the bells*, indeed. This tower is remote, and the walls so thick I cannot even hear the seagulls outside. "Is the war going well, then?"

"Very well," Balon reassures me. "The king thinks Darkfell will be conquered within the next month."

"So soon?"

"Aye. He says they are no match for our fierce warriors." There's a pause. "What of the Fellian you are trapped with? Have they been troubling you?"

"I barely see him," I admit.

"Him?" Balon sounds shocked. "You are trapped with a man?"

"No, I'm trapped with a *Fellian*," I remind him. "I would hesitate to call any of them men."

I think of the creepy glowing eyes and hulking form and try to match it with the stories I have heard of their appearances. I've heard them called devils and monsters all my life. I was told they have hideous gray skin and clawed hands and feet and that they can dwell in the shadows.

Suddenly, I'm a little anxious as my candle sputters.

"The Fellian ignores me," I say, "just as I ignore him. We have an unspoken agreement. He sticks to his portion of the tower, and I stick to mine."

"Do you have a weapon to defend yourself?"

"I do," I say, touching my bodice. My sister's knife goes with me always.

Strangely enough, I'm not worried about the Fellian. He's given me space and left me alone. Most days, it feels as if I'm in this tower by myself in the darkness. I never see him and rarely hear him moving about.

Other than his supplies in the root cellar, he might as well be a ghost.

"If he threatens your honor . . . " Balon's voice trails off.

"What?" I taunt. "If he threatens my honor, what? You'll stand outside and shake a fist in his direction?"

"Princess—"

"No, Balon. If you're so worried about my honor, help me get free from this prison!"

"You know I cannot."

"I know you *will* not," I remind him. "Cannot and will not are two very different things. You will not, so you do not get to worry about my virtue, understand?"

He's quiet for a long moment. "I am not trying to upset you, princess."

I bite back a sigh of frustration, hugging the pillow I have on the blanket with me. "I know, Balon. I'm very grateful for your company. It's just . . . it's miserable in here. You can understand me wanting to be free."

"I know." Balon pauses. "I will donate to the temples and ask the gods for a sign."

"Yes," I say eagerly, sitting up. "Do that! If the gods tell you to free me, you must act."

I want to reach through the walls and shake him with excitement. Maybe he'll get a message from the gods. Maybe they don't want me in here either. Maybe just the thought of me putting myself through this is enough. It's the slenderest of hopes, but it's all I've got.

"Ask the gods for guidance, and let me know what they say when you return." I pause and then add dryly, "I'll be here."

"I will indeed ask," Balon replies. "Just be careful around the Fellian. They are pure evil to the core."

I think about the unpleasant Fellian somewhere in this tower with me. He's definitely not someone I'm inclined to spend a great deal of time with. I think the feeling is mutual. The few times we've crossed paths, he's made it quite clear that he despises me.

Perhaps he wasn't meant to be the sacrifice for his people either.

Perhaps he feels just as trapped as I do.

"So," Balon says cheerfully. "Did I tell you I have a new horse?"

Hours later, Balon leaves, promising to return in two weeks once more. He professes his love for me and reassures me that he will ask the gods for guidance, and I'm left with that to tide me over.

When he's gone, I get to my feet and pick up my blanket and pillow, folding it and placing it atop one of the many scattered empty trunks I've left near the doors. I've been here almost a month now.

I feel just as trapped as that first day.

But I have hope now, however small.

It's this hope that makes me restless and full of energy. I grab a plank of wood from one of the trunks and pick up my guttering candle, which has melted down to a nub, and head for the kitchen.

Maybe I'll make myself more potions since I'm not ready to sleep. My mind is racing with everything Balon has told me tonight. My sister has a son. The war has started, and we are winning. He is going to pray to the gods to ask for a sign.

I wonder if I should pray too. I consider this as I descend the stairs to the kitchen. The fire is out, and I move my candle close by, tossing the hunk of wooden board into the fireplace for future use.

I've never been devout, and it feels as if it would be insincere if I tried now. But tomorrow, I decide, I will devote myself to the goddess and beg her to let me free.

I clasp my hands to my chest and bow my head. "Please, please, please," I whisper. "Please, goddess. You don't want me here."

A dirty lock of hair slips over my cheek, reminding me that it's been a while since I've washed it. I finger my hair thoughtfully.

Bathing has been difficult. For the first week or two, I struggled with getting myself dressed, medicated, and fed. There's been no energy for anything else.

I'm settling in now, though, and I've been giving myself quick sponge baths with cold water, but it's not the same as a nice, warm bath.

And I'm not ready to go to bed yet.

Excited at the prospect of a warm bath, even if it means a lot of work, I haul the tub out into the center of the kitchen and start pumping water into one of the pots to boil. I hang it over the fire, then eye my tinderbox. It's nearly empty.

Maybe a cold bath, then, before my candle dies on me entirely.

I pour the water into the tub, then continue to fill it with pot after pot of water. It must be warm outside because the water itself feels like a tepid bath. It's surprising, given that the tower stays cool at all times.

I wonder if it's because the darkness and stone insulate us from the sun. Not that speculating on the weather does me any good.

I run my hand through the water, then tug at the laces of my dress, loosening them enough that the entire thing will slide off my shoulders. It pools onto the stone floor and next to go is my sweaty chemise. I kick off my slippers and get into the water, sinking low into the tub.

It doesn't quite cover my breasts, and the water is definitely cool . . . and my soap is upstairs. But it makes me feel a little more human again to bathe. I relax and drag handfuls of water over my skin.

"What do you think you're doing?" a voice asks.

Perhaps it's only that I'm already on edge that I don't jump at the sound of that growling, furious voice.

Perhaps part of me suspected he'd emerge out of the shadows the moment I got naked.

It seems like something he'd do, just to try to rattle me. Whatever the reason, I remain calm, dragging another handful of water over my breasts. They thrust out of the water, uncovered and bare, and I wish I'd made my bath a little deeper, but there's nothing to be done about it now.

My heart flutters in my chest, but I put on my courtier's mask and give him a lazy, indolent look. "Bathing. What does it look like?"

The shadow blinks at me, nothing but a pair of shining, narrowed green eyes in the darkness. I can just make out the outline of a hulking form, but he's deliberately avoiding my candlelight, the bastard.

And he doesn't respond to my question.

I lift one leg from the water, arching my toes.

I've never bathed alone in the past, thanks to my many, many servants always being around. In fact, I've bathed with a lover before . . . but never the enemy, though.

This is a new one for me, yet I'm not afraid. If he's trying to intimidate me, he's failing.

I've got nothing left to lose. "Did you come here to watch me bathe? Should I put on a show?"

The Fellian growls, sounding slightly irritated. "I came here to talk to you."

"Did you?"

I lower my leg and sink into the bath, making the water lap at my breasts. I'm not built tall and willowy like Erynne. I'm round and plump everywhere, but I do have very nice, full breasts. In this, I feel confident.

"I think you're lying," I say. I drag a finger down through my cleavage. "You could have talked to me when I went upstairs. Surely, you can hear me when I go up the stairs. It's not as if I'm ever quiet or subtle about it. So, I have to think that this was deliberate on your part. You wanted to surprise the lady in her bath."

It's strange, but I actually feel . . . safe?

The conversation with Balon earlier made me realize that if this Fellian was as monstrous as he's supposed to be, I'd have already been assaulted. He's bigger than me and no doubt stronger. If he were going to attack me, he probably already would have.

He might be interested in seeing my tits, but I can handle a peeper. A peeper only looks his fill.

Frankly, I'm bored enough to let him look.

"I'm not here to play your games," the green-eyed shadow tells me.

Sure, you're not. I shrug and cup another handful of water over my breasts.

Why is it that I feel in control of my situation and in my element for the first time since I've arrived at this hellish tower? Is it because he's a man, and I know how to manipulate men? Or have I truly lost my wits?

Both, I decide.

I continue to bathe myself, rubbing my limbs with the cool water. When I glance up, the shadowy form is still there. "For someone who claims he doesn't want to play my games, you aren't doing a very good job of convincing me."

"You said I am not a man," he all but snarls at me. "When you spoke to your friend, you implied I was not a man. You think I am a demon? A monster? A malevolent creature who will suck your soul out if you meet my gaze?" His tone changes to insulting and dismissive. "Like the rest of your backward kingdom?"

"I confess I don't know what you are," I admit cheerfully. "Seeing as you're always hiding in the shadows and looming. What am I supposed to think?"

"I think you're an immodest, immoral creature."

"Says the creature interrupting my bath," I retort. "How many times have I interrupted yours?"

He snarls at me, his clothing rustling with an angry flap, and for a moment, I'm afraid. Whomever this Fellian is, he has a temper. And yet, he's still here.

Perhaps I'm not as safe as I thought. Goose bumps prickle over my skin, and I rub them away with a brisk motion of my hand. When I look over, those green eyes are still watching me from the shadows.

I arch a brow in his direction. "Well?"

His eyes narrow, and I get the impression that he's angry at me. "We are a people of the shadows," he finally says, tone stiff.

"Well, I am not," I say, sitting up in the tub. It makes my wet breasts bounce and sway, and his gaze dips to them again. Truly, all men are the same wherever one goes. "So, come into the candlelight if you're going to talk to me," I say. "Or go away."

I truly expect him to disappear. For those eyes to just wink out, vanish, and leave me alone with my bath.

Instead, the Fellian's gaze hardens, his eyes gleaming bright, and he takes a step forward. Then another and another. Until he comes fully into the flickering light of my candle.

I swallow hard at the sight of him.

I've never seen a Fellian for myself. I know their kingdom exists on the edge of ours and that we had a thriving trade agreement with them back when the Vestalin line was upon the throne.

I've heard that the kingdom of Darkfell is mostly underground, inside hollow mountains and winding caves.

I've also heard that they are devils, so hideous and unholy to look upon that they avoid the Absent God's light. I always thought those were foolish rumors, but as the stranger steps forward, I realize not all the stories are lies.

He does look like a monster.

The green eyes glittering in his face are the only hint of color, and even those are almost drowned out by the black sclera that surrounds them. The Fellian seems to be made entirely of grays and blacks. His skin is nothing but deep-gray muscle, and his features are not entirely human.

His oversized hands are tipped with thick, deadly claws. His feet are bare, tipped with the same claws, and formed awkwardly, a bit like an eagle's. His knees bend backward, his thighs heavy and obscured by the leather kilt at his hips—the only piece of clothing he wears.

He crosses his arms over his chest and glares down at me. I can't help but notice his upper body is far more massive than any human knight's.

Not even his face is truly human. His features are hard planes, his nose large and prominent, jutting down from his heavy brow like a blade. His jaw is heavy too, and his mouth wide.

If he were a sculpture, I'd say he'd been carved with a heavy, angry hand, and instead of using soft marble, his sculptor went with unforgiving granite.

There's no hair upon his head either. Instead, rising from his scalp where his hair should be, dozens of curving horns arch back, like a mane blowing away from his face into an unseen wind.

Something ripples behind him, heavy and dark. The sound of fabric rustles again . . . except I realize now that it's not fabric at all.

He's not human. Not even close.

"Behold," he says flatly. "Your enemy."

"Are those wings?" I ask, leaning over the edge of the tub, my breasts plumping against the metal side. Here I thought he'd had a cloak, and all this time, he had strange, leathery-looking wings. "Are you part bat?"

The snarl he directs my way is utterly scathing. "Why would I be a bat?"

"You have leathery wings, and you live in a cave. Shouldn't that make you a bat?" I taunt.

He focuses his angry gaze on me. "You live in the sunlight and walk on the ground. Does that make you a pig?"

My jaw drops. I splash at him, indignant, but he simply steps aside. "That was insufferably rude."

"Don't ask stupid questions, and you won't get rude answers."

I'm no longer having fun with this. Glaring at him, I sink back into the bath again. "Go away so I can finish my bath in peace."

"I heard you talking to your lover."

I don't look in his direction. Instead, I just shrug.

"So, what if you did? It's not against the rules. He's not entering the tower, and I don't seem to be leaving it," I say, my tone bitter.

If Balon were braver, maybe I'd be taking a bath in an inn somewhere on land instead of a cold half bath in a dark kitchen. The thought is a depressing one. Balon is a sweet man, but he's still young and not nearly foolish enough to suit my needs. If he were more impulsive, he'd have already broken me out and damned the consequences.

Instead, he shows up to tell me about his horses and how his latest hunting trip went.

I'm just a different sort of entertainment for him, I realize. The thought is a depressing one. When Balon gets bored of coming to visit me, he'll just disappear . . . and I'll still be here. Waiting.

"I won't let you escape," the Fellian says. "Not until the Golden Moon is gone once more."

"Or until your people fall in the war," I say brightly. "Which I shall hope and pray for every day." I give him a tight smile. "You did know there was a war coming to your doorstep, yes? By now, King Lionel and his knights have probably conquered your mountain . . . or whatever grimy little cave you've crawled out of."

He huffs, and I realize he's amused. "If he told you they're winning the war, he's lying to you."

I glance over at him, dismissive. I'm getting cold, my nipples tight in the chill, but I'm not going to give him the satisfaction of covering my breasts.

I rest my arms on the edge of the tub and comment, "Balon has no need to lie."

"You think not?" Again, amusement. "As a reminder, female, if you try to leave, I will stop you."

I eye him. "Are you going to stand here all night and ogle my breasts while making threats? Or can I finish my bath?"

The Fellian bares his teeth at me—fangs. *Of course, they're fangs*. Then, he melts away into a shadow.

It takes me a moment to realize that when his eyes close, he's not returning.

I sit up, shocked. That was magic of some kind. He didn't move his legs or his wings. He simply disappeared into the darkness. If that's possible, how is anyone supposed to fight a Fellian?

As if agreeing with my thoughts, my candle gutters out, and I'm left in the darkness.

CHAPTER EIGHT

Time passes faster than I expect it to and slower than I want.

Each day seems to be made up of making fires, cooking, taking my medicine, recovering from my medicine, and cleaning. Gods, so much cleaning. Why must everything get dirty once it is used? My clothes smell of sweat. The dishes are endless. The bedding is no longer fresh. And my hair is still dirty.

All of this takes a lot of work, strength, and time that I do not have. I make a list inside Riza's recipe book of all the things I need to clean, and by the time I mark one off, three more have taken its place.

How do peasants get anything done without a staff to clean up after them? It truly boggles my mind.

I wash clothes. I wash bedding and lay it out to dry. I hang my sodden linens flat on every surface possible, but they take forever to dry. I could light a fire, but I've already burned through the wood of several of my trunks, and it is not even winter.

I have to remind Balon to tell them that I need much more wood for next winter, I fret.

I'm almost out of candles too. I burn each one down to a stub, and I'm judicious with using them. But I'm still reaching the last of my supply, and I don't know how to make more.

Riza's instructions do not cover candle making, and I grow more anxious every time I light one of my tapers. Do I burn my candles and save my firewood? Or do I burn the firewood and save my candles? Or do I do neither and sit in the dark? I have no idea.

My food supplies seem to be lasting, at least. I've taken to eating less simply because it's too much effort to cook and clean. That's going to help me stretch them, but I still don't have nearly as much in the larder as the Fellian does.

Balon doesn't return in two weeks either. I've been making marks on the wall in my room each time I fully burn a candle; that's as close as I've come to accounting for a day. By the time I've burned sixteen of them, I realize he's forgotten me.

Time crawls again, and I feel lonely.

The Fellian avoids me. I bathe several times in the kitchen just to try to flush him out, but there's no response.

I fear I'm going mad already, and it hasn't even been a season. How am I going to last an entire year, much less seven of them?

It's boredom that makes me reckless.

Boredom and sheer loneliness. I can only entertain myself for so long, after all. I've spent the last week lying in the darkness, singing songs to myself. Touching my knife and asking it all kinds of questions.

Is Erynne's baby well? Is she thinking of me? Is the war over yet?

Is Balon returning soon?

None of the answers are particularly satisfying. The world outside is forgetting about me as the months pass, and the realization no longer brings me comfort.

I want Erynne to dwell on my imprisonment. I want the war to end. I want Balon to rush to the tower and pull down the bricks on the other side of the door to free me. I want him to declare his love for me and that we'll run away to the distant mountains.

Damn the crops and the people who need the food.

I want a great many selfish things.

Thinking about the mountains gets me thinking about the mysterious Fellian. He's been avoiding me since that day in my bath. It's painfully obvious.

I hear him moving about when I lie down to sleep, and I've started counting the pieces of wood he has stacked on his side of the kitchen. He's using some because it's been slowly disappearing.

It's the only sign that he's still in the tower because he's quite good at hiding from me.

Lying in bed, I toy with my knife and consider how I can flush him out. "Is the Fellian nearby?" I ask the knife.

A shiver. *Yes.*

"In his quarters?"

Yes.

"Awake?"

Yes.

Hmm. I stroke the sheath, considering. "Does he think about me?"

Yes.

A wicked smile curves my lips. "Do I annoy him?"

A hesitation and then an affirmative shiver.

Interesting. I ponder what that hesitation means. "Does he think about me in my bath?"

No hesitation that time. *Yes.*

"Does he think about my breasts?"

Yes.

I smirk into the darkness, feeling a bit childish at the line my questions are taking, but who else am I going to entertain if not myself? "Does he touch himself to the thought of me?"

Yes.

Oh. How very delicious and fascinating. "More than once?"

Yes.

Interesting.

I think about the big ugly brute. He's definitely not attractive compared to someone like Balon, who has the smooth, elegant, good looks of a courtier. I would never touch the Fellian but knowing he's fascinated with me gives me an edge of power.

To think that he touches himself to the thought of me regularly . . .

I cannot say the same. I haven't touched myself since I entered this tower. Doing so would just make me hungry for the touch of a lover, and those needs will not be fulfilled anytime soon, so it's best to ignore them entirely.

But maybe my companion is ashamed of his needs. "Is the Fellian avoiding me?"

Yes.

So, he doesn't want to find a human attractive, then. That sours the gleeful joy I feel just a touch. He's a man. Any man confronted with a pair of nice, juicy tits in a bath would jerk his cock to the sight.

I'm not special. Ah, well. "Does he hate me, then?"

Yes.

I frown at that. "Has he thought about killing me?"

Yes.

A prickle of warning brushes over my skin. "Is he going to?"

No answer. That's a no, then.

Unless he changes his mind, of course. Unless I annoy him so much that he sees no way out except to get rid of me.

As if the knife is following my thoughts, it shivers in affirmation.

Hmph. "Sometimes your answers are very annoying; you know that?"

Yes.

I dream that Balon sails off to join the war with King Lionel, heading to the distant mountains. In my dream, he meets a pretty Fellian princess, marries her, and I never hear from him again. I sit in the tower, waiting and waiting, but Balon never returns.

"Weren't you to marry a princess?" the Fellian woman asks Balon in my dream.

"What princess?" he asks, his smile wide. "Shall I tell you about my new horse?"

When I awaken, I'm covered in sweat, gasping, and in a foul mood. It takes a moment of staring into the darkness to realize it was just a dream, then I sit up, pushing my hair out of my face. It's pitch black in my chamber as always, but I feel the oppressiveness of it today. Fumbling through the bedsheets, I look for my knife.

When I find it, I grip it tight in my hand. "That was just a dream, wasn't it?"

Yes.

I exhale in sharp relief. "Does Balon ever intend upon coming back?"

Yes.

Oh. I've been afraid to ask that question before now. I was worried the answer would be an unpleasant one that would send me into a fit of depression.

"When?" I ask, and then shake my head. "Tonight?"

Yes.

I all but squeal with delight. Finally, someone to talk to. Something to look forward to.

I jump to my feet in the darkness. "Do I have time for a bath? A real one?"

Yes.

Excellent.

I tuck the knife into my dress and race down to the kitchen, counting the steps in the darkness. I'm getting better at navigating in the pitch black, but it still feels oppressive. Right now, though, I'm *choosing* to dwell in the dark. The choice isn't being taken from me. As long as I have a handful of candles, it's my choice, I reason.

It takes hours to heat my bath, wash up, and then dry my hair by the fire. Since the water's already warm, I wash a chemise, too, and wring it out by the fire.

I'm a little perturbed at how little wood I have left. I've burned through all the trunks I've broken down. Now, all I have left are the heavy sled and whatever I can find on the top floor.

I'm almost out of tinder, too, so I've been supplementing with fluff I pulled out of a pillow.

That's a problem for tomorrow, I tell myself as I dress in a fresh chemise, my wet one hanging on a hook near the fireplace. I'll have to save the rest of my supplies for winter, which should be coming soon.

After that, well, I'll figure something out.

I comb my wet hair by the flickering fire and glance over at the Fellian's supplies. His woodpile is enormous once more. He's gotten more from somewhere. Or maybe he's hiding some in his rooms?

It's impossible for me to tell. Either way, I'm jealous. I know his side of the root cellar is still packed with food, too, while mine dwindles. Does he even eat?

Meanwhile, I have to use all my fuel to make my medicine and heat my bath. Even now, I'm making a batch of medicine. I stir the small pot over the fire, the foul stink of the herbal concoction mixed with the dried organs permeate the room.

I wonder . . .

I stand, flicking my long, wet hair over my shoulder, and open the root cellar. The firelight casts shadows over the interior, making it barely visible.

I break down and light a nub of a candle I've been keeping for such an occasion. My light held high, I step down the short stone staircase and into the cellar.

He's got so much food. Every single one of his cheese wheels is untouched. I know. I've counted them a dozen times over. The container of nuts seems to be as full as ever, and the bags of vegetables look far fresher than my own. It hardly seems fair.

I've never been tempted to steal his food before, but the realization that my supplies are dwindling is making me anxious. I reach out and touch a decorated jar, wondering what the contents are.

Out of nowhere, a hand grabs my wrist and hauls it away. My candle stub goes flying and gutters out, and I let out a cry of surprise as I'm pinned against the shelf of food.

"What do you think you're doing?" the Fellian growls at me.

My wrist is held high over my head, and the Fellian looms over my pinned body. He's absolutely enormous compared to my smaller form, and I'm acutely aware of his strength and size.

"I was just looking."

He squeezes my wrist. "You think you can steal from me without me knowing? You think I am that foolish?"

My shock is ebbing, replaced with irritation. I jerk at my trapped wrist.

"I wasn't going to steal. I was just curious." When he doesn't release me, I retort, "My food is down here too. How do I know you're not stealing mine?"

"Your spells should tell you the truth of that."

"My what?" I frown up at the glittering green eyes.

"Your warding spells. They will tell you if your food has been disturbed. You know this is not the case."

I laugh. When his hand squeezes on my wrist again, I just laugh harder.

"You think I have magic?" I sputter. "Seriously? Do you truly think I'd be wandering around in the darkness all the time if I had a whit of magic in my veins? The only thing I have is a blood curse, and it's not going to assist me with anything."

He's silent, those glowing green eyes glaring down at me. "Your potions—"

"I'm *sick*," I tell him. "They're medicine. But at least now I know you're watching me." I give him an arch smile. "See anything interesting, Fellian?"

He releases my wrist so quickly that I stagger. The next moment, I'm alone again, surrounded by nothing but shadows. I rub my wrist, breathing hard. It takes me a moment to realize he wasn't rough with me; I won't have bruises.

I stare out into the darkness, wondering if he's watching me even now.

"' . . . And so,' I said to the bard, 'Surely, you can come up with a better song than that? We need smiles at court, not frowns and sadness!'"

"Mmm," I say to Balon.

I lie on my back by the door, nestled amid the pillows and blankets. I'm just so happy he's here that I don't mind him rattling on about court life and the sheer silliness of it all.

At least, I didn't at first. I was so relieved he returned that I didn't care what he talked about so long as he talked. But it's been hours now, and he's not asked about me, nor has he told me anything about my sister.

I'm starting to wonder if I'm simply a captive audience for his tales of court shenanigans.

"And do you know what he did next? He played a merry tune, just as I asked!" Balon laughs at his own story. "Isn't that marvelous?"

"Absolutely," I say, and then add, "Can I ask you a question, Balon?"

"Anything, my darling princess!"

"Where were you? It's been a month since you came by." I don't say I've been waiting impatiently because I don't want to seem needy. I am needy, of course, but I'd prefer not to show it.

There's a long pause. "I thought you couldn't tell time inside your tower."

"Not very well. But I was so excited to see you that I've been counting the days as best I can, and I know it's been a while since you were last here. Is everything all right?"

"Everything is fine, Princess Candromeda. It's just been so busy at court. I've scarce had the opportunity to get away. You do understand that it's quite an excursion for me to come out here and see you?" His tone sounds faintly reproachful. "I must keep my visits a secret, or else I would be banned from keeping you company."

"Who would ban you?" I press. "My sister? I don't think she would. She would understand your devotion. And you said Lionel is off to war."

"It's just . . . it's dangerous."

"Only if you try to break me out. Which you said you weren't going to do, right? So, what's the harm in visiting me?" I clutch the pillow close to my chest and turn toward the door. "Did you ask the gods if you could free me?"

"No answer on that front, my love," he replies cheerily.

I roll my eyes into the darkness. I wonder if he even remembered to ask.

"Please follow up with the priests," I ask, keeping my tone sweet. "You know it would mean everything to me if I could get out of here."

"You're very brave for your sacrifice," is all he says.

I'm struck by my annoyance again. Does he think I want to be here? That I had a choice? I've been trapped since the moment Meryliese died. I had no way out of my horrible destiny.

"You're too kind," I say.

"Shall I tell you more stories of court?" he asks cheerfully. "It has been quite adventuresome as of late."

"Actually, could you get a message to my sister? Tell her I'm all out of candles and wood. I need them both if I'm to last through the winter."

"My sweet princess, you know that no one can be aware of my visits here. I dare not tell a soul."

Dragon shite. He just doesn't want anyone to know that he's visiting because it doesn't suit his needs.

"Do you want me to sit in the darkness for the next year, Balon? Because if you don't tell them I need candles and wood, that's exactly what's going to happen. I have to make my medicine, and I can't if I don't have anything with which to make a fire. Understand?"

"I shall see what I can do," he says. "But I do wish you wouldn't be so angry at me, dearest. It's not my fault you're trapped."

I pinch my brow, frustrated. "I know it's not. I don't mean to be angry, Balon. I'm just scared. If I don't have my medicine, I'll get sick and die. You know this. Please, just tell Erynne I need candles and wood for a fire. *Please.*"

There's a long pause. "I will do what I can, my heart."

"Thank you, Balon. That's all I ask." I smile into the darkness. "And you'll be back soon?"

"As soon as I can get away. It is terribly difficult to get away from court, you know. Did you hear that there is a holiday ball next week? For the Feast of Pious Arthell."

It's the Feast of Pious Arthell already? I mentally go over a calendar, trying to count the days. The feast always happens during harvest season. Maybe I've been here longer than I thought already.

"I love the Feast," I say, moving into safer territory with the conversation. "What are you going to wear?"

Balon settles in with a happy laugh and proceeds to tell me all about his wardrobe choices for the upcoming festivities. When he leaves a few hours later, he promises to return "swiftly" with news of my sister and the war and to tell the others about my predicament.

I get up from the floor and straighten my blankets, folding them as I think about his promises. I don't know if he realizes just how dire my situation is.

I think of spending the long winter in the darkness, parceling out my wood so I can make my potion and eating cold, raw food. The thought is a depressing one.

"You should tell him to forget you."

I jump in surprise, my heart thudding wildly in my chest at the sound of the Fellian's voice. I clutch the pillow to my breast, glaring into the darkness where he's hiding. Only his eyes are visible.

"Gods above, you really do enjoy jumping out of corners to startle a girl, don't you?"

He chuckles, and the sound is hollow and strange yet oddly enticing. "Not trying to startle you. It's not my fault you can't see in the dark."

"Mm. I still think you're doing it on purpose."

I set my pillow atop the sled, along with the blanket. There are no more trunks left, after all. The sled is my final resort. Once I have to break it down for wood, I'll know I'm truly in danger. For now, just knowing that it's there is comforting.

"Have you come to chastise me again?" I ask. "Remind me that I'm not to touch your things? Because I'm not."

"I heard you talking to your fool of a lover," he says. "And I wanted to remind you that we are both trapped here. He cannot free you, and I won't let you leave. It's best if he forgets you entirely."

Such words of encouragement. “He’s not going to forget me,” I say, lifting my chin in a show of defiance. “Balon loves me. He’s not forgotten about me despite the fact everyone else at court has. And besides, I don’t want him to forget me. Why should I listen to you?”

“Because seven years is a long time to be alone.”

His words are simple but devastating.

My happy mood vanishes, and I’m left feeling like a hollow shell. Seven years *is* a long time. It feels like forever. It might as well be forever.

“Thanks for that. I was in a bad mood earlier, and now I’m in a worse one. You’re not very good company; you know that?”

“I know.”

Hmph.

It’s silent in the large, echoing chamber, but I don’t feel alone. I know he’s still in the shadows, watching me. Waiting for . . . something?

“What’s your name?” I ask impulsively. When it remains quiet, I add, “So I can quit calling you ‘that damned Fellian’ when I think of you.”

“Do you think of me?”

“As little as possible.”

That elicits a laugh from the shadows. “Nemeth. I am called Prince Nemeth of the First House of Darkfell, Princess Candromeda Vestalin.”

So, he knows my name. Is it because he’s researched the Vestalin line or because he’s overheard me talking to Balon? I don’t suppose it matters. “You can call me Candra.”

“You can call me Prince Nemeth,” he replies, and I can swear I hear amusement in his voice before he fades out, and I’m alone in the room once more.

CHAPTER NINE

The next morning I realize that I've lost my knife.

I wake up in bed, reaching for the blade that I keep tucked between my breasts, only to find that I'm wearing nothing but a loose chemise, and there's no bodice in which to tuck the sheath. I grope my breasts anyhow, just in case, but there's nothing to be found.

I must have set it down when I was bathing. Or when I was talking to Balon. Or when I was cleaning up, lost in a dizzy hum of happiness that my erstwhile suitor would soon be arriving. Really, it could be any number of places.

I get out of bed and run my fingers over the mattress and blankets, looking for the knife, but my fingers encounter only bedding. I do a blind search of my room as well, but it's fruitless. I head downstairs and fumble through the darkness, searching the kitchen and then by the door.

I can't find it. Not without some light to guide me.

Panicked, I return to my quarters and find my strikers and the box of candles. It's empty except for two. Two lonely candles are left to last me the rest of the year. My panic increases and I clutch the candles in my grip.

Do I dare light one for something as frivolous as finding my knife? Or do I simply wait for it to surface again? After all, I can't leave the tower, and there are only so many places it can be; I'm bound to find it at some point.

The loss of it hits me hard, though. It feels like I've just been abandoned by my only friend.

Without the knife, I can't check to see if Erynne and the baby are well. I can't ask if someone's coming to get me or if the war is over. It doesn't matter that the answers are unsatisfying. What matters is that I have some sort of connection to the outside world. I feel lost without it.

Carefully, I put the candles back down and decide to search the tower again. I go over my room as best I can, handspan by handspan, shaking out every dress and blanket. Still nothing.

It's not until after I head out of my quarters to go search the kitchen that a new idea occurs to me.

What if Nemeth took it?

He was indignant that I touched his food, after all. What if he stole my knife as some sort of petty revenge?

I pause on the stairs and sit on the landing to his floor. I've never explored it or even stopped here, not after that first day. He made it clear that the first floor belonged to him, so I've done my best to honor that and give him space.

Not today, I decide.

Hands out, I feel in the darkness, hunting for the door to his quarters. His floor should be laid out similar to mine—

A squeak of distress escapes me when my hands run into something hard, unyielding . . . and warm. Skin. Nemeth's chest. I draw back, biting my lip.

"What are you doing on my floor?" he asks, tone ominous.

"I'm looking for my knife. Did you take it?"

"Why would I take your knife?"

"Because it's magic. And because it's mine, and you know it would bother me if you stole it."

There's a pause. "You said you didn't have magic."

"I don't. I do, however, have a magic knife."

"What sort of magic?"

I sputter. "I'm not going to tell you."

"Then, I'm not going to tell you if I have it."

Infuriating, horrible man. No, not a man, a *creature*. "So you did steal it. Why?"

"I didn't say that." He puts his hands on my shoulders and spins me around. "Ten steps ahead of you are the stairs down. You should go. You don't belong on this floor."

I brace my feet, my stubborn nature rising. "I'm not going anywhere until you give me back my knife."

He tries to guide me forward, but I push back. Nemeth clearly wasn't expecting that response because I smack into his bare chest again. He grabs my shoulders, pinning me in place so I don't topple into the darkness. It's like he's pinning me against his body, and I breathe hard, thinking about the naughty questions I asked the knife: *if Nemeth touched himself to me . . . if Nemeth touched himself to me often.*

Yes, and *yes*.

"Is this all a ploy to get me here to your chambers?" I ask, voice wobbling. "Are you so lonely that you can't simply ask for company? You have to resort to stealing?"

With a disgusted sound, he pushes me away from him. That warm presence at my back is gone, and I'm adrift in the endless black. I automatically put my hands up in front of me, trying to find a wall.

"You flatter yourself," Nemeth says. "And I didn't take your paltry knife."

"Fine," I call out. "No need to be nasty about it. Prick."

I take a step forward, only to be lifted off my feet as if I weigh nothing, and then set back down, facing a different direction.

A low, silky voice murmurs in my ear, "You'd fall down the stairs if you kept on as you were."

Oh. My skin prickles with awareness at his kindness in moving me, at the easy way he hauled me into the air, but most of all, that deep, decadent voice in my ear.

Then, he ruins it. "A smart woman would be looking for her lost belongings with a candle lit instead of accusing her neighbor."

Disgusted, I make a face at the shadows and find the wall, leaving with as much dignity as I can.

I search all day and still don't find my knife.

I give up at bedtime, lighting a candle for the briefest of moments so I can administer the injection of my medicine, then blow it out again. That quick glance shows me that I'm low on my potion. I'm going to need to make a fire, and that means I'll have to burn my sled.

Then, I'll be out of wood, just as I'll be out of candles.

Things are getting desperate.

I lie in the darkness and contemplate my options. Balon won't help me. He's made it clear that he's going to show up when he pleases, talk of nothing but court gossip to me, and then leave again. I have to make things last until the solstice next year when new supplies will be delivered.

As I check the root cellar for the dozenth time in the last few days, I come to the realization that I don't have nearly enough supplies.

Either I've been deliberately sabotaged, or whoever is in charge of supplying me needs to be removed from their post. That, or I've managed my supplies so very poorly that I've gone through a year's worth of goods in a season.

It doesn't matter. What matters now is that I take action.

I can run out of everything and starve. I can let my potion run out and die. I can bargain with Nemeth for some of his supplies.

Or I can kill him, just as Erynne suggested, and take everything.

The thought sits with me all day. I don't think of myself as a murderer, but I also don't immediately dismiss the idea. I don't like the idea of starving while he sits all pompous in the shadows, but he's got a name. We've had conversations.

It's hard to kill the enemy. It's doubly hard when you know their name.

I don't have many options, though. I feel naked without my knife, even though there are other blades in the kitchen. That knife was my consultant, my companion, my advice giver.

I search for it all over again the next day as I think about Nemeth and how I would kill him.

I don't have the supplies for poison. I don't have the strength or stealth to take him by surprise in his bed.

Maybe seduction? He's dismissive of me, but he also watched me bathe and didn't seem in a hurry to leave. I could seduce his goods out of him, I decide.

And if that fails, I can invite him to my bed and then kill him.

Then, I'd have no problems with having enough food or wood to last me through the year . . . but I would be sharing the tower with a dead body.

For the hundredth time today, I want to just get up and walk out of the tower. To somehow get the doors open and unbricked and race out into the fresh air.

Damn the favor of the Golden Moon Goddess.

Damn the crops that would surely be destroyed if the goddess is angered.

Damn it all, and just take my freedom.

Thunder crackles overhead, loud and booming enough to make me jump. It's as if the gods are reminding me that I'm at their mercy. Figures.

It's the first storm I've heard since arriving, and it's violent enough to make the walls shiver each time the thunder peals or lightning strikes. Rain furiously hammers on the tower, and it seems like fate when something wet drips onto my forehead.

Because, of course, the tower would have a leak.

The goddess really isn't making me warm up to the idea of being her sacrifice. I grumble to myself as I drag my bed frame out of the way.

Once it's moved, I can hear the *plip, plip, plip* of the water dripping down from the floor above. Thunder crashes again, so loud that it shakes the tower itself.

"Yes, yes," I mutter aloud at the displeasure of the gods. "I'm staying. Don't worry."

I pick up my dress, intending to slip it over my head and lace it up before heading upstairs to check out the leak. The moment I do, though, I toss the dress back down.

Does it matter if I wander about the tower in nothing but my filmy chemise? It's not as if there's anyone to see except Nemeth, and he's already seen everything.

Even though it pains me, I light one of my precious candles and lift it in the air, heading out to the landing and toward the steps of the third floor.

Thunder crackles overhead, booming and startling me with the severity of it. It's the season of storms, so I'm not all that surprised. They'll shower down for a month, and then it's harvest time, and then comes the snows.

After the thunder dies down, I hear something downstairs. It sounds like something hitting the wall, a soft thump not made by the storm itself.

I imagine Nemeth falling down the stairs below or the storm shaking loose a brick and it landing on his head.

I imagine him lying on the floor, broken and bloodied, and when the strange, soft thump occurs again, my curiosity gets the better of me.

Instead of heading upstairs, I go down to the floor below.

Nemeth's door is closed. Another round of thunder rumbles. The stone walls practically shake, and I hear a crash from within.

I move to his door and knock. "Everything all right in there?"

The door whips open to reveal a wild-eyed Fellian. Behind him, I catch a glimpse of crowded shelves full of books and supplies.

Before I have a chance to get more than a quick look, Nemeth focuses stark eyes on me and tugs me into his quarters. "Good, a hostage."

A . . . what?

My candle sputters as I surge forward into Nemeth's room. He looks crazed, eyeing the walls with what looks like anger or resentment.

I'm confused. "What's going on?"

"They are attacking the tower," he says, grabbing me by my shoulders and eyeing the walls. "I have never heard such a din. Do they mean to tear it apart and pull us from the rubble?"

Thunder crashes overhead again, and he jerks, his wings flicking out and extending in what must be a reflexing action. He pulls me against him, his claws twisting in the voluminous folds of my chemise.

Is this big Fellian warrior . . . afraid of thunder? Surely, I am misunderstanding him.

"You do know that's a storm, right?"

His wild gaze focuses on me. "What?"

I open my mouth to speak, but it thunders again. His grip tightens on me, his gaze moving to the ceiling. Aw.

"It's a storm," I say gently. "A thunderstorm. A loud one, granted, but still a thunderstorm. We're entering the season of storms. Do you not have that where you live?"

In the light of my candle, I see his thick gray throat work. "You . . . this is normal? We are not being attacked?"

"It's a very loud storm, but no, we are not being attacked."

The rain pounds against the stone walls, and he flinches. He doesn't let go of me either.

I'm acutely aware of my candle burning, and I know I have to save it, but I also don't want to abandon Nemeth when he's clearly feeling vulnerable and doing his best to hide it.

"If it'll make you feel better," I say, "I'll stay here as your hostage until it stops, all right?"

His gaze focuses on me. "You would . . . do that?"

"I have the time," I tell him with a wry smile. I blow out my candle and then hold my hand out to him.

Absolute darkness falls once more, but his green eyes blink at me. "You want to sit in the dark?"

"I'm being conservative with my candles," I lie. He doesn't need to know that I'm down to two. "Where do you want to sit?"

He makes a sound in his throat and takes my hand in his larger one. A Fellian's hands are massive, I realize. It's like an enormous paw swallowing mine as he holds my fingers.

Nemeth leads me forward a step or two, and my leg bumps into a bed frame.

Oh. My face gets hot. I didn't think about the implications of being in the dark and in his bed with him.

"Sit on the edge?" I ask brightly. "Or do you have a chair?"

"A stool," he says. "But not enough seating for both of us."

I nod and feel my way down to the edge of the bed and sit, clasping my hands around my candle the moment he lets go of me. His large form sinks down next to me, and when thunder rumbles again, shaking the tower, something warm and leathery skims over my shoulders—a wing.

He jerks when thunder rumbles once more, shaking the bed with his movements. I set my candle to my side and offer my hand to him.

"Are storms not like this where you live?"

Nemeth takes my hand in his again. "I live deep inside a mountain. I guess it is muffled where I am." He pauses. "You are sure we have nothing to worry over?"

"I'm sure." I pause, then add, "Now, poor Balon might have a devil of a time returning to Lios, but we're fine."

That elicits a laugh from my companion, and I smile.

"I suppose you think me foolish," he says after a time. "For thinking we were being attacked."

"Not at all," I lie, glad that I'm able to keep a straight face. "I imagine with all the training you received on how to handle living here, it didn't cover everything."

He grunts, and I suppose that must be affirmation.

"My maid forgot to tell me how to clean my laundry," I say. "She was in such a rush that we weren't able to cover everything, either, but I think I've been managing fairly well. If you notice my gowns are excessively wrinkled, though, please do not point it out. Wrinkles were definitely not covered in my book."

"A book?" he asks. "You have a book?"

"I do."

I pause for a moment, wondering how much he knows about Meryliese and her untimely death.

"My sister was supposed to be the one to come to the tower. Meryliese was an acolyte at the Alabaster Citadel and had trained all her life in preparation for her time in the tower. But when she was on her way here, her ship sank, and everyone died."

Everyone died, and now I'm here in my sister's place. My throat tightens with helpless anger, and I clear it before continuing.

"I was told three days before that I was to be the one to come here. I'm not used to looking after myself, so my maid created a book for me with as much information as she could squeeze into it in such a short period of time."

"I am sorry about your sister."

"Me too. I barely knew her, but I'm sorry that I'm trapped here. I'm not supposed to be, and it's hard to move past the resentment."

"And you are sick."

"Yes." I don't say more about that. He's still the enemy, even if we're holding hands in the darkness.

"The fop that visits you. He was your betrothed?"

I snort. "Balon was *not* my betrothed."

"He is a fop, though."

It's terrible of me, but I giggle. "He's young. Hopefully, he will grow out of it. And no, definitely not my betrothed. He was just . . . a diversion."

"I see." His tone indicates that he doesn't see at all.

"What about you?" I ask. "Were you always meant to come here? Or were you a last-moment replacement as well?"

Nemeth is silent for a span.

When he finally answers, he says, "My king told me it was my duty to come here. I did not argue. I knew it was a possibility."

"Because of the bloodline," I agree. It was always something that had lurked in the corners of my mind as well. I'd simply thought that since Meryliese was to be the one sent, I was safe.

Clearly, I am a fool.

His hand warm in mine, I turn in the darkness toward those green eyes. I know he's the enemy, but it's so good to have someone to talk to. Someone who knows the frustrations that I've been going through.

Yet, I can't say too much to him. He's still the enemy. We're not meant to be friendly. I should be looking for the best way to destroy him, not making him my friend.

"Consider yourself lucky that you were prepared. I'm not having much fun learning of all the things that were missed."

"Mm." Nemeth is quiet for a moment. "You had someone to do things for you back in the palace?"

"You didn't?"

"I am a warrior," he says as if that answers everything.

"Yes, well, you can't shame me for not knowing how to do laundry or make soup. We don't know what we don't know, and I only had three days to prepare. If I had prepared better, I could have learned how to read or play a musical instrument to keep myself occupied." I shake my head. "The days are so damned long, and the darkness is maddening."

"It bothers you?"

I know I'm saying too much. I just don't care. This is the first real conversation I've had since I've been locked in the tower—other than the other run-ins I've had with Nemeth.

But each of those occasions felt like we were trying to get the upper hand over each other. This feels like something more. So, I allow myself to be vulnerable.

"I hate it. It's oppressive and just makes me feel more trapped."

"Ah."

I wonder if he's mentally cataloging how to use this against me as he withdraws his hand from mine. Thunder rumbles again; then I hear a *tap, tap.*

The room fills with light.

I gasp, stunned. It's a pale, gentle white light, and it seems to be emanating entirely from a round, white stone set upon a pedestal.

Nemeth lifts his large, clawed hand from its surface, moves farther down the room, and taps a claw upon an identical stone, making the room grow even brighter.

The bastard isn't even using candles.

My jaw hangs open in shock.

I want to memorize everything in his room now that I can see, or at least gaze my fill on the craggy, unpleasant face of the Fellian in front of me and eye his lack of clothing, but I can't take my eyes off of the shining globes that seemingly produce their own brilliant light.

One would be enough to see by. Two feels like decadence, and then the bastard goes and lights a third one.

Harsh thunder rumbles again, shaking the tower so hard that the bed quakes and the globes shiver. Nemeth turns back to me. "Better?"

I lift a finger, pointing at the globes. "You . . . how . . . how did you do that?"

"Magic," he replies as if this is the most obvious thing ever. "You do not have magic? At all?"

I shake my head, mystified. "I told you I didn't."

"You are my enemy. You could have lied." He runs his hand over one of the globes, caressing it. "But it seemed a wise thing to bring a few with me. One must be prepared for all occasions."

He gives me a pointed look that tells me he doesn't think I'm very prepared at all.

I suspect he knows I'm low on candles too. It seems like something Nemeth would be aware of. That, and he's probably guessed from my fumbling about in the darkness.

If I had one of those globes, it would save me from having to light a candle every time I needed a hint of light. It'd save me tinder too. I could keep it for my fires.

"How does that work?" I ask. "Do you say a spell over it?"

"You tap it twice, and it lights up. That's all."

"Can you make me one?" I try to keep the eagerness out of my voice, but it's impossible. The hunger is written all over my face, I imagine. I have never needed anything as much as I need one of these magic globes of light.

Nemeth hesitates and then shakes his head. "I do not have the supplies here."

Disappointment crashes over me, but only for a moment before a new idea takes place. "Can I bargain with you for one?"

"A bargain?" he looks skeptical. "What is it you think you have that I could want?"

I fiddle with my chemise, thinking. He's right that I don't have a lot in the way of supplies that would entice him. I have less food, so I can't offer him that. I have no books, and judging from the looks of his quarters, he is a great reader. One wall is filled entirely with massive tomes.

I can't even offer my knife—not that I would. I have little in the way of wood to burn, or candles, or anything . . . unless he wants a dress.

"Fabric?" I ask. "I could take apart one of my dresses, and you could use the material for . . . something?"

He snorts and gestures down at the short, leather kilt he wears that barely covers his massive thighs. Right. He doesn't wear human clothing. In fact, he wears very little clothing at all, it seems.

"Blankets? A cloak?"

Nemeth shakes his head again, those strange horns of his making the action seem exaggerated. "You have nothing."

Despair curls through me. "Please," I say, reaching out and touching his hand. "I need one desperately."

He stares down at my hand on his arm, and his wings twitch.

I don't move.

Neither does he.

Oh.

Oh.

I look down at my hand on his arm. I suppose I do have something to bargain with.

He'd stared for a very long time at my breasts, after all, when I was in my bath. How much will I be willing to do for one of those globes? To have light constantly and easily?

I'd be willing to do quite a lot.

I look up at him and carefully put my hand on his thigh. Even as I do, I use my other hand to tug down the neckline of my chemise, revealing my cleavage. "There's nothing I have that you want?"

Nemeth jumps up so suddenly that the bed shakes. "I do not want *that*."

Oh. Gods, I'm horrified and full of shame. I can't believe I just offered myself, a *princess*, for a magical light source. Worse than that, I've offered myself to the *enemy*.

My face burns and I jerk away, grabbing my neckline and hauling it up high. I snatch my candle off the bed and race out of his quarters, humiliated. I don't know what embarrasses me more—that I offered myself to a Fellian so cheaply or that he refused.

Or that I'm *disappointed*.

I retreat to my quarters, now a familiar path in the oppressive darkness, and slam the door shut.

CHAPTER TEN

The next day, I kick a trunk set in front of my door. I grab my toe, wincing at the pain, wondering what new humiliation awaits me today.

Is Nemeth going to throw it in my face that I practically flung myself upon his beastly cock? He's a hideous-looking creature and not one that I would ever consider touching otherwise. He's not attractive. He's not even pleasant.

Is this an apology? If so, I'm not interested.

But I'm also curious to see what he's offered. If it's food, I'd be foolish to turn it away.

I kneel before the box, searching in the darkness for a latch of some kind. My fingers locate it, and I flip the lid open, cautiously feeling around inside. It's something round. And cool.

Holding my breath, I tap it twice, like Nemeth did last night. The box floods with light, nearly blinding me, and I lift the globe out of its case. He's . . . giving one to me?

My heart squeezes, and I smile, clutching the round, glowing stone to my chest. It's the most generous thing anyone has ever done for me.

He's apologizing for last night. I know he is. And this is the best way to do it.

Beaming, I pull the stand out of the box. It's a lot like a candlestick, but with claws on the end that the orb can fit into so it can be carried around. I snap it into place on the end of the candlestick and smile at the light that pours through my doorway.

No more sitting in the darkness for me.

I should go down and talk to Nemeth. Thank him for his thoughtful gift and apologize for flinging myself at him last night. Clearly, my advances weren't welcome, but he wants us to remain friends anyhow. I'm fine with that.

I'm just about to close the box when I notice there's a small, cloth-wrapped bundle at the bottom. I pick it up, and the moment I do, my blood goes cold.

I don't even have to unwrap it to know what it is. That comfortable heft has been my companion ever since I entered this tower. I know the shape of my knife without even looking at it. I pull it from the wrappings, scarcely daring to breathe, and stare down at the small blade still in its sheath.

The bastard lied to me. He claimed he didn't steal it, yet he's had it all this time.

All of my goodwill disappears in a flash. Eyes narrowing, I tuck the blade into the front of my gown in its old familiar spot.

"Did he steal you away from me?" I ask the blade.

Yes.

That prick.

I've changed my mind. We can't be friends. I'll take his glowing orb, but he can go straight to the Gray God's death pits and stay there. He's made it clear that he's got the upper hand and that he's not afraid to lie to me.

Carefully, I carry my new globe inside my quarters, pleased at the light that shines over everything. I shut the door once more and crawl back into bed.

A short time later, there's a low tap at the door. "Candra?"

I don't answer.

After that, Nemeth doesn't pursue friendship with me. It suits me just fine.

The days pass, and as they do, we avoid each other. If I hear him heading down the stairs, I make sure to keep my door closed. I spend as little time in the kitchen as possible, only going down when I have to cook something or make my medicine. If I wash up, I make sure to never get undressed, lest he thinks it's an invitation. I'm making it quite clear to him that I'm not interested.

For months, I don't see those green eyes in the shadows.

I've learned a way to keep track of the passing days. Each time I rouse from sleep, I ask the knife if a new day has arrived. Through a series of yes and no questions, I'm able to determine the date, and I make counting stitches along the hem of my oldest chemise.

Riza sent a sewing kit with me, and while it took me a long time to figure out how to get the thread to stop coming out, I've mastered a simple stitch enough that I can use it to keep track of time. I count the days because it's something to do.

Balon doesn't return for three weeks. Then four. After five weeks pass, I figure he's grown bored of visiting me and stop checking for him.

The storms pound against the tower many times after that first night, and I put a pot on the floor to catch the drippings of water. I move my bed to the far side of the wall and head up to the storage area above to move the wood away from the dripping spot.

I don't go to check on Nemeth as the storms crackle and thunder overhead. I don't care if he's frightened or unnerved by their ferocity. I hope he breaks and busts his way out of the tower.

Then, I can return home and say, *See? I wasn't the problem.*

One morning (at least, I assume it's morning), I wake up, and my breath frosts in the air. My teeth chatter with cold. Winter has arrived.

On All Winter's Feast, I will have been here half a year.

Half a year and my food supplies are looking pathetic indeed. I've counted out my medicine components, making sure I have enough for the weeks that follow, and I should be fine. I should have enough to carry me through to the new year when fresh supplies will be brought to me.

That is both troubling and relieving. I'm glad, of course. The medicine is paramount. But that means they probably provided me with enough food supplies, which means I've squandered them, somehow.

Am I eating too much? The loose fit of my corsets (and the constant growling of my stomach) tells me no. I'm eating less than before. I'll just have to be smarter with my food. For all I know, Nemeth has been stealing from me all this time. I have no wards on my food as he does . . . and he's not afraid to lie to me about it.

So, I spend two days moving my foodstuffs out of the root cellar and into my quarters. I don't know if it'll do much good, seeing as how Nemeth can slink through the shadows, but it makes me feel better to know I'm watching over them.

I keep my light lit at all times, even when I sleep. It's comforting to know I have it and to be able to open my eyes and *see* my surroundings instead of feeling about in the dark.

Wood for a fire remains a problem, though, and continues to be an even bigger issue as the weather turns colder. The tower, cool in the summer, is like ice in the winter. It's miserable, and no matter how many layers I put on, I can't seem to get warm. I end up sleeping fully clothed, my hands covered in socks, with every blanket piled atop my bed, but I still wake to my teeth chattering.

The beloved glowing orb that Nemeth gifted me is truly wondrous, but it doesn't give off heat. Winter brings new problems when I wake up to my medicine frozen in its vial. I warm it by tucking it between my breasts, but without fire, my existence is growing increasingly miserable.

Keeping my food stores isn't a problem. I barely have the energy to gnaw on my half-frozen vegetables, much less to make a fire and bake something like my book advises. I spend my time scouring the storeroom upstairs for things to burn, but everything there is either moldy, made of metal, or I've already burned it.

I turn toward my sled. I've kept it by the door, as it's too big for me to move upstairs on my own. It's as large as my bed and so heavy that tugging on it only makes an offensive scrape across the floor. I've been saving it, determined to use it as a measurement.

If I need to burn the sled, it's an indication that I'm in dire circumstances, and I need to do something drastic.

It looks like that time is now.

I have two doses of my medicine left before I need to make another fire. Three, if I'm stingy. After that, I'm in trouble.

Last time, I burned one of my dresses because I was out of wood, but it burned down so quickly I ended up having to burn another, and I know that won't continue to work. I'll be running around naked before the end of the month. Besides, the ribbons and bits of fabric are what I'm using for tinder since my box is long empty.

Downstairs, I approach my sled with one of the heavy pots from the kitchen.

Most of the trunks were fairly easy to take apart. All I had to do was bang something heavy on one side until the fittings came loose or use a knife to pull out the nails. The sled is of a heavier make, though, so I'm intimidated by it.

I carefully set my light down a safe distance away, then try to turn the sled on its side. One of the runners might be easier to take off than pulling apart the entire thing.

It takes me a while to turn the heavy thing on its side, but once I manage to flip it, my back smarting, I run my fingers over the wood, feeling for joints or nails.

Nothing.

Hmm. I tilt the sled onto one side and let it crash backward to the floor, wincing in anticipation of the tremendous crash. It makes a crash, all right, but the entire thing stays in one piece.

I've heard one of the knights brag that our woodworkers are the finest in the land, and I'm finding out, depressingly, that this might be the case. I hammer at one of the runners, then the other. I try to loosen planks. I wedge my knife into a crack and try to widen it.

Nothing gives. Nothing budges. At the end of the afternoon, I'm covered in sweat, and all I've managed to do is dull my knife and give myself a backache. The sled is as solid as ever.

Without the sled, I can't have my medicine.

Without my medicine, I'll die.

I sink into a puddle of skirts near the sled and stare at it, numb. Tears of sheer frustration threaten.

You can cry about this later, I remind myself. *You can weep all you want tomorrow, once you've had a nice fire and you've made another batch of medicine.*

Normally, the pep talk works. Normally, I can put off crying. Today is not that day. Exhausted, I burst into noisy tears and sob into my hands. I feel helpless and miserable and so damned alone.

. . . And I can't make a fire to save my life.

I truly *can't.*

The realization just makes me cry harder. I let myself weep over the entire situation—over my sister's death and the destruction of my life.

Over being trapped here.

Over cold baths and meals of raw turnips and the fact that my arm is permanently bruised from my clumsy injections. The fact that even Balon has given up on me. That I've still got so far to go before I'm free, and I won't make it.

That I'm going to die in this cold, lonely tower, alone and forgotten.

I cry and cry until I've got nothing left. Then, I cry some more.

I hear the rustle of leathery wings before I see the green eyes. "Candra."

Not him. Not now. Not when I'm at my most vulnerable.

"Piss off," I choke out. "You're not wanted here, Fellian."

To my relief, he doesn't mock me. He just slinks back into the shadows, green eyes disappearing.

Good.

CHAPTER ELEVEN

I make my medicine last four days. I tap the glass tube and squeeze every droplet out, adding a bit of water to each dose to make it last. I know I shouldn't, but I'm low on options.

I don't eat much either. I just lie in bed and gnaw on a turnip when I'm hungry, sip a bit of water, and then go back to lying down again. The less I move about, the less vital my medicine is . . . or so I hope.

Nurse would have a fit if she could see me now.

Thinking about Nurse makes me lonely. I think about Nurse and Riza and all the others who took care of me on a daily basis—those whom I took for granted. I want to hug all of them and apologize for being spoiled. I want to shower them with affection and gifts so they know how much they mean to me.

I want to go *home*. I want to go home so badly it's a physical ache in my chest.

On the fifth day, I wake up and immediately lose the contents of my stomach. Sweating, dizzy, I know it's because I've been skimping on my medicine. I'm destroying myself slowly, and I need to do something about it today, I decide, sitting up.

I'm going to conquer that sled today. I'm going to make it into firewood, and I'm going to make myself a huge batch of medicine, enough to last at least a week. Then, I'll figure something else out. I'm not going to let this beat me.

I get to my feet, blackness creeping before my eyes. I blink it away and hold onto the bed frame until the shakiness in my limbs goes away. I chew on a bit of dried meat and take a bite of turnip as I tighten the laces of my dress and slip on my shoes.

Once I'm ready, I carefully pick up my glowing orb and carry it downstairs with me, my knife tucked into the bodice of my dress, safely between my breasts. I've never let it out of my sight, not since that day Nemeth stole it from me.

When I get to the bottom floor, though, I have to blink a few times to make certain my eyes aren't playing tricks on me. I walk to the spot where I left the sled . . . but there's nothing there.

It's gone.

I shine my light and walk the large room just in case I'm dizzier than I thought and I've missed something. But no, there's no sled at all. It's gone—the only proof it was ever here is the recent scratch marks on the stone floor.

Nemeth stole it. It has to be him.

He's taken the last of my firewood, and with that, he's killed me. I take a deep breath, fighting back nausea. Maybe I'm wrong. Maybe I'm overreacting.

"Knife," I say, panting as I lean against the wall. My limbs feel weak and sluggish. It'll only get worse. "Was it Nemeth? Did he take it?"

The magic blade pulses once. *Yes.*

Dragon shite. Now I have to go kill a Fellian.

My mind races. I know if I had a full dose of medicine in my veins or I'd been eating properly, I'd be able to think straight.

But all I can think of is that the Fellian has stolen the last of my firewood. He's strong enough to drag it up the stairs to his room, and that sled represents days—maybe weeks—of slow-burning fires, enough to stave off the worst of my sickness through the winter. I need it. He stole my knife from me, and now this?

He has to die.

I didn't want to kill anyone, but he's forcing me to do this. The logic of killing him makes more sense with every breath I take.

The Fellian has plenty of supplies. He has three of the globes that produce light. He's got wood. And he's got books that'll make a finer fire than my dresses, should I run out of wood. If I kill him, it all belongs to me.

It'll be more than enough to last me until the next solstice when more supplies will be delivered.

If I have to choose between the enemy or myself, I'll obviously choose myself. Setting my light down in a safe spot, I touch my bodice to make sure that my knife is in place. I can do this. I eye the stairwell hidden in shadow.

The first floor is Nemeth's. I can go up there, kill him, find something to burn, return to the kitchen, make my potion, and inject it the moment it cools. Then I'll deal with the blood and body later, once I feel better.

One thing at a time. Murder first.

I take a step onto the stairs, then another . . . and nearly collapse. I'm weaker than I thought. *It's all right,* I remind myself. *You can rest all you want once the potion is made. Go up the stairs one at a time, but you must go up the stairs. Kill your enemy, then everything will be fine.*

I go up the steps slowly. Achingly slowly. I have to pause several times, and I'm not sure if the blackness swimming in front of my eyes is because of my dizziness or the shadows. I can do this, though. I can.

I make it to the top of the stairs and sway, holding onto the wall. Panting, I wait for my breathing to calm, and then I head toward his quarters, drawing my knife from my bodice. My hand trembles with weakness, but I think I should still be able to stab his throat. That will kill a man, won't it? Or should I go for the groin? Which one bleeds more?

Pausing outside his door, I draw a breath. I can do this. He's proven himself to be my enemy time and time again. No hesitation.

My life versus his.

Before I can knock on the heavy door, it opens. A large form melts from the shadows, coalescing in the faint light emanating from his room. Nemeth's green eyes reflect and shine as he gazes down at me. "Candra?"

I stab.

It's a clumsy effort, and if I were thinking clearly, I would have tried seduction first. But I can think of nothing except my medicine and how desperately I need that wood. So, I plunge my knife toward his broad chest, toward the slabs of muscle that cover his torso.

He grabs my wrist before the blade nicks the skin, stopping me.

"What do you think you're doing, little princess?"

"Killing you," I choke out. I struggle against his grip, but it's useless. He holds me in a vise, and I can't break free. Spots swim before my eyes, and I glare up at him, defiant. "I won't let you destroy me."

"Destroy you?" Nemeth laughs as if the idea is ludicrous.

He gazes down at me, and as I snarl up at him, the lights seem to go out.

Everything dims around me, and the last thing I see before I pass out is the bright, amused glow of those great green eyes.

I'm lost in dreams.

They're terrible dreams, though, because even in my dreams, everything hurts. My body aches, and I'm sweating. The space behind my eyes throbs with pain, and I can't seem to escape any of it. I'm so thirsty too. My mouth is a desert, and I dream of cool glasses of water, only for them to be held away from me, taunting me.

Now, I'm in a desert. I stagger through the sand and come upon a large statue of the goddess. She looks angry, and when I collapse at her feet, she lifts one enormous stone hand and clutches me in her grasp, her fingers supporting my lolling head.

"Which is it, princess? Injected or imbibed?"

I have no idea what the goddess is talking about. Her face is cruel as she leans in toward mine, and I flinch back. "W-what? I don't understand, great lady."

The Golden Moon Goddess clutches me in her arms. It's like being hugged by a rock, and as she leans in, I'm terrified. "Your medicine, little fool. Which is it? How do you take it?"

"N-needles," I manage. "Needles. Injected. Please don't kill me, goddess. I'm here, aren't I? Haven't I done everything you asked?"

She makes a derisive sound and sets me down gently on the sand again, and I escape to darkness once more.

"Drink this."

A low, rumbling voice wakes me from my feverish dreams. This time, it's not the hand of the goddess lifting me up but a warm touch and a light scrape of claws as I'm pressed against a hard chest. My eyes flutter, and I catch a glimpse of gray skin and broad muscle—and a far too bright light behind him. I squeeze my eyes shut again because everything hurts.

"Princess." Nemeth's voice is cajoling. "I made this especially for you. You must get something in your belly, or you'll be sick again. Drink this for me."

I lick my lips—or try to—but my tongue is dry, and there's no moisture. I think about that blinding light. "Are we . . . outside?"

"Alas, no. Is the light too strong? You said you liked it, so I wanted it to be bright in here for you."

"Hurts my eyes," I manage. "Hurts my head too."

I'm gently set down on the bed again, and then I hear a *tap tap*, followed by another *tap tap*. Nemeth's large form sits on the edge of the bed again, the frame groaning with effort, and then that gentle hand lifts me upright once more. "Better?"

I squeeze an eye open, and there's no stab of light this time. Thank goodness. I blink, trying to focus my gaze, but all I see is Nemeth's green eyes in the darkness. His face is perilously close to mine, and I worry that he's going to kill me. A whimper escapes.

"I made you a broth," he says. "You have to drink it."

A cup is held to my lips, and I take a hesitant sip. Flavor bursts on my tongue, and I moan at how good it is. He made this for me? He's not trying to kill me? He's . . . taking care of me? I try to take a large gulp, but he pulls the cup away, and I whine in protest.

"Small sips," he tells me. "You can't have much. You've been sick, and I don't want you losing it all again."

Losing it all . . . again? Oh no. I know when I miss my potion, my stomach tends to rebel. Have I puked all over him? And he's just trying to take care of me? I grimace at the realization. He probably hates me more than ever now. I take another sip when he offers it to me, savoring the flavor and the warmth of it. How long has it been since I've had a warm meal of my own? At least a week has passed since the last time I made my potion and hastily made a quick soup of vegetables and meat while I had the fire going. Mine is never as good as this, though, and each time he lifts the cup to my lips, I drink more.

I want to protest when he pulls it away, but then I'm offered a cup of water, and that's just as delicious. I drink as much as I can and sigh with relief when I'm done. "Thank you."

There's no response to my words, and my skin prickles with awareness. He gently sets me back down onto the bedding again, and even though I'm exhausted, my mind races. The thick blanket that's pulled over me is not mine. The wide, hard bedtick I lie upon? Not mine. My weak hands brush over my chest, reaching for my knife, but it's not there. I'm not wearing my bodice or my dresses, nothing but a thin chemise.

And I'm too weak to do anything about it.

I can't decide whether he's going to kill me or exact his revenge in other ways. "I'm in your quarters," I point out unnecessarily.

"You are. It seemed a good idea since you collapsed at my door after trying to murder me. No sense in going upstairs." There's a touch of reproach in his voice. "Not that you have a lot upstairs that you'll be missing."

Terrible, horrible Fellian. "Where is my knife?"

"Safely out of reach. You can have it back when I'm assured you won't slip it into my ribs the moment I turn aside."

"It was a gift from my sister. I want it returned."

"And it will be. Right now, you just need to rest."

"In *your* bed?"

He snorts. "If I wanted you, I'd want you willing and healthy, not sickly and weeping."

I clench my jaw at his irritatingly arrogant words. "I don't weep." Of course, the moment I say that I think of how I broke down and sobbed when I couldn't tear my sled apart and that he watched me cry. Bastard. I hate that he saw me in my weakest moment.

"Next, you'll be telling me you don't get sick when the proof is all over my clothes," he says, voice dry. Those green eyes lean in close in the darkness, and then gentle fingers brush a lock of hair off my brow. "Just rest. You can pick a fight with me when you feel better."

Am I picking a fight? He's the enemy. We've been at odds since we got here. He's a thief and a liar, yet here he is, tucking the blankets around me and feeding me soup. I want to say more, but I'm exhausted, so I close my eyes.

Before I drift off, a claw rubs against my cheek. "How often do you need your medicine? So I know when to give it again?"

"Once a day," I mumble. "In the arm."

"I'll remember. Rest now."

CHAPTER TWELVE

I sleep better than I have in months. You would think that my senses would be a little on edge given that I'm in a Fellian's bed and completely at his mercy, but no. I sleep so heavily that I don't even dream, and when I wake up, my chin is covered in tracks of dried drool.

"You snore," is all the Fellian says to me when I awake.

"I do not snore," I say, indignant. "I am a princess."

"A snoring princess is still a princess."

I glare at him and sit up in the bed. I feel surprisingly good. I'm still drained, of course, but my stomach is settled, and my limbs no longer feel sluggishly heavy, nor is my mind fogged. It's a relief, and I owe my recovery all to my enemy, which is unsettling.

"Do you want the lights on, or is your head still bothering you?"

I rub my eyes and notice that there's one light on in the corner, the orb covered by a thin cloth, so it shines dimly and gives just enough light to illuminate the shapes in the room. Considering he can see in the dark, it's obviously for my benefit and a thoughtful gesture.

I look around at the absolute clutter in his room and then back to him. "The light is fine; thank you. Why are you being so nice to me?" I'm suspicious. "I showed up here to kill you."

"Did you truly think you'd succeed?" He sounds amused. I notice that he has a stool pulled up to the side of the bed, and he straddles it, his strange legs folded on each side, his wings a black cloak behind him. Those strange horns of his make him look regal even in the near darkness, as does the heavy set of his brow.

Did I think I'd succeed in killing him? It's a good question. In all honesty, no. But he doesn't need to know that. "I had to try. You have me backed into a corner."

"I don't know how you came to that conclusion." He shakes his head. "I've done nothing to you."

Is he serious? "You stole the last of my wood! That's why I came after you."

Nemeth gives me a puzzled look. "Your wood? You mean that sled?" At my indignant nod, he continues. "The sled you banged around with for a full day and got nowhere with? The sled you cried over because you couldn't break it apart?"

"I didn't cry," I hiss, embarrassed. Tears are weakness, and I hate showing weakness to this cretin.

"I saw you were having trouble with it," he says, his words slow and measured, his gaze locked on me. "So I took it apart for you and put the wood in the kitchen below, by the hearth. You would have seen it if you'd gone downstairs."

I blink, taken aback. I hadn't thought to go downstairs to look. I'd simply asked my knife if he'd taken the sled, and the answer was yes. I hadn't thought to ask why he'd taken the sled or where it was now. "You made it into firewood for me?"

"I broke it down into easily manageable pieces, yes. You should be able to burn them now." He shakes his head. "Whoever sent you your supplies needs to be drawn and quartered. To think that they sent you sixteen trunks of dresses and nothing to burn."

Rude man.

He's right, of course, but it's still rude to point it out. "I suppose your people did a lot better for you?"

"I suppose they did, yes." He gestures behind him, and I can see a massive stack of firewood, the logs jammed into place as high as the ceiling. He also has wood downstairs in the kitchen, so this must be an additional supply. It's revolting to see how well stocked his quarters are. In addition to the food downstairs, he's got some hidden away up here too. Shoved in between books and wooden cases, I see more wheels of cheese and what looks like a board full of growing mushrooms standing up in the corner of the room. There are bushels of dried leaves hanging from the ceiling too, and I've no doubt that he's got more than enough supplies to ease through the winter and spring until the next solstice.

Whereas I've been chewing on stale, raw turnips and shivering under my blankets. So, that's fun.

I sit up, and he immediately moves, fluffing a pillow behind my back. It's a rather touchingly sweet response and makes me feel guilty. Here he is, this big, vicious-looking enemy warrior, making sure I'm comfy in his bed. I glance over at him. "I don't suppose you have any more water?"

"I do. And soup if you're hungry."

I nod because I don't trust my voice not to shriek out, *yes, yes, please; I'm starving*!

He hands me a wooden cup full of water, and I force myself to take tiny sips even though I want to gulp the whole thing down. As I drink, I watch him move across the room. His fireplace is flickering, and there's a small pot over the flames. He stirs the contents with a ladle and then fills a second wooden cup with what smells like soup. My mouth waters, and at this point, if he pulled his cock out and told me I had to suck it to share his food, I'd gladly do so. I'm that hungry.

But he only sits down on that stool again and holds the soup out to me. He doesn't ask for anything.

Warily, I take the cup from him, trading my empty water cup for the food. "This isn't poison, is it? Because with my luck, it'd be poison."

Nemeth rolls his eyes at me. He crosses his arms over his bare chest—still wearing nothing but his leather kilt with the decorative metal studs—and considers me. "Why would I nurse you back to health only to poison you?"

"Because it hurts more that way."

He throws his head back and laughs. "Remind me to get tips from you on how to torture the enemy. I think my people could learn a thing or two."

I take a sip of the soup. Gods, it's good. There's a warm, spicy taste to it that I don't recognize, but the majority of the flavor is mushrooms and savory bits of meat. I don't have any mushrooms in my supplies, so this is clearly from his stock. I eye him as I take another sip. He seems relaxed and at ease, watching me with curiosity instead of resentment. And he made me dinner.

This feels like a trick.

It has to be a trick, or else I'm an absolute arse for trying to kill him. Either he truly is as kind as he's pretending, or there's an ulterior motive. Right now, I'm too tired to figure it out, though . . . and his soup is too good to worry about it.

I finish the soup quickly and hold the cup out for more. He shakes his head. "Give yourself a few hours, and then you can have more. You should eat small meals until we're certain your stomach can handle it."

It makes sense, even if I don't want to hear it. With a sigh, I nod and swing my legs over the side of the bed. "I should get going anyhow."

A big hand covers my shoulder. "What are you doing?"

I look up at Nemeth in surprise. "Getting out of your way?"

He shakes his head, and that enormous hand stays on my shoulder. "You're not going anywhere until I'm certain you're feeling better. You can sleep in my bed for another night."

It sounds like a good idea to me because not only is his bed comfortable, but I'm too tired to consider walking up all forty stairs to my room. "Where will you sleep?"

"The same place I slept last night." He nods at the spot on the bed next to me.

I should protest that it isn't seemly, but honestly, it just makes sense, and if I'm not kicking him out of his bed, I'm all for staying. "All right," I say lightly. "But if you try anything, I will projectile vomit on you."

He rolls his eyes and offers me a hand. "Do you need help getting to the garderobe, or can you manage on your own?"

Just the thought of crossing the hall to relieve myself sounds exhausting, but I will absolutely be humiliated if I have to use a chamber pot in front of him. "I can manage . . . just give me a moment."

Nemeth just eyes me. "Very well. If you need help, just ask. I know you're not inclined to do so, but I will offer it all the same."

"You're too nice," I mutter. "I don't trust it."

"Should I hold a knife to your throat as you drink your soup? Will that make you more comfortable?" His hard face creases with amusement.

"Very funny."

"I thought so. If you're feeling better, perhaps you might answer a few questions of mine." He tilts his head, regarding me, and those horns draw my attention. So strange to see hard, thick horns there instead of soft, waving hair. It reminds me that however friendly he is, he's not human.

Not even close, and I shouldn't let my guard down. "You can ask."

"Why did you want to kill me?" His teeth flash, a hint of white fang showing. "I assume that's what you were trying to do, no matter how poor of an attempt it was."

Twist the knife, why don't you? I scowl at him, hugging his blanket to my chest. "So I could keep your supplies. I thought that was obvious." I gesture down at my chemise. "Did you undress me while I was unconscious?"

"Yes. I thought that was obvious," he says, throwing my words back into my face. "If you wanted something of mine so badly, why didn't you just ask me for it? Have I proven myself so craven that I wouldn't share? That I would let you starve while I fill my belly?"

He looks so very indignant that it startles me. How can he sit there and say that I'm in the wrong? That I assumed the worst of him? Of course, I did. Not only is he a Fellian, but he's proved himself to be a thief. Twice. "You stole my sled. You stole my knife. Why would I think you were going to share anything when you're stealing what little I have?"

Nemeth sits back on his stool. He looks utterly flummoxed. "You think I stole from you?"

"I *know* you stole from me." I point an accusing finger in his face. "No one else is here, remember?"

He runs a hand down his face, and I can't help but notice that they're oversized—like boulders. His feet are overly large, his thighs massive, but I thought his hands would be normal-sized, like a human's. His proportions are all wrong, though. With both hands, he could probably span my waist, and I'm a plump, rounded sort. If he raised a fist, it'd be the size of my head. "You think I stole from you."

"You did. You stole my blade. Do you deny it?"

Nemeth reaches out and grabs the finger I'm pointing in his face. He glowers at me as he lowers it and speaks in an even, careful tone.

"After our conversation, I went looking for your blade. It had fallen into a dark corner. I didn't think you would find it on your own, so I retrieved it and kept it safe. You never came to ask for it back." His tone is dangerous. "If you would have checked with me again before jumping to conclusions, you would realize that I have never meant ill for you. After all, I gave it back, did I not?"

I swallow hard, feeling guilty. What he says is plausible . . . if I trust the enemy. Still, he hasn't acted like an enemy to me. Not truly. Have I overreacted so much, then? I know when I don't take my medicine, my thoughts get erratic, but I don't think I can blame everything on my blood curse. I've been assuming the worst about him.

"So, what is it you want?" I ask. "An apology?"

He gives me an exasperated look. "I want a truce, Candra."

"A truce," I echo, confused.

Nemeth nods, the movement proud and just a little stiff. "We are the only company allowed each other for the next seven years. I see no reason why we should be enemies. Why we should war against each other inside this tower when it would be far better to be friends."

Friends. With a Fellian.

A man I just tried to kill. A man who has quietly nursed me back to health, who simply wants a truce. It makes me suspicious, but at the same time, it also makes sense. These past six months have been long and lonely, and it's hard to do everything on my own. If we pool our resources, will it not be easier? Sitting by the fire together? Relying upon one another?

Having someone to talk to?

My throat tightens at how much I want that. But I try not to reveal too much in case there's another hidden bargain somewhere in his words. "I suppose you make a good case."

"I could ensure that you take your medication too." He reaches out and touches my arm, stroking a claw down the inside. "You've been mangling yourself."

That soft, gentle caress takes me completely by surprise. My body clenches pleasurably, and I gaze down at the sight of his dangerous-looking claw teasing over my horribly bruised arm. "It's difficult to shove a needle into yourself," I admit. "And I'm not very good at it. My nurse had gentle hands, but I guess I'm impatient."

"I'm not." He runs that claw up and down my arm one more time and then pulls back. "If you trust me, I can administer it for you."

His touch is slightly proprietary, yet not all that unwelcome. Is it because he's been caring for me? Or am I so lonely that even a Fellian is starting to look good? "And what do you want in return?"

He gives me a look of sheer exasperation. "Why do you think I always want something?"

I lift a finger into the air. "Because you're a Fellian." Another finger. "Because you're the enemy of Lios, and I am a Liosian princess." A third finger. "Because you're a man, and men always want something from women."

Nemeth leans back on his stool, his jaw clenching in a way that makes those prominent lower canines jut out. "You think I have so little control over myself?"

"You *are* a man." I raise my brows at him. "And I seem to recall someone watching me in my bath with great interest."

His craggy face creases, and he laughs, shaking his head. Amusement is written all over his expression. "I seem to recall a princess who shamelessly soaped herself in front of me, practically daring me to say something."

"That's where you're wrong." I lift my chin. "There was no soap."

He slaps his knee and laughs harder, the sound so booming that it reminds me of the thunder of last month's storms. His smile is wide and genuine, and I begin to smile too. I like his laughter. It feels like so long since I've had something to laugh or smile about, and I'm a happy person. Damn the gods! Why am I doomed to be miserable here? Why can't I be happy even if I'm trapped? Why not make the best of it?

Maybe that's possible if we're friends instead of enemies.

His smile fades a little, and he gives me a rueful look, his hands resting on his big thighs. "I have had nothing but books for companionship these last few months. While it is keeping me sane, I would prefer the company of another person. You, my suspicious princess, are low on food and fuel. I am low on people to talk to. Can we not pool our resources and spend our time together?"

He makes it sound so good. I imagine Lionel's expression when he hears I'm in the enemy's bed. That I'm friendly with a Fellian. That he's better at this "tower sacrifice" thing than I am. I would be banished from court for being a Fellian sympathizer. Not even the Vestalin bloodline would save me from his wrath. My sister Erynne would be furious at my disloyalty too. The crown must be strong and unified in order to lead the people, and the Fellians are longtime enemies of Lios. She would be disappointed that I have not yet killed Nemeth. Erynne would have. Erynne always does the right thing.

Yet Lionel is not here. My sister is not here.

This tower is our world for the next seven years. Why spend it at odds?

I look at Nemeth and then at his room, brimming with supplies and books. I compare it to my sparse pantry. "You realize I have a lot more to gain from our alliance than you do?"

"Does it matter?" He holds his hand out, palm up. "If you trust me, I trust you."

That makes me bite my lip. "That's the hard part," I confess. "Trusting you."

"Princess," he says, and his tone is exasperated. "If I wanted you dead, I could have just let you die at my doorstep instead of spending the last few days nursing you back to health."

Oh. That brings me up short. He's absolutely right.

And I'm being a suspicious ass.

"You're right," I say and put my hand into his. "I'm being unfair. Let's be friends, shall we?"

He grins, and for the first time in a long time, I have hope that all of this might turn out all right.

CHAPTER THIRTEEN

Nemeth is an annoying nursemaid.

After our initial agreement to work together, he insists I visit the garderobe and then nap again. I need to regain my strength, he says, and after my quick jaunt to relieve myself, I'm tired and decide it's not such a bad idea.

The next day, he insists I stay in bed while he fusses over me. Pillows are fluffed, blankets are adjusted, and he makes me more soup. I'm feeling much better and like myself again, but when I try to get out of bed, Nemeth is not happy with this idea.

"Where do you have to go that's so urgent?" he asks. "Stay in bed. If you are bored, I will give you one of my books. If you are hungry, I will feed you. If you need to go to the garderobe, I will assist you."

I frown at him. "I can walk on my own."

"Three days ago, you were at death's door," he reminds me.

"And now I am not. Which means I do not need you at the garderobe door." I get to my feet, smooth out my chemise, and then head for the door to his room, my shoulders straight.

Nemeth hovers over me, a frown on his face. "You will come right back?"

"No, actually. I'm going to go up to my room once I'm done." It's not that I need anything specific; I just . . . need a moment alone to think—a moment to breathe. Nemeth has been nothing but kind for these last few days, but my skin itches with the need to put some distance between us, even if it's only for a few minutes. Maybe six months alone truly has taken a toll on me.

He growls at the thought. "I do not like this. You are weak."

When he puts a supportive hand on my back, I bat it away. That's what's bothering me, I realize. I'm being hovered over. I didn't like it with Nurse and Riza, and I don't like it now. "I have survived for six months on my own. I will survive another hour. Leave me be."

With a furious look, he ruffles his wings—a sign I'm learning is agitation. Then, he stomps to the nearest table, picks up the globe on its stand, and holds it out to me. "Take a light."

And then he stomps back into his quarters again.

I stand in the doorway, frowning at his temper. He acts like he's the one who hasn't had a bit of space to himself the last few days. "I don't know why you're making a big fuss like this," I point out. "We both know you're going to just hover in the shadows and watch over me like a mother hen."

"I am not," Nemeth declares, his tone dangerous. He picks up a book and brandishes it. "I am going to read. Take as much time as you like. I care not."

Rolling my eyes at his temper tantrum, I head for the garderobe. When I'm done there, I'm tired, but in a pleasantly achy sort of way, and I'm not ready to lie in bed for the rest of the day again. Nemeth acts as if I am a fragile thing that must be protected from myself. He doesn't realize how much strength it takes to live with an illness such as mine. Every day is survival, and I am tougher than he thinks. So, I head upstairs to my quarters and open the door.

My room feels chilly and strangely vacant. It's been days since I've been in here, and it both feels like forever and five minutes ago. I take a few steps inside, and as I do, I see my knife carefully laid out on my (also carefully) made bed. My discarded dresses have been picked up off the floor and put on their hooks too. That must have been Nemeth. I can see him fussing over every detail, right down to fluffing my pillows. I want to roll my eyes, but I smile instead.

Who would have thought Fellians were so particular about tidiness? I expect a certain amount of mess from anyone born into a royal family because we have servants following behind us all day, waiting to clean up after us. I'm certainly not nearly as tidy as him. I move over to my bed, set the lamp down next to it, and pick up my knife.

I'd tuck it into the front of my dress, but I'm still wearing nothing but a chemise. "Hello there," I say to it. "Did you miss me?"

The knife is silent. Figures that I'd have a salty magic blade instead of a friendly one.

I glance around my room. The fireplace is cold, and my food supplies are exactly where I left them. Not surprising. I consider my dresses and decide I want a fresh chemise, as I'm yet too tired to go through the process of heating water for bathing. I lift the neck of my chemise and give it a sniff. "Do I smell?"

The knife pulses an affirmative.

"Thanks," I say wryly. Okay, a change of clothes, then. I eye my surroundings. "Is Nemeth lurking in the shadows?"

Silence from my knife.

Interesting. So much for my hovering Fellian nursemaid. Maybe he realizes I'm not as weak as I seem and is going to give me some space. I pull off my old chemise and exchange it for a new, fresh one that's wrinkled from washing. It's chilly inside the tower, so, toes curled against the stone floor, I pick up one of my heavier dresses and slip it over my head. It's bright green with an attached skirt, and when the bodice slides over my head, I settle it at my waist and then lace it up at the front. As fashion goes, it's a terrible choice. No one likes their dresses to lace in the front because it screams, *I am poor*. Fashion insists that other people dress you.

I wonder if Nemeth would do my laces up for me if I had a dress that tied in the back.

Once I'm dressed, my sleeves fastened and puffed, fresh exhaustion hits me. I collapse on the edge of my bed. Maybe I'll take a moment before I head back to his warm, toasty, crowded quarters again. I lie on my back in the bed and tuck my knife between my breasts, which are now lifted and plump from the bodice's support. "Is Nemeth coming up here?"

The knife does not respond.

Hmm. Thinking about Nemeth makes me think about other things. Naughtier things. I stroke my hand down the front of my bodice. "Does Nemeth still think about me when he touches himself?"

Yes.

My insides clench, and I think about that claw that skimmed up and down my bruised arm.

"Did Nemeth touch himself to thoughts of me when I was sick?"

Silence. There's that, I suppose. He's not an absolute pervert.

"Has he touched himself to thoughts of me recently?"

Yes.

"Today?" I ask, scandalized.

Yes.

"Right *now?*"

Yes.

Oh. My lips part, and I stare up at the shadowy ceiling in a mixture of shock and titillation. After giving me so much grief about wanting a moment alone, he's taking this time to quickly rub one out? To the thought of me? I stroke my hands up and down my bodice as I consider that, utterly fascinated. I picture a big, skull-sized fist wrapped around his cock, squeezing and twisting as he shuttles into his grip. I bet he'd need large equipment for that to feel good because his hands would dwarf his cock otherwise.

I realize I haven't touched myself since I arrived in the tower. Is that why I'm so fascinated with the thought of him touching himself? Or is it because he's jerking off to me? I haven't been a chaste princess. I've always known I couldn't get pregnant due to the blood curse, so saving myself for marriage seemed rather silly. I slept with my first lover when I was fifteen, and I've had a string of them since then. Sex is a craving, and I've been so preoccupied with survival in this tower that I've had no time to even think about it.

But I'm thinking about it now.

I'm thinking about him touching himself and how good it must feel to release. *Where does he come*, I wonder? Into his hand? A cloth he keeps for such purposes? Does he call my name while he's doing so?

The knife pulses between my breasts, and I shiver with arousal.

I'm tempted to follow his lead and touch myself, to give my body a quick, dirty release, but with my luck, he'd show up in the shadows the moment I put my hand under my skirts. He's probably already done.

Yes.

There goes that idea. I sit up on my bed and glance around my quarters once more. He wants me to return to his room, and it's more practical, of course. We can share fuel and meals. We can make everything go twice as far.

It's just that it also means sharing a bed. He's slept next to me for the last several days, but I've also been ill. The moment I closed my eyes, I was fast asleep and didn't notice anything out of the ordinary. Now, though, I'm going to be acutely aware of his presence. I'm going to think about him touching himself.

Does lying beside me in bed arouse him? Is he hard and aching as he lays at my side?

It's going to be a long winter.

I find a pair of thick woolen stockings and then decide to head back downstairs before Nemeth comes looking for me or before I get any ideas on slaking my own release. Composed, I shake out my skirts and then pick up the light, exiting the chamber.

When I get back downstairs, I see the door to Nemeth's room is open, warm, bright light pouring from it. He sits on his stool by the fire with a large book in his hands that's open to the middle. His expression is serene, as if he's been sitting there reading the entire time I was gone—such a liar. I smile sweetly at him, feeling a bit naughty at knowing his secrets. "See? I'm fine."

He eyes me, his gaze moving over my tight-waisted dress. "Isn't that getup uncomfortable?"

"This? Not at all." I put my hands to the bodice and give my tits a jiggle. "It keeps everything in place."

Nemeth quickly looks away again. "I see."

It takes everything I have not to smile.

It's a slow, lazy day, the first I've enjoyed in a long time. Nemeth refuses to let me help him make dinner as he cooks a thick stew of dried meat and mushrooms over the fire. I'm told to stay in bed and rest, and he gives me his book to "enjoy" while he tends to the food.

I flip through the pages, frowning. "There are no pictures in this. And the words are so tiny. Are you really reading all this, or are you just pretending to?"

He chuckles, the sound so deep and low that it does quivering things to my belly. "What is the point in pretending to read a book? Clearly, it doesn't impress you. Next time, we'll ask for books with more pictures."

I regard him as he stands near the fire. "Are you trying to impress me, then?"

"Don't be ridiculous, princess."

He doesn't turn around, though, and I wonder if he's done other things to impress me. Things like taking apart my sled for firewood, perhaps, or giving me one of his precious magical lights. Here I've been too obsessed with thinking of him as the enemy to think of him first and foremost as a lonely man.

A lonely man can be controlled by his needs. I wonder if I should try to pull Nemeth under my thumb to make him fall in love with me. It'd be diverting to seduce him and keep him begging for my favors, but it also seems rather callous, considering he's already offered to share his supplies with me and nursed me while I was sick.

I'm just . . . not used to having a man as a friend. The men I know are courtiers who want to get in my bed for a quick fling or want an alliance with my house. They want to use me to get close to the king or Erynne. No one ever just wants to get to know me simply because of me. No one spends time with me because they want to. It's all because of what I can do for them.

I flip through his book idly, not reading any of it. I'm not a scholar. Reading is difficult for me unless I concentrate, and the thought of staring at a book with such tiny lettering makes my head hurt. I watch Nemeth instead. "Tell me about your life back home."

"So you can pass it on to your people? You'll forgive me if I decline." He stirs the food. "Not too much longer now."

I make a face at his back. "Not about that sort of thing. Tell me about your family. Do you have one?"

"Me? No." He continues to stir. "I have parents and siblings, but I will not speak of them to you due to the war. I do not have a wife of my own or children if that is what you are asking." He sets the spoon down and glances back at me. "From a very early age, I knew that my destiny would be this tower. My parents sent me off to the Alabaster Citadel so I might study under the priests there."

I gasp in surprise. For some reason, I thought he'd spent all his life in the Darkfell mountain caverns. "The Alabaster Citadel? So you knew my sister? She was there too!"

He is silent for a long moment. "I did know her, but only in passing."

"What was she like?"

Nemeth turns to look at me. "You didn't know?"

I shake my head. "She was sent off when we were young, and I only have the vaguest of memories of her. What was she like? Was she happy?" Oh, I hope she was happy. It hurts me to think that she might have had a miserable life cut short. I've always had to deal with my blood curse, but overall, my life has been a joyous one. "Please tell me what you recall."

He pauses and considers this for a moment, then picks up a pair of bowls and begins to dish out the stew. "As I said, I only knew her in passing. We were kept apart because of the strain between our countries. The priests at the Alabaster Citadel didn't want discord there. But I remember her as being tall with dark hair and pale skin. Big eyes. Quiet. She liked to sing the morning hymns with the priests."

Oh. I take the bowl he offers me and picture my sister—someone with Erynne's face and form, singing and happy. I sniff at the thought, desperately missing Erynne and the sister I never had a chance to know.

He holds a spoon out to me with a wary look on his face. "Are you crying?"

"What? No. Absolutely not. Piss off." I rub a finger under my nose. "I've just got a tickle."

Nemeth grunts. He sits and eats while I compose myself, and he doesn't push me on the fact that I sniff again. *I'll cry tomorrow when I'm alone,* I decide. *I'll think about Meryliese then and whether or not she had a happy, fulfilled life.* To think that Nemeth knew my sister and I did not. "So you spent a long time at the Alabaster Citadel?"

He nods. "I actually had dreams of becoming a monk there at one point. I liked the thought of spending my life working on books."

"A monk?" I make a face at him and then giggle. "To think that they stuck me in here with a monk!" It explains why he was so frozen at the sight of me bathing . . . and why he touches himself in secret instead of flirting with me.

"I do not see what is so amusing about that," Nemeth says in a stiff voice.

"It's funny because I'm not the most virtuous of princesses," I say, tapping his arm with my unused spoon. "Back at court, I was known as a bit of a flirt and a rather determinedly frivolous sort. King Lionel was very vexed by me." I smirk. "I don't think he was sad to see me go."

"King Lionel is a monster."

"On that, we are agreed," I say cheerfully. I put my spoon into my food, stir it, and then take a tiny bite. Delicious. "You're a good cook, by the way. This is far better than anything I've made."

"I had years in which to practice my skills."

It makes sense. I imagine one of the duties at the Alabaster Citadel was to ensure that the two "sacrifices" to the goddess were self-sufficient and had no need to abandon the tower. "At least you were somewhat prepared for this." I gesture at our surroundings. "I had three days, and two of them were spent traveling. We found out about the shipwreck, and suddenly, I was being tossed into a carriage and sent here."

"I am . . . sorry." He watches me with dark green eyes. "It must have been quite a transition."

"Awful," I agree. "But I was the only choice left. The Vestalin bloodline is all but gone save for Erynne and—" I break off because I don't know if he knows that my sister was pregnant. Erynne had told me that the moment she was able to take Lionel to her bed again, she was going to try to get pregnant once more because it was so very important for our bloodline to continue. "My sister, the queen," I emphasize, deciding that's safe information. "Myself and my sister, and I'm trapped here."

He continues to eat, saying nothing.

It's difficult to know what we should speak of and what we shouldn't. I want to ask him how many are left in the Darkfell line, but I suspect he won't tell me. The gossip coming out of Darkfell's mountains is anemic at best, and our spies are few. I don't know how many are left in the bloodline there or if they yet have control of the throne as they did back in the days of my ancestors. Then again, Nemeth wasn't there all his life. He was at the Alabaster Citadel, and I had no idea. I eye him over my bowl. "You were at the Citadel but didn't travel on the same ship as my sister?"

Nemeth looks uncomfortable. "I was called home a few weeks prior to the solstice. My king wished to speak with me privately. I was supposed to be on the ship, though. I . . . think about that a lot."

I can imagine. "Well, I'm glad you're here."

He manages a smile and then gestures at my bowl. "Eat."

CHAPTER FOURTEEN

I go with Nemeth as he takes the dishes down to the kitchen and rinses them out. I offer to help, but he won't let me, so I sit on one of the counters and watch him, and we talk about the things we can't wait to eat or do once we get out of here. It passes the time pleasantly, and then we head back upstairs for bed.

I take off my overdress, tugging on the bodice laces, and to my surprise, Nemeth moves to my side and loosens the ties on my oversleeves. He helps me without saying a word, and it feels comfortable yet too intimate. "I can manage," I murmur, acutely aware of how jiggly my breasts are the moment I loosen the corset. "It's really no problem."

"I should learn how to undress you," he says.

"Is that so?"

His eyes flash, and I could swear he's blushing. "So I can know how to take care of you if you should get sick again. For your medicine."

"Of course. That's absolutely what I was thinking," I purr. "Medicine."

Nemeth looks shy as he finishes unlacing my oversleeve. Once it's off, I roll up my chemise sleeve and examine the inside of my arm. I always use the right arm because that's the one Nurse used. There are bruises and scabs from my clumsy efforts, but I don't see any sign of yesterday's dose forming a new bruise. He *is* good at this. I glance up at him as I sit on the edge of the bed and steady my arm on my lap. "How did you know how to make my potion when I was sick?"

He picks up a small pot near the fire, and I see he's already been warming the concoction. "You made the same foul-smelling mix in the kitchen over and over again, and you always stared at your book as you did. I figured it was a recipe for something important, and when you fell sick, you were delirious. You kept talking about your potion and how you needed it, so I started searching your quarters. I found your book, and when I looked inside, there were instructions." He gives me a grave look. "I hope I did not intrude."

"You saved my life. I'm fine with a little intrusion."

Nemeth fills the syringe and carefully flicks a finger against it, releasing any trapped air bubbles. "If I do something wrong, please let me know. I'm simply going off the instructions in your guide."

"So far, so good," I tell him, holding my arm out. I'm a little disconcerted when he pulls his stool up extremely close and cradles my arm in his lap. His knee moves between mine, and this suddenly feels more intimate than when I was lying in bed and he administered the needles before. I wonder if I should lie down again. But before I can, he wipes my arm down with a wet towel and gives me the dose without me even realizing he's pricked the skin. His touch is so gentle that I barely feel it. Before I know it, the medicine is rushing through my veins, and he wipes my arm again, this time to clean the blood.

He moves back to the fire as I fold my arm and hug it to my chest. "I've been boiling these before using them like your instructions say. Your nurse is quite thorough."

"She's wonderful," I agree, feeling pleasantly lightheaded with the medicine.

"If I may ask . . . you have plenty of supplies for your medicine. Why is it that you were so ill?" He glances over at me. "Was it a protest of some kind?"

As if I'd be that foolish. I shake my head. "No protest. I'm too fond of living. I was stretching the doses I had left because I'd run out of firewood. That's why I had a slight fit;" I pinch my fingers, indicating just how slight, "Over the sled."

"A slight fit," he echoes, voice dry. "You did try to kill me."

"Very slight," I agree. "I didn't try very hard. I think we both agreed on that."

Nemeth huffs, the sound both amused and offended all at once. He pokes at the logs on the fire, settling them, and then pushes them farther back into the fireplace. "I think we should get ready for sleep unless you need something else."

"You're just rushing me to bed, aren't you?" I tease.

His wings flutter. "Of course not. Tomorrow is just a busy day. Much cleaning to be done. And bathing." His wings twitch again. "I thought you might like a bath after being ill."

The man is not wrong. I would absolutely love a bath. "It sounds delightful."

"Tomorrow, then." He goes around the room, tapping the lights to turn them off, and his quarters darken. I get under the covers, checking my arm to make sure it's no longer bleeding before he turns off the final light, and then I lie and wait, scarcely daring to breathe.

This is the first night I'm truly aware that he's going to be in bed next to me—that he touched himself to thoughts of me only hours ago. I scarcely breathe as he climbs over the headrail and into bed next to me. His bed is far larger than mine, and when his wing gently brushes my arm, I realize that this bed was made for the Fellian who would be entering the tower, the sacrifice from his people. "You know, when I first got here, I thought you took the first floor just because you were being a prick," I murmur into the darkness as he settles down in bed. "I didn't realize your bed was so much larger than mine."

He goes still, and then his chuckle echoes in the darkness. I catch a glimpse of shining green eyes, gleaming like a cat's. "The furniture here seemed sized to one of my people. Perhaps I should have said something."

"We could fill the last six months with all the things we should have said," I joke. Having someone in the darkness here with me feels far less lonely than it did in the past. It's rather nice. Like when Erynne used to crawl into my bed when we were children, and we'd snuggle together as she told me stories.

Snuggling in bed with a Fellian isn't quite the same, but at least I don't feel adrift and alone any longer.

"Indeed," is all he says, and then he shifts his weight on the bed. "Pleasant dreams."

I pillow my head on top of my arm, thinking. It's obvious that Nemeth isn't going to use bedtime for flirting. I could take the lead, of course. Turn and press my body against his back—and wings—and spoon him from behind. My smaller form would be ludicrous against his larger one, but after pushing my breasts against his back, I'm sure he'd get the idea. I could run my hands over him. Play with his wings, see if they're sensitive. Rake my nails down those thick thighs that seem to be made backward from mine . . .

And then what?

Have sex with a Fellian? Would it be just sex? Or would the monk-in-training view it as a long-term commitment? As love instead of pure lust and boredom. I'm used to the men at court, where a fling is simply something to do to escape boredom. It's flirting taken a little too far in the dark corners of a room or the thrill of sneaking into a lover's quarters. That's all it is—a thrill.

But I have a feeling that to Nemeth, it would mean something much more.

I tuck the blankets under my arms and decide I'm not ready to make that leap. Not when I have a fire and a full belly for the first time in weeks. I'm not doing anything to mess this up.

For now, sleep is best.

The days start to settle in. The winter rages on, but we're tucked away in the tower; the only sign that the Gray God is in hiding is the ice that sometimes forms over the water and breath that sometimes fogs the air.

I keep track of the days on my wall just as I did before, and just as those did before me. My tally of marks looks distressingly small compared to some of the older ones, so I don't study the existing ones too much. I don't want to remind myself how much time I have here. Through asking questions of my knife, I learn that the Feast of the Good Father is coming up. That means an end to winter and that we are one season away from the solstice.

An entire season left in the first year. What a depressing realization.

But it doesn't seem as bad as before, not with Nemeth to talk to and share the hours with. We split the chores, and even cooking and cleaning don't seem so terrible when you have company at your side. At first, we're a little on edge with one another, uncertain about the other's motives, but that quickly turns into an easy friendship. Nemeth is as kind and sweet as he is oversized—a big gentle giant who does his best to bluster and seem tough, but who is truly sweet inside.

He's courteous, making sure that I have my privacy when I need it, and I try to give him his—aware of what he might be doing when he's alone. I've stopped asking the knife about such things because it seems unfair. He's my friend, and right now, I value friendship far more than a lover. Although sometimes, I truly do ache. It's worst just before my moon flow when I wake up from dreams with my hands between my thighs—feeling an aching, hollow need that can only be filled one way. Sex is a craving, and when I'm moody and irritable, I get *all* the cravings. On those days, I take to hiding in my rooms for a time, hastily rubbing out a climax so I can relax.

On the morning of the Feast of the Good Father, the air is so frigid that it hurts to breathe, and the water pump in the kitchen is entirely iced up.

"No bathing today," Nemeth says, breaking a drip of frozen water off the underside of the pump. "At least we have water in a pitcher upstairs to drink, so we will not have to go without."

"Oh, no. And today is Feast Day." I barely manage to avoid pouting. Barely. "I wanted to celebrate."

"Feast Day?" he asks. "Feast for what?"

"The Feast of the Good Father?" I blink up at him. "Do you not celebrate it? I thought we could make a small grain cake to mark the passing of time or something. It's for good luck."

He arches one of those heavy, stony eyebrows at me, leaning on the useless water pump. Now that it's colder, he's taken to wearing a heavy, enormous cloak over his wings, and I can tell it bothers him because he's constantly slapping it out of the way. Even now, he pushes it aside as he regards me. "No, we do not celebrate such a thing. Exactly who is this Good Father you celebrate?"

"Why, Mekaon Vestalin, of course. He was the king of Lios long ago, the great-grandson of the hero Ravendor Vestalin back when the Vestalin family still held the throne. His daughters were stolen away by Fellian princes. I'm surprised you haven't heard of the story." When he indicates I should continue, I do.

"Mekaon threw a wedding feast pretending he wanted to honor their marriages, but when the grooms arrived, they were slaughtered and the pieces sent back to Darkfell. His daughters were returned to him, and the gods were so pleased that they blessed each Vestalin daughter with a child and a new, noble Liosian husband, and the Vestalin line continued." I purse my lips. "Okay, I'm starting to see why you don't celebrate it."

His lips twist in a wry smile. "Celebrate the willful slaughter of my kinsmen under the false truce? No, we do not celebrate it at all."

"Fair enough, but the gods did bless them," I point out. "All four of the Vestalin daughters had children, and not one of them had the blood curse."

"And did those children have wings? How did their knees bend?"

Rude. "Are you insulting my ancestors by saying they bore the children of the men who raped them?"

"I am saying that perhaps the Vestalin daughters didn't want to return, and perhaps they were happy with their Fellian husbands until their father decided he didn't like it. I'm saying the gods had nothing to do with it, and there's no reason to feast."

I scowl at him. It's a story I've heard all my life and one that reminds all of Lios just how important the Vestalin bloodline is. I love the Feast of the Good Father. Why is he making me doubt the story? "It's not like we can celebrate anyhow. Our water is frozen; we can't cook because we shouldn't spare anything, and it's not as if we have a good deal of pepper anyhow. Or apples."

He blinks at me. "Pepper? Apples?"

Grinning, I flounce to the root cellar in a swirl of skirts. "You don't know the tradition? Okay, so after the Vestalin brides returned, a second feast was held, a betrothal feast. The brides wanted stalwart husbands, so each one took an apple and studded it with peppercorns. Each suitor would take a peppercorn, pull it free from the apple with his teeth, and bite down on it. If he sneezed or spat it out, he was eliminated from consideration." I pause. "But I guess you don't know much about the Feast traditions, right?"

"Yes, I stopped listening after the slaughter of my ancestors," he says dryly.

I make a face at him. "Well, anyhow, the tradition is that those at court flirt by studding apples with peppercorns and handing them to a man they're interested in. If he's interested back, he takes a peppercorn from the apple with his teeth. It's truly a lot of fun." I sigh, eyeing our dwindling supplies in the root cellar. "No apples left, I'm afraid."

"Sorry to disappoint, princess. If it makes you feel better, we have more stew to eat."

More stew. I bite back a sigh. While I am thrilled with every bite of it simply to have good, warm food, sometimes the monotony bothers me. "Stew is a celebration all its own," I say cheerfully. "Especially when you're cooking."

Nemeth smiles at me.

CHAPTER FIFTEEN

We head back upstairs and have a meal of leftover stew. The day is miserably cold, so I huddle under the blankets and nap while Nemeth pulls out one of his books and reads by the fire. It's a lazy day; it's too cold to do much.

I think of my sister back at Castle Lios and wonder if she's enjoying the holiday or if she misses me. Is she eating sweetcakes and drinking mulled wine? Is Balon eating peppercorns out of the apples of other ladies? Do I even care since he's abandoned me? I didn't expect him to wait seven years for me, but now that he's the one who showed up to visit, I'm annoyed that he's wandered away.

Seven years is a long time to miss out on celebrations and parties. Seven years in my prime too. When I get out, I will be thirty-one. Will flirting and dancing seem frivolous and silly? Will everyone be expecting me to settle down? My thoughts take a depressing slant, so I fluff my pillow and go back to sleep.

A hand gently shakes me awake a short time later. "Candra."

Nemeth. I inhale, stretch, and pause because I smell . . . onions? I sit up, rubbing my eyes. "What is it?"

He holds an onion out to me, the source of the smell. Studded into the surface are bits of wood serving as . . . toothpicks? No. They're attached to peppercorns! He's made me a feast apple, but since we have no apples, it's a feast onion.

I giggle at the sight of it, feeling perilously close to crying with joy. "You made me an apple."

"You were so sad at missing the holiday; I figured we could have one of our own without assigning it to a particular historical figure. Nothing says we cannot celebrate the end of winter, just the two of us." His hard face is impassive, but his eyes gleam with amusement. "I will not celebrate that man, but I will celebrate at your side."

I clutch the peppercorn-studded onion to my chest, utterly touched. "Thank you, Nemeth."

"What would you like to do for your holiday? Since there is no one to flirt with but me, you cannot play your regular games." His cloak sways as if his wings are twitching nervously underneath.

"I can't flirt with you?" I tease, hugging the onion as if it's made of gold. I'm just so happy. "You wouldn't eat a peppercorn for me?"

His wings move again, a sure sign he's nervous. I think it's his way of blushing. "If you want me to, I will."

I beam at him and wink, holding out the onion. He takes it from my hand, his fingertips brushing over mine, and then he studies it as if trying to decide which peppercorn he'll eat. Nemeth finally lifts the onion to his lips and plucks one of the peppercorns off it with his tongue, chewing.

"You did it," I crow, delighted. I clap my hands. "Now the rules say we have to be lovers."

He coughs, choking on the pepper in surprise, and I burst into a fit of laughter. Nemeth laughs, too, and the room feels full of happiness even though there's no feast to celebrate. We don't need one after all. We have each other for company and full bellies. It's enough for me.

Nemeth's cloak practically shivers, and he sits down on the bed next to me, handing back the onion. "What else do you do on this holiday?"

I stroke the stupid onion with my fingers, knowing we're not going to eat it. Ever. I'm going to keep this onion forever just because it will remind me of this moment. Nemeth doesn't realize how touched I am that he's done this for me. Other than my sister, people tend to only do things for me because they have to or because they want something from me. Nemeth just did it to make me smile. I touch the tiny splinters of wood, the peppercorns he somehow glued to the end of each one with a substance that looks like honey. It must have been a lot of fiddly work, and to think he did it all so quietly as I slept. "Some people give gifts, but it's mostly parties and food for the feast. Oh, and party games."

"What sorts of games?" he asks. "Perhaps we can do them here."

With just two people? I don't know how effective that will be, but it's sweet of him to want to try. "Well, there's a game where one of the king's rings is hidden into a cake, and everyone gets a piece. If you get the ring in your piece, you get to rule court for a day. And then there is a dessert full of minced nuts, and if you get a whole nut in your dessert, it's supposed to be lucky. It means you're supposed to be exceptionally fertile in the next year."

"Mmm. We can avoid that one, I think."

I chuckle. "It's pretty useless for one such as me anyhow."

"Why is that?"

I wave his question aside. "Most of court likes drinking games or flirting games. Things that involve kissing."

There goes his cloak again, shaking with agitation as the wings underneath move. Is he even aware that he's doing that? It's such an obvious tell that I think perhaps he has no idea. "I doubt you would want to play such things with me."

"Are you kidding?" I laugh. "I am up for any kind of game. And while I'm not a huge fan of kissing old men, I've done so in the past just because I like to win." I give him a sly look. "Did I mention that I'm competitive?"

"Gods help us both," he mutters. Nemeth gestures at me, his big hand motioning where I'm nestled in bed. "You pick the game. I will play."

I consider, turning the onion over carefully in my hands. "Do your people have games they play?"

"Ours are mostly ones of skill. Flight games." He shrugs. "I do not think you would be able to play."

No, I suppose not. I consider the games I know that can be played without additional props or people. I can't think of anything that doesn't involve rather lascivious sorts of things or court frivolity, so I decide to make one up.

"I suppose we could play . . . Secrets. Yes. I give you a challenge. Something small, like, 'Go across the room and touch the wall' or whatever. If you decide not to perform my challenge, you must tell me a secret instead."

Nemeth frowns at me, moving to sit on the stool beside the bed. "This sounds like a foolish game."

"Highly foolish," I agree. "But did you have another way you were planning on spending the afternoon?" I give him a challenging look. "Is your day full of meetings? You have many things to discuss with your advisors?" I lift a corner of the blanket and peer underneath. "Are your advisors hiding under here?"

He chuckles. "Fine. Fine. You win. We shall play your secrets game. All right?" When I beam at him with approval, he asks, "Who goes first?"

"Me because I'm the lady." He raises a brow, and I nod. "Those are the rules. I swear. All right. For my first challenge I . . . " I look around the room, trying to decide. Then, the idea hits me, and I hold out my onion. "I want you to eat another one of these peppercorns."

Making a face, Nemeth takes the onion from me and pulls another peppercorn free with his lips. They lock around the kernel in a rather impressive sort of way that fascinates me, and then he pulls the toothpick free and crunches down on the peppercorn. A moment later, he grimaces and gives his head a shake, but he doesn't sneeze once.

"Very nice," I tell him. "Now you're doubly my suitor, aren't you?" I give him a sly wink. "I suppose it's a good thing we don't have the minced nut cakes for fertility."

His cloak shakes violently even as he narrows his eyes at me. "You are trying to embarrass me."

"I am," I agree. "I find your embarrassment utterly charming."

There's a pained expression on his face, but his cloak gives another vigorous flutter.

"I told you I'm a flirt," I warn him.

"You did."

"Should I stop? I can tone myself down if you feel uncomfortable."

Nemeth shakes his head and runs one hand over his cluster of horns. "I would rather you be yourself. Pay no mind to me. I am just a blushing, bookish sort and not the type to go toe to toe with a court lady."

"So you are blushing?" I tease. "Excellent!" I shift in the bed, curling my legs underneath me as he hands the onion back once more. "Now it's my turn. Dare me something or force me to tell a secret."

He scratches at the base of one horn. "A dare, eh? Let me think."

"Don't vex yourself," I tease. Oh, I'm having so much fun.

Nemeth gives me a quelling look. He rubs his chin, thinking, and glances around the room for inspiration. "I should dare you to . . . "

"Something wicked," I encourage, practically bouncing with anticipation. "Something naughty. Make me do something naughty!"

His nostrils flare, and the cape flutters again. He looks everywhere but me and then says, "I dare you to put a finger up your nose."

I groan. "Seriously? That's all you've got?"

"It's not very ladylike," he says, drawing himself up to his full height, shoulders stiffening. "Are you going to do it?"

I roll my eyes and jam a finger up my nose, making a face at him as I do. "You need to get better at this game, friend. Allow me to show you the way." I crack my knuckles (also not very ladylike) and pretend to consider. "All right. My dare for you is that you take off your kilt."

Nemeth recoils in surprise. "What?!"

"You can keep your cloak on for modesty," I say, flicking my fingers at him. "But that's my dare. I dare you to give me your kilt."

"Absolutely not."

"Then you have to tell me a secret." I wiggle my eyebrows at him. "Make it a juicy one, please."

He puts a hand on the belt of his kilt, as if determined to protect his modesty from me, and narrows his gaze in my direction. "What sort of secret would you like?"

Is he letting me choose? Well, that's just delightful. "Tell me a secret about a past lover."

He rubs his ear. He truly is the twitchiest man when he's nervous. "There are no past lovers."

I suspected as much, and I can't help but smile. "Is that part a secret? That there wasn't anyone?"

Nemeth shrugs. "I suppose it depends on who you ask. The monks back at the Alabaster Citadel might have known the truth of it. It was a secret to you, so that counts, does it not?"

Was it truly, though? As skittish as he is, it doesn't surprise me in the slightest, especially if he grew up at the Citadel with my sister and was surrounded by monks, priests, and prophets. It's not exactly a setting conducive to sensuality. But he's clearly disconcerted at confessing such a thing to me. He looks uneasy, and those brilliant green eyes won't look at me directly. Does he think I'm going to judge him?

I sit up, reach out toward him, and touch my fingertips to his chin. "Look at me, Nemeth."

He does, and his eyes are shuttered as if he's afraid to show emotion.

"This is just a game," I say gently. "A game between friends. Whatever you tell me here in this tower remains with me and only me. I make you that promise, all right? I would never tease you about your experience or lack thereof."

Nemeth just grunts. I suppose that's some sort of agreement.

I hold my hand up. "Want to swear it in blood? I'm happy to slash my palm in dramatic fashion and mingle my blood with yours."

That makes him roll his eyes. He snags my wrist and turns it face up. "Here is a hint from a warrior to a princess," he says, and his claw brushes over the middle of my palm. "You never cut down the middle. A vow in blood doesn't mean you have to slice your hand open. If you do so, not only can you not hold your sword, but you run the risk of destroying the tendons in your hand. If you truly wish to make a blood pact, use a fingertip." His claw moves to the tip of my finger, and he rubs it, his callused hands warm over mine. "Fingers bleed. And no blood pact says that great amounts of blood must be used."

"Such an expert," I say coyly, amused that he's educating me. As if I'd ever hold a sword. "Does this mean you don't want to make a blood pact, then?"

"Oh, we can do it, little princess. You make it sound like a challenge, and I won't back down from a challenge from you." He lifts my hand to his mouth and then nicks my finger on one of his teeth.

I gasp in surprise. Unexpected . . . as was the answering pulse between my thighs.

"Did I hurt you?" he asks, lowering my hand. There's a look of concern on his face.

"No, I'm fine." Strangely aroused, but fine. I watch as the blood wells up on my fingertip, then he nips his own finger and holds it to mine.

Our blood mingles, and his eyes meet mine from across our joined hands.

"Our secrets remain ours," he says. "Nothing leaves this tower when we do."

I nod, and when he releases my hand, I automatically put my finger into my mouth to lick off the blood. Here I started a silly game simply because I wanted to tease him and have some fun, and it's turned into a strange sort of vow that feels rather weighty. Like we've just made a soul pact of some kind.

Nemeth's gaze is on my mouth as I suck on my finger. He licks his, and I watch as his tongue slithers over his skin. "Do you still want to play?"

"I always want to play," I whisper, and I wonder if we're talking about the same thing.

The game dies a quick death after the deep moment of bloodletting and finger-sucking. It's hard to find the fun mood after that, and Nemeth, clearly out of his element, returns to tending the fire. Instead of teasing him about it more, I let him retreat. If he were Balon or one of my suitors, I'd keep hounding him until I got the response I wanted—either an angry, passionate kiss or a heartfelt confession—but I'm not going to push too far with the Fellian. He's my friend, and I don't like the idea of making him so uncomfortable that he wants to retreat from my presence. Something tells me that if I keep needling Nemeth, it won't break his resolve and turn into a passionate kiss. He doesn't know how the game is played. He'd probably storm out of the room and not speak to me for a week, thinking I was teasing him out of cruelty.

I'd much rather us be friends. So, I cradle my pepper-studded onion in my hands, and we talk of nothing at all for the rest of the night until it's time for bed.

All in all, not so terrible a holiday. When we go to bed, I'm happy, even if my hands do smell like onions and pepper despite washing them.

CHAPTER SIXTEEN

I wake up in the middle of the night to a strange, jarringly loud clattering noise. It's completely dark in the room since the fire has gone out, and it's so cold it feels like my entire body is made of ice. It takes a moment for me to realize that the constant clicking sound is my teeth. I shiver wildly in the bed despite the layers of blankets and the thick dress I'm wearing.

"Candra?" Nemeth's large hand grips my arm. "Are you all right?"

"C-cold," I manage, my teeth chattering. "Why is it so c-cold?"

He shifts in the bed, and I see green eyes blink to life in the darkness. "The fire is out. I could light another, but we should conserve our fuel. Do you need another blanket?"

"H-have them all," I manage, my jaw trembling. "How is it so cold?"

"One last storm before the end of winter, perhaps?" He rubs my arm. "Do you want to get under the blankets with me? Share warmth?"

Do I?

I thought he'd never ask.

I all but fling the blankets back the moment he suggests we share warmth, tugging his blankets over me. Even though we share a bed, we've had two separate sets of blankets all this time, simply because it was more comfortable for both of us to have our own space. I don't care a bit about space tonight, though. Not when I'm freezing and my toes feel like icicles.

I plunge under his blankets, my hands seeking out his to share warmth. He's turned toward me in bed, and my seeking hands encounter bare chest and muscles. Lots and lots of muscles.

I pause, not because I'm shy, but because I know he is. "Are you naked?"

"I am wearing an undergarment." His voice is oddly tense in the darkness.

"Okay, good." I slither forward. "Because you're really warm, and I'm going to put my hands on you."

He remains still as I move against him, settling myself in. His big body is enormous against mine, dominating the bed. I press up against him, my front to his front, my hands tucking between our bellies for warmth, and I curl my legs up against his.

"Better?" he asks, a little more ease in his tone.

"Much," I murmur and lean in, breathing in his warm scent as he settles my blankets over his, enveloping us in a cocoon. My jaw unlocks, no longer shivering with distress, and all of me relaxes. He smells like herbs and woodsmoke from tending to the fire, and it's actually quite a lovely scent on his skin. I'm tempted to burrow my nose into his neck and just breathe in from there all night. "Thank you, Nemeth."

He grunts. "Your chattering was keeping me awake."

I just smile against his chest. He's trying to sound stern and grumpy, but I know him better than that. He hovers over me, watching me as if I'm some fragile thing that's going to break at any moment. I think my blood curse scares him and makes him think I'm more vulnerable than I am. As long as I get my daily medicine, I'm fine. But if he wants to fuss over me? I'll let him.

My feet are still cold, so I draw my legs up and tuck them between his. I'm wearing a heavy dress for warmth, but despite all this, our knees bump. His legs fit together with mine strangely, and he shifts his weight, trying to get comfortable. Right. Time to spoon, then. I roll over, presenting him with my back, and then grab his arm and put it around my waist, tucking myself against him once more. "Better?"

He grunts again.

This time, when I move my feet back and tuck them between his legs, it's far more comfortable for both of us. I'm half-curled, but I like it because he's curled around my back, one of his heavy hips practically over mine. I don't know if he's aware that he's pinning me to the mattress, but I like it. I like his weight over me, hugging me against him. The hand on my waist practically covers me from breast to groin, and I'm fascinated with how much larger his hand is than mine. Now that I think about it, his feet are enormous too.

I shift my weight, pressing my backside up against him.

Just as I suspected, there's a hard wedge of cock between his thighs, pressing up against my amply padded butt. The hand on my waist tightens as if he wants to hold me in place. My senses are utterly, wildly alert. I'm not sure how I'm supposed to sleep now, with his thumb claw practically brushing my breasts and his cock pushing against my buttocks. Perhaps a better woman than I could ignore this, but I've always been a bit of a mess.

I move my hips back and forth in a deliberate manner just because I'm the worst.

I'd love for him to grab me tighter. To haul my skirts up, push my thighs apart, and just claim me. To grind his cock against my backside until he comes. Heated, delicious fantasies fill my head, and I know some of it is the late hour, and some of it is my enforced celibacy, but right now? All I can think about is how good it would feel if he drove me down into the mattress and used me.

"Are you warm now?" Nemeth asks.

I burrow back a little farther just because I'm clearly the only one feeling aroused at the moment. "This is so much better. How is it you weren't freezing?"

"I'm not a puny human."

He is most definitely not. I put my hand over his on my belly, fascinated by the large size of it once more. "Why is it that your hand is so much larger than a human hand?"

"Why are yours so small?" he counters. "Go to sleep."

"Are they big because you have wings, and they're for gripping? I noticed your feet were big too."

He sighs, and his breath brushes over my hair, teasing it. "I do not know. We are two different peoples; thus, we are made differently. Are you going to ask why my knees bend in the opposite direction of yours? Have I asked you about your tail?"

"Tail?" I hiss. "I don't have a tail. Do you have a tail?" Is he hiding it under that kilt?

"Go to sleep, Candra."

As if I can sleep now. I wriggle backward against him, hoping that he'll react. Just a small groan. A hitch of breath. Something that tells me he's noticing how blatantly I'm pressing my backside against him. There's no response, though, and I fight back disappointment. He's not interested, I realize.

But if he's not interested, why does he jerk off to thoughts of me?

The man is a perplexing mystery, but I'm not going to give up—not now that I'm warm and wide awake. "Are you tired?" I whisper. "Because now I'm not tired."

"Candra." There's a hint of amusement in his voice. "You are impossible sometimes."

Am I? I'm clearly not the impossible one. His big hand is a breath away from landing between my thighs, his cock is pressing up against my backside, and I'm the one being unreasonable? I want to laugh at the irony of it. "Want to play our game? We can skip the dares and just tell each other secrets. It's too cold to get out of bed anyhow." I blow a breath out and imagine it fogging in the air.

I wait for him to give me a grumpy sigh or tell me to go to bed. Instead, his weight settles in against mine, his delicious hip heavy against my thigh. His chin presses against my hair. "What do you want to know?"

"Do you have a tail?"

Now I get the heavy sigh. His hand twitches against my belly. "Ask me something else, Candra."

"I'm going to assume that's a yes since if it were a no, you wouldn't be so fussy at me." I tap a finger on the back of his hand. "But fine. Tell me when your birthday is."

"My birthday? Do you truly celebrate such childish things?"

"Why not? Birthdays are a celebration of you. What makes that childish?"

"My people do not celebrate birthdays after you come of age."

I tap his hand again. "Well, I'm human, and I want to celebrate it, so humor me. When is it?"

He's quiet for a moment. "On the seventeenth of spring, I will be twenty-eight."

Born a short time after the last people in his family were in the tower, then. "Were either of your parents in the tower?"

"My aunt." He pauses. "She was never the same afterward."

Mine neither. My Aunt Calliope was older when she went to the tower, and my mother (Calliope's much younger sister) said she was never quite right in the head afterward. That she preferred to sit in the darkness and liked a small, quiet room. She moved to a monastery not long after she returned from the tower and died a few years later. My mother rarely spoke of her, and whenever I asked about the tower, I'd been told that it was Meryliese's duty and not to worry about it.

Now I wish I'd pressed more.

We're both quiet for a long moment, and then Nemeth's mouth brushes against my hair. "That was two questions, you cheat."

Two questions? Oh—the tower and his birthday. "Well, ask me two questions, then."

"Your birthday?"

"Alas, I am high summer, three days after the solstice." I smile into the darkness, cocooned against him. "Didn't feel much like celebrating this past year. I just turned twenty-four." I pat his hand again. "Next question."

"Did you leave a lover behind?"

Oh. I'm surprised he asked that. Perhaps he's not as detached as he's pretending to be at the moment. I stroke my fingers over his hand on my belly and consider my answer. Most men don't like hearing that a woman has experience in bed. They seem to think we don't have needs or desires like they do—that we're supposed to be pristine, virginal goddesses until they deign to stick their cocks into us and "make us whole" or some such drivel. Erynne waited for her marriage to Lionel, and she told me that her wedding night was so awful that she cried for a week.

I've never regretted being free with my favors. But I also don't want Nemeth to think less of me. "I left a great deal of lovers behind," I say, deciding to go for a teasing manner. "But if you are asking if I had my heart on someone specific, the answer is no. Court was just . . . court. Everyone there was bored, including me. You amuse yourself the best you can, and sometimes you end up in someone's bed. It means far less than you'd think. It was mostly flirting, and sometimes flirting would go a little too far. But no heart attachments, no."

I hold my breath, waiting for his response. Waiting to see if he's going to shame me for my immorality.

"So . . . this Balon . . . he is not a great love of yours?"

Oh, is he jealous? I'm thrilled to my core at the thought. "Balon? Please. He wants to marry a Vestalin."

Nemeth chuckles. "So it is not true love?"

I snort. "Very clearly not. He got bored and stopped visiting. If he really loved me, he'd be out there constantly. He's just fascinated by me because I'm an incorrigible tease and have an important family name. Even if he was in love with me, his family wouldn't allow it. Balon will need heirs."

"Ah, so you don't wish to give him heirs?"

I pause. "No one will marry me. I have the blood curse, and it makes me barren."

"This blood curse—you've mentioned it before. What is it?"

I turn my head as if I can see him in the darkness. His breath fans over my face, and it's warm and pleasant and surprisingly cozy. "How many questions are you going to ask? You're not very good at this game."

He squeezes his hand over my belly, sending a pulse of heat straight through my body. "Just tell me. I wish to know."

"Do your people not have the blood curse then? The First House of Darkfell?"

"No curse at all."

Figures. I consider for a moment, wondering if I should tell him. He's still the enemy, even if I enjoy cuddling with him—even if I'm starting to have filthy daydreams about him. Would he use this information against me in the future? But . . . we made a promise that whatever was shared in the tower would not be used against each other. I decide to trust in that.

"The blood curse dates back to Ravendor Vestalin, the First of our Line. Have you heard of her?"

"Yes, everyone has—even us monsters in Darkfell."

I poke him for referring to himself as a monster. The more time passes, the more I'm convinced he's just a man. A man with wings and fangs and weird legs and possibly a tail, but definitely a man. He has people just like I have people.

"So, if you know of Ravendor Vestalin, then you know she was the First of her Line, and she was born from starlight. She wasn't given the name Vestalin until her quarrel with the Golden Moon Goddess. Back then, they called the goddess Vestal. That was before we lost the right to call the gods by their names. Have you heard this story?"

"A version of it, but very different from yours, I imagine. Keep talking."

"Ravendor was a fierce warrior who sold her sword to whoever would pay her. The goddess was upset because Ravendor had killed the goddess's son in battle. He was supposed to be impossible to slay by any blade, so Ravendor used a club given to her by a man of the First House of Darkfell. The goddess was extremely upset and appeared in the sky as the Golden Moon for the first time. She demanded that Ravendor and the man from Darkfell pay a penance—to give seven years to the goddess. Seven years of piety and prayer, and the goddess would forgive them. Ravendor agreed, so the goddess rose the tower from the land itself—this tower—and Ravendor went inside. The Golden Moon hung in the sky for seven long years, watching over the tower to ensure that Ravendor and the Fellian did not leave. Once the seven years passed, Ravendor stepped foot outside of the tower, but the goddess was furious because Ravendor had been blessed by the Gray God during that time and had given birth to a child."

"The Gray God, eh?"

"Yes," I say. "And the goddess named Ravendor as Vestalin—under Vestal's eye—and cursed her line, so some of her descendants are born with a blood curse in their veins that will destroy them from the inside out. It was only through prayers to the Gray God that we figured out a potion that enables me to live." I shrug. "But that's why the Golden Moon Goddess rises every thirty years to harass the new generation of Vestalin and your people, and why she gets so very mad when her demands aren't met."

It's the only reason the goddess's name has survived for so long. Mankind lost the ability to refer to the gods by their names in another war another time, but the Vestalin name has remained even though the names of the Gray God and the Absent One are long forgotten.

"I see."

He sounds amused, and I cannot for the life of me figure out why. It irks me. "You think it's a funny story? That everyone in my line has a risk of death? That I have to take potions for the rest of my life because the goddess is angry with my ancestor?"

"That's not it at all." He shakes my hand against my belly as if I'm a child to be jiggled into paying attention, but instead of making me attentive, all it does is remind me that I'm pressed to his body, and we're sharing warmth, and I'm starting to ache in all the spots that most definitely should not be aching. "You are misjudging me, little princess. I laugh because your story is so different from what I have heard."

"Okay then, what have you heard?"

His breath is warm against my hair. "Well, the Fellian legends are similar in regard to the war."

"But?"

"But the human Ravendor fell in love with the Fellian Azamenth when they went into the tower. It was he who gave her the club that killed the goddess's son, and they were lovers before they went into the tower and continued as lovers when they were there."

"What?" I practically screech. "Humans don't marry Fellians!"

"She gave birth to Azamenth's child," he continues, his tone chiding. "Which is far more believable than the Gray God touching someone like her and having her give birth to a baby with no father."

I sputter. "The Gray God—"

"Are you sure she did not fornicate with a gray man? A Fellian? Because my people are gray. It is entirely possible that the story was twisted over time. My people say Azamenth was devoted to her, and it was Ravendor who betrayed him. The moment they left the tower, she abandoned him for her human lover. He killed himself out of grief and the loss of her. It is why my people do not like humans much. They have betrayed us time and time again."

I roll my eyes, plucking his hand off my stomach. All the sensual pleasure I felt about being wrapped in his embrace has disappeared, and I'm left with vague irritation. "So you're saying that I'm not born of the Gray God, but that one of my ancestors was Fellian. Do I look Fellian to you?"

"It was many generations ago. Our legends say the child looked like Ravendor, but his coloring was that of my people."

I think of my sister's dark hair and green eyes—and mine—and how we stand out in the court of blonds back in Lios. "Someone told you a story full of dragon shite," I declare. If Erynne and I were Fellian, even a drop, we'd be tossed out of the court at Lios. We'd be pariahs, Vestalin bloodline or not. "It's not true."

"Is it such a very terrible thing if it is true?" he asks, his voice soft in my ear as his breath tickles my hair.

"I'm tired," I say. "I don't want to play this game anymore."

I huddle down in the blankets and pretend to sleep. My mind whirls with what he's said. His story can't be true. Ravendor was a brave hero, the champion of Lios. She didn't seduce the enemy and betray him—garbage. All of it's garbage.

Either I disappoint Nemeth, or I disappoint my ancestors, my bloodline, and my kingdom.

CHAPTER SEVENTEEN

The story sits between us for a time, souring our conversations. Things remain awkward, and even though we're friendly, the ease between us is gone. I haven't been flirting. I haven't been teasing him when he returns to our room, dripping and wet from a quick bath, even though he looks delectable, and I find him more disturbingly attractive by the day.

It's strange because we're together in the same room, yet we could not be further apart.

The weather continues to be icy cold for another week, and we burn through far too much fuel. After a few days of this, Nemeth declares no more fires for heat, and we huddle in the blankets together, fully clothed, to share warmth. Since our conversations are fraught, he reads aloud from a book of poetry, and I pretend like they're interesting.

Poetry is truly only exciting when it's dedicated to you, and your lover has written it on your behalf. The rest of the time, it's dreadfully dull and complicated. This one appears to be a war poem of some kind, with lots of flashing spears and mighty heaves of weapons, and it takes all of my strength not to yawn and offend Nemeth, who is quite absorbed.

I have my knife again, and I hold it sometimes and think about the questions I want to ask but I'm too scared to know the answers to. I want to ask it if my sister misses me. If Ravendor really loved the Fellian she was stuck in the tower with. If Nemeth still thinks of me when he touches himself.

I don't ask, though. Perhaps the knife senses my hesitation, because it never volunteers answers. Sometimes it's easier not to know the truth. And the truth would change nothing anyhow. If Erynne doesn't miss me . . . I'm still trapped in the tower. If Nemeth is tired of me, it's not as if he can leave.

If I have Fellian blood, it doesn't change anything. It just depresses me.

I keep to safe questions. "Is Erynne well this day?" I whisper to it.

The knife vibrates with affirmation.

"And her son? Is he well?"

More affirmation.

"And Balon?"

The knife is silent.

After that, I decide to put it away.

Spring comes. At least, I assume it does. There is no hint of sunlight in the dark, oppressive tower. No sound of birds chirping or a gentle breeze or anything to tell us the seasons are passing. But my breath no longer fogs the air with cold, and when I touch the stone wall, it no longer feels like touching ice.

Another sign of spring? Nemeth is restless.

Every day, he exercises. He tells me it's to keep his strength up since he cannot fly properly in the tower. Even though he was living at the Alabaster Citadel, he had an active life. Part of his training, he tells me, is to be prepared to defend the tower. When he told me that, I laughed. Nobody comes in or out. But Nemeth was very serious and replied that it was to ensure no one tried to remove us from the tower before the seven years were up.

After that, I'm no longer laughing. I think about Balon and how I'd begged him to free me. Would Nemeth have attacked him? Or me? Simply to stop the displeasure of the goddess from falling upon us? It's a sobering thought.

I watch Nemeth one morning as he does his exercises.

"Do you want to join me?" he asks because he always asks.

"I'll just watch." I always watch. Not because I'm lazy (though I am) but because the sight is spectacular. I hold a book in my hands, but I am not a reader and have no plans of actually cracking it open. Books are boring. People are far more fascinating.

Nemeth wears nothing but an unadorned linen kilt around his hips as he exercises. It allows for movement, he tells me, but all I know is that it allows for some delicious viewing. He faces the fireplace, his back to me, and I watch as his wings ripple outward. He does a series of stretches after this, lifting his wings up and allowing me glimpses of his magnificently strong back. He's immensely broad. His shoulders are wide and taper down to a thick waist that's nothing but slabs of muscle. He's not elegant and lithe like Balon. Every bit of him is strength, and it fascinates me.

As his big thighs flex and he maneuvers, his kilt tightens across his buttocks, and I catch a glimpse of strong, tight globes of muscle and a hint of a tail between them. Aha. As secretive as he is around his tail, I feel like I've just seen his cock, and it makes me incredibly aroused.

I might need some alone time after watching him exercise.

He stretches; his fingers arch toward the ceiling, and his wings flick outward. My breath catches, and I press a hand to the bodice of my gown, fascinated at those oversized hands. He could absolutely wreck a woman with just one single finger, and the thought makes me squirm. Gods, I really need something to take the edge off. Maybe I will go upstairs after this, citing a headache and alone time needed. Something. Anything.

Nemeth stretches higher, his heels lifting off the ground. Then, he curses and thumps back to the floor, scratching wildly at the base of his neck—just above where his wings attach to his shoulders. He growls in frustration.

"Problem?" I ask, tossing aside the book I'm not even pretending to read. It's so unlike Nemeth to show irritation that it immediately gets my attention.

He makes another crabby noise and claws at his back again. "Dry skin. The winter has made me itchy. I can reach most spots but not this one."

Oooh. I watch as he scratches frantically at another spot on his shoulder before trying to reach for the place near the join of his wings again. His twisting is giving me quite a show, and I pause to watch for a moment before taking pity on him. "Would you like some help with that?"

"Help?" He turns and gives me an impatient look.

"Yes, help. I can oil your shoulders and wings for you if you'd like. I'm happy to be of assistance." I make my voice sound as innocent as possible. As if I'm just an innocent saint willing to help out. As if I haven't been salivating at the thought of putting my hands on him. I fling the blankets off the bed and get to my feet as if it's already decided. "You've got some oil around here somewhere, don't you? Or a lotion of some kind?"

He turns and faces me, still grumpy. "I guess so, yes."

We pick through several bottles of various concoctions that he's brought with him for healing. He has a number of tinctures for burns and extracts for sicknesses of various kinds, and eventually, we find a bottle that's labeled "wing oil." Nemeth hesitates to pull out the cork stopper. "I've been saving this because I'm not sure if they'll bring me more when they bring supplies. It needs to last."

"Maybe we can make our own if we run out," I tell him. "There's no point in you having itchy wings for the next seven years. I'm sure that can't be good for your skin."

"Six," he corrects absently. "But . . . yes. You are right."

Huh. In another month, it will be six years. We've almost made it an entire year. It feels like we've been in this tower forever, yet at the same time, it feels like we just got here, and we're still finding our footing. "Your birthday is soon then," I comment. "How do you want to celebrate it?"

He snorts. "The only thing I wish to celebrate is another solstice so we can be that much closer to freedom."

Good point. "I promise I'll be sparing with the oil."

I pour a tiny bit into my hands and show it to him for approval. Nemeth gives me a cranky grunt and then taps at his shoulders. "Right between here."

"Just a moment." I close my fingers over the bit of oil in my palm and, with my other hand, grab my skirts. I climb onto the bed and stand upright, then turn around to face him. "There. This should help since you're so much taller than me."

His wings flutter as he gazes up at me. "You're sure you don't mind doing this?"

"You're really going to ask that?" I give him an exasperated smile. "You, who administers my medicine to me every night?"

The wings twitch again, his shyness coming through. "You bruise so easily. I want to make sure you don't get hurt, that's all."

. . . Because he is kind and gentle. Because he doesn't like to see me suffer. Because we have this strange push-pull dynamic between us that we can't figure out how to handle. I indicate that he should turn around, then rub my hands together to warm the oil. I've had heated oil massages after my baths in the past, and it's always nice to have someone's strong hands working your muscles. It's the least I can do for Nemeth after all the kindness he's shown me.

Plus, I'm being selfish because I really, really want to touch him.

Carefully, I place one hand below his neck at the spot between his wings. It's surprisingly hard to reach because his sweeping horns jut backward like a wind-swept mess of hair, and they get in my way as I try to maneuver closer. But the moment I stroke my fingertips between his shoulder blades, he sighs with pleasure.

"Perfect. Just like that."

His low voice sends ripples of heat through me. Thighs clenching, I bite my lip as I smooth my oily hands over his back, rubbing and massaging around the base of each wing. I dig my fingers into his hard muscles, fascinated at the play of them. He's so very strong. His shoulders are enormous to give strength to his wings, but I don't find them unattractive. The opposite, really. I run my slippery hands down his spine, then back up again. "Should I do the wings too? Or just your back?"

"Wings too, if you can."

"I've never touched a wing before," I say softly. "If I do something wrong, let me know."

With careful fingers, I caress the delicate, flexible bones of his wings. I know from watching him move them that the bones here are strong but light. He's meticulous with them. He stretches the wing I'm touching out to its full length, the ripple of leather-like skin fascinating up close. I can see minor striations in the skin and veins tracing through the delicate membrane. Using my fingertips, I trace along one vein, forgetting that I'm supposed to be massaging and following my curiosity instead.

"Perfect," he groans. "Your hands . . . they're perfect."

My pussy clenches at his words and the ragged way he says them. He sounds aroused, as if the movement of my hands over his wings is the most decadent thing ever. "I don't think I'll have enough on my hands to cover your wings, but I'll get the bases well," I murmur, moving to the other wing as he extends it outward. "Tell me to stop, and I will."

He doesn't tell me to stop, though. Instead, his breath hitches the moment I touch his other wing, and just that small noise makes me clench again. I stroke and toy with the thick base of the wing, rubbing the oil on and around it, working the firm muscle on his shoulder where it's attached.

I'm having very naughty thoughts. Very naughty thoughts brought on by arousal.

Would he stop me if I ran my oily hands down his front? If I reached around his waist, gripped his cock, and worked my slick hands over him until he came?

I bite my lip again, the mental image of that driving me slightly mad with lust. Do I dare?

I know he's a Fellian. I know he's the enemy. I just . . . don't care at the moment. I'm dying to touch him.

Slowly, carefully, I slide my hands lower down his back.

Nemeth stands before me, frozen in place, his wings spread so I can administer more of the oil to his skin. I should be working on his wings. I know I should. Instead, I'm running my fingers lightly down his back. I want to touch him all over, to caress that hot, muscled, deep-gray skin and give him pleasure. I'm shameless, but I want to watch him come.

"Can I keep going?" I ask, breathless. "Or should I stop now?"

"Keep . . . going?" It takes me a moment to realize he's confused by my question. "My wings no longer itch, Candra."

"I wasn't talking about your wings." I lean in, slipping my hands around his front, and move lower down his belly. I'm being obvious. So obvious. I close my eyes as I stroke my fingers over his abdomen, waiting for him to push me away.

Maybe if he spurns me, I'll finally stop thinking hungry thoughts about him.

"I . . . I . . . " he stutters for a moment. "You do not have to, Candra. I did not mean to . . . "

He trails off. Didn't mean to what? I remind myself that he's a virgin and he's not used to flirtation. He grew up around monks, after all. "I know I don't have to. I *want* to. May I touch you?"

Nemeth groans, the sound low and ragged. "*Please.*"

Oh gods. My pussy clenches again at the sound of that single word. Has anything ever been so sinfully *delightful*? I keep my hands on him as I step off the bed, all the better to stroke my slippery hands around his waist. His wings fold in slightly, but my arms are yet underneath them. Not quite trapped, but definitely holding me in place.

I love it.

I press my cheek to his back, not caring that I'm getting oil on my skin. I close my eyes and savor the moment, my hands flexing over his stomach and then moving down to the waist of his linen kilt. Before I can even reach downward, there's something hard and urgent pressing against my hand.

His cock is already fully erect.

Oh. My lips part, and I reach down, moving my fingers over the shape to learn him. I can feel the tension bunching up in Nemeth's muscles, but he doesn't stop me. He doesn't pull my hand away. He's perfectly still except for his wings, which twitch each time I touch him.

It's the most erotic experience I've ever had . . . and I've experienced quite a bit.

Nemeth's head falls back, his horns brushing against my hair. "Candra . . . "

"I love touching you," I confess in a whisper. "I've thought about it so often—how you'd react if I got brave enough to put my hands on you. I wondered if you'd push me away because I'm human and a spoiled princess or if you'd feel anything for me." I bite my lip because I'm blurting out vulnerable things, and I hate being vulnerable. "Anything at all."

"Candra—"

"And then I decided," I continue before he can speak. "That it doesn't matter. We're trapped here, and we can do whatever we like, and no one has to know. Just like we promised, all secrets remain in the tower." I slip my hand under the waist of his kilt, and the fabric falls to the floor between us. "We can do anything at all," I whisper. "You can be my secret, and I can be yours."

I curl my fingers around his cock and stroke him.

"*Unh*." The sound Nemeth makes is primal. His hips surge up as I caress him, and I stroke him again, this time slower, learning his cock with my grip as I do.

I gasp with delight as I realize just how big he is. I drag my hand up and down his shaft, from base to tip, and it's a *journey*. He's big and thick, and I can't believe what I'm touching. "You've been hiding all this under your kilt? That's incredible. To think I've been missing out on seeing all this."

He grips my other arm, the one I have around his waist, and his hand covers mine. At first, I think he's going to stop me, that I've gone too far, but he links his fingers with mine and holds me tight.

Oh.

My heart aches. Sweetness rushes through me, and I nuzzle against his back. I want to kiss him all over. I want to make him feel so damn good. I slip my hand up to the tip of his cock, encircling it, and it's an elongated sort of tip that ends in a blunted point, less mushroom and more arrow. How very curious. I tease the tip, pressing my finger against the dip in the center. Within moments, my fingers are coated with sticky pre-cum, and I begin to work him again with a tight, shuttling grip. "Tell me if I do something you don't like."

He groans, his hand tightening over mine. "Good," he rasps. "So good, Candra . . . "

I squeeze harder, using his foreskin to work him, and add a little twist near the end of his cock, teasing the tip as I drag up and down. "I love that you say my name."

And I do. I love that I'm fulfilling his fantasies, that he's twining his fingers with mine even as I work his immense cock. I love the hot, hard feel of him in my grip. I love the trembling of his wings that intensifies with every stroke of my hand. I've daydreamed of this, but the reality is so much better.

His hips buck, startling me from my reverie.

Nemeth makes another one of those *unh* sounds that seem ripped from his throat, and when I work my hand over his cock again, it's as if he's pumping into my grip. He must be getting close. Hot excitement curls through me at the realization. "Can I make you come?"

He groans again, the sound more of a growl, and it's so intense and sexy that it makes my toes curl and my thighs clench in response. His laced fingers tighten over mine, and his other hand covers the one gripping him. He forces my hand up and down his shaft, hard, and as he does, his hips flex forward.

"Use me," I purr. "I love it."

Nemeth's breath catches again, and then he's fucking my hand roughly, shuttling his cock into my grip over and over again, twisting and using my hand for his pleasure. His breath catches again—a rough, choked sound—and I squeeze tight. There's a wet splat as his hot release spatters on the floor in front of us, and my hand is coated with his seed. I stroke over him again, slowly . . . and then pause. There's a hard bulge at the base of his cock that's new to me. It appeared just now, and I'm mystified. "What's this?"

"Knot," he wheezes. "My knot."

It feels hot and tight. There's no sound of panic in his voice, though, so it's clearly a normal thing for him, even if it's strange and inhuman to me. I stroke my fingers over the "knot" at the base of his shaft. "Should I touch it?"

His wings spasm, jerking so hard that I know the answer before he speaks. "Yes," he pants. "Yes. Feels good."

All right, then. I lightly touch, and when his cock twitches in my grasp and more seed spurts out of him, I grow bolder. I rub that hard knot, toying with it even as I whisper filthy things against Nemeth's back. I drag my thumb over the bulging ring of it, and Nemeth continues to come, his lungs heaving. Perhaps it's a lot like my clit, I decide, where I can have multiple orgasms with the right touches at the right time. The thought's an appealing one, and I keep working him with my fingers until he groans and pulls my hand away, clutching it against his chest, just like the other one.

I hug him from behind, smiling, my cheek pressed to his warm skin. Even though I didn't come, I feel good. Happy. Pleased. He sags against me, and our joined fingers are sticky with his release. He seems reluctant to let me go, and I'm content for him to hold me tight. I didn't realize how much I've missed touching until just now.

It's not about sex. It's about intimacy. I've been craving intimacy with Nemeth, and I'm so, so glad I finally took the leap.

I just hope I haven't offended him in some way. I know how to handle a human man. I don't know how to handle a Fellian . . . as the knot has blatantly proved.

"You . . . " he manages to choke out. "Why . . . ?"

What does he mean, *why*? I'm puzzled by the question. "Because I wanted to?"

He releases my hands and pulls away from me, leaving me to stagger forward. I manage to catch myself before I faceplant in the room and hold my dripping hand out from my skirts. Normally I'd just wipe my hand on my dress, but now that I'm the one who has to do the laundry, it's not worth the mess. I watch in surprise as Nemeth scoops up his discarded kilt (and yup, there is definitely a small wedge of a tail tucked above his butt cheeks) and tugs it over himself, giving me a disgruntled look.

He's acting like he's upset . . . at me? My stomach gets a little queasy, and I pick up one of my discarded woolen stockings and wipe my hand clean on it. "You said you wanted me to keep going."

"I didn't realize what a game my responses were to you." His voice is harsh, cutting. "You find Fellians revolting, remember? Was this a ploy of some kind? To have something to use *against* me? Or so you can prove that I'm weak and foolish around a pretty woman?"

Hurt spirals through me. I calmly finish wiping my hands and toss down the stocking. I smooth my skirts and wipe my cheek, still slick with oil. I want to cry, but I'm not going to show the bastard that he's wounded me. "That wasn't a game."

"Then what was it?" he bites out. "What else could it possibly be?"

"Maybe I just like you, you sodding pile of dragon shite," I bellow at him. I grab my skirts and lift my head, marching across the semen-splattered stone floor as if I were a queen. "I'll be upstairs. Don't come after me."

I head up the stairs in the darkness. I'm so irritated and hurt that I've forgotten to grab one of the lamps, but no power in all the heavens is going to make me go back into that room and face him. My jaw set, my dignity arming me like a cloak, I head up to the second floor and to my old room.

My bed is where I left it, and there's a gentle dripping into the pan that tells me it's raining outside. I lie down on the naked bed (since all the blankets are downstairs) and stare up into the darkness. Tears threaten again because I feel betrayed that something I thought was so wonderful has turned out so badly. How could he think that I touched him just to have something to use against him? Does he think I'm that cheap with my favors?

True, I have said in the past that Fellians are horrible and the enemy, but I thought he realized just how attracted I am to him. I can barely keep my hands off him whenever we're together. I watch him do his exercises like some sort of pervert. I cuddle up against him and press my body to his in bed the moment there's a hint of cold weather.

Yet he thinks the worst of me.

It hurts more than it should, and I'm not used to letting people wound me like this. If we were back at court and someone thought I was using him after I'd made him come . . . I'd probably have laughed in his face and thought nothing of it. I'm untouchable back at court. A Vestalin princess with the world in her fist.

I don't like this tower version of who I am. She's far too vulnerable. Tears threaten again, and I jab my nails into my palms until the pain makes the tears vanish.

I'll cry later. Tomorrow. Next week. When I get out of this fucking tower. Just not now.

CHAPTER EIGHTEEN

I stay upstairs and glare in silence at the ceiling for what must be hours. I don't feel like coming down from my room because then I'll have to face Nemeth, and I really don't want to. He made me feel ashamed and hurt, and it pisses me off. I'm considering just staying up here for a few weeks—maybe longer—until things settle between us. There's not as much of a need for firewood now with the weather warmer, and if I miss his company, it's my own fault for trying to entice a stupid, stubborn Fellian into liking me back.

I hear Nemeth's approach in the dark, silent halls of the tower before I hear the knock on my door. "Come out, Candra."

"Piss off." Am I being sulky and childish? Yes. Do I care? No.

"It's time for your potion."

I sit up in the darkness. "I'll do it myself."

"No, you won't." That stubborn note enters his voice. "You hurt yourself when you do. Come downstairs, and I'll administer it for you."

"Quit being a bully," I yell back. "I can do it myself."

"Not without your tools, and they're currently in my room."

Oh, is it going to be like that? Indignant, I get to my feet and feel my way across the room, finding the door. I fling it open, and sure enough, there are the brightly gleaming, narrowed eyes of my Fellian nemesis.

He puts a hand on my shoulder. "I'll guide you."

"I don't want guiding. I want to be left alone."

"I'm not going to do that," he growls.

Insufferable Fellian. I jerk away from his grip and head for the stairs, my hand out. "I've made this journey hundreds of times in the dark, have I not? I know the way."

From behind me comes a feral snarl. "Stubborn little princess." In the next moment, I'm grabbed and tossed over his shoulder, the wing moving backward to accommodate me. He smacks my butt as if I'm a child and hauls me down the stairs toward his quarters.

I'm furious.

I'm also turned on. How fucking dare he spank me? How fucking dare he act like he owns me? Like he can take care of me better than I can myself. I grit my teeth, hating that my body is responding to his, especially after he's made it quite clear that he thinks I'll just diddle any man put in front of me like a shameless tart.

And even if I did, so what? He enjoyed it. He's angrier about that than anything, I suspect. He let himself be jerked off by a human, he liked it, and now he's mad at me about it. My anger fires up, and by the time he sets me down in the pleasant, lit warmth of his supply-crowded quarters, I'm past all reason once more. I glare at him, indignant, and then race for the table where my medical supplies are kept, intending to snatch the bag and race upstairs with it.

I don't want to depend on him. I don't *need* to depend on him.

He growls, grabbing my wrist before I can reach the table. "So it's going to be like that, princess?" Nemeth hauls me over to the bed, and I struggle to break free from his grip. "You're so gods-damn stubborn."

"Me?" I sputter. "You're the arse who thinks he's the Gray God's gift to humans. Acting like you're too good for a slutty human's touch, is that it? Because I'm not some pristine virgin, you think I'll just grab any cock in front of me? You think—"

I break off because he whirls me about, and then I'm on my belly, bent over the side of the bed. He pins my arm down on the mattress next to my head, surprisingly gentle despite his strength and size.

"You, princess, will be the death of me," Nemeth snarls into my ear, his voice deadly with fury and . . . something else. A moment later, a hand goes under my skirts and skims up my leg. "The absolute death of me," he repeats, and this time his tone is hot, distracted, as his claws scrape my thigh.

I suck in a breath.

My ass is in the air, and I'm pinned to the bed, half under him, as he presses his weight over me, keeping me secured in place right where he wants me. That searching hand goes between my thighs, and I realize what he's doing a split second before he speaks.

"You can be my secret, and I'll be yours, remember? Just tell me to stop, and I will."

He practically purrs the words into my ear.

Tell him to stop?

I've never wanted anything more than for him to keep *going*.

Pinned down with Nemeth's hand beneath my skirt, I find that all of my anger disappears in a flash.

I want him to touch me. I *need* it more than I've needed anything in a long time. My lips part, and my nails dig into the blankets even as his hand skims up my backside, finding the silky fabric of my panties and tearing them apart with a quick snag of his claws. "Tell me to stop," he warns me again, breathing hard. "Tell me you don't want this, and I'll let you go, Candra."

Stop? Never. I want all of this. I want him to make me come so hard my toes curl and lights flash behind my eyes. How long has it been since I've had a good, hard orgasm? Touching myself isn't the same, and given that my arousal is heightened by Nemeth and the way I touched him earlier? I'm going to come *so* damn hard. It's going to be amazing.

"Don't tease me if you don't intend to follow through."

He growls again, the sound feral and wild. I love it. It makes my nipples prick and my body sing with awareness because I know I'm driving him past all reason. I love that I can push Nemeth—scholarly, warrior-like Nemeth who wanted to be a monk, of all things—past the brink. I love that he's pushing my skirts up to my waist and exposing my backside to the air because he's going to stare his fill at me and see just how much I want and need this.

And I'm relieved. He liked my touch after all. It's evident in the way his hand roams over my hips and thighs, his touch greedy. It's like he doesn't know how to stop caressing me, so he's just going to keep touching and touching until I demand that he stop . . . or I come. Well, I'm definitely not telling him to stop. This is the realization of every filthy fantasy I've had in the last year, ever since I stepped foot over the tower's threshold. My cunt clenches with need, and I gasp as he slides his hand over one buttock, his claw grazing along the crease of my ass.

"Naughty, beautiful Candra," he murmurs. "You're so gods-damn wet. I can smell you from here."

I moan, burying my face against the blankets because he's right—I am thoroughly, unabashedly wet. My cunt is so slippery with arousal I can feel my skin gliding against itself with every slight shift of my hips. I'm so wet he doesn't need oil of any kind to serve as lubricant. I don't think I've ever been so very slick.

His big hand grips my buttock, and it fits neatly against his oversized palm. He gives it a squeeze, and even that small touch is arousing. "How long have you been aroused like this?"

I bite my lip, squirming against his hand. Why, why, why do I desperately want those dangerous claws in naughty places? "Since I touched you earlier."

Nemeth sighs. "And I sent you away."

"You did. You're a monster," I agree breathlessly.

"You want this monster to touch you?"

"Please," I practically sob and spread my thighs apart in silent invitation. "Oh, please do."

He groans, and those delicious claws carefully skate over the seam of my cunt. I can feel him dipping them into the arousal, lubricating my pussy and thighs. "You're flushed with heat here. So warm and soft and wet. To think you've been hiding all this under your skirts all this time."

I whimper because he's still teasing me. His hand is barely brushing over me, and I'm absolutely going to lose control if he doesn't touch me properly soon. "*Nemeth*."

"Did you mean what you said earlier?" he demands, and something hard and unyielding glides through my folds. His knuckle. I groan as he rubs it up and down my pussy, barely grazing over my clit. It's the cruelest of teases. When I don't answer quickly enough, he reaches up and smacks my buttock with a hard, ringing sound. "Answer."

"I don't remember what I said," I confess, utterly distracted. The only thing on my mind right now is the hand I want between my thighs again.

"That you wanted to touch me? Was that true?"

I nod, biting my lip. *Please, please touch me again,* I silently beg.

He smacks my butt once more. "Say it out loud."

"Yes, it's true!" I should be annoyed by the spanking, but gods, it's arousing. I love this bossy, dominant side of him that only comes out at certain times. "Why would I lie?"

"To toy with me," Nemeth comments, stroking my stinging butt cheek once more. "How long have you wanted to touch me?"

His claws skate close to my pussy again, and I clench my hands into the bedsheets in anticipation of his touch. "Since . . . since winter. Since we shared heat under the blankets."

He pauses. "Truly?"

"Maybe earlier," I babble. "I don't know! I don't keep track of these things! I just know I need you to touch me."

"You want a monster to finger your cunt? A terrible, awful Fellian man? You want him to touch your pretty folds and make you come?"

I whimper because when he puts it that way, *yes, yes, I absolutely do.*

Then his fingertips gently brush over my folds again, and I cry out because it's taking everything I have not to buck my hips. "Your claws—"

"I'll be careful," he murmurs, concentration in his voice. "You think I've gone through this world with claws for twenty-eight years, and I don't know how to wield them against delicate things?" The pad of one finger strokes up my cleft and toward my clit. "You think a monster can't be gentle?"

The moment he touches my clit, I sob. His touch is perfection. To my astonishment, he knows just how to touch me too. His fingertip circles around my clit in slow, careful motions, and Nemeth makes a rumble of pleasure when I twitch against him in response.

"So soft," he purrs, the sound rumbling low and delicious in his throat. "So soft and wet and pink." He strokes the hood of my clit, nearly making me come off the bed. "I'd finger that pretty cunt of yours, but you're so small, and my fingers are so big. I think I'm too big for you."

I practically wheeze with need. Oh gods, he's saying such filthy things. I love it. I love it, and I want more.

"Should I try anyhow?" he asks, voice like silk as he leans over me and teases my clit. "Should I stretch you around one of my fingers and see if that pretty cunt can take it? I bet you can take it. I bet I can slip a thick finger inside that pink heat and work you until you're stretched wide. You'd have to be if you're going to take my knot."

Oh gods, his knot. Whimpering, I arch against his fingers. "Please, Nemeth."

"Please, what, princess? Please stop? Please give you my knot? You have to be more specific." His finger moves away from my clit and skims down toward the aching entrance to my body. "If you can't tell me what you want, I'll just . . . stop."

"Fingers," I manage. "Please . . . fingers. Fill me up."

"You only get one, naughty princess," he murmurs, and his voice fills me with heat and longing. "One until I decide you can take two. Or even three."

I've seen his fingers. I don't know if my body can handle three of them, but right now? Nothing sounds hotter than that.

"Hold still," he commands me, and his grip gets tight on my wrist again. "You don't want me going too deep." He leans in close, his breath hot on my ear. "Don't worry about my claws, Candra. I'll be safe with this pretty cunt. Wouldn't do me any good to damage it when I want nothing more than to be deep inside it."

A choked sound breaks from me because I want that too. So much.

"Hold still for me, princess," he tells me again, and then he pushes my thighs farther apart. I don't need more encouragement than that. I spread my legs wide, opening myself up for his access.

There's a pricking nudge, and then an impossibly thick finger slides deep into me. I'm stretching all right. It's a tight, delicious fit that promises so much. I whimper again, squirming because, oh, it feels incredible. It's been so long since I've been filled like this that it makes the breath escape from my lungs. I shiver, and then when he starts to slowly move that finger in and out, I moan. "Need . . . "

"Need what, princess?" His voice is hot against my ear, his weight heavy upon mine. "Tell me, and I'll give it to you."

"Need you to touch my clit too," I manage to choke out. "Need it to come."

"Do you?" That maddeningly thick finger shifts inside me, and then I feel him dragging his finger against the inside wall of my body.

Everything inside me clenches—a paroxysm of responses. I whimper again as my cunt squeezes around his finger, and I come—come so hard that my vision blurs. My muscles lock up, and I keep coming as he whispers and tells me how pretty I am while my face contorts, and I make ridiculous sounds as the climax rolls through me like a wave.

I can only breathe again when that enormous finger slips out of me, and

Nemeth nuzzles at my neck, his weight pressing me into the mattress. "Now we have both used each other."

I moan because that's all I'm capable of. I'm wrung out and exhausted, my bare ass hanging over the edge of the bed, but I can't say I'm displeased. I do feel used, but it's in the best sort of way. How in all the gods did a scholarly virgin know how to do all that? What kind of books was Nemeth reading? A laugh bubbles up inside me at the mental image of him poring through filthy tomes about how to make a woman come.

"Now you have no leverage," he tells me and then gets off of me. He gently lowers my skirts over my thighs and then crosses the room. I sit up, woozy and dazed, and watch as he licks my taste off his fingers and moves toward the fire. "I'll prepare your medicine."

Just like that?

I'm a little miffed. I don't even get a kiss or a cuddle after a fingering like that? Is that all that was to him . . . leverage? Something to use against me? A game to play?

I eye Nemeth as he stands near the fire, watching his reaction. It's calm, but he deliberately avoids looking over at me. His normal kilt is on, but I'd have to be an idiot to miss the way it's tented in the front. Touching me turned him on. He can pretend that he's not affected by me, but I just watched him devour my taste off his hand.

If he wants to play games, we can absolutely play games. This is my *forte*.

CHAPTER NINETEEN

I wake up before dawn, his hand on my stomach. We've been sharing blankets since that one fateful night, just peeling off layers as it gets warmer. Most of the time, I wake up spooned against his big body, but today he's asleep on his back, his wings tucked under him, and his hand on me as if he has to hold onto me even in his dreams.

It's achingly sweet of him, and despite the fact that things were strained between us last night after he touched me, I think it was more than just "leverage" as he claimed. I think there was far, far more to it. But if he wants to call it leverage, and he wants to treat this thing between us like a game, I can play along. I excel at this sort of challenge.

So, I slide out from under his grip and ease the blankets down his waist.

Despite the fact that he's caught me in my bath once, I've never seen him fully naked. We bathe separately, and he hasn't intruded upon me again. In addition, we've taken pains to remain fully clothed for the other person's comfort. It was easy to do in winter when it was so cold that the last thing you wanted to do was strip down. He's always warmer than me, so I suspect his layers of clothing are for my benefit. But now that it's getting warmer, I've been wearing less to bed, and I'm waiting for him to do the same.

As I tug the blankets down to expose him, I see he's wearing nothing but a loin wrap. He gets into bed after all the lights are off, so I've felt the material brush against my skin. It feels like little more than a length of fabric wrapped around his waist and between his thighs, tucked artfully to keep it in place. It should be easy enough to unwrap.

Like a festive gift, I decide and smile to myself. With careful fingers, I loosen the fabric until it falls away from his hips. Once the initial tuck is free, the rest of the linen slides away like water, and I get to feast my eyes upon Nemeth's body.

Like all men, he's nearly erect with morning wood. Unlike all men that I've seen in the past, his cock is spectacular. It's long and thick, which I expected, with velvety-looking, dark-gray foreskin and a heavy, full sac. The end of his cock is tapered and arrow-like and reminds me of one of his horns. He's wide at the base, with an extra ridge that looks like the knot that appears toward the end of his orgasm. I wonder what it's for.

Doesn't matter. As far as I'm concerned, it's for fun.

I run a playful finger along the side of his cock, tracing a dark, thick vein. He groans and shifts in his sleep, his shaft stiffening even more. Encouraged, I lean in and blow a soft breath against his skin. Gods, I love teasing him. I ponder what I should do next. What would feel good to a Fellian as opposed to a human man? More ticklish touches? Play with his sac? Rub his knot that's swelling even now?

A bead of pre-cum appears on the tip of his cock, and that decided me. I lean in and lick him, my tongue swirling over the head.

Nemeth awakens with a gasp, his eyes flaring open.

I give him a wicked smile, meeting his eyes as I tease the head of his cock with the tip of my tongue. "Tell me to stop, and I will."

He groans—the sound as starved as it is needy. Nemeth stares at me, and as he does, his hands fist in the sheets, deliberately not touching me. Not stopping me.

I give him another lascivious lick, pleased. "I thought so."

"Candra . . . "

Smiling, I lick him again and then take him in my hand. I grip the base right over his knot and then feed the tip into my mouth, lapping at him as I do. The head of him fits neatly against my tongue, but the farther in I go, the wider he gets. I can only fit a portion of him into my mouth—the rest is simply too thick.

That's all right. I have hands that can take care of what I can't manage with my mouth.

He makes one of those guttural sounds when I suck on the head, his hands flexing. I pop him out of my mouth with a lick and turn to look at him. "You can hold my head if you want. Guide me. I don't mind."

"Candra," he groans again. "You . . . your mouth . . . "

"I know. I'm good at this." I wink at him and rub the tip of his cock against my lips. "Just lie back and enjoy, yes?"

His breath hitches as I take him into my mouth again. I know just how to please a man with my tongue. I know how to flick my tongue against the underside, how to work his foreskin with my hands as I use my mouth on the tip, and how to coat him with drool so he slides against the back of my throat with a lovely friction.

I'm not surprised when Nemeth's hands go to my hair, and he starts to guide me as I bob on his cock. He doesn't push, but I can tell he likes it best when I take him to the back of my throat and suck hard, hollowing my cheeks. That makes his fingers spasm in my hair, and his hips jerk in response.

The knot under my hand hardens and suddenly balloons, and I can guess what that means. I pull back, tonguing Nemeth's cock with a wet mouth and sweeping licks of my tongue. "Do you want to come on my face or in my throat?"

He growls, his back bowing, and then he's spurting across my parted lips, the orgasm wringing from him with such violence that his claws dig into my hair. Men do love the sight of a woman tonguing their cock, and it's never failed to make a lover come in the past.

I give him small, kittenish licks as his seed fountains out, coating my hands and lips and the front of my sleeping gown. He tastes good—musky and not quite as bitterly acidic as I've had in the past, which I appreciate. I rub his knot as he comes, and each time I give it a squeeze, I'm rewarded with another burst of semen, so I work it until his arched back collapses, and he heaves a great, gusty sigh.

I give him a few more licks and then press a kiss to the top of his cock. "I'll get a towel."

"What . . . what was that?" he asks, dazed, as I get up from the bed.

I'm tempted to retort that it's more leverage to see if he'll fling me down onto the bed and give me my share. But then again, I want him to touch me because he wants it, not because he imagines he must. So, I simply smile and lick my lips. "Happy birthday."

"My . . . what?"

Clearly, when he comes, his brains get scrambled. "Your birthday," I repeat again. "The felicitous occasion of your entrance into this world. You said it was today. Do you not remember our conversation? You said you don't celebrate it after manhood, so I thought I might give you an adult sort of celebration." I flutter my lashes at him. "Did my method of waking you meet your approval?"

The look he sends my way is utterly dazed, and I think, *yes, yes, it did.*

My scholar is clearly not a great thinker once his cock is drained. I find this adorable.

Since we have nothing but time in the tower, I decide that today is a special day.

Nemeth takes care of me regularly, so today, I shall take care of him. I make a midday meal . . . poorly. And since we have no supplies to spare, we have to eat it. Somehow, though, it doesn't bother us. Nemeth is touched that I try and teases that I should actually look at Riza's book of recipes next time instead of just guessing.

I sing him a birthday song (again, badly) and work on mending the hem of his favorite cloak while he reads his favorite book aloud to me. I offer to make him dinner that night, but Nemeth prefers to cook it himself. I do the washing up instead, and he tends to his mushroom farm that grows on the strange board. He's had to move it to the storage rooms since they prefer darkness, and I need the lights.

All in all, it's a lovely sort of day. Nothing outside of the usual (other than my morning greeting to him), but pleasant anyhow.

Before bed, I present him with a cake of my favorite soap, scented with lavender. "If you ask nicely, I might even offer to wash you," I tease, earning myself a wing flutter and a smile.

We get ready for bed, and Nemeth taps the globes, one by one, turning off the lights and leaving the room in darkness. He climbs into bed next to me, and I hold my breath. Now, I wonder, will he touch me? Kiss me?

By all the gods, I would *love* for him to haul me against him and kiss the sense out of me.

Nothing happens, though, and I worry for a moment that he's not interested. That I've misjudged things somehow, and the more I chase, the less he wants me. That I'm only a convenient mouth and nothing more, and that any man would have responded to the way I woke him up.

For a moment, I panic.

Then I remember the knife and all the times it told me he was touching himself to thoughts of me. He does like me. I haven't been imagining it. Something's holding him back, though. Shyness? Maybe that's what it is. Maybe he's shy . . . or waiting for dawn so he can wake me up in a similar fashion.

I squeeze my thighs together at the thought. Oh, it is going to be so incredibly hard to sleep tonight if that's the case.

"Thank you," Nemeth says, voice soft in the darkness. "For today."

"You're welcome." I mean it too. I've enjoyed making him feel special. I can tell he's not used to anyone doting on him, and I'm not used to doting on anyone myself, but I think we both had a lot of fun today. "It's probably terrible to say this, but I'm glad you're here with me. I don't think I would have lasted this long without you, and the thought of spending the next seven years here with you at my side isn't so bad."

"Six," he corrects. "It's almost six now."

"Almost six isn't six, though. I'll celebrate when we get our next round of food." I smile into the inky black of the room, hugging the blanket to my chest. He hasn't pulled me against him yet, which means he's either not ready to sleep . . . or he's hard. I find I'm not ready to sleep yet, either, so I turn on my side and face him.

The bed creaks, and the mattress shifts; then, his green, glowing eyes blink to life in the darkness, telling me that he's facing me too.

I bite my lip, wondering if he'll kiss me now. Ever since I touched him this morning, he's been quiet. At first, I thought it was simply that he was blown away by my generosity (and by having his cock sucked for the first time in his life), but what if he's unhappy? What if that's why he's silent? "Are you all right?" I ask, unable to hold it in any longer. "You've been a little silent all day, and I worry I've upset you now that I have leverage over you again."

I keep my words teasing, but I feel vulnerable. If he's offended in some way or wants me to stop touching him, I'll definitely be hurt. Back at court, if someone bothered me, I could avoid them. Here in the tower . . . he's all I have for company. There'll be no coming back from this if I've made him uncomfortable.

Nemeth chuckles, but the sound is awkward. "It's not you. Please don't think that."

"Kinda can't help but think that."

"I know." He sighs and reaches out and rubs my arm, his big hand warm through my sleeping gown. "Today just made me realize a few things, and my thoughts went to strange places."

"What sorts of things did you realize?" I press because I'm nosy and needy, and I want him to tell me how much he liked my mouth on his cock.

His thumb rubs small circles onto my shoulder. "That I have mocked you for hating Fellians and finding them strange, yet my thoughts have been polluted with the same sorts of things. It occurred to me that if I told anyone that a beautiful human princess woke me up with her mouth on my cock, they would think I was insane for allowing such intimacy . . . that I am deviant for allowing a human to touch me. And more deviant of all, that I *liked* it."

"So, you *did* like it," I clarify. "You didn't feel I sullied your honor or something like that?"

Nemeth snorts. "If you had, I would have asked you to sully my honor at every chance. No one has ever done something like that for me . . . and nothing has ever felt so good. I think that is why it made my thoughts spin to what my people would think."

I move a little closer to him in the bed because worrying about what your people would think? I totally understand that. "My sister wouldn't understand," I confess. "She'd think I'm a tramp for touching you. She'd be horrified, and her husband, the king, would probably toss me out of court. Send me to a convent where I could pray on my 'lustful and wanton ways.'"

"And yet you still did it."

I smile at those glowing eyes. "We're the only ones here. The rest of the world abandoned us. Why should we care what they think?"

"And what about when we leave?"

"I'm not thinking about when we leave. That's too far in the future."

His eyes narrow in the darkness as if his face is creasing into a smile. "You have an excellent perspective on things."

"I've always been the useless princess. Maybe knowing that I'm unimportant except for my family name helps me not care. After all, I can be a whore, and someone will still find me valuable because I'm a Vestalin." I sound bitter, even to myself. "But I'm here for the next seven years because it's better for the rest of the world, right? We're martyrs so the fields can be full of crops, and the Golden Moon Goddess will hold back her rage. We're giving seven years of our lives up for everyone else. I think, given that, they're not allowed to judge us for finding comfort in one another."

His thumb strokes a teasing circle on my shoulder. "Is that all it is to you, then? Comfort?"

"Well, I don't know," I say, trying to keep my tone light. "What is it to you?"

"More."

Just that one simple word fills me with soft, radiant joy as if I've swallowed a star. One word, and I'm so . . . happy. "It's more to me too," I whisper. "Can I ask you something?"

"Of course." His hand slides off my shoulder, and he takes my hand in his, squeezing it. "Ask anything."

"Do your people kiss? Because I've been thinking about kissing you, and you've never even tried to kiss me. So, I wondered if you even kiss with those fangs of yours. If I'm being too nosy or forward, feel free to tell me so. It's just . . . I was thinking about it." By the Gray God's night robe, now I feel like an absolute fool. I'm a princess. Why am I begging a man to kiss me?

Because it's Nemeth, my mind tells me. *He's different.*

He is, and that frightens me a little. If things sour between us—and they always sour with me and my lovers—there'll be nowhere to hide.

"I've never kissed anyone," he confesses. "And no, it's not something my people do. We rub horns . . . but I have seen the humans at the Citadel kiss. Do you want me to kiss you?"

Do I want him to kiss me? The thought makes me want to laugh. I'm here in bed with him, our faces turned toward one another, and I'm filled with such yearning and affection for him. My heart feels both full and empty. Full because I'm with him, and I know he cares for me the way I care for him . . . and empty because I desperately need him to show me just how much he wants me.

I don't think I've ever wanted to be kissed more.

"I would love for you to kiss me," I admit. "But only if you want to."

"If you would like it, I would too." He pulls me closer to him in the bed, his gaze on me.

We're so close now that our breath mingles, warm and inviting. I don't think I've ever liked it when another lover breathed on me. They always smelled of sour wine or something worse. But with Nemeth, I like all his scents. His breath is never foul, and when I feel it against my skin, I know it's because he's close by, and it arouses me.

Then again, everything he does arouses me.

I slide a hand to his neck, stroking my thumb over his skin. He said his people rub horns. I look at the strange, sweeping cluster of horns that cover his scalp instead of hair and wonder if he'd like for me to rub them for him or if that's a Fellian-only sort of gesture. "Can I touch you?"

"Now you ask?" he teases. "You know that you can touch me anywhere."

I move closer until our noses are practically brushing. "So . . . are you going to kiss me, then?"

"You're impatient." His amusement makes me flush with warmth.

"Of course I am. I've been waiting for you to kiss me for weeks." The moment the words leave me, I know they're true. I've been waiting for him to make a move since that first night we cuddled under the blankets for warmth. The fact that he's been so very circumspect is *killing* me. "I keep thinking you're not attracted to me."

His hands clench my waist, and his nose rubs against mine. "No. Never think that. You're the most beautiful thing I've ever seen."

I smile. "Should I tell you that you're the most fascinatingly virile man I've ever seen?" Stroking his cheek, I continue. "That I've never been so turned on by wings? That I watch you exercise because it lets me appreciate every flex of your muscles? That your big hands make me breathless, just like when you pin me under your hip when we sleep?"

"You should absolutely tell me all that."

"I would, but instead of trading compliments, I'd much rather we just kiss," I whisper.

Nemeth moves closer, and then his mouth brushes against mine. His face is hard and unyielding, the planes of it surprisingly brusque against my face. There is no softness in his cheek, and his nose doesn't yield when mine brushes against it. He feels like he's carved from the stone his people dwell under, and it surprises me.

But oh, his mouth is soft.

His lips move over mine, gentle and warm. It's as if he's carefully tasting me, not certain he'll like the flavor. I hold still because I'm afraid to even breathe—afraid that it might somehow offend him. If his people don't kiss, will he even like my mouth on his? Mouths are incredibly intimate sorts of things. I've kissed men before that turned out to be unpleasant to taste, and—

His lips move over mine, breaking my chain of thoughts. One small nibble at my lower lip, teasing it, and then moving on to more light, teasing kisses. His searching mouth finds my upper lip, and he gives it the same light, feathery kisses as my lower lip. I'm utterly entranced, my eyes fluttering closed as he brushes his mouth over mine. "You're soft," he murmurs. "So very soft."

"Soft all over," I agree with a whisper because it seems I can never stop flirting.

Nemeth groans. "I'd wager you are," he murmurs, and his words are hot against my mouth. "Can I kiss you with my tongue? That's how it's done properly, yes?"

"Please do." If he doesn't, I'm going to leap from the bed, screaming in frustration.

His tongue lightly flicks over my parted lips, and then he enters my mouth. I moan at the first touch of his tongue to mine. How is it that a Fellian can taste so good? He tastes like sweetness and honey, and his tongue is strong and pleasant against mine as he dips into my mouth in light, teasing strokes. He doesn't stop after a few flicks; he keeps going, and my hands curl around his neck as he leans his weight over me, hauling me against him as his kisses grow with intensity.

Oh yes, Nemeth likes kissing. His mouth slants over mine, and the kiss grows hungrier by the moment, his tongue becoming more dominant.

I moan against his mouth because how the hell did he learn to kiss like this? He's a natural. With every slide of his tongue against mine, it makes me ache deep between my thighs. I press against him, panting and hungry. "Touch me."

He lifts his head and strokes my cheek with those thumb claws. "Candra . . . "

"I want you." I nip at his lower lip.

Nemeth groans. He presses his forehead to mine. "I would love to do nothing more than spend all night kissing you, princess, but I think we should savor it."

I bite his lower lip again and suck on it because I'm not sure he understands just how badly I want him right now. "Savor . . . it?"

Surely, I'm hearing him wrong.

"Savor," he agrees, leaning in to lightly brush my upper lip with a kiss. "Yes. After all, we have nothing but time here in this tower, do we not?"

Oh. I suppose he's right. We do have nothing but endless time. It would give us something to look forward to through the endless days. I'm disappointed, but I'm also intrigued. No one has ever wanted to "savor" me before. "What do you propose?"

"That we take our time. That we save kisses and touches for bed." He strokes my cheek and then traces my jaw, his fingertips dancing over my lower lip. Hot curls of need ripple through me, and I want to whimper a protest when he draws away. "That we make each kiss and caress count. That we savor each one for how special it is."

My aching pussy that wants desperately to be filled disagrees, but my heart adores how sweet Nemeth is. He wants to *savor* me. How can I possibly say no? "You do know my past has been less savoring and more . . . greedy."

He kisses the tip of my nose. "Then our actions will make this all the more special."

I'm not entirely convinced, but when he tugs me against him and holds me close, I'm willing to *savor* until tomorrow.

CHAPTER TWENTY

Sleeping next to Nemeth means a lot of twitching and him taking up most of the bed for his wings, so when he adjusts the blankets and the bed creaks, I only roll over and tuck my head against the pillow. "Is it morning?"

"Mmm-hmm."

"Just wondering." I don't intend on getting out of bed. It's far too pleasant, and I don't have anywhere to be. I pat the mattress without opening my eyes. "Come back and snuggle with me."

Nemeth chuckles, and I feel his weight shift on the bed. His hand grazes over my hip, and then he lifts the hem of my sleeping gown, hiking it up my thighs. "Roll onto your back for me, greedy princess."

Ooooh. A change of heart? I'm awake now. I roll onto my back as he asks and tug my gown up the rest of the way until it's at my waist. "You're not going to find a single objection to a morning wake-up such as this."

His big hands skim over my legs, warming them. "Gods, you're pretty."

I wriggle with pleasure at that. My legs are plump and pale, but I like to think they look nice. I've never had any complaints. "I have hair between my legs," I point out since he did not. "It's a normal human thing."

"I see it," he murmurs. "Such a sweet little tuft of floss."

His husky words make me clench, and I'm getting wet with anticipation. He skims his hands over my thighs again, the bed creaking . . . and then he stops.

Nothing happens.

I open my eyes, but of course, it's pitch black in the chamber without a hint of light bleeding in. "Um, Nemeth?"

"Shh," he whispers. "Do you hear that?"

I don't want to hear *anything* but the enthusiastic sounds of his mouth on my pussy. I squirm against his grip, but he's still not doing more than holding my hips in place. "Hear what?"

"Shh," he says again.

Then, I hear it.

A very faint *chink*. A pause, and then another *chink*.

Like someone's tapping away at the tower.

I sit upright at that. "Balon? Do you think he's trying to come in?"

"I don't know," Nemeth says, and there's a growl in his voice. "But if he is, I aim to stop him."

Never have I heard Nemeth so . . . possessive. So fiercely angry. I shiver with unexpected delight. "Maybe it's just birds," I say, even as I swing my legs over the side of the bed. I hear Nemeth moving about in the chamber, and two taps later, one of the lights flares to life. I catch a mouthwatering glimpse of his straining morning erection in his loin wrap, but then he turns away and picks up his kilt.

"Whoever it is, they have bloody awful timing," I mutter. To think that Nemeth woke up aroused and ready to treat me with the same wake-up that I gave him . . . and then to cruelly thwart me.

He chuckles. "It is the gods reminding me that I am to savor and not to be weak and greedy."

"I don't mind weak and greedy." But I get dressed too because I'm curious what the sound is. I throw on an ornately embroidered sitting gown, knot the seven ties across the front that act as a bodice and make it decent, and then slide my feet into my slippers. "Get the light?"

He finishes belting his kilt and picks up one of the lights while I braid my hair as I walk. I can't help but notice that Nemeth's hand remains firmly on the small of my back as if he's protecting me from Balon . . . if it even is Balon. I think about my knife's ominous silence and worry anew.

At some point, I'm going to have to tell Nemeth what the knife's magic is. Perhaps after I dig it out again. Right now, I'm not certain I want to hear its answers. For now, I'm happier not knowing.

We head downstairs to the large, empty chamber. It's been a while since I've done more than simply pass through this room, especially now that all of my wood is gone. It's so strange to me that this tower has four floors, but both Nemeth and I barely use the top floor or this one. Perhaps prior Offerings came with a larger number of things? A full suite of furniture? Musical instruments?

Or is it simply to provide enough room so that both the Fellian Offering and the Liosian Offering don't have to run into one another?

On the main floor, we can hear the steady clinking of rock and the sound of brick being chipped away. I draw closer to Nemeth because I don't know what to make of this. "Do you think it's our supplies?"

"The solstice is not for another week," Nemeth tells me, and I can hear the concern in his voice too. "It's not against the goddess's rules for the door to be opened so long as we do not step outside."

Right. The rules are clear; we have to stay in, and no one else can join us. "If it's Balon, what do we do?"

"What we have to do," Nemeth says grimly.

I glance up at him, fretting. Balon is harmless. He's a flighty, pretty idiot. I don't think he has a mean bone in his body, but what if I'm wrong? What if he's decided to liberate me from the tower like I begged when I first arrived?

I'm . . . not sure I want to be liberated anymore. I still hate the tower. I hate it, and I hate the suffocating darkness and having to wash my own clothes and all that comes with it . . . but I like Nemeth, and I like being alone with him. The moment we leave the tower, all of our closeness, our *savoring*, will be gone.

We're supposed to be enemies. I'm supposed to have killed him and stolen his food to ensure my own survival.

I'm definitely not supposed to be kissing him.

There's a loud *clink* and the sound of crumbling brick. Then, two more fast-paced *thunks* of pickaxes hit the brick. "More than one person," I whisper as the pickaxes move faster. "There's at least two."

Nemeth hands me the light. "Stay here."

I clutch it tightly, watching as he strides forward, his wings flicking with agitation. He moves toward the heavy, sealed wooden door and puts his ear to it, listening. After a moment, he pulls away and looks over at me. "They are breaking down the wall."

Well, that's obvious. "Did they say why?"

He shakes his head and stiffens, his wings flaring out behind him. A look of recognition crosses his face, and then he glances over at me. "Liosian. They have a sled. Someone just told them to bring it forward."

Oh. "That must be my supplies. They've come early? Unless we've messed the dates up?" We're still marking days on the wall, but given that we have no sunrise or sunset in here, it'd be easy for things to slide off track.

Nemeth shrugs. He touches my shoulder and then sinks into the shadows, disappearing. "I can't let them see me with you."

"Right. Of course." It makes sense. I don't know why it hurts my feelings, though. He's just being cautious. The last thing we need is for them to change their minds and not give us food. Nemeth has been judicious with his supplies and still has enough for maybe another month, but I've been down to scraps for weeks now. I need what they're bringing in, and my excitement grows with every crumble of brick and the loud *CHINK* of the pickaxes tearing away the wall in front of the door.

The doors rattle, and then there's a loud scrape as the bar is pulled away. I clutch the light to my chest—and then realize what I'm doing. Right. I can't show Fellian magic to them. I quickly tap it off and set it aside, blinking at the darkness that surrounds me.

The doors open, and the chamber floods with sunlight. I blink, stepping forward, as I see sunlight for the first time in a year. Three men stand outside in Liosian livery, wearing the leather-and-chain armor common with the court guards. They look tired and haggard, but I'm delighted to see them. "Greetings!" I call out, crossing over to them. "Are you here early? You—"

One holds a sword up. He points it at me. "I'm sorry, princess, but you have to stay inside."

"Oh, I wasn't leaving," I say, shocked. I stare at the weapon pointed at me and take a step backward. "I just wanted to breathe in the fresh air."

"I need you to stay back," he repeats again, not lowering the sword. "We won't be here long."

"Are those my supplies?" I can see a packed sled behind the men on the beach.

"They are."

"You're here early."

He keeps a watchful eye on me as if he doesn't trust me not to dart past him and race for the shore. "We came while the weather is good."

"Has there been bad weather, then?" It looks gorgeous outside to me. The sunlight pours in, warm and bright. I can hear the distant waves hitting the shore and the call of an albatross, and I ache with the need to step into the sun. I want to breathe in the sea air, if only for a few hours. I close my eyes and take a deep breath. Gods, I want to go outside. He's right to hold his sword on me because that sea breeze is divine, and I want to drink it in.

But I tell myself that I can't.

They can't come in, and I can't go out. Even if they didn't try to stop me, I suspect Nemeth would. There's more riding on my staying here than just my personal wants. I can't leave. I can't step a foot outside.

But oh, that breeze tempts me.

One of the men steps forward and tosses a long rope in toward me. It falls at my feet, a large knot at the end. The other side is tied to the front of the sled. "Pull on your side, and we'll push."

"Did you bring firewood?" I ask as I delicately pick up the rope. "Because I need wood. Last year there wasn't nearly enough."

To my surprise, the man's face contorts and hardens with what looks like rage. "You'll take what we give you and be grateful. Make demands, and we'll turn around and leave with your food."

My jaw drops. I stare at him in shock. He's . . . he's threatening me? "But you have to. That's the agreement."

Somewhere in the darkness, Nemeth growls low in his throat.

The soldier sneers at me. "Do I? You don't know what it's like—"

One of the men coughs, kicking sand against his angry companion, who stands in the doorway.

The guard holding the sword straightens as if remembering himself. "Do you want this food or not, princess?"

"Yes, of course, I want it." I hate that I have to be polite and friendly to this ass. If my sister knew how he was treating me, he'd be strung up, and his head would be put on a pike in front of the castle gates. But I'm here alone, and I need that food, as much as I need Nemeth not to lose his mind and attack the men. So, I pick up the rope and tug on it.

The sled doesn't budge; it's too weighted down. The men give me another wary look, and then all three of them line up at the back end of the sled and push it forward while I tug it inside. The moment the runners are over the threshold, the men pull back, and I grunt and drag the sled another foot or so.

The men on the other side have pronged sticks that they lean on, shoving the sled forward until it's clear of the door.

I dust off my hands, dropping the rope and stepping forward again. "Thank you for the supplies. Tell me of news back at the castle while you're here. Is my sister well? Does Allionel grow strong?"

The leader holds his sword up again, shaking his head. "Stay back, princess. You have your supplies. Now we must brick up the door again."

So soon? "Oh." I bite my lip. "You can't leave it open? Just for a few hours so I can enjoy the breeze?"

He shakes his head. "I have my orders."

The men shut the doors before I can plead again, and the darkness swallows me once more. I fight the knot in my throat, tears threatening as I'm left standing there. As I hear the men bar the door from the other side, the sand grit under my slippers reminds me of what I'm missing out on. "Get the bricks," one calls, voice muffled.

And . . . that's that.

My people are gone for another year. I blink hard, my jaw working. I didn't even get a hint of news about my sister or the war. I don't even know if they sent me firewood. All I know is they were extremely unpleasant . . . almost as if they resented me. I'm giving up seven years of my life for *that*?

I clench my jaw so I don't cry. I'll cry tomorrow so Nemeth doesn't realize just how rattled I am at that interaction. All my life, I've been treated well by the Liosians. No one's ever disrespected me like that. I wonder what it means. Did they somehow see Nemeth? Do I have love bites on my neck? I touch my throat absently, wondering what caused such disgust.

"Are you all right?" Nemeth asks, emerging from the shadows once more.

"Perfectly lovely," I say with false brightness. My gaze strays to the door as the scraping, slapping noise of the door being rebricked hits my ears. I'm truly starting to hate that sound.

"I didn't like the way they spoke to you," Nemeth tells me, a glare on his hard face as he moves to my side. His big hand goes protectively to my shoulder, and he extends a wing, curling it around me as he pulls me against him.

"I wasn't a fan of it either," I admit, then tease, "I shall have to send a sternly worded letter to my sister."

"I'm serious, Candra."

I am too. I'm helpless without the authority that my name brings. If they don't care that I'm a Vestalin, how do I have any sway? I might as well have been talking to the walls for all those men cared. They didn't want to hear from me. They simply wanted to dump my supplies and brick me back up again. I don't think I could have said anything to sway them.

And I'm used to swaying men.

I touch my hair, wondering if the lack of daylight is affecting my looks. I turn to Nemeth. "Do I seem unappealing to you? Any marks on my face? Wrinkles? Is my hair a fright?"

His wing curls even more protectively around me. "You are a vision, Candra. As I have said before, I have never seen anyone as lovely as you."

"Well, sometimes a woman needs to hear it again," I admit. "No marks on my neck? You're certain?" He inspects me, and when nothing is found, I'm puzzled. It's not because I'm with Nemeth in a carnal sense, then. It must be something else entirely. "So very puzzling. To be here early and so rude too."

"Are you truly going to write your sister?" Nemeth asks, his claws stroking over my braid.

"I don't know if it would do anything," I confess. "Provided that I could count on them to deliver it and not simply cast it into the sea the moment we're shut away, it'd still take another year to get a response."

"Exactly. So best to just ignore it." He strokes a knuckle over my cheek. "You don't know the reason behind their moods. They could be separated from their wives. They could be on duty with instructions to return quickly. Or perhaps your king is superstitious and told them not to speak to you."

Now that, I can absolutely believe. Lionel hates me as much as I hate him, and he would take any opportunity to twist the knife. He knows I would loathe being here, so it's very possible they were expecting me to break out and push past the guards. If I take one footstep outside the tower, the goddess will be furious and cast her wrath down upon all of mankind. My selfish actions would make people starve, ships wreck, and cities upon the coasts sink into the furious waters of the sea.

A year ago, I would have absolutely done it . . . but a year ago, Nemeth was still my enemy. He's saved me in so many ways. Six more years trapped in this tower seems like a lifetime, but I don't hate it as much with Nemeth at my side.

I look up at him thoughtfully. His fangs are gleaming in the light he holds, and the slant of it illuminates his strong, rocklike jaw and the harsh angles of his features. His strange nose and heavy brow cast shadows and make him look monstrous, but I see the warmth in those glowing green eyes, and the wing that's tenderly tucked around me shields my form as if he can protect me from the rest of the world.

How horrified my sister would be to know that I'm in the arms of a Fellian, and I adore it. She would view it as a betrayal and say that a Vestalin must do their duty to the kingdom first and foremost. After all, she put aside her own personal wishes so she could marry Lionel and secure the throne and the future of the Vestalin line.

Erynne would have killed Nemeth before the first month was over. Of that, I have no doubt.

I guess that makes me a bad sister because I'm ready to crawl back into bed with him and see if he wants to put his face between my thighs after all.

I smile up at him. "Shall we return to bed?"

Instead of agreement, I get a baffled look. "Now?"

"What's wrong with now?" If nothing else, I can get away from the sound of them laying bricks outside, which I'll probably hear in my nightmares. "The food isn't going anywhere."

But my fussy Fellian shakes his head. "Right now, we should get a quill and some ink and make an inventory of all your supplies so we know exactly what you have for this upcoming year, and that way, we can plan our meals accordingly. It'll give you the best chance of making it all stretch."

Ugh, so practical. I guess I'm not getting his head between my thighs after all.

CHAPTER TWENTY-ONE

The interaction with the Liosian soldiers bothers me all afternoon as Nemeth carefully catalogs each bag full of dried goods. There's an entire trunk of dried animal pancreases for my medicine, along with bushels of herbs and more vials and needles. There are a few new dresses. There are candles, and soaps, and another book full of recipes and practical advice that I clutch to my chest just because it means that Riza hasn't forgotten me. There's even a heavy trunk at the bottom filled with thick, dark-looking bricks of dirt that Nemeth calls "peat."

"Do you ever burn this in your castle?"

"No, never." I wrinkle my nose. "It looks gross."

"It can have a strong smell," he agrees. "That is most likely why. At least they sent fuel this time." Nemeth seems pleased with my supplies, weighing a bag of dried meat with his hand as if he can tell how much is in it, then making notes on his parchment.

In a chest full of herbs, there is a book—my sister's favorite epic poem—and tucked into it are several envelopes.

I gasp in delight at the sight of them, clutching them to my chest. "Letters!"

Nemeth smiles at my pleasure, pausing in his inventory to sit back on his haunches. "Who are they from? Your young lover?"

Holding the first one close to the light, I eye the handwriting. "Balon is not much of a wordsmith," I admit. "This one is from my maid, Riza." Hot tears well up in my eyes. By all the gods, I really do seem to cry a lot lately, but I'll allow myself a moment of softness for this. "And one from Nurse." I flip to the third letter. "And my sister, Erynne."

"No love notes, then?"

I'm so happy I don't even care that Balon didn't write. "Jealous?" I tease, hugging the letters against my breasts.

"Anything that can make you smile so broadly? Aye, a bit jealous."

My happiness bubbles over just a tiny bit more at his admission. "Balon probably found someone new to flirt with. He was only interested in the Vestalin name, anyhow."

The moment I say it, I think of my enchanted knife, and my happiness sours a little. When I asked if Balon was well, it was silent. He could be sick. Suddenly, I feel guilty. "He's a sweet boy."

Nemeth grunts and gestures at the letters. "Are you going to save them or read them now?"

I chuckle at that. "Now, of course. Why would I save them?"

"In case you want to savor them."

I drop my hands and give him an exasperated stare. "You and your savoring."

"You don't agree?" The look he gives me is pure innocence. "Savoring can make the pleasant moments last longer."

Dragon shite. "Or I can read it now, and if I need more pleasant moments, I can read it again. And again. Which I will probably do."

Nemeth gives me a lazy grin. "Then read, oh greedy princess."

"Thank you; I shall." I flick my finger under the wax seal of my sister's letter and unfold it, holding it close to the light. While I'm excited to read all three of my precious letters, I'm most eager to hear my sister's words. The moment I see her handwriting, that confident, swooping script that's so very familiar to me, a knot forms in my throat. I'm quiet for a moment, then clear my throat. "*Dearest Candromeda,*" I begin and then pause. Should I read this out loud if it has to do with the war? Will there be state secrets I need to keep from Nemeth? When he nudges my knee, I give him a quick smile. "She has such messy handwriting; some of it's hard to decipher."

"I'm good with script," Nemeth says, holding his hand out. "May I?"

I shake my head, resisting the urge to clutch the letter to my chest. "I've got it."

He relaxes, unaware of my thoughts, and smiles up at me.

That smile makes me ache. I feel like I'm doing something wrong as I hesitantly read out my sister's letter. "*Dearest Candromeda,*" I start again. "*It has been a year now since you left my side and went to do your duty in the tower. It feels like it has been forever, yet we still have six more years to go. The thought of not being able to see you again for that long is unbearable. I cannot imagine what it must be like in the tower. I hope you are cozy and well, and . . .* " I falter over my sister's next words.

I hope you took my advice and dispatched your enemy swiftly. There will be no judgment on my side. We must do what we must do.

"It looks like she spilled ink right here," I say, my giggle high pitched. "Here we go." I continue blithely, skipping forward. "*I trust that the supplies have held you through this first difficult year. Know that I am thinking of you daily. But enough about me worrying over you. I am sure you want to hear news of the outside instead of my muttering over how much I miss my dear sister. Nurse Iphigenia is wonderful with the baby, but she compares you to him daily. She misses you dreadfully and tells me constantly that she will be too old to tend to you when you get out, that her hands will be withered with age. Riza and I both roll our eyes. If anyone is full of determination to work all their days, it is your nurse. Even now, she's fussing at me and insisting I drink a hot posset because it will help the baby. Alas, I am pregnant again.*"

I pause, glancing up at Nemeth.

He doesn't seem overly interested, his gaze more focused on me. "Are you surprised? She is young enough."

I shrug. Part of me aches that I haven't seen her first child, and now a second one is coming. We are missing out on so much.

I continue reading. "*Alas, yes, it is Lionel's. I am not bold enough to take someone else to my bed, though the thought has occurred to me time after time. I suppose if I must sleep with Lionel, at least he is fecund. One week was all it took, though that was plenty for me.*" I chuckle over my sister's dry humor, glancing up at Nemeth from over the pages of the letter. "It is the court's worst-kept secret that my sister is not overly fond of her husband. She will do her duty to the Vestalin line, though."

"Not her duty to her husband?" Nemeth raises a heavy brow at me.

I make a face. "No. Theirs is a marriage of state." I don't mention Isabella, and I suspect my sister will not either. She protects Isabella because if anyone found out how my sister truly felt about her, Isabella would be in danger. "I don't think anyone loves Lionel."

"His men do."

Nemeth isn't wrong. "His men have poor taste," I say cheerfully. "Shall I go on?"

He nods.

I continue. My sister goes on pages about Allionel, how he's a clever baby and so very smart and already has several teeth. That he, unfortunately, looks just like his father, and Lionel is besotted with him. How Allionel was born with Lionel's golden curls, but they immediately fell out, and now he has the dark hair of the Vestalin line. He's healthy and well (no blood curse), and everyone adores him. He's become somewhat of a talisman for Lios to get them through tough times.

Of course, my sister never says what those tough times are, and it frustrates me. Her letter goes on to talk about court, some political marriages that have been made, visitors from outlying territories (that I suspect are there due to the war), and the unusually cold winter we recently went through. Her tone seems to be cheerful, and she closes her many-pages-long letter with a personal note.

I took your friendship for granted when you were at my side, Candra. Now that you're gone and out of reach for the next seven (here seven is crossed out)*—six—years, I feel very alone. I didn't realize how dear you were to me, and I think of all the times I scolded you for rolling out of some fool's bed. I would take back all those scoldings in a heartbeat just to be able to see your happy smile. Please take your medicine every day, and think of your sister, and know that she loves you and misses you dearly.*

Yours forever,

Erynne Vestalin

Tears blur my eyes again, and Nemeth's hand touches my knee. "Piss off; I'm not crying," I say as I sniffle through my tears. He chuckles and gives my knee a squeeze, knowing me too well at this point. "I just miss her. That's all. I want to see her babies, and I want to go back to court, and I hate this gods-damn tower." I carefully fold Erynne's letter again, knowing that I'm going to read it over and over while I'm trapped here in the tower. "It's just surprisingly good to hear how much someone on the outside misses me. I love my sister, but . . ."

"But she's always been the dutiful one, and you were not?" Nemeth guesses.

I nod. "Lionel almost sent her here when I refused to go." Surely it can't be a betrayal of state secrets to mention that? After all, I am here. Clearly, it didn't work. "My sister was heavy with his child, and he was still going to lock her away in this tower to prove a point to me. He's a loathsome man, and I despise that he's king of such a good nation." With a little sigh, I run my fingers over the letter again. "Oh, and it's not as if that's a secret. The entire world knows that King Lionel does not get along with his wife's squat, sickly sister."

"Squat? Sickly?" Nemeth snorts. "You are neither of those things. You are a goddess, and I have no doubt that if he would have sent your sister to the tower, he would have taken you to wife instead, all to keep his clutches on the throne. You know his family's claim to it is weak. Of course he wants a Vestalin wife at his side. It doesn't matter which one, I suspect."

Nemeth's words make me pause. He . . . isn't wrong. Lionel's family line—the Rivertree family—is a younger branch, and they are only on the throne because two generations ago, a general overthrew the puppet king and slaughtered the existing king's family, only sparing the Vestalin line due to the Golden Moon Goddess and her curse. Ever since then, Rivertrees have been marrying Vestalins. My mother was married to a Rivertree cousin, and Lionel's father was married to one of my great-aunts. I'm not sure how incestuous it makes our family line . . . I'm just glad I didn't have to marry Lionel myself.

Poor Erynne. She's just as trapped as I am; she's just not in a tower. Instead, she's being forced to make babies with that odious man. I give Nemeth a tight smile. "I suppose it's a good thing that I'm here, then, and not Erynne."

"I am glad of it," he says, a hint of fangs flashing in his smile. "Call me selfish."

Maybe it is selfish to say such a thing, but I don't mind hearing it. Not from him. And I know what he means. I wouldn't wish this tower upon anyone, but if I must be here, I'm glad to be here with him. I smile. "You're lucky it's not Erynne anyhow," I comment. "She snores dreadfully."

Nemeth laughs. "I wouldn't share my bed with your sister, Candra."

"Wouldn't you? She's quite lovely. And they probably would have given her the same amount of firewood they gave me, which is to say, none at all. She would have crawled into your bed and begged quite prettily for some warmth."

"And I would have kicked her out," Nemeth says easily. "Because a Fellian's heart is not won by pretty words and a smile."

"Oh, no?" That sounds like dragon shite to me.

"We like a challenge—like a spoiled princess who tells us to piss off."

Now that makes me laugh. I giggle at his words and have the strangest urge to fling myself over the mountain of trunks and kiss him silly. Erynne's letter has made me sad, but he's managed to cheer me up despite things. Surely, that deserves a kiss or two.

To my surprise, he holds up one of the soaps included in the trunks. "You said you wanted to try out some of the things you'd been sent. Would you like to bathe, princess?"

"It depends. Are you going to watch?"

His wings give an agitated flutter. "It depends. Would you let me?"

"I would," I say, hopping to my feet. "I'll even let you wash my back. And if you're good, I'll let you wash my front."

"Oh, I'll be good," he practically purrs.

CHAPTER TWENTY-TWO

My heart is racing as we head down to the kitchen. I don't know if Nemeth is trying to distract me or attempting to pick up where we left off this morning, but I'll gladly take it. I'm already wet with anticipation, my pussy slick enough that I can feel my folds brushing against each other as I move. He carries the lamp for light, sets it down on one of the tables, and pulls out the tub. "I'll start a fire and heat the water for you."

"It's not necessary." It's a lot of work to heat the water—distracting work—and I'd rather have him focused on me. "If I get too cold, you can always warm me up."

His reflective eyes flare with arousal. "If you like."

Oh, I *like*.

I watch in silence as he fills the tub with bucket after bucket of water. When it's hip deep, I slip off my robe and chemise and step forward, naked. My skin prickles, but it's more from awareness of his gaze than the cold. Ever since I entered this tower, my baths have been cold because it's seemed like a waste of fuel to make a fire just to heat water, so I'm rather used to the chilliness now.

Nemeth holds a hand out to me, and I place mine in his as I step into the tub. I can feel his eyes roaming over my pale limbs. I do wonder if he finds them unnaturally light or unpleasant looking compared to his own or if he's disturbed by the fact that I'm all rounded softness where he's hard planes and angles. I haven't seen many Fellians in my life, but the ones I have seen looked like him. Is that why he wants to go slow? To "savor" things? So he can get used to my appearance?

I stand in the calf-deep water and consider him, still holding onto his hand. "Does my appearance repulse you? Be honest."

"Repulse me?" He shakes his head. "You are built differently, but I do not find you repulsive."

I glance down at my legs and my knees that bend forward instead of backward. My lower half is definitely quite different from his. His kilts are short, frequently offering glimpses of the wrap that protects his cock, and his powerful hind legs flex under the skimpy shield of leather. One of his thighs is as big as my torso, and he's made large all over. Even with legs that bend backward, he's still taller than Lionel, taller than any of the men at the Liosian court. I can only imagine how massive he'd be if he was built with the same legs as us—tall as the tips of his wings that loft above his head, maybe?

I shiver with fascination picturing that.

"Cold?" His other hand slides over my shoulder, enormous and warm, and I bite my lip to smother the moan that threatens to rise. I'm so hungry for touch that I want to fling myself onto him and forget all about the bath. *Savor, Candra,* I remind myself. *Savor!*

With a little sigh, I lower myself into the water. "Not cold. Just thinking."

"About?"

"You." I slither deeper into the water. It rises now that I'm in it, no longer calf deep but brushing against my breasts. I lean back against the wall of the tub and rest my arms on the edges, which leaves my body free for his perusal.

Nemeth is silent. "So, it *was* a bad shiver."

"No such thing as a bad shiver," I reply, my tone light. "Certainly not when it comes to you. Wash me?" I raise one foot into the air.

Those wings of his give a telling shake, and he crouches low next to the tub. He picks up the bar of soap that he'd set aside and studies it, then looks at me.

I wink at him and lower my foot onto the lip of the tub, keeping it out of the water as I wait to see how he'll react.

"Do you toy with all the men who come into contact with you?" Nemeth muses as he dips the soap into the water. The cake looks ridiculously small in his huge hand.

"Only the ones I like," I tease. "Are you this shy around all women?"

"Only the ones I like," he confesses with a sly look in my direction.

That makes me smile. I wiggle my toes at him, beaming. "You can't be shy around me. I've sucked your cock and rubbed your knot. That should make you more at ease in my presence."

Nemeth groans as if pained, closing his eyes. "And when you say such things, it reminds me of those moments and makes it impossible to concentrate."

As if that's such a bad thing. "You were the one who offered to bathe me."

"So I did." He drags the cake of soap through the water again and then lifts it to my leg. Nemeth carefully runs it over my calf, and the scent of roses fills the air.

Roses. Erynne does love her roses. I sigh with contentment and close my eyes. It doesn't even matter that the water is cold. I love that someone's taking care of me, and I love that it's Nemeth.

He grunts to himself as the soap moves over my foot. "You have such small toes. No claws either. Humans really are a helpless race. I have no idea why you wish to war with mine."

"I don't want to war with anyone," I deflect as he lifts my leg by the ankle and continues to wash me.

"No," he muses. "You wouldn't. You'd kiss everyone until they got along."

"Not everyone. Only the handsome ones."

"Then it's a pity you're stuck with me." His big, wet hand trails up to my knee and rests there, going no higher.

I open one eye and scrutinize him. Why is he speaking so negatively of himself? Because I'm flirting? I thought he liked my blatant attempts at seduction. "Is something bothering you, Nemeth?"

"Aye," he says and moves to my other calf, washing it. He doesn't look me in the eye. "I am reminded how very different we are. How you must have had a lively life back at court, full of suitors who were hungry for your attention. And then I think of myself and how you must be with one such as me simply out of . . . boredom."

Boredom? Frowning, I lift my clean foot and shove it against him, catching him in the arm. "Don't be an arse."

Nemeth blinks those soulful, glowing eyes at me. "I'm not. I am a scholar. A Fellian. I am acutely aware of what I am." He holds up one hand. "I have claws. Fangs. Wings."

"A knot," I agree. "And a cute little tail."

He shoots me a quelling look. "Tails are private. Do not call mine 'cute' or 'little.'"

Oops. "If it helps, your knot is enormous."

Nemeth's wings twitch. After a moment, he admits, "That . . . does help, yes." He starts to wash my leg again. "My point is that I know you are not truly interested in me. I am no court swain. I am not Liosian. I do not know how to properly court a human woman."

Court me? I blink in surprise at that. "You want to *court* me?"

"Is that so strange?" He gestures at my legs. "I am touching you. I share a bed with you. When my people mate, they mate for life." He pauses. "I am asking if you truly wish to be mated to a Fellian. If you have thought this through."

I'm without words. "We can't just flirt and enjoy one another?"

"Is that all this is to you? A diversion?" He gives me a soulful look.

I swallow hard. I truly have no idea how to answer that. I adore flirting with him. I adore *him*. At the same time, I'm greatly aware that this flirting between us isn't allowed. If my people were to find out that I'd kissed him? That I'd sucked his cock? I'd be treated like some sort of aberrant. I'd be a filthy whore in their eyes, Vestalin princess or not. I'd be giving up everything once I got out of here. My home would no longer welcome me.

I wouldn't be a martyr and a heroine. I'd be a freak.

Yet the thought of turning Nemeth down makes me hurt deep inside. I want to kiss him more. I want to touch him more. Six more years of being with him and not being with him might be more painful than being locked in this tower.

"You're not a diversion," I say softly. "You're my friend. I care for you."

"But you wouldn't give up your people for me?"

How did we go from a lighthearted, flirty bath to defecting to the enemy? "Must it be decided today? This feels a bit like manipulation."

He gives me a stricken look, his hand hesitating on my leg. "I didn't mean for you to feel like that, Candra. I just . . . I am Fellian, I suppose. My mindset is that of my people. And I cannot think of devoting myself without asking for you to be my mate and all that that entails." His claws trail up my leg in a teasing gesture. "It's difficult for me to try to think of it in human terms."

Mmm. "Humans don't exactly think differently either. At least not the wealthy ones. All of those marriages are for wealth, land, or name. If you're a noble and you have a daughter, she's little more than a cow for you to sell off to the highest bidder." I make a face at the idea. "It's only because of my name that I have the slightest bit of freedom, but perhaps that's why I struggle. Despite the fact that I bear cursed blood, I have had marriage proposed to me seventeen times. Seventeen different people wanted to marry me, all because they desired to be tied to the Vestalin name. Because they think their magic cocks can somehow 'cure' my infertility." I snort. "And that's the problem. No one wants *me*. Candra. So when I hear a marriage proposal, I know it's shite, and I automatically wish to run straight for the hills."

"Even a proposal from a Fellian," Nemeth muses. "I understand."

"Do you?" I study him. "I've never been in control of my fate. Not as a woman, not as a Vestalin. The only reason I didn't have to marry those seventeen men who proposed was that the court astrologer said they would have no children if they married me. It was never my choice, understand? Even as the cursed Vestalin, I still would have been made to marry. The only thing I have ever had control over is my body and who I share it with. Must I give that up so easily, simply because I am fond of you and want to touch you?"

"I understand," he says again, his expression somber. "You might think I do not, but I do understand what it is like for your life not to be your own."

I realize what he means—that he is of the First House of Darkfell and thus a Royal Offering. He is a prince of his people. Perhaps he does understand. I reach for his hand and grip it in mine. "Then you know, in a world without freedoms, those that we have are more precious than ever."

Nemeth smiles at me, his expression slightly sad. He takes my hand and kisses my knuckles, then hands me the soap. "I do. And I must think on it. Can you finish your bath without me?"

And then he disappears into the shadows, melting away and leaving me alone in the room with my tepid bath, which is far less exciting without him.

Hmph. "You could have at least stayed to watch me soap my breasts," I call out. "Being horny is not a crime."

There is no answer.

—

I head upstairs after I've finished bathing, the tub emptied of its water and my soap carefully put away. I hold the light that Nemeth left for me, and when I get to his room, I find him in there reading a book. He gives me a distracted smile, kisses my palm, and then returns to reading. It's obvious that he needs some time to himself to pick through his thoughts.

That's fine. I have two more letters to dig through that sit on the corner of the bed. I glance over at Nemeth. "Should I go upstairs? Give you some privacy to think?"

He looks up at me in surprise and blinks those strange eyes at me. Then he shakes his head. "No. I would like for you to stay." The smile he gives me is a little shy, a little uncertain. "I prefer you here."

I beam back at him, pleased. Impulsively, I go to his side, to the stool he has near the cold fireplace, and I fling my arms around his neck and press a kiss to his cheek. "No matter what you decide, Nemeth, we are friends. Understand?"

Big arms go around me, and he holds me close. "You are right. Let us be friends first and foremost. I keep forgetting that we are here for the next six years. That we have many, many days and months to live through before we worry about the outside world." He squeezes me tight as if in an apology. "Forgive me for thinking too much."

"I never have that problem," I tease, and I'm rewarded with a chuckle from him.

He hugs me again, pulling me closer. I love the feel of his arms around me, so I press his head to my bosom and hug him like I would a child, stroking the horns that sweep back from his brow.

Nemeth immediately stiffens, his body growing tense against me.

Oh. I've done something improper, I suspect. I pull back, lifting my hands. "I'm sorry. Is touching your horns bad?"

"It is . . . a strong sort of touch." His voice is tight.

Oh dragon shite. He's told me that before, hasn't he? And I've completely forgotten. "As in, not the sort of touch a friend gives a friend? I'm so sorry."

Nemeth nods at me and lets me go. I'm left feeling vaguely disappointed and sad that he doesn't pursue things more. That he doesn't fling me down onto the bed and fuck me until stars burst behind my eyes.

He needs this to be a true marriage between us—a mating, as he calls it—but I am Liosian.

If I choose him, I lose everything the moment I get out of this awful tower.

I'm not sure I'm ready to make that choice yet. Picking up my letters, I move back to the bed and sit down to read. Nemeth retrieves his book, opens it to a page, and starts reading.

It's quiet between us, and it's not a comfortable quiet in the slightest.

CHAPTER TWENTY-THREE

The letters from Nurse and Riza are less guilt inducing than Erynne's letter. Both of them are sweet and full of worry over me, and they tell me all about Erynne and court—what the latest fashions are, who recently got married, and who inherited a fortune. They tell me of Allionel and his baby activities, and it's clear that both of them adore him. It seems like the entire court does. I read their letters multiple times over the next several days while Nemeth makes careful lists of meals we can make that will stretch our food and firewood.

I offer to help him with it, but he has a workbook he pores over and numbers he moves back and forth, so I give up trying to assist. He has a system worked out, and I'd just slow him down.

Nemeth's food supply is delivered in much the same way as mine. I expected them to deliver it through magical means since they have lights that shine without fuel and the ability to meld their bodies with the shadows, but Nemeth assures me this is not infallible. To move through the shadows, one must see where they are going, and with a wall in the way, no one would know where they'd arrive.

Plus, they are not allowed to step foot inside the tower, and he is not allowed to go out.

When they arrive on the Solstice (as planned), I have to hide upstairs from the Fellians. Hiding in the shadows and watching isn't enough because they can see in the dark. It makes me feel like I'm being punished even though I know Nemeth's request is reasonable. I sit upstairs and read through my letters for the dozenth time as Nemeth waits downstairs for his supplies.

We're supposed to pray to the Golden Moon Goddess on the Solstice, but I don't feel much like praying to her—or to any of the gods. They can just enjoy my presence here in the tower and know I'm doing my stupid, ridiculous duty to them. I flick through Riza's letter.

And then Nurse's.

A thought occurs to me, and I pick up Erynne's letter from the stack and read through it again.

No one has mentioned the war.

There's not a single mention of the fleet of ships that were waiting in the harbor last Solstice for a good wind. No mention of their arrival to Darkfell lands or how the conquest is going. If the Fellians are fighting back or if they have been completely destroyed. I've seen just how large the Liosian army is, and I can't imagine the war is going well, even if Fellians can blend with shadows. How very curious that they didn't say anything about it at all.

Could it be because they're afraid Nemeth would get the information? That seems the most likely reason. If so, I'm a little hurt that Erynne, Riza, and Nurse don't trust me enough not to blab about state secrets. Am I not here in this wretched tower because I love my country?

Hurt, I look to the stairs, but there's still no sign of Nemeth. He's been down on the bottom floor for a while now, and I worry that he's getting the same abrupt treatment I did. I put on my slippers and grab my skirts so they don't rustle and tiptoe down the dark stairs without a light, counting until I get to step thirty-five out of forty. Then, I sit and strain my ears to hear.

There's a low murmur of conversation, but I can't pick out the words. They must be speaking Fellian because the cadence of their voices is unfamiliar to me. Then, someone laughs.

A moment later, I hear Nemeth's booming voice join in. He laughs, too, the snake, and I frown into the darkness. Are they just standing at the door and chatting as if they're having a cup of tea? Catching up on gossip while I was treated like a prisoner by my own people? I'm irritated, and sitting on the steps, hiding as I eavesdrop, isn't helping things. When they laugh again, a stab of hurt radiates in my chest.

Nemeth's people clearly love him. They're pleased about his duty as the Royal Offering.

Mine won't tell me about the war and treat me like I'm some sort of beggar when they come to give me supplies. I'm sure there's a reason behind it, but resentment stirs in me just the same.

Nemeth is down there for hours, and I get tired of sitting on the stairs, listening to a conversation I can't understand. They seem to be jovial enough, and I wonder if they're teasing him about me. *Stuck with the fat, cursed princess? Shame about that.*

The thought irritates me, and I head upstairs. I fold up my letters and put them aside because their contents no longer bring me pleasure. Instead, all I can see is what they *don't* mention. Other than the baby and my sister, I realize that no names are given. When they mention someone at court marrying, it's a "certain someone with a forked beard," not "Bernard Athelhorn, Lord of Silver Thorpe." They're hiding information from me because of my situation. It bothers me, so I decide to put the letters away into my trunk upstairs, where I keep my knife and the secretive things I don't want Nemeth to see, like the worn-out bloomers I wear when I have my period and the supplies for such things.

My trunk is just where I left it, but I'm a little anxious each time I open it, worried that this time, my knife will be gone again. That Nemeth will have lied to me and stolen it. That he's somehow figured out its magical properties and wishes to use it against me. But when I open the small, gilded trunk, my knife is there.

I pick it up and set the letters inside. "I missed you," I joke.

The knife doesn't respond. It's either disagreeing with me or didn't realize it was a question.

I bite my lip, thinking. Should I keep it with me or put it away once more? I stare at it, hoping for inspiration. I'm afraid to ask it anything. I'm afraid to hear the answers because I'm powerless to do anything about them. "Is Erynne well?" The question comes out of me grudgingly, and I flinch, waiting for the answer.

To my relief, the knife shivers in response.

I sigh, some of the anxiety disappearing. "And the new baby? Has it been born yet?"

No answer.

"Is it a boy?"

No answer.

I smile at that. A girl, then. I hope she looks just like Erynne. Lionel will be annoyed that his second child isn't a boy, but he can just suck on eggs, as far as I'm concerned. I cross my legs and sit in front of my chest, gazing at the innocent-looking knife in my hands. "Is Nurse well? Nurse Iphigenia?"

Again, the knife shivers.

I smile once more. "And Riza?"

Silence.

The urge to vomit rises in my throat. "Is Riza alive?" I whisper. The knife shivers, and I let out a deep breath. All right. Riza is alive, but she is not well. "Is she sick?"

No response.

"Wounded?"

No response.

"Lost? Sad? Tired?"

None of these questions get a response, and I'm frustrated by my inability to close in on the proper questions. I'm filled with a vague sense of worry, and I want to fling the knife away again. It feels willful to do so, but what use are these answers? They fill me with grief and anxiety, not comfort. "Is Balon well?"

No answer.

"Is Balon *alive*?"

No answer.

I swallow hard, blinking back tears. I suppose that's my answer. He hasn't returned because he's dead. Poor Balon was so young too. "Was it sickness?"

No answer.

"The same problem as Riza?"

No answer.

"Was . . . it the war?"

Yes.

"Did he die in battle?"

Yes.

Oh. I had no idea he had joined the war. I thought he'd been considered too young. That his father didn't want him gallivanting off when he was the heir. It seems he changed his mind. "Is King Lionel alive?"

Yes.

Figures. I stare down at the knife, unhappy.

"Candra?" Nemeth calls up to me. "Are you hiding? Come and see what was brought." His voice is cheerful, and his mood a happy one. He doesn't need to know that I feel as if I'm a cake that has suddenly sunk in the middle. There's no need for both of us to be miserable.

I can do nothing about what is happening at home, so I shall not think about it at all. I tuck the knife into the front of my bodice and get to my feet, dusting off my skirts. "Coming! Are we going to feast on fresh Fellian mushrooms tonight?"

Nemeth laughs again, the sound echoing through the lonely tower, and I feel a little better after hearing it.

Just a little.

The world outside fades away from my thoughts far too easily.

Now that our supplies are flush once more, it's easy to feel happy and settled. The root cellar is full to overflowing, and the storage room on the bottom floor brims with flour for bread, dried herbs and teas, fuel, and new, warm clothing that we can use in the winter. There are fresh blankets and sweet-smelling candles. There are soaps and lotions for me and new books for Nemeth. With his ledger book, Nemeth has our food supplies plotted out to last us several weeks beyond the next Solstice, all without skimping on meals.

The tower seems a little more comfortable in the weeks past the Solstice, and I wish things between Nemeth and I were equally so.

It's not that things are bad between us. But Nemeth has erected a wall. He's stated what he wants is *a mate* and is calmly and patiently waiting for my decision. He doesn't want a fling from me, and he's perfectly willing to wait—or to decline my advances entirely. We still share a bed at night, but the kissing and cuddling ended as quickly as they began. Things are still friendly and affectionate between us, but he hasn't tried to wake me with his head between my thighs, and I'm afraid to approach him in a similar fashion once more and get turned down.

I don't know what to think.

It's hard not to feel like I'm being punished. That he's withholding until I agree to be his mate and say, "Yes, I renounce my kingdom, my sister, and everything I've ever believed in." But Nemeth is still my friend. We still laugh over passages in books and curl up together in bed to read or talk about nothing at all. We take turns making meals and playing a card game, and it's all quite lovely and sweet.

He's not trying to be an arse about it, I realize. It's just that if we take things further, Nemeth is only comfortable with one route—as a mated couple. I understand that. I respect that.

I just don't know if I can *do* that.

To his credit, Nemeth doesn't push me to accept him. It'd be easier if he did, I think. Instead, he's kind and understanding and leaves it all in my hands.

Sigh.

Why does he have to be so nice? Why can't he just grab me and pin me against the wall and have his way with me? Demand my body? Demand my kisses?

I know why—it's not who he is. He's a polite monk of a Fellian who just happens to be trapped in a tower with a princess of loose morals who really, *really* wants to ride his cock.

Weeks pass with our relationship standstill. I keep waiting for Nemeth to break, but I'm starting to realize that this anxious tension on my part might continue for the rest of the time we're here in the tower. Six years of waiting for Nemeth to push me into his arms (and his bed), and it might never happen.

And that bothers me.

I wake up in darkness, and the bed beside me is empty. "Mmm," I say aloud, sitting up and rubbing my eyes. "Nemeth?"

No answer.

I reach over and tap the light, turning it on, and the room we share—Nemeth's room—is empty. I see stacks of books and firewood by the hearth. I see the table heaped with my sewing (the only hobby I've managed) and the cards from our last card game scattered about. I see the shelves filled with supplies and Nemeth's stool near them, but no Nemeth. Frowning to myself, I reach under the mattress and pull out my knife from where I keep it when I sleep.

"Is everything all right?" I ask. "With Nemeth?"

A quick pulse reassures me.

Yawning, I put the knife back. A midnight run to the garderobe, then. I should just go back to sleep.

I don't. Instead, I get to my feet, drawn perhaps by instinct to leave our comfortable quarters and the light behind. The moment I step outside of our room, I hear a grunt.

I know that sound.

Fascinated, I follow it toward the storage room where Nemeth keeps his mushroom farm and the wood supplies. I don't have to be able to see in the dark to know that the door is slightly ajar. I can tell that from the sounds coming from inside. The slick, frantic slap of a hand working a thick cock is a familiar one to me, and heat pulses between my legs.

It's quickly followed by an ache in my heart.

I would have done this for him. I would have touched him (and thoroughly enjoyed doing so). I would give him relief and make him feel so good . . . but he doesn't want my touch unless it's that of a mate. How deeply and utterly infuriating. I'm angry and frustrated, but most of all, I'm hurt. I've offered myself with no strings attached, and he's turning me away. It makes me feel like he somehow finds my touch dirty.

Pushing away from the wall, I head back for the bedroom.

"Candra?" Nemeth's voice is startled, wary. He realizes he's been caught in the act.

"Go ahead and finish," I call back to him, not turning around. "Or don't. I don't care what you do."

I tap the light to turn it off, get back into bed, and pull the covers over my head like a child. My mouth is set in what feels like a permanent frown, and I just . . . ache. I ache because I'm dying for Nemeth to touch me, and instead, he's sneaking off to jerk his cock in the darkness, hiding his need from me. I don't think I've ever felt so low.

A short time later, the bed sinks with Nemeth's weight. He touches my blanket-covered shoulder. "Candra?"

"I don't want to talk. Go to sleep."

He tugs at the blankets I have pulled over my head. "You are upset."

"Of course, I'm upset," I grit out, frustrated. "I've offered myself to you on a silver platter, and you push me away. Finding you touching yourself in the middle of the night when I'm in bed right next to you? Just waiting for you to touch me? It makes me feel like you don't want me. You don't approve of me unless I agree to be your mate. You make me feel like there's something wrong with who I am. Like I'm *dirty* if I touch you without some stupid vows."

"Candra, no." His hand strokes my back through the blankets, and I wish it didn't feel so good. "You misunderstand me."

I suspect I'm not misunderstanding anything. Nice try, though.

He continues to rub my back. "I . . . I must relieve my body, Candra. It is the only way I can be around you without touching you."

His words make me jerk upright, all frustration. I sit up in the darkness, glaring at the glow of his green eyes, the only thing I can see. "So, *touch* me. I'm right here."

"It is not that simple." His eyes flicker. "I cannot compromise who I am, and a mate is everything to a Fellian. A woman brings honor to her mate, and I would not dishonor you."

"You weren't thinking about honor when my mouth was on your knot," I grumble.

"You woke me by surprise. No man would turn away such a thing." A long claw strokes along the curve of my jaw. "I am a strong man, but not that strong, Candra."

"So you didn't like it."

"No, that's not the problem. I liked it too much." His voice is achingly gentle. "I like *you* too much. I am just trying to love you and honor you in the best way I know how."

I go still in surprise. "You . . . love me?"

"You sound shocked. Have I not made my affection for you clear?"

Has he? It's hard to say. He's kissed me, and we've fooled around, but I didn't realize love was a factor. Or am I so used to court morals and flirting that it all seems normal to me? "I mean . . . it could be clearer."

"I asked you to be my mate," Nemeth says gently. "I do not offer such things lightly. If I took a human woman as my mate, I would be mocked before my people. They would not shun me, but they would make their displeasure very evident, and it would take many long years for my family name to return to honor. I know my brothers would be disgusted with me. I know all this, yet I still offer it to you because a life without you seems far more unbearable." His thumb pad skims over my lower lip. "Would I take myself in hand all through the night if I did not care for you?"

"All through the night, huh?" How did I sleep through this?

He gives a wry chuckle and skims my lip again. "Being near you and not being able to touch you? It is maddening. But I respect you. My people think so little of Liosians that I would have no one think I did not treat you with the utmost honor in our time here. Please do not be angry with me."

"Well . . . I can't be angry now," I say, mollified. I feel better knowing that despite his serene facade, he's desperate with wanting me.

His claws move to my chin, and he tips it up, making me meet his eyes in the darkness. "Then say you will be my mate."

I swallow hard. If I say yes, I get what I want here—him and me together. But once we leave this tower, I'll be a pariah. Not just in my kingdom, but it sounds like in his too. There will be no place for us to be happy together. "I don't know, Nemeth."

"I understand." He leans in and presses a kiss to my brow. "Take all the time you need. We have years."

Instead of reassuring me, that just makes me feel worse. Do I waste our time together worrying about the future? Or do I forget about the future and live for now?

This time, when we lie down to sleep, Nemeth pulls me against him. He doesn't kiss me again but tugs me against his chest and holds me close. If I were a strong, indignant woman, I'd say that his holding me is a little manipulative. That he's trying to pull me to his way of thinking.

But I'm lonely and needy, and his arms around me feel far, far too good. I guess he's not the only one who's weak.

CHAPTER TWENTY-FOUR

"Candra." Nemeth's voice is hushed against my ear, rousing me from sleep. A moment later, he shakes me gently. "Candra, wake up."

"Mm?" I rub my nose against his chest, drowsy and content. "Is it morning?"

"I do not know. But I hear something."

The urgency in his voice makes my sleepiness fade. I pull out of his arms and sit upright, ears straining. He's right. I hear the faint but familiar *chink, chink, chink* of bricks being broken outside. "Someone's back?"

"It seems so." He sounds uneasy.

I slide out of bed and reach for the lamp, tapping it to turn it on. "Do you suppose they forgot to give us something?"

"They forgot to give you wood to burn last year, and they never came to give you more," Nemeth points out, hauling his big body out of bed.

Frowning, I pause. He's right. Riza's letters were full of apologies about how guilty she'd felt once they'd realized the mistake. How she'd been anxious all year at the thought of me fending for myself without a basic necessity. Yet no one had thought to reopen the tower and provide me with the forgotten wood. So why return now? It's past the Solstice. The goddess's eye will be heavily upon us, watching to make sure we don't venture anywhere near the door and break our vow.

"Then what can it be?" I ask Nemeth, even as I slip my shoes on. "Is it your people, perhaps?"

"It will not be," he says to me. "I would know if they planned to return."

Hmm. Does he have a magical instrument like my knife that tells him secrets? Or is he just assuming that he would know all of his people's plans?

"It'll be humans, then." I glance down at my clothing. I'm wearing nothing but my chemise, and it seems foolish to race downstairs in nothing but that. I think about the dismissive, ugly looks the Liosians gave me and decide to look my best because clothes can be armor. "Can you help me dress? Do we have time?"

He nods. "It is not a fast process, breaking into the tower. Show me what you need help with."

I slip a deep-blue gown over my head. The bodice and decorated skirt are attached, with the laces going up the front of the heavily embroidered bodice. The sleeves attach separately to the shoulders of the bodice, as all my gowns do, so they can be removed for my potion to be administered. I have Nemeth help me with these as I lace the front of the tight gown, reaching in to adjust my tits so they bubble over the front of the bodice pleasantly. As I do, Nemeth's wings flick, and I know he's watching my breasts.

That restores a bit of my confidence in myself. After all, I might be trapped in this tower, but I'm still Princess Candromeda Vestalin, known flirt of a proud, handsome lineage. I know I'm attractive, even if I'm plump and rounded next to Erynne. I shouldn't doubt myself.

Once the laces are tied with a knotted bow just under my cleavage, I pat the swells of my tits and toy with the edges of the chemise that tease out just over the edge of the bodice. "How do I look?"

"Beautiful," Nemeth tells me, his tone reverent. "You are always beautiful."

I smile up at him, and his strange green eyes seem to be devouring me where I stand as if I'm a delicious morsel and he's a starving man. For a brief, shining moment, I'm annoyed that we have to go downstairs. I'd rather stay up here, unlace my gown again, and see how he reacts when my tits spill free.

But then the *chink, chink, chink* of brickwork reminds me that something today is different, and we can't lounge in bed.

Nemeth finishes tying my sleeves and studies his handwork. "I'm terrible at being your maid."

I glance down, and the bows he's made are clumsy and not decorative in the slightest, but it doesn't matter. I've got my mental armor on once more. I give him a coy look. "I suspect you'd be better at undressing me rather than the reverse."

His wings flutter again. "Let us go see what they want."

"Just a moment." I put my hands to my braid and smooth it, working strands back into place before looping my braid into a knot atop my head and securing it with a pin. "Ready now."

I throw my shoulders back, pick up a lamp, and carry my skirts, my head held high. Whoever is at that door is getting Princess Candromeda Vestalin, not Candra the flirt.

I head downstairs with Nemeth a step behind me and his large hand on my back in silent support. I move through the empty lower chamber and wonder again if we should make this place cozier. Bring in a few chairs from downstairs, use the hearth, maybe a rug . . . but something inside me rebels. I don't want this to be a home. It will never be anything but a prison, no matter how comfortable a prison.

I bring the light closer to the door, walking forward. Nemeth remains behind. As I head for the heavy wooden double doors, I notice voices leaking through, along with a crack of sunlight peaking in from the door's seams. The sounds are muffled, but the closer I get, the more distinct they become. "Not much more," a man calls. "We're almost through. Rally your strength, boys!"

Turning to Nemeth, I flick my fingers, indicating he should back away. "They're definitely human. You'll have to hide in the shadows again. They can't see us together."

"Have they said what they are doing here?" When I shake my head, his nostrils flare, and he looks . . . angry. "Send them away."

Then he steps backward and melts into the shadows in that unnerving way he does. His eyes glimmer in the darkness at the edge of the circle of light provided by the lamp. I fight back a flicker of annoyance. "Don't get mad at me. It's not as if I invited them."

"Just send them away," he says again. "You know the rules."

I do. I'm a little irked that he's acting like this is somehow my fault because they're human. It should be obvious that I'm just as in the dark—no pun intended—about this as he is.

Holding the lamp, I move closer to the door. I hear nothing but the sound of loose rocks. "Clear the last of it away," a man says. "Dolf, come help me with this bar."

The bar across the door? So they mean to open it, then. "Who's there?" I call out. "Who has sent you?"

There's no answer. I can make out a faint murmur of voices outside, as if they're deliberately speaking too low for me to hear.

"Did the king send you?" I call again. "This tower is sacred to the Golden Moon Goddess. We cannot have visitors."

I mean, we can, but we're supposed to be living apart from the world. Visitors just remind us to abandon our duties, like they did with some of the ancestors who dwelt in the tower before us. That's why it's bricked up now. That's why we're isolated.

I shoot an anxious look at Nemeth when my calls receive no response.

"I'm here," he says quietly, eyes gleaming eerily in the darkness. "All is well. They will not take you."

It's like we're sharing a mind. I nod and turn to face the door, inwardly wincing as the heavy metal bar on the other side scrapes against the wood as it's removed. Keeping my head held high, I remain where I am, figure proud, as the doors scrape open and harsh, bright afternoon sunlight pours in. I squint at the light from the open door, shielding my eyes with my free hand. "Who's there?"

A man steps forward, a pickaxe in his hand. He's framed by the blistering sunshine, and I can't make out his face. "Well, well," calls out a crude voice. "You must be the princess."

I don't like his tone. It sets my shoulders on edge. "How very astute of you," I say in my bitchiest princess voice. "Were you expecting someone else to be locked in the tower as the Royal Offering?"

He steps across the threshold and into the light of my magical lamp and grins at me. The first thing I notice—after I get over my initial shock—is the absolute stench of him. He's filthy, and it's clear from his reek that he hasn't bathed in ages, if ever. The smile he sends in my direction is full of blackened, yellow teeth and surrounded by a bushy, untamed beard. His clothes are crude too.

He eyes me up and down. "You look well fed, princess."

"Piss on you," I snap. "Get out of this tower. You're not supposed to be here." Even now, just seeing him step across the threshold makes me anxious. There's something about his manner that tells me he's up to no good. He's clearly not been sent by the king. He's not wearing livery, and I've never seen such a grimy individual in my life.

The man turns his pickaxe menacingly in his hand as if to remind me that he holds it. He lifts his chin at me. "Where's your food?"

I frown. "Get out."

"I will—just as soon as you give me all your food." He grins again. "We need it more than you do." The filthy man eyes me, his gaze on my prominent breasts. "You've got a bit of padding to last you, after all."

"Quit flirting and just get the food," another man calls from the doorway. He peers in but makes no move to cross the threshold as if he's worried about the goddess's wrath.

"She's going to show me, aren't you, princess," says the man with the pick-axe. He takes another menacing step toward me. "Maybe if she's real nice, I'll leave her a few bites. She's a pretty piece."

A larger man steps inside, this one almost as tall as Nemeth but thin. He looks just as grimy as the first man and just as poor.

He leers at me as well. "I'll give her something to eat."

And he grabs his crotch.

"Get your revolting selves out of this tower," I demand. "I'm not giving you anything. Those supplies are mine and are meant to last me because I must stay as part of my goddess-sworn duty."

"Piss on the goddess," the bigger one says, marching forward. "We need food."

Starving peasants? I'll treat them like they are inferiors, just to cow them a bit. I flick my fingers at them dismissively, not showing the fear that's skitter-ing up my spine. "You can't have my supplies. Get out of my tower. Go to the capital. Go to the king. He will feed you."

The bearded one moves closer to me, grinning. "You don't get to tell me what to do, princess."

Before I can react, he reaches out and backhands me, knocking me to the floor. The luminescent globe lamp in my hand crashes to the stones a moment before I do, shattering into a thousand pieces as pain blooms through my face.

I cry out as my head hits the stone. A split second later, my cry is drowned out by an angry roar.

Nemeth.

"Now, you will die." He stalks out of the shadows like a menacing demon, his wings flaring outward and making him appear enormous.

The men take a momentary step back, and then the bearded one steps over me while the tall one moves forward, holding his pickaxe. "Stand down, Fellian. We just want food."

"You will get nothing from us." I've never heard him sound so lethal. He marches toward the man with the pickaxe.

"Then we'll fight you for it," the man says, surging toward Nemeth.

I bite back a scream as the two men clash. Staggering to my feet, I try to make out what's happening in the darkness. Light pours in from the doorway, and there are more men waiting there, staring into the shadows as Nemeth scuffles with the peasant. The other, taller man jumps into the fray, and there is nothing but the snarls and thuds of fists hitting muscle. A wet, overly loud, tearing sound pierces the air, and I gasp, watching in horror to see who is going to emerge from the struggling cluster of limbs.

SNAP.

That was bone. I know it was.

Horrified, I watch as a figure tumbles to the floor. It's the man with the pickaxe and beard, his unseeing eyes staring in my direction. A brief moment later, there's another terrifying snap, and I watch in shock as Nemeth strides toward the gaping doors. He flings the other man—now limp—toward the bystanders. "I will murder all of you if you try to take what is mine," he snarls, voice unrecognizable. "Set one foot inside this tower and *dare* me!"

The men run, shrieking.

I watch in silence as Nemeth storms back in toward me. He scoops up the other dead man, returns to the doors, and flings him outside with a swing, the dead body making a loud thud on the sands. Then, he closes the doors, and the last of the sunlight disappears, shrouding us in total darkness once more.

All is quiet.

Nemeth sighs heavily.

"Candra. Are you well?"

I lick my dry lips. Am I? I just watched Nemeth brutally destroy two men without breaking a sweat. More worrisome than that was the fact that our tower was invaded at all. Everyone knows that we're trapped here, that we do this for the good of all mankind—and Fellian-kind—yet someone tried to steal our supplies. I don't understand it. "I'm all right."

"He hit you." Nemeth's voice is tight in the darkness.

"He did," I agree. "Hurts like an absolute pile of dragon shite too. But I'll manage." I glance over at the doors, vaguely outlined by a trickle of light streaming in underneath. "What do we do about the entrance?"

"We'll have to barricade it. I don't know that it would prevent anyone else from coming in, but it would slow them down, at least." Nemeth moves to my side, running his hands over me. "You are sure you're all right?"

I nod. My cheek stings like ten thousand fiery sparks, but there's nothing to be done about it. "You saved us," I tell him softly, taking his hand and bringing it to my cheek. "They were going to steal our food, leave us with nothing. And you saved us."

"I should have done more," he growls. "Should have stopped him before he hit you."

"You didn't know." How could he? It surprised me, and I was standing right next to him. "I thought I had it handled. I was apparently wrong." I pause because there's a strange scent in the air, one that's coppery and raw. "Do you smell . . . blood?"

"It's nothing."

That alarms me. "Nemeth?" I ask, squeezing his hand against my chest. "Did they hurt you? What happened? It's too dark—I can't see anything." My slipper crunches on glass, and I wince. "I broke one of your globes."

He grunts, distracted. "We should go upstairs and find some things to barricade the doors from our side. Something heavy from the top floor would work. Maybe your bed on the second floor. Anything we can jam against the doors to ensure they'll have to struggle to get in."

"Sure," I echo. "Of course. Just as soon as you tell me where you were hurt."

"It does not matter, Candra," he says, his voice low and soft. "Our safety depends on getting that door blockaded."

"We can start with some slats of wood or a couple of knives," I point out. "And some rope for the handles. I'm actually quite good at figuring out how to lock someone out of a room I don't want them in."

Nemeth chuckles, and I don't like the sound. It's flat and tired, as if all his strength is sapping out of him. "I believe you. All right. Show me your idea."

CHAPTER TWENTY-FIVE

Growing up in the palace with several pushy attendants, I learned just how to jam a door from the inside so it won't open. While I figured it out to keep Riza from walking in on me with a lover, I'm pleased to be useful now.

I gather a couple of knives and a few pieces of wood that we had sitting around for carving when we were bored. As we head back downstairs, Nemeth is quiet. He deliberately avoids the light cast by the lamp in my hands, and when I glance down at the stone floors, there's a dark trail that I don't like seeing.

He's still bleeding, the stubborn arse.

Annoyed, I work quickly as we return to the doors. I wedge the wood underneath the door itself, so it'll act as a doorstop. Then along the side, where the doors are hinged, I take a thick, short blade and jam it to the crevice, pushing it forward until the dagger is wedged so tightly that I can't pull it back out. I repeat that on the other side, and when Nemeth's done tying the door handles together, I'm fairly satisfied. I tug on the door, and it doesn't budge.

"Better," I say. "This won't keep away anyone who's incredibly determined, but it'll give us time to figure something out." I glance over at him. "Do we have a staff or a pole of some kind that we can slide through the handles to act as a bar?"

"Somewhere," he answers, that distracting sound in his voice again.

I'm tired of pussyfooting around the issue. I pick up the lamp from the floor and hold it up to him, shining it on his face. "Are you going to tell me where they stabbed you, or am I going to have to find out the hard way?"

He squints at the light, holding a hand up. "First of all, they didn't have knives. They had pickaxes—"

"Like that makes it better?"

"And second of all, I want to know what the hard way is."

Is . . . is this difficult Fellian choosing now to flirt with me? *Now*? When I'm ready to start screaming obscenities at him? I scowl as fiercely as I can. "The hard way is me getting my soaps and some water and examining every last bit of your skin until I find the damage."

"That doesn't sound so bad—"

"It won't be gentle scrubbing," I hiss. "Because right now I am so angry at you that I could scream, Nemeth. How dare you take care of me when I'm sick and not let me do the same for you? Do you truly not trust me that much?"

His eyes glimmer as he gazes down at me. We are in a standoff, he and I, where neither of us is willing to yield. I remain where I am, glaring at him.

"It is not about trust," Nemeth says after a long moment. "It is . . . not something that can be mended with ease. It will heal on its own. Or not. Regardless, you cannot help."

I scowl at him. And he thinks *I'm* stubborn? "Clearly, we are doing this the hard way. I'll go get my soap."

When I move to pass him, Nemeth grabs my arm. "Candra. Wait." To my surprise, he looks embarrassed more than anything. "It is . . . a wound that would be regarded as shameful and foolish among my people. That is why I hesitate."

Ah. It's a dick wound. I get it now. I shake my head. "Nemeth, you saved me. I don't think you can get more gallant and heroic than that. You confronted two men, snapped them like they were twigs, and flung them out of the tower. You kept us *safe*. How could you possibly think I would consider any wound you got in those efforts as embarrassing?"

He remains silent, his eyes reflecting the light of my lamp.

I decide to try another tactic. "I'll suck your cock if you let me heal your wounds."

Nemeth gapes at me. "W-what?"

"You heard me," I say calmly, even though my heart is racing at his visceral reaction to my bargaining. "You let me tend to you, and in exchange for you saving my life, I'll suck your cock. I'll suck it so hard that we'll be scraping your cum off the ceiling."

"You cannot offer that—"

"It's my mouth, and I'll offer it if I want to," I say, voice pert. "Of course, I'll save the sucking for after you're all healed up, but the offer remains. You saved my life, and I never got to thank you. Now, I'll bargain with you. Let me tend your wound for being my hero and saving my life a second time, and I'll suck your cock in sheer gratitude."

I don't point out that the sucking on him would be for my pleasure, as well. That just thinking about it is making my heart flutter with anticipation, and that the flutter has lodged itself between my thighs.

"I would not bargain for such a thing," Nemeth says, voice stiff. "I would never force you to service me—"

"Give me your hand," I say, holding mine out. I set the lamp down on the floor nearby and gaze up at him.

"Candra—"

"Give me your hand," I say again. When he sighs and does as I ask, I hike up my skirts with my other hand and guide his big palm under my layers of clothing, pressing him to the vee between my thighs. I'm slick and aching there already. "Does that feel like I'm being forced to service you?" I tilt my head up at him. "Or that I'm excited to reward a strong warrior who's saved me twice now?"

"You . . . are utterly impossible."

"Yes, I am," I agree. "Now let me see your wound so I can take care of it for you."

Nemeth grumps and fusses at me as we head up the stairs.

"You do not need to tend my wound," he says in that stuffy voice as I move into our quarters ahead of him. "It will heal on its own. Nor do you need to offer your mouth as incentive. That is not appropriate."

"Mmm. But I'm going to do both anyhow," I reply, setting the lamp on one of the tables. I tap the other one to turn it on, flooding the chamber with more light. Moving to the fireplace, I hang a pot over the empty firepit and bend down to start a fire, deliberately ignoring Nemeth. I'm going to give him time to adjust to the idea of me tending to him, however much he might dislike it. If his wound gets infected, I'll be left alone in this tower, and I refuse to let that happen.

Once the fire is lit and licking at the wood, I pour water from a pitcher into the pot so it can heat up. I glance over at Nemeth, ready to argue with him if necessary. The big Fellian is seated on his favorite stool, his posture stiff and upright, a mutinous look on his face. I don't get why he's acting like I'm suddenly the enemy. It must truly be in an uncomfortable spot, this wound, and I remind myself to be patient with him. He's a man, even if he's Fellian, and they're sensitive about their cocks.

I look him over again. He's seated upright with his thighs parted, straddling the stool. Are his legs farther apart than usual? Is that because of the wound there? Sympathy rushes through me, and I dip the cloth in the warm water, then move to his side. "All right. Lift your kilt."

Nemeth gives me a shocked look. "You . . . you are going to suck my cock now?"

Does he really think now is the time? I find it interesting he's no longer averse to such an offer, just the timing of it. "Tempting, but I'm actually going to clean your wound for you and save the cock sucking for when it's recovered. But I can't help you if you don't show me where you're hurt." When he hesitates, I step between his thighs and reach for the edge of his kilt. "I promise I'll be gentle."

He grabs my hand again, stopping me with a puzzled look on his face. "And you think it's between my thighs?"

"Where is it, then?" Where is this shameful wound if not in a private area?

Nemeth sighs heavily and runs a clawed hand down his face. Then, still covering his expression, he extends one wing out to the side.

I see it, then. A horrible, ugly gash that slices down through the delicate membrane of his wing. One of the men must have lunged at him with the pickaxe and dragged it through his wing, tearing it apart. The cut looks horrid, as long as my arm, and extends all the way down to the edge, where it continues to drip blood. "Oh," I breathe. "Oh, Nemeth."

"There is nothing to be done for it." He hangs his head. "It was my fault. A warrior knows he must always protect his wings in battle, but I wanted to frighten them with my size, to distract them away from you."

And it worked too. Once Nemeth appeared, they had no interest in me.

Tears pricking my eyes, I lean in and press my fingertips to his chin, forcing his face up so he looks at me. "Thank you," I tell him in a soft voice. "It was very gallant."

"It was pure foolishness, and now I will pay for it." He grimaces. "My father would be ill-pleased."

"He's not here." I kiss his hard, unforgiving mouth. "He doesn't know our situation." I kiss him again, nibbling on his lip because I love the feel of him against me. "And I'm grateful, even if I hate that you got hurt. May I tend to you?"

"Oh, so now you ask with sweet words?" His voice is wry as he gazes up at me. "You no longer demand?"

I cannot help but grin. "You respond best to demands. Maybe I should." But I don't. I just nip at his lower lip again, scraping my teeth over it, and then I lift my head. "I promise I'll be gentle."

Nemeth makes a choked sound as I reach for his wing. He grabs my hand, stopping me first. "Wings are . . . sensitive."

Right. And this one is wounded, and he's getting all squirmy. "You're allowed to get turned on. I won't judge you."

He scrubs a hand over his face again and shifts in his seat. "I don't think I'll get turned on, but I might get twitchy. Fair warning."

So, he's going to wriggle like a naughty little boy? I can deal with that. I move toward his wing, and he extends it out—then hisses with pain. I'm careful as I gently brush the cloth over the wound. The angle of treating him is odd and uncomfortable, but I give it a shot anyhow, wiping away the excess blood and examining the gash. The membrane looks thick enough to hold a stitch, and I wonder if I can sew it up. As I consider it, the wing stretched in front of me gives a shiver.

I glance over at Nemeth. He wears a rictus of concentration, his eyes squinted, and his nostrils flared. His fists are clenched on his lap. "Are you all right?"

He responds with a distracted grunt.

I turn back to his wing, watching him out of the corner of my eye. Sure enough, the moment he thinks I'm looking away, he reaches for the front of his kilt and adjusts himself. And when I touch his wing again? It jerks under my grasp.

"Ticklish?" I ask.

He scowls at the word. "It just . . . feels like a lot."

"It might feel like a lot more in a moment because I think I should sew it up." I set the blood-stained wet towel down and give him a calm look, even though my heart is fluttering at the thought of having to sew flesh. "You can't let it just hang open like that. Your wing will be destroyed."

"My wing is *already* destroyed."

"Not necessarily," I bluff, though I don't know anything about wings. He might be right, but that doesn't mean I want to give up hope. "I'll make very tiny stitches, and we can at least try to save it. We'll clean it daily and rub some salves on it to help with the scarring. Are you all right with that?"

His nostrils flare again, and I can tell by his expression he is very much *not* all right with it. His wing closes again. "I will think about it—"

I put a hand on his chest. "No. You're going to let me do this. There's no thinking about it. If you wait, it will almost certainly get infected, and if it scabs over like this, your scarring could be much worse." I know as much about scars as I do wings, but it sounds good to my ears. "So, you're going to let me tend to you."

"With a needle?" Nemeth sounds faint. "On my wing?"

I nod. "You're probably going to want to be numb for this. Where's that fermented mushroom brew of yours?"

"That's for cooking."

I get to my feet. "But it's alcoholic, right? Today it'll be for you."

Back when I was only allowed a cup or two of wine, there was an herb that I used to experiment with (because I'm a shameless, naughty princess). One that amplifies the sensation of being drunk. It's good for sleep, too, which is why I have a supply, but right now, it'll also help Nemeth.

I'm going to get him good and drunk so he'll let me sew up his wing.

It takes three glasses of his mushroom wine and two chewed leaves of my special herb before Nemeth loosens up. I watch him carefully, and after a while, the shine in his eyes seems to get fuzzy, and his lids get heavy. While I sit next to him, threading a needle, he reaches out for my braid and strokes a claw down it.

"So soft," he murmurs. "Like petting a kitten."

My brows go up. "How are you feeling, Nemeth?"

The smile he gives me is lazy and heart stopping, his eyes closed. "Good. Except my wing. It hurts like dragon shite. But other than that, I feel good."

Oh, is he borrowing my phrases now? Biting back a giggle, I hold three fingers up. "How many do you see?"

"I see three kitten claws," he murmurs, taking my hand in his and kissing each fingertip as if to prove it.

All right. I think the leaves are definitely working. "I'm going to clean your wing and then sew it up, all right, love?"

He groans, the sound more reluctant than pained. "Must we?"

"We must," I say firmly, amused. "This will be easiest if you lie on the floor next to me, and I spread your wing over my lap. Can you manage that?" I get to my feet and grab one of the biggest pillows off the bed. By the time I turn around, Nemeth is on the floor already, his strange legs bent and his head turned due to his sweeping horns. I tuck the pillow under his head, and he tries to kiss my fingers again. "Not now," I cajole. "You can kiss them after you're stitched up."

"Have you ever stitched up anyone before?" he asks as I make him comfortable on the floor, adjusting the pillow.

"I have not." I'm bloody nervous about it too. Terrified, really. What if I can't do it? What if I'm too disgusted by the thought that I can't pull the needle through his flesh? But if I don't, there's no one else who can. Nemeth needs me to do this right, so I must.

"Then I am proud to be your first," he says.

I snort. Now I know he is truly drunk. I settle in next to him, sitting on my knees, and I spread a towel across my lap. "Let's just get you taken care of, all right? Spread your wing for me."

He does, and I want to cry all over again at the sight of it. How am I ever going to sew it so tightly that he'll be able to fly again? I bite my lip hard enough to draw blood, determined not to panic. He needs me. He needs me.

I can do this.

"Is it very bad?" he asks in a hushed voice.

"Not so bad," I lie, wiping more blood away and then applying a cleansing ointment sent by Riza for cuts and scrapes. "I'm trying to figure out the best way to go about this. I think I can get the stitches tightest if I tack the sides together in a few spots and then go back over to the smaller stitches to pull everything together like two pieces of fabric. All right?"

Nemeth doesn't answer, and when I look over at him, he gives me a dreamy look. "You are so beautiful, Candra."

I smile at that momentary distraction. "Thank you. I'm going to sew the first stitch now."

He continues to watch me as I take the needle in my hand and brace myself. Then, holding my breath, I make the first stitch. He doesn't so much as twitch, and when I'm done, I expel a gusty sigh. All right. I can do this after all. "How are you holding up, love?"

"You called me 'love,'" he muses. "Twice now. You must really like my knot."

Chuckling, I make the next stitch. Flirty drunks, I can handle. "Thinking about that, are you?"

"Constantly," he admits.

I continue stitching his wing, hoping that I'm doing this right. I tack it in several spots to hold it together, then go back to the "beginning" of the wound and wipe away the blood. I make the first tiny stitch, wishing for the first time that I'd paid attention to Riza's needlework lessons. Still, how hard can it be? You make a stitch on one side and pull the needle through. That's all. I make a tiny cross-stitch instead since that seems more secure and glance over at Nemeth to see how he's handling the pain.

He's still watching me, his expression thoughtful.

"I'm doing the best I can," I tell him, making another stitch. "Tell me if you need me to pause so you can handle the pain."

The Fellian snorts. "Mere tickles."

I wipe away more blood. "Uh-huh."

"Is it true?"

I pause, looking over at him. "Hmm?"

"You called me 'love.' Twice now. Did you mean it?"

For a drunk, he has an amazingly sharp mind. I'm not used to being confronted on my flirting. "It's an affectionate name. I feel affection for you. Of course, I'm going to call you 'love.'"

"You feel affection for me?"

"I said that, didn't I?"

"And you enjoy sucking my cock. And you liked my knot. Those weren't lies?"

I make another stitch, wincing in sympathy as I tug it through his wing. "Where are you going with this?"

"That perhaps you have feelings for me."

I already know I do. That's not the problem. The problem is that he's forcing me to choose frolicking in bed with him over my kingdom. "I adore you," I confess. "Being with you makes me happy. You're the only reason I haven't given up a dozen times over. You're the only reason I didn't race out that door the moment they opened it."

"That and the wrath of the Golden Moon Goddess, yes?"

I'm silent because I'm not a good person. If it were up to just me? I'd probably have left. I like to think that I'd be noble and sacrificing, but I don't think I'm strong enough for that. I'm a weak coward. "I'm just glad you're here. You saved me down there." I wipe the blood off his wing again and make another stitch. "Something tells me those men wouldn't have stopped at simply taking our food. They likely would have murdered us too."

Well, after raping me.

The thought is a grim one, and it reminds me that those men were humans. Liosian humans. They're supposed to be my people. Yet every time I'm contacted with my people, they treat me with derision. Or worse. I think about the fluffy letters that Riza and Nurse sent, letters that were sweet and thoughtful but shared no information about the outside world because they did not trust me with it.

"You haven't answered," he says. "Perhaps these feelings mean we should be together after all?"

I nod absently as I stitch, focusing on the work in front of me as I think more about my people and how those men showed up early with the supplies this time. They didn't wait for the Solstice. They said they didn't have to . . . and I'm reminded of how much I struggled last year, fighting to make my candles last, fighting to make every bit of wood count. They could have brought me more at any time; Riza even pointed out in her letter that she knew I didn't have any, yet no one did anything about it.

It hurts.

Those choices, combined with the men who broke in, make me question my kingdom. I know King Lionel is a complete arse. If he fell off a cliff, I'd cheer. I've got no love for him or this war he's started. But he's married to my sister, and she's everything to me. I can't abandon her.

Yet . . . she wanted me to kill Nemeth. Probably still would the moment I left this tower.

The thought sickens me. She doesn't know him. Not like I do. She doesn't know that he takes care of me, fusses over me when I'm not feeling well. He administers my medicine to ensure that I don't bruise myself. He's shared his supplies and everything he has with me simply because he's a good person.

Erynne wouldn't understand that, and it feels like a knife in my chest. Nemeth's insistence upon an honorable mating between us means I would have to choose between him and my sister.

It's a choice I cannot make.

"It's all right," Nemeth says in a soft voice.

I glance over at him, startled. "Hmm?"

"If you don't want to be with me. I know I am not the same as your kind. To them, I am a monster." He gives me a sleepy smile. "If nothing else, I am glad I will have this time with you."

My heart aches. "I wish it were simple, Nemeth."

"It is," he says, closing his eyes. "It is all very simple. And I am content to wait."

CHAPTER TWENTY-SIX

I take great care with Nemeth's wing. When he quiets, it's easier to concentrate, and I focus all of my attention on making each stitch as tiny and perfect as I can. I visualize the seam of the scar as small and flat, well healed and painless.

I've never flown, but I can imagine how terrifying it would be to lose the ability. So I take the utmost care with Nemeth and his wing. It takes forever to finish, but when I'm done, I'm satisfied that I've given him my best effort.

Once his wing is stitched and slathered in salve, I gently help him fold it closed and then change the blankets on the bed so he can have somewhere clean to lie down. It's impossible to bandage the wound itself, so I stick a bit of cloth to the thick salve to cover the worst of it and help him to bed. Nemeth is an affectionate drunk. He tries to pull me into bed with him and kisses my neck and face over and over again until I'm breathless with need.

"I love you," he whispers, brushing my hair back from my face. "My beautiful Candra. I would die before I would let anyone harm you."

That just makes my heart hurt more. I force a bright smile to my face and give him a sassy wink that I don't feel. "You think about your reward for being a good patient. But for now, get some sleep."

He doesn't let go of my hand, and I hold it tight as he mumbles to himself and drifts off to sleep.

I stare down at our joined hands. His is easily twice the size of mine, his palm huge. His thick fingers are tipped with deadly-looking black claws, but I've never been truly afraid of him. He's always been so kind and gentle, even when it's obvious that he could crush me in his grip. I feel safe with him, and that's oddly ironic because I've never felt safe at court. I love court, and I know how to survive—and even thrive—on the games played there. But it feels like living on the edge of a knife, where the slightest wrong move could destroy you.

It's definitely not safe or comfortable, and until Nemeth, I didn't think those were things I wanted.

I toy with his fingers, tracing each dangerous claw, thinking of how Nemeth would fit in back at the Liosian court. Provided they didn't immediately toss him into the dungeon, he still wouldn't fit in. He's a scholar who delights in his books and loves to sit by the fire and discuss what he's read. He's far more suited for a monastery or a college. The court is a place where fashion is discussed, not philosophy. A place that cares about who is fucking who, and which lord is about to make an advantageous marriage, and which lord has been cuckolded. It's an aggressive, shallow place, and I think Nemeth would hate it.

And that makes me oddly sad because he doesn't fit into my world. If we weren't in this tower together, we'd have never met. If Meryliese had lived, I'd still be at court, being chased by Balon, and Nemeth would be here, reading his books and enduring quietly.

Alone.

Because I don't know if Meryliese would have been his friend. I don't know if they would have spoken. I don't know if she would have lived through that first long year in which all my wood ran out far too quickly.

I like to think that Meryliese would have shared with him, but what if Erynne had given her the same dagger she gave me? What if Erynne had given her the same instructions and told her to kill the Fellian in the tower before he killed her? Erynne is all wrong about Nemeth. He is fierce when he needs to be, but he's also a good, kind man.

I'm more torn than ever.

Placing Nemeth's hand carefully back on the bed, I pull the covers over him and get to my feet. With a lamp in my hand, I head upstairs for my trunk, where I've left Erynne's letter. Maybe reading it again will give me more clarity of mind. I head up to my old room, and again it feels oddly empty and strange. To think that there is so much life in a room shared with Nemeth and his things. I don't even mind the cozy clutter of his books because it feels like we're snug in a den together.

Or perhaps it's the "together" part that I'm so enamored with.

I sit on the floor in front of my trunk and pull it open. Erynne's letter is waiting there, and I unfold it, running my fingers over the parchment as I do. The light hits the thick paper with a strange angle, and as it does, I notice something peculiar. Certain letters seem to be bolder than others. Here is a large *C*, and in the next line, an overlarge *H*. I thought Erynne had sloppy writing, but perhaps it's an encoded message?

Holding my breath, I whisper each letter aloud.

C-H-E-S-T-L-I-N-I-N-G.

By all the gods. How could I have missed this?

I jump to my feet, frantically searching the room for the chest that the letters came in. Which one was it? The one with the brass buckles or a plain one? Have we yet burned it? I race back downstairs, heading for the first-floor storage room where Nemeth painstakingly detailed our supplies and made plans for them to last us. I find the chest in question, and panting with anticipation, I pull it free and flip it open. Still full of herbs. I pull the bags out, and when they are removed, I can see a dainty fabric with a delicate repeating pattern glued to the bottom of the chest itself. I skim my fingers over the fabric, holding the lamp up to see. Sure enough, there is a hint of a bulge, and when I run my fingers over the lining, there's a give, as if a thick sheaf of parchment is underneath.

Using my fingernails, I pry the lining up and snatch the letter inside. It's folded and sealed with Erynne's scented wax, the impression of House Vestalin's symbol staring back at me. I flick a finger under the wax and unfold the letter.

A small pouch flutters into my lap as I do.

This time, the message is brief.

Candra,

I am told the Fellian yet lives in the tower with you. The war goes badly, and we need to send a message. I've sent you the tools. Do not be a coward.

For Lios,

Erynne.

I stare at the letter and read it again.

And a third time because I cannot believe what it says. Erynne knows I didn't kill Nemeth, and now she's demanding that I do so? She's sent poison along? I push the sachet off my lap in horror and skim the note again, looking for more hidden messages. There is nothing I can see, no strange letters more pronounced than others.

The writing is unmistakably Erynne's, as well.

They know he's alive . . . how? There must be a spell of some kind that tells her of our doings. If she gave me a magical knife that answers questions, it stands to reason that she would have a second for herself. She can't see inside the tower, I don't think, or she would know that Nemeth and I share every meal. That he takes care of me. That the idea of killing him is unthinkable.

For the first time since I've arrived, I don't feel helpless guilt over my sister's commands.

Instead, I'm enraged.

How dare Erynne ask for this? How dare she demand that I kill my only company? The man who has been nothing but kind and protective of me? Who saved me from those men below? My cheek still throbs from the smack across the face I was dealt. I think of Nemeth's poor wing and how distraught he was over the wound. How he didn't want to show it to me because he felt responsible for his wing's destruction.

How wings are useless in a tower.

My heart hurts. Here I've been so focused on my own struggle that I've failed to acknowledge Nemeth's. However hard it is for me to be here, it's equally difficult—or more so—for him. I can't imagine having the freedom to fly and then being trapped here in the tower. I've always been forced indoors due to my illness, never very far away from a nurse or an assistant who can administer my potion.

A potion that I have to administer to myself tonight since Nemeth is probably going to be unconscious for the remainder of the day, drunk and relaxed.

I head for the garderobe, and I toss the packet of poison in without hesitation. Then I head to start a fire to cook a meal, brew my potion . . . and burn my sister's letter.

The gods can take Erynne's plans and send them straight to the Gray Lands. I've got plans of my own, and they don't involve killing Nemeth to send a message of any kind. She thinks I'm a coward? I'm going to show her a different sort of bravery and do the very thing I'm terrified of.

I'm going to marry Nemeth.

Provided that's still what he wants, of course. But I know a sure way to find out.

While Nemeth sleeps off the pain, I try to stay busy. It's a warm day, so I set the fire in the kitchen and watch as my sister's letter burns. I feel nothing but anger toward her. Anger and a hint of resentment. She's telling me I'm a coward? Asking me to put my kingdom first? Haven't I done that by being here in this tower? Aren't I giving the next six years to my dragon-shite-loving kingdom?

Well, they get no more than that from me.

I set my potion's ingredients to boil over the fire and then head for the tower's doors. Curiosity—and a little worry—drive me to go and stand in front of them. The knives I've wedged into the doorjambs remain in place, the ropes around the handles tight. I've brought a broom with me to shove the long handle of it through the metal of the door handles so it can act as a bar, but it doesn't feel like enough. Even now, I can feel a hint of air blow in at the hinges, and light leaks in from the tiniest cracks.

Pressing my ear to the door, I wait to hear the sound of voices—of more men coming back to attack the tower. It's quiet outside, but that doesn't mean someone won't return again. If they come back with enough men, no doors in the world will stop them. This is merely a stopgap and not much of one. Without the bricks on the other side, the tower feels open and oddly vulnerable. Anyone could get in.

I could unblock the door and leave at any time.

I put my hand on the wood. It feels warm and pleasant and not nearly solid enough. To think that the first week I was here, I was so frantic to get out that I begged Balon to remove the bricks from the doors and save me.

I could walk out right now, a year later . . . and I won't.

Not because I want to stay for the good of Lios. But because Nemeth is here, and I want to be with him.

After I give myself my injection and clean up the kitchen, I head upstairs. Nemeth is sprawled in bed, asleep, his big, thick legs taking up the majority of the mattress. I watch him for a moment, then set the lamp across the room and tap it once to dim it. I want to be able to see what I'm doing. Gathering my skirts, I slip off my shoes and crawl into bed next to Nemeth. I carefully avoid his wing, easing the blankets down his hips. By the gods, he's so beautiful. How did I think he was monstrous when I first saw him? He's nothing but thick slabs of dark grey muscle, and the strength in his body calls out to me, begging to be appreciated.

Lucky for him, I know just how to appreciate a good-looking body.

I lean over him and kiss his chest. I tell myself that he should probably wake up and eat dinner. That I need to check his wound. But those feel like excuses because, in all reality, I just want to touch him. I want to show him that I'm with him.

That I've made up my mind to be his mate.

I press another kiss to a strong pectoral. He's remained in excellent shape despite being trapped in here, and I suspect a lot of it is due to the fact that he performs his exercises daily, stretching and maneuvering, as well as carrying heavy supplies up and down the stairs constantly. I appreciate his strength, and I certainly appreciate the muscles it builds. I've always been a soft creature, coddled by my nurses, and when Erynne was out riding horses, I was told to sit by the fire with a blanket. I've always felt a little weak compared to my sister, but Nemeth doesn't make me feel like a problem. He makes me feel like I'm someone to be cherished, to be cosseted and taken care of. He appreciates me despite my shortcomings.

Well, I do have a few talents, and I plan on showing them to him. I kiss lower down his chest, hovering over his navel.

He makes a low sound in his throat, his big frame shifting on the bed.

My hands go to his belt, and I tug at it, loosening the buckle and then pulling it free. Without the belt, his kilt falls from his hips, revealing the wrap he wears over his groin. After watching him dress, I know that a tug in the right spot will pull everything undone, and I waste no time unwrapping him from his clothes like a feast day present.

And then he's naked, sprawled underneath me. His cock rests against his thigh, growing harder as I gaze down at him. I see the ridge at the base of his cock that will become his knot and the pointed tip of his shaft. Gods, he's pretty. I sigh happily at the sight of him, and his cock twitches at the sound.

"Candra?" He sounds fuzzy and confused.

"I made dinner," I tell him, lowering my head to kiss the flat plane below his navel. His cock stirs again, almost brushing my face. "And I wanted to wake you up with your reward . . . unless you want me to stop."

He rolls fully onto his back, his strangely bent legs spreading ever so slightly to invite me in. "I am no fool."

"Mmm." I grip his shaft in my hand and skim my fingers over him, loving the way he strains against my touch. He's fully erect now, the head of his cock flushed and inviting. "I've also been doing some thinking."

Nemeth's breath catches as I give the head of his cock a lick. His claws fist into the blankets, digging at the material.

I suppose that's as decent an answer as any. He's listening, that's for certain. I lick a stripe down the side of his shaft and sigh with pleasure at the feel of his hot, turgid length in my grip. There's something so delightful about an erect cock that just begs to be squeezed and nibbled on. I love the feel of it, and I love his responses too. Gripping the base of him, I rub the pad of my thumb against his knot, trying to get it to balloon. It feels hot and tight under my hand but hasn't yet descended. Fascinated, I work his cock with my tongue, trying to get the knot to extend. I tease his tip, dipping it into my mouth and slicking it with my saliva. A salty burst on my tongue tells me that he's leaking pre-cum, and I lap at him, making humming noises of appreciation as I do.

"You . . . " he groans, one enormous hand moving to the top of my head. It hesitates there, and when I suck harder on the tip of him, his hips jerk, and he drives up into my mouth. "You . . . you were . . . thinking?"

Ah. Right. I run my tongue along the underside of the head. "I was. I was thinking that my answer is yes."

He groans as I nibble down the underside of his shaft, nipping at his foreskin before running my tongue over his tight sack. "For the life of me, Candra, I cannot remember the question."

Grinning to myself, I trail my lips up to the head of his cock again and swirl my tongue around the crown. "Think very hard."

"I cannot think at all . . . "

I give him a teasing lick. "Poor thing."

He makes a choked sound, his claws tightening in my hair. "Candra . . . "

"Yeeesss?"

"Your mouth . . . "

I give him a far more lascivious lick. "Mmm-hmmm?"

"So good," he breathes. "By all the gods . . . never felt anything so good." His breath hitches when I close my mouth over the tip again, hollowing out my cheeks and sucking. "You . . . "

It's so incredibly cute how flustered he is at me working his cock. His thoughts are utterly incoherent, his hips rising up from the bed as I bob my head down over his length, taking more into my mouth before drawing back with a noisy slurp and licking him once more. "Me what, love?"

"Perfect. So perfect."

"So you want to come in my mouth, then?" I swirl my tongue around the head of his cock. "Or did you want to come on my face? Or my tits? You might enjoy that—"

I can't finish my statement because, in the next moment, my mouth is full of his hot, silky release. I hum with approval, pleased to make him come so quickly. When his wing feels better, I can take my time with him. For now, it's a quick tease with the promise of more. Making little soothing noises in my throat, I lick him clean, very aware that his gaze is locked on me as I do so.

Unable to resist, I give him one last kittenish lick before asking, "How are you feeling, love? I hated to wake you from your sleep, but I thought we should check on your wing." My lips curl into a teasing smile. "I figured this might be the best way to do so."

"You . . . " Nemeth makes a strangled sound in his throat. He looks stunned.

I have to admit, I love seeing that expression on his face. "Me," I agree, and press a kiss to the tapered head of his cock. "I said I'd suck your cock if you let me stitch you up, and really, we're both coming out as winners in this bargain." I lick him again, and I could swear his cock stirs as if trying to harden in my grasp. It makes me smile, and I glance up at Nemeth.

"Before you say that I shouldn't have done this," I quickly add, "I wanted to. And besides, it's perfectly fine. I'm going to be your mate." I sit up beside him on the bed. "So now I'm afraid you're stuck with me."

"You . . . what?" Those fascinating eyes blink at me.

"I said I'm going to be your mate. I'm not going to let worries over the future destroy my happiness for the next six years. Whatever happens outside, I'll worry about that later. For now, I want to be happy, and I want to be with you." I smile, but his dazed response isn't giving me much to work with. Is he happy? Upset?

He just keeps staring at me as if I've grown another head. I realize I've just sucked the strength right out of him, but a girl needs *something* to work with. "Have you changed your mind?"

Faster than I can blink, he grabs me and hauls me over him. "Never." His gaze searches my face. "You mean it?"

I nod, feeling a little shy. I've never been a girl for commitment, but for him, I want to try. "I do."

"Is this because I am wounded?"

"While that was terrifying, no, that's not it." *It's because my sister wants me to murder you, and I realized I'm in love with you and that my life would be empty without you. That's why.* But I can't say any of that aloud. "You saved me at no thought to yourself earlier, and it made me realize how much I love you. I don't want to spend the next six years depriving myself." I lean over and kiss him. "I'll be your mate if the offer still stands."

He groans, wrapping his arms around me and hauling me down against his chest in a hug. Of course, with the angle of our bodies, it means that my breasts are in his face, and instead of pointing this out with embarrassment, Nemeth nuzzles them. He buries his face in my cleavage, and I gasp at the exciting prickle of awareness that courses through me. "Of course, the offer stands. Just . . . say it again."

"I'll be your mate."

One of those big fangs scrapes against the swell of my breast. "No, Candra. The other part."

Oh. "The part where I said I love you?"

He gazes up at me. "Do you mean it?"

I nod, smiling shyly down at him. "I'm not all that familiar with love, so you might have to be patient with me." Back at court, love is something that can be wielded against you by a lover or a gossip . . . or by my sister, who keeps trying to get me to kill Nemeth. I push thoughts of her away and cup Nemeth's big, handsome face in my hands. "But I love you, and I'm tired of saying no. I'm a girl that much prefers a good 'yes.'" I wriggle my backside against him. "So . . . wanna have sex after I check out your wing?"

Nemeth runs his nose along the swell of my breast, sending skitters of pleasure through me. "Not until after we have the ceremony."

"There's a ceremony?" I pout.

"A Fellian ceremony," he agrees. "On the night of the new moon." He presses a kiss to the slope of my breast, and I'd give anything for him to tug my bodice down and take my nipple into his mouth at this moment. "Since we have no idea if the moon is rising, however, I'm inclined to say tomorrow is a good day."

"Tomorrow," I agree, though I'm throbbing with awareness between my thighs, and I want this to happen today. But I can wait for tomorrow. "Tomorrow, I'm yours."

"All mine," he agrees, and I love the covetous look on his face.

CHAPTER TWENTY-SEVEN

His wing is healing well, so I get out my best dress and dampen the skirts to get some of the wrinkles out, pressing it under Nemeth's heavier books to iron it. It's still pitifully wrinkled, but there are no instructions in my book on how to wash clothes without that happening. I fuss with my skirt for a bit, despairing over a wrinkle as big as a canyon right down the front where my overdress artfully parts to show my pretty, pale-blue chemise underneath. I need something heavier to smooth the wrinkles out. There's a huge book of war poetry that Nemeth often reads, and it might do the trick. Glancing around our quarters, I look for the volume . . .

And find it in Nemeth's hands.

He sits by the fire, reading, his wound slathered in ointment, the stitches an unpleasant-looking line across his beautiful wing. More than that, though, he straddles his favorite stool, his big body hunched over his book, one big hand skimming down a page, and I'm suddenly jealous of poetry.

I know we agreed to wait until tomorrow, but there's nothing that says I can't distract him right now.

"Nemeth," I call sweetly, leaving my dress and stepping across the room toward him. "Can I trouble you for a moment?"

The Fellian straightens, sliding a ribbon between the pages and closing his book. His eyes follow me as I stroll in his direction. "What is it?"

"I need to borrow your book." I bend over and pluck the tome from his hands.

"You're going to read it?"

I chuckle. "Don't be silly. It needs to flatten the wrinkles out of my skirt."

"Gods forbid that I catch you reading one of my books," he teases as I move back to my dress and set the heavy book atop the offending wrinkle. "You . . . do know that books are for reading, yes?"

"So many big words," I mock-pout, turning back to him. "You know it's too much for me to take in. And you can just read something else while I keep your book busy."

"Ah, but perhaps I was reading that one." He tilts his head at me, a smile curving his hard mouth as I saunter toward him. "What are you up to?"

"I'm bored and lonely," I say, sliding my arms around his neck. "And tomorrow seems very far away."

His hands settle on my waist. "I know. But it is important to me that we honor my people's customs." His eyes are bright as he gazes at me. With him seated and me standing in front of him, we're almost the same height. It just reminds me how very massive he is in comparison to my smaller form, and I find it incredibly appealing. "Surely one more day will not be so terrible. And then we will marry in the custom of the Fellian people."

"Very well." I can respect that, even if it isn't quite what I had in mind.

His hands slide down my back in a gentle caress. "Care to tell me of Liosian weddings? Are they very romantic?"

I grimace, thinking of Erynne's wedding to Lionel and the endless paperwork and deeds and knighthoods that followed. "They're more contractual, I'm afraid. When my sister married, there were three days of feasts in which my sister sat at one table and her groom sat at another, and priests read out the virtues of both of their bloodlines. After that, it moved on to land grants and favors to particular parties that would benefit from the union. I seem to recall that my sister was followed by three lawyers from both parties at all times, even the first night of the wedding."

I think of how Erynne handled it all bravely, even though her companion (and true love), Isabella, waited in the shadows. Erynne could never marry Isa, though. Isa was not noble, and Erynne was duty bound to give birth to more children to continue the Vestalin line. And Erynne has always, always done her duty.

I'm reminded of the letter she sent, demanding that I take action "for Lios." I'm so very tired of duty and loyalty to one's kingdom. I just want to be happy. With Nemeth, I am . . . and I'm not going to look beyond that.

"It sounds dreadful," he says, interrupting my thoughts. "But if you want something like that—"

"I do not." I hug him tighter, burying my face against his neck. "It was the opposite of romantic. So I am quite happy to have a Fellian ceremony instead." I rub my nose against his skin, feeling amorous. "Tomorrow you will claim me as your bride. What do Fellian ceremonies say about tonight?"

"Tonight, we will anticipate tomorrow," he tells me, grinning.

I'm inclined to do more than just anticipate, though. "Unfortunately for you, I'm a very impatient sort of princess." I run my hands down his broad, strong arms and then grab handfuls of my skirts. Before he can react, I climb onto his lap, and the hands loosely at my waist are suddenly clutching me tight. "There, that's better," I say as I straddle him. "Don't you think?"

Nemeth is silent. His face is impassive as I settle in on his lap, my legs hanging over his thighs, my skirts bunched up to my waist. I feel small against him like this, and it reminds me that when he covers me in our bed, he's going to truly cover me. His size is absolutely enormous, one hand practically spanning my back.

And that's not the only part of him that's enormous. I think about his cock, and the knot at his base, and I'm breathless. I flutter my lashes up at him because this is now the territory of my favorite hobby—tormenting Nemeth. Not in a bad way, of course. I just love watching the need in his eyes as he gazes at me. I love him hungrily devouring me with his eyes as if I'm a feast he can't wait to dig into.

I wriggle on his lap, carefully hooking one heel behind his back and then the other. I make sure not to brush his wings, and as if sensing what I'm doing, he lifts them out of the way, his gaze never leaving my face. "What are you doing, Candra?"

"I'm savoring," I say, voice light. "Isn't that what you want us to do? To savor the moment? Allow me to savor your body pressed to mine and think about what tomorrow will bring."

I shimmy against him, pressing my sex against the rapidly hardening cock sandwiched between us. The breath escapes him, and I smile. "I promise our clothes will stay on," I say. "But I'm afraid that's all I can promise." And I rock my hips suggestively against him. "Is that all right, or should I stop?"

Nemeth growls low, one big hand palming the back of my head and pulling me forward. "Woman, you will be the death of me."

He kisses me hard and then drags me down against his shaft. Ah, yes. I savor this moment because it's clear that for all his growling, Nemeth wants to play too. I work my hips, rubbing against him. "This is savoring, isn't it? This is just a little taste. To whet our appetites."

"This is a tease," he tells me.

"But you like it," I lean back in his arms because it puts pressure where my pussy hits his cock. "You're not telling me to leave."

"I am not," he agrees. He drags me down against his shaft again, and my eyes flutter closed.

I whimper as he thrusts upward, driving against my bloomers. It's been so long since I've had an orgasm—since that day he held me down and finger-fucked me—that I haven't realized how bad I need one until just now. I dig my nails into his skin, clinging to him. "I need you. Please, Nemeth, I need you."

He growls. "I've got you, Candra."

"Then make me come," I whisper, rocking my hips frantically against his. "Please, please make me come. I need it."

With a feral sound, he surges out of his seat and crosses the room, heading for the bed. I hold on tightly, ecstatic that we're getting somewhere. Maybe he'll rip my clothes off and fuck me senseless like I've been needing. The thought makes me want to squirm with excitement.

Nemeth pushes me down onto my back, and he's on top of me. My skirts are up to my waist, and I moan as his big, heavy body settles between my thighs. One big hand grips my hip, and this time, when he thrusts, he practically lifts me off the bed.

Oh *gods*, that's good.

He drives against me again, the hard bulge of his shaft pressing against me. I quiver, trying to hold on to him, but he's so much bigger than I am. I want to kiss him, but there's no way I can reach his lips.

"Free your breasts," he pants, thrusting against me. "Free them so I can see them."

Moaning, I fumble with the laces on my bodice, ripping the delicate ties apart. I always wear my corset tight, as I like the feeling of everything being held and caged into place, so the moment the laces are freed, my breasts spill forth, jutting from the constraining material.

Nemeth hisses at the sight, driving between my hips again. With his free hand, he reaches for me. I hold my breath, waiting for him to palm my breast, but instead, he carefully rolls my nipple against his thumb.

I wasn't expecting such tenderness, not as he drives between my legs like a ravenous beast. I cry out, my pussy clenching hard in response.

"You're going to look so pretty with my knot deep inside you," he rasps, thumbing my nipple. "You're going to be so tight around my cock, but I'll make you feel good. I'll work your pretty tits and rub your sweet cunt until you squeeze my knot and take all my seed."

Oh gods, that sounds so good. As he rocks against me again, hot need pulses through me. I whine, desperately wanting him. Urgent need is rippling through me, and this is not quite enough. I need more to send me over the edge—a finger on my clit, a finger inside me, something. "Nemeth," I pant. "Make me come."

He leans in and growls low, a dangerous, feral sound. As he does, he pinches my nipple between his claws. The jolt of pain-pleasure is surprising, and as he drives against my pussy again, I come. It's a hard, messy sort of climax, and I make choked sounds as he thrusts against me, rippling waves of pleasure shooting through me as he teases my nipple and then squeezes my entire breast tightly. The air departs my lungs as I clench and clench with my body's reaction, and when I finally unclench, a little moan escapes me.

Nemeth thrusts against me one last time and then collapses over me, his big body practically burying me in the bed. Someone else must have come too.

I giggle at how good I feel, holding him tight as he pants, his weight pressing me down into the blankets. "Now *that* was savoring. I can't wait for tomorrow."

He groans, nuzzling against the top of my head. "You're determined to exhaust me, aren't you?"

Maybe just a little. He's just too fun to be with. Even now, I can't stop smiling. I stroke a hand down his shoulder. "Tell me about a Fellian ceremony for marriage. What does it entail?"

"Mmm." Nemeth kisses the top of my head and then carefully rolls onto his back, minding his wing. I turn on my side, facing him. "The usual. A bath to cleanse yourself as you head into your new life. Vows before the gods and an offering of cake. The biting. The marking. The chase—"

"The what?" I sputter, sitting up. "Did you say biting?"

He nods, facing me. "Yes. Give me your hand."

I hold it out to him, and he traces the mound just below my thumb with one claw. "Here. We bite each other here, and then ink is rubbed into the wound so that the mate's marking remains for all time. Anyone who sees your hand will know that you are claimed, and the bite pattern is unique to your mate."

I shiver with aftershocks as he rubs his thumb over the fleshy part of my hand. "Is it painful?"

"It is a bite. I will make it as good for you as I can." His gaze slides to my mouth. "Yours will probably be more painful for me because those tiny teeth of yours don't look like they tear flesh easily. My hand will be mangled by the time you are done with me."

I laugh, slipping my hand out of his grip and batting his arm. "Be nice! I have perfectly normal human teeth. I'll do as well as I can."

"And I will enjoy it because it is my mate marking me as hers." His eyes seem to glow brighter at the thought.

"Now, what's this about a chase?"

"After the bride and groom have given their cake offerings to the gods," Nemeth continues, "The bride flees the groom. It is my duty to capture you—to prove my strength—and fly you across the threshold of our home."

Except he can't fly inside the tower. And his wing is wounded. "I assume we'll improvise?"

"Considering you're human?" He gives me a sly grin. "We must."

It doesn't matter how good I feel after my delicious orgasm or how convicted I am of my path. I have nightmares that night of King Lionel dragging me from the tower for betraying my people. Of my sister holding her child in her arms and spitting on me as the stone tower is destroyed with Nemeth still inside. Of being dragged through the streets of the capital and my people throwing rocks at me.

Vestalin whore, they cry.

I want to protest that I've always been free with my affections, that it's only now that they have a problem because of who my partner is. But dreams are impossible things, and my mouth won't work. I can only scream silently as they stone me and call me names, and somewhere behind me, the distant tower is being destroyed, with a broken Nemeth buried alive in a sea of rubble.

Vestalin whore!

I gasp awake, my body bathed in a cold sweat. It's pitch black in our chambers, and I can't see anything. My breathing rasps hard in the silence, and for a moment, the tower feels oppressive. My skin crawls with the need to escape, to drink in the sunlight, to be free—

"Candra?"

A hand strokes my arm. Nemeth's sleepy voice instantly reminds me of his presence. I look over and see two glowing green slits of eyes, the only light in the darkness.

I swallow hard. I want to marry him. I do. So why is my head full of dragon shite?

I curl up against him, letting him loop a comfortingly heavy arm around me. "Bad dream," I manage. "Just a bad dream."

"I have you. Go back to sleep."

I can't sleep, though. I don't want to dream about my sister or Lios or that I'm betraying them. Why is it so wrong to want to marry a kind, loving man? Does it truly matter so much that he's Fellian? Is my happiness not the most important thing?

Unfortunately, I suspect I already know the answer. My happiness counted for nothing the moment Meryliese died. And her happiness counted for nothing at all.

Even after Nemeth returns to sleep, I stare into the darkness at nothing. The tower feels incredibly vulnerable with the loss of the bricking outside that barricaded the door. While it was up, I only thought of how it kept me in.

Now it's far more important that it keeps the rest of the world out.

I slide out from under Nemeth's arm. He immediately stirs, reaching for me, protective even half-asleep. "I'm all right," I tell him in an easy voice, finding his hand and squeezing it. "I'm headed to the garderobe."

"Take a lamp," he tells me sleepily.

I find one in the darkness. Nemeth always keeps them in the same spot for me so I don't fumble like a child hunting for one. I hold the lamp against my sleep chemise as I step into the hall, tapping it once to light up. I don't head for the garderobe, though. Instead, I go down the stairs and toward the door, the flimsy barrier that keeps the world out.

It doesn't feel like enough. Not nearly enough.

Standing in front of the door, I raise the lamp and eye our efforts. The knives wedged into the doorjambs. The wood wedges at the bottom and down the middle of the double door. The broom slid through the handles to act as a bar. The ropes tying the two handles together. Nothing has been disturbed, but on the other side of the doors, in the sand, are two sprawled bodies. Someone's going to see them and come ask questions, surely.

Or someone else will be curious.

Or someone will think we are an easy target to rob, a princess and a Fellian alone in a tower.

I think of the men with their pickaxes. How they'd attacked Nemeth. My cheek still smarts from where I was backhanded, and there's a bit of a bruise on my face, but I've been using a hint of cosmetics to keep Nemeth from noticing. He's taken enough of the brunt of things. I remember his wing and how it dripped blood everywhere. *I should clean the floors*, I think absently.

Clean the floors and then pull down some of the junk from the third floor to stack against the door. Barricade us *in*.

I walk away from the doors, musing at how much I've changed in the last year. Back at court, I would have never cleaned a floor, much less tended to someone else's wound. I would have cried and fussed dramatically over my own small bruise until I was certain everyone knew of my pain and was feeling it with me. I would never have married a Fellian. I don't even know that I would have married at all. Perhaps I would have spent my days carousing in court, the drunken wastrel aunt of Allionel and Erynne's upcoming child.

As I head for the stairs, I pass the forgotten altar of the Golden Moon Goddess. At least forgotten by me. There are remnants of incense and herbal offerings that show that Nemeth hasn't forgotten the goddess, at least. "Was this your plan?" I ask as if the goddess will somehow answer me. "To change us down to our very beings? To make us forget where we came from?"

There's no answer.

I'm wrong, anyhow. I might be changing, but Nemeth is as steadfast as ever. I'm the only one who is being made anew.

CHAPTER TWENTY-EIGHT

I sleep late the next day, though it's impossible to be certain of the time. All I know is when I wake up, there's a scent of baked sweets lingering in the air, and Nemeth's face is buried in one of his books. One of the lights sits near his feet, giving off a gentle glow that illuminates his strong, harsh features. He looks up as I stretch, a warm smile spreading across his face, and I instantly feel better. Dreams are just dreams, nothing more. I smile at him, rumpling my tousled hair. "You should have woken me up."

"You seemed like you needed to sleep, *milettahn*."

That's a new word. I pause, tilting my head at him. "I haven't heard that before. What does that mean, *milettahn*?"

To my surprise, he looks a bit taken aback. "Mate," he manages after a moment. "It means 'my mate.'"

Such a shy man. I beam at him. "Today's the day. You're not going to back out on me, are you?"

"Never." The look he gives me is full of intense longing, his shoulders immediately tensing. "Have you changed your mind?" I shake my head, and he relaxes again. "I have already baked the cakes for our ceremony. Do not touch them when you go downstairs. We must save them for our offering." He turns a careful page in his book. "And I have readied your bath by the fire. All you have to do is add the warm water I've prepared. It's still on the hearth."

Oh, how thoughtful. I know a bath is a lot of work. I get to my feet, padding across the cold stone floor, and slide into his lap, wrapping my arms around his neck. "You are most kind."

"I am determined," he corrects, sliding one arm around my waist as he closes his book with his other hand. "I shall have you tied to me before the gods quickly so you cannot change your mind. To that end, I am ridding us of any chance of delays."

I chuckle. Who knew such intent could be so damn sexy? "If you've drawn a bath for me, I can't possibly refuse. I'm sure that's in the vows somewhere."

Nemeth rubs a hand up and down my back, watching me. "No more nightmares?"

"None. I slept quite well after I got to put my feet on you."

He grunts, his hand straying to my backside and rubbing. "You make it sound as if you don't put your feet on me every night."

I slide a little closer, my breasts loose under my sleep chemise. With my hair tousled and the fact that I'm almost naked? I feel quite frisky this morning. The bath can wait. "You don't mind."

"I never said I did." His voice lowers and grows husky as I lean in. "Go take your bath, Candra. Once the ceremony is completed, I'll be rutting atop you for hours. Save it."

Oh. *Rutting*. Such a delicious word. With a shiver, I slide off of his lap. "Let me see your wing first. If it looks bad, we're not doing anything today."

"I shall be the judge of that," Nemeth tells me, but he stands upright and stretches to his full height, his wing gently flaring outward. He doesn't stretch it all the way, just enough to let me examine the stitching.

It looks a little puffy and swollen, but it's no longer bleeding, and the color is good. Best of all, there are no red lines tracing outward from the wound. I don't know anything about healing, but I remember Riza told me her husband died because he had a tiny wound that got infected, and that redness crept up his arm in straight lines as it infected his blood. He died two days later.

Thinking about that makes me a little panicky. I swipe at some of the salve on his wound and poke one of the stitches. "Painful?"

"When you poke it, yes," he growls.

Fair enough. "But it doesn't throb? No burning?" I touch the wound again, this time gentler, and it doesn't feel hot, which is a good sign. "I need to put more salve on it."

"It is fine, Candra. I promise you." He sounds a little pissy, his wing flicking as if he wants to pull free from my grasp. "Quit stalling."

How very rude. I huff indignantly, releasing his wing. "I am not stalling."

"Aren't you?"

Scowling up at him, I wipe my salve-smeared fingers on my sleep chemise.

"I'm not stalling," I say again. "I do wish to get married. I just don't want to spend a day frolicking in bed with you if your wing is hurting."

"But our frolicking last night was fine?" He arches a heavy eyebrow at me.

Damn this man. I'm not stalling . . . am I? "Excuse me for being worried about you," I say in my most regal voice. "Gods forbid anyone should care if you're hurt."

I draw myself up as tall as I can and turn away. A moment later, he grabs my wrist and spins me around. He hauls me toward him, one big hand clenching my ass as he pulls me up against his chest and kisses me hard. His mouth is rough and possessive, but I like it. I like the scrape of his oversized fangs on my lip, and I love it when his tongue strokes into my mouth as if he's claiming me.

Then, he sets me down again and swats my backside as if I'm a naughty child. "Go bathe, or I really will think you're stalling."

Distracted, I toss my hair and try to exit the room as gracefully as possible, even though my knees are weak from that rough, wild kiss. I forget a lamp because I'm too caught up in the pleasant throb of my lips, so I have to return to retrieve one.

Stalling indeed. Doesn't this Fellian realize I want nothing more than for this ceremony to be over so I can finally get his cock inside me? Hmph.

Well . . . perhaps I was stalling a little. I'm terrified of what the future might hold when we get out of the tower, but I'm choosing to focus on the present. On Nemeth. On being happy.

So, I head down to the kitchens and to my waiting bath. Sure enough, the tub has been filled halfway with tepid water, and the fire in the hearth is banked, coals smoldering. On one of the tables, four circular cakes are cooling on racks, and they're the source of that divine smell from earlier. He's been busy, all right. I'm a little miffed that all that deliciousness is going to be an offering to the gods, but I'll let Nemeth run things as he chooses today. He wishes to do things the Fellian way, and if I become his bride, I'm telling my people that I've more or less switched sides. I'm betraying them, and they won't know for years because I don't plan on telling them until I emerge from the tower. No sense in cutting off my food supply.

I pause, worried for a moment. Is my sister going to use her magical blade to figure out what I'm up to and withhold from me? I'm tempted to race upstairs and quiz mine. If I did, though, Nemeth would know something was going on, and he'd want to know more about it. He knows it's magic. I just haven't specified what kind. Today is perhaps not the day to have that conversation, so I'll have to question my knife later, in private.

Heading for the hearth, I see the largest kettle hanging on a hook over the coals. I hold my hand close to it. Still warm. Perfection. I pour the water into the tub, and as I do, the scent of roses touches my nose. Oh, he's added scented oil to my bath? How lovely. I smile at the shadows and wonder if Nemeth is watching from them even now.

Probably not. He's such a stickler for his people's rules that he's probably just staring up at the ceiling and not even touching himself to the thought of me bathing. He's going to save all that pent-up passion for tonight.

I shiver at the thought because I'm not hating it. Not in the slightest.

I take my time and luxuriate in my bath since it is my wedding day. I might as well pamper myself. It's nice to be able to soak in a warm bath and even nicer to wash my hair without shuddering from ice-cold water being poured over my head. *When I get out, I'm not going to take a single servant for granted, I tell myself.* I'll be so thankful to Riza and Nurse for their efforts—

And then I pause because I'm giving them up if I marry Nemeth. I'm abandoning them as well as my sister, and Riza is sick . . . I sink lower in the tub, frustrated and miserable. I can't do anything about their struggles. Erynne will take care of them. My sister is nothing if not committed to duty. I can't let the thought of Riza being upset with me for marrying Nemeth stand in my way. Don't I deserve a hint of happiness after all I've done? I'm staying here in this tower, after all. I'm sacrificing seven years of my life.

No one says they have to be miserable years. Why not make them happy ones as Nemeth's mate?

Resolute once more, I finish my bath and dry off, then head upstairs with my towel wrapped around my body and another around my hair. Liosians have all kinds of traditions about the groom not seeing the bride before the ceremony at the altar, but I decide to bend the rules. I leave the water to tidy up later and return upstairs. Nemeth is seated by his large table, his horns gleaming strangely. He's wearing an unusual set of clothing—one I've only seen on him once before when we first entered the tower. Normally he wears only a leather kilt of some kind, but today he's wearing a leather kilt that's cut into jags, each one heavily studded with decorative bits of metal. His chest is covered with a leather breastplate that has straps over each shoulder and around his waist to hold it in place. The breastplate itself is studded and heavily decorated, just like his kilt, and it seems an odd choice for a seven-year peaceful stint inside the tower.

As he regards me, Nemeth carefully sharpens his claws.

"You look very dapper," I say as I enter. "Are you dressing up for me?"

His gaze skims over my body, and then he goes back to sharpening his claws. "Of course. I would only wear my finest hunting leathers for our ceremony."

"You brought hunting leathers with you into the tower?" I arch a brow at him as I unwind the towel from my hair.

"You brought cosmetics," he points out.

Fair enough. And here I thought he hadn't noticed me wearing them over my bruise. Luckily, it's almost gone now, and I won't have to fuss over covering it any longer. I drop my towel from my body and pick up a fresh chemise, shaking it out before slipping it over my head. When I glance over at him, I can see he's definitely watching me. Good.

I love when he watches me.

"Thank you for oiling my bath," I purr, putting a foot on the edge of the bed and then running my hands up my leg, hiking my skirts to reveal my calf. "It made my skin really soft and touchable."

He groans and sharpens his claws even more frantically, the metal file's loud scrapes filling the room.

Hmm. I sit on the edge of the bed, eyeing him. There's a new sort of confidence in him today, a self-assuredness that's rather erotic. "Did you oil your horns?"

"Tradition."

"I suspected as much . . . " I trail off as he flexes his hand, eyeing his fingers. Instead of a full hand of dangerous, lethal dark claws, the claws on the fingertips of the first two fingers have been cut to the quick. "Your claws!"

"Again, tradition." And he eyes me as he carefully files those first two fingers. "A Fellian who takes a mate trims down his claws for his woman."

I eye his hands. Sure enough, the forefinger and second finger of each hand have been filed down to short, blunt nails. As I realize what it's for, I blush. It takes a lot to make me blush, but Nemeth's simple determination and the naughty claw-filing will do it. I imagine him using those fingers on me, no longer worrying over his claws, and my breath escapes my throat. Oh, today is *exciting*. "My," I murmur. "I'm liking this ceremony already."

The look he gives me is scorching with heat.

Just the glances he's giving me are making me squirm with arousal. It's like he's been saving up all his pent-up needs for this day, and it's about to erupt out of him. "I suppose I should get dressed."

"Unless you want to enter your mating ceremony with your hair about your shoulders and wearing nothing but your chemise, aye."

The thought gives me a delightfully erotic shiver. As much as I love the thought, I also love pretty dresses, and I always wanted to look nice for my wedding. Plus . . . I want a few moments in private with my knife so I can question it properly. "I should dress and do something with my hair." I touch a damp lock in explanation. "I want to look good too."

"Shall we do your medicine early, then?" He puts away his sharp-looking nail file. "In case we are . . . distracted later? I've readied your potion."

My goodness, he truly is selling this mating ceremony. Heart fluttering, I nod. "Very well." Taking my medicine early will make my head a little swimmy, but it beats the alternative. "Now?"

He nods and gets to his feet. "Come."

I move closer to him, and he smells like leather in his new clothing. I'm tempted to bury my face against his chest and just breathe in the mix of scents—Fellian skin with leather armor—but I suppose that won't help him administer my potion. To my surprise, he pushes aside the books on the table and then lifts me atop it, seating me. He presses a quick kiss to my lips. "Wait here."

As if I'm going to go anywhere when he's looking so delicious and being so commanding. Nothing could drag me from his side.

I roll up my sleeve as he crosses the room to the fireplace. I didn't notice that he'd set a small fire there until just now when I realized he truly has been warming my potion. He's thought of everything this day as if he's mapped it all out in his mind as to how he wants it to go. I'm fascinated. He tests his claw in the potion and rubs it between his fingers to check the temperature. Then, he carefully pours it into one of the glass vials and screws on the specially made lid with the attached hollow needle.

With a damp towel, he rubs my arm clean, just as he's done for me these last several months. He's always incredibly gentle with me—gentler than I am with myself. Today, however, his movements are distracted yet thoughtful as he strokes my arm.

"What is it?" I ask, curious.

"Am I pushing you?" He slides the towel over my arm, caressing me clean. "Into this mating."

"Of course not. It was my decision."

"But I have been withholding my affection from you. I have pressed you to mate with me. I worry I have pushed too hard. That this isn't what you truly want."

"Nemeth." I put my hand over his larger one. "I'm a little nervous because of what our union means for the future, but it doesn't mean that I don't want this . . . or that I don't want you. On the contrary. I'm going into this with my eyes open. I know what our mating will mean." I smile, deciding to tease him a little. "Besides, are you sure you want me? I have it on good authority that I'm a bit spoiled."

"You are," he admits, a hint of a smile curving his mouth. "But I can look past that."

"Can you look past the fact that I cannot give you children?" I give him a worried look. "My blood curse prevents me from carrying. You would never have offspring of your own."

"I know." Nemeth shakes his head. "It will be the duty of my brothers to carry on the bloodlines of the First House, just as your sister carries on the Vestalin bloodline. I will be happy with you at my side. I want nothing more."

"*Nothing* more? Not even to be free of this tower?" I tease.

He gives me a somber look. "Sometimes I think I would be happy to remain here for the rest of my life if all stays as it is today."

Strangely, I know just what he means. If we could stay in this moment for all time, I would be a happy woman.

"Now, give me your arm, *milettahn*," he murmurs, picking up the needle. "I will be gentle."

As if I need reminding. Nemeth is always gentle.

After my medication is administered, I tell Nemeth I want a bit of time to myself to primp and look good. He seems skeptical, but I kiss his cheek and take a lamp with me upstairs, promising not to be gone for too long. While it's true that I've left the largest mirror upstairs on my wall, I also want some time alone with my knife so I can ask it a few questions. I need to see what Erynne knows about my plans or if she knows anything at all.

I head upstairs and close my door, setting the lamp next to my mirror. I eye the woman who stares back at me. I don't look the same as I did from my days in court. My face is incredibly pale, the sun-kissed warmth once gracing my cheeks gone completely. My hair is thick and full of split ends from my careless brushing and the fact that I don't have Riza to rub silky oils into the ends. I wear no cosmetics, and my face is a bit thinner than it used to be, my cheekbones pronounced instead of a rounded face.

Ugh. I'm vain enough for this to bother me.

Fussing with my hair, I manage to smooth it as much as possible and then work it into a clumsy set of braids that highlight the pronounced cheekbones and the stark, unhealthy paleness of my skin. I look even worse, somehow. I dig through the cosmetics on my table and find a bit of rouge and apply it to my cheeks, but I end up looking more clownish than ever.

"Happy wedding day to me," I mutter, giving up and wiping my cheeks clean. At least with the scrubbing my face is enduring, I'll have a ruddy glow.

Giving up, I move away from the mirror and begin to pace. I know I'm stalling. I don't know that I want to hear about Erynne. What if she knows of my intent to marry Nemeth and will stop the next food shipment? What then? Can I back away from what I want—to marry Nemeth—for my own good? And if I don't . . .

Biting back a frustrated whimper, I pull my knife sheath from its place, nestled deep in my cleavage. I free the blade and roll it in my hands, gazing down at it. A thousand questions surge in my mind, but I don't put voice to them, and if the knife picks any of them up, it's not indicating so.

I hesitate a moment longer and then ask, "Are you there?"

The knife shivers. *Yes.*

Here goes nothing. "Does Erynne know of my plans to marry Nemeth?"

Silence.

"Would she approve?"

Silence.

All right, then. That's answered. It's not a surprise either. My sister is blindly loyal to the kingdom, even if it's run by an absolute twat like Lionel. I think for a moment, trying to determine the best questions to ask. "Does my sister have a knife like you?"

Shiver.

"Does she know I love Nemeth?"

Another shiver. Oh no.

"Is that why she asked me to kill him?"

Shiver.

"Oh, ugh. Truly, Erynne?" I make a face at the knife as if it's the one deciding things. "Must we all be martyrs to the Vestalin name like you?"

The knife gives a confused shiver as if it doesn't entirely understand the question but wants to respond anyhow.

That response just irritates me more, though. Meryliese devoted her entire life to preparing for the tower, only to die. Erynne is queen but is miserable in her marriage, and her husband is a warmonger. And now I'm supposed to have a horrible fate as well? I don't think so.

"Has Erynne been asking about the poison?"

Shiver.

"Does she know I tossed it?"

Silence. *No.*

"Does she know I won't use it?"

Shiver.

I consider this. "Are they planning to punish me for not killing Nemeth?"

Silence. *No.*

That's good at least. "So, they plan on sending food to me next year?"

Shiver.

That's enough for now. I can't ask if it'll happen—the knife won't know the future—but if they intend to continue feeding me, that's the most I can ask for. I consider things a moment longer and then roll the blade in my hand again. "Did my sister send those men to break in?"

Silence.

Huh.

"She knows nothing about them?"

Shiver.

"Did Nemeth's people send them?"

Silence.

"So no one sent them?"

Shiver.

"They came to raid the tower entirely of their own volition?"

Shiver.

How very odd. I wonder what possessed them to attack. They wanted our supplies, they said. Surely that wasn't all of it? I wish I'd paid more attention to the tower's history so I would know if crazed peasants had ever attacked it in the past.

Yes, shivers the knife.

Well, that answers that. I move to put the knife away, back into its sheath and then pause. "My sister is well? Her son well?"

Yes.

"Her pregnancy goes well?"

Yes.

Even though I'm currently miffed at Erynne, I'm still glad she's healthy. I decide to ask about more people. Lionel is well (sadly). Nurse is well. Riza is well again (much to my relief), and my friends at court seem to be healthy. It fills me with accomplishment, as if these victories are somehow mine, and I'm in a pleasant mood when I go to sheathe the knife once more.

Then I pause. "Does . . . Nemeth love me? Truly?"

Yes, the knife shivers.

I'm beaming as I tuck it away, leaving it on my table since I don't plan on wearing my gown for very long after the ceremony. I finish my primping in the mirror, eyeing my unsatisfying reflection. Then, after a moment's pause, I reach under my skirts and tear my bloomers off.

No sense in wasting my time . . . or Nemeth's.

CHAPTER TWENTY-NINE

I race back downstairs with my lamp to greet my bridegroom, more excited than ever to get this marriage going. I don't care that I'm going to be abandoning my people or that Erynne, the only family I have left, wouldn't approve of my actions. Nemeth loves me, and I love him, and I'm excited to become his wife in all ways. I'm radiant with happiness as I enter our room . . . only to find it empty.

Hm.

I know he didn't come upstairs. I peek into the storage room, wondering if he's touching himself again, unable to wait for me to return, but it's empty as well. Curious, I take the lamp and head downstairs. "Nemeth?"

"Here," he calls. "I am readying the altar."

Right. Because the Fellians ask for the approval of the three gods when they mate. Liosians have a similar ceremony, but ours is more of standard pomp and fussiness than actual praise of the Gray God, who looks over the land of Lios and protects us from the whims of the Golden Moon Goddess.

With the lamp in hand, I head downstairs. Sure enough, Nemeth has our precious candles lit at the altar, and he has an intricate, woven prayer cloth covering the table. That's . . . new. "Where did that come from?"

"I found it upstairs," he tells me.

"Huh." I move toward the altar, fingering the delicate fabric. It's clear that whoever created this spent a lot of time on it. The stitches are exquisite and plentiful, with flowers and birds moving along the elegant vines on the borders. "I've never found anything but useless junk in there."

"It was buried under a few old books," Nemeth says, his big hand smoothing the sides of the fabric as he sets the ceremonial plates on the altar in their spots.

"Well, that would explain why I never saw it," I say brightly, though I don't recall books either. Nemeth must have snagged them before I went up and did my hunting.

I eye the altar. Even though we've been here for a year now, I've done no more than glance quickly at it. Assuming that it looked like every other church effigy I've seen, I knew it would hold images of the three gods—a triptych carving of them—ruling over their particular realms. The Absent One's face turned up to the heavens instead of gazing down at the people of the world, surrounded by sunlight and the daytime realm. Across from him, the Gray God's sorrowful face tilts toward the ground as if watching over the people of the mortal realm, his equally gray moon behind him. And between them, the Golden Moon Goddess, god of dawn and dusk—the fickle one—stares right at the person in front of the altar as if daring them not to worship her.

Normally, the Absent One is an elderly, gray-haired man, the Gray God a bearded father figure, and the Golden Moon Goddess a radiant young woman. But in this triptych, they are all Fellians. Their faces are hard and angular, noses pronounced just like Nemeth's. They have spread wings and horns that draw back from their faces just like he does. Their legs bend backward, and they do not look like friendly, familiar gods at all.

I stare in surprise at this blasphemy, then glance over at Nemeth. "Are there two altars? Have I missed one?" Perhaps this is the altar of the Fellians (who would be used to blasphemy of this sort), and there is a different one for Liosians.

"You have been here as long as I have," Nemeth says. "Have you seen another altar?"

I have not. I purse my lips, then decide to drop the matter. What do I care? It is not as if I am particularly devout, and since I am throwing my lot in with the Fellians, should I not get married at an altar with Fellian gods? Nemeth sets an offering bowl upon the altar in front of each representation of the gods, then pulls out a cushion for my knees and places it on the floor in front of the altar. "Shall we begin?"

The sight of that cushion gives me a dozen filthy ideas, none of which have to do with religion. Pinching my arm to clear my thoughts, I kneel upon the cushion and hold my hands out to Nemeth to take. He doesn't exactly kneel across from me as much as he crouches, thanks to his backward-bent knees, but the intent is the same—to make oneself lower than the gods.

He takes my hands in his and begins a quiet prayer to the gods. "We ask for your protection, oh Great Ones. We ask for abundance. We ask for your smiling eyes to look down upon us. We ask for your favor. We ask for your joy. We ask you to see this mating between this male and this female and give us your blessing." His gaze locks upon me. "We ask that you see this union of Nemeth of the First House of Darkfell and Candromeda Vestalin of Lios and grant us happiness. We seek to live our lives in the shadow of your glory and to bring honor to your forgotten names. Be with us."

"Be with us," I echo appropriately, trying not to fidget. I want Nemeth to see that I'm taking this seriously. I want him to be proud to have Candromeda Vestalin as his mate. So for the first time in my life, I don't crack jokes at a religious ceremony. I pay attention.

Nemeth bows his head and then begins to speak in Fellian, switching out of common. His words are lyrical and flowing, and I understand not a bit of them. But I watch him for clues, keeping my hands in his as he continues the ceremony. Even though he's concentrating on the prayer, I like the feel of his hands in mine.

When the prayer is completed, he smiles at me. "Candra?"

"Aye?" Did I miss an important cue?

His eyes narrow. "It's not too late for you to change your mind."

I shake my head, squeezing his hands. "I want this. I want you."

"Then let us give our offerings to the gods and complete the prayers."

"Of course," I say as if I have any clue about how our ceremony will work. "You start, and I'll follow your lead, naturally."

"Naturally," he agrees, amused. He lifts our joined hands to his mouth and kisses the back of mine. "Let us give our offerings."

He gets to his feet and helps me to mine. Nemeth stands proud in front of the altar with my smaller, ridiculous figure at his side. I cannot imagine what the gods think of our pairing. Of a short, rounded, soft human woman in a voluminous pale-blue dress with puffed sleeves and a tightly laced corset, standing next to an enormous Fellian with gray wings, glowing green eyes, wearing a leather kilt and decorated breastplate. We are a mismatched pair, to be certain, but I like to think that he enjoys the sight of me as much as I enjoy the sight of him.

And truly, that is all that matters.

Nemeth takes each cake and breaks it in half, preparing to feed a portion to the flickering candles in front of each of the triptych images. He chants the words of a prayer in Fellian, and when he places the hard cake into one of the flames, it lights up as if covered in pitch and turns to ashes in moments. He indicates I should do the same, and he patiently leads me through the Fellian prayer and the cake offering. We repeat that for each of the gods, and when there is nothing left but ashes, Nemeth takes the final cake, breaks it in half, and offers me a bite.

I eat it delicately, making sure to nip his fingers as he feeds me. Then I feed him, and his hot gaze devours mine, sending shivers of anticipation through my body.

"Now are we mated?" I ask, breathless, as I brush a crumb from his hard mouth.

Nemeth chuckles at my eagerness. "Not quite. Now we must give each other the bite of marking."

Right. The bite-y part of the ceremony. That means we're close to the end, at least. "Do you bite me first or me you?"

"You bite me," he says, and his green eyes flare as if the thought excites him very much.

"All right, but my teeth are rather blunt. Don't blame me if I gnaw for a bit." I take the hand that he holds out to me, palm up, and eye him. "I'm a little afraid I'm going to hurt you."

His lips twitch. "You will not."

Hmph. He acts like I've got a mouth full of pillows. Teeth are still teeth, and if I have to tear at his skin, it's not going to be pleasant for either party. "Do you have the ink, then?"

Nemeth pulls out a small glass bottle with a flat bottom that's full of dark, thick ink, likely used for dipping a quill pen.

I gnaw at my lip, realizing I really have to bite the man I love to show him I care. I glance up at Nemeth, but the look on his face is unafraid. If anything, he looks excited at the prospect of my bite.

Well, all right, then. "Do I just bite down whenever? Is there a particular method?"

"However you like. Just do it wide enough and deep enough so it will leave a scar pattern of your teeth."

I examine his hand and the meaty portion just under his thumb. I lift it to my face, eyeing him, and his excitement heightens visibly. I'm glad this is a turn-on for one of us, at least. I lick the meat of his palm with a little smile and then sink my teeth in before I can overthink things.

Immediately, I know I'm not biting hard enough. I can barely dig my teeth into his skin, and Nemeth shows no reaction to my bite, so I concentrate on bearing down as hard as I can. When I finally taste blood, I realize I've broken skin, and I make a noise of surprise.

"Don't let go yet," he whispers. "Bite harder so you can mark me harder."

Oh gods, why did that sound arousing? I do as he commands, and my mouth fills with a gush of his blood. Horrified, I draw back in surprise, spitting it out onto the floor, and swipe at my lips with my sleeve. "I'm sorry," I say automatically. "Is that enough?"

Rivulets of blood slide down his palm, and the look he gives his hand is pleased indeed. "It is a fine bite."

"Is it?" I grimace, still tasting copper. I scrub the sleeve over my mouth again, knowing I'm probably ruining my dress. I love the taste of Nemeth . . . but not his blood. "Can I see?"

He wipes the blood away with a brush of his fingers over the skin and shows me. Sure enough, there are the flat lines made by my front teeth and then the holes from my incisors, along with the rest of the bite that forms a ragged oval on the meat of his palm. More blood wells up, but instead of wiping it away, he picks up the bottle of ink and pours it over the wound.

I wrinkle my nose at the sight, imagining the pain. "Does it hurt?"

"It is a good hurt," he reassures me, producing a strip of white cloth and wrapping it around the fresh wound. Immediately, the cloth soaks with a mixture of ink and blood. "It is a wound I am proud to carry. May the mark last forever, and if it does not, you will have to refresh it for me."

"Of course." In that case, I hope it lasts forever. I'm going to feel the give of his flesh underneath my teeth in my nightmares; I just know it.

"Give me your hand." Nemeth holds his out, his eyes feverishly bright.

I obey, eyeing his large, sharp teeth. Surely his bite won't involve nearly as much . . . sawing. I swallow hard as he delicately turns my hand over and lifts my palm toward his mouth. "Be gentle," I whisper.

"You are not a woman who likes gentle." The way he says it is like a caress, his breath playing over my skin.

"You're right, but—" I gasp as his teeth sink in.

A hot, sharp pain shoots through me, accompanied by an odd curl of pleasure. The way he bends over my hand, his teeth deep in my flesh . . . it should not look as seductive as it does. He immediately lifts his head and swipes his tongue over the wound, lapping up the blood.

"Oh," I breathe.

"If it makes you feel any better, you are delicious," he tells me, licking my palm again as he gazes at me. Another curl of pleasure ripples through my belly at the sight, at the drag of his tongue over my tender, abused skin. "And now we are almost done."

"Will you put the ink on the bite for me?" I ask. I'm not good at applying my medicine, and I suspect I will be equally poor at this.

He nods, picking up the vial and giving my heated flesh another swipe of his tongue before dousing it with ink. I whimper as the dark ink stings at my fresh wounds. Gods, I hate pain. Hate it. But Nemeth's eyes are bright with both pleasure and wonder as he gently binds my hand, wrapping up the bite so it can have the chance to heal. "I will tend to them both in the morning."

I take my throbbing hand back and study it, the bandages soaking through with inky blood in the shape of a bite. "Now are we mated in the eyes of the gods? In the eyes of your people?"

"Almost." There's a feral light in his eyes as he regards me. "The marriage must be consummated."

"Well, now. This is my favorite part." I beam up at him and tug at the bow at the front of my dress. "Wanna do it in front of the altar? Shock the gods? Or should we go back up to bed—"

He puts a hand over mine, stopping me before I can unlace my dress. "Now, we must do the ceremonial chase."

Another hot curl of pleasure slides through my blood. "A chase, mmm?"

Nemeth nods, unable to pull his gaze from me. "A good Fellian male gives his mate a chance to run from him, and then he hunts her down and gives her his knot, claiming her as his for all time."

"It sounds positively barbaric." And absolutely filthy. I am so ready for this. He needs to be prepared for the worst chase ever because I am going to let myself get caught and caught hard. I lick my lips, and I love that his gaze flicks to my tongue. I smile, feeling powerful and sexy, knowing I'm about to be fucked thoroughly. "How much of a head start do I get?"

"Start running, and you shall find out," he all but purrs to me.

I stare at him, eyes wide. I just . . . run? Flee from him? I've never done such a thing before. It seems a little silly, but as Nemeth straightens to his full height, his wings flaring out, I can see he's deadly serious. This is part of their ceremony, and I've agreed to be Fellian.

So, it seems I must be chased.

I glance around the large, empty downstairs chamber. Other than the pillow in front of the altar and the wood wedged around the door, it's barren.

"Start running," Nemeth tells me in a soft whisper. He pulls off his belt, his movements slow and deliberate. "Make it a good chase, and the reward will be all the sweeter."

I hesitate. There's something both menacing and arousing about his stance, about the way he casually removes his vest next, his gaze locked on me. I look around again, but there's nothing to hide behind, nowhere to go. I'm trapped in this tower, and whatever fleeing I do will be quick. Even so, I grab two handfuls of my skirts and cross the room, my heart starting to pound hard in my chest. There's an exciting element of terror to this whole "chase" concept.

It should not be nearly as arousing as it is, yet I'm somehow stimulated.

I rush across the room from him, strategically placing myself nearer the stairs. I turn to look at him, and Nemeth is stripping off the last of his clothing, revealing his enormous body and straining erection. My body throbs at the sight, my breath catching in my throat. Part of me just wants to fling myself to the ground, give up on the idea of a chase, and just let myself be caught.

But the chase is important to him. Important . . . and exciting in a naughty, thrilling sort of way.

I watch as he tosses aside the wrap he wears over his loins and steps forward toward me, his movements deliberate with a hint of menace to them.

With a squeak, I turn and race up the stairs.

Going up forty steps always seems to take a long time, but today it feels like forever as I fling myself up them as quickly as possible. By the time I get to the top of the landing, I'm gasping, unable to draw a deep breath in my tight corset. I stare down the narrow, winding flight of stairs, and then I hear footsteps.

He's following me up, and he's not far behind.

With another whimper born of both excitement and dread, I turn and continue racing away—across the narrow, half-circle hall of the first floor and past Nemeth's room that we share. Past the garderobe and the storage, and onto the second floor. I can hear Nemeth's footsteps behind me, the heavy Fellian trod of his strange feet on the stones. I imagine I hear the swish of his wings as he closes in on me, and it makes me race faster, my heart hammering in my chest.

As I reach the bottom of the second flight of stairs, something tugs at the skirts of my dress. I scream and pull free, racing away once more.

I make it halfway up the stairs before I feel the tug on my skirt again. I shriek, tottering on the step, in danger of losing my balance.

Suddenly, Nemeth is there, large arms wrapped around me and shielding me against his chest. "Are you all right? Candra?"

I sag against him for a moment, breathless. I manage a nod. "Almost fell."

"Be careful, *milettahn,*" he murmurs, nuzzling the side of my neck before releasing me and placing me on my feet again. "If you are too scared to continue—"

"I'm not," I tell him, straightening my shoulders. Part of me wants him to catch me and nuzzle me again, but a greater part wants him to keep chasing me. "If I get scared, I'll say the word *ribbon,* and you'll know it's too much."

"Ribbon," he agrees, and his green eyes glow with lust. He reaches a clawed hand for my skirts.

I swipe them out of his grip once more, then turn and race up the rest of the way, heart pounding as I hear him pacing after me. This might be one of the strangest sex games I've ever played . . . but also one of the most exciting.

This time, he snags me around my waist before I get up the stairs to the third flight, and I realize he's been toying with me this whole time. He could have caught me at any point, but he let me run like a cat playing with a mouse.

Squealing, I'm hauled backward, and a big arm traps my waist. A large body hunches over my squirming one, and I feel Nemeth's breath hot in my ear. "I have you now, my mate."

A hot shudder of arousal rips through me as he growls, rubbing his face against my neck. I bite my lip, holding back a moan as one hand slides under my skirts, pushing them up and revealing my legs.

Nemeth's breath hisses as he glides his fingers up my thigh. "No bloomers?"

I shake my head.

"Naughty princess," he murmurs, and then his hand pushes between my thighs, cupping my cunt.

I whimper, collapsing against him, my cheek pressing to the first cool step of the stairs as he holds me against him.

"Knees up," he reminds me as I sag.

I do as he commands, settling my weight on my knees even as I keep my face low to the ground. Cool air brushes over my backside as my skirts climb their way up my back, and Nemeth's hand presses against my pussy. His first two fingers glide through my folds, and I cry out, wet and slick and wildly excited for more.

"My naughty, naughty Candra," Nemeth rasps, finding my clit and rolling it against his fingertips. "You are so very aroused by our chase, aren't you? As aroused as I am."

And he presses his length against my thigh, letting me feel just how hard and aching he is. I make a choked sound, spreading my thighs wider so he can have full access to my body. I love this. I love how fierce he is in this moment. He's not my shy scholar right now—he's a primal being about to claim his mate.

And by all the gods, does his mate want to be *claimed*.

He rubs a teasing finger against my clit again. "Should I make you come on my fingers before I give you my knot?"

"Yes, please," I whine, bucking my hips against his touch. "I want that. I want you, Nemeth."

A hard finger dips lower, grazing the entrance to my body. I rock with his touch, trying to get him to go deeper, to pierce me with one of those big digits. I'm greedy, and I want everything. But he only slips his hand away, and I cry out at the loss. "No fair!"

"Shh." His hand rubs my backside, and then his fingers trace between my thighs again. Something hot and hard prods at the entrance of my body, and I moan, realizing that we're skipping all the foreplay and going straight to the consummation. He teases the tip against my core, leaving me clenching and needy and whimpering with distress. "My pretty *milettahn*," he murmurs. "Do you want your mate?"

"Yes!"

Nemeth surges into me, and I let out a choked sound. Oh gods, that is so good. It's been forever since I've been filled like this, and I've forgotten just how intense and delicious the sensation of a thick cock pushing into me can feel. He thrusts into me hard, rocking me against the cool stone of the steps, and I don't think I've ever been so full. Nemeth is larger than any lover I've had in the past, and I squirm as he seats himself to the hilt, his heavy thighs bracketing mine. His breath hisses, and he remains still over me, frozen in place.

"R-ribbon?" he asks, his voice tight.

"What?" I turn my head, trying to look back at him.

"Am I hurting you?"

"Gods, no! Keep going!" I try to arch against him, lifting up my backside in silent encouragement. "Give me everything," I pant. "Give me your cock. Give me your knot."

He growls low in his throat, and his hips surge against mine once more. It's as if he can no longer control himself, and now that he knows I'm not hurt, he's free to claim me as he wants. He pounds into me from behind, rocking our bodies together and driving into me with such force that each thrust leaves me breathless. My toes curl as he pumps into me, and the sensation is so good that a low curl of pleasure starts to warm deep in my belly, a sign that I just might have an orgasm from thrusting alone.

"More," I cry out, eager to chase that sensation. "Harder, Nemeth. More!"

"Can you take my knot?"

Is he not giving me everything? "Yes." I widen my legs, trying to give him more access to my body that's already stretched tight around him. "Give me everything. Make me your mate."

"You're so tight," he hisses between his teeth and thrusts shallowly into me.

"Give me your knot," I say again, demanding. It won't feel like we're truly mated until he does.

Nemeth growls again. He clenches my hips tight and then presses forward. Suddenly, it feels like too much, and the realization is startling. He's got more to give me? But I'm not new to sex. I try to relax my body, keeping my hips loose as he thrusts into me, pushing a little harder each time.

It's no longer feeling good; my climax is pounded away as Nemeth slowly drives his knot into me.

"Unh!" Nemeth shudders over me and thrusts deep, clutching my hips tight. He spills into me, and I try to hold still as he comes. It's impossible. His knot feels enormous and like it's splitting me apart. I squirm in place, wriggling in an effort to get comfortable as I'm pinned under his heavier weight. I feel . . . stuck, oddly enough, which is a strange sensation. And when I try to slide away from him, I find that I can't; our bodies are locked together.

I whimper, distressed.

"Shh, love," Nemeth murmurs. He rolls onto his side, pulling me with him until we're curled on the floor together. "Give my knot time to recede."

Squirming, I'm trapped between the pleasure-pain moment and the realization that I had no orgasm. "How—how long does that take?" I ask, panting.

He strokes a big hand down the front of my dress, then slides that hand under my skirts. "Longer than a few breaths, that's for certain. Did I . . . hurt you?"

"Your knot feels like a lot," I confess tightly, wriggling again. I can't stop moving. "Still does."

Nemeth groans. "By the gods, you feel good. You're squeezing my knot so hard." Even now, he bucks lightly against me, and I feel another burst of his release inside my body. His hand slides between my thighs. "Did you come?"

"No," I practically wail, and I sound pouty and pathetic.

"Truly, I am a terrible mate. I will have to make it up to you," he soothes.

I'm miffed that he doesn't sound sorry. He sounds like a man who just got his knot in his woman, and he's sated.

He nuzzles the top of my head, his legs curled around mine, and I whimper pathetically again as his hand slides to my cunt. "While you milk my knot, I get to take care of you." His fingers tease my clit.

I cry out, shocked at how intense it feels. Oh gods. I've never been stuffed so full, and the combination of his fingers strumming my clit while I'm speared on his cock is explosive. I immediately clench around him, my cunt squeezing tight, and Nemeth lets out a shocked little gasp of his own.

"That's it, *milettahn*," he groans. "Milk my knot with your sweet cunt. Gods, you feel good."

I come hard, the orgasm rolling through me in waves, and then it doesn't stop. Instead, Nemeth continues to tease my clit, rubbing circles around the hood as my body squeezes tight around his cock, and I make breathless, gasping sounds as he makes me come over and over again. One orgasm rolls into the next, and I arch and writhe against him as he works my body, sending one pulse of pleasure after another until I'm breathless and spent, and still, he makes me come again. He strokes my throat and face with one big hand while the other strums between my legs like I am a lute he will never tire of playing.

By the time his cock eases from my body, I'm exhausted from having come so many times. I feel worn and dazed with pleasure, curled up against his chest. I sigh as he slips free from between my thighs, and a rush of fluid follows. He tugs me higher up against him and nuzzles my face. "Now are you pleased, my greedy princess?"

I snuggle back against him. Am I pleased? Gods, I don't think I've ever been so pleased. Sex with my Fellian has been incredible. I expected it to be good because I love him, but I was not expecting to be utterly wrung out with decadent pleasure. "I think I like your knot."

He chuckles, stroking a finger along my cheek. "I am glad you approve."

I think if I approved any more, the gods would need to scrape me off the walls.

CHAPTER THIRTY

We remain on the floor, with me tucked against Nemeth's chest. I think we're both far too tired to get up for a while, so he runs his fingers over my skin, petting me, and at some point, I fall asleep.

I wake up to Nemeth picking me up off the floor and bridal carrying me into our room. "I can walk," I tell him, yawning. "You can put me down. I'm not that tired."

"You are very tired," he argues. "But more than that, you are my mate, and I am going to carry you to our bed on our mating day."

I can't fault that logic. Plus, Nemeth is nice to snuggle against, his chest warm and bare and, best of all, mine. He sets me down in the bed, and I reach for him, only to have him kiss my fingertips and move away. He gets a bowl of water and a towel, and as I recline sleepily in the bed, he begins washing himself. And, the shameless woman that I am, I watch him. There's something so satisfying about seeing his hand move over his cock. About his hard features that ease slightly when he looks at me as if I'm all the softness in his world. He rinses the towel off and then moves to my side, parting my thighs and wiping me down with gentle, tender care.

Once Nemeth is satisfied that I'm clean of his seed, he sets the bowl aside and unlaces the front of my corset, helping me undress. Instead of our normal sleeping attire, he pulls my chemise off of me and studies my body, now as naked as his. I want to preen at his hot gaze because it's clear he likes what he sees. "It's a bit early for sleep," I tease as he climbs into bed beside me. "Are you that tired?"

"It's the day of our mating." He props up on his side of bed, watching me with a hungry, avid gaze. "Should we not spend the day in bed?"

Again, I cannot fault his logic. I immediately pull him against me, sliding an arm around his neck and bringing him down for a kiss. "This has been quite the wedding day."

His arms move around me, and he hauls me against him, pressing my breasts to his chest. He rolls me onto my back and brushes his nose against mine. Our lips meet in a brief kiss, and then he scrapes his teeth against my mouth, the moving a mere graze but oh so sensual. "And are you content?"

"Mmm. 'Content' implies that I'm done with you. And I haven't finished *savoring*." I kiss him back, letting my tongue flick against his. I'm tired, but at the same time, a warm, hungry pleasure is coursing through my veins. I wouldn't mind another, far more leisurely bout of bed sport with Nemeth. "You're always talking of savoring, after all."

"I am," he agrees, chuckling. He kisses his way across my jaw and then moves down my chest toward my breasts. "I would love the chance to savor these."

"Now's your chance," I joke. "I hear their owner just got married."

"What a lucky male to mate such a prize." He cups one breast and buries his face in my cleavage. "Gods have mercy."

I shiver with delight as he kneads my breasts, stroking my fingers over his horns. It feels strange for my lover not to have a bit of hair on his body, but I like the way Nemeth looks. I love the strong line of his nose and the harsh angles of his cheeks and brow. I even love his strangely fluid-looking horns that feel so hard to the touch. I'm so focused on caressing them that I lose track of what Nemeth is doing to my breasts until he takes the tip of one into his mouth and sucks on it.

With a whimper, my attention is solely his once more. "Nemeth!"

He flicks his tongue over my nipple, teasing circles around it. "How is it that you taste so good, *milettahn*?"

I open my mouth to reply, but all that comes out is a needy groan as he sucks on the tip hard. I arch against his devouring mouth from need and squirm in bed under him as he ministers to my breasts.

"Gods, I'm glad we're married," I pant. "You've made me wait long enough."

"I would have waited a thousand years for you," he tells me, voice husky with emotion as he presses a kiss to the tip of one breast. "You are worth waiting for, Candra."

Sweet words clearly from a man besotted with his new bride. I don't truly believe him, though. It's a pretty saying because he finally got to fill me with his seed, but he would have said it to any woman trapped in this tower with him . . .

The thought is a sobering one, and I push it out of my head quickly. It doesn't matter if I'm special or not. I'm here with Nemeth, and Meryliese (and Erynne) are not. He's mine, and I'm not giving him up. "I love you," I blurt out as he kisses his way down my belly. "I love you, Nemeth."

He grins up at me and then pushes my thighs apart. "Shall I check to see if you can take my knot again, my sweet one?" And he runs his tongue over my sore, well-used cunt.

I gasp. It's always so surprising to me how assertive Nemeth can be in bed for a virgin. His people must have incredible natural instincts when it comes to mating. He laps at my pussy with long, slow strokes and then spreads my folds, feasting upon my clit. I cry out, my legs folding with the intensity of the sensation. "Oh gods."

"I'm going to get your cunt good and slick so you can take my knot again, Candra. I'm going to fill you every day with my seed until my scent is irrevocably stamped upon your skin."

"That . . . that's a lot of seed," I breathe, whimpering as he tongues my clit with gentle circles.

"You can take it."

Gods, why is that so damn sexy? I moan as he sucks my clit into his mouth and teases it with the tip of his tongue. He works me with his mouth until I'm crying out, and this time when he mounts me, I know what to expect. I know that his first thrust will be shallow and delicious, followed by the increasing size of his cock until my body is straining to take him. I know that when I feel completely speared by his size, he's going to press farther, demanding that I should take his knot deep inside me. And it's going to be tight. And it's going to feel like too much . . . until it isn't.

This time, when he's knotted deep inside me, he gazes down at my smaller form and smiles. It's a triumphant sort of smile as if he likes the sight of me stretched around him, my body taut around his invading cock. As he leans over me, he slides a hand between us and caresses my clit, his green eyes locked on mine with such a possessive stare that it steals the breath from my lungs.

I come instantly, and this time, I come first.

When I wake up in the middle of the night, Nemeth's side of the bed is empty.

At first, I don't think much of it—a garderobe excursion, nothing more. I roll over, hug my pillow, and wait for him. Half-awake, I smile to myself and think drowsy, sultry thoughts. Maybe he'll awaken me with his head between my thighs. Maybe I'll wake up earlier and surprise him. Then again, what's the point of waiting? I might just snag him when he returns and insist that he let me try his knot one more time.

I wonder if it would be pleasurable for him if I rode him. Only one way to find out.

I stretch in bed, deliciously sore between my thighs in ways I haven't felt in ages. There's nothing quite like the stretch of well-used muscles from bed sport, and I feel wondrous. The minutes slip past, though, and Nemeth doesn't return. I frown to myself, curious. Surely, he's not touching himself in the storage room again when I'm right here and hungry for more. It doesn't seem like something he would do.

So, curious, I get to my feet and pad into the darkness, listening for the sounds of Nemeth's wings. I don't take a lamp with me. There's nothing in the darkness in the tower that can frighten me.

I'm only a few steps into the hall with my hand on the wall to guide me when I hear Nemeth's voice. It's coming from downstairs, the bottom floor. Confused, I head in that direction, wondering who or what he could possibly be talking to at this moment. Have the other Fellians returned? Are we no longer safe?

I creep down the stairs as quietly as I can, listening as Nemeth continues to talk. I can't make out his words, and I realize he's speaking in Fellian. Well, he's taught me a few words of his language in our flirty moments. Maybe I can pick a few of them out. I press my ear to the stones, listening as Nemeth's words spill through the darkness.

Wait . . . was that the word for wife?

I peer around the corner into the large chamber and see Nemeth standing in front of the altar, a single candle flickering in front of him. He does not have his hands clasped in prayer but atop the altar itself, and his expression is troubled.

The moment I look around the corner, he sees me and goes silent, a look of guilt flashing across his face. "Candra. *Milettahn*. I woke you up?"

I cross over to his side, fighting back a yawn. "I woke up, and you weren't in bed. Who are you talking to?"

He looks flustered by my question. "I . . . the gods."

I arch an eyebrow at his answer. "The gods? Truly? You have never been particularly religious before."

"Yes. It seemed like a day to pray." Nemeth strokes my cheek with his knuckle. "I am sorry if I worried you. Prayers for my people are . . . private things, and I wished a moment alone."

"I understand." I slide my arms around his waist and smile when he holds me close. I get wanting to be alone with your thoughts. "Can I ask what you were praying about? Feel free to tell me no. You did say it was private, but I am simply curious." I gaze up at him, his face cloaked in shadows. "I heard the word *wife*."

He pauses and strokes my cheek again. His reluctance is clear. "You will not get hurt feelings?"

"Well, now you have to tell me," I say, poking a finger into his stomach. "You can't just approach it like that and not expect me to worry." A new thought occurs to me, and I hesitate. "Do you have . . . regrets? Do you feel like you made a mistake?"

"What? Never." He bends over and cups my face, pressing a kiss on my forehead. There's something so very empowering about such a large, dangerous-looking man hunching over to shower gentle kisses on my face, and it soothes my worry a bit. "I am concerned that I am selfish, actually. That is why I pray."

"Selfish?" I've had selfish lovers in the past, but Nemeth is most definitely not one. "In what way?"

His expression is tormented. "In that I pressured you to mate me. I know you were hesitant. I worry I have been selfish in my need for you and pushed you more than I should have. I worry that I convinced you with caresses instead of letting you decide for yourself. That I rushed you."

I make an exasperated face. "You didn't rush me, Nemeth. It was my decision. It has been all along. I knew what I was getting into when I married you, and I decided I wanted to do so anyhow."

He caresses my face, his expression sad. "And will you abandon me when the tower doors open, like Ravendor did her mate?"

"Of course not. My love is stronger than that." I put my hand over his. "I knew what I was doing when I decided to mate you. I knew I was giving up on my people for yours. They won't accept me now because of what I've done. I've thrown my lot in with you. I suppose, in a way, I am Fellian now."

Nemeth looks sad. "Not Fellian," he says softly. "Just mine."

"That's all I need." I smile up at him. "Come to bed now?"

He blows out the candle.

Being mated to Nemeth makes me happier than I ever thought I could be. If I thought being with him was pleasant before, it is utterly joyous now. We spend several days in bed doing nothing more than touching and learning one another. I learn that if I scrape my teeth on his knot, he will come instantly. He learns that there is a spot behind my knee that, if touched, will make me go mad with need. We learn how to make each other's bodies sing, and I never tire of his touch.

That in itself is a marvel. I've grown weary of every other lover I've had in the past. Either they would grow selfish, or the sex would become routine, and I would find myself losing interest. Instead of pleasuring me, sometimes those lovers would seem as if they were interested in nothing more than making themselves come. I'd feel like an object instead of a person. Or worse—I'd feel like they were fucking the Vestalin princess and not Candra.

It's different with Nemeth. I love his touch. More than that, I love that I always feel that he sees me. Not Candromeda Vestalin. Not the princess of Lios. Not Erynne Vestalin's spoiled, useless sister. It's always Candra with him, the Candra who loves a shoulder rub when she has her period, hates epic poetry, and who some times drools on her lover's chest when she falls asleep atop him. It feels like Nemeth loves me and all my flaws, just like I love him. I love that he insists on putting basil into everything because it's his favorite, even though too much will make his stomach ache. I love that he adores epic poetry, the longer and duller the better. I love that he's fascinated with his mushroom farm and that he talks to them as he tends to the shoots.

I adore him, and every day that passes doesn't feel like torture now. It feels as if we're in our own cozy, little nest, letting the world pass us by as we snuggle under the blankets and kiss.

The weather grows cooler, and as it does, it seems to be colder than the last winter. This strikes me as particularly odd. After all, we're in the tower to prevent the Golden Moon Goddess from venting her wrath upon the people of our world, yet this doesn't feel normal. We conserve our wood and our peat bricks as best we can, and some days, we warm my potion with body heat instead of the warmth of a fire.

This winter, the water in the kitchen pump freezes for over a week. But we are prepared for such an event. We've kept several tubs and buckets full of water just in case, so it isn't anything more than a minor inconvenience, but it worries me.

"We are sacrificing seven years of our lives to make the goddess happy, and this is what we get?" I ask Nemeth on one particularly cold morning. I gesture at the walls of the tower. "This doesn't feel happy to me."

"Perhaps other things displease her." Nemeth turns a page in his astronomy book.

"Like what?"

"War."

I narrow my eyes at him. "You think the war goes badly?"

"I suppose it depends on who you ask."

"Well, if the goddess is choosing sides, I hope she realizes that everyone is suffering." I gesture at our frigid room. "Your skin is dry from the cold, and my toes feel like they are icicles. Suffering, everywhere."

Nemeth chuckles at my pouting. He arches a brow at me and puts his book aside. "You are being dramatic, *milettahn*."

I am, but I don't even care. "It's just rotten that we're devoting ourselves to the cause, and some days I can't even tell what the cause is."

"Strange things happen with the eye of the goddess on the world," Nemeth says. He pats the blankets, indicating I should join him instead of pacing near the cold fireplace. "The books say the weather can be foul and unpredictable."

"Because of the goddess," I agree.

"Because of the moon in the sky," he says, and then adds, "And the goddess too. But my point is that we do not know what the gods have in mind. It is not our job to speculate. Our job is to remain here in this tower." As I crawl into bed next to him, he slides his arm around my shoulders. "It is not so bad being here with me, is it?"

"You know it's not." Some of my grumpiness eases, and I dramatically drape myself over his lap. "What else does your book say?"

"Mmm. Nothing near as important as this." His hand slides up my skirt, and when he discovers I have no bloomers on, he arches an eyebrow. It's become a tease of mine to only wear bloomers sometimes, just to see his reaction. It never fails to arouse him. "You are letting this pretty cunt freeze to death."

"You should warm it up."

He grins, showing his fangs. "I absolutely should."

Hours later, I've forgotten all about the goddess and her theoretical anger. I've had Nemeth knotted inside me, and he made me come so hard that I wept his name as he played my body like a harp. Now I'm feeling much looser and relaxed, and I watch from my spot in bed as he feeds a log to the fire, preparing my potion. As he hovers near the hearth, he practices his stretches and extends one wing gracefully outward. I wince inwardly as the other stretches out, the flare of it tight and off center from where I stitched him. It looks uncomfortable.

"How does it feel?" I ask.

Nemeth shrugs. "It is tighter than it should be, like my wing is pinched in one spot. With time and use, I think it could stretch itself out again. The scar tissue just needs to be worked."

"And you need to fly," I say softly. "And there is nowhere to fly in here." He's tried flying downstairs, but he doesn't have enough room to spread his wingspan to its full breadth. The ceiling is too low, and the stairwell's too narrow. It's something I fret over constantly because I know how much it must bother him to be stranded here like this—to have an injury to such a vital part of him and not be able to do the proper exercises to mend it.

"It is what it is," Nemeth replies. He pauses and glances over at me. "Speaking of things we cannot change . . . we are out of your tea."

The minty concoction that Riza makes for me? She sent a bag along with our supplies last summer. But if we're out, we're out. I shrug. "I'll just drink your brew."

His wings flutter as he closes them, a sure sign that he's nervous about something. "I examined yours to see what was in it because I knew you were running low. Did you know you have pennyroyal in it?"

"I couldn't pick out pennyroyal if someone painted a portrait of it," I reply tartly. "I don't know plants. What about that one is important?"

"Pennyroyal is an herb that can prevent pregnancy. I never said anything before because I know you drink it for the taste, but now that you are out, I wondered if you wished to try to replace it with something else?" His wings flutter again. "Or shall I not give you my knot anymore?"

I snort. "Are you truly worrying over an herb? I told you, love, I can't get pregnant. I know you think your cock is impressive—and I do too—but even you cannot pound the blood curse out of my veins." I give him an amused look. "Much as I would love to try, of course."

"You are not worried about conceiving, then?"

"I'm far more worried you'll stop giving me your knot."

His eyes gleam with heat. "If my mate demands, who am I to deny her?"

Who, indeed.

CHAPTER THIRTY-ONE

"Today's the day," I say excitedly to Nemeth as I dress one summer morning. "Solstice. Year two! Can you imagine? We've made it two years so far." I give him a cheery look as I slip my dress over my head and then pull the laces of the bodice tight. "I think we should celebrate. Once our food supplies are delivered, we should splurge a little. Work that into the plans for the year. If I'm being perfectly honest, I'd give my left tit for some pie or a scone with cream."

Nemeth chuckles at my enthusiasm, reaching over and tugging at one of my laces the moment I tighten it. I swat his finger away. Normally I'd take him up on any kind of flirting because we have nothing but time, and bed sport is so very delightful, but today is not just any day.

It's the Solstice, and our food is to be delivered today.

It's a delivery that is desperately needed. Nemeth has been careful with our supplies this entire year, but we're out of our wood logs and almost out of peat bricks. My ingredients for my potion are low, and our foodstuffs are looking pathetic. I'm sure we could make it last for another month or two if we had to, but I'm very glad that we don't.

My mouth waters at the thought of a cup of tea in the blend that Riza always makes for me. Tea and a bit of honey. Oh, and fresh bread with jam. Gods, I would love that. Simple, but delicious. "Do you think they'll send jam again this year? I've completely forgotten to ask in my letters. The last jar they sent was delightful. I'm not normally a fan of yellow plums, but that jam was pure bliss on toast." I cinch my corset up tight and then fluff my tits, adjusting them in the dress. "Oh. My letters. I need to get them! Where are they?"

"Next to mine, *milettahn*," Nemeth says in that calm voice of his. My sweet scholar never gets his wings ruffled over anything (except perhaps a knot-licking). "We won't let them leave without taking the letters; I promise."

I beam at him, full of anticipation. I know I won't find out what anyone thought of my letters for a year, but it's exciting to be able to send word to someone outside, even if I must conceal everything I've done here. I've got no mention of Nemeth or our mating in the letters I've written to Riza, Nurse, and Erynne. Part of me feels guilty that I'm keeping such a large secret, but then I remember that they deliberately avoided mentioning the war in their letters to me and kept their letters full of fluff and nonsense.

I can do the same.

For the last month, I've written and rewritten my letters, obsessing over the messages I'm sending. The one to Riza is twenty pages long, and the one to Nurse is nearly as lengthy. But Erynne's is five pages. Part of me wanted to be ruthless and send her nothing because I'm still bitter over her demands that I murder Nemeth. But . . . she is my sister, and in the end, I know that sending her a chirpy letter full of absolute nonsense will make her mad with frustration. As a sister, I can't *not* send such a thing, after all.

I'm equally excited to see what the others have written to me. Even if the letters are full of nothing but recipes and weather predictions, I will savor every word.

Moving to Nemeth's writing table, I push aside his books and hunt down my letters. They're not sealed because I've got no wax to seal them with, so I've tied them with ribbons from my least favorite dress. Nemeth's stack of letters is twice as big as mine. He spends a great deal of time writing to his family and friends back in Darkfell. Letters are something he has sent frequently in the past since he spent his time locked away in the Alabaster Citadel.

I think of Meryliese and how I never wrote her a single letter, and I feel just a smidge of guilt.

"Who do you think will be here first?" I ask Nemeth, picking up my stack of letters and turning to regard him. "Darkfell's suppliers or Lios's?" I gasp as a new thought occurs to me. "Oh, I hope they don't run into each other. That will be quite ugly." I get a terrifying mental image of the two parties warring on the beach and our supplies being abandoned mere steps away from the tower. "We have to keep them apart."

"Do not borrow trouble, *milettahn*. They will avoid each other. Darkfell will make certain of that." Nemeth rises from the bed and puts on his favorite kilt. "They are familiar with how this works."

"Yes, but if they both come on the same day . . . " I pause, realizing what he's saying without being obvious. "More magic, then?"

He nods. "There are simple spells to observe others. Darkfell will ensure they do not run into Lios's contingent."

I eye my mate, leaning against the table. I never ask about magic because other than lighting a candle or two, he avoids doing it in my presence as if it'll frighten me, which is just plain silly. I don't understand magic, but that doesn't mean I'm scared of it. Most of the spells he's mentioned seem to have practical uses of some kind. "You're going to have to teach me some of those simple spells."

He gives me a fanged grin, eyeing my half-laced breasts. "They only work if you've got magic in your blood, I'm afraid."

I sigh dramatically, toying with the laces because I do so love to flirt. "And here I am with cursed blood, alas."

"Alas," Nemeth murmurs, watching me as I tease a finger over my cleavage. "Magic requires intensive studying, and you are too busy anyhow."

"Too busy?" I laugh. "Too busy doing what?"

He rumbles low in his chest as he slinks to my side, all dark wings and big slabs of gray muscle. Nemeth reaches for my laces, brushing a finger over my breasts as he does. "Busy with kissing your mate . . . taking his knot . . . licking his knot . . . "

"Truly, a packed schedule," I agree, fluttering my lashes. Then I mock-pout. "But I have had no knot today."

"Because with my luck, I will be balls deep inside you, and they will come knocking at our door." He slides a finger into the front of my dress, finding my nipple and teasing it. "And how shall I explain that I am knotted inside a human princess?"

"Perhaps I'm a particularly wicked human who seduced you. After years of me begging you for sex, you finally gave in. It's not so very far from the truth." I lean back, giving him full access to my breasts.

But Nemeth frowns at my words. "I would not have you slander yourself to my people."

Aw. "Is it slander if it all sounds wonderfully naughty?"

He pinches my nipple, sending ripples of heat through my body. "You are my mate," he chastises. "I would have you respected."

It's getting dreadfully hard to concentrate when he's teasing me like that. "Nemeth, they can't know I'm your mate."

"Even so. I do not like the thought of anyone thinking poorly of you." He frowns at the idea. "You are a Vestalin and a princess, and you deserve respect, even if it's the respect of Fellians." With that, he pulls his hand from my bodice and reaches for the laces, this time to tie them. "And that means we must save our playing for later."

I want to pout again, but I know he's right. If we want to keep receiving food from our respective peoples, it's best that no one looks too closely at our relationship—that we are seen as enemies, separate and coexisting in the tower in our own spaces. It sounds like it should be easy to do, yet I find that the more time passes, the more intertwined we become. And denying that feels wrong.

Nemeth finishes lacing my corset, and I reach in, adjusting my breasts as I always do so they look optimal. "Will you braid my hair for me? I want to look perfect. Maybe a crown looping around my head? The men Lios sent last year were absolute beasts, and I want them to remember that I'm a princess when they talk to me."

He presses a kiss on my forehead. "I can do that for you, of course."

A short time later, my hair is braided to perfection, my dress sleeves are laced and puffed artfully, and I feel every bit the princess I am. Nemeth has dressed more casually, wearing only his kilt and a knife at his waist. I'm full of excitement as I slip my shoes on, picking up one of the lamps. "Do you suppose the dead men are still out on the shore? Their presence is a little horrifying, but at the same time, I feel they're an excellent deterrent for others who might want to rob us. Still, I don't want anyone scared away at the sight of a couple of bodies upon our doorstep."

"They know their duty to us," Nemeth replies. "They will not be frightened away."

I know he's right. It's just that I'm so very excited about the influx of food and supplies. It's like a Feast Day celebration, and we have so little to celebrate or to change the monotonous passage of time that this feels momentous. Even so, I'm surprised when Nemeth moves toward the hearth and picks up his favorite stool. "Where are you taking that?"

"Downstairs." His mouth curves into a knowing smile. "I imagined you standing by the doors waiting, listening for our supplies, and I thought a seat might serve you better."

"Bend down so I can give you a kiss," I tell him, beaming. "You clever, delightful man."

He's not wrong, though. I'm fluttering with anticipation, my heart beating rapidly as we head down the stairs and toward the double doors that are the only way in and out of this tower. Will we be given more supplies this time? Will it be different from last year's batch? Will there be new letters to read and pore over? I clutch my stack of letters to my chest, wondering how we'll be greeted this time. Rude soldiers or polite ones? What will we tell them if they want to know about the bodies outside?

I ponder all of this as Nemeth sets the stool near the door and then approaches the entrance. He carefully unwinds the ropes around the handles and removes the broomstick. I pull the knives out and kick aside the wedges we've lodged in place.

"Want to look outside?" Nemeth asks.

Do I? The idea feels downright naughty, as if we're children up to no good. But there are no rules against opening the doors; we simply cannot cross through them. I nod at him. "I'd love to get some fresh air, even if just for the day."

"Just for the day," he agrees. We both know we can open the doors any time we like, but there's something about keeping them tightly sealed that reminds us of our duty. That reminds us just how dire things would be if we chose to leave . . . which is why we cannot.

Nemeth pulls the doors open and steps back, regarding the space outside.

It's raining. Not a noisy, thunderous storm because we would have heard that through the tower walls. This is a gentle, dreary rain, the skies gray and unpleasant, the water equally so. I move to Nemeth's side, peering over his shoulder as humid, fresh air slides inside, and I take a deep breath, closing my eyes at the feel of the breeze.

My throat tightens with yearning. At this moment, I want nothing more than to race outside and feel the rain on my skin. Tears threaten, but I swallow them down. I'll cry when we're free.

We stare out at the beach in silence.

"I wish it was sunny," I say after a moment. "Just so I could glimpse the sun. Rain almost feels like we're being cheated."

Nemeth stares out, and his wings flick. I touch his arm, knowing how hard this must be for him. Twice as hard as it is for me because he cannot fly here in the tower. He's doubly trapped. "I suppose we should be grateful the weather is unpleasant. It makes it that much easier to stay inside."

"Mmm," I agree, though secretly, I would still race out into that dreary rain if it wouldn't cost the world everything. I scan the shore. "I don't see boats or rafts anywhere. They must yet be on their way."

"My people will fly in," Nemeth says absently, his gaze still on the stormy-looking skies. "But yes, I do not see them either."

"Then we're early," I say, making my tone bright to distract him. "I suppose we have time to waste."

"I suppose we do." Reluctantly, he pulls his gaze away from the outdoors and focuses on me again. I hold my hand out to him, and he squeezes my fingers tightly. My heart aches for him. "Shall I fetch you a cup of tea? Do you need to sit?"

I shake my head, reluctant to move away from the doors. If I stand just so, there's a drizzle of rain that brushes inward and feels lovely against my skin. "Do you see our attackers anywhere? Their bodies? Surely, they must still be on the beach."

He squints out at the sand, then gestures. "A bit of weathered clothing there. And some bones. I imagine that whatever the elements did not finish off, the seabirds did."

Wrinkling my nose, I try not to picture that. "Horrid. Just horrid."

"It's what they deserved." His unearthly eyes gleam with remembered anger. "I will not waste a moment lamenting their fates."

Me neither. But I still don't think I'd like to be left in the sand for the birds to pick at. I hold his hand tightly and lean on his arm. "Well," I say with a sigh. "I suppose there's nothing to do but wait."

"They will be here soon enough," Nemeth reminds me. "Patience, my greedy princess."

Right. Patience.

We stand near the doors for a time, and when my feet begin to ache, I move to the stool and sit, arranging my skirts like I'm a queen and this is my throne room. Nemeth paces, moving in and out of the shadows, his gaze constantly straying to the wide-open doors. I pick at my nails and then pick at threads on my gown as the gentle rain eases and the long, gray afternoon stretches. My stomach growls, but I can't find it in me to get up and go to the kitchen for food. Some small part of my mind worries that if I leave my spot by the door, I'll miss them, and nothing will be delivered.

So, I remain where I am, watching as the sun briefly peeks out from behind the clouds, only to disappear below the horizon. It grows dark outside, and no one comes. Not the Fellians. Not the Liosians.

I chew on my nail. "Perhaps we have the wrong day? Perhaps today isn't the Solstice after all?"

But I know it is. I checked with my knife, and I've been keeping careful records of the days that pass. Nemeth has too. We both know today is the Solstice. As the sun disappears below the horizon, the great Golden Moon of the goddess rises in the sky, the surface milky and clouded like a child's marble. It feels as if the goddess is glaring down at us, and I flinch at the sight.

"They must be delayed," is all Nemeth says. "They will be here soon enough."

We wait longer, neither of us speaking as the stars come out and the air grows chilly with a night breeze.

"Perhaps the weather," I begin.

"Perhaps," Nemeth agrees. He looks over at me, and his expression is weary. Mine must be too. "Go upstairs and get your potion ready, love. If they arrive, I'll come get you."

I hesitate and then nod. I'm tired, yet it doesn't feel right to leave him here. But even if his people arrive, I can't be seen with him. And if mine arrives first, he can do that weird shadow thing and slip to my side faster than a blink.

I move into his embrace and press against his chest. He wraps his wings around me, holding me close, and before I can blink, he has me upstairs and in our room, the shadows receding as I blink in surprise. Well, now, that was a neat trick. "How did you do that?"

"Trust me; I'm just as surprised as you," he says with a chuckle. Nemeth bends down and kisses my upturned face. "I'll come wake you the moment they arrive."

He disappears in another swirl of shadows, and I absently go tap the light in the corner, dimming it. I'm too uneasy to sleep, but sitting by the door is just making me anxious. It must be making Nemeth anxious as well, and that's why he's sent me up here. I prepare my potion and inject it myself, waiting for Nemeth. Still nothing. Grr. Kicking my shoes off, I lie atop the blankets, fretting. I tell myself I'm not going to sleep. I'm just going to lie here to satisfy Nemeth if he checks on me.

It seems an eye-blink of time passes. I jerk awake, wiping the corners of my mouth in surprise. Turns out I was able to sleep after all. I scramble out of bed, excited and terrified all at once.

Nemeth didn't come and wake me. Maybe I didn't sleep for long? Maybe even now, his people are depositing food at our doorstep, and he's been so busy he hasn't come to alert me? I put on my shoes as I race for the stairs.

When I get to the first floor, my heart sinks.

There, in front of the wide-open doors, sits Nemeth. He's a few paces away from the entrance, still carefully inside. His back is to me; his face turned toward the dawn of a new day.

No one came all night.

Dragon shite.

"Nothing?" I ask as I approach. I know the answer already, though. It's evident in the slump of Nemeth's broad, strong shoulders. It's evident in the empty first floor. It's evident in the stack of letters at Nemeth's feet.

No one has come.

"It is a delay, nothing more," Nemeth says. When I get to his side, he pulls me into his arms, seating me on his lap. "They'll come today. It doesn't have to be on the Solstice, after all. Perhaps the weather delayed the shipment."

"That must be it," I reply brightly, sliding an arm around his neck. "They'll be here today."

They have to.

I didn't think there was a day that could be worse than the first day I arrived here in the tower.

I was wrong.

Waiting endlessly for supplies that never arrive is the worst kind of torture.

Watching the beach—full of sunshine this day—remain empty and seeing no one on the horizon? It feels awful. Worse than awful. I don't know what this means for the future.

Surely, we haven't been forgotten . . . have we?

Nemeth remains near the front entrance even after the sun sets on the second day.

"Please go sleep," I beg him. "You can't stay awake for days on end."

"The moment I close my eyes, they will arrive," he jokes, weariness etched on his hard face. "Is that not how these things work?"

"Then go and close your eyes!" I grab his hand and haul him to his feet. He must be tired because he doesn't resist. He lets me drag him toward the stairs. "I'll keep watch. The moment there's even a sniff of a boat, I'll come get you. There's just been a delay, nothing more. They're still coming for us."

It turns out that I'm a liar. No one comes that night or the next day. It's hard to eat or take my medicine because each time, we face our dwindling supplies. When Nemeth goes to sit by the door again, and it's my turn to sleep, I head upstairs to pull out my knife instead. I cradle it in my grasp, terrified of the answer it's going to give me, but knowing I have to ask anyhow.

"Is anyone coming?" I ask. "Anyone at all?"

The knife's silence feels like a betrayal.

CHAPTER THIRTY-TWO

After several days pass, we no longer remain by the door to guard it and watch for shipments. I don't tell Nemeth about my knife's answers, though the secret of it weighs on me more with every passing day. It's just . . . at what point do I speak up and tell him what I've learned? What if he's unhappy that Erynne has been plotting his murder since I arrived? It would look bad for the Fellians to know that the queen of Lios has been plotting murder, so I keep the secret and feel guilty that I do.

In some ways, I'm still protecting my sister, and I hate myself for that.

We leave the doors wide open. If no one's coming, there's no point in closing them. I'd actually welcome an intruder because it would mean someone remembered us. I don't understand how we could be so easily forgotten.

Everyone knows about the tower. Everyone. What about the clergy at the Alabaster Citadel? They devote their lives to the gods, and surely, they'd make sure that those of us who gave our lives to the tower would be fed.

At least, you'd think that. Turns out that's not the case.

Worse than the knowledge that we've been forgotten is what this has done to Nemeth. My strong, scholarly Fellian has not been himself. His eyes are ringed with fatigue, and his very stance is one of defeat. It hurts me to see him like this.

So, we need a new plan.

I wake up one morning with determination in my belly. We're going to get through this. I'm not going to give up. I roll over in bed to wake up Nemeth, only to see that he's already awake, staring up at the ceiling with a listless, apathetic expression. "We're not going to give up," I tell him. "It's out of the question."

Nemeth sighs. "I haven't given up, Candra. I just don't know what to do. If I could leave . . . "

"Yes, well, you can't. That's the entire crux of this situation—neither of us can leave." I keep my voice cheerful and light, my expression full of renewed energy instead of despair. If he's going to be sad, I'll be the happy, positive one until his mood changes. We're a team. Since he's feeling low, I'm going to pick him up. "Let's think of ideas. Here's the first idea. We learn how to eat books."

He snorts.

"It's the only thing we have a lot of," I tease. "Books and my dresses. And I can tell you quite honestly that my dresses taste awful."

He shoots me a sidelong glance. "This is a serious situation, Candra."

"Oh, I know it is." I sit on my knees, clasping my hands in my lap. "And since we have nothing to do with our time but think, let us think our way out of our current situation, shall we? Let's start with the obvious. You have magic. Can you send your people a message of some kind through your magic?"

"I've tried."

His admission startles me. I haven't seen him casting spells or even approaching his books in the last several days. When was this? Is he keeping secrets from me?

Then I feel guilty all over again as I think of my knife. He's not the only one keeping secrets. "You tried? In what way?"

"I attempted to contact my brother, Ivornath. He's the king of Darkfell."

"And he didn't answer you?"

Nemeth turns his head toward me. "I'm not supposed to speak of Fellian magic to outsiders."

"I'm not supposed to marry a Fellian," I reply tartly. "Lucky for you and your knot, I'm a rule breaker."

That brings a smile to his face. "You always bring up my knot."

"It's my favorite part."

He sits up halfway, propping himself up on one elbow, his wings folded behind him like a rumpled cloak. "Your favorite, eh?"

"I told you I was a lusty princess when we met." I reach out and pat his knee. "Now quit distracting me with thoughts of your knot and tell me more about Fellian magic and the message you sent."

"It's a spell," he starts slowly as if the words feel forbidden to even speak. His gaze lingers on mine. "I write out the missive and burn it in a candle upon the Gray God's altar. One of the god's sacred spirits takes it and delivers it to my brother, who must receive the message via a trained evoker. Every court in Darkfell has one. Several, actually. But when I send my messages, they go nowhere."

"Go nowhere?" I ask.

"They are not received. Whatever evoker is there at court with my brother will not receive my messages."

"Are you in trouble?"

"Not that I'm aware of." His mouth crooks into a half smile. "No one knows of the lusty princess I've mated yet, if that's what you're asking."

"Then there's no reason for them to ignore you?"

"None. That's what worries me." His expression grows direr by the moment. "Either the evoker is sick—or dead—or my brother is choosing to ignore our plight. *My* plight."

Right. Because no one knows we're a team yet. "That doesn't explain why no one would come from my people either. There must be something going on that's preventing both groups from bringing supplies to us. A problem with crossing the water, perhaps."

"Perhaps," Nemeth agrees, but he doesn't sound convinced.

"Can you pray to the Gray God to answer you? To intercept?"

He shakes his head. "The Fellians are the children of the Gray God, and he gave us his magic, but he will not interfere with mortal trifles."

It doesn't feel like a mortal trifle. It feels like a big deal for us to be forgotten by everyone. But I know what he means. Mortals lost the goodwill of the gods when we lost the ability to call them by their names. I'm surprised Fellians still have magic. Stories say that humans had it once, but it was stolen from us when the gods abandoned our kind.

And yet . . . I do have magic of a sort.

The secret of my knife gnaws at me. Do I confess it now? Do I yet keep it a secret and hope Nemeth never finds out my sister's plans? It seems unfair, given that he's shared a Fellian secret with me. "I need to tell you something, Nemeth."

He arches a brow at me. "Oh?"

I fuss with the folds of my gown. I've been sleeping in my clothes for days now, just in case someone would arrive with our supplies. "Humans don't have magic. Not really. But we do have a few magic objects."

He grunts. "Because you've stolen them from Fellian owners."

I wince. He's not wrong. Humans are the children of the Absent God, who made us from simple clay. It is the Fellians who are the children of magic, the offspring of the Gray God and his benevolent shadows. The only way we acquire magic is if it's gifted to us or we steal it. And since we're sworn enemies with the Fellian people . . . it's almost always stolen. I decide to avoid the sticky accusation part of things and go right for the meat of the topic. "I have an enchanted blade. It's the one you stole from me, actually. It has magic."

"You mentioned it before, aye."

I can't tell what he's thinking from his neutral tone, so I continue on. Best to get it all out in the open quickly, like pulling a thorn from my foot. "My sister wanted me to be able to have some sort of connection to the outside world, so she gave it to me just before I came here. If you ask the knife a question, it can answer with a yes or a no."

"I see," he says.

Hmm, that's not a good sign. "I've been using the knife to check on my sister and my friends at court. When I left, my sister was very pregnant, and I was worried about her. She had a baby boy, and now it seems she's pregnant again."

Nemeth thinks for a moment. "Kind of her to send you a gift so you can keep in touch with her. Strange that it is a knife."

"Isn't it?" I say brightly, determined not to take the bait. No matter what happens, I am absolutely not going to tell Nemeth that my sister wants him dead. "Strange indeed, but I suppose if it's a stolen item, she didn't get to choose what was ensorcelled and what wasn't. I imagine if there had been enchanted hairbrushes lying around, she would have sent me one of those, but alas."

My mate gives me a look that tells me he doesn't quite believe me. That's all right. I suspect I'd be more than a little anxious if I found out that his people were giving him special knives too. "I don't bring it up to worry you about something new. I bring it up because, well, I asked the knife about our situation. I asked if anyone was coming, and it said no."

"It said no?" he asks, surprised.

I nod. "Well, sort of. The knife pulses if the answer to my question is yes. If it's not, it doesn't do anything."

He furrows his brows. "May I see it?"

I fight back my unease. How ironic that I trust Nemeth with my body, both in bed and out of it, yet the thought of handing him my knife makes me pause. Is it because the knife reminds me that he's supposed to be my enemy? That I'm supposed to use it to kill him? Why is it that I'll let him give me a dose of my life-saving medicine every night and let him knot me, but this makes me hesitate?

It's stupidity. It's Erynne's actions poisoning my mind against my mate. Nemeth has been trustworthy and reliable ever since I arrived. He's saved my life twice now—once when I was sick and once when the men broke in and attacked us. I love him. I hate that I hesitate. I hate that I've been so poisoned against the Fellians all my life that even now, it affects me. I nod and stand to my feet. "I keep it upstairs. Let me get it."

By the time I return with my knife, I'm calm again, all worry gone. It's only that I've kept this secret for so long that it makes me fret about revealing it. I hand the knife to Nemeth, who's now seated on his stool, and then I settle myself in his lap. He puts one arm around me, nuzzling at my ear, and I feel a little better. "Thank you, *milettahn*. Show me how it works?"

I pull it out of the decorative sheath and lay it flat in his big palm. Really, it's ridiculously small compared to Nemeth's size, and I wonder what Erynne expected me to do with this knife. Poke him to death? "You ask it a yes or no question aloud. Sometimes it picks up my thoughts, but I prefer to ask aloud. It helps me focus." I lean forward, addressing the knife. "Is my sister alive?"

There's no answer.

My heart thuds for a terrifying moment.

"Which sister?" Nemeth gently reminds me. "You had two of them."

I exhale with relief. Oh gods, he's right. The knife should know, of course, but maybe it needs prompting. "Is Erynne alive?"

The knife shivers in his palm, visibly trembling.

He grunts, wrapping his fingers around it. "Let me try." He thinks for a moment and then asks, "Am I mated to Candra?"

The knife shivers again.

"Are we going to have a dozen children?"

I prickle uncomfortably at the question, and I'm not surprised when the knife doesn't move.

"Am I in love with Candra?"

Shiver.

"Do we have enough food to last for the next five years?"

Nothing.

"How can we make it last for five more years?"

Nothing.

"Do you know what I am?"

Nothing.

"Do I have wings?"

Shiver.

Nemeth grunts. He takes the knife by the tip and holds it back out to me. "I know this sort of spell. It's not a yes and no question, as you say it is."

I frown, holding the knife tightly by the handle. "It isn't?"

"The spell is more specific than that. Or rather, it is not as powerful. It is enchanted to only reply if you ask a very specific sort of question that can be answered with a 'yes.' It does not have a setting for a 'no' because that would involve a second spell to give it the ability to answer 'no,' and then a third spell to force the knife to decide between the two answers. So, in this case, a lack of response is perceived as a 'no,' but that is not always the truth. It's simply not a 'yes.' Does that make sense?"

"I guess so." I never thought of it as more than one spell . . . or any spell, really, just that it could answer me. "I asked it if someone was coming to bring us food supplies, and it didn't answer me."

"Ask it again." There's a desperate look in his gaze. "Just in case."

I hold the knife flat in my hand, extending it between us. "Is Lios sending food to me?"

No response.

"Is Darkfell sending food to Nemeth?"

No response.

"Perhaps that's too specific," Nemeth says quickly. "Ask it if anyone is sending supplies to us."

I do, and the knife is as silent and cold as before. A knot of despair forms in my throat. "There has to be a reason why," I say to him. "Something must be wrong. They wouldn't cut us off."

"They would if they knew we were mated." Nemeth's gaze is solemn. "If you reported back to your sister that you'd become the mate of the enemy, they wouldn't feed you."

I'm a little stung by his accusation. "I wouldn't report back to her. How can I?"

"You think she doesn't have a little blade just like this? You think she doesn't ask about you?"

I hold the knife up by the tip so that if the blade shivers, it'll jump out of my grip. "Have I reported back to Erynne about my relationship with Nemeth? About anything?"

The knife doesn't move.

"I am wrong," Nemeth says in a soft voice, squeezing my waist. "My apologies, *milettahn*."

"And you?" I accuse back. "Were you reporting back about me?"

He's silent.

The knife is not. It shivers in my grasp.

Oh.

I let out a shaky breath. Hurt makes my chest tight, and I stand up, wanting to get away from him. "I see."

"My life is not my own," Nemeth says desperately. His arms go around me, holding me against him. "Listen to me, Candra. Listen. Too many others have a say in things. Just because I am here does not mean that I am in charge of my life. All of Darkfell watches me, just like all of Lios watches over you."

He's not wrong. How many times has Erynne tried to push her wants on me? How many times did she explicitly state that I needed to kill Nemeth? "I understand, but . . . it's hard to hear that."

"My heart," he murmurs, his green eyes desperate as he meets my betrayed gaze. "My *milettahn*. It is true I sent them reports of you in the beginning. Bare details enough to keep them satisfied while allowing me to feel rebellious. But as I grew to care for you, I have sent them less and less. My last report was some time ago."

"Is that true?" I ask the knife.

It shivers.

"I am not your enemy," Nemeth tells me in a soft voice. "I meant it when I said that you and I were in this together. You are my mate, my heart, my comforting darkness." He strokes my cheek, his eyes full of emotion. "I love you, and I mean it when I say that I came into this tower with secrets, but it has changed me, just as I think it has changed you."

I lick my lips and then nod. He's right. We come from warring peoples. Of course, they're going to want him to spy on me and report back. I'm surprised Erynne didn't ask me the same. Then again, my sister asked me to kill him, so I suppose there would have been nothing to spy upon if he was dead. "I'm with you," I reassure him. "We will find a solution together."

"Together," he says and kisses me, his lips soft and coaxing on mine.

And because I'm in love, I adore that kiss as much as I adore every kiss he gives me. He's right. I'm not the same person who entered this tower two years ago, defiant and anxious to escape. I've changed. It's ironic that I would happily stay in this tower with Nemeth forever, given that we had the appropriate supplies.

That's the real problem here, not Nemeth. I kiss him back and then nip at his lip. "You're going to need to prove that devotion between my thighs later."

He chuckles, pressing hungry, insistent kisses to my face and throat. "Later? Not now?"

"We have the knife out," I say, even though my will is faltering under the onslaught of his kisses. Gods, he's good with that mouth of his. Even now, he tugs at my clothing as if to undress me. "Might as well use it to figure out our situation."

Nemeth groans, pressing his forehead against mine. "Right. You're right, of course. Ask it about our supplies."

I hold the blade out again so he can see the reaction to my questions. "Have we been forgotten?"

A shiver.

I make a sound of distress in my throat. "How in all the gods' forgotten names did they forget us?"

"Something must be going on outside," Nemeth says, his arms tightening around my waist. "Something terrible enough that sending food to us is no longer a priority."

This is my worst fear coming to life. Anxious tendrils flare through my body, my limbs feeling cold and numb. "Has Darkfell won the war, then?"

No answer.

"Has Lios?"

No answer.

I exchange a worried look with Nemeth. "Is the war over?" I ask.

No answer.

"It doesn't mean no," he reminds me. "Just that it's not a 'yes' to any of those questions."

"Then the war stretches on," I reply, fretting. "Maybe things have gotten so bad that whoever is in charge of our supplies is too busy to recall them. But surely my sister would remember to send me food, and your family at Darkfell . . . " A new idea hits me, and I try a new line of questioning. "Is Erynne well?"

Yes, the knife shivers.

"Is she at Castle Lios?"

No answer.

That's concerning. My sister wouldn't leave her throne behind—or the castle itself—unless she had to. She's worked too long and too hard to rule, even if it has to be at Lionel's side. "Perhaps they had to evacuate," I say to Nemeth, worried. "And in the chaos, we've been neglected. What do we do? What should I ask?"

He shakes his head, rubbing my back in sympathy. "You won't be able to ask it enough questions to clarify a response that will satisfy you. Ask it about our food instead. Ask it how long our supplies can last us. I've been saving them in case of such a situation, but I'll have to recalculate my serving portions now that we have no new supplies of food coming in . . . "

I ask the knife, "Can our food last us another month?"

A shiver.

"Two months?"

A shiver.

"Three months?"

Silence.

"Well then," I say, grimacing. "That's our answer. Maybe someone will arrive in the next three months to resupply us."

Nemeth grunts, but he doesn't look convinced.

I decide to ask the knife another question. "Will my medicine last three months?"

Silence.

"Two months?"

Silence.

Dragon shite. Nemeth's hands tighten around my waist painfully, and I make a joke. "Well, the solution is obvious. You're going to have to kill me and eat me, my love."

He growls. "That's not funny, Candra."

It's a *little* funny, but he looks quite upset. For some reason, his worry makes me feel even better. For all that I've learned today that makes me fret, I know Nemeth loves me with his whole heart. He could not feign the terror on his face. I lean forward and press a delicate kiss onto his cheek. "Someone will come before we have to resort to that. Do not worry." I pause, thinking. "Do you have any spells that can divine the future?"

Nemeth peppers me with soft, urgent kisses. "If I could tell the future, would we be in this predicament?"

Fair enough. "Then we assume the worst, and we make our supplies stretch. We make my medicine stretch."

He leans back, eyeing me. "Like you did before? When I found you weak and shivering? It doesn't work like that."

I reach up and trace one of his horns idly, trying to distract him from thoughts of my impending doom. "I did it wrong last time. I gave myself half-doses constantly. I watered them down. This time I think I should do a full dose, but only do it every other day." At Nemeth's horrified expression, I smile confidently. "It'll make my medicine last twice as long."

"That cannot be good for you."

"Oh, I imagine I'll feel pretty rotten every other day, but I would rather feel unpleasant than run out entirely." I continue to stroke his horns. Ironic how I thought I would be the one needing comforting, but I'm strangely calm. I'm the one who's easing Nemeth's worries.

"And if we don't get more medicine soon?"

"Then we'll figure something out." I shrug. "We don't have any other choices."

He holds me tight, burying his face against my breasts. "I love you, Candra," he says, his voice desperate and fervent. "Whatever it takes to save you, I'll do it. Even if it means leaving the tower—"

"No," I say quickly, pressing a finger to his lips. "We've come this far. We're not doing that. Don't even consider it."

He shakes his head, the look on his face steely. "I won't let you die."

"That's good because I have no intention of dying." I run my finger along his horn, enjoying his shudder of arousal. "We take this one day at a time, and we make things stretch. Someone will come for us. We're too important for them to neglect." I deliberately lift my hand from his horn and rub his cock instead. "Now, I don't know about you, but I could use a good romp in bed."

"Are you trying to distract me?" he growls.

"Absolutely."

He huffs but picks me up and takes me to bed anyhow.

As my lover helps me undress, I hope I'm right. I hope that this is just a minor hiccup and that someone will be arriving soon with food and enough potion for me to continue on. I don't want to think about what will happen if no one comes.

Surely Erynne wouldn't abandon me? Not when my presence here is so important to the kingdom?

CHAPTER THIRTY-THREE

Potion days are actually the worst days.

Nemeth administers my potion at night because it makes me sleepy and fatigued. I feel well all through the next day, even though I don't take another round of my medicine that night since we're stretching it. The next morning, when I wake up, though, it's rough. It always is. Between nausea, dizziness, and cold sweats, it's a long, horrible stretch of day until I get my next dose.

It's something that has to be done, but it's miserable.

It's been a month of stretching my potion. A month of good days and bad days. Or . . . bad days and bad days, really. Even the good days aren't all that great. It's been a month of feeling constantly sick, of worrying over the dwindling supplies, of waking up and hoping that today, someone will arrive at the tower. That it's all been a mistake and they're here with food and medicine.

It's been a very, very long month.

Today is going to be a bad day. I know it the moment I wake up and my mouth floods with saliva. I reach for the chamber pot under the bed and barely manage to roll out from under the covers and onto the floor before I vomit. For what feels like forever, I throw up. When there's nothing left in my stomach but bile, the vomiting eases, and I lie on the floor next to the bowl, my face pressed to the cold stones of the tower.

"I hate this." Nemeth's deep voice is an angry growl over my shoulder. He moves to my side, producing a wet cloth that he presses gently to my brow. "You're killing yourself in increments, Candra."

"It's fine," I tell him. I keep my eyes tightly closed and lie on the floor for a bit longer. Most mornings seem to start with illness lately, but it's worse on the days I've got to make it to bedtime before I get my potion. I'm eating less just because I know it'll come back up again, and I know that worries Nemeth. "I'm feeling better."

"Will you eat something?"

Damn it, he's calling me on my bluff. It's just . . . lately, breakfast has been a thin mushroom soup, and while I mentally appreciate it for being food, my stomach does not appreciate it in the slightest. "Soon."

He growls, and I hear him pacing across the room. He returns a moment later and crouches low to the floor next to me. "I have water for you. Can you sit up?"

I manage, moving slowly, and I'm relieved that everything in my stomach seems to be gone. That means no more vomiting for now, at least. "I think I'm good. I feel better."

Nemeth won't take that for an answer, though. He never does. He helps me sit up, resting me against his strangely bent thigh and giving me sips of water from my wooden cup. "How is your stomach now?"

"It's fine."

He huffs, clearly not believing me, and rubs a hand down my chemise, then pauses. "Your stomach is hard. Do you hurt anywhere? Any stabbing pains?" When I shake my head, he touches my stomach again. "Candra, I am *worried*."

"There's nothing we can do, love." I lean against him. "We just have to wait it out and see if anyone is coming."

Nemeth wipes a sweaty lock of hair from my brow, his green eyes searching my face with worry. He's been so good to me these last few weeks, taking over all the chores of our daily living because I'm too weak to help out. He helps me bathe, washes my clothes, and reads to me when I'm feeling too puny to get out of bed. I'm filled with so much love for him that it hurts sometimes. There's an endless ache in my chest that wants nothing but the best for him.

And I know I'm holding him back. If he wasn't sharing with me, his food would be lasting twice as long.

"Lie down on the bed," Nemeth tells me. "I want to examine your stomach. If one of your organs is infected, it could make your belly hard. And if that's the case, I cannot heal you."

His anguished expression fills me with guilt. "I really do feel better, Nemeth. Truly. If my stomach is hard, maybe it's just because I threw up. Or something I ate for dinner last night?"

"You did not eat dinner last night."

Right. With a frustrated press of my lips, I get to my feet and let him help me to bed. I lie quietly as he pushes my chemise up and pokes and prods at my belly, leaning close. We haven't had sex in at least a week now because I've been feeling too awful, and I miss it—and his touch—terribly. I hate being sick. I hate feeling weak. I hate puking every morning. I hate that my potion only offers a short window of relief.

More than anything, I hate that we've been abandoned.

"I do not feel any injuries," Nemeth says, stroking his fingers over my stomach. "No lumps or protrusions."

"What about lower?" I ask innocently.

He presses his fingertips to the spot just below my navel, worry all over his broad, stony face. "Here?"

"Lower."

Just above my mound. "Here?"

"Lower."

He realizes what I'm doing, and Nemeth gives me a cross look and lowers my chemise. "Candra, be serious."

"Well, I do have an ache there," I say, teasing. "And you asked if I hurt anywhere."

"I am going to have to research this," he tells me. "And we need your knife so we can rule out any sort of illness with our questions."

I nod, curling up in bed and watching him as he begins to pace in our room. Back and forth, back and forth, his wings flicking with agitation. He gets moody when he sees me sick, but today . . . I've never seen him so upset. If I didn't feel rotten, I'd be thrilled that he's so worked up. There's just something so delightful about seeing a big, tough man fretting over someone like me.

"I've decided something," Nemeth says, pausing in his brisk steps to turn and look at me.

"Oh? What's that?"

His eyes seem to glow a brighter shade of green than I've ever seen. "If it turns out you're well . . . I've decided I'm going to leave the tower."

I jerk upright, staring at Nemeth in shock. "You what? No, Nemeth. You can't do that. *We* can't do that. Think of what will happen."

He moves and sits next to me on the edge of the bed, his big body and wings taking up most of the space. I don't mind it, though. There's something about being squeezed in next to him and his wings falling over me that feels pleasant and comfortable. "That's just it, Candra. I have been thinking about it. I've been thinking about it a great deal. No one is coming for us."

"You don't know that," I protest. "Let's get the knife—"

"And see if it offers a different answer than yesterday? Or the day before? Or the day before that? We have asked it repeatedly, Candra, and every time, the answer is the same. No one is coming. Either they will not, or they cannot. All that matters is that we will starve to death in this tower if we remain here."

I hate that he's right. I hate that every option we have is a bad one. We can slowly starve to death here, serving the needs of our people and our goddess, or we can selfishly abandon the tower and hope we won't be flayed alive for doing so. "You really want us to leave?"

"No," he says slowly. "I will leave. You will stay."

"B-but," I sputter. "The goddess requires both of us to stay. The rule is broken if either one of us leaves the tower. Neither of us can leave."

"I will not let you *die*," Nemeth says, his voice low and deadly, his hand possessive as it rests upon my thigh.

I don't want to die. Not in the slightest. Not when my life feels far more meaningful now that Nemeth is in it. "My life doesn't matter in comparison to the thousands of my people—and yours—who will be affected—"

"I will not let you die," Nemeth repeats. "It is not going to happen."

"Nemeth—"

"If I leave, the pact is broken—that we cannot get around. But if it is only me who emerges from the tower, you will be spared. The anger of both of our peoples will fall solely upon my shoulders. You will be innocent . . . and you will be saved."

"Nemeth, *no*." My horror grows as I realize what he's referring to. I'd forgotten that in the past, when someone left the tower early, the people would take revenge on them. The second Vestalin to serve in the tower was martyred, stabbed a hundred and twenty times when he arrived in his homeland; his corpse hung from an ash tree. One hundred years later, Tinaria Vestalin attempted to flee the tower to see her children and was killed by an angry mob, her head placed on a pike at the gates of Castle Lios.

If we leave the tower, there is no safe place for us in this world. We will be blamed for every injustice that falls upon the land for the next generation. We cannot do it.

I'm not going to let that happen to Nemeth. "Absolutely not."

"You do not have a choice in this, Candra. It is decided."

"Dragon shite," I snap at him, pushing his hand off my leg. I get to my feet, and my head swims. Nausea rises, but I ignore it. If I get sick right now, it'll just reinforce that he's right and that I'm so weak he needs to rescue me. Well, he's the only thing that's kept me here all this time. "If you walk out those doors, I'm going to be one pace behind you."

Nemeth huffs with irritation as he stands to his feet. He looms over me, trying to look forbidding, but I know him far too well to be intimidated. "Do not be stubborn about this, Candra."

"*Me* stubborn? You're the one who's talking about walking out the door and becoming a martyr. I'm not going to let you sacrifice yourself to an ugly fate. If you go, you're not going alone." The more I roll the idea around in my head, the more I like it. I won't let Nemeth leave on his own. If he wants to leave this tower, he's going to have to take me with him.

His tone turns placating. "Candra, love. If I know you're *safe*—"

"How safe do you think I am with the doors wide open?" I gesture at the distant stairs. "How long before someone else arrives to attack me? Better yet, how long do you think I'll be able to take care of myself as my medicine dwindles? How long before I can't get out of bed? What if I die waiting for you to come back?"

He flinches as if I've struck him. His big hands fist at his sides. "Don't *say* such things."

"What, don't say the truth?" I put my hands on my hips, glaring up at him. "Don't point out the obvious? Nemeth, you've already been doing most of the housekeeping in our tower. You cook all the meals. You take care of me when I'm sick. And this is when I'm on just a half dose of my potion. What happens when I run lower? When I can only dose myself every three days? Every four?"

I don't point out that I'll probably die if it takes four days because whatever poison is in my blood will destroy me before then.

He growls furiously at me, grabbing me by my shoulders. His hands are tight but gentle. "*Stop.*"

"Stop speaking the truth? You know I'm right, Nemeth." I put my hands on his, feeling the need to touch him. To anchor him. "If you leave this tower, we need to go together. There's no point in you leaving only for me to die from being left behind." I rub his wrists. "And if there are consequences, I'd rather face them together than apart."

Nemeth sinks to a crouch in front of me, his hands sliding to my waist. His legs fold in that strange way of theirs, and then he tugs me forward into his embrace. His head rests upon my breasts, and he holds me tight. I slide my arms around him, stroking those strange, sweeping horns of his. "I feel as if I am dooming you no matter what I choose," he says, voice thick with emotion. "If I leave you or if I stay . . . I feel as if you will die either way. And if I leave *with* you, I am putting you in new danger."

"Then let me choose my fate," I say softly, fingers playing on his cluster of horns. "If we're to be risking our lives, I'd rather do so at your side. We can spend a few days preparing to leave. We can pack bags and prepare for the next step. Then we'll leave this place together, hand in hand."

"I cannot ask that of you."

My hands tighten around him. "Then let me beg you. Please don't leave me behind, Nemeth. Please." My voice breaks, and I'm perilously on the edge of tears. "I don't care if we make the entire world mad at us. I just want to be at your side. Your mate, forever . . . just like you promised me."

He angles his face up to gaze at me, his eyes tormented. "Don't cry, love. Please. We'll go together, then. If you would be with me in this—"

"I would," I say quickly.

"Then I would be honored." He leans into my touch, his eyes closing. "I will not put you in danger, though."

I don't point out that we're always in danger anyhow. Here, we're in danger of starving. Outside, we're in danger of angering the gods. "We'll prepare to leave. Pack our things. Prepare meals. Ready our clothes. Make a heaping dose of medicine. And then we'll leave together and face the future. Together."

He opens his eyes and gazes up at me with such hunger on his face. Leaning into my hand, he nips at my palm next to the bite mark—the mark that shows the world I'm his. Arousal floods my body, and even though I'm not feeling my best, I want nothing more than to be under him, tied to him with his knot, claimed by my mate. "Make love to me," I whisper. "Claim your mate."

Nemeth groans, his teeth scraping my hand again. "*Milettahn*."

I love that Nemeth uses this most intimate of nicknames, and I decide to say it back just to see how he reacts. "You are my *milettahn* too."

Heat flares in his eyes. A low, sexy growl rises in his throat. "I want to lick your cunt," he tells me feverishly as he rises from the ground, his arms locked around me. I'm lifted into the air, safe in his arms. "I want you on my tongue. I want to make you come. I want you to come so hard that your cunt traps my tongue inside it because it's squeezing so tight. And then I'm going to put my cock inside you and fill you up. And when you're full, I'm going to keep pushing and make you take my knot. I'm going to make you take all of me, and then I'm going to fill you so full with my seed that there will never be a question, ever, of who you belong to. My scent will be painted all over you for the world to breathe in."

I moan at his filthy words. "I want that. I want all of that."

He sets me down on the bed, ever gentle, and then throws my skirts up. They smack me in the face even as his hands are on my legs, pulling off my bloomers and revealing my cunt. Nemeth makes a satisfied sound at the sight of me, then eases my thighs apart, pressing hungry kisses along the inside of my knee. He works his way up, making a line for my pussy, and I spread my thighs wider in invitation. It's been weeks since we've touched, and I'm ravenous for him. I need this connection between us. I need his tongue, his knot. I need him to remind me that we're in this together, that no matter what happens, I'm his mate, and he's mine.

"I love you," I pant as his teeth scrape at the apex of my thighs. "I love you so much. I'm sorry I'm forcing us to leave."

He growls against my pussy, his tongue swiping over my folds, and I shudder with arousal. "You are forcing *nothing*, Candra. You do not apologize." With practiced ease, he finds my clit and teases it, drawing little circles around the hooded nub. "You are my mate. I would do anything for you."

"Then make me come," I breathe. "Make me come hard, Nemeth."

"You want to come? You want me to make this pussy clench?" He lifts his head, gazing up at me even as his thumb strokes up and down through my wet slit. "You want my knot?"

I choke with need. I love it when he gets demanding in bed. "Yes!"

"Then get on your belly, love."

Moaning, I do as he commands. I love it when he takes me from behind because he grips my hips so tightly. Our bodies fit together like magic in those moments, and he's able to push into me so deep that I feel undone. I move onto my belly, my ass in the air and my feet hanging over the edge of the bed.

A moment later, I'm gripped by two big hands, my buttocks clenched tight in his palms as he spreads my cheeks and buries his face there, licking at the entrance to my body. I cry out, rocking back against him, my hands fisting in the blankets. "Yes," I breathe. "Yes, Nemeth."

I love that he buries his nose into my body. I love that his tongue pushes so deep inside me. I love that he lifts my hips into the air just a bit more, as if dragging me toward his mouth so he can lap at me properly. Normally he teases me with little strokes of his tongue, edging me toward my orgasm.

Not today, though. He's ravenous, his mouth devouring me as his tongue thrusts into my channel. I make a choked sound of surprise, clenching around him, but he only works me harder. I can feel the urgency in his body. It's evident how badly he needs me in how he feasts on my cunt as if he's starving—how he guzzles at me as if he's never tasted anything so incredible before. All the while, he makes noises of pleasure in his throat, letting me know that while he's attacking my channel with his tongue, he's thoroughly enjoying himself.

It doesn't take me long to come. Today he's not coaxing a release from me. He's demanding, and I'm eager to comply. I let out a choked cry as the climax tears through me, all of my muscles tensing, leaving me weak and whimpering in its aftermath. Nemeth lowers my hips back to the bed again, his hand skimming up my back. "My beautiful mate," he murmurs. "I'm going to keep you safe. You can trust me."

I do trust him. And I want to look at him when he comes inside me. I roll onto my back and reach for him, ready for the weight of his heavy body over mine.

He fits himself at the entrance to my body, and I wriggle against him. Nemeth presses into me, and I gasp at the sensation of him filling me. It never gets old. There's always that delicious stretch that comes with fitting my body to his, followed by the tease of his knot as he pumps into me. I hold on tightly to him as he pounds into me, hard and fast.

"Yes," I moan. "Yes, *yesyesyes*."

He fucks me hard and brutal, and just when I think I'm about to come, he hooks a hand behind my knee, his other moving to the base of my neck and cradling me against him. In the next moment, he presses his knot against my core, and I squirm. It never "fits." It's not meant to fit. It's meant to push its way into me, to plug me, so I won't release his seed. It's so he can *breed* me.

And I absolutely love it. I cry out at the sensation of him thrusting, his knot working at my entrance. He rocks into me, his movements shallow and full of pressure, and then with one last pump, he's fully inside me, and tears come to my eyes at the sharp sensation of his knot filling me beyond what I feel I can take. "Oh . . . oh gods . . . "

"You've got me," he murmurs, running his hand over my leg. "You're taking my knot so sweetly, aren't you? Because you're the perfect mate, my Candra. So giving. Such a good, gripping cunt. You hold me so tight." He groans, his hips flexing as he presses into me one last time, and then he begins to come. "My mate."

"Yours," I breathe, feeling tight and clenched and overstuffed and perfect all at once.

I don't come at the same time he does. He already made me come once, and when my belly is full of his seed, and he collapses over me, he flutters his wings as if they need to stretch. Nemeth makes a satisfied sound and then rolls his hips against mine, our bodies locked. They'll remain locked for a while, and I know he especially loves this part.

I do, too, if I'm being honest with myself. It's an exquisite kind of torture to be so full of him, to have his weight bearing down on me. I'm pinned under him, his in every way, and when he strokes a hand down my hip and then between us, I whimper with anticipation. His thumb moves to my clit, grazing it with just the barest of sensations. "Squeeze me again, love. Milk my cock."

Letting out a choked sound, I clench around him as another orgasm ripples through me.

"That's right," he rumbles, clearly pleased at my reaction. He continues to stroke circles around my clit, leaving me breathless and gasping for mercy, my nails digging into his arms as he makes me come over and over again, with lazy, indolent touches against my clit while I clasp his cock and knot tightly deep inside my body. "Squeeze my knot. Milk it for its seed. Take everything I have for you."

When I come again, I wrap my arms around him, pressing my cheek against his arm. "Mercy," I wheeze. "Mercy, Nemeth."

He finally lifts his delicious, maddening finger from my pussy and licks it clean as he nuzzles at my hair. "My sweet mate." His tone is full of wonder and adoration. "How can you ever doubt that I would do anything to protect you?"

I just hold him tighter, exhausted and sated, my sweaty legs clasped around him. "You're not leaving without me. Don't even try that shadow shit."

Nemeth chuckles. "Shadow shit? What do you mean?"

I tweak his nipple because he knows exactly what I mean. "That moving through the shadows thing that you do. Don't think you're going to leave me behind by just poofing away. If you do that, I swear I won't take a single potion until you come back." I rub my lips against his sweaty muscles, loving the taste of him. "Promise me you won't try to be noble and leave me behind."

"I promise." He strokes my hair from my flushed face. "It doesn't work that way, anyhow."

"Exactly how does it work?" I tilt my head back and gaze up at him. "Can you move anywhere? Any length?" I clench around him in surprise because if that's the case, what's stopping him from just flitting over to Castle Lios and getting my potion? Would the goddess even notice he was gone?

But Nemeth shakes his head. "I can only gather the shadows about me for short distances. There must be enough darkness to cover all of me, and I must be able to see where I am going . . . or I must know the exact layout of the room I want to appear in. If I flow through the darkness into an object, it will stop my heart instantly. One small thing out of place—one piece of furniture askew—could mean my death. Most Fellians won't even risk it. That's why we don't flow through shadows for very long distances."

His words terrify me. If a single thing is out of place and he slides into it, he dies instantly? It sounds far too dangerous to even try. "I don't think I want you doing that at all."

Nemeth huffs, amused. "Like I said, most Fellians won't risk it. It's useful in combat, perhaps, but you have to know where your opponent's sword will be at all times. I would rather use my wings to fly than flow through shadows and simply hope for the best."

I hold him tighter, thinking of the time he flowed through shadows with me in his arms. Was he risking his life even then? "Great. You know I'm going to panic every time you do that shadow thing now."

He laughs, and I feel it all through my cunt, where we're still joined. "It's called 'flowing through shadows,' and if it makes you feel better, I won't do it." He rocks against me, reminding me that he's yet hard and his knot hasn't gone down. "I'm far more interested in other ways to exert myself."

"Pervert," I say breathlessly. But I'm relieved because he's *my* pervert, and he's not risking his neck. I'll happily be perverted with him.

CHAPTER THIRTY-FOUR

That night, Nemeth gives me my potion, and I feel the effects immediately. My pounding head stops swimming, a cold sweat breaks out over my skin, and I want to throw up . . . but it goes away quickly, followed by a relief so profound that I fight back tears. I laugh instead, wiping the sweat off my skin with my chemise and stripping it off as I lie in bed naked. "This is my new favorite time of day."

Nemeth chuckles, and instead of joining me in bed, he moves to the table stacked high with his books. "How is your stomach?"

"A little queasy, but it always is after my potion."

"No aches or pains? No stabbing sensations on your side?" He picks up one book—one that I know is a medical tome he brought with him in case he needed to treat himself. He begins to turn pages. "Any tingling?"

I run my hands over my stomach. Is it truly feeling harder like he says? "I'm fine."

He flicks a page, frowning down at the book. "I haven't been able to find anything about a hard belly unless it's a sick organ."

"I think I'd feel that, wouldn't I? Or something would hurt to press on?" I experimentally push my fingers into the soft rolls of my belly, but nothing feels unusual or painful.

"Mmm." He sits down with the book, reading. "There must be something here."

"I think you're just panicking," I tell him. "You're stressed, and now you're seeing problems where there are none."

"Possibly." But he doesn't sound convinced.

I cup my breasts, wondering if I should distract him with some sex before bed . . . and then pause. They feel surprisingly tender, even more so than when I have my period. That's . . . odd.

Out of nowhere, I remember a conversation my sister had with Nurse when she first got pregnant. She'd been unsure if she'd truly been with child.

"Are you ill in the mornings?" Nurse had asked her. *"Tits sore? Does your belly feel different?"*

Belly . . . different? Like hard?

I squeeze my breasts again and wince at the pain. They're extremely tender, all right. But Nemeth could have been too vigorous with them earlier in our lovemaking. That doesn't mean anything. Once he sucked on my nipple so hard that he left a mark for days, and that made it extremely sore. I'd teased him relentlessly about it too.

But I've also been sick in the mornings. I've rolled out of bed and vomited until I was weak every single morning for the last two weeks. I thought it was because we'd been doling out my potion every other day—that it was affecting my stomach like it affects all aspects of my physical person. What if it's not that, though? What if it's a baby?

That's impossible. I'm not supposed to get pregnant. I've got cursed blood.

I must be wrong. I got my period recently. It was . . .

I pause, lost in thought. When *was* the last time I had my period? I remember having it prior to the Solstice when I'd had particularly bad cramps, and Nemeth made me a cup of tea. We'd joked that it was the last of that flavor of tea until we got our supplies in and that we'd be glad to get new flavors because we were down to our least favorites . . .

And one of my favorites prior to that had been one that had an herb that prevented pregnancy, and I'd sneered that I didn't need it.

I can't be pregnant, though. I'm the Vestalin with cursed blood. I can't get pregnant, can I? That's what I've always been told.

Or is it that I *can* get pregnant, but I can't carry it to term?

The thought is a terrifying one, and I wish I'd paid more attention to what was written about the blood curse. I trail my fingers over my belly, worried. If it wouldn't make Nemeth fret, I'd get up and retrieve my knife to ask it questions. As it is, Nemeth has enough to worry about. I'll wait until I'm alone and have my knife clarify what the truth is.

I can't be pregnant.

—

Later that night, I slip out of bed.

Nemeth immediately reaches for me, stroking a hand over my arm. "Sick?"

"No, I just need the garderobe," I tell him. "I'll be right back." I pick up my dressing gown, slipping it over my shoulders and wrapping it around my body. I hope he doesn't notice the heavy pull of one pocket where I hid my knife earlier. I hate that I'm keeping secrets again, but I need to know for myself first. So, I head to the garderobe, shut the door, and then pull out the knife.

"Am I pregnant?" I whisper.

It pulses in my hand.

Panic floods through me. How? It doesn't make sense. I've been told all my life that a Vestalin with the blood curse cannot get pregnant. Haven't I been told of relatives who had the same curse and lived their lives childless and alone? I want to ask if I'll be able to carry it to term, but the knife can't see the future any more than I can. Asking will get me no answer, which feels the same as a "no," so I'm not even going to ask that. I'll ask other things instead. "Is the baby healthy?"

Yes.

Hot relief floods through me, and I sag against the door, clutching the knife. "Does Nemeth know?"

No answer.

That doesn't surprise me; I just figured it out myself. "Am I healthy enough to carry the baby the full nine months?"

No answer.

My lungs tighten. I close my eyes. Okay, okay. That doesn't mean anything. My question might be too vague. I might not be healthy enough right now because I haven't been taking the full dose of my potion. "If I eat properly and take the right dose of my medicine, will I be healthy enough to give birth?"

A shiver of affirmation, and I feel like I can breathe again.

I didn't know Nemeth could make me pregnant. I don't know what to think about the realization that I'm going to be a mother. I've never considered it. Never considered a life in which my blood curse wouldn't prevent me from carrying on my bloodline. I've been told all my life that I can't give a husband heirs. That because of my blood curse, I'll remain sick and a burden all my days.

This seems impossible. But I think about my dark hair and how everyone in Lios has pale, blond hair except for those of the line of Vestalin. I think of the stories that say we have Fellian blood and that's why our coloring is different. The Fellian rumor of Ravendor, the first Vestalin, giving birth to half-Fellian children that she hid away from the world. I've always thought that Nemeth's version of the story was ridiculous . . . but now I wonder.

"Is it true?" I ask the knife. "Do I have Fellian blood in my veins?"

The knife throbs in affirmation, and I gasp.

It seems my ancestor found a mate in this tower after all.

A week doesn't feel like enough time to prepare. There's an endless amount of work to be done.

Food must be cooked and bread baked. Our meat is already dried, but any foodstuffs that aren't portable must be made into something that is. We'll only be able to carry limited amounts of goods with us, so we take the last of our stale flour and withered nuts and make a traveling bread that's hard and dry but will last a long time. We cook up everything that won't travel and eat our fill, and Nemeth uses the last of my potion supplies to make enough doses to last me a week if I take it daily after we leave the tower. Until then, as we prepare, I'll continue on with half doses.

I sew adjustments to my clothing as Nemeth packs and repacks our bags, trying to see how much we can bring with us. He makes careful plans, determined to give us the best chances to survive. I know he's miserable about leaving his books behind. I want to tell him that we can come back for them after we get my potion—after our futures are settled—but something in me knows we're never coming back here.

Once we cross over the threshold, we've committed to our fates.

So, I sew. My dresses are frothy, silly things with tight bodices, ribbon detailing, and silken panels. They're useless for travel since I've only ever gone by carriage in the past. But when we leave this tower, there will be no horses waiting for us, no retinue to take us to our homeland. We'll be crossing on foot, and we don't know how long it will take or how unpleasant the weather will be. For the entire week as we prepare, thunder crashes, and the wind howls so loudly we can hear it even through the stones of the tower. I can only imagine what sorts of storms we'll be pummeled with when we depart and invoke the goddess's wrath.

I modify my dresses for travel as best I can. I'm not good with a needle, but I know how to make stitches, at least. And I raise the hems of my simplest dresses to above the ankles so the skirts won't drag in the mud. I remove expensive, flashy-looking ribbons and embroidery. I extend the laces in the bodice, thinking of the child growing in my belly. How soon does a Fellian pregnancy show? I still haven't told Nemeth. I don't know when the right time will be, but right now, he's frustrated and worried, and he doesn't sleep at night. He's anxious about leaving the tower—we both are.

In addition to angering the goddess, I'm worried there will be mobs of people waiting with pitchforks to tear us apart.

"We'll go to your people first," Nemeth tells me. "I'll ask for asylum in their lands. I'll tell them I've defected, and I want to join your kingdom."

I think of cruel King Lionel, who wants to destroy all of Darkfell, and of my sister, Erynne, who has urged me over and over again to kill Nemeth. "I'm not sure that's wise."

"It might not be, but it's the surest way to get your potion in your hands quickly. This fenugreek herb? The aloe vera? They do not grow under mountains. We must trade with outsiders to get such things." He's silent for a moment. "And . . . I am not sure I trust my people to get them for us. Not after they've abandoned us and left us to starve." He holds me close. "At least if we go to your people, I know you're safe."

"But what about you?"

"I can take care of myself." He presses a kiss onto my brow. "If I am not welcomed, I will go."

I shake my head. "If you're not welcomed, I'm going with you."

"We will take it one day at a time," Nemeth promises me. "But first, we must get more potion for you. We'll figure everything else out later."

As the days crawl forward and our plans near completion, I spend a lot of time at the altar downstairs. I've never been the most religious . . . or actually religious at all. But knowing that we're flagrantly disobeying the goddess feels dangerous. I kneel before the altar and clasp my hands in front of me, and my prayers are full of apologies.

"I'm sorry," I whisper. "We can't stay, and I'm sorry. I know we're not your children; I'm human, and we're the children of the Absent God, and Fellians are the children of the Gray God. I'm not sure you have children. But if you did, I can't imagine that you would want us to starve to death in your honor. Back when you had names, the Golden Moon Goddess was supposed to be a goddess of love, a goddess of families and affection." I hesitate. "And I'm pregnant. My baby doesn't deserve to die here because our people have betrayed us. So, please, please understand."

The goddess on the triptych doesn't answer. That's not surprising. No one ever answers a human's prayers, but I pray anyhow. I know Nemeth does, too, but if his prayers are answered, he doesn't tell me. We pray, and we leave food offerings with the gods because we know we're going to be disobedient.

But we're going anyhow. There's no choice in Nemeth's mind, and I'm not going to let him go without me.

Our bags are packed, our clothing ready. We pick the last of the mushrooms from Nemeth's mushroom farm and stew them for dinner. It almost feels like too much food, and then I'm reminded that we've been carefully rationing for a long time. Tomorrow, that all changes.

I'm terrified of tomorrow.

That night, we crawl into bed together, in sheets we're going to have to leave behind, our heads resting upon fluffy pillows that will also be abandoned for whoever is in this tower next. Our packs are laden mostly with food and necessities—a change of clothes for traveling, a heavy cloak, and not much else. I've sewn some of my jewelry—hairpins and earrings, mostly—into the hem of my cloak, just in case we need coin.

I can't stop thinking about tomorrow, and I suspect Nemeth cannot either. He drags me on top of him and teases my breasts until I'm whimpering, then seats me atop his cock. I rock to my climax above him and then force myself down on his knot, sheathing him inside my body and locking us together. When he's pulsing inside me, his knot hard, he flips us over, and then I'm under him, my mate's small thrusts filling me with his spend. Nemeth presses kisses onto the top of my head as we drowse, limbs entwined, bodies joined. He strokes my skin over and over, and I don't know if he's trying to reassure himself or me.

"Are you ready to do this?" I ask him in a soft voice.

I don't have to explain what I'm asking about. We're both thinking of the same thing. "I am committed," Nemeth says.

"Is that the same thing?"

"Does it matter?" He gives me a wry smile. "It has the same results."

My heart feels full, achingly so. To think that he's willing to do this for me, to doom himself (and possibly others) just to save me. I wrap my arms tightly around him and squeeze my inner walls around his cock, wanting to demonstrate everything that I'm feeling. I don't have words for how much I love him. I've never been good with words.

But I can demonstrate a little. At least tonight.

Nemeth wakes me from sleep with a caress on my cheek. "Candra."

I'm immediately awake, my senses alert. It's dark, but as I rouse, Nemeth reaches over the bed and taps the light once to turn it on. The shadowy room fills with faint light. "Is it time?"

He nods and slides out of bed, his wings tucked against his back as he gets to his feet. Normally Nemeth would stretch, letting his wings ripple outward as he yawns off the last of his slumber. Today though, he seems just as restless and uneasy as me. I didn't sleep very well last night. I was constantly on edge— worried for the dawn even as I waited for it. I know Nemeth felt the same.

It's here now, and there's no avoiding our fates.

My big, handsome mate offers his hand to me. "Can you sit up? How is your stomach this morning?"

"I think I'm good." But the moment I lift my head, my stomach rebels, and I reach for the chamber pot once more. I throw up everything in my stomach and then lean against the bed weakly. "All better."

Nemeth watches me with a worried expression. "I do not understand. You had a full dose of your potion last night. Why are you yet sick?"

I wonder how long I can hide a pregnancy from him. If he knew I was pregnant, he'd make me stay here and go out alone. I shake my head, playing it off. "It's probably just a leftover from my missed doses. It'll take my body a few days to feel right again." I get to my feet, ignoring the queasy turn of my now-empty stomach, and turn to my mate. "Shall we dress?"

"Are you sure you can travel?" he asks.

"I'm committed," I joke back, but he doesn't laugh with me.

He just sighs and presses a kiss onto my forehead. "Let us dress. We should leave before the sun gets too high. I don't want you getting overheated."

I nod, wishing for a real kiss, but I probably wouldn't want to kiss my mouth, either, not after my usual morning. So, I rinse my mouth out and braid my hair, then pin it up off my neck. I put on one of the dresses I've prepared for travel. It's a plain, boring, deep blue with all the decoration stripped off it, the sleeves plain. My shoes for the journey don't match it, as they are a sturdy pair of slippers with reinforced soles (thanks to Nemeth) in a deep black. I shouldn't care about fashion. It's just that my skirts were shortened to make walking easier, and now everyone will see my hideous footwear.

I tighten the laces on my bodice, and my breasts ache enough that I have to loosen my dress. I smooth a hand down my front. My stomach is still flat, at least. I wonder how long a Fellian carries a child. Will it be too obvious if I ask? I decide yes, it would be too obvious, and I slip my enchanted knife into the front of my dress, tucking it between my breasts.

Nemeth is dressed in his favorite kilt, with a sword buckled at his waist and our heavy packs slung over his back. "Ready to go?"

Biting my lip, I study our little chamber. "I need to make the bed." I plump the pillows, then pull the blankets up. "And then I should wash out the chamber pot and make sure the kitchen is clean—"

"Candra," Nemeth says in a gentle voice. "Leave it. Anyone who comes here will understand why we had to leave."

Will they? Or will we be reviled by both Fellian and Liosian peoples for what we're about to do? We're not supposed to leave, even if we're starving. Even if we're dying. We're supposed to sacrifice ourselves for the greater good.

Not that I've ever wanted to do that. Nobody asked me either. I've been told. Perhaps that's why I feel so damn guilty that we're leaving. We don't know what's going to happen . . . we just know that no one will be pleased. I wring my hands, anxious. He's right. No one's going to care that we left the tower a mess, only that we left the tower. "Right. Of course."

He holds his hand out to me. "Come. It's time to go."

"I'm scared," I confess, a panicky feeling settling in my stomach.

"I know," he says, continuing to hold his hand out for me. "But we must go anyway."

I nod. It's not even a question of if I should stay behind anymore. We're committed to our path. I take his hand, squeezing it tight as he leads me through the hall and toward the curving stairs. "Do we have everything?" I ask anxiously.

"I packed last night," he reminds me. "I checked my list three times."

Right, because Nemeth is nothing if not prepared at all times. I hold onto him as we go down the stairs toward the now-unlocked doors on the first floor. We've left them accessible in case someone came by. Nothing barricades us inside anymore. A simple tug on the handle will open the doors, and then we'll be on the beach, a travesty to the goddess for leaving the tower five years too soon.

"Do you think she'll strike us down?" I ask Nemeth as we pass by the altar, the remnants of our prayer offerings still upon the tiny plates. "The goddess?"

"No," Nemeth says. "If we are to believe the stories, her wrath takes the form of drought and famine or flooding and destruction. Her hand is never direct upon those who offend her."

"Because it's more fun to punish everyone, I suppose," I say lightly.

He only grunts.

"Do you think she will punish us?" I prompt. "For abandoning the tower?"

"If the stories are to be believed, aye." He doesn't let go of my hand. If anything, his grip tightens. It's as if he's afraid I'll change my mind.

I won't, but it doesn't mean I'm not terrified.

"What do Fellian stories say?" I continue as we head toward the double doors, the only path out of the tower. My voice wobbles with fear. "About those who abandon the tower?"

"Nothing good."

"They're just stories anyhow," I decide. "They could be full of dragon shite. Maybe the goddess will understand. Maybe she won't be upset." Maybe she knows I'm pregnant with Nemeth's child and that any path we take will be a difficult one anyhow.

"Mmm."

That's a nonanswer if there ever was one.

We stand in front of the doors. My hand is sweaty in Nemeth's. He reaches forward and tugs one door open, swinging it outward. There's a scrape against sand-covered stone, and then the doors fall open. Bright sunlight spills inward, and it looks like a gloriously sunny day. The air is warm, and a gentle breeze touches my face. The skies are blue, the waters less so, but still beautiful. The strip of sand that surrounds the tower is deserted and unmarked.

We stare out, but neither of us moves forward to take that first step. I breathe in the fresh air. If it's going to be bad for us, why must it smell so good? I want to stand in the sunlight and drink it in so badly, yet I'm terrified too. This isn't just my future at stake. I have a child to consider—a child I'm trying very, very hard not to think about.

"I should go first," Nemeth says abruptly, releasing my hand. He gazes down at me, his strange, sharp Fellian features resolute. "If the goddess's punishment is instant, I would rather that it happen to me and me alone. Yes?"

I sputter. "What? No, absolutely not." Grabbing his arm again, I cling to him. "We're doing all of this together, remember? That includes everything."

"Candra, let me do this," he says in a soft voice. "If the gods will only punish one person, I would rather it be me."

"I'm not going to let go of you," I say, obstinate. I loop one arm in his belt and twine the leather about my sleeve. "When you step forward, I will be dragged through with you at the same time because we're doing everything *together*. Like we promised."

"Candra—"

"I am prepared to be dragged!" I shout dramatically, anchoring myself against his waist. "Don't think that I won't hold on because I will!"

He sighs heavily. "Why are you so stubborn?"

"Because I love you, and we're doing this together."

He glares down at me with those eerie green eyes and runs a hand over his face, his two shorn claws evident. "Fine. You stubborn mule of a human, fine."

I smile at him. Not just because I'm getting my way but because it's clear he loves me as much as I love him, and he's trying to protect me even now. So, I let go of his waist and hold out my hand. "We cross together."

Nemeth growls low in his throat, frustrated. He glances at the open door and then down at me. Then, he hauls me against him and bends over me, his lips on mine in a hard, frantic kiss. "Whatever waits for us on the other side, know that you are everything to me." His mouth presses to mine over and over again. "Everything. Understand?"

I cling to him, kissing him back, trying to show him just how much I adore him. I know we're both stalling, but I don't care. I would happily have kisses from Nemeth until the end of time.

He sets me back down on my feet again with utter gentleness and sighs. He holds his hand out to me, his gaze upon the door, and I slip my hand in his. We move closer to the edge, and then he nods at me, lifting one foot.

And together, we step over the edge of the portal and outside of the tower for the first time in over two years.

CHAPTER THIRTY-FIVE

I hold my breath.

Holding my breath, tightly closing my eyes, and waiting for something to happen. Time feels as if it's slowed; my pulse is pounding in my ears. My slippers—made for walking on the even stone floors of the tower—sink into the sands of the beach. A breeze ruffles my hair, pulling a few strands loose from my braid. Somewhere in the distance, a seabird cries out.

I wait for the goddess's wrath to fall upon us. I wait for lightning to strike us down. For the skies to rumble with thunder and the wind to wail, letting us know she's displeased that we've broken our vow to remain in the tower. I wait for anything, any sign at all.

Nothing happens.

I exhale and open my eyes.

It's . . . a nice day. The sun shines down from above without a cloud in the sky. The breeze is cool for the otherwise warm day. The sandy beach surrounding the tower looks pristine and untouched, and if the waves seem to be a little high and whitecapped, it makes for a pretty scene.

Shouldn't it be . . . awful? Out here? As punishment? "I don't understand," I say to Nemeth, my clammy hand still clutched in his. "I thought we'd feel something."

"I did too," he confesses. His gaze moves over the bright blue skies, and he squints, raising a hand to shield his eyes. "Perhaps the goddess hasn't noticed yet. Or perhaps she understands our problem and forgives us."

Out of nowhere, thunder rumbles overhead, loud and crackling.

"Or not," I say tightly, clutching at his hand as I stare up at the still-blue sky. "Dragon shite."

Nemeth extends a wing over my head as fat drops of rain begin to fall from above. It seems impossible for it to rain on us without clouds overhead, but I guess the gods can do whatever they want. I peer out from under Nemeth's wing, thinking of the small pack I have on my back with my cloak and a change of clothing. Nemeth insists upon carrying everything heavy, but I don't mind carrying my fair share. I glance up at my lover and notice the rain is sluicing down his dark-gray skin in rivulets. "Do we . . . go back inside and wait out the rain, or do we just soldier on through?"

He shakes his head slowly. "It seems insulting to retreat back to the tower after taking two steps out. We'll continue onward. Let us give the rain a moment."

Sure enough, the patter of rain stops as quickly as it started, and Nemeth shakes off his wings before folding them up again. "Shall we have a look around?"

I nod, not trusting my voice when a knot rises in my throat. We really are leaving. We've done it now. There's no turning back. It doesn't matter that we had no choice. The goddess would probably argue that our choice could have been to starve. Maybe the Golden Moon Goddess has never been a goddess of kindness or sympathy, after all.

I cling to Nemeth's hand for a moment longer, and when I take a step forward, my shoe scrapes on something hard. I glance down and realize it's one of the bricks that used to cover the door. It's nearly covered in sand, and a quick look around shows that more of them are scattered against the wall of the tower and off to the side, most of them covered in grit or half-buried.

It reminds me of the dead men who should still be on this beach.

Instead of investigating our surroundings, I scan the sand for dead bodies. They would have rotted, I think, though I have no idea how much or how little would remain. I doubt they would have coin, but they might have weapons. More knives. We can always use more knives.

So, while Nemeth looks around on the beach, his mood as apprehensive as mine, I go hunting. A short distance from the door, I find what looks like a rib cage half-buried in the sand. I use my shoe to kick some of the sand away, and the moment I do, I see a dirty piece of cloth . . . and then a faded symbol embroidered on the cuff of a sleeve.

It's the cuff of one of Castle Lios's guardsmen. Surely, he couldn't have been one of the men who broke in? I remember them as skinny and disheveled, with ragged beards and a terrible need for a bath.

"Candra?" Nemeth calls. "What are you doing?"

I kick the sand back over the bit of rotten fabric. "I thought I saw a pretty shell," I call out. "It's nothing." Gathering my skirts, I return to his side, slogging through the sand. It fills my slippers and makes walking difficult, but I manage a bright smile for Nemeth. "I don't suppose you see a raft anywhere?"

"A raft?" Nemeth echoes.

Nodding, I glance around the lonely stretch of beach. There's nothing here but a few waving pieces of grass and a distant seagull on the far end of the beach. I vaguely remember the old, weathered dock on the far side of the shore and that there wasn't one on this side. "Something we can use to get across the water? I can't swim." I want to point out that the men who arrived to attack us would have needed a raft or a boat of some kind, but I don't want to bring Nemeth's attention to the dead. For some reason, I don't want him to know that they were from Lios. They were human, so it stands to reason that they were my people, but . . . still. "Any ideas?"

Nemeth chuckles. "I cannot believe you even have to ask."

It's on the tip of my tongue to ask what he means when he picks me up into his arms, grinning. My shoes stream sand, and I cling to his neck as he spreads his wings and moves into the shadows of the tower.

The world flips upside down and my stomach heaves. Everything spins, and it feels as if all gravity has disappeared.

A moment later, everything is heavy once more. The tumbling world sets itself right again, and when I blink away the confusion, I see we're still on the sandy shore, but now we're in the shadow of a cliff, and across the long stretch of water in front of us is the distant tower.

He's shifted us into shadows.

"See?" Nemeth murmurs against my ear.

I smack his arm, furious (and a little queasy). "You said you wouldn't do that! You're not supposed to risk your life."

"There was no risk. I could see the beach from here." He ignores my anger, setting me down. "And with how weak you've been, I don't want you attempting anything."

I don't point out that he has wings. We both know he does. The fact that he wouldn't fly us over the water means he doesn't trust them, which makes me ache inside. How horrible must it be to have wings and not be able to use them? To be stuck with nothing but your two feet to travel? I want to ask him how he's feeling, but I also don't want to prod an open wound. So, I give him a huffy look, straightening my rain-dampened clothes. "Next time you do that, please warn me."

"So you can panic?"

So arrogant and confident in himself. I love it, even if I want to wrap my hands around his neck and choke him right now. "So I can talk you out of it."

Nemeth snorts with amusement. His gaze moves over the rocky shore, eyeing the Liosian land. On this side of the channel, it's not nearly as mountainous. The Fellian landscape is nothing but mountains, his people living deep in the belly of the rocky giants instead of on their sloping surface. Meanwhile, the Lios lands are far more temperate. There are some steep cliffs near the waters, sure, but Castle Lios itself is tucked into a rolling green valley surrounded by a thick forest on one side and hills upon the other, with an impressive dockyard to the south leading to deep waters and a harbor constantly full of ships. Here, though, we're days away from the castle and the city it protects. There's nothing but desolate beaches that lead up to equally desolate plains. Here, there are no ships on the water and no farms for as far as the eye can see. It's remote and deserted.

It worries me a little. When I was brought out here, there was a carriage with strong horses, and it still took two days to arrive. How long will we be traveling on foot across this land? How long will it take for us to return to Castle Lios?

And how are things going to go when I arrive five years early with a Fellian at my side?

Hot panic bubbles up inside me, but I push it down. I'll worry about that when I have time. For now, I'm here with Nemeth, and we need to conquer one issue at a time.

"There's no one here," Nemeth says, gazing along the empty shore. "Is this normal?"

I shrug. "As normal as to be expected, I think. There's nothing out here."

He nods, then studies my face. "Are you tired? Do you need to rest? Your face is flushed."

Is it? "I'm just anxious." I gesture at the coast. "Castle Lios is a few days north on horseback. I suppose we can start in that direction."

"Are you all right?"

"No," I admit. "But neither are you. We're out of choices."

"Are you tired? It has been a long time since either one of us was outside. This is a lot." His voice is gentle. "If you need a moment, I understand."

I do need a moment. I also need five more years of food supplies and to have not left the tower. I need to not have a blood curse. I need to not be pregnant with a Fellian's baby. But these are not choices I have, so I shake it off. "No, I can walk. Let's go, shall we?"

I'm a terrible traveling companion. I know I am. Before we walk very far at all, my feet are hurting; my shoes are useless. My legs ache with fatigue. I'm hot and sweaty, and I dislike being hot and sweaty. Nemeth makes excuses for me because he loves me. I'm fatigued due to my illness. I'm fatigued due to years in the tower. I point out to him that I'm also a princess, and a princess never walks farther than across a ballroom. That, I think, startles him. As a Fellian prince, he has been trained in all kinds of combat, even from his days in the Alabaster Citadel. He has traveled to his homeland and back again.

But he is also a man and not one with cursed blood. I have been sheltered all my life, and even the tower was a sort of shelter.

So, traveling? Not my favorite. It's difficult and unpleasant, and I want to scream when we finally find a rutted dirt road that's more rock and mud than actual road. It stretches across the endless horizon without a single town or village in sight. I know I should be glad that we can travel without a Fellian being noticed, but then I pull the sixteenth rock out of my flimsy, useless shoe. And I would give my smallest toe for a run-down inn with a free bed. Any kind of bed, no matter how filthy. Just a bed.

No, a chair, I decide. I would give two small toes for a chair.

I want to ask Nemeth if he isn't flying because I'm with him or if he's nervous about his injured wing. He hasn't even attempted flight, despite spreading his wings a few times. Maybe we're both on edge and doubting ourselves. Certainly, our communication skills have been strained. Normally in the tower, we can't stop talking to one another, but ever since we've crossed the threshold, we've been more or less silent. It worries me.

Then again, all of this is worrying.

Like the shrines we passed as we looked for a road. Small roadside shrines to the gods are common, as travelers make offerings so they will be protected on their journeys. The shrines we've passed aren't filling me with reassurance, though. They're covered in leaves and detritus, the offerings left behind withered and ancient. The flowering bushes near each stone effigy that are tended to by travelers out of courtesy are overgrown and abandoned, and even the earthenware offering bowls on the altars themselves are cracked and look as if they've seen better days.

With how abandoned things are, if I didn't know better, I'd swear we'd been in that tower for a hundred years instead of just two.

"Not exactly a reassuring sight," I tell Nemeth as we pause in front of the latest set of altars. Whatever has been left in the offering bowl of the Gray God rotted into a pile of goo long ago. I wrinkle my nose. "Surely the gods can't be pleased with this."

"I imagine whoever was here last did the best they could," Nemeth says at my side. "Do you want to stop for a time and tend to it? Do our duty?"

I don't. I really don't. I'm tired and cranky, and I just want to sit somewhere and rest. But we're not exactly the favorites of the gods right now as it is, so I suppose it couldn't hurt to kiss up a little. "Why not."

We pause by the shrines for a time, tidying up. I brush the three altars—one for each of the gods. Then, I rid them of debris and clean the offering bowls, rinsing them out with water. Nemeth uses a knife to tend to the unkempt plants, trimming vines and cutting down overgrown branches from the flowering bushes. When we're done, the altars look less forlorn. Even though we don't have much food left, we offer a few withered vegetables from our depleted store. Part of me hates to leave those behind. We need them more than the gods—or whatever birds will pick them off because the gods won't notice or care.

But Nemeth is more pious than me. He seems happy with our contribution, smiling at me. "If the gods have noticed us at all, perhaps they'll notice our efforts too."

Noticed us? I don't see how they couldn't, given that we abandoned their tower. But I don't say that aloud. You never say the bad things aloud.

CHAPTER THIRTY-SIX

A short time later, when the sun is setting on the horizon, we come across the first structure we've seen since leaving the tower, and it makes me wonder if the gods are looking out for us after all.

Granted, it's not an inn. It's a crumbling shed that probably once housed livestock. There's no house nearby, though a large burnt spot a short distance away tells us what probably happened to it. There are no cattle, no horses, and the hay in the shed looks to be older than I am. But there's most of a roof and at least three walls, and that's better than sleeping out in the open.

Nemeth is pleased with the sight of it. "We'll stop here tonight. Do you need me to clean it out for you? Make a bed?"

I shake my head, tossing down my much-lighter pack and using it as a seat as I rest in the old, moldy hay. "Just lay down a cloak. I don't care. I'm too tired to care."

He sets down his pack and crouches near me, a worried expression on his face. "Do you feel well?"

"My feet hurt," I admit with frustration, even though I know it makes me sound like a whiny child. "They hurt, and my shoes are dreadful. Not even a charming dreadful. Just ugly and ill fitting. And my face feels hot. And my scalp does too. And I'm tired and hungry and miserable, and part of me wants to go back to the tower and just lie there and *starve* because it'd be easier."

Nemeth chuckles at my crabby response. "There's no going back."

"I know there's not." I sigh. "I wouldn't go back even if we could. I'm just tired and not used to this. And why is my scalp hot?" I touch the top of my head, wincing when it feels scorching.

"You're red," Nemeth says, touching a finger gently under my chin and tipping my face toward his. "Your face is bright red, and so is your scalp where your hair is parted. Why is this?"

I look down at my hands, and sure enough, the backs are bright red with sunburn. I'm stunned—then I laugh. "I haven't seen sunlight in two years. I must be truly pale." I flex my hands and wince at how hot and tight my skin feels. "That's going to be painful in the morning."

"What can we do about it? I do not like to see you in pain."

I think of the delicate, floral-scented lotions I have back at the tower. I didn't bring them because we only brought necessities, and why would lotion be one? But now I'm regretting it. I shrug. "Not much to do about it except wait for it to heal. Tomorrow, I'll wear a hood. It just felt nice to have the breeze and the sunlight on my face."

It was really the only nice thing about today.

"I should have left you safe in the tower," he mutters to himself. "Let me see your feet."

"I wouldn't have stayed," I retort. And I'm wrong, anyway—the sunlight wasn't the only nice thing about today. Being with him is always wonderful. I peek at him as he kneels in front of me, lifting my skirt and taking one of my aching feet in his hand.

He frowns down at them as if they've somehow failed me and then pulls one shoe off. "These are useless."

"I noticed." I wince when even more sand falls from inside the shoe, even though we left the beach hours ago. "They weren't fun to walk in."

"I will fix them for you before we leave in the morning." As if it's his job to tend to me, Nemeth wipes sand away from my toes and then rubs my foot, tsking at the red marks and blisters on my skin. "Tomorrow, when you get tired, I will carry you."

A thoughtful offer, but it's one that makes my mind spin into uncomfortable territory. We walked all day today, most of it in pensive silence. But the silence bothers me less than the fact that I have a winged man at my side . . . and we *walked*. Not once did he spread his wings except to shield me from the rain. "Can I ask you a question?"

He looks up from my foot, his eyes glowing. "What is it?"

"I hope this isn't too personal, but . . . your wings. You didn't try to fly today?"

Nemeth is silent for a long moment. He continues to rub my foot, sending skitters of pleasure up my spine. He's thoughtful as he continues to rub, and he eventually speaks. "When we first arrived in the tower, I thought of nothing but my freedom—of the day I would see wide-open skies above me and fly into the air. Most of Darkfell's mountains are hollow. Did you know that? The main caverns are hundreds of handspans high and riddled with tunnels and caves, so we can fly back and forth between each other's homes. There are very few stairs because they are not needed except for the elderly and infirm. I always flew at home. Even at the Alabaster Citadel, my room was situated in a tower on one of the highest parapets. All I had to do was open a window, and I could fly out. I flew constantly. It was as necessary as breathing. And then . . . "

He pauses.

"And then you were trapped in a horrible tower for two years because of the name you were born with," I say bitterly.

"No," Nemeth says quietly. "And then I met someone who showed me that perhaps it is not so bad to be on the ground. It is all about the company."

I reach over and flick his shoulder. "That's a lovely story."

He smiles at me.

"And we both know it's dragon shite," I continue, my voice tart.

Nemeth's smile widens into a grin. He laughs, and some of the unease I've felt all day melts away. "It's not all dragon shite. I do enjoy being with you."

"Are you afraid to try out your wing?"

He goes back to rubbing my foot, thinking. "It feels tight," he admits after a moment. "It has for some time. Like it's pulled taut in one spot. I'm afraid that I could damage it further if I try to use it without a healer looking at it. And as long as I don't try it out, I don't know how bad it could be. I can delay the truth for another day."

"Oh, Nemeth." My heart aches for him. "I'm so sorry. I wish I could have fixed it better for you."

He shakes his head. "You did the very best you could. That is all anyone could ask for." He sets my foot down and picks up my other, dusting it free of sand and then rubbing it as well. "How can I be upset? We have had to fend for ourselves for two years." Tilting his head, he studies my face. "Which reminds me. We should heat your potion soon."

"Soon," I agree, and then wiggle my foot in his grasp. It feels good, the foot rub, but it also feels like a distraction, as if he's determined to pull me away from a difficult conversation. "Tomorrow?"

"Tomorrow what?"

I wiggle my foot again to get his attention. "Tomorrow you'll try to fly? For me?"

"You must truly hate walking."

That does it. Exasperated, I pull my foot out of his grasp and lean forward to cup his face so he'll look me in the eye. Why is it this man can lick my pussy with the confidence of a court lothario but gets shy when I ask about his wings? I meet his gaze, stroking his cheek. "It's not about walking. It's about knowing our limitations so we know what we have to push past in the future. Just because your wing is tight now doesn't mean it always will be. It just gives you something to overcome."

He smiles at me, his cheeks stretching. "How is it that you can make me feel so calm? Even on a day such as today?"

"Because we're together," I tell him. "We're taking control of our destinies. Even if the Golden Moon Goddess frowns down upon us, maybe the Gray God will look after us."

Nemeth gestures at the rickety barn. "He led us to this, did he not?"

"He could have led us to an inn," I say tartly, but I let a smile curve my lips. "But this will do for now. So tomorrow morning, you'll fly for me, and then we'll see how to proceed from there. It's decided."

"Stubborn mule," he says, his voice loving. "But fine. In the morning, I will fly, and we will see how it goes."

"If you really want to speed up our travel, is it safe for you to slide through the shadows? Like you did in the tower?" I bite my lip because it feels strange to even ask. The magic of it unnerves me, but he said it was safe as long as the area was wide open and visible, and our surroundings certainly are. "But only if it's safe."

This time, the look in his eyes grows dark. He shakes his head. "I'm not certain I wish to risk it. When we crossed the water, something felt different from the last time I carried you."

"Different?" Everything inside me clenches. Has he figured it out?

Has Nemeth discovered my secret already? Does he know I'm pregnant? I keep my eyes wide with innocence, my face carefully blank. "Teleporting me feels different? How?"

He shrugs. "It's hard to explain. All I know is I don't wish to try it again. We're not supposed to shadow-glide with a human anyhow."

I want to tell him that I have Fellian blood. That somewhere down the line, one of my ancestors—likely the legendary Ravendor herself—had sex with a Fellian and gave birth to his child. I want to tell him that I'm pregnant with his child too . . . but the words won't come. They stick in my throat like honey. I'm afraid something will change between us. That he'll realize I'm more fragile than he anticipated and leave me behind.

The thought terrifies me. I grab his hand and put a smile on my face to hide my fear. "I can walk."

We gaze at each other for a long moment, and I scarcely dare breathe for fear he'll read the secret on my face.

"Your medicine," Nemeth finally says. "Are you ready for it?"

I nod. Anything to divert the conversation.

He pulls out the bag full of my carefully cleaned medical supplies—the needles, the syringe, the cloths, and finally, the vials of prepared potion that have to be warmed. I watch, wordless, as he starts a fire with a flick of magic. It burns inside the small pot we brought for such things, and he holds the vial over the flames for just a moment before attaching the needle to the end and flicking it to ensure there are no air bubbles. I untie my sleeve and roll it up, and we use a sip of our precious drinking water to wash my arm.

Nemeth readies the syringe and then gazes at me with a somber expression. "I'm sorry I cannot be a better mate to you, Candra. You deserve a prince with two working wings and stronger magic, but instead, you got me."

What? Does he think I asked about his wing because I'm mad at him for not flying?

Before he can administer my shot, I push his hand aside. "Wait a moment."

He looks surprised at my hesitation. "Are you in pain? Do you need to vomit? Shall I find a bucket?" He glances around, getting to his feet. "Give me a moment—"

I slide forward onto my knees and hold him by his leg. "Stop."

"Stop what?"

"Stop doubting yourself." I gaze up at him. "I don't care that you can't fly. I only asked because I know it's hard for you. I don't care if you don't have huge magic. I don't have any. I don't care if we have to walk every step of the way to Castle Lios. I just want to be with you. We're in this together, the both of us. Every step of the way. Understand?" I cling to his leg, pressing my cheek against his strong, strangely bent thigh. I run my hands up and down his leg. I wonder if our child will have knees that bend backward like Nemeth's or if they will be like mine. I wonder if they will have wings.

I wonder if they will have his huge, giving heart.

I brush my lips over his skin. "I love you, Nemeth. I don't want anyone but you. Understand? You and I are doing the best we can, no matter the situation. None of this is what was expected to happen. We were supposed to stay in the tower, but they were also supposed to bring us food. Now we've left, and we'll figure it out. All of it. But I don't want you to blame yourself. Not when you're the best thing in my life."

His hand lands atop my head, and I don't even mind that it brushes over my sunburn. His fingers dig into my braid, his remaining claws tugging at my hair. "I would do anything for you," he rasps. "You know that, yes?"

I love the hunger in his tone, the yearning. And even though I'm weary and sunburned, I want nothing more than to touch my mate right now, to pleasure him and show him how much I adore him. I slide my hand up under his kilt, brushing my fingers over the linen wrap underneath. "I want you."

"Now? After the day we've had?" When I nod, he groans, and as I stroke my fingers over his cock, I can feel it hardening in my grasp. "I cannot give you my knot, *milettahn*. We do not dare the enemy to find us locked together and helpless."

"Then don't give me your knot," I whisper, rubbing him through the fabric. "Just let me suck on you and give you pleasure."

Nemeth groans, and I know he can't resist.

I stroke him harder, gazing up. "Take your kilt off for me?"

He nods and quickly divests himself of his belt and then the kilt itself. The linen wrap goes next; all the while, I grab the pack I'd been sitting upon earlier and use it as a footstool. Now, when I'm on my knees, I'm the right height to pleasure my massive, tall mate. I sigh with anticipation at the sight of him naked, his cock rigid in front of me, his knot not yet full. Unable to help myself, I reach out and clasp him in my hands, rubbing my face against his shaft.

"I love this," I whisper. "Love the feel of you in my hands, your hot skin against mine." I run my cheek along his cock, just enjoying the feel of his hardness. "Love knowing that this is mine to play with." Just touching him makes me ache, my pulse throbbing between my thighs. I could cheerfully worship his cock all night long, but something tells me he's going to want more than just me rubbing on him like a kitten for hours. I grip him at the base, looking up at my mate's glowing green eyes. I love the way he watches me as I lick him from knot to tip, then swirl my tongue around the head. A burst of pre-cum flavors his skin, and I lap it up, not surprised when another droplet replaces the first. He's perfect, my beautiful Nemeth, the tapered tip of his cock all but begging for me to suck upon it.

So, I do. I'm not one to deprive myself, after all.

I take him into my mouth and love the ragged sound he makes. Love that his hand carefully tightens in my hair. Love the sharp inhale of breath when I tongue the underside of his cock and then suck him deeper into my throat. I work him with my mouth and tongue, my hand squeezing over his now-taut knot. And as I do, I gaze up at him as if he's the only thing in my world because I know he likes to watch my face when I suck on him.

Nemeth's eyes are fierce with need as he watches me. I suck him deeper, even though my jaw aches from the size of him, and the head of his cock buts against the back of my throat. My eyes water, and saliva pools at the corners of my mouth, and still, I take him, my gaze locked on his.

"Candra," he breathes, his voice reverent even as he rocks gently, shuttling into my mouth. His movements are careful, but I don't want him to be careful. I want him unhinged. I want him lost in the moment. We both need to forget about the stress of today.

So, I hike my skirts up and slip a hand between my thighs, stroking my clit even as his hand settles heavier on my head.

"Greedy thing," he mutters and then shows me that I'm not the only greedy one. He pushes on my head, forcing me to take more, and drool slides down my chin. He thrusts again, and I make a low noise around the cock stuffed in my mouth, my fingers moving faster over my clit. I can't even get close to his knot, but it doesn't matter. All that matters is that he's using me, fucking my mouth with his quick, jerking motions, and I love it. I love that he's got a firm hold on my head now, his cock hammering against the back of my throat as he works toward his release. I love the grunts he makes, love how stretched my lips are, how red-hot his knot feels under my grip. I whimper as I rub my clit harder, close to the edge. I just need a little more—

Nemeth's breath hitches, and then he lets out a low, guttural sound. In the next moment, my mouth floods with his release, his knot like a rock beneath my grasp. I immediately lose my orgasm, drawing back and coughing as his seed fills my mouth. He spills over my face and then onto the front of my dress as I draw back with one hand still on his cock, squeezing his knot the way I know he likes. I murmur his name over and over again as I milk him, not caring that my traveling dress is ruined. It's just a dress, and Nemeth's need at this moment is far more important than anything else. "I love you," I tell him, gazing up adoringly with my messy face. I'm hit with a surge of emotion so intense it brings tears to my eyes. "I love you so very much."

He groans again, then covers my hand, squeezing his cock one last time before heaving a tremendous sigh of release. His fingers stroke my cheek as he catches his breath, and I use my hem to wipe my face clean of his spend. His knot is swollen now, aching and huge, and I run my fingers over it, making him shudder with aftershocks of pleasure. It takes time for his knot to go down, and I can probably make him come again just by teasing it with light, stroking touches as he waits.

But Nemeth pulls me away with gentle hands, shaking his head. He drops to kneel beside me, pressing kisses on my face despite the fact that I've just wiped away his cum. "You are incredible," he tells me. "The most perfect, beautiful, talented creature."

"I am pretty great," I tease, running my hands over his chest. "It's all true."

He captures my mouth again and nips at my upper lip. "Did you make yourself come?"

"Not quite, alas. My fingers weren't fast enough." I'm feeling playful and more like myself despite our rather dreadful surroundings. *This is who I am,* I remind myself. A sexually confident tease who is loved by a big, delicious, winged Fellian. In or out of the tower, that won't change.

"A shame," Nemeth tells me between light, hungry kisses. "Luckily for you, I know where to find a mouth to finish the job."

"Now, that sounds like an excellent idea. Should I lie on my back?"

He looks around us, eyeing the moldy straw. With a quick kiss, he releases me and tears open one of our packed bags, digging out a blanket and spreading it over the ground. "Here," he says, voice gruff and his eyes a deep, delicious, sated shade of green. "Lie down for me."

I don't need to be told twice. In the next moment, I'm on the blanket, wriggling with anticipation when he pushes my skirts up faster than I can haul them to my waist. He tugs my bloomers down, tearing at the delicate fabric with his remaining claws, and then his face disappears between my thighs. My breath catches in my throat as his hungry mouth latches onto my clit, going straight for the best part. With a moan, I cling to the sleek horns that arc back from his brow, trying to find something to hold on to. "Just like that, Nemeth," I pant. "Gods, your mouth is so good."

"Look at how wet you are," he rasps between decadent licks of my cunt. "I love that touching me makes you so slick with need. All of this just because you sucked my cock?"

I whimper when he laps at my clit. "I like sucking your cock."

"Clearly." A thick finger pushes inside me—one of the ones he keeps shorn short so he doesn't claw me. He tongues my clit again and strokes his finger in and out of me, working me. I huff with need and rock against his hand, and this time, he doesn't lift his mouth to talk. He just keeps sucking and licking, and the orgasm that was so close crashes over me with fierce intensity. I cry out, clinging to him as the ripples of pleasure wash through me until his tongue no longer feels pleasant but too sensitive. I gently tug him away, and Nemeth crawls over me, pressing one more wet kiss to my mouth—his lips tasting of my cunt—and then collapses next to me.

I slowly tug my skirts down, thinking of all the washing I'm going to have to do. Maybe I'll just throw away this dress. I can't very well return to Castle Lios in a gown that reeks of sex and is covered in dried cum. I have another dress packed away . . . somewhere. And I won't need these gowns when we return to the castle. I'll have my wardrobe back and Riza and Nurse. I want that so badly I can taste it, and I sigh happily, turning and tucking myself against Nemeth's big form. It's probably a fantasy, but for now I'm going to live in that dream.

"Candra," my mate murmurs, stroking my braided hair.

"Hmm?"

"I . . . " He hesitates, then holds me tighter against him. "It's nothing. Just me worrying."

Well, now that makes two of us. "What were you going to say?"

"Nothing," he replies. "Nothing at all."

It takes everything I have not to touch my stomach. Has he figured it out?

. . . but no. If he knew, he'd say something, wouldn't he?

Surely?

CHAPTER THIRTY-SEVEN

I wake up to the sound of thunder crackling overhead and what sounds like rocks smashing against our flimsy shelter. Hail, I realize as I see a sprinkling of icy-looking pebbles outside. Beside me, Nemeth sits up, tense and uneasy. His wing is spread over me protectively, keeping me safe from the drips of rain that leak in through our shelter. "Good morning," I say, rising slightly. My face feels hot and tight, thanks to the sunburn. "I see we have great weather for our travel."

"The goddess has sent an angry storm to greet us," Nemeth says, and when he jerks at a faint crack of thunder, I feel a wave of sympathy for him.

He doesn't like storms, even in the protected halls of the tower. I can only imagine how loud and terrifying this must be. I reach over and touch his arm. "If this is the worst the goddess has for us, I'll consider us lucky."

"Mmm," is all he says, and I can tell he's unnerved by the ferocity of the storm. It does seem a little stronger than expected, but I also don't spend a lot of time outside in storms myself. This barn isn't much of a shelter either. The entire thing sways with a strong breeze. "We should wait the storm out," Nemeth tells me. "Hopefully, it will not last too long."

"I'm fine with waiting. It's not as if I want to go traipsing about in the mud anyhow." I hug one of the blankets tighter around my shoulders, watching the storm—and my lover. Nemeth had been in a good mood last night after our fooling around. He'd given me my medicine, and then we snuggled together in the blankets. This morning he seems on edge, though. I nudge him. "Don't think that a storm means you're getting out of flying. I want to see you in the skies."

The look he gives me is downright cranky.

I ignore it and drape his arm over my shoulders.

He gives in, tucking me under his arm and rubbing my back. "Ask your knife if this storm will last all day. We do not have enough of your medicine to linger in one place for long."

Right. We have a week of medicine. After that, I'm out, and I don't know how long it's going to take us to get to the capital of Lios and the palace itself. "If it keeps raining, we can just walk in the rain." But I pull out my knife from its sheath that I've kept tucked tight in my cleavage and hold it in my hand. "Hello, knife. Is this storm going to last all day?"

The knife is still.

I give Nemeth a smug look. "See? The knife wants you to fly too."

His expression remains grave. "Ask it if the weather is because of the goddess. If she's angry."

I bite my lip because I hate the big questions. I'm never ready for the answers. I hold the knife, squeezing my eyes shut. "Is the goddess angry at us?"

Cringing, I wait for the knife to shudder. It does nothing.

I gasp and look over at Nemeth, delighted. "That's a no, right?"

"It's not a yes. That's all." He still looks pensive, his mouth hard. "I don't understand. We disobeyed. Shouldn't the goddess be furious at us?"

But I'm giddy, my heart fluttering with relief. "I'll change the wording, then." I concentrate on the knife. "Is the goddess angry?"

Shiver. *Yes.*

My stomach plummets again. "The goddess is angry, but not at us?"

Again, a shiver of affirmation.

I look over at Nemeth. "She's angry, all right. Maybe she's furious that they forgot us and we were forced to leave?"

He doesn't look convinced. "I don't know. I don't have the answers for any of this."

Me neither. I think for a moment longer, then ask, "Does anyone know we've left the tower?"

No shiver.

I suppose that's a good thing. "Will we get to Lios in under seven days at the rate we're traveling?"

No shiver.

Oh. I fight back panic because there's no sense in it. We knew I was low on medicine. I look over at Nemeth. "I guess we need to speed up."

My mate nods. He gets to his feet and shakes his wings out. "I don't mind walking in the rain."

Me neither. I need to walk for as long as I can, for as far as I can, and then hope that Nemeth can carry me. "Once the hail stops, we can go."

It's a miserable journey. My face is hot with sunburn and hurts despite the constant rain, as do my hands and scalp. The wet weather isn't all that soothing, as it soaks our clothes and turns the road into mud. I scrub at my dress as we walk, trying to get the worst of the cum stains out using the rain. I suppose that the good news is that when it dries, it'll be so wrinkled and unsightly that no one will notice a few stains.

The land around us remains flat and rocky, with only a few scrubby bushes and very few trees to break up the landscape. It's rather unpleasant, but there are distant hills that hint at a change in scenery, at least.

"Does any of this look familiar to you?" Nemeth asks me.

I shake my head. "I was too miserable to pay attention to the scenery when I was brought here," I admit. "I vaguely recall following the coast and driving through a few little towns along the way."

"Well, we're following the coast," Nemeth agrees, gesturing at the horizon to the east, where just out of sight, the waters of the sea gleam invitingly.

"Perhaps a boat?" I ask. "To speed up our travel?" I'm all too aware that the knife says we won't get to the castle in time. We need a way to speed up somehow, to walk faster . . . something. Anything.

"Do you know how to sail?" Nemeth asks me.

"Well . . . no. Do you?"

His brows go up. "Candra . . . my people live *inside* a mountain."

"Is that a no, then?" I joke.

He stares at me, and then his big shoulders shake with laughter. A chuckle rumbles out of him, and the heavy pack on his back jostles with the force of his laughter. I smile as I walk at his side, pleased that with everything we're experiencing, I can still make him laugh. "It's not as if we're knee deep in boats anyhow," I admit. "I'm just trying to think of alternatives to walking."

"We will figure something out," he promises me.

—

After a soggy midday meal, the rain finally eases off. My clothing begins to dry, and my fingers no longer resemble dried prunes. The sun comes out, and the temperature immediately changes from cool and pleasant (if wet) to steamy and overly warm.

Doesn't matter. It's clear; that's all I care about. When I spot a large boulder by the roadside, I immediately head for it, climbing atop a few smaller rocks and then sitting down atop it with my damp skirts spread.

"Time for a rest?" Nemeth asks. "I can carry you if you're too tired to keep going."

"I'm fine," I lie because I'm tired as shite and want nothing more than to crawl back to that tumbledown shed, moldy hay and all. But I give Nemeth a bright smile and gesture at his pack. "You can take that off for now since you're going to try flying."

"I am?" He arches a heavy brow at me.

"You are," I say firmly. "You'll never know unless you try."

He doesn't look eager, though. "I could spare myself the humiliation and ask your blade if I can fly."

"Or . . . you can just do it anyhow. I promise not to laugh." I clasp my hands tightly in my lap so he doesn't see how anxious I am. It's my fault that his wing is scarred, after all. He was wounded saving me, and on top of that, I'm the one who stitched it up. If it's all wrong, it's doubly my fault. But I keep my tone bright. "After all, I can't fly a lick, so anything you do is far better than anything I could manage. Give it a try, love. There's no one here to see but me."

Nemeth scowls in my direction, but he takes the pack off and sets it down at the base of the boulder, out of the mud. I hold my breath as he takes a few steps out, rotating his arms as if he's about to enter battle and needs his muscles loose. First, one arm, and then the other. He's breathtaking, his shoulders as broad as the day I first saw him, and if he's lost any muscle, I wouldn't know it. Hasn't he done his exercises faithfully every day? Hasn't he stretched his wings constantly, trying to keep them in shape?

I hope it's not for nothing. If I could make his wings work simply by worrying, he'd be airborne right now.

Nemeth spreads his wings with a ripple, and everything inside me clenches. Gods, his wings are enormous. I stare in fascination, wondering if this is the first time I've seen him spread them like this. He's always been confined by the tower, and the ceilings and halls weren't nearly big enough for him. His wingspan is enormous, easily twice as wide as he is tall, and my heart aches at the sight of the dull, pink stripe that slashes across the membrane of one. His scar. He's right; it appears tight there, the membrane taut and unpleasant looking around it. As I watch, he strains one wing and then stretches the other out, trying to match it. The scarred wing won't go out as far as the other.

He turns to look at me, and I can see the uncertainty in his eyes. I won't show him my distress. Instead, I beam as if my heart isn't breaking inside and give him an encouraging gesture. "Go on! You'll do wonderfully."

Nemeth nods and closes his eyes. Then, his powerful legs seem to bunch up, his wings folding in, and he flings himself upward, launching into the air.

I hold my breath, watching as he immediately flicks his wings out the moment he's in the air, flapping to gain height. His movements are awkward, the one wing clearly crippling him. He flounders, listing to one side, and I press a fist to my lips so I don't scream aloud. But then he rights himself, and, wobbling through the air, he manages to keep flying. His wings beat with heavy, strong waves, and he stays in the air. I watch as he soars higher, and even though it isn't a pretty flight or a fast one, it's still flight, and I'm proud of him.

Hands clasped over my heart, I watch as he circles high in the skies, flying so far away that he looks like a drunken bird. I'm not worried—I know he'll come back for me. When he disappears from sight, I adjust my skirts to dry them in the sunlight and make sure my head is covered with my hood so I don't sunburn any more than I have.

Nemeth isn't gone for very long. When I look up again, he's returning, his flight obvious by the jerky movement of his wings. I watch him with pride, waving as he approaches. To a normal human, he might look fearsome, a dark-gray demon with bat wings come to steal them away from their home, an evil Fellian monster. But I can see the pride on his face as he comes to a clumsy landing on the boulder beside me. I can also see the sheen of sweat on his skin, and I know that flight was harder for him than he'd ever let on. "You were magnificent," I tell him proudly. "Utterly magnificent."

"Dragon shite," he says, crouching low and panting. But he grins, displaying his fangs. "It was terrible, and I'm pretty sure I strained something in my back, but I could fly. That's one worry handled."

"How did your repaired wing do?"

"It's weak," he admits. "Weak, and the damaged section pulls constantly when I beat my wings. But I'm hoping with time, it'll grow as strong as the other once more." He scrubs a hand down his sweaty face but then grins at me. "It still felt amazing."

"I'm so glad." I could burst with how happy I am for him. "I knew you could do it."

"It doesn't change anything," he admits. "I'm not strong enough yet to carry you, and we have to be careful. If any humans see me, they might shoot first and ask questions later."

That's not something I considered. Here I've been encouraging him to fly, and I never stopped to think how dangerous it might be. He's the enemy, in enemy territory, and by now, Lios would have attacked Darkfell and declared war. Lionel had been slavering to launch his army of ships and conquer the riches he imagines Darkfell's mountains hold. I should have asked my knife if the war had been successful, but I'd been too much of a coward, and now I don't have a moment to myself to inquire quietly.

I should just tell him everything I know about the war. I should. I don't know what I'm waiting for. "Nemeth . . . "

He straightens to his full height. "Speaking of humans, I saw a settlement to the north. We should head there."

"What? Why?" Hot panic flares in my chest. "Didn't you just say humans would attack you? If there's a settlement, I'm thinking we should avoid it entirely."

Nemeth shakes his head. "You need supplies for your potion. We need food. You need better shoes. We need a decent place to sleep. And if it's a small settlement, perhaps we should test the waters anyhow. See how they react to my presence."

"Liosians hate Fellians, remember?" I remind him, panicked. "You can't go into a human settlement, Nemeth. You just can't." This entire plan suddenly seems the height of stupidity. What made me think I could just stroll back to Castle Lios with a Fellian at my side and assume it would all be fine? I've got an enemy husband . . . and a baby on the way. The thought of something happening to either of them is horrifying.

This is a nightmare. Why didn't I think this through? Why am I taking him to a war zone where he's the enemy?

I grab his hands, frantic. "We should go to your people instead. We can still go back. We'll return to the tower and head to Darkfell—"

"Love," Nemeth says softly. "I know it's dangerous."

I suddenly want to cry. "I'm tired of dangerous, Nemeth."

"I know." He pats my hand. "Let us see who is in this settlement. If they try to attack, I will fly out of reach. You will be safe. They would not dare harm their princess." He pulls me to my feet atop the rock. "And we need supplies."

My head is full of old stories as we approach the village. Every Vestalin knows all the stories of those who lived in the tower, of the Royal Offerings from times past. I think of all the tales of those who left the tower early and the angry mobs that met them. I used to side with the angry villagers too. What sort of selfish piece of dragon shite would abandon the tower, knowing they were condemning the entire world to famine and flood?

But now *I* am that selfish piece of dragon shite.

And I really do not want to be killed by pitchfork-wielding villagers.

We wear our heavy cloaks despite the steamy heat of the afternoon just so we can try to hide Nemeth's wings until the last moment. I keep my magical blade tight in my hand, just in case I need to stab someone for threatening my mate.

All my worry is for nothing. The village is deserted.

No one comes out to greet us. The fields we pass are fallow and overgrown with weeds. There are no cattle, no dogs, not even a single scurrying rat to cross the muddy streets. There are no crops, and the only vegetation other than weeds is a sapling at the far end of town. It's completely empty, and what's worse, it looks as if it's been empty for a while. The thatched roofs are falling in, and a broken cart in the middle of the street looks long abandoned.

There won't be any food here.

In a way, I'm relieved. Nemeth lowers his hood, exposing the sharp planes of his gray face and his horns, and there's no one here to see. "Abandoned."

"Looks like," I agree, and gesture at the three small altars to the gods nearby. They're overgrown and covered in windblown dirt, just like the last ones. "I don't think whoever lived here left recently either."

"Then they won't mind if we search for food," Nemeth tells me. "Let's check these houses for anything we can use."

It feels wrong to even consider it, but I know he's being practical. If it was left behind, it's fair game. Our supplies must be running lower than I thought. It starts to rain again, a heavy downpour, and we wordlessly split up to look around.

I duck into the first house. I would have called it a hovel back in my court days, but I've got a new appreciation for rough living after my time in the tower. Despite the fact that these people didn't have much, everything is put away. There are no plates on the table, and the lone, sad-looking bed is made. There's no food to be found either. I check in every pot. I check the root cellar. Nothing. The next house is much the same, and bewildered, I head out to find Nemeth. He stands at the center of the cluster of houses in the heavy rain, his gaze thoughtful.

"There's nothing here," I say to him as I approach. I pull my hood over my head, annoyed by the constant rain pattering on my face. "No food. No people. They didn't leave in a hurry either. They're just . . . gone."

He gives me an uneasy look. "I found something."

Uh-oh. I don't like that expression on his face. "What?" I ask warily. "What is it?"

"Come," he says, putting a hand on my shoulder to steer me. "And . . . stay close."

Oh no.

He leads me to the edge of the small settlement, and the rain begins to come down harder. Everything around us is turning into one big, muddy puddle, but that can't be the reason everyone left. The worry of it keeps turning over in my mind, and I'm so focused on trying to understand the problem that it takes me a moment to realize Nemeth has paused.

I look up . . . and gasp.

What I thought was a sad-looking tree at the edge of town isn't a tree at all. It's a large stake, and spitted upon it is the desiccated corpse of a Fellian. His wings have been cut off, and the remnants of his kilt flutter in the breeze. The stake has been lodged between his thighs, and the tip of it protrudes from his mouth, his head bent backward, his horns shorn off.

I have no words. I just stare.

"I guess that answers if I will be welcomed or not," Nemeth says in a low voice.

"Gods," I whisper, clutching my knife tightly. "Who would do this?"

"Liosians, obviously." His tone is hard. "Who else?"

But why? I want to ask. Why be so cruel? But I know the answer already. If the supposedly erudite, learned courts of Lios considered the Fellians devils and pure evil, what must the crude, uneducated villages think? They wouldn't stop to ask if a Fellian was lost or needed help. They'd kill first and ask questions later.

Then again, how do I know he was lost and looking for help? Maybe he came here to attack and was dispatched by the village. Am I automatically just assuming the Fellian is kind and understanding because of Nemeth?

Maybe I'm more of a traitor than I thought.

CHAPTER THIRTY-EIGHT

It continues to rain on us for the rest of the day.

After the discovery of the dead Fellian—the only person we've seen, dead or alive—we don't want to stay near the abandoned village. We walk on, even though the weather is unpleasant. It continues to grow even more unpleasant throughout the day, the rain falling so heavily that I can't see farther than my outstretched hand. My teeth chatter with the cold, and walking becomes even more of a chore, the mud so thick it sucks at my feet.

Everything around us has turned into a swamp. This has to be the goddess's wrath. Just like my knife said, she's angry, and she's taking it out on the world around us. Horrible guilt sweeps through me and I feel responsible anyhow. Like it's my fault the goddess is angry. I want to cry . . . except I don't want to add to the wetness falling from the sky.

I'll cry when I'm nice and dry and relaxed, I tell myself.

That night, we sleep out in the open because there's nowhere else to go. It rains on us the entire time, and even though Nemeth spreads a wing protectively over me, I'm soaked to the bone. It's the most miserable night I've ever spent, and when it continues to pour rain in the morning, I dread taking another step in my soaked shoes.

"Our food supplies are soaked," Nemeth tells me as he hands over a strip of bloated jerky. "The vegetables are going to rot if this keeps up. Actually, everything will."

I stare at the bit of grayish jerky, and my stomach gives a queasy flip. Before I can hand it back, my mouth fills with saliva. I have just enough time to turn my head and bend over before the contents of my stomach come up. Nemeth wraps a strong arm around my waist, holding me so I don't collapse in the mud. It takes forever for the vomiting to cease, and when it does, I'm left weak and shaky.

"Candra?" Nemeth asks, worry in his voice. "Are you all right?"

I manage a nod. "I'm fine. I don't think I can eat, though." My stomach roils at the thought. "Maybe just some water."

He holds me while I sip and wash my mouth out. It takes several minutes for the nausea to abate, but then I feel much better. I straighten and give Nemeth a weary smile. "Shall we keep going?"

"You're sick, aren't you?"

"No, I'm okay."

"Candra, don't lie to me. Is it your potion? Is it not working as it should?" The look on his face is frantic. "Do you need another dose?"

I shake my head. "It's not the potion. I just . . . I don't want to eat water-bloated food supplies."

"That might be all we have left soon." He glances up at the sky. "This rain is never ending."

The goddess is punishing the world right now. Maybe she's upset about the war. Maybe she's going to rain us right out of our cities and sweep us all out to sea. Never mind that we didn't want to leave until we had to. "Let's keep going."

"I'm worried about you, *milettahn*." Nemeth doesn't let go of me. "If you're sick . . . "

"I'm sure it's just the weather," I lie. I need to ask my knife questions to make sure Nemeth won't be upset that I'm pregnant. I don't want him to feel I lied or that I'm using him. Or worse, trapping him at my side.

I have to tell him today, for better or for worse. I just need to find the right moment.

Not right now, I decide. I need to gather my courage first. Because if Nemeth is furious with me, I don't know what I'll do.

We find another abandoned town close to sunset. This one is bigger than the last but just as empty. We call out, looking for anyone who lives nearby, but our search is fruitless. The only thing we find is a recently deceased cow with stiff legs stuck in the mud. It looks so skinny and unhealthy that we avoid going near it. The one bright point in this town? No dead Fellians.

Nemeth picks out a small home in the midst of a cluster of houses. It's got a decent thatched roof, and when we step inside, the never-ending rain isn't pouring from the ceiling. "We'll stay here tonight," he tells me.

I'm too tired and soaked to protest. As weird as it is to think of spending the evening in a stranger's bed, it's warm and dry, and that's all I care about. Nemeth barricades the door and covers the windows, latching the creaky wooden shutters. Strangely enough, I find being boxed in like this comforting. It reminds me a bit of the tower and its thick, impenetrable walls.

"We can't make a fire tonight, Candra," my mate tells me. "With our luck, the rain would clear, and then everyone would see our chimney smoking." He digs through a trunk at the foot of one of the beds. "There are plenty of blankets, though. We can spread out our clothes and hope they dry a bit."

I don't need to be told twice. As Nemeth pulls out one of his lamps and taps it to turn it on, I strip off my soaked layers. The room is frigid—two days of rain has made the air chilly and unpleasant. And I shiver as I wrap myself in a musty wool blanket. I sit on the bed and watch as Nemeth spreads out our possessions around the cottage, trying to dry everything. Our foodstuffs are a pathetically small bundle, but I know from checking the cottages that there's no food here. There's no food anywhere.

As if he can read my mind, Nemeth comes to my side with a sodden bit of traveling cake full of the last of our nuts. He holds it out to me. "Eat this. You haven't eaten all day."

"Neither have you," I point out, but I take it from him.

The traveling cake is wet and unpleasant in my hand, and I wrinkle my nose. I don't want to eat it, but I know I have to eat something. Without food in my stomach, my medicine will make me dizzy. And I'm carrying a child . . .

Gingerly, I take a small, mushy bite. "Yum yum."

Satisfied that I'm eating, he turns back to the table and continues spreading out our supplies to dry. "It'll be less wet in the morning, but you can't wait that long between meals. This is hard enough on you as it is."

On . . . me? We're in this together. It's hard for both of us. I eye him skeptically as I take another wet bite. "Do you think everyone's gone because of the war?"

Nemeth pauses, thinking. "It seems doubtful. A benevolent ruler might let his people know that they'd be safe behind the protected walls of his capital. Does that seem like something Lionel would do?"

Lionel? Benevolent? The thought is ludicrous. "I once watched Lionel grind a piece of crust under his boot just so the poor wouldn't have a scrap from the king's plate."

"So that's a no." Nemeth turns to me with a wry look.

"It's definitely a no." I glance around me at the small house. It's no more than two rooms, but they're tidy rooms. Whoever lived here before was proud of their home. The wooden shutters over the windows are carved, and the quilt on the bed is clearly the result of many hours of tedious work. "Why would someone leave their home behind? With all their things?"

"Perhaps they did not have a choice." Nemeth shrugs off his cloak and hangs it over the back of a chair.

"So . . . that has to be the war, right?"

"If the war called up the men, why are the women and children not here? Where are the elders? The infirm?" Nemeth shakes his head. "Something has happened, and everyone has left this place behind."

"If I didn't know better, I'd say it's the rain," I grumble, hugging the blanket closer to my chest. "Nothing can grow in the fields when everything's a mud pit. But the goddess wouldn't have cast her wrath down on anyone until we left the tower, and that was just a few days ago. These people have been gone for a while." I run my finger on the edge of the bed frame and the dust there. "Maybe it's food. Remember the men who came to the tower?"

Nemeth turns and arches a brow at me. His scarred wing flicks. "I have not forgotten."

"Right. Sorry." I give him an apologetic smile. "I'm just thinking out loud."

"I like hearing it. Your voice is always a pleasant one." He moves to the far side of the table and unhooks his belt, removing his sodden kilt. "Continue."

I watch him undress, distracted. "Those men came looking for food. They knew we had some and were willing to try to steal it from us. And then after that, we received no supplies. Maybe there was no food to bring us? Maybe everyone's been hungry, and that's why they're all gone."

Nemeth considers for a moment. "War would definitely slow down trade, and if there was a blockade, I could see food not getting through. And then we have the weather." He wrings out the edge of his cloak, and water spatters all over the floor. "But if that's what has happened, where did all these people flee to in the hopes that they would be fed?"

I think. "They would assume the capital has food. That's where I'd go. Just show up, and even if the king didn't feed me, I'd hope someone else would. My sister Erynne is always complaining that there are people showing up from far-flung countries with their hands out."

His brow furrows. "Your sister does not sound much better than her husband."

At times, she really doesn't. I know it's because she's trying to see the big picture instead of individuals, that when more people show up at the castle needing handouts, it puts a strain on resources, but sometimes you have to think with your heart and not your head. I think about the poison Erynne sent me to use on Nemeth and wonder if she's locked her heart away permanently.

If so, that's a sad thing for a ruler. "She's probably not as bad as I make her sound."

I hope.

Nemeth glances at our surroundings. His wings give an agitated little shiver, and then he folds them tightly against his back. "This roof seems to have held together, and this cottage is comfortable enough for you, isn't it?" He touches the high back of one of the wooden chairs. "There is no seating for those with wings, but I imagine for a human, it's quite cozy." His gaze slides to me. "Perhaps you need to stay here for a few days while I travel ahead and hunt some supplies."

"What? No. Absolutely not."

"Be reasonable, Candra." Nemeth crosses the room and crouches at my side. He takes my hands in his larger ones. "This travel is unpleasant, and you're not as strong as me. If it's miserable for me, I can only imagine how awful it is for you." He rubs my hands, gazing into my eyes. "I could leave the foodstuffs with you, and you would have to administer your potion yourself for a time, but—"

I shake my head. "No, Nemeth. You can't leave me. I'm the only chance you've got. Think of what they did to the Fellian at the last village."

He grimaces. "I haven't forgotten. But I could slide through shadows, steal from people if they won't welcome me—"

"And then you'll be as bad as the rumors make Fellians sound! No. We're a team, remember? We're doing all of this together." I hold tight to his hands, squeezing them as if I can force my opinion on him. "If you leave me behind, I will never, *ever* forgive you. So get that thought out of your head."

"Candra," he says softly. "You're sick. I won't let this travel kill you. That would destroy me."

Is that what this is, then? Because I threw up this morning, now he wants to leave me behind? Telling him the truth might further convince him that I need to remain here in the cottage, but I can see the worry and stress on his face. If nothing else, maybe I can take some of that away. "Actually, we do need to talk. We need to have a long discussion and compare notes."

He tilts his head, curious. "Compare notes? About what?"

"About Ravendor. About your ancestors. About my ancestors."

He tries to pull his hands from mine. "Candra—now is not the time for a history lesson."

I shake my head, clinging to his hands and refusing to let go. "Just . . . humor me. All right? I swear I've got a point. And we're not going anywhere tonight. So come lie down with me and tell me the Fellian version of Ravendor Vestalin."

"Candra."

"Please. It's very important."

Nemeth rubs his jaw, and it's clear he wants to keep arguing with me—or rather, keep trying to convince me to stay behind in this little cottage. He looks around and then goes to the door, checking the bar over it one more time and then shoving a chair under the handle to reinforce it. After that, he comes and sits uncomfortably on the edge of the narrow bed.

"Lie down," I tell him. "You'll be more comfortable."

"This bed isn't big enough for both of us," he protests.

"Then I'll lie atop you." I beam at him as if this is the simplest of answers.

His cock twitches in response, and I know I've won. With an annoyed (but defeated) expression, Nemeth lies back on the bed, stretching out. It's a hay tick mattress and not as soft as the down ones we had in the tower, so I know it's difficult for him to get comfortable. Once he settles his large body in, I climb over his bulk and sprawl across him.

Nemeth immediately puts his hands on my hips and settles me in place, the tip of his hardening cock brushing between my spread thighs. "You're doing this to distract me, aren't you?"

"I'm not," I promise. "And you're the one who's putting me in the most distracting position." I wriggle in place, deliberately rubbing against his shaft, then folding my hands over his chest and propping my chin up on them. "I promise to be very still. Now, tell me the story."

His eyes narrow, and he watches me for a long moment as if trying to determine my goal. His hand goes to my hair, still damp from the weather, and he twines a lock around one finger. "Let me think."

"Don't hurt yourself."

He tugs on the strand of hair, a reluctant smile curving his mouth at my teasing. "Naughty thing." One hand slides down my back, his fingers trailing over my spine. "I don't know that you'll like the story."

"I don't expect to like it. I just want to hear it. I imagine the Fellian version of events is very different from the human one."

He chuckles. His expression turns vague, and he thinks for a moment. "It starts, I suppose, at the beginning of time. The gods created their children and placed them in the world to live. Humans, being the dirt crawlers made from clay, were given the mountains—"

"Hey!" I thump his chest, insulted. "Dirt crawlers? Seriously?"

"This is the Fellian version of events," he reminds me. "It's not going to be flattering. Do you wish to hear this or not?"

I scowl at him. "I do. Fine. Go on."

He clears his throat loudly and obviously, making me snort with amusement. "As I was saying, the dirt-crawler humans lived under the mountains, as they were most comfortable being clasped in the earth that they had been brought from. The children of the Gray God were crafted from the clouds and the skies, so they lived above, in the fields full of sunshine and warmth."

I try not to frown. Humans lived under the mountains? This is new to me. "Why would humans live underground?"

"Why do you think winged people do?" he replies and taps his fingers on my arm. "I am getting to that part."

Oh. I'd never realized how very impractical it would be for winged people to live underground. What he says makes sense in a disturbing sort of way. Our legends say that humans were built of clay to be adaptable and to change quickly. Not that we're from the earth itself. We're told that the Absent God decided to create one last thing before he left, so he took all the goodness in the world and pushed it into the clay, and that made humans.

Our legends also say that the Gray God was jealous and took all the evils in the world and made them into a race of his own—the Fellians. Nemeth isn't evil, though, and I know Lionel certainly isn't good, so clearly, the stories have spun away from their origins over time.

When I don't interrupt again, Nemeth continues. "Humans saw how happy the Fellians—back then, we were just called the 'sky people'—were in their homes. They resented how free we were, how the sun warmed us when we flew. So, the humans came and demanded that the sky people trade places with them—that humans live above ground and the sky people below. Naturally, we refused, and a war began.

"The war continued for a hundred years, and neither side was willing to give up. Then, a human more cunning than any other began to lead the humans. Her name was Ravendor, and she was a mercenary sellsword who first fought for the sky people, acting as a spy among her people. Then, she decided she could have more power among the humans, so she betrayed her employers and used their magical weapons in battle. She conquered the Alabaster Citadel, which is supposed to be a neutral place dedicated to all the gods, and claimed it for humankind.

"The goddess was upset and decided she wanted the war to end. Both parties were never going to see eye to eye, so she decided that it would be best for them to come to care for one another. She insisted that Ravendor, the leader of the humans, and Azamenth, the king of the sky people, enter a truce. She split the land into two continents, and between them, she erected a tower. Ravendor and Azamenth were bidden to enter and not return until they were ready to make a truce."

"And let me guess," I interject. "Seven years passed, and when they came out, Ravendor and Azamenth were in love, yes?"

Nemeth grins at me, his fingers trailing over my spine. "Something like that. At least, Azamenth believed himself to be in love with Ravendor. I'm told she was charming and beautiful, and if you are of her line, I can believe that."

I want to preen at his praise, but I know he's getting to the uncomfortable parts, so I gesture that he should continue instead. "So, what happened after they left the tower?"

"There was peace for a time." His expression grows thoughtful, his fingers slowing as he caresses my back. "Everyone lived in harmony outside of the mountains, sky people and humans together. Ravendor had four children by Azamenth—two with wings and two without, two born inside the tower, and two outside the tower. But eventually, the humans became dissatisfied with living with the sky people. Why should they share what was rightfully theirs? So, they whispered things into Ravendor's ear until she acted."

I know this part. He's mentioned it before. "She killed her mate?"

"Aye." Nemeth sighs, the sound heavy and defeated. "She slew Azamenth and drove his people from the kingdom. Anyone with wings was not welcomed in Ravendor's land. Azamenth had a younger brother, Abedon. He stole the two winged children from Ravendor and retreated with what remained of his people deep into the mountains, across the channel, and established the kingdom of Darkfell. The princes of the First House are the descendants of Abedon and of Azamenth's half-blooded children, though a thousand generations have passed. Abedon swore to avenge his brother's death, and ever since, Darkfell has not trusted a human for betraying them and stealing their lands.

"The goddess was furious with Ravendor's betrayal and the destruction of peace. She confronted both the Absent God and the Gray God and told them of the humans' misdeeds. The Absent God turned his face away from his children, and the Golden Moon Goddess and the Gray God withheld their names from the people. We are no longer allowed to use them, so our prayers are dulled because we cannot beseech them by name. The land is cursed, and the line of Ravendor and the line of Darkfell must return to the tower over and over again, or the goddess's wrath will be swift. And that is the end of the story. Does it satisfy you?"

It's a terrible story, one that paints humans as monsters. "Ours is really different."

"I remember. You told me once." His hands continue to stroke my skin, petting me. "Ravendor was a saintly hero and saved the humans from the big bad Fellians. That is your version, yes?"

"More or less."

"And which do you think is more likely?" There's no judgment in his tone, just genuine curiosity.

"My guess is that the truth is somewhere in the middle," I admit. "The humans weren't innocent saints, and the Fellians weren't martyrs. Everyone was probably fighting over land and resources because it's the same thing everyone's fighting over now."

"Why the interest in old stories?" Nemeth asks, his gaze seeking mine. "Why do you care about Ravendor or the House of Darkfell?"

My throat closes up. I don't want to tell him. He said he didn't care that I couldn't give him children, so I hope it won't be an issue that I'm pregnant. I . . . hope. I can't let him continue to worry over my health. I certainly can't let him leave me behind, thinking he's doing it for my own good. "Do you love me, Nemeth?"

"How can you ask that? You know the answer." His eyes narrow as he studies me. "You think my feelings would change the moment I leave the tower, like Ravendor?"

The parallels between Ravendor's story and my fate are a little worrisome, but I push those thoughts aside. "I wanted to hear more about the children that they had—Ravendor and Azamenth."

"They aren't mentioned except in the context of the larger story. Why do you want to hear about them?"

"Because I'm pregnant," I blurt out. "And I'm not supposed to be."

CHAPTER THIRTY-NINE

Nemeth's hands go still. He freezes under me, his expression unchanging. For a long moment, I don't dare to breathe. His hands slide up my arms, and then he grips my shoulders tight. "What do you mean you're pregnant?"

"I've been told all my life that I can't get pregnant—that because of the blood curse, I'm infertile. But I haven't had my period in weeks now, and I'm sick in the mornings. My stomach is hard, just like Erynne's was when she found out she was pregnant with Allionel." When he continues to stare at me in disbelief, I add, "I asked the knife, and it said I was pregnant."

He's utterly silent, and as the moments slide past, my skin prickles with discomfort. "How long have you known?"

I know the calm in his voice. He's angry. So angry. My heart feels as if it has stopped in my chest. "Since we were in the tower."

Those accusing eyes widen. "And you're just now telling me?"

I know I've done wrong. I sit up higher, determined to somehow explain away the guilt I'm feeling. "I didn't want you to feel as if I was manipulating you—trapping you into being with me," I babble, frantic. "I know you don't want this. I didn't even know it was possible."

"And yet you let me take you from the tower, knowing that the goddess's wrath might fall upon both of us—"

"Because I want to stay with you," I cry. "I can't let you leave me behind! I want us to face the future together!"

"Except you didn't want to tell me you were pregnant with my child," he bites out. "Until you were going to get left behind once more. You're using it as a game piece, trying to out-maneuver me."

"I'm not," I declare hotly. I'm offended by his words, more so because I understand exactly how he's feeling. In a way, I'm feeling just as betrayed as he is. I've been told lies all my life, and now I'm reaping the consequences. But he's looking at me with such accusation that I can't stand it. I want to defend myself, to make him realize I'm not trying to deceive. Instead, what comes out is even worse. "You weren't exactly clamoring to come on my belly," I accuse, near tears. This is all going horribly wrong. "You wanted to give me your knot."

He rears up under me, trying to get to his feet. "Because I thought it was safe—"

"I thought it was too! All my life, I've been told that I'm useless and barren. That I mean nothing. That I am the worst of my bloodline because I am a dead end, a loose thread that goes nowhere. How do you think I feel? The records are clear that Ravendor's descendants with the blood curse never have children, and yet here I am, pregnant. It's obvious that it's because you're Fellian."

"How is that the obvious reason?"

"I wasn't a virgin when we got together, Nemeth. I haven't saved myself for marriage. Why bother when I'm barren? I've had more than my fair share of lovers at court—"

"I don't want to hear about your past lovers." His eyes darken, his expression growing intense.

"—and not a single one of them has ever gotten me pregnant." I want to grab him by his shoulders and shake him to make him understand. "You said you could move through shadows with me, right? And that it felt different this last time, and you didn't know why you could do it. It's because of *me*. My blood. Ravendor's story must have some seed of truth in it because I have Fellian blood in my veins, and maybe that's what's poisoning me. Maybe that's what allowed me to become pregnant with your child. I don't know! I don't have the answers!" I'm babbling, but I can't seem to stop. I just need him to know, need him to understand that I didn't plan this. "All I know is that I love you, and I'm terrified you're going to hate me now because you never wanted children—"

"Shh," Nemeth tells me. He wraps his arms around me, and then a moment later, his wings slither out from under his back and envelop both of us in a cocoon. "Calm yourself, Candra."

"I'm not trying to deceive you," I choke. "I just don't know what to do. I don't want you to stop loving me because of a child I didn't know we could have—"

"Love. *Milettahn,* please." He brushes gentle fingers over my cheeks, and I realize belatedly that they're wet. I'm crying, after all. "A child doesn't change how I feel about you. You could shove a knife between my ribs, and I would still look at you with adoration because you're my mate. We are not Ravendor and Azamenth." He searches my gaze. "I never said I did not want children, Candra. Just that they are a complication."

"What do you mean, a complication?"

Nemeth pauses and then chuckles. "I think our story is complicated enough already, don't you?"

He's got a point. I manage a wobbly smile. "It's certainly not getting any easier."

He strokes his knuckles over my cheek again, wiping away my tears. The look on his face is incredibly tender. "How are you certain you have Fellian blood?"

"I asked the knife. I didn't understand how I was pregnant, and I wondered if that was why. Maybe I have more Fellian in me than others in the Vestalin bloodline, and that's why I'm 'cursed.' Maybe the two types of blood don't get along."

"Maybe you have magic," Nemeth says softly. "Fellian magic."

I snort. "I don't even know how to respond to that. There's no way I have Fellian magic. If I did, I certainly wouldn't have eaten cold turnips for half a year because I ran out of firewood."

He's not laughing with me, though. Nemeth looks very serious. "Just because you haven't been taught doesn't mean you don't have magic in your blood. Every Fellian is born with it. If you have Fellian blood, perhaps you have Fellian magic too."

He honestly thinks I have magic? "How would I have magic?"

"There are ways to tell. Tests. Trials." Nemeth looks gravely concerned. "A human with magic is what a Fellian fears most. It's our edge against your rapaciousness and cruelty."

By the gods, he's making me sound like a monster. I'm stung. It's not quite an accusation, but it's close. "Then use your magic and give me one of these tests. I can show you that I don't have any. If I did, do you think I'd take a potion every day that makes me feel like absolute garbage? Do you think I'd suffer through the illness that comes with a skipped dose? Or would I just wave a hand and cure myself?"

His hard mouth twitches. "That's not how magic works."

"How would I know?" I explode, indignant. "I'm a bloody human! Even if I had Fellian magic in my veins, who's going to teach it to me? The humans at court couldn't magic their way out of a goat pen."

Nemeth rubs my arm. "You're right. You're right. I'm not saying you do. I'm just worried things are growing more complicated. If we have to go back to my people, I don't want to give them cause to cast you out." He pauses and then adds, "I won't *let* them cast you out."

"Let's hope it doesn't come to that, then." I give him a mock pout. "I shall be very cross if that happens."

He laughs, his expression more like the Nemeth I know. "Cross, eh?"

"Excessively." His smile eases some of my worries. "I am sorry, you know. It wasn't as if I was trying to get pregnant. I've been told all my life it's impossible, yet here I am. I should be thrilled that I'm not barren since that's apparently supposed to be the worst thing ever for a Vestalin woman, but instead of being excited, I feel vaguely betrayed. Like everything I've been told is a lie."

Nemeth rubs my arm again. "I understand." His gaze strays to my stomach. "You're certain?"

"The knife gave me a 'yes' answer, so it must be true, right?"

"Aye, its magic wouldn't let it lie to you."

I tilt my head, studying him. Other than creating a spark of fire with a snap of his fingers, Nemeth hasn't done a lot of magic in front of me, but he makes it sound like all Fellians are brimming with magic energy. "Do you have lots of magic yourself?"

"I should. Most Fellians are taught spells from the time they begin schooling until adulthood, but because of who I am, I wasn't allowed to learn anything that wasn't deemed essential."

"Who you are?" I'm puzzled.

"The son of the First House bound for the tower. They worried anything I knew might be shared with humans, so they chose to keep the nonessential magic secret rather than risk teaching it to me." A bitter smile curves his mouth. "Which means I know less than most children."

I rub his chest to offer sympathy. I know what it's like to be coddled because of who—and what—you are. "What kind of magic were you allowed, then?"

"Small things. Fire spells, light spells, communication spells—"

"Communication spells, of course." I echo, my skin prickling with awareness. I think back to the time I caught him speaking aloud for no reason at all. I thought he'd been praying, but he'd probably been talking to his brother. "What exactly have you been telling him?"

An uneasy look crosses his face. "Candra . . . get dressed." He sits upright, his wings sliding off our naked bodies, and then he untangles himself from the bed, dumping me on the far side of the mattress. A moment later, he melts into the shadows, disappearing.

Just like that, I'm alone.

"Dragon shite—you do not get to end a conversation like that!" I pound a fist on the mattress. "Come back here, Nemeth!"

He doesn't come back, though. There's no one in the hut but me. I'm so annoyed with him that I jerk to my feet, grabbing at my wet chemise that's spread out on the nearby table. The moment I stand, though, darkness creeps in at the edges of my gaze. My stomach turns, and my skin gets clammy. Oh, no. This has happened before—when my dose is wrong for my medicine, or when I take it and I haven't eaten enough.

Dragon shite. I'm going to faint.

The realization hits me a moment before I go completely under.

I wake up some time later to my ass on the cold floor, a blanket tossed over me, and the sounds of eating.

Disoriented, I open my eyes and roll over to look at Nemeth, who must be ravenously devouring a meal—only to find that it's not Nemeth at all. Two strangers stand with their backs to me, eating what is left of our foodstuffs spread out on the table. I glance around the cottage quickly, but I don't see Nemeth. The front door hangs open, and one of the pretty window shutters has been destroyed, likely from an axe. Our drying clothes have been scattered about the cottage; no doubt tossed aside when the thieves entered.

And I'm only wearing a blanket.

I clutch it to myself tighter, bewildered, as I sit up. Dizziness assails me again, along with nausea. I have to lie back down, or else I'm going to pass out again. "Water . . . please."

The men turn around. I wonder if they're going to kill me, but right now, I'm feeling so lousy I might welcome a quick death. I groan as another wave of nausea hits, and to my surprise, someone lifts my head and puts a cup to my lips. "Here. Drink slowly."

Taking small sips, I'm relieved that it helps the nausea disappear. I continue to drink, and as I do, I watch the men. Both of them are of indeterminate ages, their faces unshaven and dirty. They're incredibly thin, and their clothing is ragged and faded. One is wearing a torn cloak that has the symbol of Castle Lios's guards, but perhaps it was stolen like they're currently stealing the last of our food.

I don't see Nemeth anywhere. Has he abandoned me?

He wouldn't. He loves me. Something must have happened. Worry makes my nausea flare again, and I swallow hard.

"Can you sit up?" One of the men asks, a concerned look on his face. They're being decent despite the fact that they just ate the last of our food. They even covered me in a blanket.

I manage to nod and struggle to sit upright. "Who . . . are you?"

"Might ask the same question of you," one of the men says, licking crumbs off his fingers.

The answer is an obvious one. "I was looking for food. My supplies are almost gone." I eye the table, where nothing remains. "*Are* gone."

He glances at the doorway, and I'm dismayed when a third man joins them. The newcomer looks just as thin and unkempt as the others, but this one watches me with a burning gaze as if he could stare holes through the blanket covering my nudity. He's got a long blond beard with two braids in the scraggly ends, and he strokes those braids as he sits in one of the chairs, his muddy boots tracking all over the floors. "No one else."

All three men focus on me again, their gazes skeptical and wary. "You're here alone?" one asks.

The implication in the man's tone is obvious. *What's a weak, soft thing like you doing here alone*? I don't want to tell them about Nemeth, so I decide to edge close to the truth again. "I had a companion with me, but . . . I think he left. Abandoned me when I got sick from hunger."

The first man grunts, satisfied. "Happens a lot nowadays."

"Even to a princess?" says the one with the braided beard.

I stiffen, clutching the blanket tight. The other men eye me speculatively. "I didn't say I was a princess."

He gestures at my hair. "You got the dark hair and the green eyes like the queen."

What do I say to that? I lick my lips, silent. "My name is Candra," I finally say, since I can't seem to get the upper hand. "You're right."

He narrows his gaze at me. "You the one who's supposed to be in the tower?"

The room feels positively chilly, their stares blistering. That tells me everything I need to know. "Nope," I say brightly. "I'm the sick one. You'll find my vials of medicine on the table there. Meryliese is the one who's in the tower even now."

The two relax, but the one with the long beard continues to stroke it, eyeing me thoughtfully. "Thought she died."

"You heard wrong. I hugged her good-bye even as she stepped into the tower." I sell the lie with a determined expression. "I think I would know if my sister was dead."

I hope they don't ask more questions. I hope no one points out that the weather is awful—even now it's raining again—and that I've been gone from court for years. But the one who offered me water grunts, gesturing over at the table. "She's right about the medicine. I tried to drink one. Wasn't sure if it was food or not. Tastes like shit."

"It's injected," I say helpfully. "My kit is in my bag. The medicine keeps me alive."

"There are two left," he says. "That should last you a time, yes?"

Two left? That's it? There were five yesterday. They must have destroyed more than they're letting on, and one of the men looks so guilty I wonder if that's the case. "I see."

"If you're the princess, you should go with us to the capital," one says suddenly. "We'll be rewarded for bringing you home safely."

The other two perk up. "Rewarded?"

"She's a princess, isn't she? Rewarded," he claims, nodding to himself.

Now they all watch me with speculative looks, no doubt seeing gold coins and feasts dancing in front of their eyes. Part of me wants to cry out that I can't leave without Nemeth, but the survival instinct in me is strong . . . and I need more potion. "Yes. I need to return to the castle. Please take me."

"It's settled, then. We leave in the morning." The braided-beard smiles. "To think we've been lucky enough to stumble upon a princess."

"It's your lucky day," I agree. And my unlucky one.

I'm allowed a few moments alone to quickly dress, and then one of the men sits with me at all times. They go through our bags, rifling through the small number of possessions we took with us from the tower. The magical globe in its case is tossed aside, the case emptied, and one of the men throws his filthy satchel inside it. My knife is snatched and claimed by Braid-Beard, tucked into his pocket. I don't say anything because if I tell them that it's a magical instrument, I'll be looked at with suspicion. They tear through everything we have left, looking for food or things to barter, and when the bag doesn't provide much, they hunt through the house and the rest of the village again.

There's no sign of Nemeth at all, and my heart grows heavier by the hour.

I learn a bit about the men—the two brothers are Jarvo and Corlath. Braid-Beard is their unofficial leader, and his name is Saemon. Even though they're wearing filthy guard uniforms, they're not from the army. They claim to have found the uniforms "nearby" and borrowed them, as their clothes were rotting. Outside, they have two skinny ponies that eat weeds, moss, and whatever else they can find. It seems we'll be riding back to Castle Lios.

Lucky me.

Saemon watches me closely as I give myself my potion. Out of the three, he unnerves me the most. He's constantly calculating, gazing at me as if trying to assess how he can profit from my presence. I wish I'd dyed my hair before abandoning the tower. The dark locks give me away every time because they're proof of my Vestalin heritage . . . and the Fellian blood, it seems.

I contemplate giving myself a half dose of potion to make the two vials last longer, but in the end, I go with the full dose. I'll need my strength if we're going to be traveling via horseback, and if we're truly heading for Castle Lios, then I can get more of my potion there. So, I give myself the full amount and fold my arm as I've been taught so the potion will flood through my veins faster. My head swims with the onset of it, and I feel dizzy without anything in my stomach.

"Is it true that you're cursed?"

I glance over at Saemon. "If you mean do I have the Vestalin blood sickness, yes. But it's not contagious."

"Heard you're barren."

My ears prickle at that, and I glance at him from under my lashes. I don't answer, wondering where this is going.

"Heard that you won't get pregnant no matter how many men you take between your thighs," he continues slowly. "That true?"

Ah, so that's where this is going. I'm a woman alone, so I must need some fool with a dick and balls to take care of me, and naturally, that means I'm ripe for the raping. "My, you sure seem to have a lot of information for someone who claims to have never been to the palace. Are you sure you're not a deserter?" I smile sweetly at him. "I've heard there are ever so many of them roaming the countryside."

He narrows his eyes at me. "You're lucky you're a princess. Lots of men have been looking for a woman to comfort them for a while."

"Comfort" them? What about the woman's comfort? It takes everything I have not to make a face. "I suppose I am," I continue blithely. "It would be very upsetting to my sister, the queen, should anything happen to me." I can play the game of veiled threats too.

He picks at his nails with my magical knife, and I have to resist the urge to snatch it out of his hands. "How did *you* say you ended up out here alone?" Saemon asks again.

"I didn't. How did you say you ended up out here?"

"I didn't."

Exactly. We stare at each other in a silent battle of wills, unwilling to bend.

"Get some sleep, princess," Saemon finally says in a low, deadly voice. "You'll need your strength for riding tomorrow."

I wrap a blanket around my wrinkled dress like a queen and lift my chin.

"I'm taking the bed. Wake me up when we leave in the morning. And if you find food, I expect it to be shared four ways since you've eaten the last of mine."

"Of course," Saemon says. "But there's no food anywhere. That's why we're going to the capital." He pauses and slyly adds, "That's why you're valuable to us."

I'm sure I am. If there truly is a food shortage, no one's going to give their food to a few miscreants. They need me far more than I need them . . . and then I think about the last vial of my potion and how dangerous of a position that puts me in. All right, if they've got horses and they know the way to the capital, I need them too.

But what of Nemeth? Where has my Fellian mate gone? Why has he abandoned me?

Or has something happened to him?

CHAPTER FORTY

I barely sleep that night. I'm too alert, watching the men as they take turns with the watch. I keep expecting one of them to attack me or for them to murder me in my sleep because I'm the piece of dragon shite that left the tower, and they've finally put it all together. I want to run away, to go find Nemeth, but they never give me a moment alone. There's no opportunity to slip away. Dawn approaches, and when everyone rouses, they check through my bags one last time, looking for missed food. When they find nothing, they decide to keep my dresses and belongings. "Just in case," Jarvo says. "Might need to trade it at the next village."

"It belongs to me," I point out, irritated. "Why are you stealing from a princess?"

"Because we need it far more than you do," Saemon replies. "And when you're home, if you still want your sad, wrinkled dresses back, I'll give them to you." He smiles tightly. "Until then, they go into the pool of trade items in case we run into someone who has food."

"Great," I say flatly. I'm as hungry as the next person. Hungrier, since they ate what I had and didn't share it. I want to tell them to piss off and be on their way, but with one dose of potion left and no Nemeth, I don't have a choice. I have to go with them. The unease I've been trying to tamp down flares, and I dig my nails into my palms. There's no sign of Nemeth. He'd come after me if he could. Has he been hurt? Wounded? Did these jerks stake him outside of town like the Fellian at the other village?

For a moment, my chest fills with so much pain that I can't breathe. I have to find him. I have to.

It starts to rain again, and my thoughts fill with panic. Nemeth can't slide into shadows if there's rain, can he? He can't "slide" if there's anything to interfere. What if he's bleeding out somewhere? What if these men killed him, and

I'm going along with them blindly? We head outside, the rain drenching my hair in a heartbeat, and I look around for gray wings and sleek horns, but he's nowhere.

"On to the horse, princess," Saemon says.

"Actually, you know what? I've changed my mind," I say, clutching the bag of needles and my last remaining potion. "I think I'm going to take my chances out here. Stay in this cottage for a while and see if anyone comes by."

"You're coming with us," the bearded man growls, pointing at the soaked horse at his side. "Get your sorry arse over here."

"I don't know how to ride," I protest.

"Then it's a good thing for you that I do." Saemon gives me an unpleasant smile. "All you have to do is hold on."

I cast a worried look around the village again. Everything's drenched in mud, but other than the rain, it's all so very still. Deserted. A knot forms in my throat, and I want to hitch up my skirts and just run for the hills, hoping that I'll locate Nemeth somewhere.

But if he's dead, where does that leave me?

Where does that leave our baby? I grab the front of my dress, wanting to touch my stomach to comfort myself, but knowing I shouldn't dare. Saemon watches me too closely already. My lower lip trembles. I don't want to leave.

I don't know that I would even want to live if Nemeth has been killed. I can't do this alone.

"Get on the horse, princess," Saemon says again. "Whoever you're waiting for isn't coming back."

That's exactly what I'm worried about. I'm glad it's raining because it hides the tears that fall down my face. Stupid, dragon-shite tears. I can't cry right now. I shouldn't cry. Nemeth would want me to be strong and go on. I clench my jaw, gazing up at Saemon's hated face. He extends a hand to me to help me mount, and I see the gleam of my pretty, jeweled knife in his belt.

My knife.

It could tell me where Nemeth has gone and if he's still alive.

My new goal in life is to get it back, no matter what it takes. So, I smile sweetly and take his hand, letting him help (or rather, shove) me up onto the horse's back. I sit up there awkwardly, the leather saddle and the blanket underneath making a wet, squishing sound when I'm seated. A moment later, Saemon is behind me, and he locks an arm around my waist.

I stiffen because his touch is far too casual.

"Don't worry, princess," he says and leans in close enough that I can feel his hot breath on my skin. "If you need someone to warm your bed at night, I'll volunteer."

Disgusting. I say nothing. Instead, I look down at the bite on my hand, the bite mark from when Nemeth promised to love and care for me always.

If he loves me, why isn't he here?

The entire day passes without a sign of Nemeth, and my soul feels as if it's shriveling in my body.

Nemeth would come for me if he could. The fact he hasn't tells me that something is wrong. I picture him with a wounded wing, unable to fly. I picture him melting into shadows, only to disappear forever because of some spell backfiring. I picture him slain by the very men who hold me captive right now, and my insides are ice. It doesn't matter that Saemon gropes me and whispers lewd things in my ear, things that he'd like to do to sully a princess. It doesn't matter that the rain doesn't let up for an instant, and the entire world feels like one endless wet landscape of mud. It doesn't matter that my stomach growls, and the lack of food—combined with the swaying of the horse—makes me dizzy all day long.

Nothing matters anymore. Nemeth—*my* Nemeth—is gone. I picture his face as he reads one of his boring war poetry books, and my heart feels like lead. I think of him, the heated look in his eyes as he pushes his knot into my body. The "You can take it" he always whispers to me when I squirm against him because it's too much, the best kind of too much. I picture him a thousand ways, and they all make me hurt so badly that I can't bear the pain.

Yet I have to because I'm carrying his baby, and he deserves better than the mother of his child giving up.

We pass through another deserted village, and I'm forced to stay on the horse with Saemon while Jarvo and Corlath search the town for supplies. They find nothing, but I'm not surprised. If this world is nothing but a swampy, muddy mess because of the goddess's wrath, how can anything grow?

"We'll find something at the capital," is all Saemon says while he pats me on the shoulder as if I'm his answer to everything.

That night we bed down in a stable, and at the far end of it is the carcass of a dead, rotted horse. It smells so bad my eyes water, but it's dry inside, so they won't leave. I vomit twice, then hunt my bag for an ancient sliver of soap that I packed, and put it under my nose, the thick perfume of roses drowning out the stench of decay. The men don't seem to be bothered by it, but I get sick a third time when Jarvo pokes at the dead animal to see if it's edible.

The next day is even worse. The coastline starts to look familiar, and the villages get closer together. They're all empty, and my heart hurts for the people of Lios. Did the war end them, or was it the lack of food? What's the capital going to look like with so many refugees flooding it? Erynne must be beside herself with stress. I picture my sister, but thinking of her makes me think of her orders to kill Nemeth, and it fills me with bitter anger. So, I think of Riza and Nurse instead—of their smiling, sweet faces—and I miss them both dearly. They raised me more than my mother did, and I long for my family.

Maybe Riza and Nurse will help me raise Nemeth's child.

I'm yet numb as I sleep that night, and when I wake up before dawn, I find Saemon staring down at me with a wild-eyed intensity that makes me want to tug my dress higher over my breasts. "Been a long time since I've had a woman," he comments.

"Been even longer since I've seen a gentleman," I retort. "I'm still waiting." I haul my damp cloak around my shoulders, wishing he'd go away. "Piss off with you."

But he only laughs, and the uneasiness in my stomach grows. A bitchy princess attitude will only carry me so far, and if Saemon isn't intimidated, I know it's just a matter of time before he tries something.

I hope we get to Castle Lios before he gets brave enough.

I didn't think it was possible for the rain to get heavier, but somehow it has. It's an absolute downpour, and the roads are nothing but muddy slicks. Everywhere I turn, water pools on the ground. The horses amble along, Jarvo and Corlath on one and me and Saemon on the other. It's a long, miserable day, made even more miserable as we pass through several more villages, all of them empty.

Each one makes my skin prickle with alarm. Where *is* everyone? Surely there are people left somewhere?

Surely the four of us cannot be the only ones left beyond the walls of Castle Lios? I can't imagine my sister leaving the palace, so I imagine it is absolutely packed with refugees. If that's the case, they won't mind a few more.

I scan the gloomy, wet skies, looking for signs of Nemeth, but I don't see him anywhere. The road takes us along the shore, and the beaches seem less muddy, but there are broken boards and debris along the tideline, enough for several ships. *More shipwrecks,* I figure, thinking of Meryliese. Surely no one would try to take a ship in this messy weather.

Corlath and Jarvo stay behind to raid an empty village or two. Our horse is plodding along slower than theirs, so we keep on riding, and Saemon "reassures" me that they'll catch up. His reassurances have become more handsy by the hour, and when he strokes my arm a little too familiarly, I elbow him to let him know his touch isn't welcome.

He just laughs and squeezes me harder, the prick.

That night, we stay in an abandoned manor house, the walls covered with murals of the family who once lived here. It's as deserted as everything else, and I slump in a wingback chair near the fireplace as Saemon wanders through the rooms and looks for treasures. I'm too tired and shaky to even attempt to get away. The fire in the hearth is warm, at least, and even if there's nothing to eat, the chair is comfortable enough.

Corlath and Jarvo return a few hours later with bad news. "Nothing to eat again," Jarvo says. "At this rate, we're gonna starve before we ever make it to the capital."

Saemon doesn't look overly concerned. I watch as he pulls my little jeweled knife from his belt and holds it out to Jarvo. "Go kill my horse. He's on his last legs, anyhow. He can be dinner."

I'm sickened at how much the two men light up—and I think of that poor horse, who's walked so faithfully in the mud and driving rain, carrying us. It probably deserves better than being dinner to these three cretins. My mind flashes back to last night and the half-rotted carcass in the stable and how they'd tried to eat it . . . and the smell . . .

I make it three steps before I puke.

"Are you going to keep doing that all the way to the capital?" Saemon asks, visibly annoyed.

"I told you I was sick," I manage between nauseated gasps. I lie on the floor, on cool, wooden floorboards, as I wait for the nausea to abate. Saemon moves closer. Instead of helping me, he nudges the corner of an expensive-looking rug away from me. All heart, that one. "Can I have some water?"

"I don't know. *Can* you?"

That piece of dragon shite. Gritting my teeth, I glare up at him.

He sighs and crosses his arms over his chest, studying me. "You said you were fine with your medicine."

"That was before your goons drank half of it. I only have one dose left."

"Mmm. What happens when you run out?"

I gesture at myself as if to say *this*.

"Are you going to die on us?" he asks.

"Trying not to. Water?"

With a sigh, he tosses his water skin down to me and walks out the door. It lands on my stomach with an unpleasant thunk and makes me sick anew. That prick. I manage a few dry heaves before I take a couple of sips of water. The liquid helps, and I roll onto my back, waiting for things to settle.

As I do, I realize I can hear voices outside. I can't make out what they're saying, but I know from the timbre of the voices that it's the men . . . and they're arguing. I move closer to the window in the manor house. Unlike the cottages with the shutters, this is an arrow slit high in the brickwork, and it's carrying their voices directly to me.

"I don't like this," Jarvo is saying. "She's a lady. We can't kill her."

"She's dying," Saemon's voice is flat, emotionless. "You really want to show up at Lios with a dead princess on your hands? They'll hang your guts from the castle gates."

"Maybe if we get some food into her," Corlath says. "We're going to have horse meat—"

"And she'll puke it up right on you. It won't stay down. She's got one dose of her medicine left, and she's dead after that. You think they'll welcome us with food? You think they'll welcome us with anything but a pike up the arse?"

Corlath and Jarvo murmur something too low for me to hear.

I need a weapon if they're going to try to kill me. I glance around the room. I don't see anything useful—Saemon would have taken anything that looked valuable or like a weapon. There's only some knitting left in a basket by the fire, but maybe that will have to do. Getting to my feet, I wobble back to the chair by the hearth, feeling weak and useless. The needles are wooden and thick, but I'll drive one through Saemon's ball sack if I have to. I slide it into my sleeve.

The moment I do, the door opens, and I hear footsteps. I close my eyes, feigning placidity near the fire. The men approach my chair, and then the footsteps stop. I open an eye.

Corlath and Saemon stand nearby, regarding me. Corlath looks uncomfortable, but there's a hard intensity to Saemon's eyes that worries me.

"Where's Jarvo?" I ask. Seeing as he was the only one who didn't want to kill me, that makes him my new best friend.

Corlath gives Saemon an uneasy look.

"He left," Saemon replies.

Uh-oh. Does "left" mean that they killed him? "Is he all right?"

Saemon shrugs. He moves closer to my chair, and I instinctively press back against the cushions.

"She still looks pretty alive to me," Corlath whispers, eyeing Saemon. "We could have a bit of fun with her now. While she's still warm."

"Mmm." Saemon reaches out and touches a lock of my dark hair, picking it up from my shoulder and rubbing it thoughtfully.

What in the Gray God's realm? They're not even bothering to hide their intentions. I jerk away from Saemon's touch even though it makes me dizzy. The shadows stretch and dance behind them, which means I'm probably about to faint again. "Don't touch me."

"I think she's strong enough that she'll put up just enough of a fight to make things interesting," Saemon says to Corlath. "I get to go first, though. You can hold her down for me."

An outraged sound escapes me, and when Corlath grabs me by the shoulders and jerks me up from the chair, I push at him, trying to free the knitting needle from my sleeve. He grins down at me, all cruelty—and then his head turns.

And *turns*.

And turns completely around, his bones crunching, as shadows swallow him.

I scream, the chair tipping backward and taking me with it as Saemon bolts for the door. There's no defending his friend, no fighting back. He runs like a coward, and I watch dizzily as he sprints across the manor house, the floorboards loud with his hurried steps.

As I watch from my vantage point on my back, the shadows swirl again, and I catch a flash of gray wings and sweeping horns. Green eyes flash as muscular arms lock around Saemon's shoulders and fling him to the floor with a crash.

"You dare," Nemeth growls, the sound inhuman. "You dare to touch my mate?"

Saemon crawls backward, scurrying like a rat to get away. "No—never—"

"I heard every filthy word that came out of your mouth," my Fellian snarls. He stalks forward toward his prey; his wings flared and menacing. "I heard your plans. You were going to harm her. While she was still *warm*, you said. And then you were going to cut her throat and leave her here. You thought her weak and useless to you." He smiles, showing deadly white fangs. "She's not weak because she has *me*."

And before I can take a breath, Nemeth plants a huge hand on Saemon's head and crushes it like a grape.

Blood spatters over him and the floor.

I gasp.

He turns to me, his eyes feral. "*Did they touch you?*"

"You're alive," I breathe. Hot tears flood my eyes. By the gods, I'm crying all the time now. "Oh, Nemeth, you're *alive*." I kick my legs in the air, trying to get up from the chair.

He strides to the fallen chair, where I'm still on my back, feebly trying to right myself, and plucks me out of its confines. He pulls me into the air, holding me tightly by my shoulders, but it doesn't hurt. His wild gaze searches my face and body. "*Did they touch you?*" he demands again, and his wings shiver so violently it's clear he's about to lose control.

"Nemeth. I'm all right." I search his face. "Are . . . are you?"

My Fellian groans. He crushes me against his chest, holding me tight.

Cradling the back of my head, he shudders, clasping me to him. I've never been so enveloped by him, not even when he cocoons his wings around us. "Candra. My Candra."

"I'm a little mad at you," I tease weakly. "Here you are, killing those pieces of dragon shite before I had the chance. Unfair."

He just clasps me tighter, his fingers digging into my hair as if he can somehow twine his claws into my locks and hold me forever. "I'm here," he says in a tight voice. "I'm here, and no one's going to hurt you."

His words break something inside me. I press my face against him, not caring that he's covered in Saemon's blood or that I probably reek of vomit. "I thought you died. Oh, Nemeth. I thought I'd lost you forever." I choke on a sob. "Where the fuck have you been?"

"I never abandoned you. Never. Not once." He slides a hand under my chin and tilts my head up. "You look unwell. Is it the child? Have you eaten?"

As if his reminder saps all the strength out of me, my head spins. I try to push the dizziness aside so I can gaze at his gorgeous face for all eternity because I never want to look away. "I have one dose left," I tell him. "Saving it. And no, I haven't eaten. Nothing to eat."

Nemeth shakes his head, cradling me against him again, and I find my face shoved into the crook of his neck. "I'm going to get these bodies out of here, and then I'm going to give you your potion, love. And then we're going to eat."

"You're not listening," I say, voice muffled against his neck. "There's nothing to eat—"

"There's always something to eat."

I gasp. "You want to eat the dead humans?"

Nemeth snorts, giving me a funny look. "Of course not. We're going to eat the horse they just killed."

Oh. Well, that makes a lot more sense than my theory. Even so, my stomach roils uncomfortably at the thought. "I'm not sure I can."

"I'll make it into a stew," he tells me, voice stern. "And you'll eat."

I . . . guess I'm eating horse. Because the look on Nemeth's face tells me whatever argument I have, I won't win.

CHAPTER FORTY-ONE

A short time later, I have my arm folded over, and I'm leaning back in the chair by the fire. My head is spinning, and I'm dizzy, but there's a comforting edge to it because I know it's from my potion—the very last dose I had. I don't know what we're going to do tomorrow, but I suppose that's tomorrow's problem. Nearby, Nemeth fusses with the small cook pot over the fire. We found some spices in the kitchen, along with salt, and I have to admit that even though I'm not excited about eating horse, it smells utterly divine. My mouth waters constantly, and I watch my mate with sleepy, blurry eyes.

He looks so good. I could stare at him all day and all night, just admiring the strong lines of his back. His kilt is water stained, and the leather distorted, the decorative straps no longer lying flat. They part across his backside, revealing the short stump of a tail that he's so prudish over. His wings are folded neatly, their points framing his head, and he just looks so familiar and cozy that I want to stay in this moment forever. Just me, drowsy with a hit of medication, and Nemeth fussing over a delicious-smelling meal and sneaking glances back at me while rain patters away on the roof.

"How did you find us?" I ask him when he dips a wooden spoon into the pot and tastes the stew. "Was it magic?"

Nemeth glances back at me. "I told you, Candra. I never lost you. I've been following this entire time."

The words don't make sense to me, no matter how many times I turn them over in my head. "I don't understand. What do you mean you were following?"

"We were talking, remember? In the cottage?" He licks the spoon, dips it into the pot once more, and then blows on the steaming contents to cool them. He holds it out to me, an offering, his other hand underneath. Reluctantly, I lean forward to eat. The meat is tough, but it's delicious. My stomach cramps hard with hunger, and I nod at him. He takes the spoon back and then stirs the pot once more. "Not too much longer. We'll let it cook down a bit more to soften the meat."

"Nemeth," I chide. "Don't change the subject."

"I'm not. But feeding you is first and foremost in my mind." He turns his head and gives me a wry smile. "Everything about you is first and foremost in my mind." He stirs the meat again, then lets the spoon rest against the side of the pot. "Something broke my perimeter spell, so I gathered shadows to investigate."

"Perimeter spell?" I frown. "This is the first I've heard of such a thing. What is it?"

"Magic, of course. It's a type of enchantment that allows me to watch over the periphery of an object. You know the old battle saying that you can never sneak up on a Fellian?"

"No." I give my lover an amused look. "I'm not up to date on my battle sayings, I'm afraid."

"Ah." He rubs one ear, looking embarrassed. "Well, we like humans to think it's because of our shadow magic, but it's truly due to enchantments. You can never sneak up on a Fellian because most of us have a perimeter ward upon our belt buckle." He gives his a pat. "The moment someone comes close, it makes a strident noise that only I can hear and alerts me that there's an intruder. I cast another perimeter spell upon my food stores back in the tower. You'll recall I caught you sniffing around?"

"I never stole from you!"

"Aye, I know you didn't, love. But at the time, I didn't know you well. So . . . a perimeter spell. We were in the cottage, and I heard the noise of someone approaching, so I slipped into the shadows to see who it was. When I saw it was the humans, I kept to the shadows, ready to attack . . . and then I saw that they had horses."

My stomach gives a funny, uncomfortable little flip.

Nemeth's expression is uneasy. He won't look me fully in the eye as he continues. "And I saw those horses, and it made me pause because we weren't going to reach the human settlement before you ran out of medicine. I knew I couldn't fly you there, so I made a choice."

"Nemeth, *no*." I'm horrified. He deliberately left me with those men?

"I couldn't let you die, Candra."

"You left me with those vile men? Let me worry over you? I thought you were hurt! Or worse! I thought you were dead, Nemeth, and that I'd never see you again." I shudder. "They ate all of our food and drank three of my potions before they knew what they were, and you left me with them?" I feel betrayed.

"It was a choice I agonized over," he confesses, his rich, velvety voice aching with sorrow. "And I watched from the shadows. If they tried to hurt you, I would slaughter them where they stood. But as long as they were traveling toward your city, and as long as they had the horses, they were moving faster than I could go with you, so I left you with them. I'm sorry. I thought you might be safer with them than with a Fellian who can barely fly."

I'm stiff with anger. On some level, his words make sense. The humans were moving faster than we could. Nemeth can't fly me, and we're low on supplies. But the last few days of sheer agony—of bitter worry over his absence, of distress over the situation—make it impossible for me to easily forgive. "You could have said something."

"When? They didn't leave you alone for a second, Candra." He shakes his head and nudges the spoon in the pot as if he can somehow will our dinner to cook faster. "When was I supposed to come and warn you?"

"I don't know," I say helplessly. "All I know is that you let those men eat our food and take my potion. You let me worry that you were dead—" my voice catches, and I can't speak. I shake my head, weary and hurt beyond all capacity to reason. I hate that we left the tower. I hate that Nemeth abandoned me. I hate that the world I used to know no longer exists, and I'm trapped in this rainy, deserted hellscape.

More than anything, I'm worried. My last potion is gone. We're down to eating horse . . . and every time I turn around, I feel like I'm learning something new about my mate. I stare down at the bite on my hand, and I think about the happiness I felt on that day.

It feels like a very long time ago.

"You're upset," Nemeth says, voice soft.

"I am." Upset doesn't even begin to cover the emotions I'm feeling right now.

He moves to my side and crouches low in front of the chair, gazing up at me.

Nemeth takes my hands in his, and I'm reminded of how enormous his hands are in comparison to mine. Like all Fellians, he has an oversized grip . . . a grip that squeezes my heart between his fingers and is in danger of breaking it. "I am thinking of you and our child, Candra. I know you're hurt. You have every right to be. But if I have to choose between watching you die at my side or letting some humans drag you to their city on horseback, I'm going to pick the humans." He strokes his thumb over my knuckles. "Even if it means you hate me."

"I don't hate you," I whisper, aching. "I just hate everything about this situation."

He lifts my hand to his cheek, the hard planes of his face familiar under my touch. "I've been following ever since they broke into the cottage," he tells me. "I've agonized over every moment. I haven't slept knowing that you were with them and vulnerable. Ten thousand times, I wanted to slaughter them all and take the horses, but I cannot ride either. At least this way, you could cling to one of them." He turns his face, brushing his lips against my palm, grazing the bite mark there. "I hated them. I hated them so much, and every time I nearly stole you away again, a new settlement would be on the horizon, and I was convinced that it would be the one that would have people. It would be the one where people would welcome you like the princess you are and feed you. They could give you more than a Fellian, so I watched from the shadows and held back my rage." He bares his teeth, his green eyes glinting. "I hated that they stole the food. If I had anything to slip you, I would have left it in your path. But there is nothing. The rain is washing everything away."

We knew the goddess was angry at the world—not at us—and so we should have known this would happen. We should have realized what her anger would look like. It doesn't make me feel any better, but at the same time, it's difficult for me to see Nemeth so stern and not try to make him smile. So, I manage a weak grin and stroke his strong chin. "You miscalculated, I'm afraid. We're still at least a day out from the city, and we've eaten the horse. If your plan was for them to take me to the gates of Lios, you've failed, my love."

His teeth scrape over my bite, and it sends a shiver up my spine. "I couldn't wait a moment longer. They were going to hurt you. Touch you." He bares his teeth, his lips curling back with fury. "I'd destroy every human alive before I let them harm one hair on your head."

My eyes go wide.

"You belong to me." He places his teeth over the plump part of my palm, fitting against the bite mark. "My Candra. My mate. Do you know how feral it makes me to think that they might have touched you? Do you know how much I wanted to tear them limb from limb for the way they were looking at you?" Nemeth growls, his nostrils flaring as he gazes at me. "Do you know how much effort it's taking me not to drag you to this floor and give you my knot because I need to claim you?"

My breath catches in my lungs. "Nemeth."

"I know what I did was wrong. I know, and I hated every moment of it. But I would do anything for you, Candra." The look he gives me is full of longing, full of emotion, and I'm right back there in the tower, listening to him confess his love for me. "You are everything to me."

"I love you too," I tell him. "And if I didn't feel like death warmed over at this moment, I'd ask you for that knot after all."

That brings a smile to his hard, unforgiving mouth. He kisses the mark on my palm and gets to his feet. "I may not be able to knot you, but I can feed you. Right now, that's almost as good."

"Is it? Is it really?"

He pauses. "Well, no." His wings flutter with shy agitation. "But it will have to do."

We stay that night in the manor house. Nemeth makes me eat three bowls of horse soup staggered over two hours, and then I'm so tired that I doze in front of the fire while he sets up magical wards and more perimeter spells. I want to watch him so I can see what the spells entail, but I'm so groggy after my medicine and food that my eyes won't stay open. I'm vaguely aware of the fire dying down and Nemeth carrying me to bed.

I wake up rested, no longer hungry, and curled up against Nemeth's side. His big, warm hand is palming one of my breasts through my chemise (I'm not sure how he got my outer dress off of me) as if it belongs to him. He snores, content, and I remember how he said he didn't sleep a wink while we were apart. My heart fills with love for him, and I tuck his hand tighter around me, relaxing in bed. I'll lie here and let him sleep peacefully, I decide. I'll be a good, benevolent, unselfish mate and let him sleep.

But I can't fall back asleep. Instead, I think about last night and the vicious, feral look in his eyes as he checked me all over. *Did they touch you?* he'd asked, over and over again, as if he'd lose every bit of his sanity if they had. My Nemeth, who claims to be a scholar, had almost been a feral beast.

It makes me *unbearably* aroused.

I wait for that to go away. Lately, it seems that if I'm awake, my stomach wants to vomit everything back out, and then I feel normal. So, I wait for that wave of nausea, but there's nothing. I just feel good. I feel warm. I feel aroused. Really, really aroused.

Hmm. I wriggle backward against Nemeth's groin, hoping to find him hard and erect. He snores on, oblivious to my need, and I have to decide whether I'm going to be selfish or if I'm going to let him sleep. I ponder this, even as his hand weighs heavy on my breast, and I absently shift back and forth, hoping for friction from his hand.

Stuff it, I decide. I'm going to be somewhat unselfish. I'll wake him . . . but I'll wake him my favorite way.

Decided upon my course of action, I wriggle, intending to slip out of Nemeth's grasp, when his hand tightens on my breast. His heavy thigh clamps down over mine, and he gives my breast a light squeeze. "And where are you going, princess?"

His voice is throaty with sleep, and it does something to my insides. I quiver with need. "I was going to wake you up," I pant, unbearably aware of his hand on my breast. His thumb is stroking over the thin material of my chemise, and he teases my nipple into a point. "With my mouth on your knot."

"Mmm. I have a better idea."

"Oh?" I prickle all over with anticipation.

He just keeps rubbing my nipple, teasing it to a point between his fingers and stroking it until I'm writhing against him. "How are you feeling this morning, my mate?"

"Needy," I pant. "So needy."

His big hand leaves my breast and slides down to my hip, where he tugs on my chemise. "Any sickness? Dizziness?"

"If you're asking if it's okay to fuck me, the answer is yes," I tell him, grabbing my skirts and hitching them up before his hand can. "Please, please, yes. I've missed you so much."

Nemeth's hand moves between my thighs. He cups my pussy and finds me wet, and a low growl echoes in his throat. "You have missed me, haven't you?" He pushes my gown up farther until it's bunched at my waist, and then I feel his cock pressing into me from behind.

I gasp, arching back against him.

"You can take it," he whispers against the pillows. "I'll make you wet enough that you can take all of me." His fingers dance over my clit even as he nudges my thighs apart and the head of his cock sinks into me.

Whimpering, I cover his hand with mine as he works my clit, not because I'm trying to push him away but because I desperately need to hold on to something.

"Candra," he breathes against my hair as he pushes deeper. "My sweet, perfect mate. You're so tight."

My lips part and I cling to him, desperate, as he pushes me toward a hot, frantic orgasm. "*Nemeth*."

"Your Nemeth," he says and then thrusts into me with shallow, rapid strokes. I cry out because it feels too good. He drives into me, his hand continuing to tease my clit until I'm coming and squeezing him tight. A sob chokes in my throat at the ferocity of my orgasm, leaving me dazed and breathless. He spanks my pussy as he pounds into me from behind, making me gasp. "I'm not done with you."

I moan. Gods, I love it when he gets all ferociously possessive. "Knot," I manage when I can catch my breath again. "Give me your knot."

Part of me expects him to roll me forward onto my belly and just pound into me from behind until his knot is seated inside me, stretching me tight. Just the mental image of that makes me shiver. Instead, he spanks my pussy again, making me gasp. "I'll give it to you soon enough, my greedy mate."

"Me, greedy?" I gasp. "You're the one hogging the bed. You're the one who's trying to make me last—" I choke off when he thrusts deep, sending another ripple of pleasure through my body. "I'm the one doing all the giving, and you're withholding your knot."

"You want my knot?" His hand slides up to my throat, clasping me against him as he drives into me harder. His other hand slides in under my waist, pushing toward the *V* of my legs, where he has me wide open and split with his cock. "You want this, then?" He presses into me again, this time harder than before, and I can feel it now, the bulge of his knot at the base of his shaft. It always feels like too much, but I always, always take it.

"Don't be selfish," I pant, and a whine escapes my throat when his fingers find my clit again. He hammers into me, rutting into me as he holds me in place, and I feel so protected even as he uses me for his needs. Another orgasm sweeps through me, and I clench around him as he drives harder into me.

Then, with one last hard thrust and a pinch of welcomed pain, his knot is inside me, and I'm stuffed full, so full that my pelvis aches. It's a good sort of ache, though—one that I've come to crave. I reach back toward Nemeth, my hand skimming over his face as he growls and fills me with his seed, his release ripping through him. He bites down on my thumb as I push it into his mouth, and I'm gasping and filled as he holds me tightly in place.

When Nemeth's hands loosen around me, he lets out a gusty sigh. His hand moves away from my throat and trails down to my breasts, then to my belly. It feels tight there, stretched full with his cock and seed, and I let out a noise of contentment. "That was lovely."

"Was it?" He thumps my pussy with his hand again, making me squeak. "Because I'm still knotted inside you. Neither one of us is going anywhere anytime soon."

"Nothing wrong with that," I tell him lazily. I lean back against him, loving this moment. The world outside might be a big pile of dragon shite, but here in Nemeth's arms, I can forget about everything for a moment. This is what I've chosen. This is what I'm abandoning my people for, and I'm pleased with my choice. I feel loved and needed and warm. I'm pregnant with my mate's child even though I'm not supposed to be able to carry a baby at all. I'm supposed to be barren. I still haven't figured out why things have changed, but maybe my knife . . .

Shite.

"The human who left last night," I tell Nemeth. "The one who abandoned them. They gave him my knife to kill one of the horses but he just ran off with it instead."

"Did he take your knife because it was magic?" His hand strokes my belly again and then the curve of my hip.

"No, just because it looked expensive. I don't think he knows it's magic. Should we go after him? Did you see where he was headed?"

"It's lost, Candra." Nemeth's tone is easy. Relaxed. Of course, the man *did* just come inside me, but still. "You don't need it."

"It's magic," I protest. "My sister gave it to me. It can help us—"

"If he's fleeing the two I killed, he's heading in the opposite direction of the castle. I won't spend precious time hunting him down for a blade. You don't need it."

I probably don't, but I still feel vulnerable without it. I miss the reassurance that it provided me, not for its sharp edge but for the questions I could ask. It's always been there. "I didn't get a chance to ask it much about the baby."

"Are you worried?" His fingers strum over my clit again.

I'm too sensitive, having come twice already, and I squirm in place. As I'm still locked against his knot, this only makes me pant harder, deeply aware of the press of him inside me. "Of course, I'm worried. I'm not supposed to be pregnant. I'm the one with the cursed blood."

"Maybe that's why," he muses, even as he ignores my attempts to wriggle away from his hand. This is part of the game, and I love it as much as it makes me absolutely crazy. He locks me onto his knot, and as we wait for it to go down, he continues to toy with my body, making me come over and over again. It always feels like too much.

It always makes me come so damn hard.

"Maybe your blood isn't cursed," Nemeth says lazily. "Maybe you've just got too much Fellian in you."

I moan at the double entendre.

"What do you think, *milettahn*?" he murmurs even as he rubs the pad of one finger against the side of my clit again. "Do you have too much Fellian inside you right now?"

My body squeezes around him again, and I decide that I both hate him and want to kiss him forever as he wrings yet another orgasm out of me.

I do, however, forget all about my knife.

CHAPTER FORTY-TWO

The walls of Lios are legendary.

I've seen them more or less every day of my life. Even when we'd travel, the Vestalins inevitably returned to Castle Lios. It's where we belong, in the beating heart of our country. We belong behind its tall white walls, nestled high on the cliffs above the sea. Winding roads lead up to it, surrounded by rolling farmlands and fields of all kinds of crops on one side and the blue, endless ocean on the other. The walls of Lios are high and impenetrable, as old and venerable as Lios itself. Legend says that Ravendor Vestalin had the walls built when she took the throne. The walls were there when I was born, and I always assumed I'd die behind them, sheltered like a bird in its nest.

But the next day at sunset, I see the massive hole punched through Lios's endless walls, and it feels like a hole punched through my chest.

I stare at it, numb, half expecting to see people spilling forth from the crevice in the walls, like blood flowing from a wound. It's empty, though.

Everything is just . . . empty.

It's been a miserable day and a half since we left the manor house. We spent half the day in bed, eating horse meat and gathering our strength. Then, when everything was cooked and we could no longer delay, we stepped back out into the endless rain and continued on our way to Lios.

It feels like the gods themselves are crying as the rain washes over me.

My city is gone.

I thought Lios would always be here—that even though the world has gone to pieces around us, Lios would remain. Lios would be safe, and we'd push in with all of the other refugees hungry for food. We'd collect my potion, enough to last us as we traveled to Darkfell, and I'd see my sister again. I'd say a mental good-bye to my people.

I'd be *prepared* to leave them behind.

I'm not prepared for this, though. Nothing could prepare me for this.

I've ignored all the signs up until now, believing that every village and city deserted meant nothing. That the wreckage that dots the shoreline and covers the beaches is irrelevant to the war and the fleet of mighty ships commanded by King Lionel. That the rain isn't affecting my home like it is the outlying towns and people. Lios would be fine. Lios would be there.

I cling to the wet horse, feeling drained and hopeless, as I stare at the enormous hole to the left of Lios's thick gates. "What makes a hole like that?" I ask Nemeth, my voice unsteady.

"A ballista. One with enchantments upon it."

Of course. Fellians do love their enchantments. "You could have just flown over the walls," I point out, numb, as the horse plods ever forward up the muddy road. "Why destroy the walls?"

"Because the way to win a battle is to give the enemy nowhere to hide."

Ah. Of course. And thus, they must destroy the walls so the humans can't huddle behind them. I think of Lionel, how smug he was when he forced me into the tower. So impatient, as if I was the only thing holding him back from his Great War, a war that would let him fill Lios's coffers with Fellian riches. It was a pissing stupid war. No one in Lios needs Fellian land. No one wants to live under a mountain.

Lionel just wanted to fight. He wanted a battle. Glory.

And now my home, my beautiful city, is empty. Everyone is gone. No one comes out to see a Fellian and a human on a horse limping up the mud-slicked roads.

I suspect Lios is as empty as everywhere else. Empty . . . and everyone is gone.

At least the other places were just deserted. It was easy to assume everyone had simply fled in search of food or safety. As we approach the broken wall of Lios, a different story unfolds. The signs of war are everywhere. The grass has been trampled and destroyed. With nothing to anchor to, the horse slips and slides up the muddy path toward the city. Alongside the road, I see discarded bits of armor and used arrows. There's a helm here, with a massive hole upon the back, and over there, a broken shield. A pretty altar to the gods has been destroyed and knocked over, the bushes uprooted and cast aside. As we head up the cliffs to Lios itself, I can look down at the harbor and see the broken remnants of a ship bobbing in the bay and another one farther down.

The road leading to my beautiful city is covered in the detritus of war, and I suspect it's not a war we won. If we'd won, someone would be here, right? There would be flags of victory. There would be people. There would be something other than this painful emptiness.

"You don't burn your dead, do you?" Nemeth asks suddenly, breaking the silence.

"No. We bury them so they can return to the earth that we were made from. We wait for the Absent God to return and call our spirits forth. Why?"

He gazes at what is left of the walls. "We have not seen graves. Perhaps that is a good sign?"

"If there are dead, they will be buried at the far end of the city," I say. "On the sacred grounds behind the temple."

"We can head there first if you like? To see if there's a reason no one is here?"

I shake my head. "I want to go to the palace first."

The only inhabitants of Castle Lios are rats.

They scurry across the detritus-covered floors, bold and unworried, as we step into the halls of the castle. The banners that hung showing the proud bloodlines of the nobility have been torn from the walls, and the tapestries are cut to ribbons. Lionel's golden throne is gone entirely, and my sister's elegant wooden one has been chopped to pieces and left on the dais. The massive feasting tables in the dining hall are broken, the benches scattered, and the fragile dishware a thousand pieces upon the ground. They crunch under my feet as I instinctively head toward the kitchens.

They, too, are empty, though there's a foul smell here. It smells like something's dead, and I cover my nose with my wet sleeve even as Nemeth strides toward the root cellar. He opens the hatch and peers inside, then shakes his head. "Two bodies, and they've been there a long time. You don't want to look."

I swallow hard. "My sister always said the cook would defend her kitchen to death. I guess that's true." I think of my sister—and of Riza and Nurse—and I desperately hate that my knife is gone. I want to ask if they're all right. I want to ask if they're alive. I hate that I squandered the opportunity back when I had my knife simply because I hated knowing the answers.

Not knowing is so much worse.

"I need to go upstairs," I tell Nemeth, feeling faint. "I want to see my sister's quarters. My quarters."

"Are you all right?" He gestures to the door, to the horse we left outside. "Should I get our packs—"

I shake my head, trembling. I'm not all right. Not by a long shot, but I still need to know. "I just need to see." Because if I see Riza or Nurse's dead body in my rooms, I might lose my fragile hold on sanity. It's one thing to know that the goddess will be unhappy if we leave the tower. It's another to see the effects of it.

Nemeth moves to my side, and I think at first that he's going to stop me or force me to sit down and rest. Instead, he snags me under his arms and flares his wings outward. He flies out of the great hall and down another corridor of the massive, empty palace. His flight isn't even, and I can tell he strains, but we're in the air and soaring through the empty halls. I point out directions. To turn that way, to go up that flight of stairs. To head down another hall.

And then I see the double doors that used to be mine. One is smashed, as if kicked in, the gilt design on the wood smeared with mud and broken away. A terrified sound escapes my throat.

Nemeth sets me down on the floor. Even here, there are discarded pieces of armor and torn fabrics. Shattered furniture and pieces of wood are everywhere, as if someone hacked the beautiful palace apart. The carpet under my feet that runs down the long hall is dark with stains, and I remember its bright red color. It's been destroyed, just like everything else. Even the ceiling—once dotted with beautiful stained glass—is now broken, and rain drips down from above as if the world around us is crying.

It feels appropriate.

I take a few steps toward my apartment, and then I run at a frantic speed, ignoring the squish of the wet carpet under my near-destroyed shoes. I want to go inside and see that this portion of my world hasn't changed. I want to see my bed with its beautiful draperies and elegant pillows. I want to see the thick rugs and the cozy chairs I have near the fire. I want to see my trunks and dressers full of gowns. Here, there should be something, shouldn't there?

I burst through the doors and skid to a halt, drinking in the sight of my once-bedroom.

It's worse here than below. There's a hole in the ceiling—the beams collapsed—so the rain floods in directly over my bed. The canopies are collapsed and ripped, and my mattress has been torn apart and shredded, the innards cast across the flooring and soaked. Every chest is opened, its contents destroyed. The chairs near the fire are gone; one is broken, and there's a familiar-looking charred chair leg hanging out of the hearth that tells me the other was probably burned. All my beautiful things are destroyed. There's no trace of me here, nothing left that speaks of my old life.

Beyond numb, I race back out of the room and down the hall toward Erynne's room. I know she won't be there. I know there won't be anyone there, but I still have to see it for myself. I have to know.

The doors here have fallen from their hinges, blocking the way into the room. I rip one away, tossing it aside. The interior of Erynne's room is just as wrecked as mine, the colorful glass in the big window broken and shattered, rain pouring inside. Ripped fabric is soaked and covered in mold, and the large imperial bed looks as if it was destroyed with an axe or three. I turn, looking for signs of my sister. Yes, she has betrayed me. Yes, she thinks of the kingdom before me.

But she's still my family, and knowing that something has happened to her makes me frantic.

I find the wreckage of a child's bed in one corner of the room, the pale blankets covered in mud and footprints. I pick up one corner, and as I do, I see rusty-colored splatters on it. Hastily, I drop it again and back away. The air in Erynne's room doesn't feel like enough. I can't breathe. Frantic, I race to the broken window and stare out at the view. Erynne always had one of the best views in the castle, with the sea crashing onto the cliffs below. Now there's nothing to see but more wreckage and the broken hull of a ship on the rocks.

There's nothing left of my kingdom, not even a single soul. There's nothing but broken bits and torn-apart remnants.

At this moment, I feel as destroyed as the ship that bobs in the harbor down below, the one with the hole in the hull so big that I can see it from up here.

"There's a body in the hall," Nemeth tells me, and I hear the rustle of his wings as he approaches. "It's old, but it's unpleasant. I covered it with one of the window hangings."

"Woman or man?" I ask tightly. The knife told me that Erynne wasn't here, but what if she returned only to get killed? If someone's murdered my sister and left her here to rot, so help me . . .

"A soldier," Nemeth says, his voice soothing. He moves behind me and puts his hands on my shoulders. "If you are asking if it is your sister, no. My brother is many things, but he would not murder a woman in cold blood."

"Not even if she was the enemy's queen?"

"Not even then." He rubs my arm. "Are you . . . all right?"

It seems a ridiculous question. Am I all right? Of course I'm not all right. I'm very, very far from all right. But I understand what he's asking. He's inquiring because this place has been our goal for so long, the answer to all of our problems, and it's empty and abandoned, just like the rest of my land. "I don't understand why no one is here," I say softly. I want to yell and scream. I want to rage at him and the Fellians who did this to my people, but the truth is that Lios started the war. We're just as much to blame. If the kingdom was destroyed because we lost the war, that's on Lionel.

So, I can't be angry with Nemeth. I cover his hand with mine, and then I clutch his fingers tightly as if he's a lifeline. "I don't know what to do," I admit. I'm tired. I'm cold. I'm hungry. I'm out of medicine. None of those things will be changing anytime soon because Lios is destroyed. There's no one to help us. No one to feed us.

We've left the tower for nothing. He enfolds me in his arms from behind, wrapping me in his solid, supportive presence. I want to scream and rage at him, too, but . . . I still love him. He's on my side, and I need to remember that, no matter what I'm feeling right now. "We'll travel to my people instead," Nemeth says. "To Darkfell."

Painful laughter bubbles up out of my chest. "The last place I want to go right now is Darkfell."

"Do you have a better idea?" He asks quietly.

I don't. I don't know what to do at all. "Will they kill me when I arrive? I'm one of Ravendor's descendants."

"They will not," Nemeth says firmly. "Because, first and foremost, you are my mate. You carry my bite." His hand slides to my stomach. "You carry my child. They will not touch you."

I'm not so sure. But we don't have many other choices. "How long will it take to reach Darkfell?"

He doesn't answer. His grip tightens around me, and I suddenly realize the answer. Too long. Too long, and I don't have any medicine left.

"We'll stay here tonight," he tells me. "Look for survivors and supplies. Find a decent room to sleep in. And we'll take it from there."

"You should go without me—"

"Never," he says, sharp. "I'm not leaving you."

"But you can fly," I point out. "I cannot. I only slow you down, and without my potion, I'm as good as dead anyhow."

"I'm not leaving you," Nemeth says again, and his voice is calm. Steady.

It would be better for him if he did, but I'm still foolishly glad he won't. I turn in his arms and hug him, burying my face against his chest.

My kingdom is gone. My sister is gone. And here we're deciding to head straight for those who destroyed them.

It feels like a never-ending nightmare.

We make the royal library our temporary camp. While it's been ransacked just like every other room in the palace, the ceiling is whole, so the books are undamaged by the endless rain. Nemeth makes a fire in the large stone fireplace at the far end of the vast hall, and I spread out our blankets and clothes to dry them.

Wearing nothing but my least-damp chemise, I curl up in the blankets by the fire and watch Nemeth as he picks up book after book. I can tell he's fascinated with them, turning the pages with near-reverence and a hand so delicate that you'd think he's touching my cunt instead of one of the many dusty books here. "There's so much knowledge here."

Normally I'd roll my eyes at someone fawning over books, but this is my Nemeth. I know how much he loves reading. For some reason, seeing him caress the pages of the book makes me happy. It makes me feel like things are a little more normal—like my world isn't ending. "Well, since I'm officially the last one in the palace, I declare this entire library to be yours."

He glances up at me and grins broadly. "I'm not sure you can do that."

"I can." I wave a hand at him. "Take as many as you like."

He sighs and replaces the book on the shelf he took it from. Then, he hesitates and pulls down another. "I wish we could, actually."

"Why can't we?" I roll onto my stomach on the bedding and prop my chin up on my hands, watching him.

"Because we can't waste time." Reluctantly, Nemeth abandons his newest book and gives me a sober look. "There's not enough food or medicine—"

"Don't give me that line again," I warn him. "We both know that. But if these books are important to you, they're important to me too. Why not take them with us?"

"Candra, are you listening? There's no medicine and no time to waste—"

"And there still won't be if we leave the books behind. It's not going to magically appear." I shake my head. "Let's face it, love. We're doomed with the books or without them. Take the damn books. Maybe something of Lios will remain after all of us are gone." After all we've been through, the grief is hitting me.

As far as I'm concerned, we can take all the damn books.

Nemeth shakes his head. He moves to my side, angry and determined. "You are worth a thousand books."

I chuckle because, of course I am. I'm amazing. "I know that. You know that. But the books do not expire if they don't get their potion on time. I will." My hands slide to my stomach, and I sigh wistfully. "I just hate that . . . "

I can't say the words aloud. That with my death, I'm taking our child with me. Strangely enough, I hate that thought more than I hate the one of my own death. To think that a child is something I never even anticipated, that I never even cared to have. And now that I find myself pregnant, I'm furious that I won't get to see it born.

Truly, the gods are cruel.

"Do not say it," Nemeth warns. He moves to my side and thumps down beside me. "We'll get through this. We'll go to the Alabaster Citadel. Perhaps the clergy there will have extra supplies. Then we'll head on to Darkfell."

I turn on my side, regarding him. He lies next to me on the blankets, but his body is a mass of tension. There's no fatigue in him like there is in me. Instead, he seems to be brimming with determination, his glowing green eyes hard. If I wasn't so tired, I'd be climbing all over him at this moment because there's nothing sexier than my Fellian when he's on a mission to protect me. "It's been a long time since I've gone to the Alabaster Citadel," I confess. "Is it still many days by ship?"

Nemeth nods, his eyes burning bright in his hard face. "We'll find a craft. I can enchant it with a spell that will pull us toward our destination. We can fish along the way. No matter how much it rains, there will be fish in the sea."

He's got a point. "So, we've got transportation and food. You should be fine." I give him a little smile. "You can even load the ship full of books."

"We'll kill the horse we rode here. He's not looking well anyhow, and there's nothing left for him to eat. It'll be a mercy for him and a blessing for us. We'll find some herbs, and we can use his organs as part of your potion—"

"Nemeth," I say softly, placing my hand on his arm. "Perhaps it's time for us to accept things—"

"No," he says just as swiftly. "No, Candra. I won't let you or the baby come to harm." He turns and wraps his arms around my waist, pressing his head to my stomach. "*Our* baby."

A lump of emotion forms in my throat. I stroke my fingers over the sweep of his horns. His sadness is tearing at me, and I have to improve the mood somehow. "The baby we're not supposed to have," I tease. "I guess your Fellian blood is more compatible with my cursed, awful blood than we imagined."

He chuckles against my stomach; his face pressed to my chemise. "It's because of that drop of Fellian in your ancestry. Maybe that's what's cursing your blood. You've got too much Fellian in you."

"Right now, I don't have any Fellian in me," I purr.

And then pause.

Because . . . what if he's right? What if the problem in my blood isn't a curse from the gods but because I've got too much Fellian ancestry, like he says? What if the cure for my curse is Fellian *blood*?

Nemeth sits up suddenly, staring down at me with wide eyes.

"Are you thinking what I am thinking?" he asks.

I nod, a little stunned. "I've never heard of something like this working," I confess. "But we were told the Fellian blood is a rumor. Then again, I was also told that those with cursed blood cannot get pregnant."

"Maybe you can't from a human man." He puts a large hand over my stomach; his two blunted claws strange and short against the others, marking him as mated. "But I am Fellian. Perhaps it's my blood you need." He looks up, casting his gaze around the room. "Do you have medical texts here?"

"As if I would know?"

"I just want to be certain before we try it," he says. "I don't want to inject you with something your body might consider poison."

There's no time to look through the enormous library for answers. It could take weeks, and we don't have weeks. "I say we try it. What have we got to lose?"

"Everything, Candra. We stand to lose *everything*." The look he gives me is pure anguish.

"You're wrong." I shake my head. "We have a few days at most. By tomorrow, I'll be violently ill. By the day after, I won't be able to stand. I'd rather not wait that long." I take his hand from my stomach and kiss his knuckles. "I trust you."

"This isn't about trust," he tells me, exasperated. "This is about science."

For him, maybe. For me, it's about faith. I might have lost my faith in the gods, but not in Nemeth. I give him an impish smile. "Let's try it anyhow."

He groans, and I know I've won the argument.

CHAPTER FORTY-THREE

Nemeth's blood could be my salvation or my doom. It seems strangely fitting, I think. I'm calm as I carefully plunge the needle into his arm and pull back the lever, taking just enough of his blood to fill the syringe. Nemeth wanted to do this part himself—he wants to spare me any trouble—but I can handle this.

If it works, Nemeth is the answer to my sickness. The thought that all I need is him and his blood is oddly freeing. I imagine I'd still need a dose daily, but the thought of being bound to Nemeth instead of a daily concoction of boiled animal pancreas and a mixture of herbs feels easy and right.

In my eyes, this is just another facet of our love.

Of course, if I'm wrong . . . I won't think about that. I'll focus on the positive instead. I wipe the needle carefully once I remove it, watching him from the corner of my eye as he folds his arm, pressing a bit of fabric at the pinprick of blood to staunch the flow. "How are you feeling?"

"Nervous," he grumbles. "What if we're wrong, and this makes you sicker?"

"Then it speeds up the inevitable and makes it easier for you to travel since you won't have me dragging you down." He growls, and I pat his knee. "We're out of options, love. This is the only choice we have left."

"I don't like it when you're right," he mutters. "You gloat."

"Let's just do it before we talk ourselves out of even trying." And before I'm far too sick to fight off any bad side effects. I'm confident, but at the same time, I'm well aware that I'm being effortlessly positive because we've got no other choices. Besides, Nemeth is worrying enough for both of us.

He tenderly takes my arm in his grip and hesitates. His eyes close, and I can tell he's agonizing. He doesn't want to do this. He doesn't want to risk me. I wait patiently. He braces himself, lifts my hand to his lips, and kisses my knuckles, and then picks up a towel and wipes the bend of my arm clean. When he puts the needle to my skin, he looks at me again. "I love you."

"I love you too. It's going to be all right," I reassure him. "Maybe this is what the gods wanted for me all along. Don't you think?"

Nemeth shakes his head. "I don't feel like the gods are watching us at all."

And with that cryptic statement, he pushes the needle in.

The mood is strange as we wait for the medication—Nemeth's blood—to take effect.

He holds me for hours. It's like he's afraid that if he lets me go, the worst will happen. Even though it's damp and humid in the old library, I remain locked in his arms, tucked against his chest. We're both quiet, as if speaking will somehow set things in motion. I don't tell Nemeth that when his blood enters my veins, it feels hot and a little itchy and very different from the potion.

We wait. And wait.

At some point, I fall asleep in his arms. When I wake up, I can see sunlight streaming through one of the doors into the palace, and the air smells crisp and dewy.

And I feel . . . good. Surprisingly good.

I sit up in Nemeth's arms. He immediately straightens, coming out of a deep slumber of his own with panic etched across his face. "Are you all right? How do you feel?"

"I think I'm fine?"

"Get up," he says. "Move around. Let's see if you get dizzy." There's a note of tension in his voice. "I do not think we should celebrate too soon."

Even before I get to my feet, though, I know. After years of living with my blood curse, I know what it feels like when my potion isn't strong enough. I know the waves of nausea that hit when I miss a dose. I know how it feels when things are *off*. And nothing feels off right now. I feel good. Amazing.

It feels as if some strange puzzle piece inside me has suddenly locked into place.

I push off of him and bounce to my feet. Gathering up the skirts of my chemise, I laugh and race across the library, kicking books out of the way as I do. Who cares about books at a time like this, anyhow? I feel *good*. I'm not tired.

Not drained. Not dizzy. Not feeling as if I'm going to vomit at any moment. Is this how healthy people feel every day? Like they could just run straight to the horizon and keep running? Lucky bastards.

"Careful, Candra," Nemeth warns, following after me. "Don't hurt yourself—"

I surge back toward him, running as fast as I can, and fling my arms around him. The momentum of my jump knocks us both to the ground, and I laugh and laugh and laugh. I laugh so hard I want to fling myself onto the floor and kick my legs like a child. "I'm free," I whisper, and my voice breaks into a sob. "I'm free."

"Are you well, love?" He rolls us over, his hands skimming over my body. "Does anything hurt?"

"Mmm," I say, my arms raised up above my head in a sensual stretch. I feel as if I can take on the world now. I want to both laugh hysterically and sob like a child for all that this means. "I do have one particular nagging ache."

"Gods," he murmurs, running his hands over one of my calves. "Where? Your arm? Your leg? How bad is it?"

"Higher," I tell him, helpfully pulling my skirts up a bit. When he reaches my knee, I sigh. "Keep going higher."

"Candra," he growls, and he looks utterly furious. "Do *not* make light of this."

"You don't understand, Nemeth," I say giddily. I squeeze my folded arms against my chest and shiver all over like a happy puppy. "I feel good! I feel good without the medicine! Do you know how much I've hated every dose? How much the scent turns my stomach sometimes? Do you know what this means? It means I'm *free*!" I choke on the word this time. "I'm bloody *free*."

Nemeth grunts, and I can't tell if he's pleased with me or still mad over my joke. "If by free you mean bound to me because now you must have my blood."

"Oh, pish-tosh. Being bound to you isn't a chore. I love you. I want to spend every day with you. Now I have an excuse." I beam at him. "It's the best of all worlds."

He doesn't beam back. His wings flick and then settle against his back. "You say that now, but what if you grow sick of me like Ravendor did her mate?"

Sick of him? When he's been the only thing keeping me going for so long? I shake my head and get to my knees, crawling over to him. I put a hand on his chest, pushing him back to the floor again. "I will never, ever be sick of you for as long as I live," I tell him. "You and I are in this together. There is nothing that will separate us."

"Nothing?" He arches a brow at me.

"Not even the gods." I grab the belt of his kilt and tug it off. "Now, come and kiss your wife."

"Is it kissing that's on your mind, then?" He jokes, even as my hands steal under his kilt and cup his shaft. I tease the budding knot at the base of his cock, loving the hiss of breath between his teeth. "That's not my mouth, Candra."

"I can kiss you in other places," I tell him, words coy. "But only if you ask me nicely."

Nemeth sinks a hand into my hair, his fingers curling in my mane. He holds my head pinned, and I gaze down at him, curious at the pause. But he only gazes up at me with stormy green eyes, his expression full of emotion. "This might be the best moment of my life," he tells me. "Seeing you healthy and happy."

"You're not saying that just because we're surrounded by books?"

"We're surrounded by death," he corrects. "On all sides. And yet somehow, as long as it doesn't touch you, I find I can manage. I can manage anything as long as I have you, Candra."

The look on his face is intense, vulnerable. I want to shower him with kisses and make him laugh so he'll stop looking so concerned. "Then it's lucky for you that you're stuck with me, hmm?"

"I am lucky," he agrees.

"So lucky."

He lowers me toward his face, and his lips brush against mine, just barely. "You can kiss me," he murmurs. "Or you can ride me. Your choice."

As if that's much of a choice at all. "Why can't I do both?"

"You can if you're feeling greedy." His other hand steals up underneath my chemise, skimming my thigh. "I won't judge you."

"You just want me on your knot," I tease. "Lucky for you, I'm feeling good enough to ride you for hours."

"Hours, you say?" He arches a brow at me, even as his fingers slide between my thighs. "You truly think you can last that long?"

"Is that a challenge, my mate?"

"It is."

I do so love a challenge.

I confess that we're shamelessly wasteful with the day. I know we should be focused on finding a boat to take us to the Alabaster Citadel. I know I should be hunting for my sister and the survivors of the sacked city. But we've got a bit of horse meat left, and our stomachs are full. We've got medicine for me, and for the first time in a long time, the pressing need for survival isn't quite as pressing as it usually is.

Instead of focusing on survival, we spend the day in bed.

Well . . . the floor counts as a bed. Most of the bedding that's left in the palace is soaked and moldy, but when I wake up from a delicious nap, Nemeth has found blankets for us. I don't ask what room they've come from—I don't want to know. We curl up in them, eat our horse jerky, and spend the day together, touching and kissing and loving.

I adore every moment of it, and I refuse to feel guilty. That will return soon enough. For one day, it's nothing but pleasure.

The next morning, we wake up early and head out to the deserted stable, where the sad, lone horse waits. He's skinny, searching the stalls for grass or hay, even though there's nothing to be found. The constant, incessant rain means that everything is muck, and any plants drowned long ago.

Even so, I rub the poor horse's nose and hug his neck. "I'm sorry," I tell him. "I'm sorry that it has to be you or us, friend." To think that I'm feeling guilty over the slaughter of a horse. It's just that . . . he's carried me when I was too tired to walk. He's seen the destruction of Lios and carried me this far. He's survived until now. It feels wrong to kill him.

"Remember that this is a mercy, Candra," Nemeth reminds me when I hug the horse's neck again. "We can't take him on the ship, and turning him loose here would just kill him slowly instead of quickly. There's nothing for him to eat. Better to let his death nourish us."

"I know." I do. It's just hard to watch. I bite my lip, hating that I'm so weak, but I've never been around death. It's always been hidden from me, and I don't think I can watch Nemeth slaughter the horse as it gazes at me. "Is it all right with you if I come back later? Once it's done?"

Nemeth moves to my side. He presses a kiss to my damp forehead. "Why don't you go search for mementos in the palace? Perhaps there will be something you can bring to your sister."

He's sending me away so I don't have to see the horse's death but I'm so grateful I don't even care. I give him a quick hug and then grab my skirts, hauling them clear of the calf-high muck at the entrance to the stable, and head back for the palace.

I spend most of the morning digging around in empty rooms, trying very hard to ignore all the destruction. I pointedly look away from tears in the tapestries and dark stains on the rugs. I don't find anything I think my sister would want. Whatever treasures Lios had have been taken by the conquerors, and now all that is left are scraps and memories. I head down to the library instead, determined to tuck away a few books for Nemeth. After all, if we're going to be taking a boat, we can certainly take a trunk full of books. I'm sure he'll fight me on this, but I'm good at winning fights. I pick a few of the rarer-seeming books, the ones at the top of his pile that he can't resist pawing every now and then. We don't have the luxury of staying here long enough so he can read them all, and I'm desperately glad about that.

It feels as if I'm roosting in the graveyard of my people and that if I remain here long enough, I'll be swallowed up by the dead.

Not that there has been a lot of dead. Other than a few scattered bodies, there's been nothing. I'm relieved, of course, but I'm also confused. There clearly was a battle fought here. Someone would have been killed, and the dead would have had to go somewhere. Nemeth explained to me that the Fellians burn their dead so they can be returned to the skies as ash and smoke, but that doesn't explain where the Liosian dead are.

Maybe they've all been taken captive and are currently at Darkfell. Maybe I'll see a sea of familiar faces when we get there.

Maybe.

I stack the books I want Nemeth to have into an unwieldy pile and then grimace at the mud I've tracked in. My shoes don't protect my feet as much as they simply seem to gather mud, and I've trailed a lot of it into the library. If it gets on the books, Nemeth will fuss, and while I find his fussing adorable, it does make sense to protect the books somehow. I think of a trunk my sister had in her quarters that was yet untouched. The lid's jewels were pried off, but it seemed otherwise intact and the perfect size to hold a variety of tomes for my Nemeth.

I head upstairs for my sister's quarters, and as I do, the sun comes out from behind the clouds and shines through one of the broken windows. It's such a rare occurrence that I pause in front of the windows, sighing with pleasure at the sunbeams . . .

. . . and that's when I see them.

The graves.

There are not many of them, but it's the size of each one that makes me clench the windowsill. Shards of glass embed themselves into my hands, but I don't pull away. I can't because I have to take in the sight below.

The palace once had gardens. I never cared for them much because my medicine made me sensitive to heat, and it always felt too warm to spend much time outside, but I remember my sister loved Lios's gardens. She loved the flowers that filled the beds, the vines that crept along the walls, and the scents of the herbs that flooded Nurse's herb gardens. I remember there was a maze, a sundial, and a statue of the goddess holding the moon above one shoulder like she was carrying a pot of water.

The statue of the goddess remains, but everything else is gone. The maze is gone. The hedges gone. The herb garden gone. What remains are five sunken pits in the muck, each one headed with the eye symbol of the Absent One, hastily carved out of wood. All of the sunken pits are nightmarishly big, bigger than my sister's entire suite of rooms, and I wonder just how many people were buried in each large grave.

Each one is far too big for just one body. Or even ten bodies.

This is what has happened to Lios. Tears prick my eyes, and I lean over the broken window as if pushing my face out into the light will somehow enable me to see more. I stare with sick horror at the mass graves, praying that my sister and her children aren't in any of them. That both Nurse and Riza are safe. That those I love somehow made it away from this place.

I want to leave. I need to leave.

Now.

Something flutters in the breeze. There's a heap of rags at the feet of the goddess, with a pair of swords sticking upright, the ends shoved through the rags and into the ground below. I wonder why these particular rags . . . and then I see a leg bone and the tiny bones that make up a hand, shattered and scattered in the mud. It takes me a moment longer to see the skull and realize one of the swords pierces it through the eye.

And resting upon that particular sword's hilt is a tarnished crown. I recognize that crown—recognize the spot where a fat, garish ruby sat on Lionel's brow like a giant red wart. It looked ridiculous against his pale skin and hair, and I'd spent many a night at court wishing the crown was upon any head but his.

That body—those remains—must be his.

Gods. I cannot even celebrate this death. I hated Lionel, but his death fills me with fear for my sister and their children.

"Nemeth," I cry out, turning away from the window and racing down the stairs. "Nemeth!" I fling myself down the hall, ignoring the skid of my feet on the perpetually damp floors. "*Nemeth*!"

The shadows coalesce in front of me, and then my mate is there, grabbing my arms and shaking me. There's a look of fright in his gaze. "Candra? What is it? What's wrong?"

"Good news," I choke. "We don't have to head to the far side of the city to find the dead."

And then I fall into his arms, weeping.

We don't bury Lionel. After the initial horror fades, I'm left with a deep, burning anger in my gut.

This is his fault. These deaths are upon him. Lios and Darkfell have coexisted in an uneasy truce for ages. He was the one who pushed for the war. He was the one who insisted I go to the tower, and quickly, so he could set off to conquer the mountains of the Fellians.

These deaths are on him.

While the meat from the horse smokes on racks in the kitchen (we burn the broken frame of a once-elegant poster bed), we head down to the shore and look for a ship. There are several wrecked vessels, but we manage to find a small craft with a broken mast. It's terrifyingly small for an ocean journey, perhaps the size of two horse lengths, but Nemeth assures me we don't need more than that.

We spend the rest of the day working on making her seaworthy. Nemeth replaces the mast with wreckage from another ship, and I sew a large piece of fabric that will act as a sail. As if the goddess likes the idea of us fleeing this place, the sun remains out, the rains temporarily banished. We erect a small tentlike shelter at one end of the ship that we can rest under when the sun is high, and Nemeth will cast a spell in the morning to enchant the sail itself. As long as it's on the ship, it will steer us toward the Alabaster Citadel.

And from there, to Darkfell.

I'm ready. I want answers, and all signs point to Darkfell having them.

CHAPTER FORTY-FOUR

SIX WEEKS LATER

The ship bobs on the water, the air disgustingly still and humid under the shelter at the far end of the craft. I've torn a few pages out of one of Nemeth's books and fan myself with them because sweating day and night is miserable. I'm already dehydrated, and sweating makes it worse. It rains often enough to fill the barrel we have on deck, but it's never enough to quench my burning thirst.

I thought I loathed the tower, but it turns out I loathe the sea even more. Weeks of endless travel. Weeks of rolling waves and storms that shake our tiny craft. Weeks of everything tasting like saltwater. Weeks of raw fish for breakfast, lunch, and dinner. Nemeth can spark fire with a spell, but without anything to burn, it's not very useful.

"I can see the mountains," he tells me as he lands on the front of our ship, making the entire thing sway in the water. "We should be there in a few hours."

I sit up, lacing the top of my bodice in case some Fellian flies overhead. It gets so hot on the water that I try not to wear much, but if we're going to land soon . . . "I never thought I'd be excited to see Darkfell's borders, but after spending the last several weeks on a ship, I'm more than ready for land." I glance over at my mate. "You don't think they'll treat us like the Alabaster Citadel, do you?"

Nemeth shakes his wings out, flicking away droplets of water, and then settles into a crouch next to me. "We'll be welcomed. It's different than with the citadel."

Is it? I'm not so certain. We'd hoped the Alabaster Citadel would welcome us and give us food and supplies. Instead, they'd turned us away at the harbor, keeping the holy temple closed to us.

"Traitors," the archbishop had cried, pointing a shaking finger in our direction. "It is your fault we have had two years of misery. It is your fault the goddess sends her wrath down upon us. You will receive no welcome here."

They'd refused to let us leave the docks themselves, keeping us at bay with pitchforks and angry cries. It was only later, after we'd changed the sail's spell and left the Alabaster Citadel, that we were able to think properly about what we'd seen. That's when we realized the men there had been of the clergy, and yet they'd been thin and dirty and unkempt. Whatever famine that was wrecking the land was at work at the lands of the Alabaster Citadel as well.

And their words made no sense. "Two years?" I'd questioned Nemeth. "How can they blame us for two years? We left the tower less than a month ago."

Nemeth had no answers either. "Perhaps they've been hit by misfortune since the beginning of the war, and we are an easy target to blame. We did leave the tower, after all."

He's not wrong . . . but must we be blamed for everything?

We'd sailed on from there, a tiny ship in the middle of an endless sea. We saw no other ships, and when we ventured close to land, we saw no people either.

And now we are nearing Darkfell, and I am just as unsettled as the day we left the tower. I lean forward in my seat, fanning myself with the pages. "Do you ever wonder if the gods are playing tricks on us?"

"Tricks?" Nemeth asks, rotating one powerful arm as he regards me. "How so?"

I gesture at our surroundings. "That when we left the tower, we stepped into some upside-down world, and that's why nothing makes sense? Why everyone is gone?"

Nemeth eyes me. "How does it not make sense that they are gone? They lost the war. Or is it that part that is so inconceivable?"

I shake my head because I don't want to pick a fight with Nemeth. "You know that's not it. It just feels so . . . odd. Like when we left the tower, we left our world behind too. This doesn't feel like our home. Not anymore."

He takes my hand in his. "Your home will be with me, Candra, and mine with you. Don't worry over things we cannot change."

Easy for him to say. We're sailing to his homeland because mine has been decimated. Still, I can't help but wonder what the archbishop meant when he blamed us for two years of misfortune. The goddess isn't angry at us, of course, but the rest of the world doesn't know that. Are we going to be punished for abandoning the tower after all? That's the part that gnaws at me and keeps me up at night.

That, and the endless swaying of our damn ship.

Nemeth lifts my hand to his lips, giving it a peck. "I'm going to scout some more. Do you need anything? How is the babe today?"

I put a hand on my rounded belly. Somewhere in the last month, it's swollen to double its size. It makes sense that I would have a large belly, given that Nemeth is rather gargantuan in stature, but it's not comfortable, and I wonder what I'm going to look like when I get closer to my due date. The baby is calm now, at least, and not kicking my bladder. "Sleeping, I think. And I'm good. Though if you see shore, look for berries?"

I've had the most ridiculous cravings for fruit recently. Never mind that there's no food anywhere on Lios's shores, and here I am asking for berries. But my mate gives me a wink, kisses my knuckles again, and then surges into the air with another powerful thrust of his legs. The boat rocks back and forth, and I clutch at the side, steadying myself.

Nemeth's flying has improved during our travels. He's constantly in the air, scouting or just looking for fish he can dive for and catch. I imagine that now that he's free of the tower, he has no desire to be tied down to our crappy little boat. I can't blame him. If I could leave the boat behind myself, I would in a heartbeat. The damn thing leaks, and every twitch makes it rock—it's just a wretched form of travel, especially for someone who can fly.

Sometimes I worry Nemeth will just fly away and abandon me. On my crankier days, when the baby's kicking me and the smell of raw fish makes me want to punch something, I think I'd leave myself behind too. But he always comes back, and he's always patient and gentle with me.

I sit up on the trunk that's been my seat for the last six weeks, the trunk full of books and our meager supplies. I cast out my fishing line after baiting it with the head of a minnow and ease the line into the water. Might as well fish for my lunch. I eye the mountains that have been growing increasingly dominant on the horizon with every day that passes.

I've always known that Lios is a land of rolling hills and plains and that Darkfell's people live under the mountains, but I've never really visualized the differences in the land until now. The Fellian continent looks as if it is hewn directly from rock, the cliffs steep and forbidding as the rock climbs so high that the clouds cover the tops. I can't imagine how anyone can live here. There's no place for a farm or livestock on the outside, and it makes me wonder what the interior looks like.

I don't tell Nemeth that I'm nervous. Of course, I'm nervous. After seeing what's left of Lios, it makes me wonder if my head will be on a pike before the next day. How do I know they won't spear me with a dozen swords like they did Lionel? I abandoned my sacred duty in the tower, after all. Being Nemeth's wife might not be enough to keep me safe.

My line tugs with a bite, and I jerk on it, trying to snag the fish. It goes still, and I relax, gazing up at the forbidding, looming mountains once more.

Nemeth will protect me, I remind myself. You carry his child. He loves you.

A shadow soars overhead, and I shield my eyes, glancing up as Nemeth sails through the skies, his wings outstretched, his form as powerful as it is dark. He's beautiful, and he looks at home here among the menacing, mountainous land. He's growing in strength by the day, and I feel as if I'm . . . not weaker, but more dependent.

Is this how Ravendor felt when she left the tower—like everything she'd known was different?

But Ravendor killed her mate if the stories are to be believed, and I don't think I could ever harm Nemeth.

He soars overhead again, and I wave at him, smiling brightly to hide my troubled thoughts.

Close to dark, Nemeth drops into the ship again, a worried expression on his face. "We're close enough that someone should have come out to see us."

He voices aloud one of my fears. I raise my hand to my brow, shielding my eyes as I gaze at the mountains. I've been sailing toward them all day, and they look no closer, but I've also never traveled much. I have no idea how close or far away they're supposed to look, nor do I have a clue if we should be seeing people. I don't even see a beach, just endless craggy mountains right up to the edge of the sea. "All of Lios seemed to be deserted. Do you think the same has happened to your people?"

The thought makes my stomach clench uncomfortably. If there's no safe haven for us here, either, what's left? There's a flutter in my belly that reminds me that there's more at stake than just myself and Nemeth—our child needs a home too.

"I don't know," Nemeth tells me. "I want to keep scouting and see. Will you . . . will you be all right here?" He hesitates, clearly torn between protecting me and finding out what he can. "It'll be dark soon, and I don't want you to be afraid."

I gesture at the small boat. "Afraid of what? A rogue wave? A sea monster? I would think if sea monsters existed, they would have already dined on us."

His hard mouth twitches with amusement. "There are no sea monsters on the shore. They're in much deeper waters."

"I hope for your sake that you're joking," I say tartly. Then I make a shooing motion at him. "Go and have a look around. I don't mind. I'll be fine here alone. You'll be able to find the ship? Even in the dark?"

"Always." He reaches for me, and the craft sways and bobs on the water, making my gut lurch. I hold onto the sides of the boat, grimacing, and Nemeth spreads his wings to steady himself. "I am more than ready to get off this damn ship and hold my mate again."

I'm a little surprised at his strong words. Nemeth is unfailingly cheerful when it comes to the boat, maybe because he knows how miserable it makes me. But I'm glad I'm not the only one who's tired of traveling . . . and more than ready to be in each other's arms again. It's been torture to be this close to him and not be able to sleep in his arms. We have just enough room to stretch out on the boat, but there have been no more than a few furtive touches here and there and far too few kisses. Everything is salty and damp and smells of raw fish. Every movement makes the boat sway. It's not conducive to lovemaking, especially with Nemeth's large form and my increasing belly. "Soon enough. The moment we get to your home, I'll suck your cock dry and nibble on your knot for hours, and you can feast between my legs for days. We'll be so unrepentantly amorous that people will think I've enchanted you with my evil Vestalin cunt."

He doesn't laugh at my joke.

Oh, by the gods. Surely the Fellians don't truly think I have an evil enchanted cunt? What a pile of dragon shite.

"I won't let anyone harm you, Candra. Do not worry about that. You've cast no spells on me."

"I know that," I sputter. My hands go to my belly, rounded with our child. "Don't you think if I had, it would be to travel in a less fishy environment? Or do you think I like waking up with salt in my hair and leaning my arse over the edge of the boat?"

This time, Nemeth's somber expression breaks into a grin. "I will wash every grain of salt from your skin when we get home, I promise. You'll see that Darkfell is pleasant and welcoming for all that it is underground."

Pleasant, maybe. Welcoming to one of the Vestalin name? I doubt it. But I'm out of options, and I won't leave Nemeth, so I blow him a kiss to show him how I feel. "Go do your scouting before it gets much darker, love. I'll be fine here." I gesture at my line. "Don't hold your hopes out for dinner, though. Nothing's biting."

"We'll be home soon enough, and you'll dine on the finest Fellian feasts," he tells me, a hint of excitement in his voice. "And I will return as quickly as I can. I swear it." He rubs the spot on his hand where my bite is tattooed on his skin, and it's as good as a kiss. With a wink to me, he launches himself into the air once more, and I cling to the edges of the damn rocking boat.

At this point, I'll happily run straight through Darkfell's doors if it means no more boats.

I catch nothing for dinner, and when the stars come out, I pull my line in and recline on my seat at the end of the boat, rubbing my rounded belly and gazing up at the stars. The Golden Moon is huge in the sky tonight as if the goddess is watching everything we do with a judgment-filled gaze. The stars are pretty, though. You can see them a lot better from out here in the ocean than in the palace. I gaze up at the sea of twinkling lights and hope that if the Gray God and the Absent One are watching from above, they know we're doing the best we can.

A shadow moves over the bright face of the moon. It's brief, but I catch a glimpse of wings. "Nemeth?" I call out. "Any luck?"

Heavy cloth smacks into my face, covering me like a blanket. I squawk with indignation because what a time for the sail to fall apart. In the next moment, a tight arm goes around my waist, and I'm dragged from the boat, claws digging into my skin.

I'm so surprised that I scream, only for a blow to land on the side of my head. "Quiet, human!"

That voice isn't Nemeth's. Dizzy, I flail, only for a heavy arm to push my limbs down. There's a strange puff of air, and then I'm dropped a few feet onto what feels like a cold stone floor.

"Get up," says a terrifying voice.

I don't, though. Panting, my head spinning, I try to make sense of what just happened. The air feels different. Out on the ocean, it's humid and damp, even when it's not raining, and there's a hint of salt that permeates everything. I don't smell salt now. The air is cold and dry, and when I press my hand to the floor underneath me, it's hard and chilly.

The shadow. A hood over my head. The claws that dug into my waist.

That wasn't Nemeth. Some other Fellian has kidnapped me.

A heavy boot thuds into my back, and I cry out in pain.

"I said get up," the voice tells me, impatient. "Lazy sack of shite. Stand up, or I'll make you stand."

I struggle to get the heavy hood off of my head, and when I finally pull it free, my eyes take a moment to adjust. The cool moonlight is gone. I'm inside a dark, shadowy cavern of some kind. When I look straight up, I can see a ceiling made of stone, curved high overhead. Near the ceiling are the same round magic globes that we used for light back in the tower. Nearby, I hear the slap of water against stone, and when I look around, I can see a few small ships in the distance, along with an enormous cave mouth that leads outside.

But I'm not outside. I've been taken into the depths of the mountains by a stranger. Looming over me is an unfamiliar Fellian, his face hard and unpleasant. When he glares down at me, he bares his teeth as if the hated sight of me makes him violent.

"Get up, human—"

"I'm up," I snap back. "Where's Nemeth?"

"Prince Nemeth?" The Fellian reaches out and shoves me the moment I get to my feet, nearly knocking me to the ground again. What a bully. "He's in the tower where he should be, doing his duty. Why do you care?"

I stare at him. Do I tell him that Nemeth left the tower? That I did too? That I mated to Nemeth, and I'm carrying his child? Something tells me he won't believe me. "Why did you take me from my ship?"

"Did I say you could talk to me?" He snarls, reaching out and slapping me.

I'm so shocked that I put a hand to my cheek and stare at him. He's treating me—a princess of Vestalin blood—like this? Then my anger kicks in. Because how dare he treat anyone like this? "Take me back to my ship. My mate is waiting for me there."

"Your mate," he sneers.

"Yes. My Fellian mate," I emphasize and decide to tell it all. I show him my hand with its tattooed bite. "Prince Nemeth. He's my mate."

He blinks at me. Looks at my palm. Then he throws his head back and laughs. "You humans are coming up with more and more clever ways to get out of work. I've never met a lazier lot."

"I'm not lying. Look at my hair. Look at my eyes. I'm a princess—"

He grabs my face so hard I know I'm going to have bruises, his hand covering my mouth. I let out a muffled yelp, fear flooding through my veins. For the first time, I realize that I'm just as vulnerable as any human. There's no Nemeth to protect me here. He might not even know I'm missing.

"Humans don't get to make demands of Fellians," he sneers at me. "You lost the war. Humans say 'yes, master' and 'no, master' and do as they're told." He flings me away, and I stagger backward, catching myself before I fall. He turns and glares at me. "Now . . . you tell me, woman. Who's your owner? Whose ship is that?"

"Yes, master," I say sarcastically, wiping a line of blood off my cheek from where his claws have cut me. "No, master."

His wings, tucked against his back, rattle in a way that I know means he's angry. He strides forward and grabs me by the front of my dress. "You think you're smart, human?"

"Yes, master," I jibe. I'm no longer scared. Now I'm just pissed. "I'm a lot smarter than you because you're slapping around the pregnant mate of your prince."

"You?" he sneers.

"Me." I say it with such confidence that I think it rattles him.

He stares at me long and hard and then shakes his head. "Lies." He grabs me by the shoulder. "You're going in the dungeon until we figure out who your master is. He can whip you for your impudence. I'm tired of this shite."

With that, he drags me down the hall as if I'm a piece of luggage.

I try to break free from his grip, but it's like one of iron. I'm surprised he's not flying, but I'm grateful too. Walking to the dungeon—if that's where we're going—gives me the opportunity to have a good look around at this new, strange kingdom I find myself in.

Because Darkfell—if this is indeed Darkfell—is very, very strange.

Nemeth had told me that the kingdom was a sprawling city under the mountains, but I wasn't able to visualize just what he meant. Now I can see it. The mountain itself is hollowed out, the "roof" of it so high in certain spots that it disappears into shadows. The rest of it is carved, and between the square houses that are stacked like blocks along cobbled paths, there are houses farther up, lining the high walls of the mountain. It's like a hive, and everywhere I look are homes gleaming with artificial lights at their doors. There are bright cloth awnings over what looks like street booths, and as my captor drags me forward, we pass a fenced-off area that resembles rows and rows of Nemeth's mushroom-farming board. It's all neat and tidy and industrious.

What I don't see are people.

There are a few, of course. There's a Fellian in the mushroom garden who disappears into shadows the moment they see me being dragged down the street by my captor. I see a few men in leather kilts and chest guards, dark winged and hard faced, watching as the man at my side hauls me along after him. But the streets feel strangely empty. I thought Darkfell would be crawling with people. With their limited space and so many houses, I thought I'd see nothing but Fellians on top of Fellians.

Instead, this place feels nearly as deserted as Lios. And as we head farther into the city, the sprawl continues—streets forking into narrow alleyways, buildings clustered atop one another, and even more of the nest-like homes high above—yet many of the homes have no lights on at all. Some of the houses have a strange red symbol painted on the door, and whenever we see someone, they cover their mouth and move hastily past. The mountain seems to echo all around us. Surely a crowded mountain wouldn't echo?

I turn to my Fellian captor. "Where is everyone?"

His expression grows ugly. He raises a fist at me, and I flinch, throwing my hands up to protect myself. "You'll shut your mouth if you know what's good for you, woman."

I try to wriggle out of his grip again. "Prince Nemeth—"

"—is in the tower," the man says, his claws digging furrows into my skin. He's almost bored, as if capturing humans is an everyday thing for him. As if it's no big deal to see a human near Darkfell, whose border has been closed to us for hundreds of years.

"I'm his wife," I try once more. "Prince Nemeth—he's my husband. Can't you cast a spell to see if I'm telling the truth or not? Use your magic."

The man hauls me up so quickly that I yelp. My feet come off the ground, and I dangle in midair, held aloft by the hand on my bodice. He snarls at me, showing huge fangs and a nasty demeanor. "Where did you hear that?"

"About Nemeth? He was in the tower with me. We left a few months ago—"

He pulls me closer, and I can smell his fetid breath. His pupils flick back and forth, studying me. "Who is your master?" he hisses. "Who showed you magic?"

Am I not supposed to know? "Nemeth showed me," I say again. "In the tower—"

My captor growls and flings me away. I skid across the cobbled floor, my arms protectively wrapped around my belly, and I wince when my head smacks against stone. That one's going to leave a mark. I manage to pull myself upright, panting. "If you hurt me again, he's going to kill you," I warn. "He didn't keep me alive for two years just for you to beat the stuffing out of me."

"Woman, I am warning you." He points a claw at me. "Cease with your lip and get to your feet."

If this cretin wanted me on my feet, then why'd he push me off of them?

With a huff of irritation, I stand up—and immediately get dizzy. I haven't eaten since a few bites of fish this morning, and clearly, my body has a problem with this. I shake a finger at the Fellian man. "Nemeth will not be happy about this."

And then I pass out at his feet.

CHAPTER FORTY-FIVE

I wake up with a foul taste in my mouth and a horrible headache. Groaning, I put a hand to my forehead and remain where I am, just in case the dizziness is lingering. There's a rough blanket under me, and it's very quiet, so quiet I can hear a drip of water in the near distance. I touch my belly and it seems unharmed, which is a relief. Somewhere nearby, there's a drag of chains and a low murmur of conversation.

Human conversation.

It excites me so much I almost bolt upright again, so desperate to see the faces of my people. I never thought of myself as particularly patriotic until now, when I've lost everyone and everything. It takes everything I have to remain still, and I turn my head, looking at my new surroundings.

My captor is gone. That's a good thing. He was getting far too rough and arrogant for my tastes. But his disappearance also means no one knows that I'm here or that I've been asking for Nemeth. *Panic later*, I tell myself. *Figure out where you are now.*

A quick glance around makes it obvious, though—I'm in the dungeon. The walls are narrow stone that encloses the thin pallet I'm lying upon, and there's very little light to see by. I stretch an arm out and confirm my suspicions—with both arms extended, I can touch both sides of my cell at the same time. There's a bucket near my feet that sits by the door, which has a window covered with a metal crosshatch of bars. I crawl forward on my bed and gag at the smell of the bucket—this is clearly not the first time it's been used for a toilet. I use the door to help me to my feet, leaning on it for balance, and press my face to the bars, desperate to hear more of those Liosian voices.

When I look out, I see a dark stone corridor lined with more doors just like mine. I still hear voices, though, and as I watch, a pale arm reaches out of one of the mesh grids and toward its neighboring cell, only to be met by another hand. They pass something between them—a hunk of bread—and then quickly disappear again.

They were human, though. Those fingers weren't tipped with claws.

"Hello?" I call out. "Let me out. Nemeth is looking for me."

A large, heavy figure emerges from the shadows. I know from the sound of his wings that he's a Fellian, even before those creepy green eyes meet mine. "Quiet, you."

I ignore that because being quiet never got a girl anywhere. "Where exactly am I, kind sir?" I flutter my lashes at him and lick my lips in what I hope is an enticing manner. "I fear I'm lost."

He swipes at the bars with his claws, making me yelp and surge backward. "You'll listen to me when I tell you to be quiet, woman."

"But where am I?" I stay out of reach behind the bars on the door, just in case. "My name is Princess Candromeda Vestalin, and I'm looking for Prince Nemeth of the First House. He'll be looking for me as well."

The guard's eyes narrow at me, and he sneers. "So you're royal, huh?"

"I am." I try to look as dignified as possible.

"What if I told you all the royal wenches from Lios were busy sucking cock down at the *barracks*? You still going to claim to be royal?"

My eyes go wide. Royal wenches? In the barracks? "W-what?"

"You heard me. Still claiming to be a princess?"

I say nothing.

"Good. Now, if you want your food, you'll be silent, won't you?"

My stomach growls, and I decide that maybe it's best to say nothing for now. I cross my arms over my chest protectively and glare, keeping to the shadows of my cell. I realize he can come in anytime he likes because a Fellian can move through shadows. I take another step back, twitching, in the hopes that my movements look erratic enough that he won't teleport in and bother me.

What if I told you all the royal wenches from Lios were busy sucking cock down at the barracks?

That's a lie. I know it's a lie. There are no "royal wenches" other than myself and my sister because Lionel had no siblings, and Meryliese is dead. But I've got enough sense to know that I don't want to push him. No one here believes I'm a princess anyhow. It won't do me any good.

And I'm *starving*. So hungry that my stomach feels hollow and painful. My baby needs to eat. *I* need to eat, or I'm going to become dizzy and sick. Well, sicker, considering I'm going to get sick anyhow if I don't get my medicine soon. "I would like to eat."

"Oh, *would* you?" he sneers. "What a fine lady you are. Remember that here, you're nothing but a slave."

I don't respond. Nothing I say is going to make a difference. I could tell him that I'm Candra Vestalin all day long, and he's not going to believe me. Candra Vestalin should be inside the tower, after all, devotedly fulfilling her duty to mankind and the goddess, and I'm the wretched creature that ran from it.

He grunts at my silence and then disappears in a flare of smoke. A moment later, he returns, loops a skewer full of mushrooms onto a hook just outside my cell's "window," and sets a stone cup outside on a ledge. "Your food, lady."

The guard emphasizes the word as if I'm lying.

"I need medicine too. I have to take it every day."

His reaction isn't what I expect. Instead of sneering at me, his eyes widen. He grabs a length of material loose around his neck and immediately covers his mouth with it as he takes a step back. "You're sick?"

"No, of course not." His alarmed reaction has me worried, and I decide to lie. "For my woman's time."

The look the guard shoots me is both one of relief and irritation. "Eat your food, woman. If I catch you acting up, that'll be the last meal you get for a while. Understand?"

I nod. I hate being such a weakling, but I'm no use to anyone if I'm too sick to function. Nemeth needs me—and the baby—alive and well. So, I wait in silence until the guard gives me one last glare and leaves. Then, I reach through the bars, grab the skewer with the loop at the end, pull it off of the hook, and drag it into my cell. The mushrooms were grilled hours ago and are cold, but they remind me of Nemeth's mushroom "farm" back in the tower, and those were always delicious. I gobble them down like a mannerless child and then lick my fingers. The mug is full of cold water, and I drain that, too, then replace the dishes in their spot and retreat to my pallet.

Lying down, I listen to the noises of the cells around me. There's a woman crying somewhere. A cough. A low murmur of voices. They all sound like women, except for the occasional barked command of the guard, who's a Fellian man. There's no sunlight in here; I saw only a few magic lights lining the walkways as I was dragged inside. I don't know how deep I am into Darkfell.

I don't even know if I'm still *in* Darkfell. How will Nemeth ever find me?

Pressing a hand to my forehead, I fight back frustrated tears. I just have to survive. He'll come for me. He will. He won't stop hunting until he finds me because I'd do the very same for him.

Even so, I'm frightened.

"Psst."

The sound is so low I'm not sure I hear it at first.

"Psst."

I turn on my side, staring at the brick wall next to my shoulder, where the hissing sound is coming from. A finger wiggles through a crack in the mortar.

"Psst." I hear again. "Princess. Is that really you?"

I gasp and turn on my hands and knees, pressing my cheek to the coarse blanket and mat that make up the bedding in my cell. The voice I heard, asking if I was the princess is unfamiliar to me, but they were speaking the Lios tongue. I gaze at the tiny crack in the mortar of the rock wall, where the finger slips away again. I can't see anything on the other side. It's too dark. I'm reminded abruptly of Balon and his visits to the tower, the gossip he told me through the wall, and how I'd begged for him to free me.

A wave of longing hits me. It feels like a hundred years ago since those days.

"Who's there?" I ask when the voice goes silent. I'm tempted to stick my finger through the hole to the prisoner on the other side, but what if it's a trap? So I brush chips of mortar away from the hole, trying to widen it. "Hello?"

"I'm here." It's a woman speaking softly enough that our conversation won't be heard by the guards. "My name is Senna. I worked in the palace as a washerwoman. Are you really the princess?"

"I am," I tell her, excitement racing through me. "It's me, Candromeda."

The finger appears through the rocks again, wiggling. "Give me a piece of your hair so I know it's you."

Oh. Hastily, I pull a few dark strands free of my messy braid and wrap them around the wriggling fingertip. It retreats back behind the stone walls. A quiet moment passes, and I grow impatient. "Well?"

"It's you, isn't it? You even sound all impatient like a princess."

Well, then. "I'm not lying."

"I know. I didn't think it was really you until you mentioned the medicine," the voice on the other side—Senna—says. "Riza is my friend. She told me about you and the potion you have to take daily. That you get sick if you don't get your medicine. Why aren't you in the tower?"

I bite back a sound of excitement when she mentions Riza's name. I've missed her so much. I know she's my maid, but she's also my companion and friend and a constant person in my life . . . or at least she was before I entered the tower. "Where is Riza? Is she well?"

"She's here in Darkfell," Senna whispers. "She was sold off to a Fellian master, so I rarely get to see her anymore."

Sold off? Like a farm animal? The idea is horrifying . . . but at least she's alive and well. When I get out of this dungeon, I'll have Nemeth free her. "What about my sister, the queen? Erynne? Is she here too?"

"Aye. She's the slave of one of the Fellian princes."

"Why is she a slave?" I choke, horrified. "What happened to Lios? Tell me everything!"

"She's a slave because she's pretty," Senna says, her voice bitter. "When the Fellians took the city, they slaughtered the men and took the women captive. They brought us back to this place, but it's just another tomb."

"A tomb?"

"You'll see." She chuckles as if this is all somehow funny. "So what's the princess doing in the dungeon instead of in the tower?"

"I left the tower when there was no more food," I confess.

"Mmm, aye. There's no food anywhere above ground. The goddess weeps constantly, and the rain washes everything away. At least these Fellian bastards have food." She laughs, and the sound is faintly unhinged. "Up above, we starved. Down here, there's food, but it's a different kind of hell."

I blanch. "Why are you down here?"

"Because I spit in my owner's food," Senna tells me, still laughing. "And food can't be wasted. He had to eat it or give it to me. So he sent me down here to teach me a lesson. More fool him; I'd rather be here in the dungeon than out there. At least down here, I'm safe."

"Safe from what?"

"From the goddess's wrath, of course. She's not starving the Fellians. She's got a very different punishment for them." Senna laughs again. "You can't escape the eye of the goddess, even underground! She still watches!"

My skin prickles with goose bumps. Senna doesn't sound . . . well. "About the goddess—"

"*CANDRA*!"

The bellow comes from down a distant, echoing hall, but every pore in my body pricks to attention the moment I hear it. I know that voice. I jump to my feet, forgetting all about Senna on the other side of the wall, and I press my face to the bars of my cell. "Nemeth! I'm here!"

There's a furious sound, a manly roar of primal fury, and the sound of something crashing into a wall. "*Where is she*?"

"Nemeth!" I cry again, shaking the door of my cell even as the guard swoops through the shadows toward me. "Let me out of here! Nemeth!"

"Woman," the guard hisses as I grab the empty cup from its shelf and bang it against the metal of my door. It makes a horrifically loud sound, which delights me, and even when he snatches it out of my hand and grabs me by the front of my dress, I don't care. Nemeth is *here*. He's going to save me. "Be silent—"

The shadows thicken behind the guard, and then Nemeth coalesces into the open space behind him. His eyes are wild and frantic, his teeth bared, and his wings tucked tight behind him in what I recognize as a warrior stance. His nostrils flare when he spots the Fellian man who has the front of my dress, and he grabs him by the knot of horns at the back of his head and drags him backward. "*You don't get to touch her*!"

Oh gods. Is Nemeth going to kill one of his own for mistreating me? "Wait! Nemeth, don't!"

He stops.

To my vast relief, he stops. Nemeth stares at me for a long moment as if not believing his eyes. He pushes the Fellian in front of my cell aside, and his gaze searches my face. "Open this."

The guard disappears in a flood of shadows and then returns a moment later with a key.

Nemeth doesn't move. His eyes devour me, and I know he's making a mental note of every bruise and scrape and adding them to a mental list. His wings look brittle with tension, and even though he's not fidgeting, I can feel the anger brimming through him. I reach out and touch his finger even as the guard fumbles with the keys to unlock my cell. "It's fine. I'm fine."

"You are not fine. You're in a dungeon." Nemeth's gaze darkens with fury. "A Darkfell dungeon."

"A misunderstanding," I reassure him. My indignation fades in light of Nemeth's fury. I don't want him endangering himself, and I don't know how his people will take it if he kills one of his own . . . because I absolutely believe that Nemeth would have killed the guard at that moment. There was something dark and unpleasant in his eyes when he saw I was in danger.

And I'm a terrible person because I liked it.

I keep smiling brightly at Nemeth as the guard fumbles with the keys again. It's too narrow for him to teleport in—or he doesn't trust the guard while doing so—and we have to wait as the other Fellian mumbles apologies and tries to find the correct key. When the door finally opens with a creak, Nemeth all but yanks me out of its depths and into his arms.

He wraps himself around me tightly, one hand in my hair and the other on my back, and he hugs me to his chest. I cling to him, breathing in his scent, listening to the sound of his rapid, angry heartbeat. Tears threaten my eyes, but I blink them back. I'll cry over this tomorrow. When we're settled and safe, I'll cry. Until then, the tears will have to wait. "I'm safe," I whisper to him. "I knew you'd come for me."

He steps backward and cups my face in his hands, his thumb stroking my cheek. "You are injured. Was it this guard?"

"I'm fine," I insist. "Misunderstandings are to be expected at times like this, and we can't afford revenge. I'm just glad you're here." I clutch his arms, glad for his strength and his reassuring presence. "What happens now?"

"We are leaving," he tells me in a low, furious voice.

We . . . are? When he takes me by the hand and pulls me forward, away from the other cells, it seems that, yes, we are, in fact, leaving. "Where are we going, Nemeth?"

"Anywhere but here. I won't let my mate be treated like this." The bitter fury is still in his voice.

That worries me. We've run out of places to go, haven't we? Lios is gone, a wasteland of mud and rain. There's no food to be found there, just like in the tower. The Alabaster Citadel won't have us. Isn't Darkfell all that remains?

Before I can ask about his plan, the soldier who initially captured me—the unfamiliar Fellian—appears in a nearby alcove and immediately hops down onto the floor in front of us. Right after him, a second Fellian appears, this one tall and slender, but there's something familiar about his face. He floats down next to the other, and I get a good look at his clothing. Unlike the first Fellian, this one's chest is covered with leather straps that braid and cross each other, holding an ornate chest plate over his heart. The designs on the chest plate look familiar, and I glance over at Nemeth.

"Brother," he growls. "You look unwell."

Brother?! This is the king? I stare at the taller, thinner Fellian. He has some resemblance to Nemeth, I realize upon a second look. It's there in the set of the eyes and the stubborn jaw. This one, though, looks younger than my Nemeth. And he *does* look unwell, his gray skin a sickly pale shade.

"I'm recovering," Nemeth's brother says. "And I'm surprised to see you here. It's true, then. You left the tower? Abandoned your duty?"

"What about your duty to supply us with food?" Nemeth retorts. "We had no choice but to leave." He steps slightly in front of me, just enough to put his bulk between me and the other two Fellians. It's not obvious at first what he's doing, but when they both narrow their eyes in my direction, I realize that Nemeth doesn't trust them not to attack us.

The tall one grunts acknowledgment of Nemeth's words. "You need to talk to the king."

So this isn't the king, then. This is . . . another brother? I hold tight to Nemeth's hand, wanting to ask a million questions but biting them back. There'll be time for that later.

"I'll speak to Ivornath, but only after my wife has rested. We're going to my quarters."

The brother tilts his head. "Wife?" His gaze is withering as he looks me over. "You took the other Vestalin princess as your mate? Both my brothers are fools, then." He gives an irritated shake of his wings, spreading them wide. "I will tell the king of your arrival . . . and your mate. He'll find it interesting, to say the least."

Nemeth's hand just tightens on mine.

The two Fellians fly away, taking to the tall shadowy ceiling and disappearing into its depths. I watch as they go, and it makes me wonder. Why is no one surprised or upset that we left the tower? Has something more happened?

And what did he mean by "both my brothers are fools?" What has Ivornath done with Erynne?

CHAPTER FORTY-SIX

Nemeth picks me up and flies me through the labyrinthine, dark tunnels of Darkfell. I'm too tired to protest, and though I know he must be exhausted, too, his wingbeats are strong and confident. I'm not entirely surprised when we continue to go up instead of through the bottom part of the city, and when Nemeth sets his feet down, it's upon the ledge of one of the tallest homes at the ceiling of the mountain. Beautifully embroidered banners hang outside his door, decorated in the same insignia that he wears upon his belt—the insignia of the First House of Darkfell.

The lights—the magical lamps that are so prevalent here—are on just outside his home. The double doors of metal automatically open to let us in, and then we're inside. He sets me down gently, pressing a kiss atop my head, and then he moves about the chamber, tapping lights to illuminate the inside.

And what an interior.

I'm not entirely surprised to see the massive shelf of books that immediately catches my eye. What I am surprised to see is that his home is built upward instead of outward like human homes are. The bottom floor is a visiting area with a reception table and several backless chairs near a cold hearth. On the next level, I see a small dining area and, above that, a workroom of some kind. I cannot see the very top of the house from my vantage point, but I assume that it's the bedroom. Everything is neat and tidy and screams of familial wealth. The walls are hung with silken drapes that cascade from the high ceiling, and delicate mosaics cover the floor. My feet rest upon a circle of brightly colored fish, and the wall across from me looks like a depiction of the three gods, with jeweled offering bowls set in front of each visage.

Of course, the bookshelves stretch all the way to the ceiling. This is Nemeth's home, after all.

Of course, there are no stairs. This place was made for winged people.

As if he can read my mind, Nemeth glides down to my side and lands with a thump. "Do not be alarmed, Candra. I will have workmen come and build stairs for you immediately." He takes my hand in his. "Until then, you'll be safe in my bedroom. There is a garderobe and a bathing chamber on that level as well."

I manage a nod. Fatigue overwhelms me, and I want to ask him a dozen questions, but I'm so tired that I can't think straight. All I can do is clutch his oversized hand tightly. "You found me."

Nemeth shakes his head, his jaw tight. He skims the back of one knuckle along my cheek. "They bruised you."

"I'll live."

He swallows a lump in his throat. "When I found the boat empty, I thought . . . I thought perhaps you'd fallen over. That I'd lost you for good."

Oh. I can't imagine how horrible it's been for him. "I'm glad you decided to look inside the mountain."

"I saw a scout flying, and I hoped . . . " His voice catches, and then I'm wrapped in a tight hug again, wings and everything. "By the gods, Candra. I don't ever want to let you out of my sight again."

"Then don't," I say against his chest, breathing in his scent. "Drag me everywhere like a pet. I'll sit on your knee, and you can feed me scraps. It'll be lovely."

He chuckles, and I'm glad to push some of the darkness from his gaze. He strokes my tangled hair. "You need your medicine."

"I do. And a meal."

"They didn't feed you?" He practically bristles.

"They did. A bit of mushrooms. I'm still hungry, though." I gaze up at him. "The dungeons are full of Liosian women. They thought I was just another captive who'd run away. They thought I was a slave. Your people have enslaved mine, Nemeth."

"They lost the war."

"You mean Lionel lost the war," I point out. "Lionel and his men. And now the women have to suffer?"

"It is the way of war—"

"It's *dragon shite*." I realize I'm raising my voice and press a kiss to his chest, to the side of the insignia buckle he wears. His skin tastes like salt, like the ocean. He probably hasn't had a moment to rest since I disappeared. Immediately, I feel like a selfish arse. "I'm sorry. I just have a lot of feelings right now."

"Remember that I am always on your side, Candra." His wings flare out, and he holds me tighter to his chest. "Let's get you your medicine. I won't have you fainting on me."

Nemeth's bedroom reminds me of his tower room, oddly enough. From wall to wall, it's covered with shelves of books, scrolls, and ancient jars stuffed between heavy-looking tomes. There's a reading table with a large book spread upon it and a round, circular glass that magnifies the words underneath so he can read even the tiniest script. His rich-looking furniture is squeezed in between shelves and book-laden tables, and the sight of the scholarly clutter makes me smile.

Nemeth is less pleased, though. He makes an unhappy sound at the sight. "I'd forgotten how many books I have up here. My rooms are probably not up to a Liosian princess's standards."

I snort at that. "The floor doesn't rock, and I'm not being splashed with seawater, so it's automatically better than the ship. I don't mind in the slightest."

He fusses over me, insisting I sit on the bed, and wraps me in blankets. "I'm going to have servants bring food. Wait here."

As if I can leave. I'm on the top floor of his house, which is against the ceiling of the hollow mountain's insides, perched like a bird's nest. I'm not going anywhere. But I nod, and he disappears for a long moment, drifting into the shadows. When he returns, he appears a short distance away in a circle drawn onto the mosaic floor. It's not the first time I've seen that circle on the floors here in Darkfell, and I wonder about it.

"Someone will be up with a tray shortly," he tells me, stepping off the circular platform and moving to my side. "How do you feel?"

"Better," I admit. Nemeth's blood is coursing through my veins, vivid in its potency, and I feel better than I have in a while. "So, this is Darkfell."

He grunts, his expression distant. "It is not the same as I left it."

"What is?" I joke softly, thinking of my own home.

Nemeth moves to my side and takes my hand, giving it a sympathetic squeeze. "I am not making light of your homeland's fate. It is only that . . . it feels off here. Strange. The halls are so deserted, and everyone seems . . . " He pauses. "Reserved? No, that's not right. Downtrodden, I suppose. But that makes no sense. We were the victors of the war. So why is the mood so somber?"

"Maybe a lot more went on than we know."

He opens his mouth to speak, but a woman—a Fellian woman with a longer swoop of horns and a lighter gray shade to her skin—enters the room. Nemeth is silent as the woman moves about, wearing a short tunic with a skirt not unlike Nemeth's kilt, but made of linen instead of leather. She seems sulky, too, as if she's displeased to be serving, and I suspect that has a lot to do with me. No one here likes humans. I can't say I blame them, not if we started the war.

The woman sets down a tray filled with mushrooms and cheeses and a carafe of wine. She sets out a few bowls, pouring oil and spices into them, and then slices a slender loaf of crusty bread. That done, she executes a quick bow, her hands fisted over her breast as she bends at the waist, and then flits out, disappearing into the shadows.

"She didn't look happy," I point out, getting to my feet and approaching the tray, lured by the sight of the bread. How long has it been since I've had bread? Flour always ran out quickly in the tower. But by the gods, this bread is fluffy and fresh, and it smells divine. I take one fresh slice and lift it to my nose, inhaling deeply. "This shouldn't make me nearly as happy as it does."

Nemeth grins, dragging two of the stools away from the wall and setting them at the table. "Enjoy it. I can ask for more if we need more."

I wave a hand at him, dismissing that. After being hungry for what feels like forever, stuffing my face with bread seems wasteful, no matter how much the idea appeals to me. I sit down on the stool he gives me, and we eat, soaking the bread in oil and spices and devouring the mushrooms and cheese. It's quiet; the only sounds that of chewing.

Nemeth's expression is distant, and I can tell he's worried.

I nudge him with my foot. "Tell me about your home."

"What do you want to know?"

"Do you have quarters high up because you're important or because they want to forget you exist?" I twirl a finger, gesturing at his sumptuous apartment.

He gives me a narrow-eyed look. "Both, I imagine. My younger brother, Ajaxi, is quick to agree with Ivornath's plans, no matter how strange or convoluted. I am the one who protests, and thus I am not nearly as loved by my brothers." Nemeth's mouth curves up in one corner, and he pops a bite of cheese into it. "I was never here much anyhow. I would visit a few times a year, but I lived at the Alabaster Citadel up until a few months before entering the tower."

"Why?"

"Why what?"

"Why did you leave the citadel a few months before you were supposed to enter the tower?" I think of Meryliese, who never visited court to see Erynne or me. She stayed in the citadel up until the very end, only to die in a shipwreck. My conscience twinges, and I wonder how she felt, trapped in one place, waiting to be trapped in yet another. We should have reached out to her more. Should have written more. Visited. Something.

Nemeth's expression grows shuttered, and he holds a piece of cheese out to me. "Family matters. Eat more. Remember, you're carrying our child."

I know a deflection when I see one. "As if I could forget. All right, what's that circle, then?" I point at the one that Nemeth appeared in when he teleported back. It is the same one the servant teleported in through. "Why does everyone come through there?"

He nods as if this is an easy question. "Remember when I said that a Fellian can die if they teleport into a spot and something is in the way? The circles prevent that. They are safe spots, spelled to ensure that if someone is standing in place, no one else can come through until the circle is vacated. Each house and building in Darkfell has such a circle."

Makes sense. I nibble on the cheese he gave me, wondering if it'd be too greedy to snag another piece of bread. There's a tasty-looking end near his side of the table that he's ignoring, and I have a powerful lust for it. "Very well. So circles are for travel. What about the red swirl? The one on so many of the doors?"

"I wasn't looking at the doors," he tells me.

I dip my finger in the oil and take the last piece of bread, drawing the door symbol on it. It's almost snakelike, if the snake was eating its own tail, and each one I saw had been a bright, vivid red. "I saw that mark on several doors. Do you know what it means?"

Nemeth stares down at the bread. He picks it up . . . then rips it in half, and offers half to me. "I'll have to ask when I speak with my brother."

Hm. It's strange that Nemeth—as learned as he is—wouldn't know a symbol like that. But I don't press. I'm just thrilled to be here with him, safe inside Darkfell. For once, it feels like we can stop running in search of our next meal. We can breathe. I smile at him and lick the oil off my finger, then finish off my piece of bread. "The brother that I met?"

"No. That was Ajaxi. Ivornath is king. He is the one I must speak to."

"When?"

"As soon as possible." He rubs his jaw.

He's right. Best we get this taken care of as quickly as possible. One day that my sister spends in slavery is a day too many. I don't care about our differences—she was doing what she thought was best for Lios, for our bloodline. I can disagree with her, but I can't be angry, not after everything that's happened. "Good idea," I tell him, fighting back a yawn. "Let me wash up, and I'll go with you."

"No," Nemeth says immediately. At my surprised look, he continues in a gentler voice. "It's better if it's just me for now, love. You might not be as diplomatic in your thoughts as you could be." I want to argue, but Nemeth looks tired. So tired. I remind myself that while I was sitting in a dungeon, passed out on a mat, he was searching frantically for me. That he didn't know if I was alive or dead. My heart softens. "Tomorrow, then."

"Tomorrow." He rubs his face and gives me a weary smile, reaching for my hand. "You'll be safe here, even without me. There's a stone carving by the teleport circle. Put that in the circle once I'm gone, and no one will be able to slip in without coming through the front door. And I will lock the front door with a spell that will only allow me to cross the threshold."

Once again, I marvel at the cleverness of the spells. A stone—or any object—placed in the circle stops the teleportation and gives someone privacy. It's genius. "So we're all alone up here?" When he nods, I get to my feet and move toward him, tugging at the leather straps on his chest. They're bloated with seawater, and the metal buckles are tarnished, but he's here, and he's gorgeous . . . and he's mine. "So that means if I decide I can't go another moment without licking your knot, no one would interrupt?"

His eyes grow heated. "*No one.*"

Well, now, that sounds lovely. "Good because I've missed you dreadfully," I tell him, aching with the truth of it. It's been forever since we've touched each other intimately. Forever since we've gotten to caress one another. Forever since we've eased the hungry ache of need.

Our bond feels like the only thing that's constant in this shifting world. I want to touch him, and I want to be touched.

Now.

I tug at one seawater-soaked strap that crosses his chest. "Would it be inappropriate of me to take my Fellian husband's knot into my mouth and suck it until he comes?"

Nemeth's breath grows ragged. "I . . . I haven't bathed."

I pretend to look around his quarters. "I thought I saw a bathing pool around here. I'm happy to bathe you first." Personally, I've swallowed enough seawater in the last few weeks that I don't care if his skin tastes like salt and sweat. I don't care about anything except touching him. He could drag his dick through mud in the next moment, and I'd still want to lick him clean. I want him so badly.

He groans and jumps to his feet. Before I can ask where he's going, he shadow-teleports over to the circle and kicks the stone carving into it. A moment later, he's back at my side, pulling me into his arms and then teleporting us both to the bathing pool. With a hungry growl, he rips at the front of my dress.

That makes me squeak in distress. "It's my last gown—"

"I'll get you new ones," he promises, tearing the worn fabric away. My breasts spill out, bouncing in the cool air.

I gasp, but I'm aroused at his ferocity. I love this side of Nemeth. I love that he's here. I love that he came for me, that he's just as hungry to touch me as I am to touch him.

He captures one breast in his hand, dropping to a crouch and nuzzling at the tip of the other. I whimper, heat sizzling through me as he rips the rest of my dress off, even as he tongues my nipple, teasing the other with his thumb. "I thought I was going to suck on your knot—"

"Patience," Nemeth growls. "I need to claim you first."

I bite back a whimper because I need that too. Gods, do I need that. He gets to his feet and flips me around onto my belly, pushing me over the edge of the pool. I scramble to hold onto something as he kicks my feet apart because I know what's coming next, and I'm so damn ready for it that I could scream. Big hands grip my hips, hauling me up slightly, and in the next moment, the tip of him brushes against my entrance.

That's the only warning I get before he plunges deep.

With a cry, I shudder and brace myself against the steps to the pool. He thrusts into me again, surging our joined bodies forward, and his knot—rock hard and insistent—presses against my entrance. Nemeth pounds into me, growling. "Take my knot. Take it, Candra."

He's never been so fierce. So relentless as he hammers into me, pressing against my core as if he can somehow work his knot in with sheer determination. Gods, it's so sexy. I love that he's using me. "Make me come," I pant. "Then you can knot me."

Nemeth pumps into me again, and his big hand slides between my thighs. He spanks my pussy, stretched tight around him, and I squeal in surprise at the sensation. That should not have felt nearly as good as it did, but when he does it a second time, I clench up in a burst of pleasure.

"You're mine, aren't you?" he demands. "My mate. My bride."

He spanks my pussy again, then massages my clit with his thick fingers. I come, choking on my breath at the sheer force of my climax, and with a roar, he presses his knot into my slickened heat, claiming me as his. I pant through the tight sensation, more pleasure prickling up and down my spine as he comes, our bodies locked together. He clutches me in place, holding me tight, and I try to catch my breath as curls of pleasure drift through my body. I'm dimly aware of the absolute stretch of his cock inside me, of his knot pulsing just within my channel, and the pleasure keeps flowing, pulsing in time with our heartbeats.

"So much for a bath," I manage.

"Oh, we've just begun," my mate purrs, rubbing a big hand down my spine. "I can bathe you while knotted inside you, my pretty human."

I whimper because that sounds both obscenely delicious and like far too much. Nemeth is determined, though. He tugs me upright, our bodies still locked tight, and when I flail, he wraps a big arm around my waist, holding me anchored in front of him. With that, he spreads his wings for balance and climbs into the pool.

And I moan as the heat of the water soaks into my bones. "It's warm. Gods, this is amazing."

"Here I thought you were tired of water," Nemeth murmurs, sinking our joined bodies deeper into the bath.

"I am absolutely sick to death of the sea," I point out. "A nice, clean, *hot* bath is a completely different thing." I lean back against his broad chest contentedly . . . or at least, as contented as one can be when knotted by their Fellian lover. Every twitch of his body ripples through mine, making my cunt clench tight around his thick knot. A repeat of our furious lovemaking is not far from my thoughts.

Nemeth must be thinking the same sorts of things because he cups one hand, dribbling water over my breasts, and then begins to wash them as if they're the dirtiest part of me. I moan when he drags his thumbs deliberately over my nipples, causing me to squirm atop his cock. "Unfair," I pant. "I can't get away from you."

"That's why this is the best time to do this." His hand slides lower to my belly, caressing it. "How do you feel?"

I know the question is more than how I feel. He's asking how the baby is too. "I think everything is fine."

"Does anyone suspect . . . " He brushes his fingers over my stomach again.

I snort. "Please. I couldn't even get them to believe that I was Princess Candra. You think anyone stopped to look at me closely?" I lean back against his chest, closing my eyes as he pours more water over me in the laziest, sexiest bath ever. "It's weird, actually. I thought we'd have people throwing rocks at us the moment we showed up, but no one seems to believe me when I tell them who I am. They think Princess Candromeda Vestalin is still in the tower. But if that's the case, wouldn't they notice the weather? How awful things are? Surely the goddess's wrath is a noticeable change."

"Aye," Nemeth says in a quiet voice, his fingers skimming down my arm. "I'm not sure I understand it myself. Darkfell is . . . different. Quiet. Empty. I don't understand it. I hope my brother can give me answers."

"You need to tell him to free my sister," I say. "And Riza. And—"

"One thing at a time," Nemeth interrupts. "I know you are worried, but Ivornath does not like to be told what to do. I will have to be careful when dealing with him." He drags a wet finger up and down my arm and then shifts his weight, seating me more heavily upon his knot. "I do not want to think about my brother right now. I want to think about pleasuring my beautiful mate so hard that she will never entertain the thought of leaving me."

I nearly choke at that. Pleasure me so hard I won't leave? Where, by all the gods, would I *go*? There's nothing left. "I don't think you have to worry about that."

Nemeth's arms tighten around me, and he holds me close. "I never planned this."

Planned what? There's such frustration in his voice. "Nemeth—"

"I never imagined we'd come to Darkfell," he tells me, one arm locking around my waist and the other skimming up my throat in a possessive gesture. His hips twitch under the water, pushing him deeper into me, and I suck in a breath. "I thought that when we left the tower, I would follow you. I'd follow you anywhere. You know that, don't you, Candra?"

I whimper because his cock is swelling inside me, his words a teasing whisper against my ear.

"My plan was always to return with you. To be yours."

Is that what he's worried about? I know Nemeth is a plotter. I know he likes to have everything thought and figured out in advance. "This isn't your fault," I breathe, biting my lip when he shudders, and I feel every bit of it. "Fuck the plans. We'll make new ones."

"Just . . . never lose faith in me, Candra. Everything I do is for you. For us." His arms harden around me, that hand gripping my throat just tight enough that I feel the prick of claws. It sends a shiver of arousal down my spine. Nemeth lets out a ragged breath that sounds curiously close to a sob. "I thought I'd lost you yesterday. I thought I lost you, and there was nothing left for me . . . "

I reach behind me, caressing his jaw. "You're stuck with me, I'm afraid."

And I wriggle against his cock in a very deliberate manner. He doesn't need to dwell on the past, I decide. For now, we think of the future. And when he bends me over the edge of the tub again, his hand on my clit, I can't think of anything at all.

CHAPTER FORTY-SEVEN

I wake up sometime later, my hair dry, my body clean, and I'm alone in the bed in Nemeth's chambers. Yawning, I sit up and eye the statue sitting in the center of the teleportation circle. There's a note on the bed, and I squint at it, my exhausted mind pausing over each word.

Have gone to speak to my brothers. Stay here. There is a food tray in the antechamber. I will return soon.

Hmm.

I move around Nemeth's home, eyeballing his belongings. It's strange because this place is absolutely not built for humans. The bed is large and circular and low, designed for wings and thick legs that bend backward. There's a lavatory on this floor, along with the bathing pool, but other than that, I can go nowhere. I pick up a mushroom from the tray and eat it like a piece of fruit, moving to the ledge and eyeing the spread of rooms below. I know he spent most of his life at the Alabaster Citadel, preparing for a life inside the tower. Did he come home often? Was this a refuge for him or just another prison?

More than that, is he glad to be back?

I wander around his quarters for a bit longer, then dig into the tray. There's a bitter cheese and some bread, and a handful of nuts, along with more mushrooms. I eat everything and avoid the wine carafe, drinking water instead. When Nemeth doesn't return, I yawn and retreat back into the bed.

Nemeth must be meeting with his brothers. He's rarely ever mentioned them to me. While I'd bring up Erynne regularly, he never talked of his family. At first, I thought it was because he was deliberately hiding information from me, but I think he's just not close to them. After all, I rarely speak of Meryliese.

Still, I hope they are being kind to him. I hope they don't rage at him for leaving the tower.

I wish I was there. Nemeth is too polite, too kind. I'd let his brothers know what I truly think of them and the fact that they left us to starve in the tower.

Perhaps that's why I'm here alone while he's visiting them.

I doze throughout the afternoon, only to awaken again to a large body sliding into bed next to me. I roll over to my side, and Nemeth tucks me against him, spooning my smaller form against his. He holds me tight for a long moment, then sighs heavily.

"It went that well, hmm?" I ask, tucking my arms against his.

"My brothers can be very stubborn."

Not surprising, given that one is the king. "What did you talk about?"

He hesitates, then presses his mouth against the back of my head, breathing in my scent. "They were surprised I left the tower. They said they sent a delegation with food, but they must not have made it."

"Dragon shite," I mutter, rolling over to look at him. "Do you buy that?"

He thinks for a moment. "No."

I study his face. He seems as if he's aged in the last day. Nemeth's expression is worn and tired, as if the weight of the world is suddenly upon his shoulders. For what feels like the millionth time, I wish we were back in our tower, alone and oblivious to the world outside. "What else did they say?"

Nemeth's mouth twists slightly. "They do not believe you're my mate. A Fellian should never marry one of our ancient enemies." His voice is bitter. "They called me a fool and said I was lying."

I sit up and take his hand in mine, turning over his palm to display the bite mark tattooed there. "They said this was a lie?"

"They said it didn't count."

"Did you tell them about the baby?"

He shakes his head. "I don't want to tell them any more than I have to. I don't trust them, Candra. I know they're my brothers, and I know we must try to get along so we have a safe place, but I just want to grab our things and leave." His expression is hard. "Tonight."

Leave? I stare at him. "And go where?"

Nemeth shrugs. "Get supplies and return to our tower. Stay there for the rest of the seven years and wait out the goddess's anger. Perhaps she will be appeased if we return."

I shake my head at him. "And my sister? My people? What am I supposed to do? I can't leave them behind. I can't abandon them to slavery and just run off as if I don't know what's happening here." I lean in. "Nemeth, is what they say about the humans true? That they're forcing them to have sex with Fellians? The women? I can't leave them."

"Candra—"

"No," I tell him firmly. "I don't care about the war. I don't care about who won or who lost. I want to see my sister and her children. I want to see Riza and my nurse. I want to know if my people are all right. I can't bury my head in the sand and pretend everything is fine and go back to the tower, Nemeth."

He sighs, the sound heavy and defeated, and sits up. His hand scrubs down his face, and he looks so, so tired. I feel guilty for pushing him, but I don't know what else to do. "The women of Lios have been enslaved, yes. I have not heard if they are serving sexually, but they were brought here as spoils of war."

"Well, we need to free them, then."

"How am I to do that?" Nemeth shakes his head at me. "My brothers do not believe me when I say I have a human wife. They believe I should put a collar on your throat and enslave you. That it's what Liosians deserve after picking a war. That it's what they deserve because—"

He cuts off abruptly, his jaw clenching.

"Because of what?" I prompt.

"Nothing," he mutters. "I am forbidden to speak of it."

"Forbidden by who?" When he doesn't look me in the eye, I bend forward, trying to shove my face in his sight. "Forbidden by who, Nemeth? I'm your wife. I'm your partner. What's going on?"

But he only shakes his head again. "I cannot say, Candra. Please leave it at that."

I stare at him as he gets out of bed and heads across the room to pick up a book. He's changed his clothing, I realize. Gone is the simple leather kilt, replaced by something far more ornate and gilded, a symbol of the First House slung around his neck in a thick decorative chain.

Who is this man I married? "How can you side with them? Over *slavery*?"

"Do you mean, how can I condone my people for claiming women left behind by the men who came to murder us? Those women did not stop their bloodthirsty husbands when they headed off to war to kill the Fellian people. But that is acceptable because we are the enemy, yes?" Nemeth's voice grows hard. "Candra, you are my mate and the thing I love most in this world, but your people attacked mine. Demanding that my brothers release their war prizes will not go over well. I must pick and choose my battles, and right now, I am most concerned with us staying *alive*."

Alive? I stare at him, uncomprehending. "You truly think they would kill you? They're your brothers."

His jaw clenches, and he looks away. "All I know is that they did not send us food. They did not believe in our mating. They will not give you status among our people. I have done everything they asked, and—" His mouth snaps shut. "No more."

"What did they ask you to do?" I whisper.

"To spy inside the tower, of course. To report back." He rubs a hand on his jaw. "I am tired of the throne controlling my life, Candra. When I say they cannot be trusted, I am not overreacting or exaggerating. They are my brothers, but . . . I feel as if I do not know them."

There's such despair in his eyes that I feel like an absolute arse for my demands. He's trying as hard as he can to make this work. I know he is. I move forward and cup his face in my hands.

"All I have is you," Nemeth says, voice hoarse. "You may think I have my home and my family, but my home is you. My family is you, Candra. You're everything, and I'm navigating this the best I can because I want nothing more than to keep you safe."

I reach up and stroke his horns because I know they're sensitive. It's the touch of a lover, one that I hope distracts him a little from the worries he carries. "I love you, Nemeth. We're a team. And if it takes me wearing a collar in order to talk to your brothers, then that is what I shall do. It's a trinket. It means nothing to me."

Nemeth doesn't look reassured, though. If anything, he looks more worried.

The king calls for Nemeth the next day . . . and for him to bring me.

The missive comes to Nemeth's door, delivered in an ornate parchment sealed with wax. I watch over the ledge as Nemeth takes the note from the small box by the door and frowns as he reads it. "Ivornath," he growls. "I should have known."

"Is that a summons? Didn't you see him yesterday?"

He shakes his head. "I said I visited both but in truth, I only saw Ajaxi. Ivornath refused to see me."

Well, that makes me nervous. I'm a little surprised he hid it, but then again, I know how a royal family works. Refusing to see Nemeth is a direct insult. I suspect that my mate is trying to smooth things over, to make me worry less about our future. It's sweet, but I know how court works and I'm no fainting flower.

Still, this might work out better for us. I'd wanted to see Ivornath, hadn't I? This is my chance. I'm good at court games, at wheedling and ingratiating myself—at flirting and making someone feel appreciated. I'm confident I can handle Ivornath. A little flattery, a little awe tossed his way, and then when he sees I'm nothing to be frightened of, we pitch for my sister's freedom, along with Riza's and everyone else's.

He just needs a bit of ass-kissing, I suspect. Even Lionel wasn't immune when I turned on the charm.

I can handle this. Nemeth might be his brother, but he's said before that he's not a diplomat. "Perfect," I tell him. "Show me what we have to wear."

A few hours later, my hair is pulled back into an elaborate rope braid decked with golden chains and anchored over one shoulder, my eyes rimmed with a bit of green cosmetic to show off their color. My bruises are covered with a pale powder, and my new dress is courtesy of the trunk of clothing (along with the cosmetics) that were brought in by Fellian servants.

It's proof that Nemeth has some pull around here, at least, no matter what he thinks.

The Fellian clothing for women is a little different from what I'm used to. There are no tight decorative sleeves and no ornate belts to show off the curve of the hips. Instead, the dress is a sack of glossy, flowy material with a square neck and no sleeves. There are two thin ties that can be fastened over the neck, leaving the back bare for wings. A quick look in the mirror shows me that I look short and dumpy in the long dress. It's not a flattering look, but it hides my belly well, thanks to my large breasts. It's not a very warm outfit for the cold under-mountain—more proof that Fellians run hotter than humans. Luckily for me, Nemeth takes pity on my shivering and gives me a thick, woolly wrap for my shoulders that is covered with his family symbol.

A thick plain metal collar is fastened around my neck, and I decide I hate it.

Nemeth is dressed finely too. I'm struck again by how handsome he is. He puts on a jeweled breastplate of hammered metal, the sigil of the First House displayed across the front and held onto his shoulders and waist by straps of thick leather so as to avoid his wings. His kilt is heavily gilded as well, and a heavy ceremonial hammer is hung at his waist—the ancient symbol of the First House and the symbol of the weapon Ravendor Vestalin used to smite her Fellian husband.

I decide I hate that too.

"Are you ready?" Nemeth asks me, taking my hand in his. He turns my palm over, rubbing his thumb across the bite mark. "Say the word, and I will leave you here. We will tell them you feel unwell. That you ate something that disagrees with you."

I shake my head. "I'm going with you, and I plan on charming your brother, so he'll have no choice but to let my sister and the other Liosians go. They're just women. His war wasn't with them."

"And if he doesn't?" Nemeth asks.

I won't even consider such a thing. "He will."

As I'm mentally getting back into my "court" personality, Nemeth wraps his wings around me and tucks me under his chin. One dizzying moment later, we've teleported onto a circle in front of the home of the king. If I was expecting a palace, I've been mistaken. It looks more like a fortress hewn from stone but narrow and climbing up the walls of the mountain itself. Rock pillars frame a metal double door, and two guards stand outside. Above the first floor, windows cluster like lines of grapes growing in a row, each covered in ornate stained glass. The rooms look small compared to Castle Lios's expansive quarters and winding halls, but there are so many windows that there's no question in my mind that this is where Darkfell's ruler lives.

The guards cover their mouths with scarves as we appear in the courtyard, and I could swear they flinch. Not a good sign.

Nemeth releases me, and I step dutifully behind him, pretending to be subservient. As I do, I eye our surroundings. We're in a gated courtyard on the "bottom" floor of the mountain, surrounded by high stone walls. There are plants growing here, strange twisty-looking things climbing and growing under the anemic light of magical lanterns that cast their glow. I look down at our feet, and there are a dozen circles in the tile mosaic floor as if people might teleport in and slowly gather here. There's no red symbol painted on the door here either.

"Prince Nemeth, here to see my brother," Nemeth declares in a booming voice as he approaches the guards. I trot behind him, trying to look cute and helpless.

The guards cross their spears over the doors, barring him from entering. "No humans. She will have to wait nearby." One gestures at the far side of the courtyard, where I see a small gazebo-like structure heavily encrusted with pale green vines and more of the strange lighting. "The king's orders."

Nemeth growls furiously, one hand nudging me behind him. "The king has asked for both of us—"

"Aye, and he changed his mind," the second guard says. "And if you go in, you must cover your mouth. King's orders."

My mate reaches for his hammer.

I put a hand on his arm. "Nemeth, it's fine. Just go talk to him. I can wait out here for a bit."

He turns toward me, frowning. "I should take you home—"

"No," I say quickly, giving his arm a pat to soothe him. "We've come this far and dressed up to visit. Go in and talk to him. Tell him I wish to speak to him too. I'm sure it'll be fine. Just ease the topic of your wife into the conversation." I take his hand in mine and kiss the back of it. "I can sit in a garden and wait. I don't mind."

He sighs heavily, glancing over at the guards. It's clear he doesn't like this.

"I'll be safe," I reassure him. "Unless you think the guards will hurt me?"

We both glance over at the two men in front of the doors. They're watching me hold Nemeth's hand with looks of revulsion, which is odd. I mean, I know humans and Fellians look different, but the disgust is a new take. Nemeth notices it too. He turns back to me, leaning in. "I don't like this, Candra. There should be more guards here."

"More?" That surprises me.

"Aye. The palace has always had ten guards at its doors. I don't understand this." He shakes his head. "Just as I don't understand why Ivornath would change his mind about seeing you."

"Well, go and change it back," I joke. "I'll wait here."

He nods and pulls me close, pressing a kiss to the top of my head. Then, he leads me toward the gazebo in the midst of the garden and pauses in front of the latticed door there. I can see another figure waiting in the deep shadows inside. Probably another human left behind by someone since we're being treated like rabid dogs. I turn and smile brightly at Nemeth, showing him that I'm fine with this.

With one last longing glance, he leaves me and heads for the door. The moment he does, a guard steps forward with a waterskin. "Wash your hands and face. King's orders."

I watch as Nemeth mutters something unpleasant to them, does as he's bid, and then disappears inside when the doors finally open for him.

By the gods, I knew Darkfell would be strange, but I didn't realize just how strange.

I turn around to the gazebo door and pause. There on the delicate lattice of wood, just above the door handle, is another one of those swirling red marks. *Does it mean* human? I wonder. I push the door open and head inside. "Hello," I call out to the other occupant. "May I sit with you?"

"Good," says a hard voice that makes me gasp in recognition. "You're finally here."

CHAPTER FORTY-EIGHT

I stare in shock as the woman inside the gazebo lowers her hood.

It's my sister, Erynne.

She's thinner than I remember, her face hard, and there are lines at the corners of her mouth as if she's permanently frowning now. But Erynne is still beautiful and regal, and she's family. With a choked sound, I launch myself at her, hugging her tight. "By the gods," I weep. "Erynne!"

"Tears do no good," my sister says in a brittle voice. "Save them for someone else."

I pull back in surprise, gazing up at her. Erynne's always been taller than me and svelte. She seems hard now, though, as if all her softness has disappeared. She smiles at me, but there's no affection in the expression, and I swear I can see every tendon in her throat when she does.

"Erynne," I breathe. "I'm so glad to see you. But you're so thin—"

"And you're not. I shouldn't be surprised. Even when Mother tried to make you watch your food, you always looked plump."

I flinch at her cruel words. She's angry, I realize. Angry that I've left the tower—that I've failed in a Vestalin's duty. That must be it. "How did you get here?" I ask, determined to ignore her anger. "Is it true that Lios is destroyed and the humans here are enslaved?"

Her gaze goes blank for a moment, and then she focuses on me again. "I should be asking how you got here. When did you arrive? Has it been seven years already?"

That worries me. Surely, she would know if seven years had passed? And if she thinks it's been seven . . . then why is her gaze filled with such hatred toward me? "It's only been a little more than two."

"Ah. So you abandoned your duty." Her smile twists. "You fool. It still took two years, did it? How witless you must feel."

"We stayed until we had no supplies left. No one arrived to bring food for either of us, so we left and traveled to Lios . . . or what was left of it. Is it true? Tell me it's not," I beg. "Tell me what happened." Maybe I'm wrong. Maybe, despite the odds, Lios has somehow survived. Maybe the people retreated farther into the mountains and created a settlement there. Maybe they're thriving on plants that grow abundantly in mud and excessive rain.

Something. Anything.

"You don't know what happened?" My sister's hard expression changes ever so slightly. "You truly don't know what occurred?"

I shake my head. "I've been in the tower for the last two years. I know nothing beyond the doors that closed behind me." I decide I won't bring up the destroyed shell of Lios and the villages leading to the capital. If she doesn't know about them, it might send her into madness. "Please. Tell me everything."

She touches the collar at her neck—a slave collar, just like mine, but hers is a real one. "Lionel set sail the moment you crossed into the tower," Erynne says in a distant voice, her gaze distracted. "It didn't matter that the winds hadn't yet died down or that the weather was foul. He'd sent you, and he expected the goddess to shower him with fair weather. He was such a reckless idiot." She sounds almost affectionate. "I'm told he lost half his ships before they even made it to Darkfell, and then he set siege to the mountain. Can you imagine? Waiting outside a stone mountain in a boat?"

Erynne laughs, and the sound makes my hackles rise. I try to picture Lionel laying siege to Darkfell, but all I can see in my mind's eye are the impossibly high cliffs that frame the waters of the sea on Darkfell's borders. It seems a foolish place to siege, but I am no soldier.

"He lost, of course," my sister continues. "Nine months he fought and came back like a dog with a tail between his legs. Just long enough to kiss his baby son and impregnate me again. And then it was off to war once more, taking all men who could stand upright with him and leaving me in charge of a people who were running out of food. Did you know that when all the men go off to war, there's suddenly no one to till the fields or mind the cattle? Did you know that a woman can only do so much with a baby hanging off of her? We tried to make up the slack, but in the end, there still wasn't enough food. And then the rains just made it worse. It rained, and it rained, and we starved, and we starved. I envied you in the tower, you know."

That takes me aback. "You did?"

"Yes." Her expression grows dreamy. "It seemed like the perfect escape. Just sit in a tower on a bed of cushions, eating food and ignoring the world outside as it goes to shite. Sheer bliss. You didn't have to worry about anything. You could be proud that you were doing your duty to the gods. Meanwhile, I was outside trying to hold everything together."

I feel a twinge of guilt.

"But at least I had my babies," Erynne continues. She won't look at me as she speaks, as if it's too much for her mind if she sees me. "My strong little Allionel and my darling Ravendor."

I jerk at the name, an uneasy feeling in my gut. "You named your girl Ravendor?"

She's not listening to me, though. Her expression is vague. "They're such good children too. Strong and brave." Erynne blinks hard and then turns back to me. "Isabella died, you know. During the famine. She gave her last bites of food to me so I could nurse my baby."

"Oh gods, Erynne." I reach for her hands. My youngest memories are of Erynne and Isabella always together. They were closer than I was with Erynne. I also know they'd been lovers for some time. I can't imagine my sister's pain. "I know how much you loved her."

"Nurse died too," she tells me. "Iphigenia. She was one of the first to die from weakness when there was nothing to eat."

It's a punch in the gut. I choke back a sob, horrified. All this time I've been excited to see both Nurse and Riza—sometimes more excited at the prospect of seeing them than my own sister—and to realize that I've lost Nurse breaks me. Hot tears slide down my face. "Please, no."

"Yes." Erynne's voice is cold. "She was lucky. She didn't live to see the destruction of our kingdom. After we starved for two full seasons, it was easy for the Fellians to take over. Our navy was destroyed. Our men were gone. The people left in the capital were weak, and Lionel thought he was some great commander. They captured him on the first day of the siege, and after that, I knew it was just a matter of time. But I held out for as long as I could because I knew Allionel needed a kingdom."

A sick feeling grows in my stomach. "Where is he? Where's the baby? Where are both of your children, Erynne?"

My sister turns her cold, unblinking eyes on me. "You don't know?"

I shake my head.

"The Fellians stormed our castle, destroying everything in sight. They put every man to the sword. It didn't matter how old or how young he was. If he was inside the walls, he was killed. They saved my Allionel for last, though. I held him tight in my arms, and they—they pulled him free—" She chokes.

"Don't say it. Please don't say it—"

"They took him from my arms and flung him from the walls, Candra. Because a male human was a threat to them. He was a baby. He . . . "

I wrap my arms around my sister, hating every word she says. I hate them because I know they're true. I hate them because they've broken my sister. While I sat safe and sound in the tower, my sister was fighting for her life. My sister had her baby ripped from her arms and murdered. "Ravendor?"

I'm terrified to find out the answer, but I know my sister has two children. If Allionel is dead . . .

"I don't know." Erynne chokes on the words as if they're difficult to say. Her arms tighten around me. It's not a hug, not quite, but I'll take it. "Once they stormed Lios, they put a collar on me. They took the women. They gave my baby to another woman. I don't know where Ravendor is, Candra. I don't have my babies." A sob breaks from her. "My arms are empty. My kingdom is destroyed. And I—I—I need a knife."

The change in conversation is so sudden I'm certain I've heard her wrong. I pull back. "You what?"

"I need a knife," she tells me, frantic.

"The enchanted knife you gave me?" I shake my head. "It's lost, stolen—"

"Any knife. Do you have one?"

"No. What for?"

A smile curves my sister's lips. "I'm going to cut Ajaxi's throat while he sleeps. He keeps me chained to his bed so I can serve him whenever he wishes. So, I'll kill him and anyone else who tries to stop me from leaving this place."

I stare at my sister in horror.

The rational part of me knows that she's gone through hell recently. That she's not herself. Her husband and her kingdom are destroyed. Her true love—Isabella—has died. Her son has been murdered, and her other child given away. She's been given to the enemy as a slave. Any of these things would break me, yet my sister has endured all of them.

But the way she's looking at me now is terrifying. The calm, rational Erynne Vestalin is gone. The Erynne who would do whatever it took to ensure the Vestalin line and the safety of our kingdom has been destroyed, just like Lios itself. I cannot stop staring at her dead eyes, at the look on her face.

I know at this moment that if I had a knife on me, she truly would murder as many people as she could, as long as they were Fellian.

"Erynne, *no*. That's not the answer."

She laughs. "Yes, it is. They murdered everything I cared about. Give me a knife, and I'll make them pay." Her eyes gleam with an unhinged light, and she studies my clothing. "Do you have one on you? Hidden somewhere?"

"No!" I slap at her hands when she grabs at my dress. "Stop it!"

Her hand brushes over my rounded belly, and she goes still.

Dragon shite. She *knows*.

Erynne draws back. Her shoulders straighten, and she looks at me—really looks at me—for what feels like the first time. "How did you get out of the tower, Candra?"

"We waited for as long as we could. We waited for food. No one came, and Nemeth and I had to make a decision—"

Her eyes narrow the moment I mention Nemeth's name. "The Fellian. You didn't kill him, then. I knew you were too weak. Too blinded by cock. Is it good? Does that monster have a fine cock? It must be excellent for you to betray your people just like that whore, Riza."

"Riza! She's alive, then?"

"She should be dead," Erynne spits, hatred contorting her face. "Cavorting with the enemy. Flirting with him. Pretending like he's something other than a Fellian monster." Her lip curls as she looks down at my belly. "And you . . . you're no better. Unless . . . did he rape you?"

I feel sick. Sick at how hopeful her expression is. She'd rather have me brutalized by the enemy than happily married. I shake my head. "Nemeth is kind." When she snorts, I continue, ignoring her. "He's a scholar. He's good to me. I—I married him, Erynne."

"You always were a fool for cock," she says in a bitter voice. "You should have killed him when you had the chance. Unless you still have that poison I sent you . . . ?"

I get up from the bench. "You're scaring me, Erynne. I'm not going to give you the tools to murder people."

"Because you're on their side now. Is that it? You've turned your back on your name. Your heritage. Your people." Her eyes fill with tears. "Oh, Candra. You're such an idiot."

I want to cry. I want to bury my face in Nemeth's arms and just weep for hours. This isn't my sister. This bitter, hateful shell that wants to kill and hurt and destroy isn't the Erynne I knew. The sister who always looked out for me and wiped away my tears is gone, replaced by this vengeful stranger. "It's my fault," I realize. "We never should have left the tower."

My words trail off as Erynne begins to laugh. I watch her, confused, as she holds her sides and laughs as if this is the funniest thing in the world.

"Oh, Candra," she wheezes. "Even after all this, you still think it's about you? Hah. If only it were." She laughs harder. "We've been lied to this entire time, you poor fool. And you've gone and married a Fellian. I had no idea you were so stupid."

"What do you mean? Who's lied?"

Erynne gets a catlike look on her face, a smirk that makes my skin crawl. "Your husband can tell you. After he does, bring me the knife. I'll do it if you don't have the stomach for it."

She turns away from me, hiding her face as one of the Fellian guards approaches the gazebo, and a moment later, she's led away. I'm torn between clinging to her hand and begging them not to take her and relief that she's gone. It isn't until Erynne is out of sight that I realize she's never asked about my medicine or how I'm staying alive without it.

She hasn't asked how I got pregnant. Me, who is supposed to be barren.

She doesn't care. I realize that. Everything she told me was to make me as broken and empty and full of hate as she is. She wants me to hate Nemeth and his people. I know that. I do.

But I can't stop wondering what she meant when she said we were both lied to.

Nemeth returns a short time later, his mood foul.

"Went well?" I halfheartedly joke. I can tell it didn't. He's vibrating with tension, his mouth set into what looks like a permanent frown.

"He refuses to see me," Nemeth says. "He's having Ajaxi run messages between rooms and speaks to me from across the hall. It is madness. My brother has lost his wits."

"Ajaxi?" My natural instinct is to tease a laugh out of him because if we're laughing, we're not crying at least . . . and I definitely feel like crying at the moment.

He snorts. "Ajaxi has never had wits. Ivornath is the one who has lost his."

That sounds more like my Nemeth. I wonder if I should tell him about my run-in with my sister. About all the awful things she told me. About the fact that she says I've been lied to. I don't know how much was truth and how much was Erynne's bitterness and her wanting to destroy my happiness with Nemeth. "So, what is our next approach?"

Nemeth wraps his wings around me. "Now we return home."

We slide through shadows, and my vision tilts dizzily. I cling to him, waiting for things to settle again. It's silent when we're back in his apartments, and I rub my skin, feeling safe. "Why does it feel different in here? Better?"

He grunts. "Ivornath has spells on the courtyard. He watches everything."

Weird. "He sounds paranoid."

"Paranoid but alive," Nemeth agrees. "You won't be watched here. You're safe." He touches my shoulder. "But I must leave you here again. Ajaxi wishes to speak to me privately."

Ajaxi—the one who's enslaved my sister. I swallow hard. "Take me with you?"

Nemeth shakes his head. "It's best if you remain here. Until we know what's going on, I don't trust anyone. The longer we keep the news of our child from them, the better. Let me go and speak to Ajaxi. He's not very smart; perhaps he can be coaxed into seeing things our way."

"And what *is* our way?" I ask, wanting to make sure we're on the same page. "What is it we're asking?"

He gazes down at me, his expression puzzled. "What do you mean?"

"I mean, what is our goal? What do we want from these people? What do we want from your king?"

His frown deepens. "To accept you as my mate and give you the honor you deserve."

"And then what?" I gesture around us at his apartments. "We live down here, and I just ignore that all my people have been murdered and my sister enslaved?"

"What would you have me do, Candra?" His expression is patient. "I am taking things one step at a time. For now, I just want to ensure your safety."

My safety . . . but no one else's. I've never thought of myself as particularly altruistic, but I can't sit back and just ignore the fact that those who lived in Lios have become slaves of the people here. "Nemeth, I saw my sister when you were in the palace earlier. She was waiting where I was. Did you know your brother Ajaxi has taken her captive? She's his bed slave."

Nemeth's expression doesn't change. "I knew she was taken as a spoil of war. I found out earlier. It is to be expected that the queen of the enemy is kept as a trophy, Candra."

"Did they tell you that my nurse is dead?" My voice wobbles and tears threaten, but I push them back. I don't have time to cry about them today. When we're safe and there's no more to worry about, then I'll grieve Nurse's passing. "Did they tell you that the people left in Lios were starving and broken when they raided the city and put every man to the sword? Did they tell you that they killed my nephew Allionel? He was a baby, Nemeth. A *baby*. And your brothers murdered him."

"I don't agree with what they're doing," Nemeth says gently. "I would never agree to kill innocents. Soldiers are one thing, but old men and children are another." He strokes my cheek. "But I cannot right all the wrongs from a place of no power, *milettahn*. You want me to race to my brother and demand that he free his captives when I cannot even convince him that my mate is my equal? That you should be safe with me instead of given to one of his generals—"

I gasp. "What?"

His mouth goes flat. "It won't happen, Candra. I won't allow it. Don't be afraid. But know that I'm doing everything I can. Once Ivornath listens to me, I can work to have your family freed. Until then, we must be patient. Understand?"

It's frustrating, but I do understand. I want to stomp my foot like a spoiled little girl, but that won't solve anything. "I hate this. I hate all of this."

"I know. But will you trust me a bit longer? Please? Even you cannot woo someone in the space of a day. It took you over a year to seduce me."

My mouth twitches, though I try not to smile and fail. "It's because you're far too honorable."

"Then trust my honorable nature."

"Ugh." I do stomp my foot this time. "I hate your honorable nature sometimes. I think I'd prefer if you'd rush in and cut their throats."

"Would you do the same to your sister?"

I glare at him because he knows the answer to that. I might defy my sister, but at the end of the day, she's still my family. "You—"

There's a knock at the door below.

Nemeth immediately pulls me behind him, his wings flaring protectively. I duck under his arm, worried. "Who's here?"

"I don't know. They cannot come in. I have my home warded. No one can come in through the front door without my express permission." He frowns darkly at the offending door below. When there's not a second knock, he touches my shoulder, pulling away. "Wait here, love."

It's not as if I can go anywhere, I want to point out. There are no stairs. But when he strides off the ledge and extends his wings, floating down, I move to the edge and kneel, peering below. I watch as he heads to the doors at the front and opens them. Even though I can only catch a glimpse of Nemeth's head and his array of horns, I can tell by his reaction that there's no one at the door. He reaches to pull something from a box next to the door, then frowns and tucks it under his wing.

When he shuts the door and turns away, I call out. "Who was it?"

"Just a message," he says and sets the missive down next to the door. It's sealed with wax, a square of parchment with a splash of blood red on the center and a scrawl on the front that looks suspiciously as if it begins with a *C*.

"A message from who?"

He hesitates, and I get the sinking feeling that he doesn't want to tell me. "Commander Tolian from Second House," he admits after a long pause. "He is a rival. No doubt he is seeking information."

"Is that my name on it?"

Nemeth disappears from below, and a moment later, he's next to me. He helps me to my feet, rubbing my arm. "It's nothing, Candra. I promise."

Dragon shite it's nothing. His reaction is bothering me.

He knows it too. He leans in, searching my gaze with his. "Trust me for a bit longer? Please?"

I nod. How can I not? We've had each other's backs from the beginning. I don't like it, but I do trust Nemeth.

I trust him with my life.

CHAPTER FORTY-NINE

The baby twitches and flutters all night long, making me toss and turn. Nemeth takes pity on my sleeplessness and makes me an herbal potion. "This is made from a mushroom here in Darkfell," he tells me, adding a bit of honey to the small cup. "It is boiled and distilled down, a bit like your potion. One drop will make you sleep peacefully. Never take more than that." He gives me a crooked smile. "Ironically, it doesn't work on Fellians."

"It doesn't?" I sip the drink, and it has a sweet, pleasant taste.

"Just humans." He kisses my brow. "Sleep well, my love."

I curl up in bed with him, and despite my worries and the active baby, I do sleep . . . for a time. I wake up in the middle of the night, however, and the bed is empty.

Nemeth is gone.

Hugging the covers to my chest, I wait in the darkness. I tell myself he's at the lavatory. Then I tell myself he's taking a walk. Then I stop lying to myself and just wonder what he could possibly be doing in the middle of the night.

Sometime near dawn, I drift off again, and when I wake up, Nemeth is in bed with me, naked, as if he's been there the entire time. He tugs me against him, rubbing my hip. "You feel good this morning."

I push him away and sit up, disturbed. "Where did you go last night?"

He frowns, sitting up as well. "You woke up?"

"Your potion must not have worked well on me, thanks to my Fellian blood and my curse. So, spill it. Who's the lover?"

Nemeth looks so aghast that I immediately know there's no one else. "Why would I take a lover?"

"I don't know. Why are you acting so suspicious? Where did you go last night?"

His expression grows defeated. "To see my brother. Or to try to. King Ivornath yet refuses to see me. I thought maybe if I went in the middle of the night, when all was quiet, that perhaps he'd relent." Nemeth hangs his head. "I am failing you."

I reach out and take his hands. "You're not. Maybe I can somehow sneak in and see him. Try to wheedle my way in. I'm good at getting my way—"

There's a knock downstairs, just like yesterday.

Nemeth stiffens, and in the next moment, he disappears in a swirl of shadows. Damn it! I race toward the ledge just in time to see him flinging another note away. This time, I clearly see my name on the missive. "That's for me," I call out. "Bring it to me."

"It's nothing, Candra. Leave it be."

I stare down at my husband in shock. Several floors separate us, and the irony is not lost on me. I've never felt farther away from him. Is this how Ravendor felt after she left the tower? Did her husband keep a hundred secrets—poorly—and make her wonder about his motives?

But Ravendor murdered her lover . . . and I am not her. I love Nemeth. I love him. I know him . . . or at least I thought I did. This secretive Nemeth feels like a stranger. "Why won't you let me see those messages?"

Nemeth gazes up at me, his eyes glimmering. He looks as deflated as I feel. "Because I cannot."

It's impossible for me to hide my hurt. "Why won't you talk to me, Nemeth? I feel as if I'm losing you."

He's standing right below me, a few floors away, and yet I feel as if we've become strangers all over again.

"Candra, no." He disappears from below, and a moment later, his warm hand is upon my shoulder. He's appeared behind me, holding a hand out. I take it automatically, but I can't help but give him a wary look. The pain in his eyes deepens, and he takes both of my hands in his. "Please, please trust me, *milettahn*. Everything I do, I do for us. For our future. But you have to trust me a little longer."

"I do trust you," I tell him softly, searching his face. "I just wish I understood."

"I will tell you everything when the time is right." He presses a kiss to the back of one hand and then the other. "For now, I just ask you to put your faith in your mate. Believe in me."

"Blindly?"

He flinches, and then his shoulders sag. "Aye, even if it must be blindly."

I don't understand this—any of it. I don't understand why he won't tell me what's going on or what's so terrible a secret that he has to hide it from me. Is there a listening spell cast upon his home? Some sort of enchantment that forbids him from speaking certain things aloud? I wish desperately that I understood.

But I do know that I trust Nemeth. "Then blindly it is."

A worn smile creases his face. He looks so tired, my beloved mate. So world-weary. When he pulls me into his arms, I hug him and press kisses to his chest, my hand reaching under his kilt. I'm determined to make him forget, even if it's for just a little while. To make the darkness lift from his eyes.

We make love, and afterward, Nemeth holds me against him so tightly it's as if he fears he'll lose me forever. I say nothing about it, of course.

But the next morning, when I find him gone again? I move to the teleportation circle and nudge the placeholder stone out of the way.

I'm not sure who I'm expecting to come through the teleportation circle, but I suspect it has something to do with the notes that have appeared on the door twice now. So, I prepare myself. I comb and braid my hair, dressing it with gold chains twined throughout. I put on my finest Fellian gown and slippers, and I wait.

When a large, deep-gray, unfamiliar Fellian steps through and looks around, I rise from the bed and hold myself like the princess I am. "You've been looking for me?"

"You're Princess Candromeda?" he asks. "From Lios?"

I incline my chin, holding a shawl around my shoulders as I do, pretending to be chilled but more so I can hide my belly. "Were you expecting other humans to be hidden away in Prince Nemeth's apartments?"

He does the wing-flutter thing that tells me he's embarrassed and gives me a quick bow. "I have been sent by a friend. Do you know Riza?"

Even though I'm not entirely sure that this isn't a trap, just hearing her name makes me burst into tears. "Is she with you? Is she safe?"

"Aye," the Fellian says. "She's been trying to contact you for the last two days. Have you not received her missives?"

I shake my head, a knot in my throat. I don't want to betray Nemeth, but if

Riza is the one sending me notes, how can he keep them from me? He knows how much I miss her. "Can you take me to her?"

He gives me an uncertain look. "I will have to fly you through Darkfell itself—"

"You can teleport me," I blurt. "I have Fellian blood."

He looks utterly shocked. "You . . . what?"

"I have Fellian blood," I state again. "Nemeth can teleport me."

"How is this possible?"

"I shall be happy to tell you everything," I say in my loftiest princess voice, "but only in the presence of Riza. If she's truly here as you say, you'll take me to her right now."

The man nods immediately and holds out his hand. "Then come with me, princess."

This might be a mistake. This man, for all his polite manner, might be Nemeth's enemy. I could be walking into a trap. And yet . . . Riza. I think of the notes she's sent, notes that Nemeth has withheld from me.

I trust Nemeth. I trust him with my life. But I need to know what's going on. So, I put my hand in the stranger's grasp and let him teleport me away.

The world tilts, my vision fogging like it always does when Nemeth teleports with me. I blink rapidly until everything settles again, and when I can see, I notice we're in an unfamiliar place. It's a house, but it's unlike Nemeth's. There's a winding set of stairs, for one. But everything seems more spread out, more sprawled and open. There's a stone ceiling high above me, covered with frescoes and held up by carved marble columns, and a fresh airiness to the rooms that I didn't feel deeper inside the mountain.

There's also the scent of salt. "Are we near the ocean?"

"Aye," the Fellian says. "This is my family's waterfront home. We have another deeper inside the mountain, but my mate prefers it here."

"Your mate?" I ask as he moves forward, opening a pair of delicate double doors to reveal a balcony outside. It's raining because, of course, it is, but there's a canopy protecting the balcony itself from the downpour.

And standing under the canopy in the gray sunlight is my once-servant, Riza.

Even though I knew I was coming here to meet her, I still gasp at the sight.

There's a gray streak in her dark blond hair now, and it frames her face. Her hair is soft and loose instead of the tight bun she always wore back at the palace. She wears a dress similar to mine, a shawl around her arms, and she turns as the Fellian approaches.

Her gaze turns to me, and she staggers, leaning against the stone railing of the balcony. "Oh . . . gods!"

"Riza," I weep, surging forward to hug her. She puts her arms out, and I fall into them, just as I did as a child. "It's you!"

"Thank the gods," she breathes, clinging to me tightly. "Oh, Candromeda. You look so different! You're so thin and pale." She pulls back and studies my face, cupping it in her work-roughened hands. "I don't like it!"

I manage a wobbly laugh. "Starving in a tower will do that to you."

She flinches. "You were starving?"

"Among other things." I study her dear face. More than even Erynne, Riza is my family. She's the one who taught me to be a lady, the one who read stories to me at night when I was a child. She's the one who wiped away my tears and bandaged my scrapes. She's the one I remember giving me my potion when I was a child, and then Nurse, who came in later on. I remember gentle hands and loving eyes. Her face is tired and a bit more timeworn, but she's still the same beloved Riza. "I missed you so."

"You sweet, foolish thing," she chides. "I'm no one."

"You're my family," I tell her.

Her mouth trembles, and she smiles, then pulls me in for another long hug. "Tell me what happened," she says. "Why are you here in Darkfell and not in the tower?"

So, I tell her my story. I want to be brief, but there's so much to cover. I tell her of how I ran out of supplies the first year and how Nemeth rescued me. How we became friends and then something more. She and her mate exchange a look when I mention that we've married. Perhaps they're thinking of their own vows.

I keep speaking. I tell Riza of cold and lonely stretches in the tower. The men who broke in to rob us. How we ran out of supplies when no one brought us any and we had no choice but to leave. I tell her of our journey back to Lios, the abandoned villages we found along the way, and her eyes well with tears.

"It's been so hard for the last two years," she says. "The villages were empty long before Darkfell came to the capital's walls. So many starved to death through the long winter." She shakes her head. "We were broken by the time Darkfell arrived, and some of us were glad. At least here in Darkfell, there are things to eat. Nothing can grow above. The goddess's tears are never ending."

I shake my head, my hands tightly clasped in hers. We've moved to chairs just inside the doors, and the large Fellian lurks nearby but doesn't speak. Instead, he brings drinks and a plate of fresh mushrooms for us to nibble on as we talk. I ignore the food, focusing on Riza. "I swear to you, we stayed in the tower up until the very last moment. It's only been weeks since we left. I don't know why the goddess is so angry."

Riza exchanges a look with the Fellian and then turns back to me. "We have a theory."

"What is it?"

She shakes her head, then gives my fingers a gentle squeeze. "I should tell my side of the story first."

"Of course." I try to hide my unease. I don't know how long Nemeth will be gone, and I worry what will happen if I'm found speaking to Riza. I don't want to endanger them . . . but I also don't know if they're my enemy or not.

If I had to choose between Riza and Nemeth, it would wound me to my soul . . . but I would still choose Nemeth.

Riza takes a sip of the mushroom-and-spices tea that the Fellian has brought to us. She speaks slowly, as if the memories are painful, and tells me of Lios. What it was like after I first left. My sister had fallen into a depression, only relieved by the birth of Allionel, her son.

In the beginning, no one thought there was a problem. King Lionel's fleet had sailed off to war, and if it was a little rainy, the weather always changed patterns slightly with the arrival of the Golden Moon Goddess. Spies had reassured the queen that Princess Candromeda was safely ensconced in the tower and all was well. Without Candra to tend to, Riza attended to the queen and her baby.

And then came the army's return, battered and broken. And the rain kept falling, turning to snow in the winter. It was a lean and hungry time, the villages emptying out as people sought food and shelter at the capital. Lionel took the men and went to war again, and the women and elderly stayed home.

And starved. Nurse died in that time, along with so many others.

The next year, Erynne gave birth to another baby, the girl Ravendor, shortly before Lionel returned once more, Darkfell hot on his heels. The enemy appeared at Lios's gates and conquered them in a pitifully short amount of time . . . only to put all the men, no matter how young or old, to the sword. The women were collared and taken as slaves to Darkfell to serve the Fellian victors.

"Allionel's death broke your sister. How could it not?" Riza wipes a tear from her eyes. "He was such a bright, wonderful boy, and the king slaughtered him because if there was an heir, the people would rise up." She shakes her head. "Erynne wasn't even allowed to keep little Ravendor. The baby was given away to another, and your sister enslaved to Ajaxi. I was given to Tolian."

She turns and smiles up at the Fellian hovering nearby, and he gives her a warm, affectionate look before heading to the balcony, giving us some semblance of privacy.

"And are we . . . glad about that?" I ask in a low voice. "Or are we wanting our freedom?"

My friend blushes, smoothing her long hair back. As she does, I see a bite on the inside of her palm, just below the thumb. "I'm happy. He's a good man and kind. But I know many of the women here see me as a betrayer for finding some small bit of joy among this misery."

I lift my hand, pointing to my claiming bite as well. "You won't find judgment from me."

Her eyes brighten, crinkling at the edges. "I'm glad that you've found contentment, Candra. I just wish it wasn't with one of the First House. I fear the king has lost his mind. We both fear it." She glances past me, her gaze settling on her mate, Tolian. "Something must change. Quickly."

"What sort of change?"

"Darkfell is cursed," Riza says in a low voice.

"Don't tell me you have to give it a potion daily so it won't be sick," I joke.

Riza makes a face at my attempt at humor. "I'm serious, Candromeda. Everything that could go wrong in the last two years has. I thought we'd be safe under the mountains here in Darkfell. Even if we were captives, we'd be alive, yes?" Her smile turns brittle. "But the goddess remains displeased. If she cannot kill us with the weather and starvation, she will kill us in other ways. There is a plague here."

I swallow hard, all levity gone. "Did you say plague?"

She nods. "It began sweeping through Darkfell shortly after the human captives arrived. You've seen the doors with the red symbols? It's an old Fellian symbol that marks a house stricken with plague."

I bite back a gasp. I've seen those doors, all right. I've seen them . . . and Nemeth refused to tell me what they were. Said that he thought he knew the answer but wasn't sure. It's just more that he's been hiding from me.

"We are suffering through a purging, just as the Liosians did," Tolian says, moving to Riza's side. She reaches for him, and he puts a large hand on her shoulder.

I also cannot help but notice that he's missing the first two claws upon his hand, filed down, and I feel as if I suddenly know too much about Riza's sex life.

"The plague hits quickly," Tolian continues, unaware of my indiscreet thoughts. "One day, a person will be fine, and then the next, they cannot get out of bed. Their lungs fill with fluid, and by the time their skin is covered in a dark rash, it is too late. Those who are lucky die quickly. Those who are unlucky . . . "

"It touches Fellians and destroys entire families in the space of days," Riza adds. "Everyone is afraid it will move to their house next. That is why the streets are empty. That is why the doors are marked. That is why people cover their faces when humans are near. They think we brought this upon them."

"And that is why," Tolian says in a grim voice, "We must stop Ivornath. Because he too believes humans have brought this to Darkfell, and there is talk of a purge."

A sick feeling clenches in my gut. "A . . . purge?"

Riza nods. "Some Fellians have been killing their human slaves or sending them back outside to starve. Unrest grows by the day, and Ivornath hides inside his palace. It's understandable, given the plague, but if he does not speak up to condemn the destruction of the human captives, I worry we will all be slaughtered."

Tolian's hand tightens on her shoulder. "You know I will not let you come to harm, *milettahn*."

I'm startled to hear the sweet endearment from another's lips. It makes me achingly lonely because I think of Nemeth. I think of how much I love him and the secrets he keeps from me, and it hurts. "Nemeth has been trying to speak to the king," I say, clearing my throat. "Surely he can talk sense into his brother."

They both give me pitying looks.

"Tolian and the Second House are rising up against the First House," Riza says, her tone delicate, her expression careful. She leans forward. "We need the support of the Vestalins to bring the humans to our side. They are afraid, but if their leader speaks up, it will make all the difference in the world."

Me? Lead? "Erynne—"

"Is unstable," Riza says. "I cannot speak to her without her becoming unhinged. She does not like the idea of humans and Fellians working together. We can only push her in small increments, no more. It *must* be you."

My mouth hangs open. "I can't work against Nemeth's family. I don't agree with them—or even particularly like them—but Nemeth has my loyalty. He's trying to work things out with them. He's visiting his brothers. Speaking with them. Trying to make them understand. I can't betray him."

Riza shakes her head at me, incredulous. "Candra, you know I love you and want the best for you. But I don't understand this. How does he command such loyalty from you after what he's done?"

Every muscle in my body tightens. My stomach churns, and I feel sick. "What do you mean? Whatever his brothers have done, that's on them. Nemeth is innocent."

She continues to shake her head, her movements slower and slower. "Oh, Candra. No, love. I'm sorry. Nemeth is just as guilty as the rest of them. They sent Prince Nemeth to the tower to seduce you and win you over to Darkfell's side. He doesn't love you. It's all been a plot to get you to betray your people."

I . . . What?

CHAPTER FIFTY

I stare at Riza, at her familiar, worn face. Her words sink in, but I can't make sense of them. They float in my head, dancing and circling like flames at a bonfire.

They sent Prince Nemeth to the tower to seduce you and win you over to Darkfell's side.

Impossible.

Isn't it?

I think of our interactions in the tower. How we'd both wanted nothing to do with each other at first. How Nemeth had saved my life and I'd found it puzzling. How annoyed he'd seemingly been at sharing space with me . . . until we'd fallen in love. How he wouldn't touch me unless we were mated. He'd *insisted.*

And then I think of all the times I'd woken up to hear him talking to the altar, "confessing" to the gods.

How he'd openly admitted to me that he'd spied on me at his brother's command.

All those little memories flit through my mind and fill me with terror. Have I been betrayed? Played like a musical instrument by the person I love most in this world? But if that's the case, why did he save me so many times? Why did he let the intruders attack him in order to protect me if it's all a farce? His wing was torn. He'd thought he'd never fly again.

He'd done that for me. Sacrificed himself for me.

Time and time again, Nemeth had shared his food with me, even when it meant we'd both go hungry. How could this possibly be his plan? I shake my head. "You're wrong. He loves me."

Riza bites her lip and glances up at Tolian.

"Prince Nemeth was sent at a very young age to the Alabaster Citadel so he could learn how to be the Royal Offering," Tolian says, voice neutral. "A short time ago, it was decided that Nemeth was too scholarly to woo a princess. That the Princess Meryliese of Lios viewed him as a friend and not a potential lover. So he was sent home, and Ajaxi was to take his place in the tower. For whatever reason, they changed their minds a month prior to the solstice, and Nemeth was sent back to the Alabaster Citadel once more as the offering."

Ice spreads through my veins. Nemeth had mentioned that. Had mentioned that he'd been sent back to the Alabaster Citadel and chosen once more.

"His training at the Citadel included courtship and human wooing customs," Tolian continues. "How to please a woman. I'm told he wasn't a good student at these particular lessons, preferring to read war poetry instead, but I'm sure some of it sank in."

I think of the onion he'd made me, studded with peppercorns. He'd acted like it was such a silly custom. He'd asked me to tell him about our customs . . . had he already known them? Was he just toying with me?

"Apparently, Ivornath was quite happy when he learned you were sent in place of Meryliese. It was rumored that Meryliese was cold and temperamental, and you were considered . . . "

He pauses.

"Easy?" I ask, trying to keep the bitterness from my voice. *This isn't true,* I tell myself over and over again. It's not true. It's all a lie to pull me away from Nemeth. To turn me against him.

"Yes," Tolian says. "That you were a less, ah, virtuous sort. That you enjoyed flirting games. My spies tell me that the brothers instructed Nemeth to be standoffish for a time because that would intrigue you, and then you'd fall into his arms—"

"Stop. Please, stop." I close my eyes. I'm dying inside. I'm dying because all of the little things Tolian says that were part of their plans are matching up with my memories, and I'm withering, my heart turning to ash in my chest.

Nemeth loves me. He does.

"They wanted you on their side in case of war," Tolian continues, heedless of my plea. "A Vestalin princess sympathetic to Darkfell's cause would be a blow to the Liosian king. It would sow doubt among the commoners. It would bring them to our side. You have always been a tool that the First House intended to use, Princess Candromeda. I am sorry to be the bearer of such messages, but they are the truth."

Messages.

Nemeth wouldn't let me see the messages from Riza. He wouldn't tell me why either.

He knew.

He's been hiding me ever since we arrived here. It's like a knife in my heart.

"He's always been their creature, Candra. I'm sorry." Riza's gaze is full of sympathy. Her hand brushes against her mate's. "I didn't realize you trusted him so. I thought you were with him simply because you had no other options. That you were using him and not the other way around."

I flinch at her words because I feel incredibly stupid. I've always prided myself on being flirty and seductive, winsome and appealing despite my barrenness that makes me so ineligible for marriage. Said that it didn't matter because I could make men want me regardless . . . yet I've been completely taken in by a scholarly Fellian who pretended to be reluctant.

Pretended to be falling for me.

This is why he didn't want me to see Riza. He didn't want me to know everyone was laughing behind my back. "I need to talk to Nemeth."

"Wait," Riza blurts, jumping to her feet. "Please, Candra. Before you return to his side, I must beg a favor of you. Don't tell him of our plans. Don't tell him that you've spoken to me or to Tolian."

"If the First House knows that Second House is plotting against them, we will be executed for treason," Tolian says in a grave voice. "And if I am killed, there will be no one to protect Riza."

My friend trembles, her eyes pleading.

As if I could sell her out? As if I have not dreamed of seeing her again, hugging her? Do they truly think me so capricious? But I suppose I have been in the past. That spoiled, gossipy Candra of old seems so very far away. Now I am simply tired. Tired and defeated.

My mate is using me. He doesn't love me.

My sister is a shell of herself, her children gone.

My kingdom is in ruins.

All that I have left is Riza. "I would never put you in danger," I vow to her. "You have my word."

She gets to her feet, searching my face as if seeking her answers there. As if she doesn't believe me. "Will you join us, then? Join Second House to take down First House? With a Vestalin on our side, we can convince the people that Tolian and his house are truly with us. If we let First House stand, Ivornath's madness will destroy us all."

"I can't let Nemeth be hurt," I confess. "Even if this is all a lie, I still care for him. I still need to talk to him. There's more at stake than just my life."

And I run my hand over my rounded belly to show her just what I mean.

Riza's eyes widen. A faint smile touches her lips, and she nods in understanding. "Ajaxi and Ivornath must be destroyed. Nemeth can be exiled."

"But—" Tolian begins to protest.

He's silenced by a shake of Riza's head. "If nothing else, he can be sent back to the tower."

My heart aches at the thought of Nemeth, alone and miserable in the tower once more, without room to spread his wings and fly. *How can I have so much sympathy for someone who has hurt me and used me at every turn?*

I still love him, and I hate that about myself. I want to be as cold and hard as Erynne . . . but I can't.

I wonder, absently, what the goddess will do if there are no Fellians of First House to fulfill their half of the Royal Offering. If there are only Vestalins left. I suppose if there are no Fellians left in First House, no one can be sent to the tower . . .

Except my child. I rub my belly, hating that their fate has already been decided. "I'll speak to Nemeth tonight and will let you know my answer in the morning. I will let you know if I am with you."

"If you are not, I fear we are all doomed," Riza says.

She might be right, and yet I cannot make a choice without speaking to Nemeth first. I must find out from him if all that Riza says is true . . . and I will find my answers, I suspect, in what he does not tell me.

A short time later, Tolian returns me with a quick teleport back to Nemeth's quarters.

There is still no sign of my mate, and my heart aches with the realization that he is going behind my back . . . or so it seems. They could be wrong, I reason. Nemeth's actions might be lumped in with Ajaxi and Ivornath, but perhaps he's not working with them, and that's why they sent him back to the tower.

There could be any number of reasons why Nemeth was sent to the tower, and they don't necessarily have to do with me. It could be anything, I tell myself. Anything at all.

And if Nemeth would just be straightforward with me, I'd feel so much better. I'd trust him again. Truly, all he needs to do is throw me a bone. Just one. Just a morsel.

I put the stone back in the teleport circle and pace around the room restlessly. I can't explore the rest of the house, so I'm more or less confined to our bedroom, and I hate it. I hate that it makes me feel trapped, like when we were in the tower. I hate that it makes me feel as if I'm an afterthought in Nemeth's life. Like I'm a pretty bird to be caged until it's time for me to sing.

I hate all of this so much.

Eventually, the door opens down below, and I all but fly to the edge of the bedroom and peer down. "Nemeth?"

"My mate." His voice is as warm and delicious as ever, and my heart aches painfully. In the next moment, he's behind me, pulling me away from the ledge, and his arms go around me. "Do not stand so close to the edge, *milettahn*. It would break me if you were to fall and hurt yourself."

He nuzzles the top of my head, as loving and sweet as ever, and I want to cry with the agony of it. *Why is he so good at pretending if he truly doesn't care for me*? "I'm glad you're back," I manage. "Where did you go?"

"Where I always go," Nemeth says, a hint of wry humor in his tone. "To stand at my brother's doorstep and beg for an audience."

I turn in his arms, trying not to frown. "He still won't see you?"

He shakes his head. "Being stubborn. Ivornath grew up knowing he was to take the throne, and it made him impossible to budge when he had an idea in his head. Acquiring the throne has made him less willing to listen and aging even more so. Willful fool."

Nemeth strokes my cheek, his expression full of the same humor and intelligence I've grown to love over the past few years. I see no deception there, no distaste, only the same affection he's always shown me. Maybe Riza and Tolian are wrong. Maybe my sweet Nemeth has nothing to do with Ivornath's plans.

"I'll try again tomorrow," Nemeth promises me.

"What if we leave?" I say brightly.

His mouth turns down at the corners, and he tilts his regal head at me as if he's misheard. "Leave?"

I nod. "It's clear we're not wanted here. What if we leave? Just head back out and go back to the way things were before when it was just you and me. We can fish—I've gotten pretty good at catching my own dinner—and we can grow mushrooms. We can live off the coast or even head back to the tower, though we won't have to stay inside forever. We can just come and go as we please!"

Nemeth stares at me, hard. "Candra . . . "

I grip his hand in mine. "Please, Nemeth. Say you'll go with me."

"What about your sister? What about the people enslaved here?"

He's stalling. I know he is, and it breaks my heart. "I've changed my mind. I want to leave. I don't want our child born here. I'd rather go back to the tower. Please."

My mate's bright green eyes fill with pain, and he slowly shakes his head. "We cannot, Candra. Even if I wanted to, I don't think it's the best thing for our child. There are physicians here. Herbalists. Midwives. You need them for our baby. And even if you can forget about your people, I cannot. Things are just as wrong here as they were back in Lios. It's my duty to do what I can. Once I get to see my brother—"

I fling his hand away. "I thought you loved me."

I know I'm being dramatic, but more than anything, I need him to show that his allegiance is with me. That I matter above all else. That nothing has changed, and we're still in this together, the two of us against the world. I need him to prove to me that Riza is *wrong, wrong, wrong* because my heart is shattering into a thousand pieces with every moment that passes.

Nemeth's expression is defeated. "You know I do, *milettahn*. But I cannot abandon the people here for my own selfish wants and needs. Can you?" He grips my shoulders, forcing me to gaze at him. "Look me in the eye and tell me that you would be content with abandoning all those here in Darkfell. All the humans. All the Fellians who have nothing to do with my brother's machinations. You would abandon them?"

"That's not fair."

He shakes his head. "None of this is fair. And yet it is the fate we have been given."

I stare up at him, mutinous. "Fine. If you want to stay, then get me in to see your brother. The king."

"I've been trying to see him—"

"No, not you. Me. Let me talk to him."

Nemeth's jaw sets in that stubborn way of his. "You're not going to see him until I have."

"Then I guess that answers that," I manage to say, my voice light despite my heartbreak. Tonight has proved one thing to me: Riza was right. Nemeth has some plan with his brothers, and he won't let me in on it.

Whatever he might feel for me falls secondary to duty.

The rest of the day is full of tension. We're silent over our meal, and afterward, I declare a headache and take to bed. It's not as if I can go anywhere else, after all. I pretend to sleep, the covers pulled over my head, while silent tears trickle down my cheeks.

I'm going to allow myself a tiny bit of crying, but that's all. If Nemeth has used me, I can't trust him. If I can't trust him, then I have to make my own plans.

I have to think about my baby. I have to think about my people. It feels strange to say that to myself. I've never been the most devoted of princesses, not in the slightest. But Nemeth is right that there is something wrong here. He just refuses to see that it's his brother.

So, I have no choice but to work around my mate.

He holds me that night, his hand on my belly, and our child kicks and flutters in my stomach, reminding me that I have more to think about than just myself, than just Nemeth. The baby inside me is going to need a safe place to live, and I don't care if that place is Darkfell or Lios.

Right now, neither one is safe. Darkfell is full of plague, slavery, and intrigue, and Lios is full of mud and empty of people and food.

"Give me another day," Nemeth whispers into my hair as I pretend to sleep. "We must go carefully when we approach my brother."

As if I have a choice? In a strange sort of way, I do know that he's trying.

I just don't know if it's enough. If he's lying to me and deliberately stalling, dragging our feet could mean the death of so many Liosians. Even if he's not lying and his brother truly is pushing him off, we cannot afford to wait.

I go to sleep that night with the terrifying word *purge* echoing in my head.

It's a tense breakfast the next morning. I glare at Nemeth over the food.

"I cannot today," he tells me, his expression grim but determined. "I must speak with my brother first. I will not put you in front of Ivornath before I know if you will be safe or not. I cannot get the sight of Lionel's dead body out of my mind. I will not let that happen to you."

I hate that he sounds logical. It's almost believable. If I didn't know what I know now, I'd be a much happier woman. A fool, but happier. "May I have the letters that were sent to me, then?"

He gets to his feet. "We'll talk about those when I return."

"Am I your prisoner?" I ask him. "Am I no longer your wife? Your mate? Because right now, I feel like a prisoner, Nemeth." I gesture at my surroundings. "Even a golden cage is still a cage."

He moves to my side. I don't get up from the table with the strange stools and continue to mutinously glare at him from my spot by our breakfast. He strokes my cheek with his knuckle, sighing. "I know this is difficult. I wish you could understand."

"Then tell me," I exclaim. "Tell me what's going on so I *can* understand."

"I'm trying."

"Are you? Because I feel like you're keeping secrets from me. Why can't I go with you to the palace? Why can't you let me see those letters? Why won't you tell me what the red symbols are on the doors? Where is everyone? Why won't your brother see you? What's he hiding?"

Nemeth flinches at my torrent of accusations. "Once our safety is secured, then I'll explain it all. I promise." He leans down and presses a kiss to my brow. "I'm sorry, Candra. Give me one more day."

"Do I have a choice?" I gesture at my surroundings. "It's not as if I can go after you."

"Think of this as the tower, and we are yet in waiting once more," he offers.

"In the tower, we didn't keep secrets from one another, did we?"

Nemeth is silent, and at that, my heart breaks. He leaves, and I pick at my food, no longer hungry. To think that I'd been thrilled to eat anything such a short time ago, and now my heart is so heavy that I can barely bring myself to eat the expansive plate of food in front of me.

How is it that we were so happy in the tower, yet the moment we're around others, everything turns to dragon shite? It's unfair.

I finish my meal and remove the stone from the teleport circle. I suspect Tolian will come again today or at least bring a message from Riza. If they're lying to me, they're very good lies with far too much truth embedded in them for me to be able to pick out the differences. I know Riza, though. I've known her since I was a child. She wouldn't lie to me. Not about something as important as this.

So either she's being lied to as well, or Nemeth is the one not speaking the truth.

Tolian appears in the teleport circle a short time later. I'm dressed and waiting for him, and when he holds his hand out, I take it. It feels like a betrayal of Nemeth . . . and yet I have no choice.

If Nemeth is hiding things from me, it's my duty as the mother of his child to find out what those things are. I have to make sure that my baby is safe.

This time, we don't return to the seaside villa. To my surprise, Tolian takes me deep inside the mountain to a strange storage building that reeks of mushrooms and sour wine. Barrel after barrel is stacked to the ceiling here, and as I look around, Riza appears from the shadows.

"You came back," she says, relief in her voice.

"I worry that you're right," I confess, hugging her.

"I hate that I am." Riza gives me a miserable smile. "More than anything, I want your happiness, but I cannot remain quiet if I know that he's lying to you."

I nod, not trusting my voice. Glancing around the storage building, I sigh. "So, what now?"

"I want you to see for yourself what's happening to the survivors of Lios," Riza tells me. She opens a bag and pulls out a cloak and a scarf. "You need to see how they're being treated. You need to see our fates if we don't rise up."

I slip the cloak on over my clothes, noticing that the patterns on it are similar to the ones Tolian wears on his breast and on the buckle of his belt. The sigil of Second House, then. Riza covers her face with the scarf and indicates I should do the same. "We won't be allowed to move through the city without a covering. Even Tolian would not be able to save us from a beating if we were caught. We are considered plague bearers."

Ugh. Right. I cover my face as instructed, and when we're ready, I follow her out.

We move through the city quietly, walking through what must be a main thoroughfare. Again, I'm reminded eerily of Lios, the empty streets there, and the echoing palace. The streets here are empty as well. When we do see someone, they hurry away and keep their distance. Up above us, the occasional Fellian flies overhead, but it's still far too quiet.

So many doors are marked with red too. It's terrifying to see.

"Once, the air here was filled with wings," Tolian says in a low voice. "You would look up and see a hundred people in the air at any time, moving from house to house or crossing to the harbor. Now it feels abandoned, and I worry the goddess will not stop taking lives until the mountain is completely empty."

"There," Riza says, steering me. "The field up ahead."

We pause near a stone fence, turning to see a field up ahead. It is well lit, with bright, magical lights studding the fields and giving the pale plants some light to grow by. Walking the rows are human women, their mouths covered as they pick what looks like grapes. The women look tired and thin, and their clothing is ragged. As I watch, a woman falls to the ground, only to have a Fellian overseer roughly grab her and haul her to her feet. He shakes a whip in her direction, and I have to turn away.

"The women work the fields because there are not enough healthy Fellians to do so," Riza says in a low voice. "And because the plants here are fragile and growing through false light and not the sun, the fruit and vegetables are puny. A farmer must work twice as hard to get the same amount of food. Now, of course, he has human slaves to do so."

I purse my lips. "What about . . . when I was captured, one of the men said that women were serving the Fellians in their beds. That the noblewomen were taken to a district for whores and were being forced to pleasure men for food."

Her unhappy look tells me everything.

"We are not bad people," Tolian says. "But the war has soured many hearts on Lios and its people. The king should put a stop to the abuse of the human slaves, but he is silent, so the worst run rampant with abuse because there is no one to stop them. Many are not inclined to help humans either. The plague is far reaching. Last night, Fourth House was struck down, and they cast their humans into the streets. I'm sheltering them at Second House, but I worry that the next group of humans will not be so lucky."

I turn to Tolian. "And how did you decide that this was wrong? How did you come to this when your people seem to think it's all right?"

He gives me a faint smile and glances over at Riza. "I fell in love."

That makes me ache all over again because Nemeth fell in love with me, yet it wasn't enough. I wasn't enough.

"All right," I say, resolute. "What's the plan?"

CHAPTER FIFTY-ONE

The plan is a simple one, it turns out.

A few humans with connections will go through the city and spread the word of an uprising—that Second House is with them and will be attacking the king. Weapons will be distributed so all can help Second House take control of the palace, and when the king is ousted, things will change in Darkfell.

"There is enough food for everyone," Tolian says. "And Fellians and humans do not have to be enemies. We can live together in peace, but not as things are. Ivornath must be taken from the throne and a new ruler established."

"You?" I ask.

"If I must," Tolian replies. "I do not want it, but if there are no other options, then I will serve as best I can."

More plans are made. I lunch with Riza and her husband, and we discuss guards and how to get past them. I suggest the mushroom potion that Nemeth gave me to sleep. Perhaps if we knock out the guards, we can slip into the palace with little bloodshed.

"That brew only works on humans," Tolian reminds me. "And it does not matter. We can take the guards. There are only a tenth of the warriors there were before the plague hit. They cannot cover all of the palace. We will attack from multiple sides and storm our way in."

And once inside . . . the throne will be taken.

Ivornath will be put to death, but Nemeth is to be spared. I refuse to work with them otherwise. Ajaxi's fate will be decided by my unstable, vengeful sister, who has also been plotting with Riza and Tolian.

"When?" I ask.

"Three days from now," Tolian says. "We must move quickly before Ivornath gives the order to have the humans purged from Darkfell entirely. With every day that passes, another house falls ill, and the risk increases."

So soon.

That evening, I'm restless with fear. I've never participated in a palace coup before. Oh, sure, I disliked Lionel intensely, but as a princess, I'm normally one of those in danger if the powers that be are usurped. This time, though, I'm with the "enemy."

I'm going to betray the man I love, who might only be pretending to love me. The thought is terrifying. *What if something goes wrong, and Nemeth is hurt? What if the baby is hurt?* I rub my belly. This is more than just breaking out of an empty tower.

This is the forceful taking of a kingdom.

Nemeth doesn't return until late, and when he does, he's tired and wan. He staggers to the bed and flops into it next to me, throwing an arm over his eyes.

"You don't look so good," I tell him, worried. Betrayer or not, I love him. "Are you feeling all right?"

"Just exhausted. I spoke with Ajaxi tonight. For hours." He casts me a wry look. "I told him I was tired of being pushed off. I'm First House as well, and Ivornath should see me. It's not right that he will only visit with Ajaxi. I know there is fear of my loyalties, but I am his brother too."

"What did he say?"

Nemeth grins, and my heart flips. "We have been invited to dine with the king tomorrow, the both of us."

Finally, we're getting somewhere. Relieved, I fling my arms around him and hug him tight. *Maybe it won't come to an uprising. Maybe Ivornath will listen to reason.*

And if he doesn't, maybe I find a knife and *make* him listen.

I'm nervous the next day for the dinner. Nemeth doesn't leave, so I can't send a message to Riza. In a way, I'm glad. It feels less like I'm betraying him this way and more like we're a team once more. We move around in his quarters, pointing out spots that might be good for staircases to be added, and he's affectionate and sweet, and I feel like the biggest arse in all of Lios.

Has he been on my side all this time? Are Riza's words lies? But Riza doesn't have to lie to me. She's been my family since I was born, even if we're not related by blood. It fills me with turmoil, and I'm tempted to pick at Nemeth—to pry at him and try to get him to admit his secrets.

But I'm tired. So tired. So, I opt for an easy day instead. We eat together and nap together and talk about the future as if nothing has changed. We lie in bed, and he puts a hand on my belly, feeling our child kick. And when the dinner hour nears, we prepare.

Nemeth wears his First House regalia, the metal-embossed kilt and finely engraved breastplate. He throws a bright red cloak over his wings, the material sliding down the center of his back like a waterfall. "For show," is all he says when I arch a brow at him. "Ivornath likes a production."

Ivornath sounds a bit too much like Lionel for my tastes, but I can put on a show too. I dig through the case of jewelry that had been brought for me and deck my braid with strand after strand of pearls and gold. My ears are adorned with heavy pendulums of jewels, and I wear more at my throat. My dress is the simple Fellian garb, but I pick out the most ornate-looking shawl and wrap several necklaces around my wrists in makeshift bangles.

I look very rich and very garish, which I think is the point. Gazing into the mirror, I run my pinky along a pot of lip tint and rub it onto my mouth as Nemeth comes to stand behind me. "Well?" I ask, putting the finishing touches on the cosmetic. "Do I look fit to see a king?"

"You always look like a dream to me," he confesses, taking my jewel-encrusted braid in his hand and rubbing his finger along it. "You grow more beautiful every day."

"My beauty isn't the question," I tease, keeping my voice light even as my heart aches. "It's whether or not I will impress your brother. He's been so difficult to reach that I worry we won't have another chance."

"I just hope he's finally willing to be reasonable," Nemeth says. He gently sets my braid back on my shoulder and gives me a thoughtful look. "I've thought about what you said. About leaving. If it comes to that, then we will go. But while there is food and safety here, we must give Ivornath a chance."

"Safety?" I wipe my fingers on a towel. How can he speak of safety when there's a plague here? I'm about to blurt that out when I remember I'm not supposed to know there's a plague. Dragon shite. "Do you, ah, feel we're safe here? Even though this place feels wrong to you?"

Nemeth shrugs, his wings shifting. "There is food and protection from the storms. For now, that counts as safety."

I'm not so sure I agree. Not if there's a plague striking Fellians down. "Well, I'm ready. Shall we go?"

"We should cover our mouths," Nemeth says, handing me a length of cloth. "King's orders."

"Any particular reason why?"

"Ivornath can be eccentric."

Oh come *on*. And he still won't tell me there's a plague? I give him a disappointed look but manage a smile anyhow. "Well. Shall we do my potion before we leave?"

A short time later, my pulse is singing, thanks to the infusion of Nemeth's blood, and I'm feeling good enough that despite the wooziness that a quick teleport provides, I recover quickly. We appear at the front gates as we did before, but this time, instead of the guards directing me to the gardens, they cover their faces and step away, eyeing me with distaste.

"My, how odd!" I exclaim to my traitorous mate, even as I cling to his arm. "They act as if we're sick."

Nemeth stiffens but then pulls me closer. "You're safe, Candra. Rest assured that you're safe."

I bite my lip, hating that he's giving me more nonanswers.

The large, jewel-encrusted doors of the palace open on their own, letting us in. When we step inside, it's dark and shadowy, the hall itself enormous and stretching up into the shadows as far as the eye can see. A few magical globes shed light, but I can't see enough to make out much of my surroundings. It echoes in here, our footsteps loud with every step forward. There's a set of stairs tucked along one wall, which I find curious, but we pass them quickly and head deeper inside. Shadowy shapes lurk at the edges of the darkness. I'm pretty sure they're statues, but it's unnerving anyway. "Just so you know, I hate that it's dark in here."

Nemeth chuckles. "There is not much to see other than the posturing of my relatives. Each king has made himself a very grand statue, including my brother."

"Charming."

"Indeed." He leans in as if sharing a secret. "I'm told most of the ancestors gave themselves extremely prominent portions of anatomy so no one would doubt the virility of First House. I grew up hating to visit this hall every time I visited because I always felt inadequate."

I stifle a giggle, burying my face against his arm. "If it makes you feel any better, I do not find you inadequate in the slightest."

His laughter rumbles through his body, and I ache with how much I adore him in moments like this. If we'd never left the tower, I'd still have utter faith in him. I'd still think he was madly in love with me.

We'd be dead, but I'm focused on moping at the moment, not on reality. The truth is, if Nemeth has never loved me, I suppose it's best to find out. If his idea was to turn me to his side, he's failed. I hug his arm tightly and glance around as we head down the hall. "So, where is your brother?"

"We're meeting him in the official dining hall."

"Shouldn't there be servants around?" I ask, eyeing the empty, shadowy palace with a bit of unease. "The palace at Lios was always crawling with people."

"Aye, this is unusual. But I'm told Ivornath has been retreating more and more these last months. It's one reason he's been so difficult to contact." He pats the hand I have on his arm. "Ajaxi says that it's temporary. That most of those who have been dismissed from the palace will be reinstated again soon."

Or not, because they'll be dead of the plague. But if he trusts Ajaxi, I guess we have to go with it. "Funny that your brother will see Ajaxi but not you."

"They've always been close," Nemeth confesses, and I hear a familiar wistfulness in his tone. "While I was being raised at the Alabaster Citadel, my brothers took their training together. I've always envied them for their kinship. I was more or less forgotten."

In that, I feel a kinship to Nemeth. I was the forgotten princess too. Because of my blood curse and my inability to bear children, I was considered useless for the Vestalin line. The focus was entirely on Erynne, and I spent my time with nurses and servants. "You're still their brother," I remind him. "Growing up in the citadel shouldn't change anything."

Even though I know it does. I just never thought about it much until I met Nemeth.

Another set of fine double doors opens, and a soft, yellow light pours into the hallway. There's a sumptuous feast laid out on a long, cloth-colored table. The scents of delicious food waft toward us, and my stomach growls. Here, there is a pair of servants pouring wine, and Ajaxi, Nemeth's younger brother, sits at the far end of one table and holds a goblet up in a mocking salute. "Brother. I see you brought your plaything."

"My wife," Nemeth says in an even voice. "My mate. You will speak to her with respect, Ajaxi. She is a princess of Lios."

"And Lios is dust," Ajaxi continues merrily, drinking from his goblet. Some of it runs down his chin, and he swipes it away with one big hand.

I look at him in disgust as Nemeth leads me toward the table. How can two Fellians look so alike, yet one be so very revolting to me? Ajaxi seems very much like a spoiled boy. He wears similar clothing to Nemeth's, but his are festooned with chains and fobs across one shoulder—medals of some kind for battle. He slouches in his chair, and the heaviness of his eyelids suggests he's been drinking for a while.

As we approach, he smirks in my direction and lifts his goblet, scratching at his collarbones with long claws. "Vestalin princess of nothing, greetings."

Turd. I manage a tight smile as Nemeth pulls out a seat for me. "Where is the king? We're here to see him, not you."

"Ivornath will be along shortly," Ajaxi says, shaking his goblet at one of the servants. The woman—a Fellian—hurries forward with the pitcher and pours him a fresh glass, the lower half of her face covered with a veil like mine. Ajaxi wears no face wrap, though, and I unwind mine, gazing at the delicious food. Stewed, spiced mushrooms. Braised fish from the harbor. Fresh fruit and nuts. A sinful number of olives and dates. Pickled eggs. Three kinds of bread. My mouth waters at the sight.

"Ah, ah," Ajaxi says as I touch my scarf. "Keep the human covered. They're filthy things."

"We're here for dinner," I reply sweetly, though it takes everything I have not to snarl at him. "One cannot eat when one's mouth is covered."

He snorts and chugs more wine, scratching at his neck.

I decide I'm going to charm Ajaxi, so it hurts more when he's betrayed. I give him my most coquettish smile and slide a hand over my braid, tugging it toward my cleavage. His gaze goes there automatically, and I lean forward. "You must be very close to your brother, the king, for him to trust you with so much."

Ajaxi grunts and leans in, gazing at my breasts. "Truth be told, I'm running things around here—"

Nemeth seats himself between us, clearly not understanding my play. He glares at his brother and ruffles his wings. "Ivornath will be joining us soon, yes?"

"Soon." Ajaxi shrugs, toying with his wine cup. I flick my braid and give him a sultry smile. "This one seems more pleasant than her sister. I see why you have her in your bed."

Bastard. It takes all that I have to keep smiling as if his words are a compliment.

"This one is my mate," Nemeth practically growls.

"Huzzah," Ajaxi says, smirking. "To a lovely human in your bed. Wine for my brother and his human."

"Mate," Nemeth corrects again.

"Oh, no wine for me," I tell the servant who sets a cup in front of me. "Perhaps milk or water?"

"Are we a toddler?" Ajaxi asks.

I titter with fake laughter, sliding my wine toward Nemeth. "No! But after so long of not eating properly, my stomach fusses at strong tastes. You know how it is. I have to be *so* careful with what I put in my mouth."

"Is that so," Ajaxi murmurs. Nemeth puts a hand on my thigh as if warning me. I ignore it. If Ajaxi truly is in control of things, it's best for me to get him on my side. I flutter my lashes in his direction and lick my lips. He flicks a hand at a servant. "You heard her. She prefers a . . . mild mouthful."

"I don't want to seem too greedy," I say coyly, giving Nemeth a teasing look. "But my mate has kept me well fed and my cheeks stuffed—"

"Candra," Nemeth says in a sharp voice. "Please."

"Oh stop," I say, tapping his arm with my hand. "I'm just trying to get to know your brother. He has my sister, you know. That practically makes us family." I tilt my head and give Ajaxi a bright look. "How *is* my darling Erynne? Have you been taking excellent care of her?"

He huffs and rolls his eyes, then returns to drinking.

"Where is Ivornath?" Nemeth asks again.

"Late." Ajaxi shrugs. "He'll be along soon. Eat. Drink."

I sip the milk that a servant brings me. It's ice cold and creamy, and I nearly moan at how delicious it is. I drink the full goblet and then pluck a sweetened roll from the table. "If he's anything like Lionel was, he'll make us wait out here while he lounges in bed."

Ajaxi laughs at that, perhaps harder than he should have. I pretend to ignore it, nibbling on the food. "Ivornath is indeed lying about. As for your sister, she is . . . not happy. But political prisoners seldom are."

"Nemeth and I could use a few servants now that we've returned to his home," I say brightly. "You could give Erynne to me." I lower my voice and wrinkle my nose. "She would truly hate that, which means it would be quite fun."

Maybe he's stupid enough to give Erynne over to me without much fuss, and if that's the case, he'll be easy to lead around. Maybe no uprising will be needed.

A servant hands me another goblet of milk, and I lift it to my lips.

"I'm keeping her for now. Though I must say, meeting you, it's a shame we haven't talked before now."

I give him my best I'm-a-hussy smile and lick the milk froth from my lips. "Why is that?"

Ajaxi takes another gulp of his wine and points a clawed finger at me. "I was supposed to be the one sent to the tower to seduce you—"

"Ajaxi!" Nemeth snaps, going stiff beside me. He jumps to his feet.

I stare at the brothers.

Ajaxi lounges in his chair, eyeing me. "Might have been fun to bounce you on my cock. Not at the expense of going to war, but it's a thought. Instead, they sent this one." He flicks a hand at Nemeth. "My scholarly brother who refuses to play well with others."

"Excuse me?" I say, keeping my voice pleasant. "Did you say Nemeth was sent to seduce me?"

"No," Nemeth hisses, a hand clenched at his side.

Ajaxi just shrugs drunkenly. "Might as well tell her now." He lifts his chin at me, giving me a knowing look. "It's true. It was supposed to be me sent to the tower, but then . . . plans changed." His expression grows vague, and he stares into his goblet. "Ivornath made Nemeth go instead. I might have fought harder if I knew a prime tart like you was going to be there."

I should be more upset. Panicking more. Instead, I just feel . . . tired. Drained. As if all the energy has left my body. This is confirmation of what I feared, isn't it? I shoot a glance up at Nemeth to see if he's still pretending to deny it.

"It's . . . true," Nemeth confesses after a moment. His gaze is tortured as he looks down at me. "But it's not the whole truth. Yes, I was sent to the tower with instructions to woo you. But I fell in love with you instead. That is very much the truth."

I shake my head slowly and drink a bit more milk, though my stomach is starting to feel unpleasant. My head pounds. "That seems rather convenient, don't you think?"

"It's the truth." He kicks his stool aside and drops to a crouch beside me, taking my cold hand in his. "Believe me, Candra. Think back to my actions. Of how we've worked together."

Ajaxi makes a disgusted sound as Nemeth pleads with me. "Don't debase yourself to a human, brother. Slap a collar on her and use her like the betrayer she is—"

Nemeth roars with fury, turning and rounding on Ajaxi. His wings spread, and he flies toward him. The brothers crash into a wall nearby, knocking dishware to the ground and sending the servants scattering.

I jump to my feet—and nearly pass out. Darkness swims in front of my eyes, and I press a hand to my brow. Oh gods, why am I so tired and weak suddenly? I clutch at the table as the two men brawl, and as I step away, I see another set of stairs at the back of the room.

More stairs. Huh.

I wonder if I can find Ivornath on my own.

I stagger toward the stairs, dizzy. My steps feel heavy, and something feels vaguely wrong. I should stop, go back to the table, and sit down until the dizziness passes, but we've waited so long to see Ivornath that I'm not about to stop now. Clutching the railing, I haul myself up the flight of stairs slowly, vaguely aware of the two Fellians brawling and shouting at each other. The stairs are new, the wood scent fresh, and splinters stick up from the railing, the wood so recent it hasn't yet been worn down. This seems important, but I can't get my mind to focus.

Something is definitely wrong.

In a haze, I stagger to the landing and then down a corridor lit with magic globes. There's a pair of double doors at the end of the hallway, and I push toward them. Dimly, I'm aware of them opening to let me into a room that smells sickly sweet, thick with incense and something foul. The edges of my vision fill with black, and I know I don't have much time. I fall to my knees and crawl toward the large, curtained bed in the center of the room and pull back the hangings. Sure enough, a large form lies there in bed.

Lazy shite king. With a snarl, I grab the blankets and rip them off of his body. I lose my balance and tumble to the ground with the blankets, and as I do, the smell in the room grows stronger.

The smell of dead and dying things.

Gagging, I crawl to my knees and haul myself upright, using the bed to support myself. As I do, I stare down at Ivornath's dead body. Maybe once, he was a man in the prime of his life, but now, he's simply a desiccated corpse, his neck and chest marked with a dark, putrid rash. His mouth hangs open as if he screamed in his last moments, and his wings are shriveled underneath him.

Dead.

Long dead, probably from the plague. How . . .

"It's a good thing you're already poisoned because now you have to die."

The feminine voice is light and confident, familiar yet strange. I turn, and as the darkness envelops my gaze, I can just barely make out a face similar to my own, with green eyes, long black hair, and a haughty smile.

"M-Meryliese?" I manage before I collapse to the floor.

CHAPTER FIFTY-TWO

My vision is fading, my head foggy.

Meryliese. My sister. She's alive . . . and she's here in Darkfell.

Meryliese was supposed to be the one in the tower. Instead, she perished in a shipwreck, and I was sent to her fate. I don't understand. "H-how . . . you're dead?"

She folds her hands at her waist and gives me a sly look. "Am I? I don't feel dead." She adjusts the cuff on one of her sleeves. "The shipwreck was a good story, wasn't it? Such a tragic tale too. All people on board died." She clicks her tongue. "At least, all people who didn't have a Fellian waiting to rescue them from the open water. I bet they never found my body."

I stare. My eyes slide shut, and I have to struggle to force them open again. My limbs are cold, and I can't feel my fingers. I reach for her, and she neatly sidesteps in a swirl of crimson silk.

"I love that after twenty years of my life was devoted to preparing me for the tower, they sent you in the space of three days. That must have been quite shocking for poor, pampered little Candromeda. So sad." She mock-pouts, her lower lip thrusting out. "Did you stay inside like a good little Vestalin?"

I roll onto my back, but I can't get up from the floor. Dimly, I remember her words. Poison? Someone poisoned me? I think of the milk I drank at dinner—how Ajaxi had paused when I skipped the wine. Was it him who poisoned me? I pant, trying to pull enough air into lungs that feel like ice. "Why . . . "

"Why what? Why is the curse upon us?" Meryliese leans over my dying body, studying me. "You did stay inside the tower, didn't you? What was it, at least two years now? My, my." She chuckles. "And all that time, you didn't wonder at the weather? It was Ivornath's idea, you know. The Golden Moon Goddess brings a wealth of angry storms to show her displeasure, but the Fellians are safe underground. It was a simple thing to visit the tower the day of the Solstice, step over the threshold, and quickly leave again. With the curse activated, Lios and its fleet were doomed, and Ivornath and I were cozy here inside Darkfell." Her face falls momentarily. "At least, until Ivornath went and died on me. But not to worry, his brother Ajaxi is an absolute cretin. He's dancing to my tune already."

I groan in pain, unable to believe what I'm hearing. It can't be true. Meryliese deliberately sabotaged the tower before we ever stepped inside. She and Ivornath wanted Lios to fall, wanted all this misfortune. It's horrible to think about.

"I hear you went and fell in love with your sweet Fellian. Is that true? Nemeth is not my type, you know. I like them more ruthless and vengeful." She chuckles and leans down, pinching my cold cheek. "Don't worry, older sister. I'll keep him alive. I need at least one of First House if I'm to rule Darkfell."

I want to bat her hand away, but I can't move. My limbs are stiffening as if I'm a corpse. My vision has faded to a blur, and I'm only dimly aware of Meryliese straightening and turning.

"You should be downstairs entertaining your brother," she says in a sharp voice. "Where's Nemeth?"

"I knocked him out," Ajaxi slurs in a wine-soaked voice. There's a crash of dishes and the sound of furniture being shoved across the floor. "He's . . . real, *real* mad."

"He can be mad," Meryliese says impatiently. "It won't make her less dead. With no one left, his loyalty will be to us." She leans over me again, a blur of dark hair and green eyes. She slaps my cheek, and I don't even feel it. "This one is taking a long time to die. Did you give her enough poison?"

"Lots. Lots and lots."

"Hm. Well, take her to the root cellar. Dump her body there until we can figure out a better place to store it."

I fade out.

I drift for some time.

I dislike death intensely. It's cold, and it smells like garlic and onions. Here I'd always thought death would be peaceful, but it's oniony. And someone's arguing nearby, and it's all very irritating. I growl, and someone reaches out and slaps my face.

This one, I feel.

"Ow," I manage. My lips feel heavy and tingly. "Not . . . s'pose . . . to slap . . . the dead."

"You're not dead, fool," comes Erynne's acerbic voice. "Wake up."

"Can't," I mumble. "Dead . . . just like Meryliese."

"Yes, well, she's not dead either," Erynne retorts. "So quit playacting at being a corpse and wake up."

Not . . . dead? Hm. Vague memories flicker through my sludge-filled brain. Of a woman dressed in scarlet who looks a bit like Erynne and a bit like me. Of Ivornath's dead body, still marked with plague and stinking of rot. Of Nemeth at dinner.

It was the truth, but it was not all of the truth, Candra. I swear it.

"I'm not dead," I manage, and I'm honestly surprised that I'm not. My mouth feels strangely tight, and when I try to lift my head, I can't. My neck is stiff. All of me is stiff. I can twitch a finger but nothing else, and the realization makes me whimper. "Can't move."

"Stay still," comes a kinder voice. Riza. A hand brushes my hair from my forehead. "Drink this and wait for it to pass."

A warm vial of something bitter is pressed to my lips. I cough and sputter. Some of it runs down my cheek, but I manage to drink most of it. Riza makes soothing noises and continues to stroke my hair and face. I close my eyes, drifting and dizzy.

"What if it doesn't work?" Erynne whispers.

"I don't even know how she's alive," Riza murmurs. "The cook said that they dosed her with enough to kill her twice over, yet she lives."

"It's our Fellian blood," Erynne says. "That potion doesn't work as well on us. I drank it when I got here. I was furious when it didn't kill me. It's because somewhere in our ancestry, someone married a Fellian. That blood is still in our veins."

And I have more Fellian blood than most. I have Nemeth's blood in my veins too. Maybe that's how I lived. Does he know what they did to me? Was he in on it? I have to think he wasn't. He wouldn't have given me his blood ahead of dinner if he'd known what had been planned.

What Meryliese had planned.

My bitch of a sister is alive.

"I hope that's it," Riza says in a low voice. "I don't know what we'll do if she can't walk."

"I can hear you," I whisper. "I'm right here."

"You're not asleep, then." Riza's tone is brisk as she pats my shoulder. "Good. That means you're recovering quickly."

"Cold," I manage. Everything feels like ice.

A warm hand takes mine and rubs my fingers. "I know," Riza says. "Not too much longer, and when you can walk, we'll leave the root cellar together."

"Is . . . that where we are?"

"Aye. They can't exactly dump you with the rest of the trash, or the humans will rise up. So, they're waiting to dump you when no one is looking." Riza pauses. "Or to burn you in the ovens."

Well, that's chilling. I try to move my feet to hurry things along. My eyes feel heavy, but I can keep them open with effort. "Meryliese," I manage. "How . . ."

"I had my suspicions, but nothing confirmed." Erynne hovers over me, her face blurry. "I've been hearing strange things for a while. People kept saying they would see me with Ivornath when I was not. Or they would catch sight of a dark-haired woman. I thought they were tales, but then Ajaxi started to call me 'Meryliese' in bed, and I put some of it together."

Riza makes an unpleasant sound in her throat.

Erynne just laughs. "Oh yes. It's as bad as you think it is, but I'm just waiting for the right moment to kill him. Never fear." She rubs my hand harder as if she can work her frustration into my veins to warm them. "Our bitch sister brought down Lios by activating the goddess's curse. She thought she'd be safe here in Darkfell, but I think the goddess's wrath has followed her under the mountains. I've heard some of Ajaxi's mumblings in his sleep. He wants to overthrow Ivornath and claim the throne for himself, but he'll have to get rid of both of his brothers first, and something tells me Meryliese doesn't want that."

I whimper, trying to sit up. "Nemeth—"

"Safe," Erynne says even as she puts a hand on my shoulder. "Ajaxi has him imprisoned in the palace. I don't know how he managed it because Ivornath wouldn't approve, but—"

They don't know? I groan, trying to force my unresponsive body to work. "Dead. Ivornath is dead."

"He what?" Riza leans over me, her face full of urgency. "Tell us what you know."

Even though my face feels numb, I tell them what I can of that dinner. Of Ajaxi sabotaging Nemeth with comments to make me angry. Of Nemeth attacking his brother. Me heading to the stairs—of course, there are stairs because Meryliese is there—only to find Ivornath's dead body in his room and Meryliese lurking in the shadows.

Both Riza and Erynne make unhappy noises when I'm done.

"It makes sense," Erynne says. "Ajaxi's been getting bolder lately. He won't let Nemeth live, though. As long as he's alive, the throne passes to him. I knew he was furious when Nemeth arrived, but at the time, I thought it was because of the goddess's curse. Now I know it's because he wanted him to die. I have no doubt that Ajaxi didn't send the shipment of food to the tower, expecting Nemeth to starve to death like a good, honorable prince."

Except he didn't because he fell in love with a shameless, self-centered Liosian princess. I'm a little proud of myself at that moment. "He's not with them," I tell my sister and Riza. "We have to help him."

"He's safe for now. But if Ivornath is dead and Ajaxi is getting bold enough to poison Candra, we need to act quickly." Riza's face is full of urgency as she gazes at Erynne. "We must act soon. If he's taking out his rivals, Second House is next."

And that means Nemeth is in danger no matter what they say. "Then help me up," I tell them. "Because the sooner I'm on my feet, the sooner we can take Ajaxi down."

And the sooner I get my Nemeth back and we can talk about the secrets he's been keeping.

It's still hours before we're able to leave the root cellar. No one wants to teleport me because they're afraid that in my weakened state, it'll kill me or harm the baby. So we wait, and then, extremities numb, I stagger between Erynne and Riza out of the root cellar and into the kitchens. From there, a human slave leads us down a twisting hall and a secret passage that takes us all the way to a storage shed. Then, from there, Second House meets us.

Plans are discussed, but the poison in my veins exhausts me, and with no Nemeth to give me his blood, I'm forced to rely on Riza to make me a potion. We're missing some of the ingredients, so it doesn't quite do the job I want it to, and I collapse into bed, exhausted.

I'm missing the uprising, but I don't have the energy to protest, much less carry a weapon. Erynne will be the figurehead they need for the humans, which is fine because I'm not much of a leader.

I just want Nemeth.

I'm so weak that I can't get out of bed for what feels like forever. I'm vaguely aware of the others in Tolian's home, of a cacophony of voices arguing over when is the best time to storm the palace. Of human voices mixed with Fellian. Of my sister, Erynne, speaking angrily, followed by Riza's more measured tones.

Some hero I am. I sleep and can't rise even to relieve myself. Someone has to come in and drag me to the nearest garderobe because my legs are still numb and weak. The only comfort I have is that the baby in my belly bounces and dances against my bladder as if it has taken all my energy for itself.

I doze in and out of dreams of Nemeth, dreams in which I'm still in the tower. Dreams in which I'm oiling his wings as he reads his atrocious war poetry by the fire, and we're so happy and content that it feels physically painful to wake up and find myself alone, muscles stiff and aching from my near death.

At some point, I wake up to see Riza's face near mine. She's dressed in pants and a cloak, her expression worried as she presses her fingers to my brow. "You feel warm."

"I'm fine," I manage, even though I'm very clearly not. For the first time in what feels like days, the house is silent. Second House practically echoes with how empty it is, and something about that makes my skin prickle. "Where is everyone?"

"They've gone ahead," Riza says. "Tonight is when we take over First House. Your sister will be overthrown. Ajaxi will be captured."

"Nemeth," I whimper, sitting upright. It takes a great deal of effort, but I manage. "What of Nemeth?"

"They have instructions to leave him be. We've made it as clear as we can to the others that he's not to be harmed."

I don't trust it. I've seen how incensed Erynne can be around Fellians. And if Second House wants to take over, they have to get rid of First House. What's to stop any of them from harming Nemeth? They can say it's an "accident," and no one would be the wiser. They could say that something happened during the uprising. Ajaxi could decide he's safest if he kills Nemeth before he can fall into the wrong hands.

Nemeth needs me. If nothing else so I can shield him from the other humans. So I can warn him to be wary of his poisonous brother and my vile sister Meryliese.

So, I get to my feet. Or I try to. I stumble and flop onto the floor, breathing hard.

"Princess!" Riza gasps, bending over me. "You must rest!"

I shake my head. "Nemeth needs me. We have to go find him."

"You're not well—"

I manage to pull myself off the floor, clutching at her clothing. "Do you think anyone's going to wait for me to feel better?" When she hesitates, I have my answer. "I don't care if it takes me all day and all night to get to Nemeth, I have to. I'm the only one who can stop them if they're determined to hurt him."

Riza hesitates and then purses her lips at me. "Wait here. I'll get a cart."

CHAPTER FIFTY-THREE

If I ever doubted Riza's loyalty, ever, I need to be smacked upside the head. My former servant and forever friend tirelessly hauls my cart through the empty streets of Darkfell. She's panting and sweaty but doesn't complain. I hold her weapons in my numb arms and feel grateful for her loyalty. If I could hug her, I would.

The palace rises in the distance, and as it does, so do the voices. There are shouts of anger, followed by crashes of what sound like pottery. Colorful hangings are on fire, ash drifting through the still air as we approach the mob of human slaves and Fellian defectors.

I can't help but notice there aren't many Fellians with us.

I also can't help but notice that every door we pass has a red mark on it, the mark of the plague. It's terrifying, and it makes me even more afraid for Nemeth. I can protect him from an angry mob, but if the plague is in the palace . . .

"Make way," Riza cries as she carts me closer. "Make way for Princess Candromeda! We must get inside!"

A Fellian wearing a bright red scarf over his horns storms toward us. "Riza! You cannot be here. Tolian wants you safe—"

She shakes her head, pushing past him. "Tell Tolian Candra needs my help. He'll understand. Where's Princess Erynne? Where is my mate?"

The Fellian glares at me as if I'm the problem (and I suppose I am) before following behind Riza. "They are deep inside the palace, hunting for Ajaxi and his whore." He glances at me again and then growls, taking the handle of the small, rickety cart I'm seated in. "Let me do that for you."

"We need to get to the dungeons," I tell him, my words slurred because I'm exhausted, and it's taking all of my strength to stay upright. "Can you take us there?"

He looks to Riza, and she nods.

"Follow me," he says. "And arm yourselves."

We push into the fray inside the building, and everything is chaos. Many of the Fellians are wearing the bright red scarves over their horns; they battle with others with bare heads and fight on the ground, their wings tightly protected behind them. The human women surge through the halls, destroying everything they can reach and shouting obscenities I've never heard come out of women's mouths. I don't blame them, though. I'd be mad as shite, too, if I'd been enslaved. They attack everything with a vicious enthusiasm that tells me they're avenging more than themselves. They fight for the memory of every person who was destroyed in Lionel's awful war and the Fellian vengeance that followed.

Even if they free themselves, we haven't won. No one *wins* in any of this. We're all coming out of this battered and shaken, the world far grimmer than it was two years ago.

Me? I just want Nemeth back. If I must spend the next five years back in the tower again, I'll do so gratefully. I just want him whole and well. I want to talk to him and understand the machinations behind what he did. I want to hold him close and know that we're all right.

But as Erynne, my once-gentle sister, attacks a guard with a wild, vicious light in her eyes, two other human women spattered with blood at her side, I wonder if anything will ever be all right ever again.

"Over here," Riza calls to the Fellian pulling my cart through the madness. She points at a side door, and he shoves his way forward, the cart rattling as he pushes fighters aside—both Fellian and human—with his shield.

The cart rocks, and I let out a yelp, only to have Riza come to my side. She grabs a short sword from the bundle of weapons I'm clutching and uses it to stab at a Fellian hand that grabs at the cart. I cry out again as she chops at the hand as if it were a vegetable and not attached to a body. Hot blood splashes my face, and I flinch backward.

Our guard moves away from the front of the cart and sinks his axe into the back of the Fellian attacking us, then kicks his corpse away as I stare.

"We can't let anyone stop us, my lady," Riza says in a hard voice, stepping over the dead man. "If we stop now, you're dead. Understand? We won't be able to carry you out. Not in this mob."

I swallow hard, looking around. It's madness everywhere, but no Fellian is using his wings or teleporting. Those things must be too dangerous. I nod at Riza. She's seen too much of war, and I haven't seen enough, perhaps.

The guard straightens our cart again and hauls it down the side hall, surging forward until we come to another door and then a staircase heading down. "The dungeons," is all he says. "Now I must rejoin the fight."

"Thank you, Raxus," Riza says in a sharp voice. "If you see Tolian, tell him to be careful."

He grins, showing the fang-like teeth of the Fellian men, and adjusts his shield and axe, then runs down the hall back toward the chaos.

Riza studies me, pulling out another weapon, a dagger. "Can you walk?"

No, I want to complain. My legs still feel shaky and weak, and I'm pretty sure my toes remain numb despite everything. But if Nemeth is in the dungeon, that's where I need to be. "Aye."

It takes far too long to get to my feet, but I manage. Weaving unsteadily, I take the blade she offers me and tuck it between my breasts like I used to with my enchanted dagger. It doesn't want to remain in place, thanks to my filmy Fellian-make dress, so I hook the crossguard on the neckline of my dress and wrap my shawl tightly around my shoulders, winding it twice so I won't have to hold it in place. Just those small tasks make me feel utterly exhausted, but I force myself to stand straight.

Riza nods at me and heads down the stairs, her blade in hand.

I follow. The stairs wind down, narrow and circular, and it's pitch black inside. It reminds me of my days in the tower when I was desperately preserving wood and matches for fire. I lean heavily against the inside wall, my hand pressed to the stone to guide me, and I slowly move down, counting steps.

When we get to twenty-three, there are no more steps. Riza grabs my arm, and I hear the rustle of her clothing. "I'll find a lamp of some kind. Wait here."

She moves away, and I wait in the darkness, my eyes closed. Again, I'm reminded of my time in the tower, and when I hear Riza's clothing rustling as she searches for a light, I think of all the times I got by with nothing. I think of how I recognized Nemeth by the sound of his wings as he moved and the heft of his steps upon the floor. Can I find him now?

I take a step forward, and my slipper-covered feet encounter straw on the stone floor. Rushes, I realize. Rushes that are meant to keep the floor warm and somewhat clean. The straw here smells moldy when I step forward, though, and something drips on me from above. It's cold and wet and damp in here, and I think of Nemeth and how much he'd hate it here. He loves a warm fire.

A light flares somewhere behind me, and Riza sighs with relief. "There we go."

The dungeon is horrifying. It's far more cramped than the rest of the rooms above, with multiple doors clustered tightly in a row, all of them seemingly too small for the large Fellians and their wings. I suppose that's part of the punishment, but I shiver at the sight. Each door has only a small hole to look inside, and these dungeons seem far worse than the ones I was kept in. More than that, it's foully dark down here, the ceiling low and oppressive, and the walls damp. Between that and the gross straw, I want nothing more than to leave.

But if Nemeth is down here . . .

I stagger toward the first cell. It's small, no bigger than a garderobe. Riza shines a light into it and shakes her head. "Empty."

I peer inside just in case, but she's right. I don't see anyone inside. "How does one keep a Fellian prisoner if they can slide through shadows?" I ask her, trying to distract from the fact that I'm nearly collapsing with exhaustion. "Won't they just leave?"

"Magic," Riza says. "Everything is always magic with Fellians. Tolian told me that the king's dungeon is enchanted so that all magic is nullified down here. No one can teleport in; no one can teleport out."

Makes sense, even if it makes things harder.

Riza shines her light into the next cell and then shudders. "That one is dead. Recent too."

"How recent?" My voice is hoarse with terror. Before she can answer, I peek inside because I'm unable to stand it. There's a dead Fellian all right, curled up on the ground, his limbs twisted. An ugly dark rash covers his chest and face, but it's not Nemeth.

I bite my lip because I saw that rash on another dead man. That's the plague. It's not safe for Nemeth to be down here. We have to get him out, and soon.

Riza surges ahead, and I follow after her. Most of the cells are empty, though a few have dead men—all Fellians—inside them. I'm horrified that the dead have been left to rot down here, forgotten, but I think of Ivornath's body above and wonder if that's Meryliese's awful doing. I hate her more with every moment that passes.

If we're lucky, Erynne will find her and stab her once or twice or twelve times and save me the effort of killing her myself.

In the second to the last cell, there's a large Fellian with his back to the small viewing hole in the door. His wings are wrapped tightly around him as if he's using them as a blanket, and his entire body quakes.

"Nemeth?" I call, my heart racing.

No answer. Whoever's in the cell can't hear me, either by magic or by the fever that has him trapped.

"Is that him?" Riza asks. "Can you tell?"

I open my mouth to speak when the figure turns slightly, and a long, ragged scar is revealed on one wing. A whimper of agony escapes me. It's Nemeth, all right, and he's sick with the plague. "Oh gods, we have to get him out of there, Riza."

She thrusts the light into my hands, the magical globe held in place by a large wooden base with a finger hole, much like an oil lamp. Riza tugs on the door as I hold up the light, my arm trembling with exhaustion.

The door doesn't budge, and she casts a look around. "Locked. The key has to be here somewhere. Wait here, Candra."

"I won't leave." I'm not going anywhere without Nemeth. I stare at the sight of my poor mate. How long has he been down here? How long has he been sick? My heart aches and aches, and I fight back a surge of panic. Even if we get Nemeth out, how do we cure the plague? If there *was* a cure, surely Darkfell wouldn't be so empty?

I'm terrified that I might lose him after all.

Riza checks a guard station by the door, digging through a desk and then searching the rushes on the floor. She goes over the first few cells again, but all their doors are locked as well. Lips pressed together with frustration, she glances up at the stairs. "The key might be above."

"Go," I tell her. "I'm not leaving Nemeth."

She hesitates and then nods. "Be safe. I'll return as swiftly as I can."

I watch as she races up the winding, narrow staircase again. I'm alone in the dungeon with my sick mate, and I turn back to gaze at him, watching with helpless frustration as he quakes, his wings shivering, and then claws and scratches at his neck.

"Hold on, Nemeth," I tell him in a low voice. "I'm here. I'm going to save you. I promise."

He stills at my words, and I hold my breath, waiting for him to turn and look at me. To speak. Something.

"When we get out of here, we'll go wherever you like," I promise him. I think he likes the sound of my voice. Perhaps it comforts him, even in fever dreams, so I keep talking. "I don't care if we stay or if we go, just as long as we're together. Everything works out better when we're side by side. It's the world that keeps pulling us apart. We won't let that happen anymore. You and I will raise our child somewhere safe and quiet. I'll even let you read war poetry to him or her, though you know I hate that drivel. You can teach our baby Fellian poems and magic, and I'll teach them Liosian dances and our holidays. More than anything, we'll just be happy because we're together."

"So sweet," coos a hard-edged voice. "A baby, you say? You'll have to tell me if I'm invited to witness the birth of the next Vestalin."

Why am I even surprised Meryliese is here? Of course, she's here. She keeps showing up like a pimple on the night before a dance. As I stare at her, Meryliese twirls a key on a chain, toying with it.

That bitch. She's got Nemeth's key. I lift my chin and give her a dismissive look, all the while trying to figure out how I'm going to get it away from her. I set my lamp on the sill of a nearby door so I can free my hands. "Hiding, dear sister?"

Her mouth twists in a smile. "Ajaxi's idea. While he protects his throne, I'm hiding. Or so he thinks. More like I'm protecting my interests by keeping his brother alive." She makes a face. "Or at least I thought I was until he started shaking with sickness. Now I've got to figure out who inherits Darkfell if all of First House dies." She sighs dramatically. "These Fellians are truly such a bother."

I've never hated anyone as much as I hate Meryliese at this moment. "Why are you so evil? Why are you doing this?"

"Me? Evil? For trying to take control of my own life for once?" She gives me an incredulous look. "You can't be serious."

"You don't think your actions are evil?" I slide my hand under my shawl, trying to reach for my knife without seeming like I'm reaching for a weapon. Keep Meryliese talking, I remind myself. Keep her focused on her anger.

My sister gives me a withering look. "I think I'm being selfish for once in my life, and I'm enjoying it. How do you think it feels to grow up knowing that your life isn't your own? That your head is filled with prayers to a goddess who demands all of your time and that people insist upon training you on the right prayers to give and how to make your food stretch, all so you can be an obedient lump in a tower to a jealous goddess? So I can save everyone else in the world while sacrificing myself?" Meryliese shakes her head, her eyes blazing with righteous indignation. "It's shite, sister. No one ever asked me if I wanted to do *any* of this. No one ever asked me if I cared about the fate of the rest of the world. I wanted to be a princess. I wanted to marry a king and have babies." She sniffs haughtily. "And I don't see why they didn't make you take my spot."

"Because I was *sick*—"

She waves a hand, dismissing that. "Yes, but they figured out how to treat it. *You* could have been the sacrifice, and I could have gone to court, and everything would have been perfect. We could have lied. Said you were the youngest. But no. Mother kept you instead of me, and then Erynne never suggested we switch. I was forgotten. No one wanted me . . . until Ivornath arrived." Her eyes flare with intensity. "The Fellians wanted to work with me. And when I suggested we trigger the curse to destroy Lionel's fleet, Ivornath thought it was an excellent idea. He was going to make me his queen, you know."

Her cold expression flares with something like hurt, the first real emotion my sister has shown other than pure viciousness.

I can't help but push just a little more. "But he *didn't*."

"He was going to!"

"When?" I press. "You've been here for over two years. When was he going to marry you? When was he going to give you his bite?" I show her my hand, the mark on my palm, just under my thumb. "I was with Nemeth for no time at all, and he took me as his—"

"Silence!" my sister cries. "You don't know our situation! You don't know anything!"

I give her a smug look, hoping it hides the hammering in my heart. Hoping it hides the fact that I'm reaching for the dagger tucked into the front of my dress, hidden by my shawl. "I know he would have mated you if he'd wanted to—"

"Stop it!"

"I'm just saying that this could have been you." I rub my stomach with one hand. "If he'd really wanted you, that is. It sounds to me like he was just using you too—"

Meryliese snarls and lunges for me.

I let her grab me, using the moment to pull my knife free from my dress. It falls into the folds of my gown, and, panicked, I claw for it even as my sister pulls my hair and claws at my face.

"Bitch," she cries. "You don't get everything! You—"

The moment my fingers close around my dagger, I thrust upward into Meryliese. She grunts, and then hot liquid splashes over my hands. Blood.

She stares down at me; her mouth tinged with red, her eyes still filled with hate. She reaches for my neck, her nails scratching at my skin. I shove the knife in deeper, hating the wet resistance I feel against it. "I'm sorry," I whisper to her. "But Nemeth is mine, and I'm going to save him."

Her hand rests against my throat. For a long moment, I think she's going to recover and choke me, and I've got no strength left either. We stare at each other, and then Meryliese's body slumps over mine, heavy and limp.

I tremble.

I just killed my own sister. I just stabbed a person, Meryliese, who should have been dead. Who never had her own life to begin with. I want to understand her—and some part of me does. After all, I left the tower too. Does she deserve to die for that? Do I?

Doesn't matter. She tried to come between Nemeth and me, and I'd kill her a thousand times if it meant saving him.

I bite back a sob, pushing at my sister's dead weight. For all that she was slender like Erynne, Meryliese feels as if she weighs a thousand pounds at this moment. I thrust her off of me with my last bit of strength, and her body crashes into the door. The light I perched precariously on the ledge of the door's window crashes to the ground and breaks, splintering into a thousand pieces near my head.

"Shite," I mutter aloud to the darkness.

But I'm no longer terrified by the pitch black. I sit up, brushing blood and glass off my clothes as best I can, and then I reach for my sister's dead body. With searching fingers, I find the necklace with the key on it and yank it free. I get to my feet and visualize the doors. I just need to find the one that has Nemeth behind it.

"Nemeth?" I call in the hopes my mate will answer. "Are you here?"

There's no response. But I have the key now, and I know he's close. I touch each door, and when I find the wall, I backtrack. He was in the second to the last cell, if I'm correct. I run my fingers over the door, looking for the lock. When I find it, I pull the padlock off, toss it aside, and then step in.

"Nemeth?" I take a step forward. "If you're not in this cell, and I touch a dead body, I'm going to be really mad at you."

There's a rustle of wings close by, and then green eyes flare to life, shining in the flat darkness around us. They look fevered and cloudy, but they're still my Nemeth's.

Before I can say anything, his familiar hand curls around my neck. "Good," he says in a thick voice. "A hostage."

And then he collapses to the floor at my feet.

"Nemeth!" I squeak, moving to his side. He quakes on the ground, his entire body trembling. I hear the sound of scratching and grasp his hands in mine, stopping him before he can claw at his neck. "I'm here, love. It's me. Candra. Are you with me?"

He groans, and for a moment, I think he's unconscious again. Then, ever so softly . . .

"Milettahn."

Hot tears spring to my eyes. "That's right," I say. "It's me. I'm here, and I love you, and nothing is ever going to separate us again."

"Dying . . . "

I shake my head, flinging my arms around him and hugging him tightly. I can feel the roughness of his skin from the rash, the heat blazing through his form, and the quaking of his body. "You're not dying," I whisper. "Your blood saved me, you know. Meryliese tried to poison me, but your blood and my Fellian blood saved me from the poison."

A brilliant idea flashes through my mind. If his blood saved me . . . maybe my blood can save him.

CHAPTER FIFTY-FOUR

For three days and nights, I lie in the bed next to Nemeth as he tosses and turns, caught in the grip of the plague. His skin is covered in a terrible rash, and he sweats constantly, moaning and delirious. He has to be strapped down so he doesn't hurt himself in his thrashing, and a magical collar was placed around his neck to nullify his ability to teleport so he doesn't do something dangerous while lost in the fever.

I give him blood several times a day. I don't know if human blood will kill him or not, but maybe the thread of Fellian that runs through my veins will be enough to save him. I watch my mate struggle with the plague, and I pray to the Golden Moon Goddess for what feels like the first time.

Strangely enough, my resentment for the goddess is gone. I no longer hate her or feel trapped in a fate I want no part of. Fate is just that—fate. It happens, and sometimes we're in control of it, and sometimes we're not. It's a relief in an odd way to know that the goddess's anger has never been focused on Nemeth or me. That the constant storms and flooding and the wrath of the goddess were focused solely on Meryliese, who deliberately woke the tower's curse to punish a people she felt had betrayed her since birth.

But Meryliese is dead now. Ajaxi too. He'd barricaded himself in the highest reaches of Ivornath's palace, only to be shivering and scratching frantically at his neck when he was found. Caught in the grips of the plague, he faded faster than Nemeth did.

We tried giving him some of my blood, too, just because it was the right thing to do. Erynne refused. It didn't matter, though—the plague tore through him twice as fast as Nemeth, and I can't say I'm disappointed that he died.

I've been told the uprising is a success, with Second House in control of the palace and the humans freed from their bonds. Things are chaotic right now as Second House tries to establish order. The humans are looting and being a menace, stealing food and whatever they can. I don't blame them—I'd be an absolute arse to my former slaveowners as well—but eventually, things will settle, and we'll have to figure out how to live together again, Fellian and Liosian, under the mountain. This is the only place with food and shelter from the incessant rain, so, like it or not, we're going to be companions for the next few years.

I gaze over at my mate, who is covered in sweat with a thin blanket over him. "Please wake up," I whisper. "Please talk to me."

"How are you feeling today, my lady?" Riza asks, bustling into our quarters.

I turn toward her, managing a smile. "Tired. Weak. Waiting for Nemeth to open his eyes."

She beams at me, a tray in her arms. "I've got food and your medicine. Eat something; we'll get you fixed up, and I'll tell you the news from the palace."

Riza gives me my medicine, and I obediently fold my arm up, listening as she chatters. She has a thick, savory porridge for me, made (again) with mushrooms, but I don't mind the taste. I eat it and sop it up with bread, knowing that I need my strength if I'm going to keep giving blood to Nemeth.

"Two new houses are infected with plague," Riza tells me as I finish my meal. "Your sister's blood doesn't seem to do as much for them as yours, so we're going to need more vials when you feel you can donate."

I nod and take another thick chunk of bread. "I don't think Erynne has the same amount of Fellian blood in her that I do. I think it's related to my curse."

"Whatever it is, we gave them the last of your blood, and it seems to be helping. They're sweating but have no rash so far, so the healers are hopeful. They've been quarantined, and only humans are allowed in to see them, so the spread should be minimal." She nudges a bit of meat toward me. "Eat more. You need to produce more blood as quickly as you can."

I make a face but put a slice of braised fowl on my plate. If I make more blood, I can give more to Nemeth. "How is Second House coping?"

"Not well," Riza admits with a tiny smile. She props her chin on her hand and gives me a dreamy look. "I love Tolian with all my heart, but he doesn't have the patience to lead. Says he's a willing sword, but he's not a king. And if one more person asks him about stairs, I think he's going to lose his mind."

I manage a smile at that. "Stairs are important. No one wants to feel like things are off limits to humans and not Fellians. It makes humans uneasy."

She nods. "That's what I told him, and that he's going to have to be patient. Made such a face too."

"How are the human quarters coming?"

"Very well. It's a process, but you can see moods improving all around." Riza smiles. "You were right that no one would want to move into the abandoned plague houses. I don't know why Tolian suggested it."

"Because this is his home. He means well, but he doesn't understand that the Liosian survivors need a fresh start and, by that, a place to call their own. The city will get sorted in time. For now, the women need homes where they can feel safe to be themselves and not be reminded that someone died there recently. I wouldn't be able to sleep there myself."

She grunts. "He's a man and a soldier. He can sleep anywhere." Riza gets to her feet, wiping her hands. "Feel well enough to give blood to your lover, or do you want to wait a few moments more?"

"Now," I say. It's always my answer. Any time I'm allowed to give Nemeth more blood, I will. Riza won't let me donate too much because she worries about my health and that of the baby, but we'll manage. Nemeth needs me more than anything.

Riza just nods and then gets out the needles. She takes blood from my arm, moves to him, and injects it. I lean against him, rubbing his bare skin as if my touch will somehow make it circulate faster in his body.

"I'll leave you alone with him," she tells me in a soft voice. "The healers will come by again shortly. Call if you need anything."

I nod, pressing my cheek to his shoulder. Is it just me, or is the rash on his neck fading? Or am I seeing that because I desperately want to see that? He's still sweating and unconscious, his wings trembling against his back.

He needs to awaken.

Forcing myself to sit up, I find the bowl of water Riza's left nearby. It's still warm, so I dip the towel in and wipe Nemeth's skin down. "I know you're sick, and you probably want to join the Gray God in his realm, but allow me to tell you all the reasons I think that is a terrible idea." I keep my tone light and flirty, so perhaps he'll hear it somewhere deep inside and respond. "First and foremost, you're needed here. You're the only one of First House who remains, which makes you the king. I know you probably don't want to be the king, but I think you'd make an excellent one. You'd be kind and sympathetic to the humans because you married a particularly fantastic one, and the Fellians would follow you. Truly, if you were on the throne, it'd be ideal for both parties."

I lean over the bed and continue bathing him, even though I'm so tired I want to curl up next to him and sleep for a week. But if I don't bathe him, one of the nurses will come in and do so, and I'd rather it be my hands that he wakes up to instead of those of a stranger. I want him to be touched with love. If everything that's happened is true—and I suspect it is—Nemeth broke ties with what his family wanted because he loved me.

That's why he hid me when we arrived. Even then, he was protecting me.

So now I'm going to protect him. I stroke the damp cloth over his chest, then move to his other arm. "Let me tell you a bit of what it'll be like if you decide to die on me. First of all, I have it on great authority that there is no war poetry allowed in the Gray God's realm. You know how much he loves peace, and I'm afraid that war poetry is simply out of the question."

I move the cloth over his fingers, my heart stuttering when I come across the bite on his palm. Mine hasn't the sharp outline that his does, but he's always been so proud of it. If he was truly using me, he'd have never had me give him my bite. He could have omitted it from our mating, and I would have been none the wiser.

All the signs have been there all along that he truly has loved me. I lean in and press a kiss to his knuckles, then continue.

"Second of all, your brothers are probably in the Gray God's realm as we speak. All the more reason to stay here with me a while longer." I gaze down at him, but he's so very still he makes my heart ache. Why won't he wake? It's been three days. Most who die of the plague die within a day or two. The fact that he's survived over three days with the sickness is a good sign, I hope. But I won't know for certain until he opens his eyes and smiles at me.

So, I continue.

"Third, the Gray God loves storms, and I know you do not." I slump onto the edge of the bed, tired and a little defeated. I towel his chest, forcing a smile to my face that I don't feel. "Remember when we were back in the tower, and you heard storms for the first time? You were convinced we were under siege, and you were going to take me captive as leverage." My voice breaks, and I catch a ragged breath. "I guess they don't have storms at the Alabaster Citadel, what with it being in the desert. You were so unnerved by the noise, and I never stopped to think that a storm might sound different above ground. Here I thought I was being so very brave, and I never stopped to think how difficult it might be for you too. That you were getting pressured by your family over me. You could have let me die a half dozen times and solved the problem, yet you always took care of me. You always looked out for me. If you were sent to seduce me, you did a shite job of it, love. I seduced you, remember? I was the one who pushed for us to have sex. For us to play together. For us to just enjoy each other's bodies. And I guess that leads me to the biggest reason why you have to stay." I suck in a ragged breath. "You can't leave me behind."

A knot forms in my throat, tight and hot, and I clutch his hand in mine, waiting for the stupid tears to pass so I can speak. I swallow hard and try to continue.

"I know it's been tough since we arrived here in Darkfell. I know you kept some secrets from me. But you're not allowed to leave me behind. You're not allowed to leave our child behind. I love you. I love you, and I need—more than anything—to talk to you right now. So I'm going to need you to come back to me as soon as possible. I'm probably going to stomp my foot at the secrets you were keeping, and you're probably going to tell me that you had no choice, and then we'll fall into bed together and kiss, and we'll be together again."

That stupid knot in my throat returns. What if the last memory he has of me is that awful scene at the dinner? What if he dies thinking I hate him? Tears spill down my face, and I press desperate kisses to his knuckles.

He's not allowed to leave me behind. That was never part of the plan.

"Don't . . . cry . . . "

I gasp, clutching his hand tighter. Nemeth's eyes are open, just a slit. "Oh! Nemeth!" His eyes flutter shut again, and I want to yank them back open, want him to sit up and talk to me. Something. Anything. "Nemeth?"

"This . . . is the part where . . . I should . . . be groveling at your feet . . . "

A sob escapes me. "You should, it's true. But I'm in a magnanimous mood." I cradle his hand to my chest. "You look like shite, love."

He grunts. "Candra . . . "

"I know. Don't spend your strength trying to explain to me."

Nemeth frowns. "But . . . "

"You need to explain? Let me try to help you." I bring his hand to my cheek, pressing a kiss to his thumb. My heart overflows with joy. "Your brother Ivornath concocted a plan with Meryliese to destroy the Liosian army, and they triggered the curse and sent you to the tower anyhow. Am I right?"

He shakes his head. "Didn't know . . . never saw your sister. Just knew Ivornath was up to something."

I pat his stomach. "Then we amend that. All right then. Your brother was up to something. He sent you to the tower with instructions to seduce me and win me to Darkfell's side. And when you met me, you hated the idea."

Nemeth's eyes flutter closed again. His skin is such a strange shade of gray, blotched with the plague's rash, livid and dark against his neck. "Didn't hate . . . idea. Liked it . . . liked you . . . too much."

"Dragon shite," I tell him in a wobbly voice, near tears again. "They might have told you to seduce me, they might have told you to report back on me, but you didn't have to take me as your mate. I would have been happy to be your paramour. Instead, you wanted us together. You wanted us to be mated, to give me your bite. To make me your wife. You didn't use me like Ivornath used Meryliese. You loved me."

"Still do." His fingers lift from my cheek, and he traces my mouth. "Understand . . . if you . . . no longer love . . . me."

"Dragon shite," I say again.

"Or trust me."

"More dragon shite. You're going to get better. I'm going to keep giving you my blood, and you're going to get better. You know my blood is the cure for the plague? It's been keeping you alive. We're going to get you well, my love. And then we're going to rule Darkfell together. We're going to combine our kingdoms and make the world a better place for those of us who have survived."

He smiles at me, tired, but the most gorgeous thing I've ever seen.

I press yet another kiss to his fingertips. "Now hurry up and get better so I can ride on your knot once more."

The rumbly, rusty laughter that erupts from Nemeth's chest is the best thing I've ever heard.

—

Nemeth sleeps quietly, but I can't bring myself to leave his side. Riza has seen him, along with the Fellian medics, and have pronounced him on the mend. Riza plastered his chest with an onion poultice to make it easier for him to breathe, and even though it stinks bad enough to wake the dead, I cling to Nemeth's arm, breathing in the stink.

It means that he's going to get better. Dead men have no need of poultices.

I watch him sleep, his chest rising evenly. His fever is gone, but I can't relax. Not yet. Not when things could turn just as quickly again. I press my fingers to his brow, feeling for warmth, but Nemeth always feels warmer than I do.

When I set my hand down again, Nemeth reaches for me and twines his fingers with mine. "I'm better."

"I know."

His eyes open a slit. "I can feel your tension. I can feel you watching me while I sleep too."

I chew on my lip. "Sorry. Should I leave you alone?"

"You should come into bed with me." He gestures at the open space on the side. "Lie down. You must be tired."

"I don't know if I am," I confess. I stare down at our joined fingers, at the claws he keeps shorn to show he has a mate. I bite my lip again, because I don't want to worry him. "I feel uneasy."

He struggles to sit up, and I immediately press a hand to his shoulder again. "No, no. Nothing's wrong," I reassure him. "Don't get out of bed." When he eases back, a wary look on his face, I continue. "That's just it. There's nothing wrong. I feel like we've been on the run, or stressing about something for months on end, and I don't know how to rest. I don't know how to tell myself that no one else is going to try to kill us. That there's enough *food*. Enough medicine."

His eyes widen. "Your medicine—"

"It's handled," I reassure him, stroking his knuckles. "Riza had the ingredients of a potion saved in her trunks, just in case. She's kept it with her for years now. I didn't want to take your blood without your permission."

"You *always* have my permission. Always."

I smile at him. "You see what I mean? It takes nothing but a few words and suddenly we're both panicking. I don't know how to relax, and you don't either."

"Then come rest in the bed with me and we will both try." He tilts his head, indicating I should climb in next to him.

Maybe he's right. I release his hand and gather up my skirts, climbing over him to his far side. I settle in against him and curl myself around his big arm. It doesn't matter that he smells like onions. I love the feel of him and I'm immediately a bit more comfortable. All is fine in my world when I'm with Nemeth. "Better."

"I smell of onions."

"You do," I agree, breathing deep. "I don't care."

He turns his head and looks at me, his eyelids heavy with fatigue. I should tell him to go back to sleep, but I need him in this moment, and I suspect he needs me too. "Enjoy this moment, Candra. The moment I can leave bed is when the real work begins."

I ignore that and what it could portend. "Go to sleep."

"My brothers are dead. Your king is dead, and your sister is unfit to rule. You know what this means."

"Don't say it."

Nemeth sighs heavily. "We're in charge."

Dragon shite. "Don't remind me."

"If you want to run away from responsibility, I understand." He gives a weak chuckle. "I want to run too."

Oh please. I tighten my grip on his arm and rest my cheek on his shoulder, staring up at the stone ceiling. "I'm not leaving you behind."

"That's very good, because I'm too tired to chase you." He sighs. "I'm sorry I wasn't more honest with you upfront."

In a way, it's a weak apology. In another way, it's not needed at all. I grew up at court. I know all about lies and half truths. I've certainly had my share, both giving and receiving. "We both come from a people that love intrigues. I should have expected it."

"Perhaps." He turns his head and rubs his face against my hair. "I fear this is our new home. Does it make you . . . unhappy?"

I wonder what he'd do if I said yes. Abandon both of our peoples and return to the tower with me? I suspect he would, and the thought fills me with a sweet joy, even though I know it's not meant to be. "This place has food, does it not?"

"What the underground gardens do not provide, the ocean will, aye."

"Then it's smarter than staying above where the goddess vents her wrath. We just need stairs." I pat his arm. "Lots and lots of stairs."

"Mmm, yes. Stairs." He sounds weary, so weary that I worry about him all over again.

"We'll talk about this when you're better. For now, all I'll say is that humans need to be welcome here, love."

"Of course they're welcome. Their queen is human."

"Beside a Fellian king. A union their ancestors would have been outraged over." I smile at the thought. "Though I do wonder if this is what Ravendor and Azamenth envisioned when they left the tower together. Kingdoms combined . . . before the world around them ruined their love."

"We're not going to let ours get ruined," Nemeth says, voice fierce.

"No, we're not." And I link my fingers with his once more. Nemeth is mine, and nothing in this world or the next is going to take him from me.

Not Lionel. Not Meryliese. Not the Golden Moon Goddess.

No one.

CHAPTER FIFTY-FIVE

ONE WEEK LATER

Nemeth is a terrible patient.

I glare down at my mate from my spot over his bed, my hands on my hips. "I am going to grab the nearest chamber pot and pummel you over the head with it if you don't lie back down right this instant, you absolutely infuriating Fellian."

He ignores my scowl, trying to push himself up on his feet. "I can't lie in bed all day long, Candra. There's too much to be done."

"Let someone healthy do it, you rock brain," I tell him, planting my hands on his chest and giving him a not-so-subtle nudge back into bed. "You're still recovering from the plague. Your rash has just now healed. Do I need to cover you with another poultice of herbs and onion plaster?"

Nemeth makes a hideous face at that, but he doesn't try to get out of bed again. "If you come near me with more of that plaster, I am going to scream, Candra."

"And I am going to scream if you try to get out of bed," I reply tartly. "So much screaming." I give his shoulder another nudge, and this time, he goes down without complaint, relaxing in the bed once more. I pull the sheets up to his chest and beam, pleased. "That's better."

"You are an absolutely impossible woman."

"I really am. Please don't tell me that you're surprised by this." I tuck the blankets tighter around his legs, ignoring his grumbling. "You should count yourself lucky that you have my undivided attention. Fancy lords have given trunks full of jewels for less—"

Nemeth grabs my hand and pulls me down onto the bed next to him. I tumble onto the blankets, my breasts pressed against his side, and let out a squeak of surprise.

"That's better. Now you're quiet." His arm slides around my waist, pinning me in place.

I poke his chest. "Very funny. Let me up."

He shakes his head, gazing down at me thoughtfully. "You look tired, *milettahn*. I worry about you."

"I'm fine," I protest, though I am exhausted. The constant blood draws are taking their toll on me. Maybe I can lie here next to him for a moment. I close my eyes, snuggling against his broad chest. "It's nice to be able to touch you without you smelling like onions."

"Those damned poultices of yours."

"Not mine, Riza's. And they worked, so you hush." I'm just so happy that he's getting better by the day. Every time I see him and his eyes are open, shining bright with impatience to be out of bed, my world feels a little more right. "How are you feeling today?"

"Better. Annoyed that my fragile wife is exhausting herself trying to take care of everyone." His hand goes to my belly, caressing the bulge of it. "Glad that our child is well."

"Your child is dancing upon my bladder," I retort, rolling onto my back a bit so he can rub my belly with ease. "He is more than well. And I'm not exhausting myself. Riza's keeping a close eye on me. It's just that the blood draws take a lot out of me. What would you have me do, tell those who are sick that no, I just don't feel like giving them a portion of my blood today?"

Nemeth makes an unhappy growl in his throat. "Just because I know it is necessary doesn't mean I like it." He rubs the curve of my belly. "How is the plague?"

"No new infections today," I tell him, my eyes fluttering closed. It's nice to just lie here next to him for a moment and not think about the day. There's so much to be done and so many to talk to who need advice that I fall into bed every night utterly drained, but we're making such progress that I can't be annoyed. "Sixteenth House hasn't lost anyone, so we're hopeful that they've passed through the worst of it."

"Good. How is your sister faring this week? Has her hatred of my people lessened?"

I lick my lips because I'm not sure how to answer that. "She's fine. She's Erynne."

And Erynne is both good and bad. She's still filled with an understandable hatred toward the Fellians for destroying Lios and murdering her son, but she's finally acknowledging that this was the work of Ivornath and Ajaxi and that most Fellians simply want to live in peace. Even so, I worry that Darkfell is going to be hard for her. That being here is going to remind her of everything she's lost.

Last night was a changing point, though. A Fellian woman approached as my sister and I went over plans for where to put more stairs. The woman had a baby in her arms and handed her to Erynne. It took me a moment to realize that the baby was human.

And when I saw Erynne's face, I realized it was tiny Ravendor being returned to her mother. For the first time, I saw my sister break down and weep, clutching her baby tightly. Some of the hardness disappeared from her eyes, and I know this morning she's visiting with the Fellian wet nurse who was watching over the baby to make plans since Erynne's milk has dried up.

It's not perfect, but it's progress. I saw my sister smile this morning, and there was no malice in it, nothing but pure joy.

"She's fine," I say to Nemeth again, and I mean it.

My bored, bedridden mate presses for more details. "And Tolian? Anything new to report?"

"Not since he was in here to see you this morning. Give the man a chance." I poke Nemeth again. He says he doesn't want to be in charge, but he's taken to it quite well. He's got a caring heart, which means he's truly invested in both the Fellians and the Liosians settling in and making a home out of the ruins of our two kingdoms. "I will say that your idea for the transport is brilliant. We just need the Fellians to come around."

"They'll come around once the plague slows more." He pats my stomach. "And when they get tired of building stairs. I'll be the first volunteer."

"I hope you're right." I put my hand over his, smiling. There's definitely been a lot of stair-building and grumbling. Right now, Tolian and Second House are leading the charge to make Darkfell more human-accessible. We're meeting a bit of resistance because of the plague and the fear that humans are the ones infecting Fellians, so it's natural to keep the two apart for a bit. Nemeth had the brilliant idea of having Fellians volunteer to fly humans back and forth in exchange for pay (or food), but it's a work in progress.

We'll get there. We need the Fellians to no longer be in fear of the plague and the Liosians to no longer be in fear of being enslaved. It won't happen overnight, but it'll happen.

"What about the fishing?" Nemeth prompts. "Some of the human women were going to try fishing alongside my people?"

"It's coming along," I tell him with a yawn, being deliberately vague.

"I could head out to the bay with them, supervise—"

"No," I say firmly.

"—I won't overtax myself. If it makes you happy, I'll sit the entire time," he continues. "I've read several treatises on the best fishing methods in rainy seasons, and—"

"No."

"—I can be of assistance. Candra, why are you so *stubborn*?"

"Because you almost died," I retort. "You're not getting out of this bed until I'm convinced you're healthy enough."

He chuckles. "So, you need convincing? Why didn't you say so?"

His hand slides under my skirts.

I suck in a breath, opening my eyes to look up at him.

"It's been a while," he says, his hand playing on my thigh. "Tell me if this is something you don't want, and I'll understand."

Not want? Is he mad? "Why would I not want this?"

"Because it's me. Because Fellians are responsible for so many wrongs that have been done to your people. Because you put your trust in me, and I broke that trust."

I cover his hand with mine and move it directly between my thighs. "You're my husband and my mate. And Lios lost the war, true, but it's a war that we started, so I cannot say we're blameless. As for trust, you were willing to abandon your people to go to Lios with me. Whatever your brother demanded you do in the tower, did you do it because you wanted to destroy me or because you loved me and you wanted me?"

"I loved you. Loved you from the moment I saw you in your bath."

"Then there is your answer. Just because Ivornath commanded it doesn't mean that it was what you wanted. I can't think of how many times Erynne bade me to kill you—"

"What?" Nemeth draws back, startled.

Oops. Did I not mention that? I pat his hand. "We can talk about that later. Are you going to touch your mate or not?"

With a frustrated growl, he leans in and nips at my ear, sending a shiver through my body. "You and I are going to talk about that later. For now, open your pretty thighs for me."

I thought he'd never ask. Sighing, I do as he commands. His hand is under my skirt, hidden from view, but I don't need to see his actions. I tilt my face toward his, and he rubs his nose against mine. In bed, we're close to the same height, which makes the nuzzling possible (and delightful).

"My beautiful Candra." Nemeth's fingers sweep over the mound of my pussy, stroking my curls. "It's been far too long since I've touched you."

"Yes, it has," I agree, closing my eyes. He'll find no argument here.

His lips brush over my cheek, even as his fingers slide through my rapidly dampening folds and caress me. "You're not wearing undergarments."

"I'm not," I agree. "They're a chore with a big belly, so I go without."

"I like this. I think you should go without all the time. Then you can just be ready for your mate's touch at any moment." One finger brushes against my clit, even as his teeth graze my jaw. "I like knowing that you're ready to take my knot. But this pussy needs to be much, much wetter."

I whimper in agreement.

The breath hisses from my throat when he strokes through my slick folds again. He works his finger up and down my cleft, dipping into my core and then moving back up to my clit to circle it slowly. I arch against his touch while he murmurs filthy things in my ear.

"I bet you can't wait for me to stretch you with my knot again," he says. "Do you need it? Do you ache inside to feel me locked inside you, giving you so much cock that your body has to work to take it all? Is that what you like?"

"Yes," I moan. "Gods, yes, Nemeth. Please. I need you so badly."

He teases a finger inside me again, his thumb rubbing my clit as he fucks me with his hand. I cling to him as he works me to a climax, coming hard and fast. My big Fellian holds me tightly as my legs tremble and my pussy clenches with the force of my release, and he nuzzles my cheek as I come down again. "My perfect, sweet mate. My *milettahn*. I love you so much."

I lift my chin so he can kiss me, and our lips brush. A drowsy, contented feeling drifts through my body, and when he pulls his hand away to lick his fingers, I roll onto my side and gaze up at him. His warm gray coloring is still a bit paler than I'd prefer, and his cheekbones are more prominent as he's lost weight from his sickness, but I love the sight of him. I love knowing that he's mine and that he's coming back to health.

I also love the hard length pressing against my lower leg, reminding me that he hasn't enjoyed his own release. "How would you feel about staying abed a bit longer?" I ask, my hand playing on his bare chest.

Nemeth guesses my game immediately. "What sort of enticement do I get?"

"A wife that pins you to the mattress and has her way with you . . . and your knot?"

His teeth flash in a wicked grin. "You're fascinated with my knot."

"I really am. Is that a no, then?"

He chuckles, his hand going to my thigh to grip it. "My darling Candra, for you, it is always and forevermore a yes."

Excellent answer.

EPILOGUE

MONTHS LATER

"My lady, if you don't get back in bed this instant, I am going to tell your husband," Riza says when she encounters me in the hall.

It's the same argument she gives me every time she sees me out of bed. I'd swear that no one had ever had a baby before me with the way Riza's been fussing. And sure, my little Bodahn was a large baby with an oversized head and teeny tiny wings curled around himself, but we both sailed through the birth easily. "Then get the cart, Riza, because if I'm not allowed to walk on my own, someone had better pull me along."

She grumbles as she moves to my side, trying to offer an arm for support. I shoo her away. Riza thinks that I'm fragile and made of glass.

"I'm heading to the throne room anyhow. Bodahn needs to be fed. You can come with me if you like."

Riza sighs as if I'm being difficult, then licks her finger and smooths out a lock of my hair by my temple. "If you're heading to the throne room, let me get you a better robe. This one has wrinkles. Wait here."

"What, do you think I'm going to start sprinting the moment you turn your back?" It's only been a few days since I gave birth. Walking around is difficult enough.

She swats my arm and heads down the hall. I continue toward the throne room, my steps slow and steady. She'll catch up with me anyhow. As I walk through the halls of the palace, I pass by the women and Fellians working on the construction. We're expanding the lower floors so the palace can be accessed by all who need to, and the upper rooms will only be used as storage. Everything's a mess right now, but all the reconstruction of the city gives people focus and something to do. We're making this a place for both humans and Fellians so no one feels like an interloper.

At least, that's my hope.

I get to the end of the hall and eye the stairs. That sure seems like a lot of walking. Turning to the nearest Fellian, I pull out a freshly minted coin. "Can I persuade you to carry me down to the bottom floor instead of making a poor tired woman who's recently given birth walk on her own?"

He rolls his eyes but snatches the coin from my hand. "Come with me."

"Wait, my lady," Riza screeches, running down the hall behind me. "Your robe!"

A short time later, I'm wearing the new (and far fussier) robe, Riza at my side. My Fellian companion took a coin for Riza's ride as well and then went back to work. I'm pleased that the coins seem to be working. Fellians get coins for giving people rides, and humans harvest the food from the fields (or cook, or build stairs, or fish) and receive coins from Fellians for their work. So far, so good.

I move into the main hall, a bright smile on my face to hide my exhaustion (when did this hall get so far away?), and head toward the dais. On one of the twin thrones at the front of the room, my mate Nemeth sits, a bored expression on his face, and our baby in his arms. He rocks the fussy child against his chest, trying to soothe him, and looks relieved when I appear. "Our son is hungry."

"I noticed." My breasts have been leaking ever since I woke up from my nap. I take Bodahn from his father and sit on the throne next to him. Riza immediately moves to my side, settling a blanket over my shoulder as I loosen the front of my robe and tuck Bodahn's head inside so he can nurse. The moment he latches, I relax in my chair and eye the room. "Busy today."

Nemeth grunts, his gaze affectionate as he regards me. "More weather reports. Still raining outside, though I suppose that's not a surprise."

It's not. "It won't stop raining until the goddess leaves the skies again."

"You missed all the fun," Nemeth tells me. "There was a scholar here earlier from the Alabaster Citadel. He had an outrageous theory about the weather. You should have heard it."

"Oh?"

"Aye. He said—listen to this—that it's not the goddess's wrath bringing the foul weather at all. That it's caused by the moon in the skies. That the presence of another heavenly body changes the tides and the weather patterns, and that's why it's such chaos." Nemeth snorts. "Pure dragon shite."

I blink at my husband. "You sound just like me."

"You're a wise woman." He takes my hand in his and leans over it, kissing my knuckles. "Is it so wrong that I listen to you?"

"Not in the slightest. Please, continue to praise me and my wisdom. It's vastly flattering."

He gives me a roguish grin and rubs my hand, then turns back to the waiting audience. I see smiles on a great deal of faces. They like Nemeth as a king because not only is he First House, but he's also a good listener. He's willing to entertain new ideas and to try new things . . . unless they're about the weather, of course. My presence as his Liosian (and Vestalin) wife eases human tensions, and I make sure everyone sees Nemeth with our sweet baby regularly. No one can be intimidated by a king who has a shoulder covered in milky drool and is desperately trying to jiggle a baby back to sleep.

The throne room has become part of our routine lately. We eat dinners with everyone who comes to visit us, I feed Bodahn out in the open, and Nemeth and I are affectionate with each other in front of everyone. It's a huge change from my sister's icy politeness at Lionel's side and Ivornath's secrecy. I want everyone to feel like they are part of our family because, in a way, they are. We're starting over, all of us. For the next few years, while we wait for the goddess's wrath to die away, we'll live here in Darkfell, where the weather won't soak us out of house and home.

And after that, perhaps we'll spread out. Perhaps we'll stay here under the mountain. As long as there's peace, I don't mind.

I stroke Bodahn's fuzzy head. Unlike Nemeth, he's got my dark hair and no horns. He does have his father's wings and tiny tail, about which I tease Nemeth mercilessly. We've already started talking about what another child between us would look like, and if it's a girl, I want to name her Iphigenia after my nurse. She would have loved Bodahn.

"You're just in time," Nemeth murmurs to me. "We've had human refugees arrive."

"Oh?" I sit up with interest, scanning the throne room for unfamiliar faces. The newcomers are obvious to see, their clothing soaked and muddy, their forms thin and emaciated. They look exhausted, and my heart wrenches at the sight of them. Maybe I've become soft ever since giving birth, but I know how hard it is outside, how difficult a struggle to find food. I want them to know they're welcome here.

I open my mouth to speak just as the first one steps forward and lowers his wet hood.

I gasp. "I know you!"

The man stares at me in horror. I do know him. It's one of the men who kidnapped me. The one who left when his companions were going to murder me. The one who stole my knife and took off.

I even remember his name. "You're Jarvo, aye?"

He cringes, bowing his head. "My . . . my lady. I am."

"You know this man?" Nemeth asks, practically bristling from his throne with fierce protectiveness.

"I do. He was one of the ones who robbed us when we were on our way to Lios." The room gets quiet, and Jarvo cringes even lower. He's thinner than I recall, his eyes hollow, and instead of anger, I feel nothing but pity. "It was difficult out there with nothing to eat, wasn't it? How did you manage?"

He looks at me in surprise, then glances at Nemeth. "I-I-I found kind strangers. They took me in and shared their supplies until they were gone."

I glance at the people behind him. "Are they with you now?"

"Aye." He gestures at an elderly couple with him. They have lined faces and white hair, their clothing ragged, but they don't look terrified for their lives, just exhausted.

Bodahn makes an unhappy noise at my breast, and I switch him to the other side, where he grizzles and latches once more. I stroke his tiny head, thinking about the past. I know what it's like to feel that food insecurity, and I know what it will drive people toward. "Was he a good friend to you?" I ask the older couple. "No robbing or stealing?"

They shake their heads, and the woman speaks up. "Jarvo has been like a son to us. There were days we had nothing to eat, and he would share the fish he caught. He would hunt down ravens so we could have something to eat. We would have died without him."

I glance back at Jarvo. He still looks defeated, as if fate has decreed his death. "Well, you are all welcome here. Someone in Second House will assist you with getting settled and explain the rules of our city. All we ask is that you treat both Fellian and Liosian kindly. There are no more wars. We are a city of survivors now, and there is no difference between us. Understand?"

"Yes, my lady. Thank you, my lady," Jarvo stammers, dropping to his knees on the floor. He catches himself, and then his head jerks upright. "Oh! I have your blade!"

"My blade?" I echo, though I know exactly what he means.

Sure enough, he pulls out the enchanted dagger that Erynne gave me so long ago. The one that is enchanted to give answers. The one that I relied upon so heavily once upon a time. It looks the same, small and benign, with a few jewels in the hilt.

I debate its presence for a moment. With it, I could ask questions about the future. I could suss out enemies before they strike. I could predict everything before it happens . . . and base every decision off of its answers.

But I'm tired of living in fear of what the future could bring. I look at my handsome husband, who sits on a throne. I hold my child, my best friend standing behind me. Somewhere in our city is my sister with her daughter and a thousand other faces that have become friends in the last few months.

I'm no longer cursed. If anything, I'm the luckiest Vestalin ever. So, I smile at Jarvo and shake my head. "You keep it. I'm good."

AUTHOR'S NOTE

Hello there!

Thank you so much for reading! This book holds a special place in my heart for a variety of reasons. I'm very proud of how Candra and Nemeth's story turned out, and I hope you enjoyed reading all the twists and turns as they make their way to their happy ever after.

Thank you so much to Eliza Swift and Jenny Bustance on the Yonder team. When I originally started writing this story, I knew it would be long and slightly epic, and the Yonder app seemed a fantastic place to try it out. Thank you also to Margot Mallinson at W by Wattpad Books for the gorgeous print edition! Another thank-you over to Emily Wittig, who designed the lovely cover. I'm so excited to be able to hold a print copy of this in my hands.

If you read the serial on the Yonder app, there are no significant changes in this print edition. Also, because I've been asked a million times—no, this is not related to the Aspect and Anchor series.

(Funny story, we were bouncing titles with marketing because my original title was *Tower Book* and clearly that wouldn't work. Someone suggested *Bound to the Shadow Prince* and I was like, oh, what a great title! It took me at least a week to realize that it was very similar to my self-published *Sworn to the Shadow God*. Whoops! Mea culpa and apologies for the confusion. Please be assured they are completely different books and I sometimes forget my own street address.)

A lot of the time, a story comes into my head because I hit upon a micro-obsession and I want to keep playing with it. I'll read everything that I can get my hands on about that topic and keep turning it over in my head until I've worn it to pieces . . . and figured out a way to include it in a book. This particular story features a few micro-obsessions of mine.

The biggest influence in this story was the Trojan War. I know what you're thinking: random, right? But for a while, I read every book—fiction, nonfiction, classics—I could about the topic. I watched every television special and mini-series. I have no particular clue as to why the Trojan War gripped the heck out of me like it did, but I knew some of the themes would make their way into a book. If you're unfamiliar with the Trojan War, the Greeks attacked the city of Troy because a guy stole another guy's wife (Helen of Troy). Like most wars, it wasn't really all about just one thing (Helen). And like most wars, there was a winner on paper—the Greeks. I'm going to go ahead and decide that's not a spoiler, as the story has been out for three thousand years or so. They razed the city of Troy to the ground, enslaved the women and children, and killed the men. Then the Greeks went home and . . . well, it wasn't a happy ever after. Several of them lost their kingdoms and one king was murdered by his spouse. Basically no side ends up winning and sailing off into the sunset. Two of the characters that inspired me the most were Andromache and Iphigenia, both of whom got completely screwed over by the war. You'll see a couple of Easter eggs in regard to those two characters in the story.

One of the big themes in the Trojan War (from my perspective) is how other people's choices end up suddenly becoming *your* problem. That's a theme with both Nemeth and Candra—both sides are pulled into existing problems, some of them centuries old. I can't imagine the resentment one must feel when they're told they have to sacrifice a huge chunk of their lives because of something their ancestors did. (Or I guess I *can* imagine it, because I wrote a book about it.)

Another micro-obsession that inspired this book was Candra's "blood illness." Initially, I inflicted this upon Candra because I wanted to have a character with a major ongoing health issue that affected her life—yet was still sexy and flirty and not tragic. I started out thinking she would have the fantasy-world version of diabetes, but it ended up being some weird morph of diabetes and the Rh factor in blood. I read a fascinating book called *Blood Will Tell: A Medical Explanation of the Tyranny of Henry VIII* by Kyra Cornelius Kramer and a lot of it is theory on how Rh factor affected Henry and the pregnancies of his wives. It got me to thinking how a human body would handle Fellian blood and how the family's curse was not really a curse as much as a recessive blood trait . . . which was also why she was able to have Nemeth's baby without it being "SURPRISE MAGICAL

BABY." (It still kind of is, but I as a reader need a better explanation than "he's got amazing sperm" for her to get pregnant.)

I was also inspired by the Maid Maleen fairy tale. It's a lesser known one in which a princess enters a tower and has to stay there for seven years. When she gets out, the world she knew is gone. Clearly I paid homage to this in my story, but I found myself getting swept up in the day-to-day mechanics of how it would work to live in a tower. In Maid Maleen, she has her maid with her to tend to the everyday life details, but that seemed too easy for Candra. She'd have a friend with her. She'd have someone to make her meals and draw her baths and clean her rooms. That's the tower on "easy mode." I wanted to see how Candra would handle having to make her own food, draw her own water, manage her own supplies, and entertain herself. Obviously it goes poorly for our heroine, which is another reason she and Nemeth find themselves thrown together.

At any rate, I sincerely hope you enjoyed reading the story as much as I enjoyed writing it!

Ruby Dixon
November 2023

ABOUT THE AUTHOR

Ruby Dixon is an author of science fiction and fantasy romance. She likes fated mates, baby-filled epilogues, and cinnamon roll heroes. She also likes to write biographies of herself in the third person, because it feels more important that way. Ruby also loves coffee and dirty books and will probably be a cat lady at some point.